The Best Stories of Wilbur Daniel Steele

BOOKS BY

Wilbur Daniel Steele

THE BEST STORIES OF WILBUR DANIEL STEELE

THAT GIRL FROM MEMPHIS

STORM

LAND'S END

SHAME DANCE

ISLES OF THE BLEST

THE TERRIBLE WOMAN

TABOO

URKEY ISLAND

THE MAN WHO SAW THROUGH HEAVEN

MEAT

TOWER OF SAND

SOUND OF ROWLOCKS

POST ROAD (with Norma Mitchell)

The Best Stories of Wilbur Daniel Steele

DOUBLEDAY & COMPANY, INC.

Garden City 1946 New York

PRINTED IN THE UNITED STATES
AT
THE COUNTRY LIFE PRESS, GARDEN CITY, N. Y.

FIRST EDITION

To Henry O'Neil

WITHOUT WHOSE FRIENDLY AND PHILOSOPHICAL GUIDANCE THIS COLLECTION WOULD HARDLY HAVE BEEN GOTTEN TOGETHER. THE CHORE OF CHOOSING WAS, INDEED, LARGELY HIS.

Contents

The Best Stories of Wilbur Daniel Steele

*For Where Is Your Fortune Now?**

MANY IS THE TIME MY MOTHER has stood at that window in the dead of a stormy night, when the roof rattled over our heads, and the wet shone on the cobbles, and boats came ashore on the beach; by the hour she has stood there in her bare feet and her nightgown, so still and ghostlike you wouldn't know it till you touched her in the dark. I've heard the Portugee grumbling, half in his sleep, to know what was up, and I guess she would be there again at the window, keeping an eye out for my father.

Since the first I can remember, she was always fearful my father would be turning up again. It haunted her. Maybe it was a dream or some kind of a sigh. She never had much learning, and she put faith in things she couldn't understand, like signs and cards and printed words.

I'm sure that was the reason she never got married to the Portugee. When my mother got a thing into her head, it was there to stay —she made a lot of it, and brooded over it, and sometimes, seeing she had no learning, it came out a queer thing in the end. It was so about getting married to the Portugee. Somebody told her once there was a law against a woman's being married to two men at the same time, and that a woman could be taken away and locked up in jail for it. She never forgot that. The law was a thing she never saw head or tail to, and when she thought about it, it got to be a terrible thing, as terrible as a ghost or a dragon. She was more fearful of the law than she was of the church, for she could see the church, but she couldn't see the law. And even when the stone set up in the graveyard for all our men that went north in the *Magnolia* had been standing there as much as eight years—even then, she said, you never could tell. One might have got clear, she said, and that one might be my father.

The women down at the fish-flakes where she worked were always making game of her one way or another, because she would believe anything. Scarcely a day passed but one of them pretended she made out a strange sail opening the Head, like the *Magnolia* coming home again, and never once did my mother fail them. It lay on her mind, that's why. For a wink each time she stood there with her hands empty, and her eyes running everywhere over the water, and her heart in her throat.

"What would he do to me?" she was thinking.

She was a strong, big woman, my mother, with dark hair and red cheeks and slow blue eyes. I can see her standing there on the pier now, with her skirt tucked up over her rough, red stockings, and her sleeves cut short below the shoulders, and her hair blowing about her head, the blue water beyond her, and the boats, and all around her the fish flakes like steps of snow, and the other women cleaning fish with her, and the slop and gurry from the tubs making the planks shine like the sky above. She stood like that, I say, looking for the loom of a ship that lay long years in the bottom of the sea, and her heart was in her throat.

She was never mad when they laughed, but afterward she would look at her tub awhile and shake her head and say, "I got a feeling here, girls"—and she would put her hand on her bosom—"I got a feeling here, girls, Ben Ring's never dead. That's all."

She made no secret of it. She wasn't the woman to make a secret of anything, nor was ours the village. She would say it no matter who was there, no matter even if the Portugee was there himself, and he often was, for he liked to watch folks work.

Sometimes he worked himself, though not often. Once he drove cart awhile for Haley, who put up travelers, and one summer he took it into his head to go to the weirs with John Briar's crew. That was hard on my mother and me. Though all the other weirmen went empty to the traps, my mother would get up at half past two to make the Portugee's breakfast, and with the two of them bundling about the kitchen where I slept, my sleep was broken, too. I used to lie there no more than half awake and watch them and their big shadows, my mother in her nightgown and wrapper fussing over the stove, with an eye peeping sideways as if she wondered if he wouldn't ever be tiring of it, and the Portugee getting his head through his shirt and hauling on his boots, one after the other, every motion slow and important, as if a great deal depended on it. And sometimes I used to wonder, lying there, what my father looked like, how my father used to pull on his boots, and get his head through his shirt, and wipe his mouth after he had drunk his coffee, and whether his footsteps sounded like the Portugee's going off down the cobbles toward the beach, smaller and smaller till they died away, and my mother yawned and sat down on the foot of my bed and began to think about dressing.

It made a change in the Portugee, too, having money coming in each week. Very often after supper he was out at Haley's, and sometimes he came home the worse for it. Once he hit my mother, though I don't think it hurt her much. She thought everything he did was right, just as she used to think everything my father did was right. All the same she brightened up and things were better every way when the weather came on cooler with fall and the Portugee tired of going to the weirs.

He was a good man in lots of ways, the Portugee. Very often he went clamming with me, and lay on the turf bank at the edge of the marsh, watching the clouds sail by, while I filled my bucket. When I came home from playing I could almost always count on finding him waiting somewhere in the lane, sitting on someone's doorstep with his hands behind his head and his round, black beard in the air. And then he would walk home slowly with me, and if my mother wasn't there yet he would do what he could toward getting supper ready, peeling potatoes or something. He never talked much unless it was about work, but he loved to talk about work.

He seemed to take pleasure in tales of great pieces of work men had done, like the man who stood the wheel fifty hours in a gale of wind and had to have his hands cut off, and the like of that. Yet he always seemed a little sickly to me, and his eyes weren't strong.

And how faithful my mother was! She was the kind that's meant to be faithful, though, and not to live alone. And perhaps she was more right than wrong to put faith in dreams and signs.

Everything in the Bible goes to prove it's the simple and the faithful that see God, and I've no doubt they see other things as well—angels and devils and fairies and the meaning of omens.

It's certain my mother had an omen of some kind, and if she read it just the opposite, it makes no difference. For it was on the very day my father came back that my mother had the first sure feeling he was dead and gone forever.

The night before there was a big gale of wind and rain, the kind you'll remember a long while if you live by the sea. That night we heard trees and chimneys coming down and the surf was thunder, for when the wind lies in the northeast the seas come clear of the Head mountain-high, and the beaches are one long lather of white. My mother was on foot all night, it seemed.

Around midnight a pane blew out in the front room, filling the place with wind and wet, but she would go back there for all of it. She was so restless. I don't know how many times I opened my eyes and saw her face by the light in the hall, like a dream.

It must have been about two when she gave a big groan. It was an unnatural sound. I jumped up in a wink, but then I was fearful of going in and sat still till the Portugee came leading her out to the kitchen. She sat beside me wringing her hands.

"The sea's heaving up the dead," said she. She looked daft, with her eyes set and her hair all down around her.

The Portugee couldn't make head or tail of it, and kept asking if there wasn't something he could do or somebody he could get.

My mother didn't seem to hear him at all.

"What'll he do?" she kept on saying, wringing her hands and staring at the stovepipe. "What ever will Ben Ring do to me?"

The Portugee put on his shirt and boots by and by and said he was going out to get some woman, but in the end he didn't get far.

The tide began to go a little before daylight, and that broke the wind. All of a sudden, just at sunrise, my mother began to laugh.

"I been so foolish," she laughed, "so foolish, so foolish!"

She laughed so hard and so long and her face got so red that I don't know what would have come of it had she not turned to crying in the end. She lay on my bed and cried for ten minutes, I should say, as if her heart was broken. And then she got up and got breakfast.

You'd never have thought she had been up all night to see her at breakfast time. Everybody was out in the lane having a look at the wreckage, and a neighbor woman came running in to talk it over, leaving the door open behind her and letting the sun in all over the floor, and the warm air of spring. She brought up short, seeing my mother.

"Why—why, Annie," she said. "Why, Annie, you look like a girl!"

She forgot all she was going to say, wanting to know what was up with my mother.

"It's all right," said my mother. "I been so foolish all these years, so foolish. But now I've seen him dead with his mates in the bottom of the sea. I've seen him sure as the sun in the sky."

"Where?" said Mrs. Hendie, sitting down and full of surprise.

"In here I've seen him." And my mother laid her hands on her bosom.

She didn't go to work that morning, seeing the gale had put things out of sorts at the pier. All morning she went around the house half daft, it seemed, picking things up and laying them down again without knowing why. If anyone spoke to her she went red and white and said, "What?" and by her eyes you'd say she didn't know yet whether to laugh or cry. Toward noon she grew quieter. For as much as a quarter of an hour she stood in the kitchen, brooding at the Portugee's boots behind the rocker in the corner, and all the while the color coming and going and a queer look around her lips.

"I guess," said she by and by, "I guess I'd like to get married."

The Portugee was lying on my bed; seeing her so still, and his mind relieved by it, he was almost off to sleep when she spoke up. It surprised him. He didn't know what in the world to do. He began to wander all around the house, coming back now and then on the chance she had got over it. She was beyond him.

"What would I wear?" he wanted to know.

He didn't seem to have anything to hang to. After he'd wandered about a bit more he said he thought she ought to talk it over with somebody.

"No, no," said she. "I wouldn't want to."

I can't say whether she thought better of it, but late that day she put on her shawl and started to go out. She got only as far as the front door, though, and in place of going out we heard her turning the key and throwing the bolt to. She came back and stood still in the doorway, with all the color gone out of her cheeks.

"He's standing out there in the lane," said she.

We couldn't make her out at all.

"Looking at the house," said she.

"Who?" said the Portugee.

"Him," said my mother. "Ben Ring in the flesh."

"What you saying?" cried the Portugee, starting up. But then he gave a sigh. She had got beyond him with her moods and visions.

"I saw him there in the lane," said she again.

"That's foolish," said the Portugee. But all the same he was taken aback more than a little to see her so deathly white and shivering from head to foot, and so was I. We went into the front room, both of us, and peeped out of the window. The sun was getting low by then, and the lane right away down to the water was red with it, and empty.

The Portugee looked down at me and I looked up at him and he shook his head with a despairing air.

"She's awful queer," said he. He told my mother she had better lie down awhile when we came back, but she would have none of it.

"I saw him there in the lane," said she, "as plain as I see you and Benjie now." She stood with her eyes fixed hard on us and her head nodding slowly. "He had on a gray suit and a brown felt hat, and in his left hand he had a bag and in his right hand he had a stick. He stood there abreast of June Sukie's step, looking up at the house here.

"And he knows," said she. "He knows. Else he would have come in, same as it would have been natural for a man to do."

It was well after dark before we had our supper, my mother was so distracted. And, seeing I had been up the night before, I was in bed and fast asleep before even the dishes were cleared away.

When I woke up it was the red of dawn. My mother was sitting on the foot of my bed, and on the floor with his legs sprawled out and a blanket thrown over them lay a man, sleeping like the dead. He was a large man, handsome in face, with hair turning grizzled above the ears, and when I saw the brown hat crumpled up beside him and the gray suit he had on I remembered my mother's words the night before, and the fear of him struck to my heart.

"That's my father?" said I in a whisper.

My mother turned to me with a queer, odd stare.

"Yes," said she. "He come in around two."

"What'll we do?" I asked, lying still for fear of him.

"I don't know," said she. "I don't know whatever."

"Why's he laying there? What's the matter of him?"

"He was to Haley's 'most all the night, drinking ale. He come in here on his hands and knees, and that's how he come, Benjie, and he went off straight to sleep like that."

She leaned down to smooth out the quilt a little and pull it over his feet, and I wondered to see her so gentle.

"When he wakes up," I wanted to know, "will he carry on?"

All the answer she gave me was to sit with her cheeks between her hands brooding at the floor. The sun was up now; it came in white at the window, and it seemed queerer than ever to see my strange father sleeping there like the dead. I pinched my mother's sleeve.

"Let's run away," said I. Then I had another thought.

"Where's *he* gone to?" said I, thinking of the Portugee.

"He'll be halfway to Squoisett by now," said my mother. "We thought it best he should go somewheres else, and so he took his things and a dollar I gave him, and he was out on the highroad by three, and that's the last of him. We thought it best on account of your father."

And she had no more than got the words out of her mouth when the door opened and there came the Portugee himself, shuffling in with a bundle over his back and his eyes on his boots.

My mother rose up on her feet, and I never heard her so sharp.

"What you doing here?" she wanted to know.

He let the bundle down on the floor and shifted from one foot to the other and hung his head.

"Where would I go to?" said he. He never looked at my mother. "If only you'd tell me where I'd go to," said he.

He sat down in the rocker and my mother sat down on the bed and everything seemed hopeless enough.

"Well," said my mother by and by, "seeing you're here, you'd best lend me a hand and we'll fetch him in onto the bed, for the floor's no place to be sleeping."

And they did that, the Portugee taking his shoulders and my mother at his feet, and they laid him on the bed in the other room.

My mother took me along when she went to work that morning, for we were both fearful of what my father would do when he woke up. Everybody at the pier knew all about it, of course, my father having been at Haley's the night before, and they were asking my mother a hundred questions.

"I don't know," she had to answer. "I don't know, and I don't know."

Her hand was tight on mine when we came up the lane for dinner that noon, and mine was tight on hers, the two of us wondering hard enough whether he had come back to his senses yet. And when we got to the door we found my father up in his stocking feet, playing pitch with the Portugee.

"I've twenty-eight for game, and be damned if you can beat it!" he was crying, with a huge bang of his fist on the table. And when my mother heard that, the strength went out of her hand, and she stood there leaning all her weight on the side of the door, for it was never the voice of a man who came with harm in his mind.

He was a big man, as I've said, and a handsome man. He sat there for a minute, taking her in from head to foot and never saying a word, and then he give the table another bang with his fist, crying:

"By the good God, Annie, girl, what a fool a man is?"

He pushed back his chair with a clatter, and striding across the floor he took hold of my mother's shoulders and held her off from him. He had a way with women, my father did.

"And what a block of wood I've got on my shoulders after all!" he cried. "Or else I'd have been here in my own house these eight years past, and be damned to all the slim waists and bad luck in the world!"

You should have seen my mother then. For what with this sudden turn to all her frights, and what too with the look of my father's admiring eyes, the red was chasing the white over her face and tears were raining down and her knees were gone. It was beyond belief, beyond belief. She had never looked to see him reasonable, and that was why.

"I've done you a great wrong," my father went on, drawing off and looking at her mournfully. "You'll never forgive me, Annie, never."

That was all. Not a word of her and the Portugee, and the Portugee sitting right there in the flesh all the while and hoping everything would come out right.

"That's Benjie, is it?" said my father, and crooked a finger to me.

"Benjie," said he, laying a hand on my hand, "Benjie, I've done you both a great wrong. I've give up my rights to everything a man would want, and I can never look to have you forgive me, and that's my deserts, that's my deserts."

He blew his nose, and I saw tears in his eyes.

All the rest of the day that mood was on him, and though he ate a great deal of fried whiting at dinner, and made himself comfortable, and played endless games of pitch with the Portugee, yet he would never be presuming, never a hint of reproach crossed his lips.

He gave us no word of how he had come to get clear of the *Magnolia* when she went down, but then the news was old with him and he'd had to answer so many questions at Haley's the night before that I suppose he was tired of it. That isn't to say he didn't talk. He talked the better part of the time, but mainly in scraps, jumping here and there—how he had missed one fortune by a hair at such a time, or been done out of another at another time. Bad luck had followed his footsteps no matter where he chose to go. He had done more than a few big pieces of work out in the world, but others had got the name for them; every time, it seemed, there was somebody or other ready to step in at the last minute and get a name and a pot of money, and bad luck sat on my father's shoulders. Though that wasn't to say it always would.

The Portugee never got enough of listening to him, nor I, for they were all strange tales to me. To hear my father talk, you would think our village was nothing; he was all for the huge, high cities, and the big rivers, and plains a hundred miles across.

"A man's got a chance there!" he cried, pounding the table. "Down here," said he, "when a man turns out of a morning, he knows pretty well what he'll turn in at night, ain't that so? But out there a man can never tell. Turn out a pauper and, like as not, turn in a millionaire. That's right! I've known 'em to!

"Not to say that's everything," he went on after a minute in a soberer voice, shaking his head. "Millions ain't everything. No—no."

And after supper, when everybody fell silent for some reason, and uncomfortable, and did nothing but stare at the lamp on the table, he said the same thing again, "Millions ain't everything. No—no."

He looked at my mother sidewise and then at the Portugee and bit his lips.

"I've done a great wrong," said he with a sigh. "It's my just deserts." He felt around in the dark under the table till he found his shoes.

"Well," said he, his face all red from stooping, "it's getting late, I guess." He put on his hat and took it off and coughed once or twice. Then, seeing my mother still staring at the lamp like a dumb one and her fingers picking at the edge of the plate, he said, "Well, I guess I'll be turning in." And with that he went out and down the lane to Haley's, to put up for the night.

The Portugee took to wandering about the room, out of ease as anyone could see, scratching himself and coughing and rubbing his wrist across his mouth, thinking of the good ale down at Haley's and my father so good-natured all that day and ready to stand him a glass, no doubt. In the end he couldn't bear it, and saying he guessed he'd have a look around, he put on his hat and went off down the lane, too.

Through it all, from first to last, not a word did my mother say; not a look did she give a one of us. But after she had washed up the supper things and got the kindling in from the woodhouse she sat on the foot of my bed with her hands clenched on her knees and a red spot standing on the white of her cheek and her eyes half closed, staring at nothing whatever.

How long she sat there I can't say, for I was off to sleep in a minute, and it was only the sound of her crying woke me up again. It seemed like a dream to see her lying there on my bed with her hands in her eyes and her shoulders working up and down, the lamp burning low and all the house so still I could hear the beach awash and the breeze blowing in the trees.

"What's the matter of you?" I wanted to know, but she wouldn't take her hands away to look at me, and said, "Be still, Benjie!"

"What you crying about?" said I, for I couldn't be still.

"I don't know—I don't know!"

"Is it my father or something?" said I. And with that another notion came into my head. "And if he's my father," said I, "then why doesn't he come to live to home, same as other folks' fathers?"

"Be still and go to sleep, Benjie," said she, and I saw the red creeping up between the fingers on her cheeks. "Go to sleep," said she.

I suppose the thought came to her then that she'd best be doing the same herself, for after a minute she got up and started off across the kitchen, fumbling at her buttons. But she had got no more than half the way when she brought up of a sudden and stood there listening.

There were footsteps in the yard, and we heard my father going on to the Portugee.

"Who are you?" he wanted to know. "Who are you, anyway?"

He sounded good-natured enough now, as if Haley's ale lay well on his stomach.

"If I've changed my mind," said he, "what business is it of yours? Who the devil are you, to be coming between man and wife?"

"You're a good fellow, all right!" said he, and we heard him give the Portugee a good round slap on the back that made him cough and scatter pebbles with his boots. And after another minute we heard the hinges squeaking out on the woodhouse where the Portugee went in, and my father's voice from the kitchen step, "That's the man, now. I've slept in worse places myself, and plenty's the time."

All the while my mother stood there with her hands on her bosom and her lips half open to her breath. When my father opened the door and saw her there so still in front of him, he seemed taken aback, and for a minute it was touch-and-go whether he would come in or not.

"Oh!" said he, kind of laughing and out of ease. "You were sitting up?"

He stepped in and closed the door, pulling it to several times before it seemed to latch, and all the while his face was red as a beet and his eyes everywhere.

"Hello, Annie!" said he. He cleared his throat, and then he smacked his hands together, making a great fuss, and seeing my mother hadn't stirred yet, nor so much as made a sound, he began patting her shoulders with both hands. "My, my!" said he. "What a handsome girl! What a handsome, dear girl, Annie!"

And the next thing I knew, there was my mother laughing and crying at once, and her arms around my father's neck.

You should have seen her the next day. She was so happy and her eyes were so bright. All the time you'd say she was just getting ready to sing a song, or her feet to fall into a dance. Yet there was a shyness about her, and a way of turning red at nothing whatever. And what a fine day it was for it all, with the sun shining bright, and the sea as blue as blue, and the willows breaking out in a feather of leaves, and a wind blowing.

My father went with my mother to her work, for he couldn't leave her a minute. He sat there all the morning on a salt cask with a pipe between his teeth, telling tales to the Portugee, and it's hard to say whether it was at him or at my mother folks looked the more.

That was splendid that morning, but my father wasn't the man to put up with it long. He didn't think it right my mother should go out to work. He was ready to do anything, any sort of work a man could turn an honest hand to, and he wanted the Portugee to stand on his own feet, what was more, and earn his own salt. The two of them went around the village next day, and my father talked with a great many men, only a few words with some, while with others he went on at a great rate in his loud, good-natured way. But with all of them it came to the same. He just couldn't help laughing at them.

"What you think I am?" he kept asking them, and one of them said:

"What you want is the earth, Ben, with a gold fence around it."

At dinner he was still laughing and carrying on at the lot of them. "My, my! Old Harriott, and his 'dollar a day'—imagine! Ha, ha, ha! That makes me laugh. And I've seen the day when I've put up my nose at—well, I won't say. My, my!"

My mother watched him with a cloud in her eyes.

"By God!" he cried, banging the table. "What chance has a man got in a hole like this?" He waved his hand behind him. "Out there," said he, looking at my mother, "—out there where I come from it's another thing!"

My mother's eyes went down to her plate again, and all the recent brightness was gone from her face.

"Oh well, I'll have another try around," said my father, but if my mother didn't shake her head she might have, for she knew as well as anyone that my father was wasting himself in a village the size of ours.

You wouldn't say any more that she was going to sing a song. All afternoon and evening she kept quiet, and when my father was shifting about from window to window and staring out at the sky for minutes at a time, my mother was looking the other way.

I can't say what time it was that night when I woke up to see her on her knees by the bed, watching me with the saddest look on her face.

"What is it?" said I in a whisper, for it was all queer in the weak light from the moon.

"Nothing," said she.

"What you crying about?" said I.

"I don't know," said she. "I don't know."

But she kept on looking at me as if her heart had been broken, and her eyes wouldn't let me go.

By and by, after we had been quiet awhile, she said:

"Oh, Benjie, I want you should be a fine, great man when you come to it; it's not right you shouldn't have the chance. But what chance has anyone got in a hole like this? It's not the same as it is out there, Benjie—not here it ain't—and I know it well."

I wondered to hear her go on so, and to see the round tears droping out of her eyes.

"What's the matter of you?" said I.

"Your father wouldn't be staying here a great while," said she. "And you'd best go along with him when he comes to go," said she, "and make yourself a fortune out there in the world, Benjie, boy." And before I could catch her nightgown even, she was off running in the dark.

In the morning it seemed my mother had been foolish enough, for the first thing my father did was to put on his hat and coat.

"Let's have another try," said he to the Portugee, "and see what side of their mouths they sing today." And then, seeing Haley coming into the yard, he gave a laugh. "Well, here's one of them already."

Haley was a smallish man with glassy eyes, always going about in his apron and talking short with everyone.

"I come to see about that little bill," said he, when the door was opened, and he stood with his fists on his hips looking at my father.

"Little bill?" said my father.

Haley had it in his hand, figured on a bit of paper.

"Yes," said he, "little bill! There's one night's lodging, with supper, for one thing, and there's seventeen glasses of ale first and last I've carried on the board, and three half plugs of Hayo's, the same, figuring two thirty-five, all told."

"*Two thirty-five!*" My father put his head back and roared with laughter. "Haley, on my word you'd think 'twas two hundred and thirty-five dollars, the way you act. *Two thirty-five!* Dear, dear!"

Haley kept standing as he was, with a sour look on his face.

"That's all right," said he. "It's easy enough to say 'Two thirty-five!' It's easy enough to say 'Remember it, will you?' It's easy enough to say 'Chalk that up, that's the boy!' "

"Look here!" cried my father, growing purple and shaking a finger in Haley's face. "By God, Haley, you'd best take care. When ever have I robbed a man or woman? Say! Stand there and tell me the date when Ben Ring's word wasn't good for whatever he asked of any man. Sing out!"

In place of answering, Haley closed his lips tighter and looked beyond him where my mother stood by the table, her face red and her eyes down.

"Come Saturday I'll 'tend to it," said she, hardly over a whisper.

"That's enough," said Haley. He bowed double over his apron. "That's all I want to know, all I want to know. Good day to you, ma'am."

I never saw a man so mad as my father was. It was just as well Haley was quick into his cart and quiet about it, for my father stood at the gate like a wild one, his face the color of meat, cursing him by every oath I ever heard.

"And as for you!" he cried at my mother, who was out behind him. "And as for *you*——" He stopped and pinched his forehead hard between his thumb and forefinger, to get the better of himself.

"It's no use, Annie," he went on in a kindlier voice. "You can see for yourself, Annie. Them and their ways are beyond me, beyond me, and I guess I'm beyond them, too. It's no use, Annie, girl."

And with that, giving her a kiss, he was out in the lane before my mother could say "Jack Robinson."

My heart went down and down. I began tugging at my mother's hand.

"Ma!" said I. "Oh, Ma–*you* know!"

That seemed to bring her wits back; we were out of the gate in a wink and my mother calling: "Ben! Ben!"

"Ben," said she, when we came up with him. "Take Benjie."

My father was dumfounded.

"Take *Benjie?*" He began to laugh and shake his head. "What on earth would I do with *Benjie*, say?" Then he turned soberer. "There, there," said he. "It's ten chances to one I'll be back again before you know it, bringing a pot of money for you both. There, there!"

"Take Benjie," said my mother in the same tone.

It took my father aback to see her standing up to him. Her hand was so tight on mine it hurt, but she wasn't fearful of him nor of anybody now, and her face was like a doll's face or a dead person's, so calm it was.

"Take Benjie!" said she, and that was all she said.

I could see my father didn't know how to take her, nor what to do, and with that my heart was going up again.

"Ma," I whispered, "how about my clothes and everything?" But she gave my hand a fierce grip.

"S-s-s-h! They don't amount, they don't amount. Go! Hurry now. Go! Go!" said she, seeing my father moving off, half of one mind and half of another.

She never kissed me; never so much as a "God bless you!" did she have to give me; you'd think she had no feeling in her. All the while my father and I were climbing the hill to the highroad she stood there in the same spot watching us, quiet as a stone, her face like a doll's with the pink washed out, or a dead person's.

It was a fine day, that day I started out to make my fortune in the world. The highroad runs along the ridge there with all the world spread out below, and that morning a big soft wind was blowing across it, the sky was full of little puffs of white cloud, like the ships we saw sailing far out to sea, and along the road the bushes were in bloom.

My father was like another man. At first he paid me no heed, but walked on straight and stiff. After that he seemed put out to find me still tagging at his heels, and I was of two minds about turning back. But in the end he couldn't help it; he started whistling and swinging his arms with the tune, and then he gave me a good slap on the back and said that he and I would show them what was what.

We walked on so all morning. Toward noon we stopped in a lonely part and he had me take off one of my shoes and put a pebble in it.

"That's all right," said he, when I complained how it hurt to be walking so, and he clapped his hands and cried "Fine! Fine!" to see me limping and groaning. And we had no more than come around the next bend when there was a farmhouse by the road and a kindly, white-faced woman who gave us a good dinner and made all manner of me, calling me a lamb and a poor baby and the like. When we came to go, after she had kissed me, she gave my hand a shake, and I found a shiny half dollar left in my fingers. I gave it to my father, once we were on the highroad again, for my pockets were full of holes, and then he took the pebble out of my shoe, laughing merrily all the while and thinking more and more that I was a fine fellow.

So we walked on, and when my father wasn't whistling or singing a song, he was telling me tales of the great cities and of what he was going to do and how we were going to show them what was what. It made me feel good to see him so big and handsome and able, and to know he was my father and I was his son. It made him feel good too, for he told me as much. Once he grew sober. We were having a rest, stretched out in the grass above the road where a hill ran down into a valley full of farms, and the sea at the other end like a blue teacup. We lay there awhile watching the clouds, and then my father began in a solemn way.

"You ought to do well, Benjie," said he. "You keep right at it and tend to your knitting and you ought to have a name and a pot of money one day—when I'm dead maybe, and you're a man."

He told me he was unlucky. He lay on his back staring at the sky and running on like a man talking more to himself. He said he was born to be unlucky, and that was all there was to it. The world was full of chances, he said, for a man that was lucky and had his eye out all the while and kept clear of women.

"Take a man's word on it," said he, "and keep clear of the unlucky animals. Never let yourself get tied up with a woman, Benjie; not with any woman, good or bad, good or bad."

By the time we came to Squoisett, where the railroad is, I was tired to death and my feet so sore there was no need of pebbles to make me limp. There wasn't any farmhouse there either, nor any kind woman to give us a meal, but we had that money now and we walked into a lunchroom, bold as you please, and ordered coffee and doughnuts of the girl.

My father's spirits had come back again. We were the only ones in the lunchroom, and there wasn't a minute when he wasn't laughing or talking with the girl, even when she seemed sharp with him, or made a face, or turned her back and paid him no heed.

He took a great while to finish his doughnuts, and then he ordered some more, and when the girl set the plate down he got hold of her hand.

"Fresh!" said she. She jerked it back and tried to give him a slap, but he only roared with laughter, and after she had made a face at him she began laughing too and patted her red hair up and asked him which way he was bound.

"Oh," said he, "just out for a walk."

"Oh, you like to walk?" said she.

"Do you?" said my father. His eyes were bright as water, and a smile was on his face. As for me, I might as well have been in Tophet for all the heed they paid to me.

"I'm through already," I whispered to my father, wishing he would come now. But all he did was put his elbows on the table and look at the girl.

"Do *you?*" said he again.

"Oh, it's all according," said she, looking at her fingernails.

"All according to what?" said he.

"Oh—to the weather," said she, with a toss of her head.

"It's elegant weather," said my father. "And what a nice road out there beyond the freight yard, don't you think? What?"

"Fresh!" said she. She wouldn't answer anything but "Fresh!" or "Smart Aleck!" after that until we went. But all the same my father was in the highest spirits, humming a dance tune under his breath, while we walked off through the little street. There was scarcely anyone about, for the sun was going down and people were at their suppers, and everything quiet and peaceful in the glowing light. Just beyond the last houses some freight cars stood on a siding, red as blood.

"Here's where we get our train," said my father.

"Our private car," said he, with a laugh and a thumb over his shoulder at one of the boxcars that stood with its door open, looking black enough inside. And after that he fell silent.

It came on cooler with the sundown, and there was a feel of rain in the air. Everything was so still. The sky turned from red to yellow and then to green, darker and darker all the while till the stars came out, very faint for the mist in the air. Across the road lay a broad field with a wire fence around it and woods beyond; you could almost see the dark coming out of the woods and creeping in across the field.

I tried to think of something to say. I wished my father would talk and carry on the way he had that afternoon, and give me a good slap on the back. Everything was so still here; there wasn't any surf here, and the only light was a red light burning down the track a way.

After a while I saw somebody coming out along the road under the embankment, and I didn't want my father to see, for I knew as certain as anything it was that girl from the lunchroom.

"Pa," said I, taking hold of his hand, "let's talk about what you and I are going to do."

"Sure," said he. "Sure we'll talk about it. By and by we will."

He dropped my hand and got up on his feet.

"You sit here quiet and I'll be back in a few minutes," said he. "It's all right, all right; no harm will come to you here."

And with that he was stepping down into the road and coughing a little against his sleeve.

"Whither goest thee?" I heard him saying in a comical kind of a voice.

"Oh, I don'test know," said the girl. And then they both laughed and started walking off along the road side by side, growing smaller and smaller, and dimmer and dimmer, till the trees came around them and I couldn't hear them any more.

Oh, but how I hated my father! And how lonely I was, and fearful, sitting there all by myself in that strange land with the empty field in front, and the empty boxcars behind, and that one red light looking at me like an eye from down the track. And how I cried, with my face in the grass, and my backbone running chills, and my heart full of bitterness and the awful longing to be home. I wanted to be home.

By and by I got up and started home. I ran at first. I ran through the town of Squoisett, with people staring at me from their doorsteps and calling after me, some of them, and I kept on running along the highroad till my breath gave out and I had to walk. I had been tired to death; now I wasn't tired any longer, nor lame, nor anything.

How I kept to the road I can't for the life of me say. What with the darkness and a passing shower of rain and all, I might have come out on a dozen by-roads and been no wiser. The moon rose late, and then it was better, even if I could see how long the blue road lay before me. I began to be tired again, my legs ached, and the soles of my feet were raw. And once I grew ashamed, and wondered what my mother would say to me, coming home so soon with never a fortune to my name.

But then I didn't care. A wind came up a valley from over the sea, carrying the smell of salt and wood, a wind with a shine of pearl in it, and there I was on my toes again and pounding along with all my might. For I was coming near now, coming near, and I could see the hills before me rolling down and rolling down to the shores I knew.

The moon stood high and pale, and the gray of dawn was coming up the east. The wind blew stronger; I never knew so sweet a wind, full of the ocean and flowers. And when I came along the ridge over our village, where the highroad branches to go winding down and a big dark rock stands in the elbow of it, whom should I see but my mother sitting there in the gray with her back to the wind and her hair blowing.

I never would have looked to see her there at such an hour; for a minute I was fearful something had happened to her.

"What ever you doing here?" I cried, and that was the first she knew I was there.

She sat there looking at me.

"What ever is it?" said I, going closer to her.

"I don't know," said she. "I don't know."

But, then all of a sudden, she began to cry as if her heart had been broken, and the next thing she had picked me up in her strong arms, crying: "You shouldn't have come back, Benjie, you shouldn't, you shouldn't," and there we were going down the hill with the pebbles spattering away in front and the sun up red on the roofs and the Portugee sitting at the bottom of the hill, waiting, with his hands behind his head and his round black beard in the air.

"You shouldn't have come back," my mother kept whispering over and over all the while. "Oh, Benjie, Benjie, you shouldn't have come back to me," and her tears fell wet on my face. But yet her eyes were shining with the light of heaven, and it was more like a song she sang in the morning wind.

"You shouldn't have come back to me, Benjie, never, never; for where is your fortune now?"

*The Woman at Seven Brothers**

I TELL YOU SIR, I WAS INNOCENT. I didn't know any more about the world at twenty-two than some do at twelve. My uncle and aunt in Duxbury brought me up strict; I studied hard in high school, I worked hard after hours, and I went to church twice on Sundays, and I can't see it's right to put me in a place like this, with crazy people. Oh yes, I know they're crazy—you can't tell *me*. As for what they said in court about finding her with her husband, that's the inspector's lie, sir, because he's down on me, and wants to make it look like my fault.

No, sir, I can't say as I thought she was handsome—not at first. For one thing, her lips were too thin and white, and her color was bad. I'll tell you a fact, sir; that first day I came off to the light I was sitting on my cot in the storeroom (that's where the assistant keeper sleeps at the Seven Brothers), as lonesome as I could be, away from home for the first time and the water all around me, and, even though it was a calm day, pounding enough on the ledge to send a kind of a *woom-woom-woom* whining up through all that solid rock of the tower. And when old Fedderson poked his head down from the living room, with the sunshine above making a kind of bright frame around his hair and whiskers, to give me a cheery, "Make yourself to home, son!" I remember I said to myself: "*He's* all right. I'll get along with *him*. But his wife's enough to sour milk." That was queer, because she was so much under him in age—'long about twenty-eight or so, and him nearer fifty. But that's what I said, sir.

Of course that feeling wore off, same as any feeling will wear off sooner or later in a place like the Seven Brothers. Cooped up in a place like that you come to know folks so well that you forget what they *do* look like. There was a long time I never noticed her, any more than you'd notice the cat. We used to sit of an evening around the table, as if you were Fedderson there, and me here, and her somewhere back there, in the rocker, knitting. Fedderson would be working on his Jacob's ladder, and I'd be reading. He'd been working on that Jacob's ladder a year, I guess, and every time the inspector came off with the tender he was so astonished to see how good that ladder was that the old man would go to work and make it better. That's all he lived for.

If I was reading, as I say, I daren't take my eyes off the book, or Fedderson had me. And then he'd begin—what the inspector said about him. How surprised the member of the board had been, that time, to see everything so clean about the light. What the inspector had said about Fedderson's being stuck here in a second-class light—best keeper on the coast. And so on and so on, till either he or I had to go aloft and have a look at the wicks.

He'd been there twenty-three years, all told, and he'd got used to the feeling that he was kept down unfair—so used to it, I guess, that he fed on it and told himself how folks ashore would talk when he was dead and gone—best keeper on the coast—kept down unfair. Not that he said that to me. No, he was far too loyal and humble, and respectful, doing his duty without complaint, as anybody could see.

And all the time, night after night, hardly ever a word out of the woman. As I remember it, she seemed more like a piece of furniture than anything else—not even a very good cook, nor over and above tidy. One day, when he and I were trimming the lamp, he passed the remark that his *first* wife used to dust the lens and take a pride in it. Not that he said a word against Anna, though. He never said a word against any living mortal; he was too upright.

I don't know how it came about; or, rather, I *do* know, but it was so sudden, and so far away from my thoughts, that it shocked me, like the world turned over. It was at prayers. That night I remember Fedderson was uncommon long-winded. We'd had a batch of newspapers out by the tender, and at such times the old man always made a long watch of it, getting the world straightened out. For one thing, the United States minister to Turkey was dead. Well, from him and his soul, Fedderson got on to Turkey and the Presbyterian college there, and from that to heathen in general. He rambled on and on, like the surf on the ledge, *woom-woom-woom,* never coming to an end.

You know how you'll be at prayers sometimes. My mind strayed. I counted the canes in the chair seat where I was kneeling; I plaited a corner of the tablecloth between my fingers for a spell, and by and by my eyes went wandering up the back of the chair.

The woman, sir, was looking at me. Her chair was back to mine, close, and both our heads were down in the shadow under the edge of the table, with Fedderson clear over on the other side by the stove. And there was her two eyes hunting mine between the spindles in the shadow. You won't believe me, sir, but I tell you I felt like jumping to my feet and running out of the room—it was so queer.

I don't know what her husband was praying about after that. His voice didn't mean anything, no more than the seas on the ledge away down there. I went to work to count the canes in the seat again, but all my eyes were in the top of my head. It got so I couldn't stand it. We were at the Lord's Prayer, saying it singsong together, when I had to look up again. And there her two eyes were, between the spindles, hunting mine. Just then all of us were saying, "Forgive us our trespasses . . ." I thought of it afterward.

When we got up she was turned the other way, but I couldn't help seeing her cheeks were red. It was terrible. I wondered if Fedderson would notice, though I might have known he wouldn't—not him. He was in too much of a hurry to get at his Jacob's ladder, and then he had to tell me for the tenth time what the inspector'd said that day about getting him another light—Kingdom Come, maybe, he said.

I made some excuse or other and got away. Once in the storeroom, I sat down on my cot and stayed there a long time, feeling queerer than anything. I read a chapter in the Bible, I don't know why. After I'd got my boots off I sat with them in my hands for as much as an hour, I guess, staring at the oil tank and its lopsided shadow on the wall. I tell you, sir, I was shocked. I was only twenty-two, remember, and I was shocked and horrified.

And when I did turn in, finally, I didn't sleep at all well. Two or three times I came to, sitting straight up in bed. Once I got up and opened the outer door to have a look. The water was like glass, dim, without a breath of wind, and the moon was going down. Over on the black shore I made out two lights in a village, like a pair of eyes watching. Lonely? My, yes! Lonely and nervous. I had a horror of her, sir. The dinghy boat hung on its davits just there in front of the door, and for a minute I had an awful hankering to climb into it, lower away, and row off, no matter where. It sounds foolish.

Well, it seemed foolish next morning, with the sun shining and everything as usual—Fedderson sucking his pen and wagging his head over his eternal "log," and his wife down in the rocker with her head in the newspaper, and her breakfast work still waiting. I guess that jarred it out of me more than anything else—sight of her slouched down there, with her stringy, yellow hair and her dusty apron and the pale back of her neck, reading the society notes. *Society notes!* Think of it! For the first time since I came to Seven Brothers I wanted to laugh.

I guess I did laugh when I went aloft to clean the lamp and found everything so free and breezy, gulls flying high and little whitecaps making under a westerly. It was like feeling a big load dropped off your shoulders. Fedderson came up with his dust rag and cocked his head at me.

"What's the matter, Ray?" said he.

"Nothing," said I. And then I couldn't help it. "Seems kind of out of place for society notes," said I, "out here at Seven Brothers."

He was the other side of the lens, and when he looked at me he had a thousand eyes, all sober. For a minute I thought he was going on dusting, but then he came out and sat down on a sill.

"Sometimes," said he, "I get to thinking it may be a mite dull for her out here. She's pretty young, Ray. Not much more'n a girl, hardly."

"Not much more'n a *girl!*" It gave me a turn, sir, as though I'd seen my aunt in short dresses.

"It's a good home for her, though," he went on slow. "I've seen a lot worse ashore, Ray. Of course if I could get a shore light——"

"Kingdom Come's a shore light."

He looked at me out of his deep-set eyes, and then he turned them around the lightroom, where he'd been so long.

"No," said he, wagging his head. "It ain't for such as me."

I never saw so humble a man.

"But look here," he went on, more cheerful. "As I was telling her just now, a month from yesterday's our fourth anniversary, and I'm going to take her ashore for the day and give her a holiday—new hat and everything. A girl wants a mite of excitement now and then, Ray."

There it was again, that "girl." It gave me the fidgets, sir. I had to do something about it. It's close quarters for last names in a light, and I'd taken to calling him Uncle Matt soon after I came. Now, when I was at table that noon, I spoke over to where she was standing by the stove, getting him another help of chowder.

"I guess I'll have some, too, *Aunt* Anna," said I, matter-of-fact.

She never said a word nor gave a sign—just stood there kind of round-shouldered, dipping the chowder. And that night at prayers I hitched my chair around the table, with its back the other way.

You get awful lazy in a lighthouse, some ways. No matter how much tinkering you've got, there's still a lot of time and there's such a thing as too much reading. The changes in weather get monotonous, too, by and by; the light burns the same on a thick night as it does on a fair one. Of course there's the ships, northbound, southbound—windjammers, freighters, passenger boats full of people. In the watches at night you can see their lights go by and wonder what they are, how they're laden, where they'll fetch up, and all. I used to do that almost every evening when it was my first watch, sitting out on the walk-around up there with my legs hanging over the edge and my chin propped on the railing—lazy. The Boston boat was the prettiest to see, with her three tiers of portholes lit, like a string of pearls wrapped round and round a woman's neck—well away, too, for the ledge must have made a couple of hundred fathoms off the light, like a white dogtooth of a breaker, even on the darkest night.

Well, I was lolling there one night, as I say, watching the Boston boat go by, not thinking of anything special, when I heard the door on the other side of the tower open and footsteps coming around to me.

By and by I nodded toward the boat and passed the remark that she was fetching in uncommon close tonight. No answer. I made nothing of that, for oftentimes Fedderson wouldn't answer, and after I'd watched the lights crawling on through the dark a spell, just to make conversation I said I guessed there'd be a bit of weather before long.

"I've noticed," said I, "when there's weather coming on, and the wind in the northeast, you can hear the orchestra playing aboard of her just over there. I make it out now. Do you?"

"Yes. Oh—yes! *I hear it all right!*"

You can imagine I started. It wasn't him, but *her*. And there was something in the way she said that speech, sir—something—well—unnatural. Like a hungry animal snapping at a person's hand.

I turned and looked at her sidewise. She was standing by the railing, leaning a little outward, the top of her from the waist picked out bright by the lens behind her. I didn't know what in the world to say, and yet I had a feeling I ought not to sit there mum.

"I wonder," said I, "what that captain's thinking of, fetching in so handy tonight. It's no way. I tell you, if 'twasn't for this light, she'd go to work and pile up on the ledge some thick night——"

She turned at that and stared straight into the lens. I didn't like the look of her face. Somehow, with its edges cut hard all around, and its two eyes closed down to slits, like a cat's, it made a kind of mask.

"And then," I went on, uneasy enough, "—and then where'd all their music be of a sudden, and their goings on and their singing——"

"And dancing!" She clipped me off so quick it took my breath.

"D-d-dancing?" said I.

"That's dance music," said she. She was looking at the boat again.

"How do you know?" I felt I had to keep on talking.

Well, sir—she laughed. I looked at her. She had on a shawl of some stuff or other that shined in the light; she had it pulled tight around her with her two hands in front at her breast, and I saw her shoulders swaying in tune.

"How do I *know?*" she cried. Then she laughed again, the same kind of a laugh. It was queer, sir, to see her, and to hear her. She turned, as quick as that, and leaned toward me. "Don't you know how to dance, Ray?" said she.

"N-no," I managed, and I was going to say "Aunt Anna," but the thing choked in my throat. I tell you she was looking square at me all the time with her two eyes and moving with the music as if she didn't know it. By heavens, sir, it came over me of a sudden that she wasn't so bad-looking, after all. I guess I must have sounded like a fool.

"You—you see," said I, "she's cleared the rip there now, and the music's gone. You—you—hear?"

"Yes," said she, turning back slow. "That's where it stops every night—night after night—it stops just there—at the rip."

When she spoke again her voice was different. I never heard the like of it, thin and taut as a thread. It made me shiver, sir.

"I hate 'em!" That's what she said. "I hate 'em all, I'd like to see 'em dead. I'd love to see 'em torn apart on the rocks, night after night. I could bathe my hands in their blood, night after night."

And do you know, sir, I saw it with my own eyes, her hands moving in each other above the rail. But it was her voice, though. I didn't know what to do or what to say, so I poked my head through the railing and looked down at the water. I don't think I'm a coward, sir, but it was like a cold—ice-cold—hand, taking hold of my beating heart.

When I looked up finally, she was gone. By and by I went in and had a look at the lamp, hardly knowing what I was about. Then, seeing by my watch it was time for the old man to come on duty, I started to go below. In the Seven Brothers, you understand, the stair goes down in a spiral through a well against the south wall, and first there's the door to the keeper's room, and then you come to another, and that's the living room, and then down to the storeroom. And at night, if you don't carry a lantern, it's as black as the pit.

Well, down I went, sliding my hand along the rail, and as usual I stopped to give a rap on the keeper's door, in case he was taking a nap after supper. Sometimes he did.

I stood there, blind as a bat, with my mind still up on the walk-around. There was no answer to my knock. I hadn't expected any. Just from habit, and with my right foot already hanging down for the next step, I reached out to give the door one more tap for luck.

Do you know, sir, my hand didn't fetch up on anything. The door had been there a second before, and now the door wasn't there. My hand just went on going through the dark, on and on, and I didn't seem to have sense or power enough to stop it. There didn't seem any air in the well to breathe, and my ears were drumming to the surf—that's how scared I was. And then my hand touched the flesh of a face, and something in the dark said, "Oh!" no louder than a sigh.

Next thing I knew, sir, I was down in the living room, warm and yellow-lit, with Fedderson cocking his head at me across the table, where he was at that eternal Jacob's ladder of his.

"What's the matter, Ray?" said he. "Lord's sake, Ray!"

"Nothing," said I. Then I think I told him I was sick. That night I wrote a letter to A. L. Peters, the grain dealer in Duxbury, asking for a job—even though it wouldn't go ashore for a couple of weeks, just the writing of it made me feel better.

It's hard to tell you how those two weeks went by. I don't know why, but I felt like hiding in a corner all the time. I had to come to meals. But I didn't look at her, though, not once, unless it was by accident. Fedderson thought I was still ailing and nagged me to death with advice and so on. One thing I took care not to do, I can tell you, and that was to knock on his door till I'd made certain he wasn't below in the living room—though I was tempted to.

Yes, sir; that's a queer thing, and I wouldn't tell you if I hadn't set out to give you the truth. Night after night, stopping there on the landing in that black pit, the air gone out of my lungs and the surf drumming in my ears and sweat standing cold on my neck—and one hand lifting up in the air—God forgive me, sir! Maybe I did wrong not to look at her more, drooping about her work in her gingham apron, with her hair stringing.

When the inspector came off with the tender, that time, I told him I was through. That's when he took the dislike to me, I guess, for he looked at me kind of sneering and said, soft as I was, I'd have to put up with it till next relief. And then, said he, there'd be a whole house-cleaning at Seven Brothers, because he'd gotten Fedderson the berth at Kingdom Come. And with that he slapped the old man on the back.

I wish you could have seen Fedderson, sir. He sat down on my cot as if his knees had given way. Happy? You'd think he'd be happy, with all his dreams come true. Yes, he was happy, beaming all over—for a minute. Then, sir, he began to shrivel up. It was like seeing a man cut down in his prime before your eyes. He began to wag his head.

"No," said he. "No, no; it's not for such as me. I'm good enough for Seven Brothers, and that's all, Mr. Bayliss. That's all."

And for all the inspector could say, that's what he stuck to. He'd figured himself a martyr so many years, nursed that injustice like a mother with her first-born, sir; and now in his old age, so to speak, they weren't going to rob him of it. Fedderson was going to wear out his life in a second-class light, and folks would talk—that was his idea. I heard him hailing down as the tender was casting off:

"See you tomorrow, Mr. Bayliss. Yep. Coming ashore with the wife for a spree. Anniversary. Yep."

But he didn't sound much like a spree. They *had* robbed him, partly, after all. I wondered what *she* thought about it. I didn't know till night. She didn't show up to supper, which Fedderson and I got ourselves—had a headache, he said. It was my early watch. I went and lit up and came back to read a spell. He was finishing off the Jacob's ladder, and thoughtful, like a man that's lost a treasure. Once or twice I caught him looking about the room on the sly. It was pathetic, sir.

Going up the second time, I stepped out on the walk-around to have a look at things. She was there on the seaward side, wrapped in that silky thing. A fair sea was running across the ledge, and it was coming on a little thick—not too thick. Off to the right the Boston boat was blowing, *whroom-whroom!* Creeping up on us, quarter-speed. There was another fellow behind her, and a fisherman's conch farther offshore.

I don't know why, but I stopped beside her and leaned on the rail. She didn't appear to notice me, one way or another. We stood and we stood, listening to the whistles, and the longer we stood the more it got on my nerves, her not noticing me. I suppose she'd been too much on my mind lately. I began to be put out. I scraped my feet. I coughed. By and by I said out loud:

"Look here, I guess I better get out the foghorn and give those fellows a toot."

"Why?" said she, without moving her head—calm as that.

"*Why?*" It gave me a turn, sir. For a minute I stared at her. "Why? Because if she don't pick up this light before very many minutes she'll be too close in to wear—tide'll have her on the rocks—that's why!"

I couldn't see her face, but I could see one of her silk shoulders lift a little, like a shrug. And there I kept on staring at her, a dumb one, sure enough. I know what brought me to was hearing the Boston boat's three sharp toots as she picked up the light—mad as anything—and swung her helm aport. I turned away from her, sweat dripping down my face, and walked around to the door. It was just as well, too, for the feed pipe was plugged in the lamp and the wicks were popping. She'd have been out in another five minutes, sir.

When I'd finished, I saw that woman standing in the doorway. Her eyes were bright. I had a horror of her, sir, a living horror.

"If only the light had been out," said she, low and sweet.

"God forgive you," said I. "You don't know what you're saying."

She went down the stair into the well, winding out of sight, and as long as I could see her, her eyes were watching mine. When I went myself, after a few minutes, she was waiting for me on that first landing, standing still in the dark. She took hold of my hand, though I tried to get it away.

"Good-by," said she in my ear.

"Good-by?" said I. I didn't understand.

"You heard what he said today—about Kingdom Come? Be it so—on his own head, I'll never come back here. Once I set foot ashore—I've got friends in the Brightonboro, Ray."

I got away from her and started on down. But I stopped. "Brightonboro?" I whispered back. "Why do you tell *me?*" My throat was raw to the words, like a sore.

"So you'd know," said she.

Well, sir, I saw them off next morning, down that new Jacob's ladder into the dinghy boat, her in a dress of blue velvet and him in his best cutaway and derby—rowing away, smaller and smaller, the two of them. And then I went back and sat on my cot, leaving the door open and the ladder still hanging down the wall, along with the boat falls.

I don't know whether it was relief, or what. I suppose I must have been worked up even more than I'd thought those past weeks, for now it was all over I was like a rag. I got down on my knees, sir, and prayed to God for the salvation of my soul, and when I got up and climbed to the living room it was half past twelve by the clock. There was rain on the windows and the sea was running blue-black under the sun. I'd sat there all that time not knowing there was a squall.

It was funny; the glass stood high, but those black squalls kept coming and going all afternoon, while I was at work up in the light-room. And I worked hard, to keep myself busy. First thing I knew it was five, and no sign of the boat yet. It began to get dim and kind of purplish gray over the land. The sun was down. I lit up, made everything snug, and got out the night glasses to have another look for that boat. He'd said he intended to get back before five. No sign.

And then, standing there, it came over me that of course he wouldn't be coming off—he'd be hunting *her*, poor old fool. It looked like I had to stand two men's watches that night.

Never mind. I felt like myself again, even if I hadn't had any dinner or supper. Pride came to me that night on the walk-around, watching the boats go by—little boats, big boats, the Boston boat with all her pearls and her dance music. They couldn't see me; they didn't know who I was; but to the last of them, they depended on *me*. They say a man must be born again. Well, I was born again. I breathed deep in the wind.

Dawn broke hard and red as a dying coal. I put out the light and started to go below. Born again; yes, sir. I felt so good I whistled in the well, and when I came to that first door on the stair I reached out in the dark to give it a rap for luck. And then, sir, the hair prickled all over my scalp, when I found my hand just going on and on through the air, the same as it had gone once before, and all of a sudden I wanted to yell, because I thought I was going to touch flesh. It's funny what their just forgetting to close their door did to me, isn't it?

Well, I reached for the latch and pulled it to with a bang and ran down as if a ghost was after me. I got up some coffee and bread and bacon for breakfast. I drank the coffee. But somehow I couldn't eat, all along of that open door. The light in the room was blood. I got to thinking. I thought how she'd talked about those men, women, and children on the rocks, and how she'd made to bathe her hands over the rail. I almost jumped out of my chair then; it seemed for a wink she was there beside the stove watching me with that queer half smile—really, I seemed to see her for a flash across the red tablecloth in the red light of dawn.

"Look here!" said I to myself, sharp enough; and then I gave myself a good laugh and went below. There I took a look out of the door, which was still open, with the ladder hanging down. I made sure to see the poor old fool come pulling around the point before very long now.

My boots were hurting a little, and, taking them off, I lay down on the cot to rest, and somehow I went to sleep. I had horrible dreams. I saw her again standing in that blood-red kitchen, and she seemed to be washing her hands, and the surf on the ledge was whining up the tower, louder and louder all the time, and what it whined was, "Night after night—night after night." What woke me was cold water in my face.

The storeroom was in gloom. That scared me at first; I thought night had come, and remembered the light. But then I saw the gloom was of a storm. The floor was shining wet, and the water in my face was spray, flung up through the open door. When I ran to close it, it almost made me dizzy to see the gray-and-white breakers marching past. The land was gone; the sky shut down heavy overhead; there was a piece of wreckage on the back of a swell, and the Jacob's ladder was carried clean away. How that sea had picked up so quick I can't think. I looked at my watch, and it wasn't four in the afternoon yet.

When I closed the door, sir, it was almost dark in the storeroom. I'd never been in the light before in a gale of wind. I wondered why I was shivering so, till I found it was the floor below me shivering, and the walls and stair. Horrible crunchings and grindings ran away up the tower, and now and then there was a great thud somewhere, like a cannon shot in a cave. I tell you, sir, I was alone, and I was in a mortal fright for a minute or so. And yet I had to get myself together. There was the light up there not tended to, and an early dark coming on and a heavy night and all, and I had to go. And I had to pass that door.

You'll say it's foolish, sir, and maybe it *was* foolish. Maybe it was because I hadn't eaten. But I began thinking of that door up there the minute I set foot on the stair, and all the way up through that howling dark well I dreaded to pass it. I told myself I wouldn't stop. I didn't stop. I felt the landing underfoot and I went on, four steps, five—and then I couldn't. I turned and went back. I put out my hand and it went on into nothing. That door, sir, was open again.

I left it be; I went on up to the lightroom and set to work. It was bedlam there, sir, screeching bedlam, but I took no notice. I kept my eyes down. I trimmed those seven wicks, sir, as neat as ever they were trimmed; I polished the brass till it shone, and I dusted the lens. It wasn't till that was done that I let myself look back to see who it was standing there, half out of sight in the well. It was her, sir.

"Where'd you come from?" I asked. I remember my voice was sharp.

"Up Jacob's ladder," said she, and hers was like the sirup of flowers.

I shook my head. I was savage, sir. "The ladder's carried away."

"I cast it off," said she, with a smile.

"Then," said I, "you must have come while I was asleep." Another thought came on me heavy as a ton of steel. "And where's *he?*" said I. "Where's the boat?"

"He's drowned," said she, as easy as that. "And I let the boat go adrift. You wouldn't hear me when I called."

"But look here," said I. "If you came through the storeroom, why didn't you wake me up? Tell me that!" It sounds foolish enough, me standing like a lawyer in court, trying to prove she *couldn't* be there.

She didn't answer for a moment. I guess she sighed, though I couldn't hear for the gale, and her eyes grew soft, sir, so soft.

"I couldn't," said she. "You looked so peaceful—dear one."

My cheeks and neck went hot, sir, as if a warm iron was laid on them. I didn't know what to say. I began to stammer: "What do you mean——" but she was going back down the stair, out of sight. My God, sir, and I used not to think she was good-looking!

I started to follow her. I wanted to know what she meant. Then I said to myself, "If I don't go—if I wait here—she'll come back." And I went to the weather side and stood looking out of the window. Not that there was much to see. It was growing dark, and the Seven Brothers looked like the mane of a running horse, a great, vast, white horse running into the wind. The air was awelter with it. I caught one peep of a fisherman, lying down flat trying to weather the ledge, and I said, "God help them all tonight," and then I went hot at sound of that "God."

I was right about her, though. She was back again. I wanted her to speak first, before I turned, but she wouldn't. I didn't hear her go out; I didn't know what she was up to till I saw her coming outside on the walk-around, drenched wet already. I pounded on the glass for her to come in and not be a fool; if she heard she gave no sign of it.

There she stood, and there I stood watching her. Lord, sir—was it just that I'd never had eyes to see? Or are there women who bloom? Her clothes were shining on her, like a carving, and her hair was let down like a golden curtain tossing and streaming in the gale, and there she stood with her lips half open, drinking, and her eyes half closed, gazing straight away over the Seven Brothers, and her shoulders swaying, as if in tune with the wind and water and all the ruin.

And when I looked at her hands over the rail, sir, they were moving in each other as if they bathed, and then I remembered, sir.

A cold horror took me. I knew now why she had come back again. She wasn't a woman—she was a devil. I turned my back on her. I said to myself: "It's time to light up. You've got to light up"—like that, over and over, out loud. My hand was shivering so I could hardly find a match; and when I scratched it, it only flared a second and then went out in the back draft from the open door. She was standing in the doorway, looking at me. It's queer, sir, but I felt like a child caught in mischief.

"I—I—was going to light up," I managed to say, finally.

"Why?" said she. No, I can't say it as she did.

"*Why?*" said I. "*My God!*"

She came nearer, laughing, as if with pity, low, you know. "Your God? And who is your God? What is God? What is anything on a night like this?"

I drew back from her. All I could say anything about was the light.

"Why not the dark?" said she. "Dark is softer than light—tenderer—dearer than light. From the dark up here, away up here in the wind and storm, we can watch the ships go by, you and I. And you love me so. You've loved me so long, Ray."

"I never have!" I struck out at her. "I don't. I don't."

Her voice was lower than ever, but there was the same laughing pity in it. "Oh yes, you have." And she was near me again.

"I have?" I yelled. "I'll show you! I'll show you if I have!"

I got another match, sir, and scratched it on the brass. I gave it to the first wick, the little wick that's inside all the others. It bloomed like a yellow flower. "I *have?*" I yelled, and gave it to the next.

Then there was a shadow, and I saw she was leaning beside me, her two elbows on the brass, her two arms stretched out above the wicks, her bare forearms and wrists and hands. I gave a gasp:

"Take care! You'll burn them! For God's sake——"

She didn't move or speak. The match burned my fingers and went out, and all I could do was stare at those arms of hers, helpless. I'd never noticed her arms before. They were rounded and graceful and covered with a soft down, like a breath of gold. Then I heard her speaking, close to my ear:

"Pretty arms!" she said. "Pretty arms!"

I turned. Her eyes were fixed on mine. They seemed heavy, as if with sleep, and yet between their lids they were two wells, deep and deep, and as if they held all the things I'd ever thought or dreamed in them. I looked away from them, at her lips. Her lips were red as poppies, heavy with redness. They moved, and I heard them speaking:

"Poor boy, you love me so, and you want to kiss me—don't you?"

"No," said I. But I couldn't turn around. I looked at her hair. I'd always thought it was stringy hair. Some hair curls naturally with damp, they say, and perhaps that was it, for there were pearls of wet on it, and it was thick and shimmering around her face, making soft shadows by the temples. There was green in it, queer strands of green like braids.

"What is it?" said I.

"Nothing but weed," said she, with that slow, sleepy smile.

Somehow or other I felt calmer than I had any time. "Look here," said I. "I'm going to light this lamp." I took out a match, scratched it, and touched the third wick. The flame ran around, bigger than the other two together. But still her arms hung there. I bit my lip. "By God, I will!" said I to myself, and I lit the fourth.

It was fierce, sir, fierce! And yet those arms never trembled. I had to look around at her. Her eyes were still looking into mine, so deep and deep, and her red lips were still smiling with that queer sleepy droop; the only thing was that tears were raining down her cheeks—big, showing, jewel tears. It wasn't human, sir. It was like a dream.

"Pretty arms!" she sighed, and then, as if those words had broken something in her heart, there came a great sob bursting from her lips. To hear it drove me mad. I reached to drag her away, but she was too quick, sir; she cringed from me and slipped out from between my hands. It was like she faded away, sir, and went down in a bundle, nursing her poor arms and mourning over them with those terrible, broken sobs.

The sound of them took the manhood out of me—you'd have been the same, sir. I knelt down beside her on the floor and covered my face.

"Please," I moaned. "Please! Please!" That's all I could say. I wanted her to forgive me. I reached out a hand, blind, for forgiveness, and I couldn't find her anywhere. I had hurt her so, and she was afraid of me, of *me*, sir, who loved her so deep it drove me crazy.

I could see her down the stair, though it was dim and my eyes were filled with tears. I stumbled after her, crying, "Please! Please!" The little wicks I'd lit were blowing in the wind from the door and smoking the glass beside them black. One went out. I pleaded with them, the same as I would plead with a human being. I said I'd be back in a second. I promised. And I went on down the stair, crying like a baby because I'd hurt her, and she was afraid of me—of *me*, sir.

She had gone into her room. The door was closed against me and I could hear her sobbing beyond it, brokenhearted. My heart was broken too. I beat on the door with my palms. I begged her to forgive me. I told her I loved her. And all the answer was that sobbing in the dark.

And then I lifted the latch and went in, groping, pleading. "Dearest—please! Because I love you!"

I heard her speak down near the floor. There wasn't any anger in her voice; nothing but sadness and despair.

"No," said she. "You don't love me, Ray. You never have."

"I do! I have!"

"No, no," said she, as if she was tired out.

"Where are you?" I was groping for her. I thought, and lit a match. She had got to the door and was standing there as if ready to fly. I went toward her, and she made me stop. She took my breath away. "I hurt your arms," said I, in a dream.

"No," said she, hardly moving her lips. She held them out to the match's light for me to look, and there was never a scar on them—not even that soft, golden down was singed, sir. "You can't hurt my body," said she, sad as anything. "Only my heart, Ray; my poor heart."

I tell you again, she took my breath away. I lit another match, "How can you be so beautiful?" I wondered.

She answered in riddles—but oh, the sadness of her, sir.

"Because," said she, "I've always so wanted to be."

"How come your eyes so heavy?" said I.

"Because I've seen so many things I never dreamed of," said she.

"How come your hair so thick?"

"It's the seaweed makes it thick," said she, smiling queer, queer.

"How come seaweed there?"

"Out of the bottom of the sea."

She talked in riddles, but it was like poetry to hear her, or a song.

"How come your lips so red?" said I.

"Because they've wanted so long to be kissed."

Fire was on me, sir. I reached out to catch her, but she was gone, out of the door and down the stair. I followed, stumbling. I must have tripped on the turn, for I remember going through the air and fetching up with a crash, and I didn't know anything for a spell—how long I can't say. When I came to, she was there, somewhere, bending over me, crooning, "My love—my love——" under her breath like, a song.

But then, when I got up, she was not where my arms went; she was down the stair again, just ahead of me. I followed her. I was tottering and dizzy and full of pain. I tried to catch up with her in the dark of the storeroom, but she was too quick for me, sir, always a little too quick for me. Oh, she was cruel to me, sir. I kept bumping against things, hurting myself still worse, and it was cold and wet and a horrible noise all the while, sir; and then, sir, I found the door was open, and a sea had parted the hinges.

I don't know how it all went, sir. I'd tell you if I could, but it's all so blurred—sometimes it seems more like a dream. I couldn't find her any more; I couldn't hear her; I went all over, everywhere. Once, I remember, I found myself hanging out of that door between the davits, looking down into those big black seas and crying like a baby. It's all riddles and blur. I can't seem to tell you much, sir. It was all—all—I don't know."

I was talking to somebody else—not her. It was the inspector. I hardly knew it was the inspector. His face was as gray as a blanket, and his eyes were bloodshot, and his lips were twisted. His left wrist hung down, awkward. It was broken coming aboard the light in that sea. Yes, we were in the living room. Yes, sir, it was daylight—gray daylight. I tell you, sir, the man looked crazy to me. He was waving his good arm toward the weather windows, and what he was saying, over and over, was this:

"*Look what you done, damn you! Look what you done!*"

And what I was saying was this:

"*I've lost her!*"

I didn't pay any attention to him, nor him to me. By and by he did, though. He stopped his talking all of a sudden, and his eyes looked like the devil's eyes. He put them up close to mine. He grabbed my arm with his good hand, and I cried, I was so weak.

"Johnson," said he, "is that it? By the living God—if you got a woman out here, Johnson!"

"No," said I. "I've lost her."

"What do you mean—lost her?"

"It was dark," said I—and it's funny how my head was clearing up—"and the door was open—the storeroom door—and I was after her—and I guess she stumbled, maybe—and I lost her."

"Johnson," said he, "what do you mean? You sound crazy—downright crazy. Who?"

"Her," said I. "Fedderson's wife."

"*Who?*"

"Her," said I. And with that he gave my arm another jerk.

"Listen," said he, like a tiger. "Don't try that on me. It won't do any good—that kind of lies—not where *you're* going to. Fedderson and his wife, too—the both of 'em's drowned deader 'n a doornail."

"I know," said I, nodding my head. I was so calm it made him wild.

"You're crazy! Crazy as a loon, Johnson!" And he was chewing his lip red. "I know, because it was me that found the old man laying on Back Water Flats yesterday morning—*me!* And she'd been with him in the boat, too, because he had a piece of her jacket tore off, tangled in his arm."

"I know," said I, nodding again, like that.

"You know what, you *crazy, murdering fool?*" Those were his words to me, sir.

"I know," said I, "what I know."

"And *I* know," said he, "what *I* know."

And there you are, sir. He's inspector. I'm nobody.

Footfalls *

THIS IS NOT AN EASY STORY; NOT A road for tender or for casual feet. Better the meadows. Let me warn you, it is as hard as that old man's soul and as sunless as his eyes. It has its inception in catastrophe, and its end in an act of almost incredible violence; between them it tells barely how a man, being blind, can become also deaf and dumb.

He lived in one of those old Puritan sea towns where the strain has come down austere and moribund, so that his act would not be quite unbelievable. Except that the town is no longer Puritan and Yankee. It has been betrayed; it has become an outpost of the Portuguese islands.

This man, this blind cobbler himself, was a Portuguese, from St. Michael, in the Western Islands, and his name was Boaz Negro.

He was happy. An unquenchable exuberance lived in him. When he arose in the morning he made vast, as it were uncontrollable, gestures with his stout arms. He came into his shop singing. His voice, strong and deep as the chest from which it emanated, rolled out through the doorway and along the street, and the fishermen, done with their morning work and lounging and smoking along the wharfs, said, "Boaz is to work already." Then they came up to sit in the shop.

In that town a cobbler's shop is a club. One sees the interior always dimly thronged. They sit on the benches watching the artisan at his work for hours, and they talk about everything in the world. A cobbler is known by the company he keeps.

Boaz Negro kept young company. He would have nothing to do with the old. On his own head the gray hairs set thickly.

He had a grown son. But the benches in his shop were for the lusty and valiant young, men who could spend the night drinking and then at three o'clock in the morning turn out in the rain and dark to pull at the weirs, sing songs, buffet one another among the slippery fish in the boat's bottom, and make loud jokes about the fundamental things, love and birth and death. Hearkening to their boasts and strong prophecies, his breast heaved and his heart beat faster. He was a large, full-blooded fellow, fashioned for exploits; the flame in his darkness burned higher even to hear of them.

It is scarcely conceivable how Boaz Negro could have come through this much of his life still possessed of that unquenchable and priceless exuberance; how he would sing in the dawn; how, simply listening to the recital of deeds in gale or brawl, he could easily forget himself a blind man, tied to a shop and a last; easily make of himself a lusty young fellow breasting the sunlit and adventurous tide of life.

He had had a wife, whom he had loved. Fate, which had scourged him with the initial scourge of blindness, had seen fit to take his Angelina away. He had had four sons. Three, one after another, had been removed, leaving only Manuel, the youngest. Recovering slowly, with infinite agony, from each of these recurrent blows, his unquenchable exuberance had lived. And there was another thing quite as extraordinary. He had never done anything but work, and that sort of thing may kill the flame where an abrupt catastrophe fails. Work in the dark. Work, work, work! And accompanied by privation; an almost miserly scale of personal economy. Yes, indeed, he had "skinned his fingers," especially in the earlier years. When it tells most.

How he had worked! Not alone in the daytime, but also, sometimes, when orders were heavy, far into the night. It was strange for one, passing along that deserted street at midnight, to hear issuing from the black shop of Boaz Negro the rhythmical tap-tap-tap of hammer on wooden peg.

Nor was that sound all: no man in town could get far past that shop in his nocturnal wandering unobserved. No more than a dozen footfalls, and from the darkness Boaz's voice rolled forth, fraternal, stentorian, "Good night, Antone!" "Good night to you, Caleb Snow!"

To Boaz Negro it was still broad day.

Now, because of this, he was what might be called a substantial man. He owned his place, his shop, opening on the sidewalk, and behind it the dwelling house with trellised galleries upstairs and down.

And there was always something for his son, a "piece for the pocket," a dollar, five, even a ten-dollar bill if he had "got to have it." Manuel was "a good boy." Boaz not only said this; he felt that he was assured of it in his understanding, to the infinite peace of his heart.

It was curious that he should be ignorant only of the one nearest to him. Not because he was physically blind. Be certain he knew more of other men and of other men's sons than they or their neighbors did. More, that is to say, of their hearts, their understandings, their idiosyncrasies, and their ultimate weight in the balance pan of eternity.

His simple explanation of Manuel was that Manuel "wasn't too stout." To others he said this, and to himself. Manuel was not indeed too robust. How should he be vigorous when he never did anything to make him so? He never worked. Why should he work, when existence was provided for, and when there was always that "piece for the pocket"? Even a ten-dollar bill on a Saturday night! No. Manuel "wasn't too stout."

In the shop they let it go at that. The missteps and frailties of everyone else in the world were canvassed there with the most shameless publicity. But Boaz Negro was a blind man, and in a sense their host. Those reckless, strong young fellows respected and loved him. It was allowed to stand at that. Manuel was "a good boy." Which did not prevent them, by the way, from joining later in the general condemnation of that father's laxity—"the ruination of the boy!"

"He should have put him to work, that's what."

"He should have said to Manuel, 'Look here, if you want a dollar, go earn it first.' "

As a matter of fact, only one man ever gave Boaz the advice direct. That was Campbell Wood. And Wood never sat in that shop.

In every small town there is one young man who is spoken of as "rising." As often as not he is not a native, but "from away."

In this town Campbell Wood was that man. He had come from

another part of the state to take a place in the bank. He lived in the upper story of Boaz Negro's house, the ground floor now doing for Boaz and the meager remnant of his family. The old woman who came in to tidy up for the cobbler looked after Wood's rooms as well.

Dealing with Wood, one had first of all the sense of his incorruptibility. A little ruthless perhaps, as if one could imagine him, in defense of his integrity, cutting off his friend, cutting off his own hand, cutting off the very stream flowing out from the wellsprings of human kindness. An exaggeration, perhaps.

He was by long odds the most eligible young man in town, good-looking in a spare, ruddy, sandy-haired Scottish fashion, important, incorruptible, "rising." But he took good care of his heart. Precisely that; like a sharp-eyed duenna to his own heart. One felt that here was the man, if ever was the man, who held his destiny in his own hand. Failing, of course, some quite gratuitous and unforeseeable catastrophe.

Not that he was not human, or even incapable of laughter or passion. He was, in a way, immensely accessible. He never clapped one on the shoulder; on the other hand, he never failed to speak. Not even to Boaz.

Returning from the bank in the afternoon, he had always a word for the cobbler. Passing out again to supper at his boarding place, he had another, about the weather, the prospects of rain. And if Boaz was at work in the dark when he returned from an evening at the Board of Trade, there was a "Good night, Mr. Negro!"

On Boaz's part, his attitude toward his lodger was curious and paradoxical. He did not pretend to anything less than reverence for the young man's position; precisely on account of that position he was conscious toward Wood of a vague distrust. This was because he was an uneducated fellow.

To the uneducated the idea of large finance is as uncomfortable as the idea of the law. It must be said for Boaz that, responsive to Wood's unfailing civility, he fought against the sensation of dim and somehow shameful distrust.

Nevertheless his whole parental soul was in arms that evening when, returning from the bank and finding the shop empty of loungers, Wood paused a moment to propose the bit of advice already referred to.

"Haven't you ever thought of having Manuel learn the trade?"

A suspicion, a kind of premonition, lighted the fires of defense.

"Shoemaking," said Boaz, "is good enough for a blind man."

"Oh, I don't know. At least it's better than doing nothing at all."

Boaz's hammer was still. He sat silent, monumental. Outwardly. For once his unfailing response had failed him, "Manuel ain't too stout, you know." Perhaps it had become suddenly inadequate.

He hated Wood; he despised Wood; more than ever before, a hundredfold more, quite abruptly, he distrusted Wood.

How could a man say such things as Wood had said? And where Manuel himself might hear!

Where Manuel had heard! Boaz's other emotions—hatred and contempt and distrust—were overshadowed. Sitting in darkness, no sound had come to his ears, no footfall, no infinitesimal creaking of a floor plank. Yet by some sixth uncanny sense of the blind he was aware that Manuel was standing in the dusk of the entry joining the shop to the house.

Boaz made a Herculean effort. The voice came out of his throat, harsh, bitter, and loud enough to have carried ten times the distance to his son's ears.

"Manuel is a good boy!"

"Yes—h'm—yes—I suppose so."

Wood shifted his weight. He seemed uncomfortable.

"Well, I'll be running along, I—ugh! Heavens!"

Something was happening. Boaz heard exclamations, breathings, the rustle of sleeve cloth in large, frantic, and futile graspings—all without understanding. Immediately there was an impact on the floor, and with it the unmistakable clink of metal. Boaz even heard that the metal was minted, and that the coins were gold. He understood. A coin sack, gripped not quite carefully enough for a moment under the other's overcoat, had shifted, slipped, escaped, and fallen.

And Manuel had heard!

It was a dreadful moment for Boaz, dreadful in its native sense, as full of dread. Why? It was a moment of horrid revelation, ruthless clarification. His son, his link with the departed Angelina, that "good boy"—Manuel, standing in the shadow of the entry, visible alone to the blind, had heard the clink of falling gold, and—and Boaz wished that he had not!

There, amazing, disconcerting, destroying, stood the sudden fact.

Sitting as impassive and monumental as ever, his strong, bleached hands at rest on his work, round drops of sweat came out on Boaz's forehead. He scarcely took the sense of what Wood was saying. Only fragments.

"Government money, understand–for the breakwater workings–huge–too many people know, here, everywhere–don't trust the safe –tin safe–'Noah's Ark'–give you my word–heavens, no!"

It boiled down to this–the money, more money than was good for that antiquated "Noah's Ark" at the bank–and whose contemplated sojourn there overnight was public to too many minds–in short, Wood was not only incorruptible, he was canny. To what one of those minds, now, would it occur that he should take away that money bodily, under casual cover of his coat, to his own lodgings behind the cobbler shop of Boaz Negro? For this one, this important, night!

He was sorry the coin sack had slipped, because he did not like to have the responsibility of secret sharer cast upon anyone, even upon Boaz, even by accident. On the other hand, how tremendously fortunate that it had been Boaz and not another. So far as that went, Wood had no more anxiety now than before. One incorruptible knows another.

"I'd trust you, Mr. Negro" (that was one of the fragments which came and stuck in the cobbler's brain), "as far as I would myself. As long as it's only you. I'm just going up here and throw it under the bed. Oh yes, certainly."

Boaz ate no supper. For the first time in his life food was dry in his gullet. Even under those other successive crushing blows of Fate the full and generous habit of his functionings had carried on unabated; he had always eaten what was set before him. Tonight, over his untouched plate, he watched Manuel with his sightless eyes, keeping track of his every mouthful, word, intonation, breath. What profit he expected to extract from this catlike surveillance it is impossible to say.

When they arose from the supper table Boaz made another Herculean effort. "Manuel, you're a good boy!"

The formula had a quality of appeal, of despair, and of command.

"Manuel, you should be short of money, maybe. Look, what's this? A tenner? Well, there's a piece for the pocket; go and enjoy yourself."

He would have been frightened had Manuel, upsetting tradition, declined the offering. With the morbid contrariness of the human imagination, the boy's avid grasping gave him no comfort.

He went out into the shop, where it was already dark, drew to him his last, his tools, mallets, cutters, pegs, leather. And having prepared to work, he remained idle. He found himself listening.

It has been observed that the large phenomena of sunlight and darkness were nothing to Boaz Negro. A busy night was broad day. Yet there was a difference; he knew it with the blind man's eyes, the ears.

Day was a vast confusion, or rather a wide fabric, of sounds; great and little sounds all woven together, voices, footfalls, wheels, far-off whistles and foghorns, flies buzzing in the sun. Night was another thing. Still there were voices and footfalls, but rare, emerging from the large, pure body of silence as definite, surprising, and yet familiar entities.

Tonight there was an easterly wind coming off the water and carrying the sound of waves. So far as other fugitive sounds were concerned it was the same as silence. The wind made little difference to the ears. It nullified, from one direction at least, the other two visual processes of the blind, the sense of touch and the sense of smell. It blew away from the shop, toward the living house.

As has been said, Boaz found himself listening, scrutinizing with an extraordinary attention this immense background of sound. He heard footfalls. The story of that night was written, for him, in footfalls.

He heard them moving about the house, the lower floor, prowling here, there, halting for long spaces, advancing, retreating softly on the planks. About this aimless, interminable perambulation there was something to twist the nerves, something led and at the same time driven, like a succession of frail and indecisive charges.

Boaz lifted himself from his chair. All his impulse called him to make a stir, join battle, cast in the breach the reinforcement of his presence, authority, good will. He sank back again; his hands fell down. The curious impotence of the spectator held him.

He heard footfalls, too, on the upper floor, a little fainter, borne to the inner rather than the outer ear, along the solid causeway of partitions and floor, the legs of his chair, the bony framework of his body. Very faint indeed. Sinking back easily into the background of the wind. They, too, came and went, this room, that, to the passage, the stairhead, and away. About them too there was the same quality of being led and at the same time of being driven.

Time went by. In his darkness it seemed to Boaz that hours must have passed. He heard voices. Together with the footfalls, that abrupt, brief, and (in view of Wood's position) astounding interchange of sentences made up his history of the night. Wood must have opened the door at the head of the stair; by the sound of his voice he would be standing there, peering below perhaps; perhaps listening.

"What's wrong down there?" he called. "Why don't you go to bed?"

After a moment came Manuel's voice, "Ain't sleepy."

"Neither am I. Look here, do you like to play cards?"

"What kind? Euchre? I like euchre all right. Or pitch."

"Well, what would you say to coming up and having a game of pitch then, Manuel? If you can't sleep?"

"That'd be all right."

The lower footfalls ascended to join the footfalls on the upper floor. There was the sound of a door closing.

Boaz sat still. In the gloom he might have been taken for a piece of furniture, of machinery, an extraordinary lay figure, perhaps, for the trying on of the boots he made. He seemed scarcely to breathe, only the sweat starting from his brow giving him an aspect of life.

He ought to have run, and leaped up that inner stair and pounded with his fists on that door. He seemed unable to move. At rare intervals feet passed on the sidewalk outside, just at his elbow, so to say, and yet somehow, tonight, immeasurably far away. Beyond the orbit of the moon. He heard Rugg, the policeman, noting the silence of the shop, muttering, "Boaz is to bed tonight," as he passed.

The wind increased. It poured against the shop with its deep, continuous sound of a river. Submerged in its body, Boaz caught the note of the town bell striking midnight.

Once more, after a long time, he heard footfalls. He heard them coming around the corner of the shop from the house, footfalls half swallowed by the wind, passing discreetly, without haste, retreating, merging step by step with the huge, incessant background of the wind.

Boaz's muscles tightened all over him. He had the impulse to start up, to fling open the door, shout into the night, "What are you doing? Stop there! Say! What are you doing and where are you going?"

And as before, the curious impotence of the spectator held him motionless. He had not stirred in his chair. And those footfalls, upon which hinged, as it were, that momentous decade of his life, were gone.

There was nothing to listen for now. Yet he continued to listen. Once or twice, half arousing himself, he drew toward him his unfinished work. And then relapsed into immobility.

As has been said, the wind, making little difference to the ears, made all the difference in the world with the sense of feeling and the sense of smell. From the one important direction of the house. That is how it could come about that Boaz Negro could sit, waiting and listening to nothing, in the shop and remain ignorant of disaster until the alarm had gone away and come back again, pounding, shouting, clanging.

"Fire!" he heard them bawling in the street. "Fire! Fire!"

Only slowly did he understand that the fire was in his own house.

There is nothing stiller in the world than the skeleton of a house in the dawn after a fire. It is as if everything living, positive, violent, had been completely drained in the one flaming act of violence, leaving nothing but negation till the end of time. It is worse than a tomb. A monstrous stillness! Even the footfalls of the searchers cannot disturb it, for they are separate and superficial. In its presence they are almost frivolous.

Half an hour after dawn the searchers found the body, if what was left from that consuming ordeal might be called a body. The discovery came as a shock. It seemed incredible that the occupant of that house, no cripple or invalid, but an able man in the prime of youth, should not have awakened and made good his escape. It was the upper floor which had caught; the stairs had stood to the last. It was beyond calculation. Even if he had been asleep!

And he had not been asleep. This second and infinitely more appalling discovery began to be known. Slowly. By a hint, a breath of rumor here; there an allusion, half taken back. The man whose incinerated body still lay curled in its bed of cinders had been dressed at the moment of disaster; even to the watch, the cuff buttons, the studs, the very scarf pin. Fully clothed to the last detail, precisely as those who had dealings at the bank might have seen Campbell Wood any weekday morning for the past eight months. A man does not sleep with his clothes on. The skull of the man had been broken, as if with a blunt instrument of iron. On the charred lacework of the floor lay the leg of an old andiron with which Boaz Negro and his Angelina had set up housekeeping in that new house.

It needed only Mr. Asa Whitelaw, coming up the street from that gaping "Noah's Ark" at the bank, to round out the scandalous circle of circumstance.

"Where is Manuel?"

Boaz Negro still sat in his shop, impassive, monumental, his thick, hairy arms resting on the arms of his chair. The tools and materials of his work remained scattered about him, as his irresolute gathering of the night before had left them. Into his eyes no change could come. He had lost his house, the visible monument of all those years of "skinning his fingers." It would seem that he had lost his son. And he had lost something incalculably precious—that hitherto unquenchable exuberance of the man.

"Where is Manuel?"

When he spoke his voice was unaccented and stale, like the voice of a man already dead.

"Yes, where is Manuel?"

He had answered them with their own question.

"When did you last see him?"

Neither he nor they seemed to take note of that profound irony.

"At supper."

"Tell us, Boaz, you knew about this money?"

The cobbler nodded his head.

"And did Manuel?"

He might have taken sanctuary in a legal doubt. How did he know what Manuel knew? Precisely! As before, he nodded his head.

"After supper, Boaz, you were in the shop? But you heard something?"

"Yes."

He went on to tell them what he had heard, the footfalls, below and above, the extraordinary conversation which had broken for a moment the silence of the inner hall. The account was bare, the phrases monosyllabic. He reported only what had been registered on the sensitive tympanums of his ears, to the last whisper of footfalls stealing past the dark wall of the shop. Of all the formless tangle of thoughts, suspicions, interpretations, and the special and personal knowledge given to the blind which moved in his brain, he said nothing.

He shut his lips there. He felt himself on the defensive. Just as he distrusted the higher ramifications of finance (his house had gone down uninsured), so before the rites and processes of that inscrutable creature, the law, he felt himself menaced by the invisible and the unknown, helpless, oppressed; in an abject sense, skeptical.

"Keep clear of the law!" they had told him in his youth. The monster his imagination had summoned then still stood beside him in his age.

Having exhausted his monosyllabic and superficial evidence, they could move him no farther. He became deaf and dumb. He sat before them, an image cast in some immensely heavy stuff, inanimate. His lack of visible emotion impressed them. Remembering his exuberance, it was only the stranger to see him unmoving and unmoved. Only once did they catch sight of something beyond. As they were preparing to leave he opened his mouth. What he said was like a swan song to the years of his exuberant happiness. Even now there was no color of expression in his words, which sounded mechanical.

"Now I have lost everything. My house. My last son. Even my honor. You would not think I would like to live. But I go to live. I go to work. That *cachorra*, one day he shall come back again, in the dark night, to have a look. I shall go to show you all. That *cachorra!*"

(And from that time on, it was noted, he never referred to the fugitive by any other name than *cachorra*, which is a gender of dog. "That *cachorra!*" As if he had forfeited the relationship not only of the family, but of the very genus, the very race! "That *cachorra!*")

He pronounced this resolution without passion. When they assured him that the culprit would come back again indeed, much sooner than he expected, "with a rope around his neck," he shook his head slowly.

"No, you shall not catch that *cachorra* now. But one day . . ."

There was something about its very colorlessness which made it sound oracular. It was at least prophetic. They searched, laid their traps, proceeded with all their placards, descriptions, rewards, clues, trails. But on Manuel Negro they never laid their hands.

Months passed and became years. Boaz Negro did not rebuild his house. He might have done so, out of his earnings, for upon himself he spent scarcely anything, reverting to his old habit of an almost miserly economy. Yet perhaps it would have been harder after all. For his earnings were less and less. In that town a cobbler who sits in an empty shop is apt to want for trade. Folk take their boots to mend where they take their bodies to rest and their minds to be edified.

No longer did the walls of Boaz's shop resound to the boastful recollections of young men. Boaz had changed. He had become not only different, but opposite. A metaphor will do best. The spirit of Boaz Negro had been a meadowed hillside giving upon the open sea, the sun, the warm, wild winds from beyond the blue horizon. And covered with flowers, always hungry and thirsty for the sun and the fabulous wind and bright showers of rain. It had become an entrenched camp, lying silent, sullen, verdureless, under a gray sky. He stood solitary against the world. His approaches were closed. He was blind, and he was also deaf and dumb.

Against that, what can young fellows do who wish for nothing but to rest themselves and talk about their friends and enemies? They had come and they had tried. They had raised their voices even higher than before. Their boasts had grown louder, more presumptuous, more preposterous, until, before the cold separation of that unmoving and as if contemptuous presence in the cobbler's chair, they burst of their own air, like toy balloons. And they went and left Boaz alone.

There was another thing which served, if not to keep them away, at least not to entice them back. That was the aspect of the place. It was not cheerful. It invited no one. In its way that fire-bitten ruin grew to be almost as great a scandal as the act itself had been. It was plainly an eyesore. A valuable property, on the town's main thoroughfare—and an eyesore! The neighboring owners protested.

Their protestations might as well have gone against a stone wall. That man was deaf and dumb. He had become, in a way, a kind of vegetable, for the quality of a vegetable is that, while it is endowed with life, it remains fixed in one spot. For years Boaz was scarcely seen to move foot out of that shop which was left him, a small, square, blistered promontory on the shores of ruin.

He must indeed have carried out some rudimentary sort of a domestic program under the debris at the rear (he certainly did not sleep or eat in the shop). One or two lower rooms were left fairly intact. The outward aspect of the place was formless; it grew to be no more than a mound in time; the charred timbers, one or two still standing, lean and naked against the sky, lost their blackness and faded to a silvery gray. It would have seemed strange, had they not grown accustomed to the thought, to imagine that blind man, like a mole, or some slow slug, turning himself mysteriously in the bowels of that gray mound—that time-silvered "eyesore."

When they saw him, however, he was in the shop. They opened the door to take in their work (when other cobblers turned them off), and they saw him seated in his chair in the half-darkness, his whole person, legs, torso, neck, head, as motionless as the vegetable of which we have spoken—only his hands and his bare arms endowed with visible life. The gloom had bleached the skin to the color of damp ivory, and against the background of his immobility they moved with a certain amazing monstrousness, interminably. No, they were never still. One wondered what they could be at. Surely he could not have had enough work now to keep those insatiable hands so monstrously in motion. Even far into the night. Tap-tap-tap! Blows continuous and powerful. On what? On nothing? On the bare iron last? And for what purpose? To what conceivable end?

Well, one could imagine those arms, growing paler, also growing thicker and more formidable with that unceasing labor; the muscles feeding themselves omnivorously on their own waste, the cords toughening, the bone tissues revitalizing themselves without end. One could imagine the whole aspiration of that mute and motionless man pouring itself out into those pallid arms, and the arms taking it up with a kind of blind greed. Storing it up. Against a day!

"That *cachorra!* One day . . ."

What were the thoughts of the man? What moved within that motionless cranium covered with long hair? Who can say? Behind everything, of course, stood that bitterness against the world—the blind world—blinder than he would ever be. And against "that *cachorra*." But this was no longer a thought; it was the man.

Just as all muscular aspiration flowed into his arms, so all the energies of his senses turned to his ears. The man had become, you might say, two arms and two ears. Can you imagine a man listening, intently, through the waking hours of nine years?

Listening to footfalls. Marking with a special emphasis of concentration the beginning, rise, full passage, falling away, and dying of all the footfalls. By day, by night, winter and summer and winter again. Unraveling the skein of footfalls passing up and down the street!

For three years he wondered when they would come. For the next three years he wondered if they would ever come. It was during the last three that a doubt began to trouble him. It gnawed at his huge moral strength. Like a hidden seepage of water, it undermined (in anticipation) his terrible resolution. It was a sign perhaps of age, a slipping away of the reckless infallibility of youth.

Supposing, after all, that his ears should fail him? Supposing they were capable of being tricked, without his being able to know it? Supposing that that *cachorra* should come and go, and he, Boaz, living in some vast delusion, some unrealized distortion of memory, should let him pass unknown? Supposing precisely this thing had already happened!

Or the other way around. What if he should hear the footfalls coming, even into the very shop itself? What if he should be as sure of them as of his own soul? What, then, if he should strike? And what, then, if it were not that *cachorra* after all? How many tens and hundreds of millions of people were there in the world? Was it possible for them all to have footfalls distinct and different?

Then they would take him and hang him. And that *cachorra* might then come and go at his own will, undisturbed.

As he sat there sometimes the sweat rolled down his nose, cold as rain.

Supposing!

Sometimes, quite suddenly, in broad day, in the booming silence of the night, he would start. Not outwardly. But beneath the pale integument of his skin all his muscles tightened and his nerves sang. His breathing stopped. It seemed almost as if his heart stopped.

Was that it? Were those the feet, there, emerging faintly from the distance? Yes, there was something about them. Yes! Memory was in travail. Yes, yes, yes! No! How could he be sure? Ice ran down into his empty eyes. The footfalls were already passing. They were gone, swallowed up already by time and space. Had that been that *cachorra?*

Nothing in his life had been so hard to meet as this insidious drain of distrust in his own powers; this sense of a traitor within the walls. His iron-gray hair had turned white. It was always this now, from the beginning of the day to the end of the night; how was he to know? How was he to be inevitably, unshakably sure?

Curiously, after all this purgatory of doubts, he did know them. For a moment at least, when he had heard them, he was unshakably sure.

It was on an evening of the winter holidays, the Portuguese festival of Menin' Jesus. Christ was born again in a hundred mangers on a hundred tiny altars; there was cake and wine; songs went shouting by to the accompaniment of mandolins and tramping feet. The wind blew cold under a clear sky. In all the houses there were lights; even in Boaz Negro's shop a lamp was lit just now, for a man had been in for a pair of boots which Boaz had patched. The man had gone out again. Boaz was thinking of blowing out the light. It meant nothing to him.

He leaned forward, judging the position of the lamp chimney by the heat on his face, and puffed out his cheeks to blow. Then his cheeks collapsed suddenly, and he sat back again.

It was not odd that he had failed to hear the footfalls until they were actually within the door. A crowd of merrymakers was passing just then; their songs and tramping almost shook the shop.

Boaz sat back. Beneath his passive exterior his nerves thrummed; his muscles had grown as hard as wood. Yes! Yes! But no! He had heard nothing; no more than a single step, a single foot pressure on the planks within the door. Dear God! He could not tell!

Going through the pain of an enormous effort, he opened his lips. "What can I do for you?"

"Well, I–I don't know. To tell the truth––"

The voice was unfamiliar, but it might be assumed. Boaz held himself. His face remained blank, interrogating, slightly helpless.

"I am a little deaf," he said. "Come nearer."

The footfalls came halfway across the intervening floor, and there appeared to hesitate. The voice, too, had a note of uncertainty.

"I was just looking around. I have a pair of–well, you mend shoes?"

Boaz nodded his head. It was not in response to the words, for they meant nothing. What he had heard were the footfalls on the floor.

Now he was sure. As has been said, for a moment at least after he had heard them he was unshakably sure. The congestion of his muscles had passed. He was at peace.

The voice became audible once more. Before the massive preoccupation of the blind man it became still less certain of itself.

"Well, I haven't got the shoes with me. I was—just looking around."

It was amazing to Boaz, this miraculous sensation of peace.

"Wait!" Then, bending his head as if listening to the winter wind, "It's cold tonight. You've left the door open. But wait!" Leaning down, his hand fell on a rope's end hanging by the chair. The gesture was one continuous, undeviating movement of the hand. No hesitation. No groping. How many hundreds, how many thousands of times had his hand schooled itself in that gesture!

A single strong pull. With a little bang the front door had swung to and latched itself. Not only the front door. The other door, leading to the rear, had closed too and latched itself with a little bang. And leaning forward from his chair, Boaz blew out the light.

There was not a sound in the shop. Outside, feet continued to go by, ringing on the frozen road; voices were lifted; the wind hustled about the corners of the wooden shell with a continuous, shrill note of whistling. All of this outside, as on another planet. Within the blackness of the shop the complete silence persisted.

Boaz listened. Sitting on the edge of his chair, half couching, his head, with its long, unkempt white hair, bent slightly to one side, he concentrated upon this chambered silence the full powers of his senses. He hardly breathed. The other person in that room could not be breathing at all, it seemed.

No, there was not a breath, not the stirring of a sole on wood, not the infinitesimal rustle of any fabric. It was as if in this utter stoppage of sound, even the blood had ceased to flow in the veins and arteries of that man, who was like a rat caught in a trap.

It was appalling even to Boaz; even to the cat. Listening became more than a labor. He began to have to fight against a growing impulse to shout out loud, to leap, sprawl forward without aim in that unstirred darkness—do something. Sweat rolled down from behind his ears, into his shirt collar. He gripped the chair arms. To keep quiet he sank his teeth into his lower lip. He would not! He would not!

And of a sudden he heard before him, in the center of the room, an outburst of breath, an outrush from lungs in the extremity of pain, thick, laborious, fearful. A coughing up of dammed air.

Pushing himself from the arms of the chair, Boaz leaped.

His fingers, passing swiftly through the air, closed on something. It was a sheaf of hair, bristly and thick. It was a man's beard.

On the road outside, up and down the street for a hundred yards, merrymaking people turned to look at one another. With an abrupt cessation of laughter, of speech. Inquiringly. Even with an unconscious dilation of the pupils of their eyes.

"What was that?"

There had been a scream. There could be no doubt of that. A single, long-drawn note. Immensely high-pitched. Not as if it were human.

"God's sake! What was that? Where'd it come from?"

Those nearest said it came from the cobbler shop of Boaz Negro.

They went and tried the door. It was closed; even locked, as if for the night. There was no light behind the window shade. But Boaz would not have a light. They beat on the door. No answer.

But from where, then, had that prolonged, as if animal, note come?

They ran about, penetrating into the side lanes, interrogating, prying. Coming back at last, inevitably, to the neighborhood of Boaz Negro's shop.

The body lay on the floor at Boaz's feet, where it had tumbled down slowly after a moment from the spasmodic embrace of his arms; those ivory-colored arms which had beaten so long upon the bare iron surface of a last. Blows continuous and powerful! It seemed incredible. They were so weak now. They could not have lifted the hammer now.

But that beard! That bristly, thick, square beard of a stranger!

His hands remembered it. Standing with his shoulders fallen forward and his weak arms hanging down, Boaz began to shiver. The whole thing was incredible. What was on the floor there, upheld in the vast gulf of darkness, he could not see. Neither could he hear it; smell it. Nor (if he did not move his foot) could he feel it. What he did not hear, smell, or touch did not exist. It was not there. Incredible!

But that beard! All the accumulated doubtings of those years fell down upon him. After all, the thing he had been so fearful of in his weak imaginings had happened. He had killed a stranger. He, Boaz Negro, had murdered an innocent man!

And all on account of that beard. His deep panic made him light-headed. He began to confuse cause and effect. If it were not for that beard, it would have been that *cachorra.*

On this basis he began to reason with a crazy directness. And to act. He went and pried open the door into the entry. From a shelf he took down his razor. A big, heavy-heeled blade, made long ago for a beard which turned the jaw black again an hour after shaving. And the old, brown, polished strop. His hands began to hurry. And the mug, half full of soap. And water. It would have to be cold water. But after all, he thought (lightheadedly), at this time of night . . .

Outside, they were at the shop again. The crowd's habit is to forget a thing quickly, once it is out of sight and hearing. But there had been something about that solitary cry which continued to bother them, even in memory. Where had it been? Where had it come from? And those who had stood nearest the cobbler shop were heard again. They were certain now, dead certain. They could swear!

In the end they broke down the door.

If Boaz heard them he gave no sign. An absorption as complete as it was monstrous wrapped him. Kneeling in the glare of the lantern they had brought, as impervious as his own shadow sprawling behind him, he continued to shave the dead man on the floor.

No one touched him. Their minds and imaginations were arrested by the gigantic proportions of the act. The unfathomable presumption of the act. As throwing murder in their faces to the tune of a jig in a barbershop. It is a fact that none of them so much as thought of touching him. No less than all of them, together with all other men, shorn of their imaginations—that is to say, the expressionless and imperturbable creature of the Law—would be sufficient to touch that ghastly man.

On the other hand, they could not leave him alone. They could not go away. They watched. They saw the damp, lather-soaked beard of that victimized stranger falling away, stroke by stroke of the flashing, heavy razor. The dead denuded by the blind!

It was seen that Boaz was about to speak. It was something important he was to utter; something, one would say, fatal. The words would not come all at once. They swelled his cheeks out. His razor was arrested. Lifting his face, he encircled the watchers with a gaze at once of imploration and of command. As if he could see them. As if he could read his answer in the expressions of their faces.

"Tell me one thing now. Is it that *cachorra?*"

For the first time those men in the room made sounds. They shuffled their feet. It was as if an uncontrollable impulse to ejaculation, laughter, derision, forbidden by the presence of death, had gone down into their boot soles.

"Manuel?" one of them said. "You mean *Manuel?*"

Boaz laid the razor down on the floor beside its work. He got up from his knees slowly, as if his joints hurt. He sat down in his chair, rested his hands on the arms, and once more encircled the company with his sightless gaze.

"Not Manuel. Manuel was a good boy. But tell me now, is it that *cachorra?*"

Here was something out of their calculations; something for them, mentally, to chew on. Mystification is a good thing sometimes. It gives the brain a fillip, stirs memory, puts the gears of imagination in mesh. One man, an old, tobacco-chewing fellow, began to stare harder at the face on the floor. Something moved in his intellect.

"No, but look here now, by God——"

He had even stopped chewing. But he was forestalled by another.

"Say now, if it don't look like that fellow Wood, himself. The bank fellow—that was burned—remember? Himself."

"That *cachorra* was not burned. Not that Wood. You damned fool!"

Boaz spoke from his chair. They hardly knew his voice, emerging from its long silence; it was so didactic and arid.

"That *cachorra* was not burned. It was my boy that was burned. It was that *cachorra* called my boy upstairs. That *cachorra* killed my boy. That *cachorra* put his clothes on my boy, and he set my house on fire. I knew that all the time. Because when I heard those feet come out of my house and go away, I knew they were the feet of that *cachorra* from the bank. I did not know where he was going to. Something said to me, 'You better ask him where he is going to.' But then I said, 'You are foolish.' He had the money from the bank. I did not know. And then my house was on fire. No, it was not my boy that went away; it was that *cachorra* all the time. You damned fools! Did you think I was waiting for my own boy?

"Now I show you all," he said at the end. "And now I can get hanged."

No one ever touched Boaz Negro for that murder. For murder it was in the eye and letter of the Law. But the Law in a small town is sometimes a curious creature; it is sometimes blind only in one eye.

Their minds and imaginations in that town were arrested by the romantic proportions of the act. Simply, no one took it up. I believe the man, Wood, was understood to have died of heart failure.

When they asked Boaz why he had not told what he knew as to the identity of that fugitive in the night, he seemed to find it hard to say exactly. How could a man of no education define for them his own but half-defined misgivings about the Law, his sense of oppression, constraint, and awe, of being on the defensive, even, in an abject way, his skepticism? About his wanting, come what might, to "keep clear of the Law"?

He did say this, "You would have laughed at me."

And this, "If I told folks it was Wood went away, then I say he would not dare come back again."

That was the last. Very shortly he began to refuse to talk about the thing at all. The act was completed. Like the creature of fable, it had consumed itself. Out of that old man's consciousness it had departed. Amazingly. Like a dream dreamed out.

Slowly at first, in a makeshift, piece-at-a-time, poor man's way, Boaz commenced to rebuild his house. That "eyesore" vanished.

And slowly at first, like the miracle of a green shoot pressing out from the dead earth, that priceless and unquenchable exuberance of the man was seen returning. Unquenchable, after all.

*Out of the Wind**

MOLLY WAS HARDLY A YEAR OLD when her sister Ray was born; they might almost have been twins. As they grew the one was light, the other dark. Molly's eyes, under the golden drift of her hair, were the gray eyes of fathers watching the ocean's rim for whales that came; Ray's eyes had in their darkness the bedeviled vigilance of mothers watching the ocean's rim for ships that never came.

These two were sunshine and shadow hand in hand. Like the whiteness of sheep on the dark mat of the island moor that was their playground, like the slowly tumbling arabesque of little cloud shapes drifting across the sand cliffs on a summer wind, neither was anything without the other. It was the other that was pretty as a picture. It was the other that made play fun, that brought dolls to life, sweetened the breath of the arbutus in springtime and reddened the huckleberry brakes in the fall. It was the other, when their swift quarrels were dissolved, that had been the harmed.

They lived out of town, to the southward, on Candle Hill. All they could see of the village from Candle Hill was the tower of Center Church and the masts of vessels lying at the upshore wharves. Their father's house was plain, square, and high to the eaves, in the fair proportions of the days when boys had killed their whales off Chile, danced with the maidens of the Marquesas, and seen the mountain of Africa, before ever they had set foot on the continent of America, visible on a clear day across the Sound.

Behind the house and on either side of it were locust trees and poplars, and a wistaria vine, as big around at the base as a man's thigh, climbed to the chamber windows at the front. In leaf time all this arborescence kept up a rustle like another and airier surf even in the stillest night; in the winter, when the winds rushed in from the dark Atlantic, trunk and bough and twig, the trees made harps, and the harps made a giant and wild and mournful music that came through the clapboards to the girls hidden in the walnut bed in the southeast chamber, their hearts thrilled, their arms about each other, safe.

This room of theirs was big and square, like the house, and plain and uncrowded. Paper with figures of little flowers on it covered a portion of the walls, but the greater part was done in paneling, expanses ivory white and serenely subdivided in low relief, solid-looking, and, were an ember left to redden on the hearth, warm-looking, so that though the sound of the gale came in to the sisters nothing else of it could come; nothing from the outside could get them once the shutters and the doors were closed and the four strong walls complete around them, the comfort pulled up dark over their heads and their secrets told.

Here they were secure not only from the world of the wind out of doors, but also from the world of the father and mother (or when their father had died, of their mother alone), who sat downstairs. And this is no little thing.

Ray was seventeen, Molly was eighteen, Eddie Franklin was twenty. Eddie's grandfather, starting around the globe as third mate in a nor'westman at seventeen, had returned at Eddie's age her master in broadcloth and buttons and beaver hat, with a roll of money, a chest of hyson, a set of Canton, and a wooden leg. Eddie, gone as far south as the Delaware Breakwater in a mackerel netter, was home with a roll of money, a hairline serge, a derby, and a crocheted four-in-hand.

Times and styles may change, but never the light of stars and never the heart of youth. The same stars that had shone on the broad shoulders of one sea conqueror shone on the shoulders of another now, as Eddie leaned on the post of the steps at the house on Candle Hill, content in the eyes of the pretty Coffin girls.

It was Maytime, Maytime. On the clapboard rise of the house the wistaria, looking black in the little light, gave off a perfume of flowers that got into the throat and into the heart. And Ray, when she had sat there for a long time on the top step, her fingers locked tight in Molly's and her eyes wistfully on the strong, adventurous beauty of the man, decided, and bit her lip, and turned her face.

She turned her face and looked at Molly, the elder, the lovelier, the first, the golden girl whose stillness was like the earth that bore the two of them secure through space. Tears, sudden and burning hot, filled the black eyes under the black lashes. Taking her hand out of Molly's, she got down the steps and walked to the corner of the house, leaving the princess and the prince alone.

"Where you going, Ray?"

"I just remembered, Molly, I didn't shut the chicken pens tonight."

Once out of sight she ran, a sob in her throat and salt on her lips. She ran through the shallow grove of locusts and poplars; she ran on out across the open plain.

But then she was astonished; her pulse leaped with dismay. "But no!" she began to cry to herself. For where there should have been only the whisper of wind-bowed grasses behind her she heard the footfalls of Eddie following. "But no, no, no!" She should have had the swiftness to fly on a wind he could never follow; bewildered, she had no strength at all. "But yes, yes, yes!"

When the girls were in bed that night, the lamp out and the fragrance of the vine under the sills of the open windows hanging like a sick oppression in the room, they both lay quiet and straight for a long while. By and by it was Molly that spoke.

"Did he kiss you?"

"Why, Molly! As if——" Ray lay as still as ice. "What a thing!"

It was the first time in their lives that a lie had crept into that bed between them.

Oh, for one thing! Oh, that it weren't spring; that it were deep in winter, with a cold gale blowing, and the four walls whole around them to shut it out!

It was more than Ray could bear. One lie wants another lie, and another. "I don't like him very much, Molly. They do say he's a wild kind; you've heard that yourself. I like fellows like George Dunker better. They've got some manners and some sense."

All this time Molly was saying nothing. Presently, still wordless, she slid an arm under Ray's neck and made a pillow of her shoulder for the hot, dark head.

"There, go to sleep."

It was Molly's arm that went to sleep. And the pain in Ray's neck that came from holding her head just so, so long, grew almost intolerable. But neither one, for her life, would have let the other guess.

The next time Eddie Franklin came to Candle Hill, Molly wasn't there, and Ray, waiting and waiting, felt her cheeks growing dark with shameful happiness when it became plain he wasn't even thinking of asking where the absent one kept herself.

Maytime, deeper Maytime than ever under the flowering vine; and a cool little silver shallop of a new moon riding above the fires of sunset beyond the western sea.

Molly was out there, not near the shore, but on the broad emptiness of the commons, where the trillion new green things pressed up from the earth, where evening birds delighted, two by two, weaving bright circles away overhead in the last red heights of day, and where, flat on the plain to the east, the road from town came past.

When she saw George Dunker come out from behind Ginny Silva's windbreak, sitting bolt up on his bicycle, a tiny figure far off in the dusk, she came to a stop and for a moment laid the palms of her hands over her closed eyes. Then, letting the deep breath out of her breast, taking her hands down and opening her eyes, she walked at a pace unhurried but unlagging in the direction of the road.

George left his machine beside the ruts and came toward her.

"Good evening, Molly; I'm glad I saw you. I see you're out for a pleasant evening stroll."

He was a good-looking fellow, spare and above the medium height, almost as blond as Molly, and grayer, if smaller, eyed. He had, as Ray said, "some manners and some sense." He never swaggered, and he never laughed out loud. In his early twenties he was already able to look out for himself; already they were saying, "The man that gets the best of old man Dunker's young 'un'll have to stay up all night." It was technically his father who owned the hardware store and the third interest in the bank, but the old gentleman was failing; the blood in the business was the son's.

A curious thing happened when, two weeks later, George put his arm around Molly and kissed her on the cheek, saying, "I want you to be my wife." It seemed to change him in her vision. Looking at him in the lamplight thrown out beside the steps from the parlor window, Molly saw him transfigured and magnified.

Eddie Franklin! What was an Eddie Franklin, after all? A thought withered to a ghost, a little wistful in disdain, saying good-by forever to her soul.

Here before her was the man of men. Where in another's sight there might have been a look of hardness about those eyes, she saw only their resolution; in the economy of his word and gesture she discovered a grave reticence; in the line of his thin lips there was nothing so plain as the promise to cherish and protect her indomitably. She perceived all this with the clairvoyance of a love that seemed to have waited only for that caress of his to spring full-grown and to pass out from her and enwrap him, a garment woven of a woman's tenderness, a girl's inchoate hunger, a child's dependence and loyal faith.

It was a strange thing, after clearing their secrets in the dark under the covers each night of their lives for seventeen years, the enormous secrets of their engagements the sisters told each other only after days and through a third one's ears. And their mother, when she had heard them, and when she had sent them packing upstairs at last to their oddly unfamiliar room and their shrunken bed, sat for an hour of the night, the lamp behind her, her eyes, clouded with years, fastened on her own shadow on the wall. In her hand she held tight a hand, but it was only her other one. Alone at one stroke, she felt creeping toward her a harm against which she had no longer the power to defend her own.

She knew more than they thought she knew, those girls of hers. She had heard more than they had imagined an old isolated woman would ever hear. But day before yesterday there had been an unpleasantness in town, a fist fight in a twine shed between two boyhood enemies, young Franklin, the netter, and young Dunker from the hardware store. What it was all about the little bird had neglected to tell her. Which one had beaten the other she hadn't learned either, but this was because, unfortunately, neither had won.

Molly and Ray were aware of it, naturally, but neither would have known that the other knew. Its effect was only to draw them together in a nervous, outward closeness; for a few days it was as if they clung to each other's fingers with a grip so fearfully tight that their hands and arms grew frozen, without any feeling any more. But they loved each other so. Molly, brooding over her strange young sister secretly, cried to herself: "Poor Ray, poor Ray! My man has had to give your man a thrashing. I'm so sorry, dear!"

And Ray was hiding this from Molly, "Poor Molly, I'm so sorry; Eddie has given George the beating of his life."

Nothing had happened; that was agreed without words. But being women and in love, still without words they set themselves to the desperate task of salvage. It is extraordinary how much can be done without common scheming, when there is a common will. And if George and Eddie were not by any stratagem to be brought together on the same calling night at Candle Hill—then what if the Coffin sisters, in town of a summer evening themselves, each with her lover's arm secure in hand, chanced upon each other innocently just before the door of the ice-cream place?

Four sundaes in a row on the marble bar, two pineapple, two chocolate. Rollicking, carefree voices, Molly saying this, Ray that, Ray trilling, Molly laughing in her melodious contralto, bending her neck, soft at the nape with a faint golden down, over her dainty. "Isn't that right, George?" "Now, Eddie, wouldn't *you* say so?"

Eddie wouldn't say anything till the cream was low in the plates. But then, rising from his stool in a large and careless way, a princeling eye on George down the line, "Take it out of that, Harry, my boy!" he cried to the fountain tender, slapping down on the counter a yellow-backed bill.

"You think you mean the whole of it?" said George. "All four?"

"Gosh, yes! What you think?"

George shook his head, his lips flat on his teeth. "Not on your tintype; not my share you don't pay. Harry," he turned with a quiet emphasis, "don't you take but two out of that bill; put my two down to profit and loss." And after that, fair Molly a little bewildered on his arm, he stalked out of the shop with his head in the air.

Left behind him, Eddie was red with fury and white with rage. "Harry Foggar, if you don't take the whole of them sundaes out of that there piece of money——"

"Golly, Ed, I dassent, if George Dunker says no. I ain't the boss here, remember. Him and his pa took title to this prop'ty yesterday afternoon."

Turned back to back in the walnut bed that night, with the distant surf and the gossip of nearer leaves mingling in what ought to have been a lullaby, the sisters lay as still as sleep. But on the one pillow the blond head was thinking, "Poor Ray, she must have been mortified to see him making such a big show of himself with his money—trying to set up a man like George." And the dark head, hot and hurt on the other pillow, was thinking, "Poor Molly, if I'd been her I'd have given him a slap, the strait-laced, stingy old smart-Aleck stick-in-the-mud!"

Both weddings were in the fall. Old Mrs. Coffin died soon after Ray's, leaving the house on Candle Hill to the girls.

George Dunker, who didn't need the money, advised his wife to sell it. And Molly thought that that was wise. Eddie Franklin, who did need the money, swore from the bottom of his chest that the property could tumble in on itself before he would see "that slick-haired bloodsucker feel the heft of one red penny of it in his hand!" And Ray adored him more than ever for just that.

One day the girls got together to go out and clean and close the house. It was early December, but the island autumn still hung on, making a broad world and a high sky. They had been parted for little more than nine weeks, but already, walking each in her rut of the wheel track, in each there was half a sense of embarrassment. It was almost shame. No, it went deeper than that; in each loyal heart there rankled a hurt.

It didn't come out until they had let themselves in and stood in the hall, at the foot of the stairs leading to the chamber where, waiting through nearly eighteen years for their lives to come and take them, they had slept in each other's arms in peace. And now, amazingly, it was Molly, the mild, that began it, a frown like George's on her brow.

"But, Ray, Eddie didn't need to do that."

"Do what?"

"Say that—tell that lie of his—that led up to the fight. About it was lucky for the storekeep the sailor didn't ask me first."

"Lie, you say? *Lie?*"

"Oh, Ray!"

"Oh-Ray me all you want to, it's true. What the *lie* was—and you can say it to your husband as coming straight from Edward Franklin's wife—was what George said about its being lucky for you the sailor *didn't*, then, seeing's you'd hardly have been very gay on the living a *mortgaged roustabout was ever apt to make*. So there!"

It was out. It was done. They stood in the light of the pink panes flanking the door, their breasts distended, their fists tightened, staring at each other in loyal fright. In the mind of each sat wonder, sat helplessness. "What's happened? *We* aren't doing this. This isn't *us*." They didn't clean the house. They locked the door, and, leaving it as it was, wilted flowers still in their pickle jars and an undertaker's helper's gray glove on the parlor floor, they returned by separate paths across the plain to their husbands' homes in town.

Ray lived in a house in the lower end, in what used to be called the Marsh. Here they were near the mooring of Eddie's boat, their neighbors other fishermen, and more and more with each decade Portuguese Negroes from the Cape Verde. Ray's house had a picket fence around it, however, a crimson rambler over the front trellis, and geraniums flowering in the window boxes—at least for the first few years.

Molly lived in the Dunker residence in the Brick Walk, the "little city" where for three generations there had been no room for an outsider to creep in. Cobbles and brasses and tubbed box trees, wrought-iron railings at the doorsteps, and fanlights over the doors. When Father and Mother Dunker had passed on, Molly made an ideal mistress for this early-Victorian mansion, matching its fine solidity, lighting its shadows with her serene and luminous presence, and making a grace even of saving, as that wise man, her husband, would have her save.

It was a house in a hundred for doing that, saving pennies gracefully. Built in the flush days of whaling, of granite, of never-rusting brick and never-weathering slate, everything sturdy to begin with and lastingly right, it wanted little a year in the way of upkeep and brightening; it wasn't like a jerry-built shingle cottage in the Marsh district, where, between the wind from over the flats and the smoke from the gasworks, paint stayed decent so short a time it grew hardly worth the labor and expense of freshening, and where, between the neighbors' children and one's own, there was no keeping all the pickets always on the fence in front.

"Poor Ray!" thought Molly, when in the press of those fruitful days she ventured to think of her at all.

But Molly was mistaken; Ray was far from poor. Ray was rich in the thing that mattered, the play of life. Not in boxwood to be kept clipped, nor brasses to be shined, nor chandeliers to be dusted, not in painted ancestors to be lived up to, nor in stodgy Daughters of Dorcas to be entertained at tea—but in the simple things her big, wild, gallant husband loved she took her joy.

Better than the clink of silver and the feel of silk it was to see him striding, admired and feared, across his domain, the Marsh; or to behold him, back from a trip with the salt rime on him and the smell of the wind still in his hair, seated on the parlor sofa with his first-born on his knee, the fairy Meg, whose eyes were as blue and curls as fair against his swarthiness as had been her grandma Coffin's, for whom she was named. And braver than anything in a book it was to hear him, whacking fist on thigh, cry passionately: "If ever once I catch that lily-gutted storekeep not moving out of my way on the sidewalk again! If ever once I haul off and hand him one!"

And gayer than any starched-up social in the Brick Walk it was when, to forget a poor trip or celebrate a big one, a keg of beer was tapped in the kitchen, with men who knew how to tell stories telling them in the parlor and girls who knew how to dance dancing in the shed. But best of all, better than any easy inherited wealth, was the knowledge that, with Eddie's brave heart what it was, and her faith what it was behind him, the day was coming when they would all be saying, "If you please, sir," to her husband, and George Dunker the humblest of them all.

"Poor Molly, with that life to live," mused Ray sometimes with a curling lip, "and that dried-up penny squeezer of a man, and that flounced-up, ailing child."

The son that was the light of Molly's world wasn't really ailing; he was simply retiring, stamped from the first with the arrogant shyness of the dreamer, the playfellow of passions and of doubts. Of fair-skinned parents, he grew up dark, black-haired, and black-eyed —as Molly would say, like his grandpa Coffin (for whom he was *not* named; he was named for his father and his father's father, George).

The darkling heir of the blond Dunkers. The blond daughter of the dark Franklins of the Marsh. The two cousins, hardly aware each of the other's existence, waiting at the two poles of childhood for life to throw for them with loaded dice. In the years when they might have played together naturally they were still strangers, Meg in the Western School and George in the Whittier. By the time they reached the common ground of high school they knew enough to know that they were enemies.

It happened like lightning, a crackle out of a cloud long ago almost forgotten down in a corner of the sky.

Dunker, the merchant, was standing in the door of his shop on a slack April afternoon. Franklin, the netter, was coming up the street.

Dunker still stuck to his store these years, weighing nails and counting cod hooks over the counter early and late, as though his next day's very bread depended on it. The thin green shadow of the leafing elms fell on his head today without affecting him with its vernal virus; he was thinking of next winter's stock, and the head was bald. Franklin's head wasn't bald, but the hair was grizzling over the ears, adding the last touch of romantic weight to his bigness, his open-handed, open-throated exuberance, his devil-may-care.

There was blood under his skin as he came to a stand, fists on hips, in front of Dunker in his door.

"You keep your brat away from my girl!"

There was no blood under Dunker's skin.

"W-h-a-t?"

"You keep your brat away from my daughter!"

"So, eh? Well, you can bet your bottom dollar I *will.*"

Thus Canute to the tide.

When a girl "gets in trouble" in a town that size it's not long hidden. It's the kind of news that can fly in the air or swim in the water or burrow underground. "Hear about Ed Franklin's girl?" "Not Meg, don't tell me!" "They do say, yes, Meg."

Franklin was away at the Block Island grounds, swordfishing, when this came to light. This time it was the mothers that faced each other.

Again it was surprising. It wasn't the injured Ray that went up with her wild black hair and her wilder and blacker heart to call a Brick Walk to the reckoning, as one would have thought to see. It was mild Molly that came down. Standing before Ray's gate, as strange an intruder as ever the Marsh denizens saw (from behind their hen houses and wash lines where they listened and watched), she put a question three days old to her sister in the yard:

"Where's my son?"

"Where's my daughter?" But Ray's voice was no lady's voice; it came out tearing. "Where's my girl?"

"Where is my boy, I say?"

"What do I care where your boy is? In the devil's pit, I hope. And another thing I hope is, I hope your brave husband is satisfied, now he's got back at Eddie Franklin the only way he dared, sicking his dirty pup on to smirch a better man's pride, while the better man's away."

For answer to such as this the lady of the Brick Walk only turned her head slowly, to the right, to the left, on her proud white neck. Surveying the blistered shanties and their unkempt, half-bred spawn, the look on her face said: "If anything here can be smirched, I'm surprised. As well try to say that the hand dirties the clod it picks up in the road, when in truth it does no more, honoring the clod, than very slightly to dirty itself."

Turning her face back to her sister, she reopened her lips.

(But even between that and the words a thought ran like queer lightning through the back of her mind: "What are we doing, Ray and I? What are we doing *here?*")

She reopened her lips and said: "I came to you simply to ask for information. Be so good as to tell me, where is my son?"

Ray ran and put her hands on the posts of the gateless gate, her eyes murderous, her voice almost soft.

"You can go to hell and find him for yourself, Mrs. George Skinflint Dunker. And while you're there you might ask him what he's done with my daughter, and when you find out you might send me word by a messenger; don't come yourself. And don't let your husband come; Edward Franklin might be here to wring his neck. Now turn your back and go!"

(And presently and weirdly, to herself, "Molly, you look so strange; you act so queer!")

The reason the children weren't to be found was that they had left the island. They had stopped long enough in Taunton on the mainland to be married, before going on, wherever they were bound. That word coming back was the last one the island of Urkey was ever to hear of them.

George wasn't the only child Molly had; she had a daughter, Beatrice. Besides Meg, Ray had young Eddie, young Ray, Harriet, and Paul, life finding her flesh more usable than her sister's as in the ratio of five to two. But neither the one nor the four that remained filled the torn place in either mother's heart left by the first-born that had deserted her. Wounds, those were, wrapped from sight perhaps, but kept open under their wrappings with a salt compounded of sorrow and anger, of chagrin and jealousy.

The twelve years following were different from the eighteen that had gone before. Little by little as the children grew up and the need of her lessened, each woman was given time and leave to open her eyes.

When Ray opened hers and looked at her husband, aswagger with his hat on the back of his head and a laugh on his lips, across the dowdy stage of their existence, she saw him not its hero, but its buffoon, its time-licensed windbag. A slovenly worker and a spendthrift, she saw him now not marching up the years, but drifting down them, poorer in spirit and in pocket with every one. But what was worst of all, she saw the fire breather a braggart, the daredevil a poltroon, so that sometimes when, with a flashing eye, he would thunder, "If ever I haul off and hit that dog a lick!" she had work to keep from crying, "Why don't you ever do it, then?"

Because of this secret shame she began to feel lonely. Another keg of beer on the kitchen table, then, loud stories in the parlor, dancing in the shed to break the floor, and the illusion of valor and aspiration and youth recaptured for a little while. "Eddie, old fellow, things are beginning to come our way at last."

But for all the brave beer and dancing there was something that wouldn't be downed. "Poor Ray," she seemed to hear Molly whispering with a lifted lip, "I told you so."

Now how she hated Molly, of the clear gray eyes!

Clear, yes. The press of her errand in the world let up, Molly's eyes were quite clear. She looked at the father of her children as he sat through the empty evenings, his head shining under the lamp, his eyes, supported by little pouches, half closed over his newspaper, the wheels in the adding machine in his cranium still going around as he drowsed; and bitterly, there in the outer shadow with her, she felt the mordant black eyes of another beside hers; she heard Ray saying, "So now you begin to see."

One would never have thought that Molly could hate, but she hated Ray.

She would set herself to think of George's virtues, his success. But then she would have to cry in her brain: "What are your virtues and your success and money, when I'd give them all for one moment in you of human grandeur; yes, gladly, for one whole, generous gesture, were it only of generous rage?"

The winter her hair turned (dully, as blond heads do) she spoke out at last.

"Why do you, George, let Franklin go around this town saying the things about you he says?"

She couldn't let it alone. Oftener and oftener she reiterated the question, and with deepening venom. But Dunker would never rise to it with anything more than a dry, deprecatory "Well, we'll see."

He wasn't the kind to do violence to any man, least of all to a man like Franklin, broad-shouldered, big-fisted, red-blooded, and full of fight. There's something in the Bible about turning the other cheek. Dunker went along quietly, giving Eddie's vessel credit when gear was needed, and seeing that his more and more frequent little catchpenny notes went through smoothly at the bank.

But once (it was at the dinner table on a dark noon in March, two months after Beatrice was married to Tom Burgess) he gave a fuller answer to Molly's "Why don't you show folks you've got some spirit? Why don't you close his mouth?"

"I guess," he said, "I've closed it today."

He hadn't done it himself, of course; that was the sheriff's affair. Once the court had given the papers, it was the sheriff's business to "plank 'em on."

The schooner, the *Ray II,* ready-painted for going South, her gear overhauled, and a new engine under her afterhouse, lay at her mooring off the Marsh, the pride of any owner's heart. But Eddie Franklin wasn't her owner any longer; she belonged to the bank. And the house he sat in, frowning stupidly, belonged to the hardware store.

It seemed hard for Franklin to understand, and the whisky ebbing in the bottle before him no longer helped. What had happened was a shrewder thing than the attachment of his house and vessel; it was the pricking of the bubble of himself. Now his audacious arms hung down like so much deadwood, his buttocks clove to the sofa, he was an old man.

No! Hell, no! From time to time he made an effort to shake himself clear of this silly seeming. Like a cast stallion he heaved, bowing his back and shoulders; the listening neighbors, friends in the kitchen, and enemies outside the windows, but all bald-necked as vultures today, trembled with stage trembles to hear him swearing: "That's the end, by God! By God, if I don't go and show him a thing for this!"

"When? Now?"

He had almost forgotten Ray, and there she was alone in the

room with him; there were her eyes, unescapable. No matter which way he turned they were after him. "When, Ed? Now?"

"D'you think I'm scared?"

"Do you, Ed?"

"D'you think I'll let him put it over me?"

It was Ray's eyes that put it over *him*. He fled them at last. She should see. All those bums around there that he could lick with his little finger, they too should see. Holding his chest out before him and making it rumble, he swung his deadwood legs up the lane toward town, throwing his empty bottle into the top of a Brava's shanty as he went.

"There he goes, be dogged if he don't!" This was another matter. "Should we get hold the sheriff?" Consternation!

In the dusk in front of the hardware store Franklin stood rocking from side to side like a man on the deck of a ship in an angry sea. Dunker was alone in his shop, the rat alone in his trap, unconscious of the disaster overhanging that dry, bright head of his, bowed at its calculations under the single gas jet in the rear.

The whisky played with the boy's brain under the grizzled pate outside. "Thinks he can break me, does he? I'll break *him!*"

It only wanted a rush to carry it off. One rush, once, at last.

Franklin opened the door, entered, and shut it behind him. But already, with the closing of the door, the rush had died. The chest had collapsed. For there was the truth and you couldn't beat it; Eddie was already broken. He was an old man.

Old men have wild flurries of hope, like children, and a little whisky with them does no harm.

"I'll put it up to him. We were kids together, Georgie and Eddie. He'll remember that. He'll call off the bank; he'll hold off on the house another spell."

Dunker had got up to peer. Seeing who it was, he stood back a little toward the corner, folding his arms.

"That windbag," he told himself. "That overgrown, loud-mouthed do-nothing. We'll see."

But it was his flesh—the flabby meat of him blanched by three decades of safe money-hunting, robbed always to pay the head, undervalued, undisciplined—out of Dunker's flesh there came a squeak.

The rat in the trap! So, after all! The sound of that squeak worked magic in the other's heart. This hard, gray-eyed rich man, of whom Franklin had always stood in secret awe—well, here was the truth—here was the cat out of the bag at last—he was so deathly terrified of big Franklin that he squeaked.

"Ah, now we're somebody! Scared, is he? Well, we'll give him something to be scared about. We'll pile it on."

A Portuguese bogman had lately chosen between two mattocks; the one he hadn't taken still lay on the counter, its handle reaching out to Franklin's hands. It was good in the hands; it had a murderous balance, swung aloft as the feet tramped forward.

Of a sudden the storekeeper fell down on the floor. He lay quiet there in the shadow of his desk, a Z-shaped string of bones, like a patent two-foot rule.

"Dunker's dead!"

Now what was the whisky doing? The front door was open, full of people; the windows were spotted with noses, turning blue. Run for your life, you fool!

Franklin ran for the door beyond the desk, standing open to the dark back room, which in turn would give escape to the alley in the rear.

When they got to Dunker they found him without a mark on him. The heart of his spirit had been willing, but the heart of his flesh was too weak. They found Franklin ten feet below the trap door left open in the back room, lying on a pile of pig-iron ballast in the cellar, with a broken neck. Neither man had touched the other, and both were dead.

Molly sat in the big room in the residence in the Brick Walk, dry-eyed. Others about her, listening to the words of the minister over the casket, wept, dabbing their cheeks with their handkerchiefs. The widow alone had no tears. She was too busy with her thoughts.

In haste, as it were to keep ahead of the minister, she reconstructed the man lying hidden in the box. He and she had been happy together; their years had been fruitful; she was proud of him for his continence, his patience, his unobtrusive will. None but she knew really what he had done for the community's ordered maintenance. No man could ask for a better townsman, no child for a better father, no wife for a better husband than George Dunker had been. And now he was gone.

She seemed to realize it for the first time. For the first time the whole of sorrow forced an entrance into her soul, a weight of bereavement, a widow's dismal wonder, a loyal pain. What she didn't know was that it was for the last time as well.

For George Dunker was finished. Of a sudden she heard "George Dunker" as simply a name. On queer impulse she turned her gaze to the dead man's daughter, Beatrice, a few feet to the right of her, seated close to her new husband.

"Beatrice Dunker Burgess." Another name. Not a few feet, but miles on miles away. It came to Molly with a clearness now, she had never known that woman; no, not even in the months when she carried her within herself. "Beatrice," "George," what were they? Ships in truth that had passed Molly Coffin in the night, and the night a dream.

And now her eyes, curiously daunted, stole about the strange, thronged, stately, somber room. "What's it all about? How do I, Molly Coffin, come to be here? Who invited me? Isn't it nearly over? Isn't it—isn't it almost time for me to be going home?"

Among the chairs in the rear, where they dared, one whispered to another: "There, there, poor thing! The tears are coming now."

In the wet wind on the hill Ray listened to the earth falling on the pine boards in the open hole. "Dust to dust." It was more like mud. Little by little on the hollow wood it fell, covering up the human glory that had been; the big, generous, adventurous figure; the man of whom, even in his failure in the commerce of life, one could be fiercely proud, as one is uplifted by the memory of a beloved great soldier dying defeated in exile. Eddie had been good to her, and Eddie was going.

Now the sound was no longer of earth on wood; it was earth on earth; the wood was covered. Eddie was gone.

Ray's eyes were fixed in space beyond the grave. In the space there was a row of willows not far away, the windbreak at Ginny Silva's farm. Beyond, farther and higher toward the sky and blurred by the water in the wind, there was a square house flanked by naked trees. The strangest feeling grew in Ray. She passed a hand across her eyes and looked out over the moor again.

It was like this. It was as if there were a young girl half nodding in a mill, her fingers feeding the moving iron with a mechanical aptness of habit, her ears gone deaf to the clank of rods and the enormous song of wheels. It was as if, between two winks, she started up, confused. "What's happened?" All that has happened is a sudden silence. The rods and the wheels are still. And it was as if a foreman, moved by a passing pity, laid a hand on her shoulder, saying: "It's a day, kid. Listen, there; there's the whistle. Time to go home and play."

Someone was speaking near Ray's ear. "Look at Ma, Harriet; she's crying at last."

They were all about her, when Ray turned her head; four of them, all bigger than she; six of them, counting Harriet's husband and young Ed's wife; seven, counting the baby in Harriet's shawl. Seven from far away, hemming her about with their somber curiosity.

She walked down the hill rapidly. They followed her. They followed her all the way to the Marsh; they came behind her into the house. The only time she was free of them was when she was up in her room, taking off the stiff black veil she found about her head. Seeing a bag on the closet floor, she stuffed a nightgown into it, and some other things.

Under their silent compulsion, downstairs again, she fried them meat and potatoes and brought from the pantry a cold pie. She sat down at the table with them; they appeared to expect it.

But presently, despite them, she was gone. They heard her climbing the back stairs. A moment and she was down the other way, a hat on her head, a bag on her arm, the front door open in her hand.

"Where you going, Ma, for pity's sake?"

"I'm just going out a little while."

"Well, we all got to be going soon, unless Paul will stay. Yes, Paul will stay."

What a queer place for people to want to live, down here on the cluttered flats! What a funny house!

The wind had increased with the coming of the night. In the open beyond the Ginny's farm it passed unbroken from ocean to ocean across the black plain; or at least but once broken, far out, by an upthrust of roof and boughs. There, as though the air had been water and the obstruction a reef awash with surf, it was heard before it was seen in the thickness; and, hearing it, Ray shifted the bag that grew heavy to her other hand and quickened her steps for the last time along the ridge between the wheel ruts full of dead grass.

She wasn't tired. They needn't think she wasn't wiry and able. Life had used her all it wanted to, but it hadn't used her up. There was plenty left.

Becoming visible, the tree trunks ran about her, and their roaring passed over her head. In the gale piled up against the windward side of the house she hesitated. "Look at me; I've come without a key." But then the queer part was that she couldn't make it seem important. "If I'd needed a key I'd have thought to remember it." Passing around the southeast corner of the building, she brought up in the lee.

There was a light in the hall. Without any more hesitation, without wonder even, she mounted the steps, lifted the latch, and went in.

Molly, halfway up the stairs with the lamp in her hand, turned and peered over the railing.

"That you, Ray? You're awful late."

"I've been hurrying, though."

"Had your supper?"

"I've had a bite. Had enough."

"Don't take your wraps off *there;* it's dank as anything. There's a fire upstairs." Molly held down a hand. "Come."

It was warm in their room, and blankets drying before the blaze.

"Do you suppose that'll be enough covers, Ray?"

"Oh yes. And I got some pillowcases in my grip."

"Well, you must get those duds off. Mercy, look at your shoes!"

Molly got down on the floor to help with Ray's shoes, and then Ray's stockings, soaked to the knees. She looked out for Ray because she always had. The younger, darker, more emotional sister was as impractical about earthly details as a princess in a fairy tale. That's why they were as close as shadow and sunshine; as the shadows of little clouds on the shine of the sand cliffs before the house when summer came.

Once they were in bed and the lamp blown out, the glow from the coals in the chimney falling around the walls no longer showed the mildew; it showed the old white paneling warm and whole.

There was one strange thing about tonight. In the dark under the clothes where till now they had always cleared their hearts and told their secrets before they slept, tonight there seemed nothing to clear their hearts of, no secrets to be told. There was nothing behind them; everything was before them.

"We'll put Canterbury bells and foxglove in the oval, won't we, Molly, again this year?"

"And snapdragons too, yes. And we'll put coreopsis and marigolds out the side way, and nasturtiums in the boxes, Ray?"

By and by, the blond one's arm around the dark one's shoulders, they slept Out of doors, trunk and bough and twig, the trees made harps, and the harps made a giant music of the wind. But nothing of the wind but the music could come in. Nothing could get them in their bed.

*For They Know Not What They Do**

WHEN CHRISTOPHER KAIN TOLD me his story, sitting late in his dressing room at the Philharmonic, I felt that I ought to say something, but nothing in the world seemed adequate. It was one of those times when words have no weight; mine sounded like a fly buzzing in the tomb of kings. And after all, he did not hear me; I could tell that by the look on his face as he sat there staring into the light, the lank, dark hair framing his waxen brow, his shoulders hanging forward, his lean, strong, sentient fingers wrapped around the brown neck of "Ugo," the 'cello, tightly.

Agnes Kain was a lady, as a lady was before the light of that poor worn word went out. Quiet, reserved, gracious, continent, bearing in face and form the fragile beauty of a rose petal come to its fading on a windless ledge, she moved down the years with the steadfast sweetness of the gentlewoman—gentle, and a woman.

They did not know much about her in the city, where she had come with her son. They did not need to. Looking into her eyes, into the transparent soul behind them, they could ask no other credential for the name she bore and the lavender she wore for the husband of whom she never spoke.

She spoke of him, indeed, but that was in privacy, and to her son. As Christopher grew through boyhood, she watched him; in her enveloping eagerness she forestalled the hour when he would have asked, and told him about his father, Daniel Kain.

It gave them the added bond of secret sharers. The tale grew as the boy grew. Each night when Christopher crept into his mother's bed for the quiet hour of her voice, it was as if he crept into another world, the wind-blown, sky-encompassed kingdom of the Kains,

Daniel, his father, and Maynard, his father, another Maynard before him, and all the Kains—and the Hill and the House, the Willow Wood, the Moor under the cloud, the Beach where the gray seas pounded, the boundless Marsh, the Lilac Hedge standing against the stars.

He knew he would have to be a man of men to measure up to that heritage, a man strong, grave, thoughtful, kind with the kindness that never falters, brave with the courage of that dark and massive folk whose blood ran in his veins. Coming as it did, a world of legend growing up side by side with the matter-of-fact world of Concord Street, it was made to fit in with all things natural, and it never occurred to him to question. He, the boy, was not massive, strong, or brave; he saw things in the dark that frightened him, his thin shoulders were bound to droop, the hours of practice on his violin left him with no blood in his legs and a queer pallor on his brow.

Nor was he always grave, thoughtful, kind. He did not often lose his temper; the river of his young life ran too smooth and deep. But there were times when he did. Brief passions swept him, blinded him, twisted his fingers, left him sobbing, retching, and weak as death itself. He never seemed to wonder at the discrepancy in things, however, any more than he wondered at the look in his mother's eyes, as she hung over him, waiting, in those moments of nausea after rage. She had not the look of the gentlewoman then; she had more the look, a thousand times, of the prisoner led through the last gray corridor in the dawn.

He saw her like that once when he had not been angry. It was on a day when he came into the front hall unexpectedly as a stranger was going out of the door. The stranger was dressed in rough, brown homespun; in one hand he held a brown velour hat, in the other a thorn stick without a ferrule. Nor was there anything more worthy of note in his face, an average-long face with hollowed cheeks, sunken gray eyes, and a high forehead, narrow, sallow, and moist.

No, it was not the stranger that troubled Christopher. It was his mother's look at his own blundering entrance, and, when the man was out of hearing, the tremulous haste of her explanation.

"He came about some papers, you know."

"You mean our *Morning Posts?*" Christopher asked her.

She let her breath out all at once, and color flooded her face.

"Yes," she told him. "Yes, yes."

Neither of them said anything more about it.

It was that same day, toward evening, that Christopher broke one of his long silences, reverting to a subject always near to them both.

"Mother, you've never told me where it is—on the *map*, I mean."

She was looking the other way. She did not turn around.

"I—Chris—I—I haven't a map in the house."

He did not press the matter. He went out into the back yard presently, under the grape trellis, and there he stood still for a long time, staring at nothing in particular.

He was growing up.

He went away to boarding school not long after this, taking with him the picture of his adored mother, the treasured epic of his dark, strong fathers, his narrow shoulders, his rare, blind bursts of passion, his newborn wonder, and his violin. At school they thought him a queer one.

The destinies of men are unaccountable things. Five children in the village of Deer Bay came down with diphtheria. That was why the academy shut up for a week, and that was what started Christopher on his way home for an unexpected holiday. And then it was only by one chance in a thousand that he should glimpse his mother's face in the down train halted at the Junction where he himself was changing.

She did not see him till he came striding along the aisle of her coach, his arms full of his things, face flushed, eyes brimming with the surprise and pleasure of seeing her, lips trembling questions.

"Why, Mother, what on earth? Where are you going? I'm to have a week at least, Mother; and here you're going away, and you didn't tell me, and what is it, and everything?"

His eager voice trailed off. The color drained out of his face, and there was a shadow in his eyes. He drew back from her the least way.

"What is it, Mother? *Mother!*"

Somewhere on the platform outside the conductor's droning "— *board*" ran along the coaches. Agnes Kain opened her white lips.

"Get off before it's too late, Christopher. I haven't time to explain now. Go home, and Mary will see you have everything. I'll be back in a day or so. Kiss me, and go quickly. Quickly!"

He did not kiss her. He would not have kissed her for worlds. He was too bewildered, dazed, lost, too inexpressibly hurt. On the platform outside, had she turned ever so little to look, she might have seen his face again for an instant as the wheels ground on the rails. Color was coming back to it again, a murky color like the shadow of a red cloud.

They must have wondered, in the coach with her, at the change in the calm, unobtrusive, well-gowned gentlewoman, their fellow passenger. Those that were left after another two hours saw her get down at a barren station where an old man waited in a carriage. The halt was brief, and none of them caught sight of the boyish figure that slipped down from the rearmost coach to take shelter for himself and his dark, tempest-ridden face behind the shed at the end of the platform. . . .

Christopher walked out across a broad, high, cloudy plain, following a red road, led by the dust feather hanging over the distant carriage.

He walked for miles, creeping antlike between the immensities of the brown plain and the tumbled sky. Had he been less implacable, less intent, he might have noticed many things: the changing conformation of the clouds, the far flight of a gull, the new perfume and texture of the wind that flowed over his hot temples. But as it was, the sea took him by surprise. Coming over a little rise, his eyes focused for another long, dun fold of the plain, it seemed for an instant as if he had lost his balance above a void; for a wink he felt the passing of a strange sickness. He went off a little way to the side of the road and sat down on a flat stone.

The world had become of a sudden infinitely simple, as simple as the inside of a cup. The land broke down under him, a long, naked slope fringed at the foot by a ribbon of woods. Through the upper branches he saw the shingles and chimneys of a pale gray village clinging to a white beach, a beach which ran up to the left in a border flight of cliffs, showing on their crest a cluster of roofs and dull green gable ends against the sea that lifted vast, unbroken, to the rim of the cup.

Christopher was fifteen, and queer even for that queer age. He had a streak of the girl in him at his adolescence, and, as he sat there in a huddle, the wind coming out of this huge new gulf of life seemed to pass through him, bone and tissue, and tears rolled down his face.

The carriage bearing his strange mother was gone, from sight and from mind. His eyes came down from the lilac-crowned hill to the beach, where it showed in white patches through the wood, and he saw that the wood was of willows. And he remembered the plain behind him, the wide, brown moor under the cloud. He got up on his wobbly legs. There were stones all about him in the whispering wire grass, and like them the one he had been sitting on bore a blurred inscription. He read it aloud, for some reason, his voice borne away faintly on the river of air:

MAYNARD KAIN, ESQUIRE
1809–1839
This Monument Erected in His Memory
by His Sorrowing Widow,
HARRIET BURNAM KAIN

"The windy Gales of the West Indies
Laid Claim to His Noble Soul
And Took him on High to his Creator
Who made him Whole."

His gaze went on to another of those worn stones.

Here Lie The Earthly Remains Of
MAYNARD KAIN, SECOND
Born 1835–Died 1863. For the Preservation of the Union.

There was no moss or lichen on this wind-scored slope. In the falling dusk the old white stones stood up like the bones of the dead themselves, and the only sound was the rustle of the wire grass creeping over them in a dry tide. The boy had taken off his cap; the sea wind moving under the mat of his damp hair gave it the look of some somber, outlandish cowl. With the night coming on, his solemnity had an elfin quality. He found at last what he was looking for, and his fingers had to help his eyes:

DANIEL KAIN
Beloved Husband of Agnes Willoughby Kain
Born 1860–Died 1886
"Forgive them, for they know not what they do."

Christopher Kain told me that he left the naked graveyard repeating it to himself, "Forgive them, for they know not what they do."

conscious less of the words than of the august rhythm falling in with the pulse of his exaltation.

The velvet darkness that hangs under clouds had come down over the hills and the great marsh stretching away to the south of it. Agnes Kain stood in the open doorway, one hand on the brown wood, the other pressed to her cheek.

"You heard it *that* time, Nelson?"

"No, ma'am." The old man in the entrance hall behind her shook his head. In the thin, blown light of the candelabra which he held high, the worry and doubt of her deepened on his singularly unlined face.

"And you might well catch your death in that draft, ma'am."

But she only continued to stare out between the pillars where the lilac hedge made a wall of deeper blackness across the night.

"What am I thinking of?" she whispered, and then:

"There!"

And this time the old man heard it; a nearer, wind-blown hail.

"Mother! Oh, Mother!"

The boy came striding through the gap of the gate in the hedge.

"It's I, Mother! Chris! Aren't you surprised?"

She had no answer. As he came she turned and moved away from the door, and the old man, peering from under the flat candle flames, saw her face like wax. And he saw the boy, Christopher, in the doorway, his hands flung out, his face transfigured.

"Mother! I'm here! Don't you understand?"

He touched her shoulder. She turned to him, as it were lazily.

"Yes," she breathed. "I see."

He threw his arms about her, and felt her shaking from head to foot. But he was shaking, too.

"I knew the way!" he cried. "I knew it, Mother, I knew it! I came down from the Moor and there was the Willow Wood, and I knew the way home. And when I came, Mother, it was like the trees bowing down their branches in the dark. And when I came by the Beach, Mother, it was like a roll of drums, beating for me, and when I came to the Hill I saw the Hedge standing against the sky, and I came, and here I am!"

She expressed no wonder, asked no question.

"Yes," was all she said, and it was as if she spoke of a tree coming to its leaf, the wind to its height, the tide to its flood.

Had he been less rapt and triumphant he must have wondered more at that icy lassitude, and at the cloak of ceremony she wrapped about her to hide a terror. It was queer to hear the chill urbanity of her: "This is Christopher, Nelson; Christopher, this is your father's servant, Nelson." It was queerer still to see the fastidious decorum with which she led him over this, the familiar house of his fathers.

He might have been a stranger, come with a guidebook in his hand. When he stood on his heels in the big drawing room, staring up with all his eyes at the likenesses of those men he had known so well, it was strange to hear her going on with all the patter of the gallery attendant, names of painters, prices, dates. He stood before the portrait of Daniel Kain, his father, a dark-skinned, longish face with a slightly protruding nether lip, hollow temples, and a round chin, deeply cleft. As in all the others, the eyes, even in the dead pigment, seemed to shine with an odd, fixed luminosity of their own, and like the others from first to last of the line, it bore upon it the stamp of an imperishable youth. And all the while he stood there, drinking it in, detail by detail, his mother spoke, not of the face, but of the frame, some obscure and unsuspected excellence in the gold leaf on the frame.

More than once in that stately tour of halls and chambers he found himself protesting gaily, "I know, Mother! I know, I know!"

But the contagion of his glory did not seem to touch her. Nothing seemed to touch her. Only once was the fragile, bright shell of her punctilio penetrated for a moment, and that was when Christopher, lagging, turned back to a door they were about to pass and threw it open with the happy laugh of a discoverer. And then, even before she could have hushed him, the laughter on his lips died of itself.

A man lay on a bed in the room, his face as colorless and still as the pillow behind it. His eyes were open, but they did not move from the three candles burning on the high bureau, and he seemed unconscious of any intrusion.

"I didn't know!" Christopher whispered, shocked, and shamed.

When the door was closed again his mother explained. She explained at length, concisely, standing quite still, with one frail, fine hand worrying the locket she wore at her throat. Nelson stood quite still too, his attention engrossed in his candlewicks. And Christopher stood quite still, and all their shadows. . . . That man was the caretaker, the man, Christopher was to understand, who had been looking after the place. His name was Sanderson. He had fallen ill, very ill. In fact he was dying. And that was why Christopher's mother had to come down, posthaste, without warning. To see about some papers. Some papers. Christopher was to understand . . .

Christopher understood. Indeed there was not much to understand. And yet, when they had gone on, he was bothered by it. Already, so young he was, so ruthless, and so romantic, he had begun to be a little ashamed of that fading, matter-of-fact world of Concord Street. And it was with just that world which he wished to forget that the man lying ill in the candlelit chamber was linked in Christopher's memory. For it was the same man he had seen in the doorway that morning months ago, with a brown hat in one hand and a thorn stick in the other.

Even a thing like that may be half put aside, though—for a while. And by the time Christopher went to his room for the night, the thought of the interloper had returned into the back of his mind, and they were all Kains there on the Hill, inheritors of Romance. He found himself bowing to his mother with a courtliness he had never known, and an "I wish you a good night," sounding a century old on his lips. He saw the remote, patrician figure bow as gravely in return, a petal of color as hard as paint on the whiteness of either cheek. He did not see her afterward, though—when the merciful door was closed.

Before he slept he explored the chamber, touching old objects with reverent finger tips. He came on a leather case like an absurdly overgrown beetle, hidden in a corner, and a violoncello was in it. He had seen such things before, but he had never touched one, and when he lifted it from the case he had a moment of feeling very odd at the pit of his stomach. Sitting in his underthings on the edge of the bed, he held the wine-colored creature in the crook of his arm for a long time, the look in his round eyes, half eagerness, half pain, of one pursuing the shadow of some ghostly and elusive memory.

He touched the C string by and by with an adventuring thumb. I have heard "Ugo" sing, myself, and I know what Christopher meant when he said that the sound did not come *out* of the instrument, but that it came *in* to it, sweeping home from all the walls and corners of the chamber, a slow, rich, concentric wind of tone. He felt it about him, murmurous, pulsating, like the sound of surf borne from some far-off coast.

And then it was like drums, still farther off. And then it was the feet of marching men, massive, dark, grave men with luminous eyes, and the stamp on their faces of an imperishable youth.

He sat there so lost and rapt that he heard nothing of his mother's footsteps hurrying in the hall; knew nothing till he saw her face in the open doorway. She had forgotten herself this time; that fragile defense of gentility was down. For a moment they stared at each other across a gulf of silence, and little by little the boy's cheeks grew as white as hers, his hands as cold, his lungs as empty of breath.

"What is it, Mother?"

"Oh, Christopher, Christopher—— Go to bed, dear."

He did not know why, but of a sudden he felt ashamed and a little frightened, and, blowing out the candle, he crept under the covers.

The afternoon was bright with a rare sun, and the world was quiet. Christopher lay full-spread on the turf, listening idly to the "clip-clop" of Nelson's shears as the old man trimmed the hedge.

"And was my father *very* strong?" he asked with a drowsy pride.

"No, not so very." Nelson stopped clipping and was immediately lost in the past.

"Only when he was *that* way five strong men couldn't turn him. I'll say that. No, if they had to get him with a shotgun that day, 'twas nobody's fault nor sin. If Guy Bullard seen Daniel there on the sand with an ax in his hand and foam-like on his lips, and the little ones cornered where he caught them between cliff and water—Guy's own baby amongst them—and knowing the sickness of the Kains as he and everybody else did—why, I'm free and willing to say 'twas his bounden duty to hold a true aim and pull a steady trigger on Daniel, man of his though I was, and man of his poor father before him. . . ."

Nelson was a queer fellow. His age was really greater than his unlined face would have told, and his mind, laden with the burden of misty years, had grown tired. It is charitable to think that, once launched on the river of memory, the dreaming fellow forgot where he was and to what audience he spoke, that audience lying quiet, so very quiet, in the deep grass behind his back.

"No, I can't make it right to lay blame on any man for it, no more than I can on them, his brother officers, that broke Maynard's neck with their tent pegs the night after Gettysburg. No, no . . ."

It was evidently a time-worn theme, an argument, an apologia, accepted after years of bitterness and self-searching. He went on with the remote serenity of age that has escaped the toils of passion, pursuing the old, worn path of his mind, his eyes buried in vacancy.

"No, 'twas a mercy to the both of them, father and son, and a man must see it so. 'Twould be better of course if they could have gone easier, same as the *old* Maynard went, thinking himself the Lord our God to walk on the water and calm the West Indy gale. That's better, better for all hands round. But if it had to come so, in violence and fear, then nobody need feel the sin of it on his soul—nobody excepting the old man Bickers, him that told Daniel. For 'twas from that day he began to take it on.

"I saw it myself. There was Daniel come home from other parts where his mother had kept him, out of gossip's way, bright as you please and knowing nothing wrong with the blood of the Kains. And so I say the sin lays on the loose-wagging tongue of Bickers, for from the day he let it out to Daniel, Daniel changed. 'Twas like he'd heard his doom, and went to it. Bickers is dead a long time now, but may the Lord God lay eternal damnation on his soul!"

Even then there was no heat; the curse had grown a formula. Having come to the end, the old man's eyes tumbled down painlessly out of the void and discovered the shears in his hand.

"Dear me, that's so," he said to himself. One thought was enough at a time. He fell to work again. The steady "clip-clip-clip" moved off slowly along the hedge. Not once did he remember; not once as the indefatigable worker shuffled himself out of sight around the house did he look back with any stirring of recollection at the boyish figure lying there as still as a shadow cast in the deep grass.

A faintly lopsided moon swam in the zenith. For three days now that rare clarity had hung in the sky, and for three nights the moon had grown. Its benign, poisonous illumination flowed down steeply through the windows of the dark chamber where Christopher huddled on the bed's edge, three pale, chill islands spread on the polished floor.

Once again the boy brought the bow home across the shivering strings, and, as if ears could be thirsty as a drunkard's throat, he drank his fill of the 'cello's deep, full-membered chord. The air was heavy with the resonance of marching feet, ghostly feet marching and marching down upon him in slow, inexorable crescendo as the tides ebbed later among the sedges on the marsh and the moon grew big. And above the pulse of the march he seemed to hear another cadence, a thin laughter.

He laughed too, giving himself up to that spectral contagion. He saw the fat, iridescent bubble with the Hill in it, the House of his dreams, the Beach and the Moor and the Willow Wood of fancy, and all the grave, strong, gentle line of Kains to whom he had been made bow down in worship. He saw himself taken in, soul and body, by a thin-plated fraud, a cheap trick of mother's words, as, before him, his father had been. And the faint exhalations from the moon patches on the floor showed his face contorted with a still, set grimace of mirth.

Anger came over him in a white veil, twitching his lips and his toes and bending his fingers in knots. Through the veil a sound crept, a sound he knew well by this time, secret footfalls in the hall, faltering, retreating, loitering, returning to lag near the door.

How he hated her! It is curious that not once did his passion turn against his blighted fathers; it was against the woman who had borne him, the babe, and lied to him, the boy—against her, and against that man, that interloper, dying in a room below.

The thought that had been willing to creep out of sight into the back country of his mind on that first night came out now like a red, devouring cloud. Who was that man?

What was he dying of—or *supposed* to be dying of? What had he been doing that morning in Concord Street? What was he doing here, in the house of the men who would never grow old? Why had his mother come down here, where he was, so queerly, so secretly, so frightened?

Christopher would have liked to kill that man. He shivered and licked his lips. He would have liked to do something bloody and abominable to that face with the hollow cheeks, the sunken gray eyes, and the forehead, high, sallow, and moist. He would have liked to take an ax in his hand and run along the thundering beach and catch that face in a corner somewhere between cliff and water. The desire to do this thing possessed him and blinded him like the kiss of lightning.

He found himself on the floor at the edge of the moonlight, full of weakness and nausea. He felt himself weeping as he crawled back to the bed, his cheeks and neck bathed in a flood of painless tears. He threw himself down, dazed with exhaustion.

It seemed to him that his mother had been calling a long while. "Christopher! What is it? What is it, boy?"

He had heard no footsteps, going or coming; she must have been there all the time, waiting, listening, her ear pressed to the thick old paneling of the door. The thought was like wine; the torment of her whispering was sweet in his ears.

"Oh, Chris, Chris! You're making yourself sick!"

"Yes," he said. He lifted on an elbow and repeated in a voice which must have sounded strange enough to the listener beyond the door. "Yes!" he said. "Yes!

"Go away!" he cried of a sudden, making a wide, dim, imperious gesture in the dark.

"No, no," the imploring whisper crept in. "You're making yourself sick—Christopher—all over nothing—nothing in the world. It's so foolish—so foolish—foolish! Oh, if I could only tell you, Christopher—if I could tell you——"

"Tell me what?" He shuddered with the ecstasy of his own irony. "Who that man is? That 'caretaker'? What he's doing here? What you're doing here?" He began to scream in a high, brittle voice: "*Go away from that door! Go away!*"

This time she obeyed. He heard her retreating, soft-footed and frightened, along the hall. She was abandoning him—without so much as trying the door, just once again, to see if it was still bolted against her.

She did not care. She was sneaking off—down the stairs. Oh yes, he knew where.

His lips began to twitch again, and his fingernails scratched on the bedclothes. If only he had something, some weapon, an ax, a broad, keen, glittering ax! He would show them! He was strong, incredibly strong! Five men could not have turned him back from what he was going to do—if only he had something.

His hand, creeping, groping, closed on the neck of the 'cello leaning by the bed. He laughed.

Oh yes, he would stop her from going down there; he would hold her, just where she was on the dark stair, nerveless, breathless, as long as he liked; if he liked he would bring her back, cringing, begging.

He drew the bow, and laughed higher and louder yet to hear the booming discord rocking in upon him from the shadows. Swaying from side to side, he lashed the hollow creature to madness. They came in the press of the gale, marching, marching, the wild, dark pageant of his fathers, nearer and nearer through the moon-struck night.

"Tell me *what?*" he laughed. "*What?*"

And abruptly he slept, sprawled crosswise on the covers, half clothed, disheveled, triumphant.

It was not the same night, but another, whether the next or the next but one, or two, Christopher cannot say. But he was out of doors.

He had escaped from the house at dusk; he knew that. He remembered the wide, hushed mystery of twilight as he paused on the door-sill between the fading pillars, the death of day running crimson in the west; in the east the still, white travail of the sea and the moon—the queer moment.

He had run away, through the hedge and down the back side of the hill, torn between the two, the death, warm and red like life, and the birth, pale, chill, and inexorable as death.

Most of that daft night-running will always be blank in Christopher's mind; moments, and moments only, like islands of clarity, remain. He brings back one vivid interval when he found himself seated on his father's gravestone among the whispering grasses, staring down into the pallid bowl of the world. And in that moment he knew what Daniel Kain had felt, and Maynard Kain before him; a passionate and contemptuous hatred for all the dullards in the world who never dreamed dreams or saw visions or sang wordless songs or ran naked-hearted in the flood of the full-blown moon. He hated them because they could not by any possibility comprehend his magnificent separation, his starry sanity, his—kinship with the gods. And he had a new thirst to obliterate the whole creeping race of dust dwellers with one wide, incomparably bloody gesture.

It was late when he found himself back again before the house, and an ink-black cloud touched the moon's edge. After the airless evening a wind had sprung up in the east; it thrashed among the lilac stems as he came through them and across the turf, silent-footed as an Indian. In his right hand he had a bread knife, held butt to thumb, daggerwise. Where he had come by the rust-bitten thing no one knows, least of all himself. In the broken light his eyes shone with a curious luminosity of their own, absorbed, introspective.

All the windows were dark, and the entrance hall, when he slipped in between the pillars; but across its floor he saw light thrown in a yellow ribbon from the half-closed door of the drawing room.

It took his attention, laid hands on his imagination. He began to struggle against it.

He would not go into that room. He was going to *another* room. To stay him, he made a picture of that other room in his tumbled mind—the high, bleak walls, the bureau with the three candles burning wanly, the bed, the face of the man on the bed. And when his rebellious feet, surrendering him up to the lure of that beckoning ribbon, had edged as far as the door, and he had pushed it a little farther ajar to get his head in, he saw that the face itself was there in the drawing room.

He stood there for some time, his shoulder pressed against the doorjamb, his eyes blinking.

His slow attention moved from the face to the satin pillows that wedged it in, and then to the woman that must have been his mother, kneeling beside the casket with her arms crooked on the shining cover and her head down between them. And across from her leaned "Ugo," the 'cello, come down from his chamber to stand vigil at the other shoulder of the dead.

The first thing that came into his groping mind was a bitter sense of abandonment. The little core of candlelight hanging in the gloom left him out. Its unstirring occupants, the woman, the 'cello, and the clay, seemed sufficient to themselves. His mother had forgotten him. Even "Ugo," that had grown part and parcel of his madness, had forgotten him.

Bruised, sullen, moved by some deep-lying instinct of the clan, his eyes left them and sought the wall beyond, where there were those who would not forget him, come what might, blood of his blood and mind of his own queer mind. And there among the shadowed faces he searched for one in vain. As if that candlelit tableau, somehow holy and somehow abominable, were not for the eyes of one of them, the face of Daniel, the wedded husband, had been turned to the wall.

Here was something definite, something Christopher could take hold of, and something that *he would not have*.

His mother seemed not to have known he was near till he flung the door back and came stalking into the light with the rusty bread knife in his hand. None would have imagined there was blood enough left in her wasted heart, but her face went crimson when she lifted it and saw him.

It brought him up short—the blush, where he had looked for fright. It shocked him, and, shocking him, more than by a thousand labored words of explanation it opened a window in his disordered brain. He stood gawking with the effort of thought, hardly conscious of his mother's cry.

"Christopher, I never meant you to know!"

He kept on staring at the ashen face between the pillows, long (as his own was long), sensitive, worn; and at the 'cello keeping incorruptible vigil over its dead. And then slowly his eyes went down to his own left hand, to which that same old wine-brown creature had come home from the first with a curious sense of fitness and authority and right.

"Who is this man?"

"Don't look at me so! Don't, Chris!"

But he did look at her. Preoccupied as he was, he was appalled at sight of the damage the half-dozen days had done. She had been so much the lady, so perfectly the gentlewoman. To no one had the outward gesture and symbol of purity been more precious. No whisper had ever breathed against her. If there had been secrets behind her, they had been dead; if a skeleton, the closet had been closed. And now, looking down on her, he was not only appalled, he was a little sickened, as one might be to find squalor and decay creeping into a familiar and once immaculate room.

"Who is this man?" he repeated.

"He grew up with me." She half raised herself on her knees in the eagerness of her appeal. "We were boy and girl together at home in Maryland. We were meant for each other, Chris. We were always to marry—always, Chris. And when I went away, and when I married your—when I married Daniel Kain, *he* hunted and he searched and he found me here. He was with me, he stood by me through that awful year—and—that was how it happened. I tell you, Christopher, darling, we were meant for each other. John Sanderson and I. He loved me more than poor Daniel ever did or could, loved me enough to throw away a life of promise, just to hang on here after everyone else was gone, alone with his 'cello and his one little memory. And I loved him enough to—to—— *Christopher, don't look at me so!*"

His eyes did not waver. You must remember his age, the immaculate, ruthless, mid-Victorian teens; and you must remember his bringing up.

"And so this was my father," he said. And then he went on without waiting, his voice breaking into falsetto with the fierceness of his charge. "And you would have kept on lying to me! If I hadn't happened, just happened to find you here, now, you would have gone on keeping me in the dark! You would have stood by and seen me—well—go *crazy!* Yes, go crazy, thinking I was—well, thinking I was meant for it! And all to save your precious——"

She was down on the floor again, what was left of the gentlewoman, wailing.

"But you don't know what it means to a woman, Chris! You don't know what it means to a woman!"

A wave of rebellion brought her up and she strained toward him across the coffin.

"Isn't it something, then, that I gave you a father with a *mind?* And if you think you've been sinned against, think of *me!* Sin! You call it *sin!* Well, isn't it *anything at all* that by my 'sin' my son's blood came down to him *clean?* Tell me that!"

He shook himself, and his flame turned to sullenness.

"It's not so," he glowered.

All the girl in him, the poet, the hero-worshiping boy, rebelled. His harassed eyes went to the wall beyond and the faces there, the ghosts of the doomed, glorious, youth-ridden line, priceless possessions of his dreams. He would not lose them; he refused to be robbed of a tragic birthright. He wanted some gesture puissant enough to turn back and blot out all that had been told him.

"It's not his!" he cried. And reaching out fiercely he dragged the 'cello away from the coffin's side. He stood for an instant at bay, bitter, defiant.

"It's not his! It's mine. It's—it's—*ours!*"

And then he fled out into the dark of the entrance hall and up the black stairs. In his room there was no moonlight now, for the cloud ran over the sky, and the rain had come.

"It isn't so, it isn't so!" It was like a sob in his throat.

He struck on the full strings. And listening, breathless, through the dying discord he heard—the liquid whispers of the rain, nothing more. He lashed with a wild bow, time and again. But something was broken, something was lost; out of the surf of sound he could no longer fashion the measure of marching feet. The mad Kains had found him out and cast him out. No longer could he dream them in dreams or run naked-hearted with them in the flood of the moon, for he was no blood of theirs, and they were gone. And huddling down on the edge of the bed, he wept.

The tears washed his eyes and, falling down, bathed his strengthless hands. And beyond the fantom windows, over the Marsh and the Moor and the Hill that were not his, the graves of strangers and the lost Willow Wood, lay the healing rain. He heard it in gurgling rivulets along the gutters overhead. He heard the soft impact, like a kiss, brushing the reedy cheeks of the Marsh, the showery shouldering of branches, the aspiration of myriad drinking grasses, the far whisper of waters coming home to the waters of the sea—the long, low melody of the rain.

And by and by he found it was "Ugo," the 'cello, and he was playing.

They went home the following afternoon, he and his mother. Or, rather, she went home, and he with her as far as the Junction, where he changed for school.

They had not much to say to each other through the journey. The boy had to be given time. Five years younger, or fifteen years older, it would have been easier for him to look at his mother. You must remember what his mother had meant to him, and what, bound up still in the fierce and somber battle of adolescence, she must mean to him now.

As for Agnes Kain, she did not look at him, either. Through the changing hours her eyes rested on the transparent hands lying crossed in her lap. She seemed very tired and very white. Her hair was done up less tidily, her lace cuffs were less fresh than they had been wont to be. About her whole presence there was a troubling hint of letdown, something obscurely slatternly, a kind of awkward and unlovely nakedness.

She really spoke to him for the first time at the Junction, when he stood before her, slim and uncouth under the huge burden of "Ugo," fumbling through his leave-taking.

"Christopher," she said, "try not to think of me—always—as—as—well, when you're older, Christopher, you'll know what I mean."

That was the last time he ever heard her speak. He saw her once again—two days later—but the telegram was delayed and his train was late, and when he came beside her bed she said nothing. She looked into his eyes searchingly—for a long while—and died.

That space stands for the interval of silence that fell after Christopher had told me the story. I thought he had quite finished. He sat motionless, his shoulders fallen forward, his eyes fixed in the heart of the incandescent globe over the dressing table, his long fingers wrapped around the neck of the 'cello.

"And so she got me through those years," he said. "Those nip-and-tuck years that followed. By her lie."

"Insanity is a queer thing," he went on, still brooding into the light. "There's more of it about than we're apt to think. It works in so many ways. In hobbies, arts, philosophies. Music is a kind of insanity. I know. I've got *mine* penned up in the music now, and I think I can keep it there now, and save my soul."

"*Yours?*"

"Yes, mine. I know now—now that it's safe for me to know. I was down at that village by the Beach a year or so ago. I'm a Kain, of course, one of the crazy Kains, after all. John Sanderson was born in the village and lived there till his death. Only once that folks could remember had he been away, and that was when he took some papers to the city for Mrs. Kain to sign. He was caretaker at the old 'Kain place' the last ten years of his life, and deaf, they said, since his tenth year—'deaf as a post.' And they told me something else. They said there was a story that before my father, Daniel, married her, my mother had been an actress. An actress! You'll understand that *I* needed no one to tell me *that!*

"One told me he had heard that she was a *great* actress. Dear God, if they could only know! When I think of that night and that setting, that scene! It killed her . . . and it got me over the wall . . ."

*"La Guiablesse"**

ONCE UPON A TIME HE HAD BEEN white; you knew that. Gazing down idly from the eminence of the Royal Mail in some azure roadstead of the islands, you may have seen him gazing back at you idly from the blistering deck of his schooner.

As long as you cared to stare at him he stared at you. He had nothing else to do. He would be waiting for lighters and lighterboys, his business interrupted by the coming of your huge, smoke-grimed, iron-skinned *bom*-ship from the north; waiting silently and without pain till God chose to move you on again over the purple rim of the world—as one learns to wait in the Caribbees.

Or again, you may have seen him as I saw him once, passing across the trade wind in the swift splendor of a tropic dusk, his sails amazingly pink against a sea colored like a peacock's breast, his deckload of fruit—limes and mangoes and shaddock from the Guiana river bottoms—giving back the level rays in a thousand tones of vert and chrome, a Negro, his blue-black torso naked to the waist, standing at the wheel behind him, and another as red as raw gold paring yams on the house. Like another argosy of gold and gossamer she passed swiftly away and vanished in the deepening shadows where the mountain of Grenada burned faint and fainter above the onrushing night.

And to the last, I am sure, Johnson leaned there unstirring, his forearms crossed on his sleeping box and his large, brown, heavy-lidded eyes fixed upon us with an expression of somnolent disdain.

He had been a white man once upon a time, and in his own country he had loved and been beloved of a woman. Frailty was her name. It had taken him an absurdly long time to find this out. He might have done something violent. In place of that he vanished. First there was the briefest sort of an interview, in which he pointed out to her with a passionate and prophetic clarity the inevitable course of all her future career, and then, as I say, he vanished, quietly, completely, and came away to be a white man all alone. Had you told him now that he was no better than a Quashie black man, that already he had fallen under another, the darker and yet more blighting dominion of a ship, I am sure he would have laughed at you.

As to the schooner, she, too, was an exile. I cannot say where she had come from, precisely, but from the curve of her cutwater and the set of her masts, dividing the room fairly, like the eyes in a man's face, I can make a guess that in her early days she had gone home to Provincetown or Gloucester with her black hull of ground-fish and the rime of the Georgias frosting her bows.

But now she was white, as white as a northern snowbank from water to tops, as befits an exile trading in the islands of pitiless light. He kept her well, that must be admitted. He used to say of her that many men had had her; that now, when the charm of her youth was gone and she had come to him in a far land where no one knew her, a bit the worse for wear, just a bit passé, you understand, he would be good to her. And as he said this he allowed a faintly ironical smile to play about the corners of his lips and shrugged his shoulders ever so slightly, as if he were thinking perhaps not quite of her, but of someone else.

A ship, at best, is a queer kind of woman. I am inclined to believe there was never a queerer one than this schooner of Johnson's. Lovely, yes; illogical, crotchety, stubborn, and (as it turned out) infinitely jealous. One has heard of man-killing ships, of ships with a taste for a certain wind and a distinct aversion to all others, of ships willing and unwilling, faithful, treacherous, and of ships prone to nostalgia. But I, at least, have never heard of another craft that, taking an unaccountable dislike to a certain place, refused consistently thereafter to be lured or dragged or driven into the neighborhood of that place.

Call it coincidence, if you will. Johnson did, at first. But the fact remains that for a space ranging upward of fifteen months the British island of Dominica was dropped from the schooner's more or less regular route of call; the coco palms parading the beach looked out no longer in the dawn to find her slim, snowy presence at rest upon the mirror of the roadstead, nor was the voice of "Bigboy" Johnson heard again over the tinkling glasses in the green sepulchral cavern of Sutro's warehouse on the quay of Roseau.

Neither was it any fault of Johnson's, nor of his factor's. Indeed, Sutro's last words as he stood on the beach were, "I say, old man, you won't fail me?" And to him, from the dinghy that drew away swiftly under the strong oar strokes of black Siza and gold-red 'Ti Josef, Johnson's words came rolling back: "My word on it, Sutro! Look for me the first week in July!"

When it came as far as the *third* week in July, the factor took himself to the corrugated-iron cable office. But send where he might—Bridgetown, French Islands—Port of Spain—no one could give him news of Johnson and the schooner. None of them was aware that at that moment, in the blind, white loneliness of the Grenadines, Johnson and his boys were "sweating blood" to get the vessel off the sandy beach where, most unaccountably, on the brightest of moonlit nights, she had somehow managed to run herself aground.

Late that year, toward the end of the rains, Sutro sent a cablegram which found Johnson lying behind the mole at Bridgetown, Barbados. It read:

IMPORTANT YOU SHOULD CALL HERE EARLIEST OPPORTUNITY.

The same evening he had an answer:

AM SAILING IMMEDIATELY. JOHNSON.

It is not a long run from Barbados—sixty hours at the worst. Little more than that had elapsed when he received the wire:

DISABLED; HAVE PUT IN FORT-DE-FRANCE.

The factor began to lose patience. Three days later the cable gave him to know, briefly, that Johnson, with a broken steering gear, had taken a tow back to Barbados.

Once after that, when winter was gone and the rains set in again, Sutro went up the pig-littered alley to the cable office.

MOST IMPORTANT YOU SHOULD CALL HERE IMMEDIATELY

he sent into the unknown.

IMMEDIATELY.

This time Johnson answered from the waterfront at Demerara in British Guiana, on the mainland:

JUST NOW LOADING JUTE FOR DOMINICA. WILL SAIL IN THREE DAYS.

And this time it was the whip end of the spring hurricane that caught him off the coast of St. Vincent and the schooner limping home, ragged and splintered, and her cargo fit only for the ministrations of the underwriters, into the basin at Bridgetown.

This time, at least, you will say it was not her fault. A matter of coincidence, pure and simple, a catastrophe which would have occurred to the schooner had she been steering to any one of a dozen other islands in the archipelago. . . . I am sure Johnson called it nothing but that as yet. No, as yet his proud, disdainful spirit would "have no truck with niggers." He probably laughed to himself in that indolent, sardonic way of his as, lying full length on the deckhouse through the watches of a white night, he listened to 'Ti Josef, the red boy from Catholic Guadeloupe, and John Bull, the brown boy from Episcopalian Grenada, comparing murmurous theories and suspicions in the waist below him.

The good Protestant expressed it as his opinion that the island had been "dressed"; that some old black witch doctor had set a sorcery against the schooner's coming—a long, low, heathen-hearted rigmarole of "Obeah-bags" and "spell-water" and the bodies of drowned cockroaches.

At all of this the good Catholic would shake his head and lift his eyes to the topsails swimming small and pale against the moon-struck sky. And then, moved, perchance, by a sense of her soaring and majestic mien, he would begin to recite the dogma of the "devil woman"—*La Guiablesse.*

As he spoke, making the sign of the cross from time to time over his naked breast, his voice seemed to emerge by degrees from his throat and hang before his palate, advancing and receding in the bony roof of his mouth with a monotonous beat of syllables, like the rhythm of a wide and shallow drum pounding in the heart of a jungle night. . . .

And one saw the tall, sleek, satiny woman, the goblin woman, moving soundlessly in the white hush of noon. . . .

"*La Guiablesse! Ah oui!*"

Squatting on the moonlit deck, his gold-red body swaying slowly, his head thrown back and his eyes fixed upon the gossamer flesh of that towering and lonely creature, the ship, the grandchild of the Congo repeated it again and again: "*La Guiablesse! La Guiablesse!*"

Johnson, sprawled on the house, laughed silently to himself and shook his large, unkempt head, as much as to say, "Can you beat that, now? A white man will never be able to get at the bottom of these children of darkness–never!"

But once, when on a night like this the schooner was standing north for Marie-Galante, and a little to the west of them Dominica itself lay outspread in full, pale view, Johnson forgot to laugh.

He had been watching it for an hour, perhaps, his eyes half closed and his chin propped in the heels of his hands. Buried in fancy, he had been thinking how like an animal it looked, sleeping there on the sea; one protruding, velvet hip, a gaunt barrel, a high bulwark of shoulder, a short, thick paw shielding the slumbering head. Beyond the veil of his reverie the voice of 'Ti Josef carried on and on, advancing and receding, touching with its colorless and insidious pulsations the nervous fibers of the man who had been white. . . .

Johnson roused himself with a half-strangled oath and thrust his head over the edge of the house.

"Quit it!" he yelled. "I tell you, quit it!"

In the bland light he saw their faces lifted, their thick brown lips half parted, their disconcerted eyes scrutinizing him palely.

"Good God Almighty! All this infernal claptrap! This jungle-nigger babble that never ends!"

His discomfort increased.

"Look here! I've had enough of it. I'll show you. When we're cleared in Marie-Galante I'll bring her back here and go in to that island. Understand? I'll run her into the roads there, fair and square, and we'll hear the end of this. Now that's enough!"

Turning away, he rolled over on his back again and stared at the sky. His face reddened slowly under its tan.

"Say!" he muttered. "I'll be getting as bad as a nigger."

He was ashamed of himself without quite knowing why, and altogether uncomfortable.

"What the devil? What's ailing me?"

I have the story of what happened in Demerara six months later from a man named Malverde. Malverde, a mulatto, half owner and manager of a large chandlery establishment in River Street, is a person of education and of considerable native acumen. Of his shrewdness in the way of judging character it is enough to say, perhaps, that he has prospered in a credit business on a tropical river. When he says that there had been a great change in Johnson since his last appearance in the river (some eight or nine months before), one may be sure he knows what he is talking about.

He says he was shocked. After the custom, he had Johnson up to the cool Captains' Room on the second floor of his emporium. There, ministered to by the soft-footed China boy, it was their habit to talk, lazily and at large, surrounded by the wide, uneasy hush of the city noon, toying halfheartedly with the mist-rimmed glasses of lime and rum till the breeze sprang up again and business affairs became tolerable.

Malverde had always liked Johnson; that is to say, he had always trusted him, admired him, and perhaps envied him a little that quality of aloof disdain, of cool and painless separation from the ambitions and complexities of life, and especially from that particular group of human aspirations conveniently symbolized in "wine, women and song."

"But he was not the same chap, sir. Jolly quick I saw that. . . . By two o'clock in the afternoon, I give you my word, he was drinking like a lord, like a lord, sir."

He had not begun his lordly drinking right away, it seems. For a while, in the languorous twilight of the room, he had sat in his long chair listening to Malverde's small talk curiously mute, gray, inattentive, relaxed. So he had continued according to the evidence, until Malverde began to "talk business." Of course, the ship chandler had something in train for him (had been awaiting his arrival for a month, in fact).

"I understand," he said to Johnson, "that your factor, Sutro, is on the lookout for a deal in jute just now. I happen to have the goods in hand. You could take it on in the stream and be at Dominica in six days' time, and a jolly pretty thing for all concerned. What?"

Johnson, still stretched out in his attitude of somber separation, gazed at the ceiling and answered, slowly.

"No," he said. "You're one jump too late, Malverde. Sutro's had that fixed up in Barbados—almost a month ago. Thom & Knight handled it."

The ship chandler was surprised and disconcerted. He was more deeply shocked than before. Having Sutro's week-old letter in his pocket, he was in a position to know that Johnson had told a lie. Being a businessman and at the same time a gentleman, he could do no more than mention the fact of the letter as casually as possible, with the still more casual comment that there must have been some mistake—somewhere or other—on Johnson's part. And now, the misapprehension having been cleared up, what did he say to the proposition?

But Johnson had got up and gone to the balcony. There he stood staring out over the housetops to where his schooner lay at anchor in the stream, staring at her (as Malverde expresses it) "in the rummest way imaginable." The ship chandler began, as he says, to be "a bit fed up with it."

"Well," he persisted, coughing slightly behind a hand, "and what do you say?"

Johnson heard him. Coming back from the balcony, he resumed his chair and lifted the glass of lime and rum which the China boy had just refilled. His face was the color of ivory, and his teeth seemed to be knocking gently together.

"What do I say?" he echoed. "I say that this is damn good stuff, Malverde, old man!"

With that he drained it and clapped his hands for the boy again. His course from then on may best be left to the ship chandler's words and the gesture with which he accompanies them:

"You may imagine, sir. I was quite helpless. I am not prepared, here, in my own house, as you might say, to—well—to put a lock on the sideboard. . . . And by two o'clock, as I say, sir, he was quite thoroughly befuddled."

In the end Malverde had to ask him to go. Some of his more respectable clients were coming into the place, and Johnson had begun to mumble into his glass—an interminable, half-coherent rigmarole about a woman named Minna, a woman who had deceived him, "double-crossed" him, and, somehow, incomprehensibly, driven him out to this God-forsaken hole of the world. When he had been sober he had stared at his ship; when he was drunk he talked about a woman. He continued to talk about her when the ship chandler, having received no reply to his request that he get out, and being withheld by some remnant of friendly shame from having the China boy do it, led him in person down the dark back stairs of the establishment.

In the close, sticky gloom of the descent his voice echoed, loud and full of self-pity. It was evident that his mind had relapsed into the past. He told this imagined woman that she might go the way she had chosen, that it might be nice now with this one, but that there would be a next one not quite so nice, and a next one, and so on, down and down and down, till she came to the end of her rope.

Malverde had him out of the back door by that, and into the blank sunlight of the dock. But he was not yet done with him. Johnson, holding the door open with one hand and imprecating him wildly with the other, addressed him with glazed and evidently unseeing eyes.

"And when you come to the end of your rope, I know how it'll be, Minna, my girl! You'll come crawling back to me, and I'll have to be good to you. Yes, damn my soul——"

Malverde tells me he got the door closed then.

"Shameful? Rather! We had always been friends. I give you my word I should jolly well rather have lost a hundred pounds—a thousand!"

But as it turned out, the rupture in that five-year-old friendship, distressing as it had been, was not complete. On the evening of the day following, Malverde met Johnson on the sea wall, where he had gone to hear the band.

I say they met. In reality it was not a question of meeting. Johnson, overtaking him from the rear, gave him a friendly greeting and fell in step. It became evident to Malverde that one of two things had happened: either Johnson had been so far gone yesterday that the whole episode had failed to leave a trace in his memory, or else he had come so low that it made no difference. Perhaps the truth lay between them.

If he recollected anything, Johnson's only reference to it was hidden in the casual bit of information which he offered as they walked along.

"I've had the fever. Don't know whether you knew, Malverde. Yes, seven weeks of it. Bad time. I don't amount to much these days."

The other, always a gentleman, and not entirely certain as to what was expected of him, murmured that he was sorry to hear it. "But then," he went on, "it was long overdue you. You're apt to be a jolly sight better for it in the long run. Cleans the blood out."

"Yes." Johnson nodded his head thoughtfully. They walked on in silence, their white-garbed figures floating ghostlike through the gloom. "Yes," he repeated, "it's cleaned my blood out, I guess; washed out all the old red things that trouble a man, that keep him restless and uncomfortable, and—well—white. Yes, I suppose I'm all right now. I suppose I'm branded now—as good as a Creole now, I guess."

He said this, not with his old laugh and shrug of irony, but as matter of fact, wistful, and at the same time acquiescent. Put rather more at his ease by the tone, the ship chandler suggested that they take a seat. They found one not far from the bandstand, where an artificial twilight flowed over them from the clustered arcs.

"I say," Malverde returned to the subject which, as a man of business, he could not very well afford to abandon, "and what about the little matter for our friend Sutro? You'll remember we were speaking of it yesterday when—ah—we were interrupted, you know."

"No, I didn't know." Johnson looked at him calmly. "I didn't know we were interrupted. And I had it in my head, somehow, that I told you I couldn't do it—couldn't go to that island."

"Ah?" Malverde was taken by surprise. "By Jove! I did not know. There has been some trouble with Sutro? I had not heard."

"No, no trouble with Sutro. It's a simple matter of geography. Being an island, a man's got to go there in a ship, and if a man's ship won't go to that particular island, why——" He lifted his palms, as much as to say, "Why, there you are."

Malverde was at a loss. As he puts it: "Fancy my position. We had been friends. . . . Well, sir, to make a long story short, I told him quite frankly that he had been drinking too much."

Even at this charge, bald as it was, Johnson betrayed no anger. His calm grew, if anything, deeper, more solicitous, more indecent. Leaning over and tapping Malverde's knee with a forefinger, he went on:

"Do you know what happened the last time I tried to go there in the schooner? No? Well, I'll tell you. She tried to kill me, in broad daylight, in cold blood. No doubt of it. There were witnesses. Ask Siza. Ask John Bull."

He paused, not so much for effect, but as if to pin the other down the more firmly with his long, solicitous forefinger.

"It was like this," he went on. "I was coming out of Marie-Galante in ballast. I said to myself, 'Now I'll see what there is in all this claptrap about that island and this ship and me.' I don't know whether you knew, Malverde, but there had been a lot of talk. Among the niggers. I had a little boy from the French Islands called 'Ti Josef. He was the worst. He called her *La Guiablesse*. Well, it's hard to make you understand; I haven't the words. But you got the feeling anyhow, to hear him, that that schooner was really a woman, or more like the spirit of a woman, a tall, white, beautiful, and bedeviled woman—and that *I* was the one bedeviled. That she wanted me to herself; that she kept her woman's eye on me; that she had me, well, let's say, pretty well under her thumb. And that, womanlike, there was something in Dominica she mistrusted—in connection with *me*, you understand. Sounds silly! But hang it!"

Johnson edged an inch or so nearer on the bench.

"Listen, Malverde. I came out of Marie-Galante and laid south by east, thinking to fetch around the south'ard end of Dominica. 'Once for all!' I said. 'Ti Josef came to me. 'Don't do it!' he said. He was scared—you could see that, Malverde, scared to death. You could see it in his eyes. If a red boy could grow white, he was white. He fell to work crossing himself; got down on his knees and begged me not to do it.

"I wouldn't listen. I'll never forget I wouldn't listen to him. I thought I knew everything. Coming clear of the south'ard end of Dominica, I hailed all hands to stand by to luff. I put the helm hard aweather. 'Once for all!' I said.

"Well, she came around—slow—too slow. I remember the French boy begging, 'Don't do it, sir!' but just then my eye fell on a free end of the main-boom lacing afoul the galley pipe. I didn't want the galley pipe carried away when she jibed over, you know, and I yelled at Josef to clear it, he was nearest. He looked at the house, but he never moved. I was mad. But there was no time. She was still coming around—slow. Seeing him still standing there, scared stiff, I suppose, I ran and jumped on the house myself. I guess that jarred him, for he was right after me, squealing something about his *Guiablesse*, his interminable *Guiablesse*.

"Well, she must have come faster all of a sudden. I didn't see, but I heard Siza yell. I knew. I fell flat, right flat down on the house. And as I went I felt the boom going over me; I felt the wind of it, I tell you, on the back of my neck—*whish!* Wicked! Yes, I was too quick for her. But if you knew how wicked it was—and how deliberate!

"When she fetched up I thought she'd tear the mast out of her. I got on my feet and looked around. 'Where's Josef?' I asked. Siza and John Bull were looking alee with their mouths open. And when I looked there I knew where 'Ti Josef had gone. *He* hadn't been quick enough, you see.

"We never got him. That boom must have broken his back like a wheat straw. We came about and looked for him, but we never got him. He had begged me not to do it, begged me on his two knees. And I wouldn't listen. And he got what was meant for me! . . . I laid a course for Bridgetown. That was where I had the fever. . . ."

In the following silence, filled with diffused and inconsequential sound—the vagrant, brassy pulse of music, the slow slapping of surf, the shuffling of feet, and low confusion of promenaders' voices—Johnson sat staring down at his own knees.

"Why?" he asked, at length. "What is it in that island?"

"Perhaps it's a woman." For the first time in their acquaintance a hint of irony crept into the mulatto's voice.

Johnson lifted his eyes and looked at the ship chandler, calmly. "A woman? No, there's nothing in that, Malverde. I— It sounds like the cheapest sort of melodrama, I know, but I guess I'm done with women, Malverde."

He went on without passion or especial emphasis:

"Have you ever heard of what they call the 'double standard of morality'—the one for men and the other for women? Well, anyway, I used to be down on it. I used to argue for hours; it seemed to me unfair and abominable and indecent. Until I ran up against it—well—much nearer home. No, Malverde, I guess I'm done with women. And so . . ."

His voice died out. He got to his feet abruptly, awkwardly, his face flushing in the faint light.

"By jingo!" he stammered. "Well, I—I'll be damned!"

Looking up, Malverde beheld a stranger turning out of the crowd. He saw a typical British colonial padding forward in his slightly bulging linen suit, a large white Panama pushed back on his thinning hair, a cigarette dependent between his drooping mustaches, and the never-failing black-cotton umbrella tucked under his arm. And he too was exclaiming: "By Jove!" and, "I say, Bigboy! I'll be damned!"

"See here," he went on, as he shook Johnson's hand. "I've a bone to pick with you. You had my letter?"

"Letter?" Johnson echoed.

"At Grenada. I heard you were looked for there in June."

"No, I was down with the fever in Barbados. No, I didn't get your letter." Johnson shook his head. "By the way," he shifted, "you know Malverde, don't you? Malverde, you're acquainted with Sutro?"

At the name of the Roseau factor Malverde was on his feet.

"Oh, by George! Surely!" He smiled, showing his extremely white teeth. "By correspondence, though—in a business way. Charmed!"

And then, breaking in smoothly on the other's return of the compliment:

"I say, Mr. Sutro, you'll be glad to know I have that little matter of jute in hand now. As I was saying to Bigboy——"

"Yes, yes, indeed!" It was Sutro's turn to interrupt. "Quite right, surely; but tomorrow—tomorrow! Thanks, awfully. And now, Bigboy, I'm amazed. I—— That puts another light on the matter, altogether. So you hadn't my letter—at all! Mmmm! So! By Jove!"

Naturally the ship chandler's feelings were not of the pleasantest, but being a gentleman and feeling himself "quite obviously a bit in the way," he made his excuses and departed. As he moved off, however, down the turf-covered embankment in the shade of the double row of mahogany trees, he could not help catching the sound of Johnson's voice.

"*W-h-a-t?*"

It was not loud. Against the background of all the small, chaotic murmurings of the night it sounded scarcely more than a whisper. And yet it had in it a quality, somehow, of stentorian and commanding appeal:

"*W-h-a-t? S-u-t-r-o!*"

Malverde took a tram home to his lodgings in Queen Street and went to bed and to sleep. It could not have been more than five in the morning, tree frogs piping and the night mist still overhanging the canals, when he was aroused by a voice and a thumping on his blinds. At such an hour the complaisance of even the most complaisant man is apt to be at its lowest ebb.

Nor was Johnson's proposal, called in through the blinds, calculated to restore it, being no less than this: that he, Malverde, should turn out, dress himself, and come down to his warehouse in River Street. At five in the morning! What Johnson wanted was salt fish (a small quantity), two hams, a dozen of tinned milk, and fifty kilos of yams. And all this immediately! In an hour's time, he said, he must be out of the river.

"But my—my *dear chap!*" The ship chandler, pale-pajamaed and irate, let out his exasperation. "But my *dear chap!*" he called through the blind. "You can't be serious. You can't be off like this. My jute! What of my jute? For of course it's Dominica?"

"Who said so? Who said it was—that island? Hush up! My men are here, waiting; so for heaven's sake don't go off half-cocked like that any more. And get a move on. Come!"

"But my jute!" the other continued to insist. "And Sutro! Take my word for it, when Sutro hears of this——"

"Sutro is here with me."

Malverde, peeping through the blind, was disconcerted, puzzled, and more than ever "fed up with it all." He began to dress hastily, calling out from time to time: "Yes. Well, well! Presently! Presently!"

About the departure of any ship, any fragile, man-made shell whatever of skin or wood or iron, wheeling outward, withdrawing, diminishing, merging by imperceptible degrees with the mystery and the brooding and implacable immensity of the ocean, there can never fail a sense of romance, a moment instinct with the illusion of wild and adventurous heroism touched with pathos. . . . About the departure of Johnson's ship in the heart of the dead-hot tropic dawn there was all this, and there was something more, a kind of an especial pomp and circumstance of mystery, of blind presumption and confidential haste.

Even to Malverde there came a momentary sense of poetic and uneasy wonder as he stood with Sutro on the mud-caked dock watching Johnson away. It crowded out even his resentment at what he called "being kept so infernally in the dark about the whole bally undertaking." For a moment, as the schooner, swinging slowly across the stream, came in strong silhouette against the flaming mountain of dawn, he was moved by a sense of admiration, foreboding, and pity. For she rode high on the water, as light and unreliable as a feather.

Johnson had come into the river laden down. Now, in his haste, he had not so much as a bag of sand in her.

Malverde mentioned it to Sutro in a tone half petulant, half awed.

"It's quite mad! He'll be jolly lucky, you know, not to lose her before he's half there—and himself in the bargain."

"Yes," said Sutro, not removing his somber gaze from the schooner. "But after all, I can't say that it matters much—blast it!"

And Malverde, glancing around, was dumfounded to see a large, bright, perfectly spherical teardrop trembling in the corner of the man's eye. The ship chandler was embarrassed. The thing was so unexpected, so (as it were) uncalled for, in a paunchy, leathery, bald-pated island factor like Sutro. Sutro struck the moisture away with a pudgy hand.

"Confound it, Malverde, but I liked that chap! No end! I shouldn't have told him, Malverde!"

"I beg pardon? Shouldn't have told him—*what?*"

"Why, bless my heart!" Sutro blinked his eyes with an apologetic recollection. "You *don't* know, do you? I say, the sun begins to tell a bit. If we could get under cover somewhere—where we might talk. . . . What? . . . Oh, thanks. Quite right!" And, giving a last look at the schooner, already no more than a vague loom on the farther reaches of the muddy, red-flecked river, he turned and followed the other into the shadow of the great cool warehouse. "Yes, a blasted awkward, deplorable business—for all concerned!"

For an hour his voice could be heard, occasional and fragmentary, floating down from the latticed balcony of the Captains' Room. . . .

". . . But you may fancy my position. My responsibility. . . . An island of that sort. And for upward of a year. . . . Yes, that was all quite natural. I was her only point of departure. She had been to the Royal Mail in New York. Quite natural. It was known there that I was her husband's factor in the islands. What more logical? . . . But you must see, Malverde, I was always looking for the beggar to turn up any moment. And so I would tell her: 'This week,' I would tell her, or 'Sometime within a fortnight, surely.' . . . Yes, a blasted awkward bit of business for the lot of us, I say. . . . Thanks! Make the better part soda if you will. . . ."

It grew toward night of the third day. The sun had set, or, rather, swinging low to the western water, it had seemed of a sudden to let go and plunge, a sullen, red, lopsided plummet, beneath the surface of the sea. For a moment a dome of pinkish light stood up halfway to the zenith in the eastern heaven; for a moment its effulgence warmed the windward slopes of the waves and touched with rose the spiring canvas of the schooner; then abruptly it was gone, too, and an immeasurable shadow overlay the ocean.

John Bull, the brown boy, came aft along the weather side of the house.

"Yes, sah," he began, addressing himself to the master at the wheel, his head bowed in the extremity of diffidence—"yes, sah. Beg pahdan, sah; but thaih was a land, sah—some land, sah. I can't rightly say, sah, but just when the sun he da go set I think I see a land thaih to leewud? Yes, sah?"

From his seat on the wheelbox Johnson gave him the grudging and watchful assent of a nod. He had seen the land himself, a tiny pyramid of rose glimpsed for a moment on the western sky line, their first landfall among the islands. And since then he had been waiting to hear of it, preparing himself for the inevitable, recurrent question.

The brown boy returned to the shy attack:

"I can't rightly say, sah, but that land thaih he da go look very much like Morne Agarou, sah. Very much like St. Vincent, sah. Yes, sah?"

And again, evading his eyes by staring hard at the deck, Johnson gave him the constrained assent of a nod. When he looked up he saw that Siza, the Barbadian, had come noiselessly to stand behind his mate. The black had more dignity and self-assurance by half than the mixed-blood; he had gone to the board schools in Bridgetown and his English was excellent, with a strong flavor of Piccadilly.

"We would be obliged, sir," he said, speaking quietly over John Bull's shoulder, "to know where we are bound, sir."

"Bound, eh?" Johnson regarded them angrily. "Bound, eh?" He got to his feet. "By heavens," he muttered, "if you *will* have it out of me, why——" And then, for perhaps the tenth time in the course of the voyage, the determination went out of him, and, lifting an arm, he waved it savagely toward the bows. "To the north'ard! We're bound to the north'ard, I tell you! Now look here, the two of you. I don't want you loafing around. Do something! Take a lick at the pump. The pump. D'you hear?"

He turned his back on them.

"They're like children," he told himself. The thought gave him no comfort.

Letting himself down on the wheelbox once more, he fell into prolonged sardonic reverie.

"What a damned fool I am!" he muttered from time to time.

At rest so, he looked worn and emaciated. His face was bloodless under its tan, lending the skin a yellow cast. A three-days' growth of beard deepened the hollows under his cheekbones. The fever, not wholly gone out, had returned a little during the voyage, giving to his mind at times a queer slant of flightiness, and this reverie, into which he had fallen on each succeeding night, followed on each succeeding night the same unvarying course to the same invariable end.

The darkness deepened. The schooner's wake became visible, stretching away, glimmering, coruscating, a dozen cable lengths to the south. From the waist came in monotonous pulsations the clank and sough of the bilge pump, and the muffled, melancholy chanty that went with the work.

"What a damned fool I am!" Johnson repeated from time to time, nodding his head in the same self-pitying, sardonic abstraction.

He got up and, leaving the wheel, went forward. At the break he paused to tell Siza to take the helm, and then he continued on his way, past the foremast and the capstan, picking his path over lines and gear till he came where he could lean with one arm on the rail and the other over the smooth barrel of the bowsprit. There, with his eyes brooding into the empty darkness ahead and his ears filled with the soft thunder of the cutwater beneath, he fell into the second phase of his reverie.

"What a damned fool I am!"

They were the same words as before, but between the sense of them now and the sense before there lay a distance not to be measured by the mere ship's length his body had traversed. Whereas, before, he had spoken in ironical self-mockery, as much as to say, "What a fool I am *to come!*" now in his tone there was nothing but the bitterest of self-abasement, self-reproach: "What a fool I am *not to have come before!* To have let myself be hoaxed and bullied and turned back by—well, by nothing at all!"

It was as if he said all that. . . .

And into his mind there came a small bright picture. He saw a room bathed in a frank, incandescent glare. He saw it vividly, in detail—the maroon-and-silver wallpaper, the gilded steam radiator, the let-in sideboard, the photograph of his senior crew framed above the gas grate. He saw the table laid for dinner, the white cloth, the broken bread, the spot where last Sunday's gravy had spilled, the untidy pile of shameful letters. He saw her facing him across the table. She was standing, just as he was standing, leaning forward with her hands on the table as he was leaning, her cheeks flushed, her eyes defiant, as were his. And in that heavy brightness, as in an intolerable vacuum, he heard his own voice crying, faintly: "And then, when you've come to the end of your rope, I know how it will be; well enough I know. You'll come crawling back to me, Minna, and I'll be good to you—yes—damn my soul to hell for a poor, soft fool!—I'll have to be good to you!"

He stirred and passed his bare forearm over his eyes. And then he seemed to hear another voice, her voice this time: "That's very fine, very fine. And yet who knows if it won't be *I* that will have to be good to *you.* There may be an end to *your* rope, too. Stranger things have happened."

Yes, far stranger things indeed had happened.

Again he stirred, and again he passed his forearm over his eyes. And immediately, without apparent transition, he was in the third phase of his reverie. Leaving the bow, he began to pace the deck, all the way aft and forward again, his hands locked behind him, his head thrown back, his eyes fixed in the towering, dim cloud of the schooner's rigging.

"Tomorrow!" he said to himself, aloud. "By this time tomorrow we shall see!"

In the sunlight each day he had been able to keep it out of sight in the background of his mind. But as night drew on, as the brightness and all the visible amplitude of sky and sea went out, casting him back inexorably upon the companionship of the vessel, under the thrall, as it were, of this mistress and sharer of his exile; then, pacing back and forth, back and forth in the starlight, he began to feel the weight of the oncoming event, the inevitable, oncoming moment of struggle, of anger, perhaps, and violence, when one of their two wills, his or the ship's, must be definitely and forever broken.

As the day of the voyage might be, he had said to himself: "Three days! By this time, three days!" or, "The day after tomorrow!"

Now it was "tomorrow"!

Leaning in the bows, he had had a vision of a woman. Now he had another vision, of another woman. He saw the ship as another woman, a woman with pale, long-curving, diaphanous flesh, a woman too wise to be any longer young or any longer profligate, a woman in the last full flower of desire, spending her loveliness now with a fierce singleness of eye, a late, twilight chastity, an extortionate faithfulness to the one love, the love that must not be let go, since it could not be other than the last.

"*La Guiablesse!*" It was almost as if he heard the whisper of the golden boy wandering the star-filled spaces of the rigging. "*La Guiablesse! Ah oui, La Guiablesse!*"

For the moment he felt the utter hopelessness of struggling against that. . . .

He had slept poorly each night. Tonight he did not sleep at all. A dozen times he was out of his sleeping box for a restless circuit of the decks. At three o'clock, driven by some obscure gnawing of apprehension, he relieved the brown boy at the helm.

In reality there was no need of anyone at all at that helm. The voyage had been remarkable, almost too remarkable. Not once since leaving the Guiana coast had the trade wind veered or fallen; a steady topsail breeze against which, on the one long reach, the vessel stayed herself impeccably from one day's end to another, helm one point aweather and headsails hauled. It had been remarkable. The day's runs had been big—almost too big.

Johnson took the wheel "for a couple of hours." He had held it for fifteen of them before he was through. Sitting there on the box, his weight eased against the metal rim, he saw the dawn, like a vast, silent explosion, half hidden by the blue wall of Martinique and the shoulders of Pelée.

The French island went away slowly, withdrawing its velvet headlands little by little and folding up its purple valleys till it became a cloud, and then no more than the shadow of a cloud hanging for a moment on the sky line far astern.

On the horizon beyond the bows there lay the shadow of another cloud. John Bull, going into the forward works, studied it for a long while from beneath his shading palm. Then he came aft. He said nothing. But in the flat white tide of the sunlight Johnson felt him standing there at the corner of the house, waiting. He aroused himself.

"Get Siza out," he said.

When the Barbadian had come abovedecks, blinking with sleep, Johnson had the two of them stand before him. With their eyes on the blazing deck they heard what he had to say. He spoke in a low tone, without especial emphasis.

"And now we'll have no monkey business," he concluded. "No more of this heathen rubbish, you understand. You at least, Siza, ought to know better. All that has happened has just happened to happen. You'll see. It will be perfectly simple, perfectly easy. All I want you to remember is that I'm master of this vessel—and that I won't stand any monkey business; not for a minute. Now go. Both of you can turn in if you want to."

It was evident that they did not want to. They went off forward, out of sight beyond the house. If they conversed, it must have been in whispers, for Johnson heard nothing more of them.

Noon came. The slow, hot, early hours of afternoon began to tick away on the ship's clock under the companionway hatch. And then, as slowly, the later hours. . . .

At half past five, feeling a slight lurch of the deck beneath him, Johnson lifted his head. Although he had been under its lee for an hour, to the casual glance it might have seemed that he was now, for the first time, conscious of the island's proximity—as if, had it not been for that sudden, soft flaw in the wind under the shelter of towering Diablotin, he might have passed it by and gone on sailing to the northward unawares.

He had not been there for upward of fifteen months. Unconsciously he brushed a hand over his eyes. As it were but a long stone's throw across the gently stirring water, he saw the curve of the white beach, the even feathering of palms, the yellow stucco of the customhouse; beyond them the town itself half buried in the immense inundation of its greenery; behind and above all, the majestic presence of the mountain, hiding its head in a cloud that sent gray tentacles of mist and sudden wind feeling down its deep, jungled ravines.

"Well," he said to himself. It was only a whisper. He found that his lips were dry, and wet them with his tongue. "Well, here we are," he said. "That's simple enough."

He felt tired. An extraordinary sensation of inertia came over him, and of a sudden it seemed that the simple act of bringing the schooner about on the other tack to come up into the roadstead was too much to think of. It became better just to sit there, saying to himself, "Well, here we are, here we are."

He had to take hold of himself, for already they were beginning to draw past. He got to his feet with an effort, and calling, "John! Siza!" whirled the spokes.

"Hard alee!" he shouted. "Stand by! Stand by!" His voice sounded high and tenuous in his own ears. Perhaps it was the fault of his ears. "Too much quinine," he muttered. He was conscious of Siza and the brown boy staring at him across the roof of the house, just their heads showing, sullen, inert.

"To the devil with them!" he muttered.

She came up to the wind, swinging slowly and more slowly to starboard; or rather, it seemed that while she remained stationary, the visible world—the island, the mountain, and the cloud—swept slowly and more slowly to port. He heard the first flutter as the throat of the mainsail lost the wind, and then the foresail slatting and banging, slatting and banging. It kept on slatting and banging too long. And then he saw that the visible world had ceased revolving.

He understood, and a groan came out of his throat. He was caught there "in irons." She hung there in the eye of the wind, stock-still, looking at the shore. And now that she had lost her momentum nothing he could do, nothing in the world, indeed, but some chance flaw of cross wind, would bring her over on the other tack.

"She's too light," he groaned. "Too high, I tell you! Too high in the water! Give me a flaw!" he cried.

A flaw came, but it was on the wrong hand. The vessel fell away, slowly, less slowly, on the old tack; slowly and then less slowly the island, the mountain, and the cloud swept back again. Another flaw, stronger yet and chill with a breath of mountain rain, bellied the canvas. White crept into the wake. And as if she had given enough of her precious time in that passing gesture, that brief and scornful obeisance to the land, the schooner stood on swiftly again toward the loom of Guadeloupe and the islands to the north.

"Too light!" he kept repeating to himself in a thick whisper, as it were in absence of mind. "Too high in the water! Too much free-board!"

His hands lay idle on the wheel. Somewhere in the back of his brain the thought kept drumming: "Look here, if you're to try again you've got to be quick about it! Look here, if you're to try again . . ."

But all he could seem to think of was that monotonous reiteration: "Too light! Too high! I might have known."

His heavy eyes left the shore and went up to the soaring fabric of the ship. The moment of evening had come again; the sun, distorted and sultry, hung a handbreadth over the sea, and in its level rays the canvas burned with a lambent flame, like the flush of a woman transfigured by a swift and painless triumph.

Johnson's face grew red, too, redder than the sun. His eyes narrowed, and into them came a new kind of a light. His teeth chattered and he began to shiver.

"You will? You will, eh?"

Behind him the mountain had been swallowed quite suddenly by the cloud. Broad, dark-blue arrows ran here and there over the water. Squalls make quickly in the lee sides of these high islands, quickly and without warning. The broad arrows collided; lost themselves in a broader, darker sheet. But Johnson did not see.

The shivering fit passed.

"You will, eh?" His lips drew back against his teeth. "We'll see. If you won't go one way, then you'll go the other. If you won't tack, by God, you'll *wear!*"

His voice rose of a sudden, powerful, strident:

"Hard aweather! Stand by to luff! *Mainsheet!*"

What happened in the moment while the vessel's head was swinging away from the wind will always remain fragmentary and confused in the telling. For one thing, you know, Johnson was not quite himself. And for another, his eyes were half blinded by the reclining disk of the sun.

At least this time the Negroes were on the move. He seemed to see John Bull making terrified gestures astern, and to hear his voice, thin and high: "Don't do it, sah! Fo' dearie God, sah!" And then there was Siza. Siza had to be dealt with. The large, glossy creature was laying hands on the wheel; actually striving, with the silent arrogance of panic, to tear his, Johnson's, away.

Johnson struck him, driving his knuckles with all his strength into the black meat of the Negro's face. He saw him falling away in a slow, sick arc. And after that he saw no more. A sudden shadow engulfed the ship. For an instant she stood perfectly upright, breathless; then, as if under the blow of another hand, she jibed over on the striking squall.

Johnson felt the main boom cutting the air over his bent head, and, as if in the same instant with it, the splintering crash of the thing fetching up on the sheet. He felt the deck turning over. He felt himself carried clumsily through the opaque air. And that was the last he felt.

Johnson was insensible for eight minutes and some seconds. The ship's clock had been striking four bells—that is to say, six o'clock—at the moment when he had put the helm aweather. And when he opened his eyes again it was precisely nine minutes after the hour. It is strange that he should remember it so definitely. Perhaps not so strange, though; for lying on his shoulder in the break of the companionway, against the side of which his flying head had struck, his first conscious sight was of the chronometer's face staring down at him, its broad brass hands pointing to nine minutes after the hour of six.

There was a welter of rain in the wind. It made a thunder along the decks. Johnson sat up. So he found himself face to face with Siza, who was also sitting up. For a moment they stared at each other.

"Where are we?" Johnson asked.

The Barbadian shook his mauled head.

"What beats me," Johnson resumed, in a dull, querulous fashion—"what beats me is why we didn't go right on over, bottom up."

Siza nodded aloft. "Mainsail went instead, sir."

Craning up, Johnson saw the boom stripped naked, sagging at the end of the topping lift. That seemed to bring him around. He jumped up, brushed the water from his eyes, and, turning forward, took stock of the schooner's condition. She had been pretty well swept clean. The mainsail, the tops, and all the headsails were gone, blown tidily out of their ring bolts. Only the foresail remained. And after he had looked at the foresail for a moment or so he wiped his eyes again.

"Good Lord alive!" he said to himself. He turned to glance over the stern. As far as he could see under the blanket of the squall, the schooner's wake made off, boiling and white. Yes, they were making way. There could be no doubt of it, they were making way, considerable way, and on the right tack, what was more. In the streaming wind, with only one sail left and the helm holding her up, she stayed herself with a kind of drunken rectitude and swept forward swiftly and blindly on the landward course—*his* course.

The pain in his head became nothing. He felt himself of a sudden heroic, puissant, indomitable. He sprang here and there, shouting strong commands.

"Siza! On your feet! Get forward with the lead, my boy. The lead! Look alive, or we'll run the island down. . . . Where's John Bull? John Bull! Ai! There! Look up, boy; it's all over! Get out of this! Confound your hide! Get out of this and tumble forward there. Stand by to lower away on the foresail when Siza sings! . . . Siza, look here! When you have four fathom, sing out, and sing out loud! . . ."

So his voice continued to ring along the decks above the tumult of the wind and rain, questioning, commanding.

"Five fathom, Siza? Keep an eye! Four fathom? All right, my boy! Lay aft at the double now and give John a hand with the fore. Let her run! Let her run! . . . Now clear that starboard anchor, quick! Plenty of chain, plenty of chain. . . ."

So it rang over the decks while the cloud tumbled to pieces and the wind went out. These leeside squalls are gone as abruptly as they come. One moment there was a black veil, a voice half drowned by falling water, the long-drawn rumble of chain paid through an iron hawsehole. . . . And, as if it were the moment following, a crystal clarity poured through the sky, and in the long afterglow of day the coco palms on the beach looked out to find a shape at rest upon the waters of the roadstead three cables off the beach, the loom of an island trading schooner half naked and half wrecked and somehow vaguely familiar.

Johnson, looking back at her from the customhouse landing over the bare shoulders of his oarsmen, felt for a moment a pang of pity. He had a vision of the warm yellow years that were done and of the strange, deep bond in exile that was broken. Just for a moment as he gazed back at her across the darkening mirror of the water, her will subdued, her passionate spirit conquered, her body stripped of its old extortionate loveliness, he felt the tragedy and the pathos of the thing.

He shook himself uneasily. "But, all the same," he muttered, "it had to be."

And, turning his back on her, he walked through the shadowed arch that cut the customhouse in half.

"Minna!" He lifted his arms impulsively in the gloom. "Minna! Oh, my Minna, my Minna!"

Yes, stranger things indeed had happened. It did not sound, somehow, as if he had come "to be good to her."

In the squalid darkness of the street beyond he caught a black boy by the shirt.

"Where is the lady? You know, the American lady from New York who has been here for a year perhaps? The lady called Mrs. Johnson? . . . What? At the Callends' place under the Morne Bruce? You're sure of that? Well, son, here's a black penny for you. I know the way."

The boy stared after him as with long, swift strides he vanished among the little houses of mud and thatch. Others, too, as he passed their dimly lighted doorways, stared after him. He had meant to shave, but he had forgotten it. He had meant to shift to his shore things, but he had forgotten that, too. He had no hat on, his feet were bare, and his thin, drenched shirt lay open at the breast. And the blood from his scalp wound, mixed with water and dried, spread a pinkish blur over one side of his fever-wasted face.

Nothing of this occurred to him until, done with the crowded darkness of the town, he found himself on a hillside, climbing a gravel roadway between thick, heavy-scented banks of foliage. An oppressive silence lay here, ruffled only by the infinitesimal whine of mosquitoes and the rare flicker of bats.

"I wonder," he said, and his pace grew a hint less headlong. His hands, groping blindly, touched his damp garments here and there, his stubbled, sunken cheeks, his unkempt hair.

"I wonder, Minna——" And then it came out, what he had studied so long to keep hidden away in the darkness of his heart. "I wonder —if you—what you will think—of *me*."

He had come to a wider place overtopping a thick-grown cliff. In the warm night he felt cold. He saw the house across the graveled dooryard. On the second floor there was a long, dark gallery with blinds, on the ground floor nothing but a wall of stucco, all blank save for a door in the center buried under a deep arch of twining bougainvillea. The door was open. In the doorway, shadowed against a dim interior glow of candles, he saw a figure waiting.

Johnson walked forward slowly, as if his feet had become lead. All the while he said to himself: "It can't be you! It can't be you!"

His hands were held out the least way in front of him, their palms upward. And he said, "No, no, it can't be Minna."

The figure left the shadow under the vine and came to meet him, moving slowly, too. And then in the faint sheen of the moonlight he saw that it was the figure of an island priest!

He stopped, with a sudden sense of suffocation.

"But—but I have *come!*"

The priest, startled and mystified by this extraordinary outburst, regarded him in silence.

"But she is here!" Johnson protested, huskily. "I—I am *he!* I am the man! I am Johnson—Albert M. Johnson! Don't you understand? I was—I am—her husband!"

The priest, moved perhaps by habit, or perhaps altogether by compassion, bowed his head.

"My son," he murmured, "she waited a long while."

Turning on his heel, he moved back slowly into the house. Johnson followed him. He saw her lying on the bed under the light of two tall candles. By the look on her dead face he saw that the priest had spoken the truth, perhaps more of the truth than he knew. For she had waited a very long while indeed.

The man lifted his face from the coverlet of the bed, where for a time it had lain hidden and motionless. There had been no sound in the room save the ticking of a nickel clock on an ant-bitten shelf in the farther corner; Johnson thought that the priest was gone. When he saw the dark-robed figure standing at the bed's foot the muscles of his gaunt face moved with a scarcely perceptible spasm.

"What time was it, Father?"

"What time?"

"When she—went. When she died."

"I have said, my son, but just now. Had you been but a little sooner——"

"Yes, yes, Father; but what hour? What minute of the hour?"

"Ah, but my son!" The priest lifted his hands in a gesture of deprecation. "As to the hour and minute——"

"Never mind," said Johnson.

He got to his feet and, without looking again at the priest or at the figure of the woman lying on the bed, he passed out of the door. Crossing the level bit, he came to the edge of the jungled declivity. With his hands locked behind him he stood there gazing out across the dark huddle of the town to where, shadowed forth with the faintest silver penciling of the sickle moon, the schooner lay at rest upon the water. And as he remembered the moment of pity he had felt for her his face grew paler yet and his teeth nipped tighter into the flesh of his lip. For now across the dim-lit space between them he seemed to catch the gesture of her quiescence, the sense of her mute and tranquil mockery.

"I might have known," he said, in a whisper, "when she didn't fight. And I can see now that she didn't fight; she came."

"Yes," he repeated, after another moment, "she came of her own will. She had me down. And then something happened, and she came."

He turned at sound of a gentle cough behind him.

"Were you still curious as to the time, my son?" The priest studied him thoughtfully. "For if you are, the maid who was with her has just now come in."

"Thank you, Father, but you needn't trouble." Johnson turned back to the cliff again. "For I know now," he said. "Minna died just after six–sometime between six and nine minutes after six o'clock this evening."

"Ah!" murmured the priest. "Yes, so I was told. . . ."

I am aware that it would make a better story if I could tell how Johnson took vengeance on his ship that night; how he rowed out to her alone, opened a seam with his own hands, and sent her reeling and bubbling down under the black waters of the roadstead. Or how, with a finer irony of imagination, he slipped her cable and let the wind take her out and away into the immeasurably empty spaces of ocean, to wait, as the other had waited, till a lonely derelict went down.

But the truth of the thing is that I have seen them both within a year. As I was coming into the bay at Barbados she was making out, full before the wind. And as she passed under our counter I saw him leaning on the wheel, gazing up at us (apparently) as he always had, with at least a ghost of that same old somnolent expression of disdain.

I don't know how it really was, but outwardly there seemed little change in either of them. Neither of them seemed much older. In the sanguine air of dawn I had the bizarre thought that they had somehow found their way to the far land and drunk of the waters of eternal youth. I don't know. Only one real change was apparent. As she passed close by I saw that the name under her taffrail had been changed. It caught the sun and glittered when she careened to our bow wave:

La Guiablesse.

*The Shame Dance**

STORIES OF NEW YORK LIFE PREFerable."

Well, then, here is a story of New York. A tale of the night heart of the city, where the vein of Forty-second touches the artery of Broadway; where, amid the constellations of chewing-gum ads and tooth pastes and memory methods, rise the incandescent façades of "dancing academies" with their "sixty instructresses," their beat of brass and strings, their whisper of feet, their clink of dimes. . . . Let a man not work away his strength and his youth. Let him breathe a new melody; let him draw out of imagination a novel step, a more fantastic tilt of the pelvis, a wilder gesticulation of the deltoid. Let him put out his hand to the Touch of Gold. . . .

It is a tale of this New York. That it didn't chance to happen in New York is beside the point. Where? It wouldn't help you much if I told you. Taai. That island. Take an imaginary ramrod into Times Square, push it straight down through the center of the earth; where it comes out on the other side will not be very many thousand miles wide of that earth speck in the South Seas. Some thousands, yes; but out here a few thousand miles and a month or so by schooner make less difference than they do where the trains run under the ground. . . .

"Glauber's Academy" . . . "Einstein's Restaurant" . . . "Herald Square" . . .

I can't tell you how bizarrely those half-fabulous names fell from Signet's lips in the turquoise and gold of the afternoon. It was like the babble of some monstrous and harmless mythology. And all the while, as he kicked his bare heels on the deckhouse and harassed me with his somnolent greed for "talk," one could see him wondering, wondering, in the back of his mind. So he would have been wondering through all the hours of weeks, months—it had come to the dignity of years, on the beach, in the bush—wondering more than ever under the red iron roof of the Dutchman: "What in hell am I doing here? What in hell?"

A guttersnipe, pure and simple. That's to say *im*pure and unpleasantly complex. It was extraordinary how it stuck. Even with nothing on but a pair of cotton pants, swimming out to me among the flashing bodies of the islanders, men, women, girls, youths, who clung to the anchor cable and showed their white teeth for pilot biscuit, condensed milk, and gin—especially gin—even there you could see Signet, in imagination, dodging through the traffic on Seventh Avenue to pick the *Telegraph Racing Chart* out of the rubbish can under the Elevated. . . .

I hadn't an idea who the fellow was. He burst upon me unheralded. I sail out of west-coast ports, but once I had been in New York. That was enough for him. He was "pals" in ten minutes; in fifteen, from his eminence on the deckhouse, with a biscuit in one hand and a tumbler of much-diluted Hollands in the other, he gazed down at his erstwhile beach fellows with almost the disdainful wonder of a tourist from a white ship's rail. . . .

"Gi' me an article you can retail at a nickel—any little thing everybody needs—or gi' me a song with a catchy chorus—something you can turn out on them ten-cent records. . . . That makes *me*. Don't want any Wall Street stuff. That's for Rockefeller and the boobs. But just one time le' me catch on with one little old hunch that'll go in vaudeville or the pi'tures—get Smith and Jones diggin' for the old nickel. . . . That makes *me*. Then the line can move up one. That's the thing about New York. . . . Say, man, len' me a cigarette. . . . But that's the thing about Broadway. When you make, you make *big*. I know a guy turned out a powder puff looked like a lor'nette—a quarter of a dollar. You know how the Janes'll fall for a thing like that."

It was completely preposterous, almost uncomfortable. It made a man look around him. On the schooner's port side spread the empty blue of the South Pacific; the tenuous snowdrift of the reef, far out, and the horizon. On the starboard hand, beyond the little space of the anchorage, curved the beach, a pink-white scimitar laid flat. Then the scattering of thatched and stilted huts, the red, corrugated-iron store, residence and godowns of the Dutch trader, the endless Indian file of coco palms, the abrupt green wall of the mountain. . . . A twelve-year-old girl, naked as Eve and, I've no doubt, thrice as handsome, stood watching us from the mid-decks in a perfection of immobility, an empty milk tin propped between her brown palms resting on her breast. Twenty fathoms off, a shark fin, blue as lapis in the shadow, cut the water soundlessly. The hush of ten thousand miles was disturbed by nothing but that grotesque, microscopic babbling:

"Say you play in bad luck. Well, you can't play in bad luck *f'rever*. Not if you're wise. One time I get five good wheezes. Good ones! Sure-fire! One of 'em was the old one about the mother-'n-law and the doctor, only it had a perfectly novel turn to it. Did I make? I did not. Why? Well, a good friend o' mine lifts them five wheezes, writes a vaudeville turn around 'em, and makes big. Big! What does that learn me? Learns me to go bear on friendship. So next time I get an idea . . ."

The girl had put the milk tin down between her toes on deck and turned her head.

"Digger!" I called to the mate. "Clear the vessel! Shove them all overboard! Here comes the Dutchman!"

Before the advance of the trader's canoe, painted vermilion like his establishment and flying over the water under the paddle strokes of his six men, Signet took himself hastily overboard with the rest. There was no question of protest or false pride. Over he went. Rising and treading water under the taffrail, and seeing the trader still some fathoms off, he shook the wet from the rag of a beard with which long want of a razor had blurred his peaked chin and gathered up the ends of the conversation:

"No, Dole, you can't play in bad luck *f'rever*. One sure-fire hunch, that's all. That makes me. When I get back to Broadway . . ."

A paddle blade narrowly missed his head. He dived.

The Dutchman told me more about him that evening. I dined at the trader's house. He was a big-bodied, tow-haired man who spoke English with the accent of an east-coast Scot, drank like a Swede, and viewed life through the eyes of a Spaniard—that is, he could be diabolical without getting red in the face.

"No, my dear sir, that Signet shall not 'get back to Broadway.' Too many have I seen. He is too tired. Quite too tired."

"But how in the world did he ever come here, Mynheer?"

"That is simple. This Signet got drunk in Papeete. He was on his way to Australia with a pugilist. How should he be in a pugilist's company, this crab? Because he plays a good game of pinochle—to keep the pugilist's mind bright. At any event, the steamship stops at Tahiti. This Signet gets drunk. 'Soused!' And the steamship is gone without him. No more pinochle for the pugilist, what? . . . From then, my dear sir, it is what it shall always be; one island throws him to another island. Here he shall stay for a while——"

"Till you decide to 'throw' him to another island, eh, Mynheer?"

"No, but I am alone. Sometimes to amuse myself I will invite him to dine with me. I put on him a suit of the evening clothes which belong to my nephew who is dead. But I will not allow him the razor, since his absurd beard is amusing to me. Afterward, however, I take away the evening clothes and I will kick him out. But he is talking continuously."

"I believe you, Mynheer."

"But at last I will say: 'My dear sir, suppose that you should have the most brilliant idea; that "hunch" of yours. "Sure-fire." What advantage will it do you here in the island of Taai? You are not here on Broadway. You are too many thousand miles. You cannot come there. You are too tired. It takes money. Now, my dear sir, I am putting a trench about the godowns. If you wish, I will let you work for me.' "

"What does he say to that, Mynheer?"

"He says, 'Do you take me for an *I*talian?'

"Then I will say: 'No; you see you are too tired. Also you are too soft. You are a criminal. That's natural to you. But you think of police. You have a wish, say. Well, my dear sir, but would you kill a man—three—ten men—to have that wish? No, you are too tired, and you must have the police. But here there are no police. I am the police. Why do you not kill *me?* Ha-ha-ha! Then you could take my property. Then you would "make big," as you say. My dear sir, that is a "hunch"! That is "sure-fire"! Ha-ha-ha!' . . . Then I will kick him out in his coolie pants."

After coffee the trader said: "One gallon of the Hollands which you sent me ashore has disappeared. The kitchen boys are 'careless.'

Also I wink one eye when a schooner arrives. Of course they will dance tonight, however. You would care to go up, my dear sir?"

Of course we went. There's no other amusement in an islet like Taai but the interminable native dance. The Dutchman led the way up a narrow, bushy ravine, guiding me by sound rather than by sight.

"Up this same very path," I heard him saying, "has gone one uncle of mine. They pulled him to the advance with one rope around his arms. Then they cut him up and ate him. But that was many years ago, my dear sir. Now I am the law. Maybe there shall come, now and then, a Dutch gunboat to have a look-in. I raise up that flag. The captain shall dine with me. All is good. But, my dear sir, I am the law."

The "music" began to be heard, a measured monotone of drums, a breath of voices in a recitative chant, slightly impassioned by that vanished gallon. The same old thing, indeed; one of the more than fifty-seven varieties of the hula. Then that had died away.

The light from the "place" grew among the higher leaves. And the trader, becoming visible, halted. I saw him standing, listening.

"No, my dear sir, but that is a new thing."

He started forward. He stopped again. I heard it now. Out of the familiar, hollow tautophony of drumbeats there began to emerge a thread of actual melody—an untraditional rise and fall of notes—a tentative attack, as it were, on the chromatic scale of the West. No he-goat's skin stretched on bamboo would do that.

We pushed on, curious. We came out into the "place." The scene under the candlenut torches was as familiar to us as the Ohio River of Uncle Tom to the small-town schoolboy; the meager rows of three-quarters-naked Kanakas, yellow with saffron and blue with tattooer's ink; the old women in the background of sultry lights and enormous shadows compounding endless balls of *popoi* for the feast; the local and desceptered chieftain squatting on his hams and guarding the vanished gallon between his knees; this was all as it should have been. This was the convention. . . . But what was really happening on that sylvan, torchlit stage that night was something as new as anything can be under the sun, because it was something that had not happened in ten thousand years. . . .

We who are worn with novelty can never reconquer for ourselves the thrill of an unmitigated wonder. We have sold the birthright.

But imagine the toppling of a hundred centuries! You could have seen it in the eyes of those watchers, in their rapt, rapacious attention, in the conflict that went on within them visibly; traitorous applause pent and pitted against all the instinctive protest of an established art. . . .

"Yes, but this isn't *dancing!*"

Yet their bodies, one here, one there, would begin to sway. . . .

Three Kanaka men, strangers to the island, sat cross-legged on the turf. One had taken over a drum from a local musician. The other two had instruments fashioned of dried gourds with fingering pieces of bamboo and strings of gut—barbaric cousins to the mandolin. So, on this one night in history, the music of another tribe had come to Taai. It just escaped being an authentic "tune." How it escaped was indefinable. The sophisticated ear would almost have it, and abruptly it had got away in some provoking lapse, some sudden and bizarre disintegration of tone. And the drumbeat, bringing it back, ran like a fever pulse in a man's blood.

In the center of the sward, her back to the musicians, a solitary female danced; a Kanaka woman, clothed in a single shift of the sheerest crimson cotton, tied at one shoulder and falling to mid-thigh. Not from Taai did this woman come; one saw that; nor from any near island or group. Her beauty was extraordinary, like that of the Marquesans, with that peculiar straightness of all lines, at once Grecian, austere, and incalculably voluptuous. . . .

The dance, as I saw it for the first time that night, I will not speak of. I have traded to many islands in many groups—even the Low Archipelago—but the island where that dance was indigenous I am sure I've never touched. Compared with any of the hulas, set and fixed in each locality as the rites of Rome, it was sophisticated; it gave an illusion of continuous invention and spontaneity; it was flesh swept by a wind and shattered; it ravished the eyes.

I don't know how long I watched; how long all the immortal flame in me lent itself to the histrionic purposes of that woman. But I shall never forget it. Never! Never!

I looked away. I saw two faces. One of them hung over my shoulder. It was the trader's. It was the face of a man who has lived a very long while wielding power of life and death over unsatisfying satisfactions. A man awakened! The toppling of a hundred centuries, indeed!

The other was Signet's. Scarred by leaf shadows, thrust like a swimmer's from the meager sea of heads and naked shoulders, it held as still as a death mask minute by minute, except that, in the penumbra cast by the veil of goat tuft on his chin, the Adam's apple was convulsed at intervals, as if he were swallowing, as if he were *drinking!*

The night grew. The torches were consumed, the "place" deserted. Somewhere the amazing voyagers had taken themselves to rest. A half-moon mutilated the island—long stripes of palms, shadow-scars of defiles, mottles of bushes. It was like a sleeping animal, a tiger of deep blue and blue-white.

We sat on the veranda at the Residence, the trader and I. By and by, soft-footed, Signet was there, occupying the lowermost step.

The Dutchman talked. Like the able administrator he was, he had already the data to be procured. Into his ears had poured the whispered trickles of a score of informants.

"You are right, my dear sir. Marquesan. You have been there?"

"No."

"She is called, in Polynesian, 'Queen Daughter.' My people, who know nothing as a rule, of course—but they tell me the woman is in actuality the daughter of a queen. But what is a Kanaka queen? After all, Signet, my dear sir, down there, what is one queen, out here?"

The trader was obviously in a good humor. He had not been excited for years. The man was alive. I've said he was like a Spaniard in that he could be diabolical without getting red in the face. Diabolically devious and strategic! Before he resumed he blew three mouthfuls of cigar smoke out into the moonlight, where they burst from the shadow under the roof like mute cannon shots, round and silvery. Beneath them, from the step, Signet's eyes were fixed upon the trader's face, dry, rapt, glazed with some imperious preoccupation.

"But they tell me this woman has danced in a great many islands. She will go from here to another island to dance. The three men are her husbands. But she is no wife. A maid, that woman! They have the hardihood to tell me that. Ha-ha-ha! But, then, she is daughter to a queen. With those 'husbands' she crosses a hundred leagues of sea in her sailing canoe. That royal canoe! To dance at another island. . . ."

As the Dutchman talked, blowing his smoke bursts into the moonlight, the vision of that Marquesan woman came again before me. I perceived her, under the heavy procession of his words, a figure of astounding romance, an adventuress incomparable, a Polynesian bacchante. No, I saw her as the missionary of a strange thing, crossing oceans, daring thirst and gale and teeth of sharks, harrying deeper and deeper into the outseas of mystery that small, devoted polyandrous company of husbands, at once her paddlers, cooks, flunkies, watchdogs, music makers. "Queen Daughter!" Royal and self-anointed priestess of that unheard-of dance, the tribal dance, no doubt, of some tiny principality rearing a cone in the empty hugeness of the sea. . . . I couldn't get away from my time and race. I found myself wondering "what she got out of it"—in some jungle-bowered, torchlit "high place," to feel again the toppling of ten thousand years? Was it something to feel the voluptuous and abominable beauty of that rhythm going out of her flesh, beat by beat, and entering into the flesh of those astounded and half-hostile watchers? Perhaps. . . .

"They tell me that she has also danced at Papeete—before the white men of the steamships," the Dutchman was informing us.

At that, from the step, from the moon-blue huddle of the castaway, there came a sound. With a singular clarity of divination I built up the thought, the doubt, the bitter perturbation in the fellow's mind. The woman had danced then at Papeete, the crossroads, the little Paris of mid-seas. And before the white men from steamers —the white men that go back!

Moved by projects deeper and more devious than ours, the Dutchman made haste to cover up what seemed to have been an overshot. Frankly he turned his attention to the outcast.

"By the God, then, my dear Signet, have you considered?"

He knew well enough that Signet had "considered." He could see as well as I that Signet was a changed man. But he must "pile it on."

"There, my dear sir, you have it. That 'hunch'! That 'sure-fire'! Do you think I do not know that New York of yours? Such a dance as that! You must believe me. If you were but a man of energy, now . . ." With the utmost deliberation he launched upon a tirade of abuse. "But no, you are not a man of energy, not a man to take things in your hands. The obstacles are too big. Those three husbands! You might even take that woman, that lovely, royal dancing woman—you, my dear sir, a common street snipe. What would a woman like that, with that novel, impassioned, barbaric, foreign dance, be worth to a man on your Broadway? Eh? But obstacles! Obstacles! You have her not on Broadway. It is too many thousands of miles, and you have no money. But see, if you were a man to grasp things, a man to 'hit the nail in the head,' to 'boost,' to 'go big'—then would not a man like me, who turns everything to gold—would he not say to you quickly enough, 'See here, my dear sir, but let me put so much money into the undertaking myself'?"

Under the explosions of cigar smoke, Signet continued to hold the trader with his eyes; seemed to consume him with the fixed, dry fire of his gaze. Not fathoming, as with a singular intuition I had fathomed, the profound purposes of the Dutchman, Signet saw only the implied promise in his words. . . . The trader broke out once more with a sardonic and calculated spleen:

"But no! Obstacles! A sniveling little animal sees only obstacles. The obstacle not to be mounted over—those three husbands. There they lie tonight on Nakokai's platform—this beautiful, incredible 'Queen Daughter'—this gold goddess of the 'Shame Dance'—and about her those three husbands. Ah, my dear sir, but their big, lithe muscles! That is too much! To imagine them leaping up at the alarm in the moonlight, the overpowering and faithful husbands. No, he cannot put out his hand to take the gift. *Pah!* He is a criminal in nature, but he is afraid of the police, even here. He is not a man for the big life in these islands. He will never do anything. Those faithful, strong watchdogs of husbands! Those strong destructive muscles! Dear, good God, that is too much to think of. . . . Look, my dear sir!"

He was speaking to me, as if Signet were less than the very pebbles at the step. He got up, striking the floor heavily with his boots, and I followed him into the house, where he took a lighted candle from a stand. Buried in our shadows, silent-footed, Signet pursued us as the trader had meant him to do. I persist in saying that I perceived the thing as a whole. From the first I had divined the maneuver of the Dutchman.

"Look!" he repeated, flinging open a door and thrusting in the candle to cast its light over ranks and ranges of metal. It was the gun room of the Residence. Here dwelt the law. Shotguns, repeating rifles, old-style revolvers, new, blue automatics. An arsenal!

"Big brown muscles!" he cried, with a ponderous disdain. "What are they? What is the strongest brown man? *Puff!* To a man of purpose and indomitable will like me! Obstacles? Three husbands? *Puff-puff-puff!* Like that! . . . But all that will never be of use to *him.* That Signet! No, he is a street snipe who will steal a pocket-book and call it a crime. He is afraid to grasp. . . . But it is close in here, is it not?"

It was too bald. He stepped across the floor, unlatched and threw open the blind of the window, letting the candlelight stream forth upon a mass of bougainvillea vine without.

"I keep this door locked; you can imagine that," he laughed, returning and shutting us out of the gun room. He twisted the key; put it in his pocket. And there, at the back, that window blind stood open.

He stared at Signet, as if the beachcomber were just discovered. "You are hopeless, my dear sir."

"Let us have a drink," he shifted.

For Signet he poured out a tumblerful of raw gin. The fellow took it like a man in a daze—the daze of a slowly and fiercely solidifying resolution. It shivered in his hand. A habit of greed sucked his lips. Into his mouth he took a gulp of the spirits. He held it there. His eyes searched our faces with a kind of malignant defiance. Of a sudden he spat the stuff out, right on the floor. He said nothing. It was as if he said: "By God, if you think I need *that! No!* You don't know me!"

He stalked out of the door. When we followed as far as the veranda we saw him making off into the striped light to the left. . . .

"Why did you call it the 'Shame Dance,' Mynheer?" We were seated again.

"Of course, my dear sir, it is not that, but it has a sound so when the Kanakas speak it. The woman spoke the name. If it is a Polynesian word I have not heard it before. 'Shemdance.' Like that."

"A good name, though. By jingo, a darn good name! Eh, Mynheer?"

But the trader's head was turned in an attitude of listening. Triumphant listening—at the keyhole of the striped, moonlit night. I heard it, too—a faint disturbance of the bougainvillea foliage around two sides of the house, near the window standing open to the gun room.

Of course the amazing thing was that the man fooled us. In the Dutchman's heart, I believe, there was nothing but astonishment at his own success. Signet, on the face of it, was the typical big talker and little doer; a flaw in character which one tends to think imperishable. He fitted so precisely into a certain pigeonhole of humankind. . . . What we had not counted on was the fierceness of the stimulus —like the taste of blood to a carnivore, or, to the true knight, a glimpse of the veritable Grail.

All the following day I spent on board overseeing the hundred minor patchings and calkings a South Sea trader will want in port. When I went ashore that evening, after sundown, I found the Dutchman sitting in the same chair on the veranda, blowing smoke out into the afterglow. There was the illusion of perfect continuity with the past. Yesterday, today, tomorrow. Life flowed like a sleeping river, it would seem.

But this was the status of affairs. The three brown music makers, sons-in-law to an island queen, lay on a platform somewhere within the edge of the bush heavier by ounces with .32-caliber slugs, awaiting burial. And Signet, guttersnipe, beachcomber, and midnight assassin, was lodged in the "calaboose," built stoutly in a corner of the biggest and reddest of the Dutchman's godowns. As for the royal dancing woman, I was presently, in the trader's phrase, to "have a look at her."

At his solicitation I followed around the house, past the gun-room window (locked fast enough now, you may be sure), and up steeply through a hedged, immaculate garden which witnessed to the ordered quality of the owner's mind. At the upper end, under a wall of volcanic tufa, we came to a summerhouse done in the native style, stilts below, palm thatch above, and walled on three sides only with hanging screens of bamboo. Striking through this screen from the west, the rose and green of the afterglow showed the woman as in a semiluminous cavern, seated cross-legged in the center of the platform, her hands drooped between her knees, and her large, dark eyes fixed upon the sea beyond the roof of the Residence below.

Was it the perfect immobility of defiance and disdain? Not once did her transfixed gaze take us in. Was it the quiescence of defeat and despair—that level brooding over the ocean which had been to her, first and last, a cradle and a roadway for her far, adventurous pilgrimages? She sat there before our peering eyes, the sudden widow, the daughter of potentates brought low, the goddess of an exuberant and passionate vitality struck with quietude; mute, astounded by catastrophe, yet unbowed. The beauty of that golden-skinned woman abashed me.

It did not abash the Dutchman. His was another and more indomitable fiber. It is fine to succeed, beyond expectation, detail by detail of strategy. His hands were clean. He remained the perfect administrator. Had there been no other way, he would not have flinched at any necessary lengths of wholesale or retail butchery. Still, it was nice to think that his hands were spotless. For instance, if that gunboat, with its purple-whiskered Amsterdammer of a captain, should just now happen in.

His face glowed in the dusk. His eyes shone with frank calculations. Fists on hips, head thrust out, one saw him casting up the sum of his treasure-trove. . . . But he was an epicure. He could wait. It was even delightful to wait. When I turned away he came down with me, his hands still on his hips and his eyes on the gently emerging stars.

The man was extraordinary. Sitting on the veranda, bombarding the direction of the foreshore with that huge, deliberate fusillade of cigar smoke, he talked of home, of his boyhood on the dike at Volendam, and of his mother, who, bless her! was still alive to send him cheeses at Christmas time.

It was midnight and the moon was rising when I got away and moved down toward the beach where the dinghy waited. The horizontal ray struck through the grating of the "calaboose" at the corner of the godown I was skirting. I saw the prisoner. The upright shadow of an iron bar cut his face in two, separating the high, soiled cheeks, each with an eye.

"You mustn't leave him get at her!"

I tell you it was not the same man that had come swimming and sniveling out to the schooner less than forty hours before. Here was a fierce one, a zealot, a flame, the very thin blade of a fine sword.

"Listen, Dole, if you leave that devil get at her—"

His eyes burned through me. He failed completely to accept the fact that he was done. His mind, ignoring the present, ran months ahead. With a flair of understanding, thinking of those three travesties of husbands and the wife who was no wife, I perceived what he meant.

I left him. He was a wild man, but the quality of his wildness showed itself in the fact that he squandered none of it in shaking the bars, shouting, or flinging about. His voice to the last, trailing me around the next corner, held to the same key, almost subdued.

"By God, if that bastard gets at her, I'll–I'll––"

"You'll what?" I mused. You see, even now I couldn't get rid of him as the drifter, the gutter Hamlet, the congenital howler against fate. "You'll what?" I repeated under my breath, and I had to laugh.

I got the vessel under way as soon as I came aboard. The Dutchman's shipment of copra was arranged for–a week, two, three weeks (as the wind allowed)–and I was to return from the lower islands, where my present cargo was assigned, and take it on.

As we stood offshore under the waxing moonlight, as I watched the island, gathering itself in from either extremity, grow small and smaller on the measureless glass of the sea, the whole episode seemed to swell up in my mind, explode, and vanish. It was too preposterous. Thirty-eight hours chosen at random out of ten thousand empty Polynesian years–that in that wink of eternity five human lives should have gone to pot simultaneously–a man wasn't to be taken in by that sort of thing.

Through twelve days it remained at that. Discharging cargo in the furnace of Coco Inlet, if my thoughts went back to Taai, it was almost with the deprecating amusement a man will feel who has been had by a hoax. If those minstrel husbands were murdered and buried; if that Broadway imp sweated under the red-hot roof of the godown; if that incomparable, golden-skinned heiress of cannibal emperors sat staring seaward from the gilded cage of the Dutchman, awaiting (or no longer awaiting) the whim of the epicure–if indeed any one of them all had ever so much as set foot upon that microscopic strand lost under the blue equator–then it was simply because someone had made it up in his head to while me away an empty hour. I give you my word, when at noon of the thirteenth day the mountain of Taai stood up once more beyond the bows, I was weary of the fantasy. I should have been amazed, really, to find a fellow named Signet housed in the Dutchman's private jail.

As a matter of fact, Signet was not in the jail.

When I went ashore in midafternoon, wondering a little why no naked biscuit beggars or gin swallowers had swum out to bother me that day, I found the trader of Taai sitting on his veranda, blowing puffs of smoke from those fine Manila Club perfectos out into the sunshine. Beside him leaned a shiny, twelve-gauge pump gun which he jostled with an elbow as he bade me by word and gesture to make myself at home.

I'm quite certain I looked the fool. My eyes must have stuck out. Half a dozen times I started to speak. With some vacant, fatuous syllable I tried to break the ice. Strange as it sounds, I was never so embarrassed in my life.

For the trader of Taai, the blatantly obvious proprietor of the island's industry and overlord of its destinies—sitting there before me now with a pump gun touching his elbow—was this fellow Signet.

Till now I don't know precisely what had happened; that is to say, none of the details of the act, horrid or heroic as they may have been. All I seemed to have was a memory of the Dutchman's voice: "Why do you not kill *me?* Ha-ha-ha! Then you could take my property." And again an echo of his disdainful laughter at that fool, "Ha-ha-ha!" as, on some midnight, he had kicked his dinner guest and his "coolie cotton pants" out into the rain. . . . Why not, indeed? But who now was the "fool"?

Signet, in the course of the afternoon, brought forth gravely a bill of sale, making over in an orderly fashion to B. R. Signet, U.S.A., the real and personal property of the trading station at Taai, and "signed," in the identical, upright, Fourteenth Street grammar-school script, by "the Dutchman.". . . I understood Signet. Signet understood me. The thing was not even an attempt at forgery. It was something solely formal—as much as to say: "This is understood to be the basis of our mutual dealings. You will see I am owner of this place."

As for the Dutchman:

"Oh, the Dutchman? Well, he decided to go away. Go home."

Before the incalculable *sang-froid* of this railbird, movie usher, alley dodger, and hanger-on at dancing academies, I could not so much as summon up the cheek to ask what he had done with the body. You'll say I ought to have acted; that I ought at least to have got up and left him. That shows two things—first, that you've never been a trader in the islands; second, that you cannot at all comprehend how—well, how *stunning* he was. Sitting there, a single fortnight removed from cotton pants and the beach, crime-stained, imperturbable, magnificent! Spawn of the White Lights! Emperor of an island! How's that?

"It's a rich island," he impressed upon me with an intention I was yet to plumb. "Dole," he exclaimed, "it's a gold mine!"

"Is—is *she* here?" I ventured to demand at last.

"*Is* she? Say! Come and have a look."

I was between laughing and wincing at the identical "have a look."

Going up the garden, Signet let we know that the woman was in love with him. I might believe it or not. She would do anything for him.

"*Anything!*" he exclaimed, standing squarely still in the path. And in his eyes I was somehow relieved to find a trace of wonder.

Obstacles! All his life had been a turning back from small, insurmountable obstacles. Of a sudden he beheld really vast obstacles tumbling down, verily at a touch. Here was just one more of them. By a lucky chance this "Queen Daughter" did not know by whose hand she had been made thrice a widow; it was the simplest thing to suppose it the trader, the same big, blond, European man who had presently removed her "for safety" to the summerhouse behind the Residence. . . . And from the trader, by a gesture of melodramatic violence, the other and slighter man had set her free. . . . Perhaps even that would not have intrigued her essentially barbaric interest as much as it did had it not been for his amazing attitude of, well, let's say, "refrainment." His almost absurdly fastidious concern for what the West would call "the sanctity of her person." You can imagine—to a Marquesan woman! That! She was not ugly.

As her gaze, from the platform, dwelt upon the shrewd, blade-sharp features of the man beside me, the elementary problem in her eyes seemed to redouble the peculiar, golden, Aryan beauty of her face. Let me tell you I am human. Perhaps Signet was human, too. Standing there, encompassed by the light of that royal and lovely woman's eyes, there was surely about him a glow—and a glow not altogether, it seemed to me, of "Smith's nickel and Jones's dime." I could have laughed. I could have kicked him. The impostor! Even yet I had failed to measure the man.

Back on the veranda again, dinner eaten and dusk come down, Signet brought out an old guitar from among the Dutchman's effects (it had belonged probably to that defunct nephew of the dress clothes), and as he talked he picked at the thing with idle fingers. Not altogether idle, though, I began to think. Something began to emerge by and by from the random fingerings—a rhythm, a tonal theme. . . . Then I had it, and there seemed to stand before me again the swarded "high place," with torches flaring over upturned faces and mounting walls of green. Almost I sensed again the beat in my blood, the eye-ravishing vision of that gold-brown flame of motion, that voluptuous priestess.

"Oh yes. That!" I murmured. "It's got something–something–that tune. . . . But how can you remember it?"

"*She* helps me out. I'm trying to put it in shape."

Indeed, when I left that night, and before my oarsmen had got me a cable's length from the beach, I heard the strumming resumed, very faintly, up in the dark behind the Residence; still tentatively, with, now and then through the flawless hush of the night, the guiding note of a woman's voice. (A woman profoundly mystified.)

A rehearsal? For what? For that almost mythical Broadway half around the bulge of the world? Had the fool, then, not got beyond *that?* Yet?

Here he was, lord of the daughter of a queen, proprietor of a "gold mine." For Signet was not to be hoodwinked about the commercial value of Taai. All afternoon and evening, as through the two days following, while my promised cargo was getting ferried out under the shining authority of the pump gun, he scarcely let a minute go by without some word or figure to impress upon me the extent of his "possessions." To what end?

Well, it all came out in a burst on the third evening, my last there. He even followed me to the beach; actually, regardless of the Dutchman's nephew's boots and trouser legs, he pursued me out into the shallows.

"A gold mine! Don't be a damned boob, Dole. You can see for yourself, a big proposition for a guy like you, with a ship and everything——"

Upon me he would heap all those priceless "possessions." Me! And in exchange he would ask only cabin passage for two from Taai beach to the Golden Gate. Only deck passage! Only anything!

"Set us down there, me and her, that's all. I'll give you a bill of sale. Why, from where you look at it, it's a *find!* It's a lead-pipe cinch! It's taking candy away from a baby, man!"

"Why don't you keep it, then?"

The soul of his city showed through. I saw him again as I had seen him swimming out in his cotton pants, with that low-comedy whisker and that consuming little greedy nickel hope of paradise. Even the gestures.

"No, but can't you see, Dole? I got a bigger thing up my sleeve. God'l'-mighty, d'you think I'm a *farmer?* You could go big here; *I* don't go at all. I ain't that kind. But put me down in New York with that woman there and that there dance—and that tune—— Say! You don't understand. You can't imagine. Money? Say! And not only money. Say! I could take that up to Glauber's Academy, and I could say to Glauber, 'Glauber,' I could say . . ."

I had to leave him standing there, up to his knees in the inky water, heaping me frankly with curses. I shall not repeat the curses. At the end of them he bawled after me:

"But I'll get there! You watch me all the same, all the same, you damn . . ."

The reason I didn't up-anchor and get out that night was that when I came aboard I discovered not far from my berth the unobtrusive loom of that Dutch gunboat, arrived for a "look-in" at last.

The only thing for me to do was to sit tight. If, when the state of the island's affairs had been discovered, there should be want of explanation or corroboration, it would be altogether best for me to give it. I wasn't yet through trading in those waters, you understand.

But Signet was no fool. He, too, must have seen the discreet shade of the visitor. When the morning dawned, neither he nor the royal dancer from the Marquesas was to be found. Sometime in that night, from the windward beach, ill-manned and desperate, the royal sailing canoe must have set forth tumultuously upon its pilgrimage again.

I sat in a place in Honolulu. Soft drinks were served, and somewhere beyond a tidy screen of palm fronds a band of strings was playing. Even with soft drinks, the old instinct of wanderers and lone men to herd together had put four of us down at the same table. Two remain vague—a fattish, holiday-making banker and a consumptive from Barre, Vermont. For reasons to appear, I recall the third more in detail.

He let me know somewhere in the give-and-take talk that he was a railway-telegraph operator, and that, given his first long vacation, an old impulse come down from the days of the Hawaiian hula phonograph records had brought him to the isle of delight. He was disappointed in it. One could see in his candid eyes that he felt himself done out of an illusion, an illusion of continuous dancing by girls in rope skirts on moonlit beaches. It was an intolerable waste of money. Here, come so far and so expensively to the romantic goal, he was disturbed to find his imagination fleeing back to the incredible adventure of a Rock Island station, an iron-red dot on the bald, high plain of eastern Colorado—to the blind sun flare of the desert—to the immensity of loneliness—to the thundering nightly crisis of the "Eleven-ten," sweeping monstrous and one-eyed out of the cavern of the West, grating, halting, glittering, gossiping, yawning, drinking with a rush and gurgle from the red tank—and on again with an abrupt and always startling clangor into the remote night of the East. . . .

He shifted impatiently in his chair and made a dreary face at the screening fronds.

"For the love o' Mike! Even the rags they play here are old."

The consumptive was telling the banker about the new co-operative scheme in Barre, Vermont.

"For the love o' Mike!" my friend repeated. "That ain't a band; it's a historical s'ciety. Dead and buried! Next they'll strike up that latest novelty rage, 'In the Shade of the Old Apple Tree'! . . . Now will you listen to that. Robbin' the cemetery!"

He needn't have asked me to listen. As a matter of fact I had been listening for perhaps a hundred seconds; listening, not as if with the ears, but with the deeper sensatory nerves. And without consciously grasping what the air was, I had suffered an abrupt voyage through space. I saw a torchlit sward, ringed with blue and saffron faces and high forest walls; I saw the half-nude, golden loveliness of a Polynesian woman shaken like a windy leaf. And the beat of a goat-hide drum was the beat of my blood. I felt my shoulders swaying.

I looked at the young man. His face expressed a facetious weariness, but his shoulders, too, were swaying.

"What tune is that?" I asked, in a level tone.

His contemptuous amazement was unfeigned.

"Holy Moses, man! Where you been?"

He squinted at me. After all, I might be "stringing" him.

"That," he said, "is as old as Adam. It was run to death so long ago I can't remember. That? That's 'Paragon Park.' That is the old original first 'Shimmie' dance—with whiskers two feet long."

"The original what?"

"Shimmie! *Shimmie!* Say, honest to God, don't you know——?" And with his shoulders he made a wriggling gesture in appeal to my wits, the crudest burlesque, it seemed, of a divinely abominable gesture in my memory. . . . "That?" he queried. "Eh?"

"Shimmie," I echoed, and, my mind skipping back: "*Shemdance! Shame Dance!* . . . I see!"

"Why?" he demanded, intrigued by my preoccupation.

"Nothing. It just reminded me of something."

Then he lifted a hand and smote himself on the thigh. "Me, too! By jinks! Say, I'd almost forgot that."

He hitched his chair upon me; held me down with a forefinger.

"Listen. That was funny. It was one night—last fall. It was just after Number Seventeen had pulled out, westbound, about one-forty in the morning. There wasn't anything else till six-one. Them are always the hardest hours. A fellow's got to stay awake, see, and nothin' to keep him—unless maybe a coyote howlin' a mile off, or maybe a bum knockin' around among the boxcars on the sidin', or, if it's cold, the stove to tend. That's all. Unless you put a record on the old phonograph and hit 'er up a few minutes now and then. Dead? Say, boy!

"Well, this night it was a bum. I'm sittin' there in the coop, countin' my fingers and listenin' to Limon calling off car numbers to Denver—just like that I'm sittin'—when I hear somethin' out in the waitin' room. Not very loud. . . . Well, I go out there, and there's the bum. Come right into the waitin' room.

"Bum! If he wasn't the father and mother and brother and sister of the original bum, I'll eat my hat. Almost a Jew-lookin' guy, and he'd saw hard service. But he's got a kind o' crazy glitter in his eye.

" 'Well,' says I, just like that, 'Well, what do *you* want?'

"He don't whine; he don't handle the pan. He's got that look in his eye.

" 'My woman is out in them boxcars,' says he. 'I'm goin' to bring her in here where it's warm.' That's what he says. Not '*can* I bring her in?' but '*goin'* to bring her in'! From a *hobo!*

"Can you imagine? It makes me think. It comes to me the guy is really off his trolley. To keep him calm I says, 'Well——'

"He goes out. 'I'm shed o' *him*,' I says to myself. Not a bit. About three minutes and here he comes trottin' back, sure enough, bringin' a woman with him. Now, mister—what's y'r-name—prepare to laugh. That there woman—listen—make up your face—she's a *nigger!*

"He says she ain't a nigger.

" 'Mexican?' says I.

" 'No,' says he.

"I give her another look, but I can't make much out of her, except she's some kind of a nigger, anyhow. She's sittin' on the bench far away from the light, and she's dressed in a secondhand horse blanket, a feed sack, and a bran'-new pair of ar'tics. And she don't say a word.

" 'Well,' says I, 'if she ain't some kind of nigger, I'll eat my——'

"But there he is, all of a sudden, squarin' off in front o' me, his mug stuck up and his eyes like a couple o' headlights. Imagine! The guy ain't got enough meat on his bones for a rest'rant chicken. Honest to God, he looked like he'd been through a mile o' sausage mill. But crazy as a bedbug. And there's somethin' about a crazy man——

" 'Hold y'r gab!' says he. To *me!* That gets my goat.

" 'Just for that,' says I, 'you can get out o' this station. And don' forget to take your *woman* along with you. Get out!'

" 'Get out *hell!*' says he. He sticks his mug right in my face.

" 'That woman you speak so light of,' says he, 'is a queen. A Canuck queen,' says he.

"I had to laugh. 'Since when was there queens in Canada?' says I. 'And since when has the Canuck queens been usin' stove polish for talcum powder?'

"The guy grabs me by the coat. Listen. He was strong as a wire. He was deceivin'. A wire with ten thousand volts into it.

" 'Look at me!' says he, breathin' hard between his teeth. 'And take care!' says he. 'I'm a man no man can monkey with. I'm a man that'll go through. I'm stained with crime. I've waded through seas o' blood. Nothin' in heaven or earth or hell can stop me. A month from now rubes like you'll be glad to crawl at my feet—an' wipe their dirty mugs on the hem o' that there woman's skirt. . . . Now listen,' says he. 'Get the hell into that there box o' yourn over there and be quiet.'

"Crazy as a loon. I hope to die! the guy was *dangerous*. I see that. It come to me it's best to humor him, and I go into the coop again. I sit there countin' my fingers and listenin' to Denver tellin' back them car numbers to Limon again. By and by I'm jumpy as a cat.

I get up and stick a record in the old machine. . . . That's what brings the whole thing back to mind. That record is this 'Paragon Park.'

"First thing I know I'm out in the waitin' room again. And what you think I see? I give you a hundred guesses. . . ."

"I'll take one," I said to him. "What you saw was the finest exhibition of the 'Shimmie' you ever clapped an eye upon. Am I right?"

The young fellow's mouth hung open. He stared at me.

"Half undressed! Honest! That nigger woman! Horse blanket, feed sack, ar'tics—where was they? Shimmie? Say! Can you imagine, in that there prairie depot at three in the mornin', and a wind howlin' under the floor? Say! Well, I can't tell you, but talk about *Shimmie!* Say, she's like a dead one come to life."

"Yes," I agreed, "yes. . . . But what about the man?"

"Well, that man, now. The record's comin' to the end and I go back in to start it over. And here's this hobo, come in behind me.

" 'What's that?' says he, pointin' to the record I got in my hand.

"Then he grabs it and looks it over. He keeps turnin' it round and round and round, starin' at it.

" 'I hope you'll know it again,' says I, with a laugh.

"My laugh seems to set him off into a shiver. Then down he throws that record o' mine onto the floor and stamps on it; busts it into a million pieces under his boots. I've been tellin' you he's crazy.

" 'Here there!' I yell at him.

"He looks at me. Looks right through me, it seems, and beyond, with them there red-rimmed eyes.

" 'Seas o' blood,' says he. That's all. 'Seas o' blood!'

"Then he turns around, walks out into the waitin' room, and sits down in a heap in the farthest corner. Never another peep. There he sits till daylight, and the nigger woman, with the horse blanket on again, she sits there beside him, holdin' his hand.

" 'What's up with him?' I ask her.

"She says somethin' in Mexican—or some language, anyway. But I see she don't know any more'n me. . . . It's just like this. The current's gone out o' the wire. . . . Last I ever see of 'em, she's leadin' him off in the sunrise toward the boxcars—leadin' him by the hand. . . . Now did you ever hear a funnier experience than that to happen to a man?"

"No," I said, "I never did."

"You had to pity him," he added.

"Yes," I agreed. . . . And I could think of her leading him by the hand.

I saw Signet again. It was on my first and last voyage to the Marquesas. Under the shadow of a mountain, on a stone platform facing the sea, sat Signet, quite nude save for a loincloth, and with an unequivocal black beard falling down on his breast. There was a calmness about him.

"How did you come here?" I asked, at length.

"She wanted it," he said.

"She's a wonderful woman," he said to me, "a wonderful woman. She would do anything for me, Dole. *Anything!* We've got a kid."

I made shift to get in a question I had carried long in mind. "Somebody beat you out at Papeete, then, after all?"

He turned upon me a faintly quizzical look.

"I mean, somebody saw her—some tourist—that time she danced at Papeete—remember?—and got away with it?"

The thing seemed already so remote that he had to grope back. Then he laughed.

"Lord, no. Look here, Dole. It was her herself seen the thing at Papeete. On board a tourist boat. I found out about it since I learned her language good. Her and some others went aboard to dance the hula—same as always, you know. Then some of *them*, the tourists, understand—well, they have to spring the latest thing from Broadway. And then this woman of mine—well, you can imagine. Like a woman with a new hat. Got to run right off and show it to the whole damn length and breadth of the South Seas. That's all. . . . And once upon a time I thought I was bright. . . ."

Out of the half house at the rear of the platform came the daughter of a queen, bearing under one arm a prince of this island valley, and in the other hand a bowl of coconut wine for the visitor. And for her lord. For you will see that at last, despite the malignant thrusts and obstacles of destiny, this guttersnipe of Gotham had come to a certain estate.

When I left, he accompanied me slowly to the beach.

"You ought to like it here," I said. "After all, the city could never have given you so much."

"No," he said. Wide-eyed, he took in the azure immensity of the sea. "No. Here a guy has got time to think, think, without any hurry or worry. . . . I been thinking, Dole, a lot. I ain't going to say nothing about it, but Dole, I believe I got an idea coming along. No flivver this time. A real, sure-fire hunch. Something that'll go big in the city. Big!"

And so I left him there in the shadow of the mountain, staring at the impassable sea. . . .

*The Marriage in Kairwan**

KAIRWAN THE HOLY LAY ASLEEP, pent in its thick walls. The moon had sunk at midnight, but the chill light seemed scarcely to have diminished; only the limewashed city had become a marble city, and all the towers turned fabulous in the fierce, dry needle rain of the stars that burn over the desert of mid-Tunisia.

In the street Bab Djedid the nailed boots of the watch passed from west to east. When their thin racket had turned out and died in the dust of the market, Habib ben Habib emerged from the shadow of a door arch and, putting a foot on the tiled ledge of Bou-Kedj's fry shop, swung up by cranny and gutter till he stood on the plain of the housetops.

Now he looked about him, for on this dim tableland he walked with his life in his hands. He looked to the west, toward the gate, to the south, to the northeast through the ghostly wood of minarets. Then, perceiving nothing that stirred, he went on, moving without sound in the camel-skin slippers he had taken from his father's court.

In the uncertain light, but for those slippers and the long-tasseled *chéchia* on his head, one would not have taken him for anything but a European and a stranger. And one would have been right, almost. In the city of his birth and rearing, and of the birth and rearing of his Arab fathers generations dead, Habib ben Habib bel-Kalfate looked upon himself in the rebellious, romantic light of a prisoner in exile—exile from the streets of Paris where, in his four years, he had tasted the strange delights of the Christian—exile from the university where he had dabbled with his keen, light-ballasted mind in the learning of the conqueror.

Sometimes, in the month since he had come home, he had shaken himself and wondered aloud, "Where am I?" with the least little hint, perhaps, of melodrama. Sometimes, in the French café outside the walls, among the officers of the garrison, a bantering perversity drove him on to chant the old glories of Islam, the poets of Andalusia, and the bombastic histories of the saints; and in the midst of it, his face pink with the Frenchmen's wine and his own bitter, half-frightened mockery, he would break off suddenly, "*Voilà, messieurs!* You will see that I am the best of Mussulmans!" He would laugh then in a key so high and restless that the commandant, shaking his head, would murmur to the lieutenant beside him, "One day, Genet, we must be on the alert for a dagger there, eh?"

And Genet, who knew almost as much of the character of the university Arab as the commandant himself, would nod his head.

When Habib had laughed for a moment he would grow silent. Presently he would go out into the ugly dark of the foreign quarter, followed very often by Raoul Genet. He had known Raoul most casually in Paris. Here in the Tunisian *bled*, when Raoul held out his hand to say good night under the gate lamp at the Bab Djelladin, the troubled fellow clung to it. The smell of the African city, coming under the great brick arch, reached and closed around him like a hand—a hand bigger than Raoul's.

"You are my brother; not they. I am not of these people, Raoul!"

But then he would go in, under the black arch and the black shade of the false-pepper trees. In the darkness he felt the trees, centuries old, and all the blank houses watching him. . . .

Tonight, stealing across the sleeping roofs, he felt the starlit mosque towers watching him in secret, the pale, silent espionage of those who could wait. The hush of the desert troubled him. Youth troubled him. His lips were dry.

He had come to an arbor covered with a vine. Whose it was, on what householder's roof it was reared, he had never known. He entered.

"She is not here." He moistened his lips with his tongue.

He sat down on the stone divan to wait, watching toward the west through the doorway, across which hung a loop of vine, like a snake.

He saw her a long way off, approaching by swift darts and intervals of immobility, when her whiteness grew a part of the whiteness of the terrace. It was so he had seen her moving on that first night when, half tipsy with wine and strangeness, he had pursued, caught her, and uncovered her face.

Tonight she uncovered it herself. She put back the hooded fold of her haik, showing him her face, her scarlet mouth, her wide eyes, long at the outer corners, her hair aflame with henna.

The hush of a thousand empty miles lay over the city. For an hour nothing lived but the universe, the bright dust in the sky. . . .

That hush was disrupted. The single long crash of a human throat! Rolling down over the plain of the housetops!

"*La illah il Allah, Mohammed rassoul 'lah! Allah Adbar!* God is great!"

One by one the dim towers took it up. The call to prayer rolled between the stars and the town. It searched the white runways. It penetrated the vine-bowered arbor. Little by little, tower by tower, it died. In a fonduk outside the gate a waking camel lifted a gargling wail. A jackal dog barked in the Oued Zaroud two miles away. And again the silence of the desert came up over the city walls.

Under the vine Habib whispered: "No, I don't care anything about thy name. A name is such a little thing. I'll call thee 'Nedjma,' because we are under the stars."

"*Ai, Nedjmetek*–'Thy Star'!" The girl's lips moved drowsily. In the dark her eyes shone with a dull, steady luster, unblinking, unquestioning, always unquestioning.

That slumberous acquiescence, taken from all her Arab mothers, began to touch his nerves with the old uneasiness. He took her shoulders between his hands and shook her roughly, crying in a whisper:

"Why dost thou do nothing but repeat my words? Talk! Say things to me! Thou art like the rest; thou wouldst try to make me seem like these Arab men, who wish for nothing in a woman but the shadow of themselves. And I am not like that!"

"No, *sidi*, no."

"But talk! Tell me things, about thyself, thy life, thy world. Talk! In Paris, now, a man and a woman can talk together–yes–as if they were two friends met in a coffeehouse. And those women can talk! Ah, in Paris I have known women––"

The girl stirred now. Her eyes narrowed; the dark line of her lips thinned. At last something comprehensible had touched her mind.

"Thou hast known many women, then, *sidi!* Thou hast come here but to tell me that? Me, who am of little beauty in a man's eyes!"

Habib laughed under his breath. He shook her again. He kissed her and kissed her again on her red lips.

"Thou art jealous, then! But thou canst not comprehend. Canst thou comprehend this, that thou art more beautiful by many times than any other woman I have ever seen? Thou art a heaven of loveliness and I cannot live without thee. That is true. . . . Nedjma, I am going to take thee for my wife, because I cannot live without thine eyes, thy lips, the fragrance of thy hair. . . . Yes, I am going to marry thee, my star. It is written! It is written!"

For the first time he could not see her eyes. She had turned them away. Once again something had come in contact with the smooth, heavy substance of her mind. He pulled at her.

"Say! Say, Nedjma! . . . It is written!"

"It is not written, *sidi.*" The same ungroping acquiescence was in her whisper. "I have been promised, *sidi,* to another than thee."

Habib's arms let go; her weight sank away in the dark under the vine. The silence of the dead night crept in and lay between them.

"And in the night of thy marriage, then, thy husband—or thy father, if thou hast a father—will kill thee."

"*In-cha-'llah.* If it be the will of God."

Again the silence came and lay heavy between them. A minute and another minute went away. Habib's wrists were shaking. His breast began to heave. With a sudden roughness he took her back, to devour her lips and eyes and hair with the violence of his kisses.

"No, no! I'll not have it! No! Thou art too beautiful for any other man than me even to look upon! No, no, no!"

Habib ben Habib walked out of the gate Djelladin. The day had come; the dawn made a crimson flame in the false-pepper trees. The life of the gate was already at full tide of sound and color, braying, gargling, quarreling—nomads wading in their flocks, Djlass countrymen, Senegalese soldiers, Jewish pack peddlers, Bedouin women bent double under their stacks of desert fire grass, streaming inward, dust white, dust yellow, and all red in the dawn under the red wall.

The flood ran against him. It tried to suck him back into the maw of the city. He fought against it with his shoulders and his knees. He tried not to run. It sucked him back. A wandering Aïssaoua plucked at his sleeve and held under his nose a desert viper that gave all metallic rose glints in its slow, pained constrictions.

"To the glory of Sidna Aïssa, master, two sous."

He kept tugging at Habib's sleeve, holding him back, sucking him back with his twisting reptile into the city of the faithful.

"In the name of Jesus, master, two copper sous!"

Habib's nerves snapped. He struck off the holy mendicant with his fist. "That the devil grill thee!" he chattered. He ran. He bumped into beasts. He bumped into a blue tunic. He halted, blinked, and passed a hand over his hot-lidded eyes. He stammered:

"My friend! I have been looking for you! *Hamdou lillah! El hamdou 'llah!*"

Raoul Genet, studying the flushed, bright-eyed, unsteady youth, put up a hand to cover a little smile, half ironic, half pitying.

"So, Habib ben Habib, you revert! Camel drivers' talk in your mouth and camel's-hide slippers on your feet. Already you revert! Eh?"

"No, that is not the truth. But I am in need of a friend."

"You look like a ghost, Habib." The faint smile still twisted Raoul's lips. "Or a drunken angel. You have not slept."

"That's of no importance. I tell you I am in need——"

"You've not had coffee, Habib. When you've had coffee——"

"Coffee! My God, Raoul, that you go on talking of coffee when life and death are in the balance! For I can't live without—— Listen, now! Strictly! I have need tonight—tomorrow night—one night when it is dark—I have need of the garrison car."

The other made a blowing sound. "I'm the commandant, am I, overnight? *Zut!* The garrison car!"

Habib took hold of his arm and held it tight. "If not the car, two horses, then. And I call you my friend."

"*Two* horses! Ah! So! I begin to perceive. Youth! Youth!"

"Don't gibe, Raoul! I have need of two horses—two horses that are fast and strong."

"Are the horses in thy father's stable, then, of no swiftness and of no strength?"

It was said in the patois, the bastard Arabic of the Tunisian *bled*.

A shadow had fallen across them; the voice came from above. From the height of his crimson saddle Si Habib bel-Kalfate awaited the answer of his son. His brown, unlined, black-bearded face, shadowed in the hood of his creamy burnoose, remained serene, benign, urbanely attendant. But if an Arab knows when to wait, he knows also when not to wait. And now it was as if nothing had been said before.

"Greeting, my son. I have been seeking thee. Thy couch was not slept upon last night."

Habib's face was sullen to stupidity. "Last night, sire, I slept at the casern, at the invitation of my friend, Lieutenant Genet, whom you see beside me."

The Arab, turning in his saddle, appeared to notice the Christian for the first time. His lids drooped; his head inclined an inch.

"Greeting to thee, O master!"

"To thee, greeting!"

"Thou art in well-being?"

"There is no ill. And thou?"

"There is no ill. That the praise be to God, and the prayer!"

Bel-Kalfate cleared his throat and lifted the reins from the neck of his mare.

"Rest in well-being!" he pronounced.

Raoul shrugged his shoulders a little and murmured: "May God multiply thy days! . . . And yours, too," he added to Habib in French. He bowed and took his leave.

Bel-Kalfate, sitting his saddle stolidly in an attitude of rumination, watched him away through the thinning crowd. When the blue cap had vanished behind the blazing corner of the wool dyers, he threw the reins to his Sudanese stirrup boy and got down to the ground. He took his son's hand. So, palm in palm, at a grave pace, they walked back under the arch into the city. The market-going stream was nearly done. The tide, against which at its flood Habib had fought and won ground, carried him down again with its last shallow wash—so easily!

His nerves had gone slack. He walked in a heavy white dream. The city drew him deeper into its murmurous heart. The walls pressed closer and hid him away. The *souks* swallowed him under their shadowy arcades. The breadth of the bazaar, fetor of offal, stench of raw leather, and all the creeping perfumes of Barbary, attar of roses, chypre and amber and musk, clogged his senses like the drug of some abominable seduction. He was weary, weary, weary. And in a strange, troubling way he was at rest.

"*Mektoub!* It is written! It is written in the book of the destiny of man!"

With a kind of hypnotic fascination, out of the corners of his eyes, he took stock of the face beside him, the face of the strange being that was his father—the broad, moist, unmarked brow; the large eyes, heavy-lidded, serene; the full-fleshed cheeks, from which the beard sprang soft and rank, and against which a hyacinth, pendent over the ear, showed with a startling purity of pallor; and the mobile, deep-colored, humid lips—the lips of the voluptuary, the eyes of the dreamer, the brow of the man of never-troubled faith.

"Am I like that?" And then, "What can that one be to me?"

As if in answer, bel-Kalfate's gaze came to his son.

"I love thee," he said, and he kissed Habib's temple with his lips. "Thou art my son," he went on, "and my eyes were thirsty to drink of the sight of thee. It is *el jammaa.*[1] It is time we should go to the prayer. We shall go with Hadji Daoud today, for afterward, there at the mosque, I have rendezvous with his friends, in the matter of the dowry. It is the day, thou rememberest, that he appointed."

Habib wanted to stop. He wanted to think. He wanted time. But the serene, warm pressure of his father's hand carried him on.

Stammering words fell from his mouth.

"My mother—I remember—my mother, it is true, said something—but I did not altogether comprehend—and—— Oh, my sire——"

"Thou shall be content. Thou art a man now. The days of thy learning are accomplished. Thou hast suffered exile; now is thy reward prepared. And the daughter of the notary, thy betrothed, is as lovely as a palm tree in the morning and as mild as sweet milk, beauteous as a pearl, Habib, a milk-white pearl. See!"

Drawing from his burnoose a sack of Moroccan lambskin, he opened it and lifted out a pearl. His fingers, even at rest, seemed to caress it. They slid back among the treasure in the sack, the bargaining price for the first wife of the only son of a man blessed by God. And now they brought forth also a red stone, cut in the fashion of Tunis.

"A milk-white sea pearl, look thou; to wed in a jewel with the

[1]Friday, the Mohammedan Sabbath.

blood-red ruby that is the son of my breast. Ah, Habib, my Habib, but thou shalt be content!"

They stood in the sunlight before the green door of a mosque. As the hand of the city had reached out for Habib through the city gate, so now the prayer, throbbing like a tide across the pillared mystery of the court, reached out through the doorway in the blaze. . . . And he heard his own voice, strange in his mouth, shallow as a bleat:

"Why, then, sire—why, oh, why, then, hast thou allowed me to make of those others the friends of my spirit, the companions of my mind?"

"They are neither companions nor friends of thine, for God is God!"

"And why hast thou sent me to learn the teaching of the French?"

"When thou settest thy horse against an enemy it is well to have two lances to thy hand—thine own and his. . . . And it is written, Habib, son of Habib, that thou shalt be content. . . . Put off thy shoes now and come. It is time we were at prayer."

Summer died. Autumn grew. With the approach of winter an obscure nervousness spread over the land. In the dust of its eight-month drought, from one day to another, from one glass-dry night to another, the desert waited for the coming of the rains. The earth cracked. A cloud sailing lone and high from the coast of Sousse passed under the moon, and everywhere men stirred in their sleep, woke, looked out—from their tents on the cactus steppes, from fonduks on the camel tracks of the west, from marble courts of Kairwan. . . . The cloud passed on and vanished in the sky. On the plains the earth cracks crept and ramified. Gaunt beasts tugged at their heel ropes and would not be still. The jackals came closer to the tents. The city slept again, but in its sleep it seemed to mutter and twitch. . . .

In the serpent-spotted light under the vine on the housetop Habib muttered, too, and twitched a little. It was as if the arid months had got in under his skin and peeled off the coverings of his nerves. The girl's eyes widened with a gradual, phlegmatic wonder of pain under the pinch of his blue fingers on her arms. His face was the color of the moon.

"Am I a child of three years, that my father should lead me here or lead me there by the hand? Am I that?"

"Nay, *sidi*, nay."

"Am I a sheep between two wells, that the herder's stick should tell me, 'Here, and not there, thou shalt drink'? Am I a sheep?"

"Thou art neither child nor sheep, *sidi*, but a lion!"

"Yes, a lion!" A sudden thin exaltation shook him like a fever chill. "I am more than a lion, Nedjma, I am a man—just as the *Roumi*[2] are men—men who decide—men who undertake—agitate—accomplish . . . and now, for the last time I have decided. A fate has given thy loveliness to me, and no man shall take it away from me to enjoy. I will take it away from them instead! From all the men of this Africa, conquered by the French. Hark! I will come and take thee away in the night, to the land beyond the sea, where thou mayest be always near me, and neither God nor man say yes or no!"

"And there, *sidi*, beyond the sea, I may talk unveiled with other men? As thou hast told, in France——"

"Yes, yes, as I have told thee, there thou mayest—thou——"

He broke off, lost in thought, staring down at the dim oval of her face. Again he twitched a little. Again his fingers tightened on her arms. He twisted her around with a kind of violence of confrontation.

"But wouldst thou rather talk with other men than with me? Dost thou no longer love me, then?"

"*Ai,* master, I love thee. I wish to see no other man than thee."

"Ah, my star, I know!" He drew her close and covered her face with his kisses.

And in her ear he whispered: "And when I come for thee in the night, thou wilt go with me? Say!"

"I will go, *sidi. In-cha-'llah!* If God will!"

At that he shook her again, even more roughly than before.

"Don't say that! Not, 'If God will!' Say to me, 'If *thou* wilt!'"

"*Ai—ai*——"

There was a silence.

"But let it be quickly," he heard her whispering, after a while. Under his hand he felt a slow shiver moving over her arms. "*Nekaf!*" she breathed, so low that he could hardly hear. "I am afraid."

[2]Romans—i.e., Christians.

It was another night when the air was electric and men stirred in their sleep. Lieutenant Genet turned over in bed and stared at the moonlight streaming in through the window from the court of the casern. In the moonlight stood Habib.

"What do you want?" Genet demanded, gruff with sleep.

"I came to you because you are my friend."

The other rubbed his eyes and peered through the window to mark the Sudanese sentry standing awake beside his box at the gate.

"How did you get in?"

"I got in as I shall get out, not only from here, but from Kairwan, from Africa—because I am a man of decision."

"You are also, Habib, a skeleton. The moon shows through you. What have you been doing these weeks, these months, that you should be so shivery and so thin? Is it Old Africa gnawing at your bones? Or are you, perhaps, in love?"

"I am in love. Yes. . . . *Ai, ai,* Raoul *habiby*, if but thou couldst see her—the lotus bloom opening at dawn—the palm tree in a land of streams——"

"Talk French!" Genet got his legs over the side of the bed and sat up. He passed a hand through his hair. "You are in love, then . . . and again I tell you, for perhaps the twentieth time, Habib, that between a man and a woman in Islam there is no such thing as love."

"But I am not in Islam. I am not in anything! And if you could but see her——"

"Lust!"

"What do you mean by 'lust'?"

"Lust is the thing you find where you don't find trust. Lust is a priceless perfume that a man has in a crystal vial, and he is the miser of its fragrance. He closes the windows when he takes the stopper out of that bottle to drink its breath, and he puts the stopper back quickly again, so that it will not evaporate—not too soon."

"But that, Raoul, is love! All men know that for love. The priceless perfume in a crystal beyond price."

"Yes, love, too, is the perfume in the vial. But the man who has that vial opens the windows and throws the stopper away, and all the air is sweet, forever. The perfume evaporates, forever. And this, Habib, is the miracle. The vial is never any emptier than when it began."

"Yes, yes–I know–perhaps–but tonight I have no time––"

The moon *did* shine through him. He was but a rag blown in the dark wind. He had been torn to pieces too long.

"I have no time!" he repeated, with a feverish force. "Listen, Raoul, my dear friend. Today the price was paid in the presence of the cadi, Ben Iskhar. Three days from now they lead me to marriage with the daughter of the notary. They lead me like a sheep to kill at a tomb. . . . Raoul, for the sake of our friendship, give me hold of your hand. Tomorrow night–the car! Or, if you say you haven't the disposal of the car, bring me horses." And again the shaking of his nerves got the better of him; again he tumbled back into the country tongue. "For the sake of God, bring me two horses! By Sidna Aïssa! By the Three Hairs from the Head of the Prophet I swear it! My first-born shall be named for thee, Raoul. Only bring thou horses! Raoul! Raoul!"

It was the whine of the beggar of Barbary. Genet lay back, his hands behind his head, staring into the shadows under the ceiling.

"Better the car. I'll manage it with some lies. Tomorrow night at moonset I'll have the car outside the gate Djedid." After a moment he added, under his breath, "But I know your kind too well, Habib ben Habib, and I know that you will not be there."

Habib was not there. From moonset till half past three, well over two hours, Genet waited, sitting on the stone in the shadow of the gate or prowling the little square inside. He smoked twenty cigarettes. He yawned three times twenty times. At last he went out, got into the car, and drove away.

As the throb of the engine grew faint a figure in European clothes and a long-tasseled *chéchia* crept out from the dark of a door arch along the street. It advanced toward the gate. It started back at a sound. It rallied again, a figure bedeviled by vacillation. It came as far as the well in the center of the little square.

On the horizon toward the coast of Sousse rested a low black wall of cloud. Lightning came out of it from time to time and ran up the sky, soundless, glimmering. . . . The cry of the morning muezzin rolled down over the town. The lightning showed the figure sprawled face down on the cool stone of the coping of the well. . . .

The court of the house of bel-Kalfate swam in the glow of

candles. A striped awning shut out the night sky, heavy with clouds, and the women, crowding for stolen peeps on the flat roof. A confusion of voices, raillery, laughter, eddied around the arcaded walls, and thin music bound it together with a monotonous count of notes.

Through the doorway from the marble entresol where he stood, Habib could see his father, cross-legged on a dais, with the notary. They sat hand in hand like big children, conversing gravely. With them was the caid of Kairwan, the cadi, Ben Iskhar, and a dark-skinned cousin from the oases of the Djerid in the south. Their garments shone; there was perfume in their beards. On a rostrum beyond and above the crowded heads the musicians swayed at their work—*tabouka* players with strong, nervous thumbs; an oily, gross lutist; an organist, watching everything with the lizard eyes of the hashish taker. Among them, behind a taboret piled with bait of food and drink, the Jewish dancing woman from Algiers lolled in her cushions, a drift of white disdain. . . .

He saw it all through a kind of mist. It was as if time had halted and he were still at the steaming *hammam* of the afternoon, his spirit and his flesh undone, and all about him in the perfumed vapor of the bath the white bodies of his boyhood comrades glimmering luminous and opalescent.

His flesh was still asleep, and so was his soul. The hand of his father city had come closer about him, and for a moment it seemed that he was too weary, or too lazy, to push it away. For a little while he drifted with the warm and perfumed cloud of the hours.

Hands turned him around. It was Houseen Abdelkader, the caid's son, the comrade of long ago—Houseen in silk of wine and silver, hyacinths pendent on his cheeks, a light of festival in his eyes.

"*Es-selam alekoum, ya Habib habiby!*" It was the salutation in the plural—to Habib, and to the angels that walk, one at either shoulder of every son of God. And as he spoke he threw a new white burnoose over Habib's head, so that it hung down straight and covered him like a bridal veil.

"*Alekoum selam, ya Seenou!*" It was the name of boyhood. Seenou, the diminutive, that fell from Habib's lips. And he could not call it back.

"Come thou now." He felt the gentle push of Houseen's hands. He found himself moving toward the door that stood open into the street. The light of an outer conflagration was in his eyes. The thin music of lute and *tabouka* in the court behind him grew thinner; the boom of drums and voices in the street grew big. He had crossed the threshold. A hundred candles, carried in horizontal banks on laths by little boys, came round him on three sides, like footlights. And beyond the glare, in the flaming mist, he saw the street Dar-el-Bey massed with men. All their faces were toward him, hot yellow spots in which the black spots of their mouths gaped and vanished.

"That the marriage of Habib be blessed! Blessed be the marriage of Habib!"

The riot of sound began to take form. It began to emerge in a measure, a *boom-boom-boom* of tambours and big goatskin drums. A bamboo fife struck into a high, quavering note. The singing club of Sidibou-Said joined voice.

The footlights were moving forward toward the street of the market. Habib moved with them a few slow paces, without effort or will. And again they had all stopped. It could not be more than two hundred yards to the house of the notary and his waiting bride, but by the ancient tradition of Kairwan an hour must be consumed on the way.

An hour! An eternity! Panic came over Habib. He turned his hooded eyes for some path of escape. To the right, Houseen! To the left, close at his shoulder, Mohammed Sheriff—Mohammed the laughing and well-beloved—Mohammed, with whom in the long, white days he used to chase lizards by the pool of the Aglabides . . . in the long, white, happy days, while beyond the veil of palms the swaying camel palanquins of women, like huge, bright blooms, went northward up the Tunis road. . . .

What made him think of that?

"*Boom-boom-boom-boom!*" And around the drums beyond the candles he heard them singing:

"*On the day of the going away of my Love,*
When the litter, carrying the women of the tribe,
Traversed the valley of Dad, like a sea, mirage,
They were like ships, great ships, the work of the children of Adoul,
Or like the boats of Yamen's sons. . . ."

"*Boom-boom!*" The monotonous pulse, the slow minor slide of sixteenth tones, the stark rests—he felt the hypnotic pulse of the old music tampering with the pulse of his blood. It gave him a queer creeping fright. He shut his eyes, as if that would keep it out. And in the glow of his lids he saw the tents on the naked desert; he saw the forms of veiled women; he saw the horses of warriors coming like a breaker over the sand—the horses of the warriors of God!

He pulled the burnoose over his lids to make them dark. And even in the dark he could see. He saw two eyes gazing at his, untroubled, untroubling, out of the desert night. And they were the eyes of any woman—the eyes of his bride, of his sister, his mother, the eyes of his mothers a thousand years dead.

"Master!" they said.

They were pushing him forward by the elbows, Mohammed and Houseen. He opened his eyes. The crowd swam before him through the yellow glow. Something had made an odd breach in his soul, and through the breach came memories.

Memories! There at his left was the smoky shelf of blind Moulay's café—black-faced, white-eyed old Moulay. Moulay was dead now, many years, but the men still sat in the same attitudes, holding the same cups, smoking the same chibouk with the same gulping of bubbles as in the happy days. And there between the café and the *souk* gate was the same whitewashed niche where three lads used to sit with their feet tucked under their little *kashabias*, their *chéchias* awry on their shaven polls and their lips pursed to spit after the leather legs of the infidel conquerors passing by. The *Roumi*, the French blasphemers, the defilers of the mosque! Spit on the dogs! Spit!

Behind his reverie the drums boomed, the voices chanted. The lament of drums and voices beat at the back of his brain—while he remembered the three lads sitting in the niche, waiting from one white day to another for the coming of Moulay Saa, the Messiah; watching for the Holy War to begin.

"And I shall ride in the front rank of the horsemen, please God!"

"And I, I shall ride at Moulay Saa's right hand, please God, and I shall cut the necks of *Roumi* with my sword, like barley straw!"

Habib advanced in the spotlight of the candles. Under the burnoose his face, half shadowed, looked green and white, as if he were sick to his death. Or, perhaps, as if he were being born again.

The minutes passed, and they were hours. The music went on, interminable, "*Boom-boom-boom-boom* . . ." But now Habib himself was the instrument, and now the old song of his race played its will on him.

Pinkness began to creep over the green-white cheeks. The cadence of the chanting had changed. It grew ardent, melting, voluptuous:

"... *And conquests I have made among the fair ones, perfume inundated,*
Beauties ravishing, that sway in an air of musk and saffron,
Bearing still on their white necks the traces of kisses. . . ."

It hung under the pepper trees, drunk with the beauty of flesh, fainting with passion. Above the trees mute lightning played in the cloud. Habib ben Habib was born again. Again, after exile, he came back into the heritage. He saw Paradise in a walking dream. He saw women forever young and forever lovely in a land of streams, women forever changing, forever virgin, forever new; strangers intimate and tender. The angels of a creed of love—or of lust!

"Lust is the thing you find where you don't find trust."

A thin echo of the Frenchman's diatribe flickered through his memory, and he smiled. He smiled because his eyes were open now. He seemed to see this Christian fellow sitting on his bed, barefooted, rumple-haired, talking dogmatically of perfumes and vials and stoppers thrown away, talking of faith in women. And that was the jest. For he seemed to see the women, over there in Paris, that the brothers of that naïve fellow trusted—trusted alone with a handsome young university student from Tunisia. Ha, ha, ha! Now he remembered. He wanted to laugh out loud at a race of men that could be as simple as that. He wanted to laugh at the bursting of the iridescent bubble of faith in the virtue of beautiful women. The Arab knew!

A color of health was on his face; his step had grown confident. Of a sudden, and very quietly, all the mixed past was blotted out. He heard only the chanting voices and the beating drums:

"*Once I came into the tent of a young beauty on a day of rain . . .*
Beauty blinding . . . Charms that ravished and made drunkards of the eyes . . ."

His blood ran with the song, pulse and pulse. The mute lightning came down through the trees and bathed his soul. And, shivering a little, he let his thoughts go for the first time to the strange and virgin creature that awaited his coming there, somewhere, behind some blind house wall, so near.

"Thou hast suffered exile. Now is thy reward prepared."

What a fool! What a fool he had been!

He wanted to run now. The lassitude of months was gone from his limbs. He wanted to fling aside that clogging crowd, leap, arrive. How long was this hour? Where was he? He tried to see the housetops to know, but the glow was in his eyes. He felt the hands of his comrades on his arms.

But now there was another sound in the air. His ears, strained to the alert, caught it above the drums and voices—a thin, high ululation. It came from behind high walls and hung among the leaves of the trees, a fantom yodeling, the welcoming "*you-you-you-you*" of the women of Islam.

Before him he saw that the crowd had vanished. Even the candles went away. There was a door, and the door was open.

He entered, and no one followed. He penetrated alone into an empty house of silence, and all around him the emptiness moved and the silence rustled.

He traversed a court and came into a chamber where there was a light. He saw a Negress, a Sudanese duenna, crouching in a corner and staring at him with white eyes. He turned toward the other side of the room.

She sat on a high divan, like a throne, her hands palms together, her legs crossed. In the completeness of her immobility she might have been a doll or a corpse. After the strict fashion of brides, her eyebrows were painted in thick black arches, her lips drawn in scarlet, her cheeks splashed with rose. Her face was a mask, and jewels in a crust hid the flame of her hair. Under the stiff kohl of their lids her eyes turned neither to the left nor to the right. She seemed not to breathe. It is a dishonor for a maid to look or to breathe in the moment when her naked face suffers for the first time the gaze of the lord whom she has never seen.

A minute passed away.

"This is the thing that is mine!" A blinding exultation ran through his brain and flesh. "Better this than the 'trust' of fools and infidels! No question here of 'faith.' *Here I know!* I know that this thing that is mine has not been bandied about by the eyes of all the men in the world. I know that this perfume has never been breathed by the passers in the street. I know that it has been treasured from the beginning in a secret place—against this moment—for me. This bud has come to its opening in a hidden garden; no man has ever looked upon it; no man will ever look upon it. None but I."

He roused himself. He moved nearer, consumed with the craving and exquisite curiosity of the new. He stood before the dais and gazed into the unwavering eyes. As he gazed, as his sight forgot the grotesque doll painting of the face around those eyes, something queer began to come over him. A confusion. Something bothering. A kind of fright.

"Thou!" he breathed.

Her icy stillness endured. Not once did her dilated pupils waver from the straight line. Not once did her bosom lift with breath.

"*Thou!* It is *thou,* then, O runner on the housetops by night!"

The fright of his soul grew deeper, and suddenly it went out. And in its place there came a black calm.

The eyes before him remained transfixed in the space beyond his shoulder. But by and by the painted lips stirred once.

"*Nekaf!* . . . I am afraid!"

In the house of bel-Kalfate the Jewess danced, still, even in voluptuous motion, a white drift of disdain. The music eddied under the rayed awning. Raillery and laughter were magnified. More than a little *bokha,* the forbidden liquor distilled of figs, had been consumed in secret. Eyes gleamed; lips hung. . . . Alone in the thronged court, on the dais, the host and the notary, the caid, the cadi, and the cousin from the south continued to converse in measured tones, holding their coffee cups in their palms.

"It comes to me on thought," pronounced bel-Kalfate, inclining his head toward the notary with an air of courtly deprecation—"it comes to me that thou hast been defrauded. For what is a trifle of ten thousand *douros* of silver as against the rarest jewel (I am certain, *sidi*) that has ever crowned the sex which thou mayest perhaps forgive me for mentioning?"

And in the same tone, with the same gesture, Hadji Daoud replied: "Nay, master and friend, by the Beard of the Prophet, but I should repay thee the half. For that is a treasure for a sultan's daughter, and this *fillette* of mine (forgive me) is of no great beauty or worth——"

"In saying that, Sidi Hadji, thou sayest a thing which is at odds with half the truth."

They were startled at the voice of Habib coming from behind their backs.

"For thy daughter, Sidi Hadji, thy Zina, is surely as lovely as the full moon sinking in the west in the hour before the dawn."

The words were fair. But bel-Kalfate was looking at his son's face.

"Where are thy comrades?" he asked, in a low voice. "How hast thou come?" Then, with a hint of haste: "The dance is admirable. It would be well that we should remain quiet, Habib, my son."

But the notary continued to face the young man. He set his cup down and clasped his hands about his knee. The knuckles were a little white.

"May I beg thee, Habib ben Habib, that thou shouldst speak the thing which is in thy mind?"

"There is only this, *sidi;* a little thing: When thou hast another bird to vend in the market of hearts, it would perhaps be well to examine with care the cage in which thou hast kept that bird.

"Thy daughter," he added, after a moment of silence—"thy daughter, Sidi Hadji, is with child."

That was all that was said. Hadji Daoud lifted his cup and drained it, sucking politely at the dregs. The cadi coughed. The caid raised his eyes to the awning and appeared to listen. Then he observed, "Tonight, *in-cha-'llah*, it will rain." The notary pulled his burnoose over his shoulders, groped down with his toes for his slippers, and got to his feet.

"Rest in well-being!" he said. Then, without haste, he went out.

Habib followed him tardily as far as the outer door. In the darkness of the empty street he saw the loom of the man's figure moving off toward his own house, still without any haste.

"And in the night of thy marriage thy husband, or thy father, if thou hast a father——"

Habib did not finish with the memory. He turned and walked a few steps along the street. He could still hear the music and the clank of the Jewess's silver in his father's court. . . .

"*In-cha-'llah!*" she had said, that night.

And, after all, it *had* been the will of God. . . .

A miracle had happened. All the dry pain had gone out of the air. Just now the months of waiting for the winter rains were done.

All about him the big, cool drops were spattering on the invisible stones. The rain bathed his face. His soul was washed with the waters of the merciful God of Arab men.

For, after all, from the beginning, it had been written. All written!

"*Mektoub!*"

*From the Other Side of the South**

THE DAY HAD BEEN DEAD HOT. Under the weight of the afternoon one would have thought it could never be cool again in the Mzab. But immediately the sun had dipped behind the cliff that guards the western rim of the oasis the thin air emptied itself, and the night chill, penetrating and treacherous, flowed over the dry bottom of the *oued*.

The town stirred. Under my gallery there came and went a word fight between Berber muleteers from the north. After that I heard the evening call of muezzin dropping down from the mosque tower on the crowded hill, arid, sinuous, like the note of another wooden well wheel shrilling above the desert floor. Then somewhere under a house arose the hollow voice of a tambour struck with a thumb, and a man sang. In a rift of silence a wandering breeze threshed all the date fronds in the *oued* bottom with a fantom of distant applause. Nearer at hand a foot scuffled in the dusk. A choked laugh. And all around in the heavy shadows of that quarter the subdued giggling, the rustling, and jewel clanking of the women of dark delight.

"What's wrong with the Ouled Nail girls tonight?" I asked along the gallery. Abd, son of Abdallah the Mozabite, rose to his feet on the tiles near the stair, a white wraith.

"*Kain kairouan ja, sidi* [There is a caravan come]."

Drums banged; women scurried. The momentous night was established and stars sprinkled the sky, large and restless stars, always flickering a little to the eye in that air without body.

I sat at an island crossroads of the western Sahara, where the pale, blurred sand courses, like the wakes of ships, come up the bald skin of the globe from the green mysteries that lie months away on the other side of the south.

"Abd!" I called. "Where does the caravan come from, east or west?"

Abd was gone. On the tiles I heard the fall of a Christian boot. Borak, the Englishman, came toward me in the shadows.

"I wonder you're not out," he said. "The caravan comes from the south."

"Not——"

"Rather! This is a real one—like the old days again. Right away up from under. You'd better have a look at the beggars; you're romantic, you know. Might not have another chance in a year."

I put on my coat and went with him. Borak has been too long in Africa, one part and another. He has forgotten that it is the Dark Continent. As we walked he went on in his habitual vein of banter.

"It's a tidy lot of heroes for you. You may imagine. Seven 'moonlights' on the trek, and I lay a pound sterling not a man in the crowd has washed in the thirty weeks."

"Thirty weeks!" I couldn't help echoing it. "Lord!"

"There ought to be a story there, eh? As a matter of fact there isn't. I insist again that there's more story, more poetry and romance in the life of a Whitechapel coster than you'll hear in a year listening to these people. They lack imagination. They want the mental whip of civilization; that's it in a nutshell."

I felt like saying "Bosh!" Borak is too dogmatic.

We were passing into the thick of the "low town," and on our right loomed the ugly oblong of the *douane*, the French customhouse that stands at the converging of the deep-Sahara routes. Borak looked at it and chuckled.

"Old Arnauld" (the customs official) "is in a fair pother. There's a frightful mixture in the trek, blacks and browns from a dozen different basins down below, and you may imagine there's a lack of passports. So that's Arnauld's job; to divine. Or rather it's Bou Dik's job, for the orderly has all the work. When I passed the market coming to you, Bou Dik was tackling an old chap who claims to be Senegal but looks away east of that, a potbellied old swine, black as a chimney pot, solemn as an archbishop, and blind as a bat. I gather all he wants is to be let pass quietly on his way to Holy

Mecca, where he hopes to die. Bou Dik, though, is full of wild and horrid notions. He has crossed the trail lately of a dervish man who has the word that Moulay Saa[1] is now booked to descend in the guise of a blackamoor, and naturally, having a fat berth with the Infidel, Bou Dik isn't going to let the Deliverer into *his* department—not if he can help it. So just now Bou Dik is death and leprosy on niggers. I wish you could have heard the row."

I was to hear it presently. We had arrived at a chain swung across the black street and, ducking under it, we came into the open market square. I had seen the place a hundred times, by sun and moon and stars, and still familiarity had not quite worn off my first sense of it as a haven between the winds, the anchorage of a remote white port of call lost in the ocean of stone. Tonight that illusion was deepened a dozenfold. There is no other metaphor in speech so true as "ships of the desert." They were here. Tonight I knew that I had known before only the small fry of that dry-sea world, only the shore huggers, the humble brotherhood of the coastwise trade. Here tonight was the creature of the main, the deep-sea squadron, the tall fleet.

From where we stood, clear to the further shore of dim arcades, the ground was hidden under the mass of kneeling beasts and heaped bales, a tumbled thing, monstrous in sleep. We picked our way through the ruck, lighting matches from time to time when we found ourselves trapped in blind alleys between bales and humps, or felt our way barred by the hairy neck of a camel curving waist-high across the night. Mountains whisked fat tails at us; sleeping legs sprawled from beneath hills of cargo like dead men pinned under wreckage. Borak took hold of my elbow.

"This way," he said. "I hear the voice of Bou Dik."

I heard it too, impassive, obstinate. There was a small fire of brush roots throwing a glow around a ring of specters in the center of the field of ruin. The burnooses, all the same color of desert dust, might indeed have been winding sheets; the hooded faces, gaunt, bone-built, played upon by the weak and tricky illumination from beneath, might have been skulls. And in the midst of the communing dead, Bou Dik, enveloped in his red robe of authority, was the devil himself presiding.

His voice had ceased. As we settled behind him a man got to his

[1]The Napoleonic Messiah of Mohammedan prophecy.

feet on the side beyond the fire. With a gesture which had in it something of the trained orator he put back the hood of his burnoose, baring his strong neck and his round, blue-black, kinky-polled Negroid head.

"Thou hast demanded, *sidi*, who is this man who is the father of my father. Thou hast demanded whence he comes, whither he goes, what he desires. Now I will tell thee all these things, I, Belkano, who am not without power in the country which is under Kalgou."

He spoke a quaint Arabic in which all the throat sounds were brought forward and softened—such a tongue, Borak told me, as black boys pick up in the Mohammedan *zaouias* at Sikasso and Timbuktu—quaint, and yet more easily understood in the Mzab than dialects not so far away, in Tunis, say, or the Moroccan uplands.

"The father of my father," he said, "is a very great and holy man."

In the pause that followed all the eyes turned upon the object deposited at the speaker's feet. It was discerned to be human.

"Black as a chimney pot, solemn as an archbishop, blind as a bat." Like many of Borak's observations, that one had everything in it but the essential. The essential thing was the man's enormous separation. Whether it was the infirmity of his great age or whether it was his "holiness" (which may account for many things), he was removed to a distance which could not be measured. He lived on another planet. He lived within another sky, the sky of his own skin.

There was something majestic in the completeness of his immobility. Save for a faint, slow, rhythmical pulse of his swollen lower lip there was nothing visibly alive in him. Not once did the dead eyeballs, sustained in little cups of rheum, shift from the line of dead ahead. From the first to the last of that audience he remained in the attitude in which I imagine he must have been deposited, a sphinx thing in ebony, content with memories. Memories gorgeous or infernal. His lip fascinated me. I could not get my eyes away from that pendulous and extraordinary tissue, throbbing with faint, ordered convulsions in the orange light. It was as if the creature's heart, appalled by something under the black sky of skin, had broken prison and escaped so far, only to be caught on the threshold and hang there eternally, beating.

I had to shake myself. In a whisper, to Borak: "What's that he was saying? The tall one."

"He says that his grandfather is bound on the pilgrimage to Mecca because he is tremendously holy, and he is tremendously holy because he has a huge sin on his soul. Not bad, eh? It has happened before."

Bou Dik's voice was heard. "What then is that sin?"

The dark orator looked around the circle beneath him.

"It is known in Andiorou and Adar. It is known in Damagarin country and even in Manga country in the east." He looked at Bou Dik. "Now I will recount thee that history, *sidi*."

His gaze returned to the fire. I shall not soon forget him as he stood there against the stars of the desert night, tall, glossy, vibrant, speaking out in a strong voice the story of the moribund flesh beside him.

"Know thou then that it was in the years before the missionaries of God (to whom be the prayer) and of his Prophet (be his bliss eternal by the streams that never cease!) had brought to my tribe the Word and the Flame of Islam. Glory to the One God!"

"Glory to the One God!" the echo rustled around the ring.

"In those days then the men of my people lived in darkness. They performed no ablutions. Their prayers were to images made with their hands. The strongest and bravest of the young men of that tribe was Djeba, who was later called Djim, as I will recount to thee, *sidi*, and who was to become the father of my father, and who is this man. The young man who was next to Djeba in strength and courage was Moa. These two were brothers of the milk. Of these two, each was the other's breath. When these two went into the bush to hunt, the animals said to one another, 'Strike if thou wilt among seven men, but avoid the Brothers of the Milk!' So lived Djeba and Moa in those days. Djeba was the spear of Moa; Moa was Djeba's shield.

"In those days then came a war party from the south, from the country of Gando under Sokoto, the country of braggarts and thieves. They came out of the bush in the morning and moved toward the village, casting their spears aloft and beating on drums. The warriors of my people did not fail to answer them. They advanced out of the stockade. Nikato, the Headman, was in the forefront, and at his two shoulders went Djeba and Moa. That sunrise Djeba slew five of the sons of Gandoland. Moa slew five. Neither cut nor bruise was on their bodies. *Sing the valor of the Brothers of the Milk!*"

The apostrophe rang out, absorbed, deep-throated, across the sleeping caravan. My eyes went to the flesh on the ground. Into that dark house had those words been able to penetrate? Had their ringing set some hidden echo ringing? How could one say? The lip that was like the man's drawn heart pulsed in the same laggard imperturbable count; the dead eyeballs did not shift. But perhaps they were dead only that they might see the better the sunlight of that vanished and heroic myth.

"*Sing the valor and the victory of the Brothers of the Milk!*

"That war party was beaten; its dead soiled the ground; its living fled into the bush. That day the drums were beaten in the village and muttons were killed; that night a feast was made. The young men danced and the old men made sacrifice to their images.

"But the images of those days were idolatrous and had no power over good and ill. *La illah il allah!*[2] Accordingly then it was written that the survivors of that war party, gathering again in the bush and being drunk with the desire of revenge, fell once more upon the village in the hour when the young men were full-fed and their weapons away. So in that night many of my tribe were slain. The stockades were thrown down; the houses were given to the flame. In the light of that flame many virgins were desecrated, many old men disemboweled, many children spun on spears. But those of good growth and being were taken away. Djeba and Moa were taken away.

"How can I recount to thee, *sidi,* the days of that march? Am I then another Errendi, that the words of my lamentation should fall like burning oil on a new wound? But the history is well known in all the country above the River, for my father's brother, Ahmed ben Djeba, he who had it out of the mouth of Djeba, has made it a chant at a hundred feasts and sung it under a hundred council trees. He has sung the days of that going, the weeks, each week after the other through the hotness of that bush trail. He has told the tale of the moons. In the roof of his mouth he has recalled the song of the lash that fell on those men's shoulders and made of their flesh the flesh of goats that is hung on the stockade to cure. He has stirred the dung heaps to bring in memory the meat that was given them at evening before they fell down to sleep. With his tongue he has made the clank of the chain that bound them together, the heavy chain of iron that bound together even those

[2]There is no god but God.

two who were bound by the strong bond of the breast that gave them suck!

"Many among them died. When they died their bodies were cut from the chain with swords. Djeba and Moa grew thin. When Djeba looked at Moa he saw a skeleton that he did not know. When Moa looked at Djeba he saw a thing which filled him with terror. At night each bade the other farewell, saying, 'In the morning I shall be dead.' But they were strong and they did not die. Only their minds became empty.

"Then they came at last to the banks of a great lake. This lake was so great that when they had been sold to a white boatman and when they had come out in the boat so far that they could no longer see the bank behind them, then they could yet see no bank before, and the water was all about them to the sky like the sand in the desert of Djouf. To my father's brother Djeba has recounted that they were more than the length of a moon in that going, but it must be recalled that his mind was empty, since no lake to be compared with that is in our knowledge. A wind arose on that lake and water came into the boat. They were athirst, but when they drank of that water it was sour and their thirst consumed them tenfold after. What man is there master of words sufficiently bitter to recount that going upon the lake of those men who were captive?

"Then they came at last to the other bank of that lake, and they were taken up swiftly into the bush of the country beyond, for there were war boats of other white men on the water. And on another day they came to a great *ksar* of a hundred shelters, and in the market place of that *ksar* they were exposed for sale. They were nine. Nine men left out of sevenscore strong men! What battle in the memory of the tribes so disastrous as that going! What ambush so bloody as that march of the companions of the Brothers of the Milk!"

For a moment after the outcry the orator's lips closed over the firelit sheen of his white teeth. I suppose that he (like his paternal uncle) had recited this tropic saga a hundred times in the villages of the black south. I doubt not that at this point he had been accustomed to pause, to receive for a moment the sweet applause of a groan.

"And so," he resumed, "they were sold that day into labor. And of the Brothers of the Milk, those whose eyes saw a single thing and whose lips spoke the same, Moa was taken one way and Djeba another, and their hearts died. Djeba, the blood child of chieftains, was driven like a bullock up into the bush by a white driver, and when his weakness grew on him and he stumbled that driver struck him with a thong.

"That country beyond the great lake is a fat country, full of planting of maize and cotton in the uplands where the bush is cleared. It is known by the name of Djoja, and in extent it lies from the banks of the lake into the interior many marches away. Djeba was taken to a certain planting and thrown into a *dar* in a stockade as great as a small *ksar*. There he had the company of other captives from the River, from the Camaroun, and from the River Greater than the River in the south. Some there were who had been there so great a time that they had forgotten their own tongues and knew only the Djoja speech, and some had been born in that stockade.

"Then they were driven into the fields to labor. In his weakness the sun beat upon the head of Djeba and made him forget. Then he was driven back to the stockade, and the rain came through the thatch of the *dar* and wet his body and fever consumed his heart. But already his heart was dead; only when he slept and saw Moa in a dream did he live.

"And that driver said to him, 'How art thou called?' And he said, 'Djeba.' And the driver laughed and cried, 'That is no name for a black boy; I christen thee Djim; and Djim thou art!' And he went away, still laughing as if he had turned a word of wit. So a hate of him came into Djeba, and Djeba would have killed him, only that he was a tall, great-bodied man, and Djeba, who had been worth five warriors in his strength, was like a child in weakness now.

"That fever burned his heart and his bowels. He was given to eat of a couscous made of sour maize and swine flesh. Then his stomach turned over. He vomited. He said, 'Now at last I am to die.'

"But then a woman came in that *dar*. She laid a hand on his head and called him Djim, but the hand was cool, and the anger went from his heart. She gave him milk to drink and his pain ceased. His sickness passed. In the darkness of that shelter that woman was like the healing benignity of the moon when it has come an hour high in the east. She spoke in tones of compassion, and he was made whole.

" 'Who then is that woman?' he asked of the men, 'and how is she called?'

" 'She is Mis'us, and she lives in the *dar kebir* [the Big House].'

" 'Is she then the woman of that driver?' he asked.

"His companions laughed. 'Nay, she is the woman of Maas Djo.'

" 'Who then is Maas Djo?'

" 'Maas Djo is the Maasa, the Headman. It is his silver with which thou wert got.'

" 'Why then have I not seen this Headman?'

" 'For the reason that since thou hast come he has been gone with a war party to fight the Yankis to the north.'

" 'He has gone then to take other captives?'

" 'Nay, he has gone to save those he has got.' And then they recounted to Djeba: 'The war parties of the Yankis who come from behind the rivers of the north choke the trails. The bush never sleeps for the sound of their drums. Their torches are among the settlements. The long peace of the white men is broken; new confederations are formed; terror is loosed abroad. The lust of booty and of blood is aflame in the Yankis. It is said that they devour babes; it is known that when they make prayer in their holy places their ablutions are performed in the blood of a lamb. Such are they!'

"Then they recounted to Djeba how Maas Djo and the other Headmen, the holders of plantings, all the young men, how they had gathered to the war drums in the trails, how they had chosen chiefs and gone away into the bush, and how the sky above them was that day the color of gore.

"And Djeba asked them, 'Which then is the stronger?' And they answered, 'The party of Maas Djo is the stronger. Mayhap even now it has driven the Yankis back across their rivers. Mayhap tomorrow he will return home!'

"But one among them who had been born into labor in that stockade in Djoja and who was now an old man said, 'Mayhap not.' That same man, who was called by the name of Moz, came into the *dar* at night and said in a low voice to Djeba, 'The Yankis are like the leaves of the pepper tree; they are small, but their number is beyond count. Hark thou well when the bush is sleeping and thou wilt hear their powder guns in the north.'

"Then Djeba hearkened, but he heard no guns. Nevertheless he sharpened his reaping tool. But he was not yet strong from his sickness.

"From time to time that woman from the *dar kebir* came to bring him sweet milk and speak in tones of compassion. And it was written that the heart of Djeba, the son of chieftains, should grow soft and meek. But when that driver perceived Mis'us ministering to the captive's weakness he jeered with mocking laughter, and the woman cowered before it as though she had been afraid and fled away to the Big House. And Djeba's hatred of that man grew like a pain.

" 'When I am stronger I will kill him,' he said.

"So he grew stronger.

"On another night that man called Moz came in secret and said to Djeba, 'Hark thou well in the night, and before another moon has gone thou wilt hear the drums of the tribesmen of the north.' And when he saw Djeba take up his reaping tool he said, 'Rather shouldst thou sing for joy. For these men here who are ignorant *niggahs* have told thee things apart from the truth. Thou hast spoken to me of thy milk brother who is called Moa, who was sold into the planting of Maas Djoj Blaak. It has come to my knowledge that Moa has fled from that planting, and with others from other plantings has gone to fight in the war parties of the Yankis, where they are received with honors. Is it probable that such men eat babes? No, Djim, I repeat to thee, these here are child-headed *niggahs*, who know not that the Yankis come to set them free out of labor in the plantings. No, Djim, rather shouldst thou sing for joy, for when thou see'st the Yankis thou wilt see thy milk brother in their train.'

"Then Djeba's heart sang for joy.

" 'Again, again I shall see my brother!' he cried. 'Again our eyes shall behold one thing and our breaths shall be one!' And he said to Moz, 'Now I too will run away from the stockade and I will go to meet Moa.'

"And Moz said, 'But the driver will prevent thee.'

"And Djeba said, 'No, for I will kill the driver before I go.'

"And Djeba waited, feeding his heart on the thought of Moa and on the promise of the death of that white man who had laughed.

"There came an evening when he watched and saw the driver going out of the stockade into the edge of the bush. So Djeba took up his sharp reaping tool and followed, creeping near the ground. He came near to the driver. He saw him very clearly. The driver was dressed in finery, with a hat like a deep drum fashioned of fur, and a tunic of blue cloth with buttons of silver. Djeba saw him against the light of dusk in the sky. But the driver was not alone. Mis'us was there, where she had stolen for solitude. It was she that the driver had followed, as the desert hyena slinks slavering after the lone gazelle. The fear was in Djeba that if he struck the man, then the woman would give the alarm and he would be taken again. He might have struck both. But his heart was softened by the compassion of the woman, and what was written in the book of the future he was not given yet to read. Had he known! Had he but known to strike—the driver afterward, perhaps—but the woman first.

"But while he hesitated, already it was too late. He saw the driver step forward and grasp the woman's arm, uttering words he could not understand. He saw the woman, standing quietly, turn her head and spit once and spit twice in the driver's face.

"She continued to stand quietly, like stone. But the driver flung off toward the stockade, laughing terribly in his deep chest.

"Then Djeba would have returned and awaited another chance of the man. But the thought of Moa was strong on him, and the bush was at his back. So he said to himself, 'I will return with Moa,' and he crept away.

"All that night he walked swiftly. He hid himself and slept in the day and advanced by night again. He did not know where he went, but the image and affection of his milk brother were so powerful in Djeba that it seemed he would come truly to Moa. Because of that he remained strong. His stomach was empty but his heart was fed, and he penetrated the bush with the swiftness of a panther. He would have wished to speak with others and know his way, but if he saw slaves in the fields then he saw with them a white driver, and he was afraid.

"There came a time when he saw a Senegal man working at the edge of a maize planting, and no driver was in sight. So he showed himself, and he asked, 'Where then are the Yankis?' And the man answered him, 'Go thou to Tlaanta. I know nothing, but at Tlaanta all things are known.'

" 'Where then is Tlaanta?' Djeba demanded. And the man said, 'If thou knowest not Tlaanta then indeed thou art an ignorant *niggah*. Turn thy face to the north, and at nightfall thou wilt behold a great *ksar* which is Tlaanta, which is the chief place of Djoja, where all things are known . . .'

("Tlaanta." Something queer was happening down in the subconscious regions of my brain. "Tlaanta, the chief place of Djoja." The equatorial forest walls were trying their hardest to topple over in my dull brain. But there was no time. I had to get back to the saga unfolding in the strong voice of the orator in that emberlit Sahara night.)

" . . . And when the night fell Djeba saw before him in the sky a pillar of light. And he came on a hill and saw a great settlement in flames. And then all about him came people fleeing in confusion through the dark bush, carrying on their heads their mills and cooking pots and crying, 'The Yankis! The Yankis are come!'

"Then Djeba was glad. He went down toward burning Tlaanta. The flame was in his face and his heart was hot, and he stood and called aloud the name of his brother of the milk. But he saw no man. A lad ran out of a shelter that took fire. Djeba caught that lad by the arm and cried, 'Where are the Yankis?' And the lad screamed, 'Gone! Gone!' and he fell down with his eyes wide open, and Djeba saw that he was dead.

"And Djeba said to himself, 'If the Yankis are gone and Moa with them, then it will be his thought to lead them to that planting where I was a slave, to kill that driver and set me free.' So he turned his back on the burning *ksar*. He ran all through that night. Others ran with him; other slaves freed by the war party's passage. They turned this way and that in the darkness, chanting the war chants of the Yankis, and their paths through the bush were ruin. In the night they pillaged and burned stockades, in the morning they marched in bands, in the afternoon they slept along the trails. But by day and by night their minds were turned with freedom, and when Djeba ran among them demanding word of Moa their answers were without sense.

"There was a night when Djeba came upon a clearing. He saw a stockade in flames. The light of those flames showed him the fields, and then he recognized that planting and his spirit leaped with joy. He said, 'Now Moa has come here seeking me, and his revenge is before my eyes!'

"And Djeba ran bounding across the fields and came into the

flame of the stockade, and he called Moa's name. He shouted the war call of their tribe. He shouted the hunting call that had been fixed between the milk brothers in the old day in the bush.

"Then it seemed to Djeba that he heard the answer to the hunting call, but in the crackling of the flames he could not say whence it came. Then he bounded on in the stockade. In that circle of fire he saw a man standing. It was a white man he had never seen. His breast was black with blood, his head hung down, and he wept. Djeba went toward him boldly.

" 'Tell me, then, where is Moa?'

"The man looked at him with dull, heavy eyes from which the tears ran down, and for answer he said, 'Where is my wife, boy? Where are my servants? I am Maas Djo. I have come home.'

"Then Djeba perceived that the man was possessed, so he did not harm him, but ran on. He leaped like a panther through all the stockade. He bounded through the wall and stood in the lighted field, and there was nothing there but his shadow. Then he ran toward the bush, and there he saw a figure. He pursued, and the figure ran into the bush, but Djeba was too swift, and overtook it, and he saw it was that woman, who crouched like a terrified gazelle and watched his coming with large eyes.

"And he said, 'It is I.'

"When the woman heard that she trembled with relief and took hold of his arm and whispered, 'It is thou, Djim! I thought it was *he*. I thought thou wert that drunken monster pursuing me still!'

"When he heard that, there came into Djeba's mind the memory and the hate of that driver. And he said, 'Where is he now?' And the woman, grasping his arm more tightly at that instant, whispered, 'Hush, thou, and hark! He comes!'

"Then near them Djeba heard the fall of feet and he saw the man advancing through the bush. He saw his shape plain and black against the glow beyond the leaves; the shape of that fur hat he remembered, in the form of a deep drum, tilted wildly; the shoulders thrust out with that tunic of silver buttons, the elbows swaggering. And he saw that the figure was drunk and lustful and that he came in cunning silence among the leaves, and he knew that the time of his revenge was at hand.

"So Djeba sprang through the leaves and caught the man's neck in his fingers. They fell down in the dark on the ground, and there they fought. But Djeba's powerful hands were about the man's throat, and the man lay quiet and breathed no more. Then Djeba went back, but the terrified woman was gone.

"Then Djeba returned across the field toward the stockade, calling Moa's name again, and in the field near the stockade he saw lying the body of a man. The man was despoiled of his clothes and naked, and his head cut three-quarters from his trunk. And Djeba looked and saw that it was that driver.

"Then Djeba said to himself, 'The night is full of infernal creatures, witches and *djinoun*. I have slain the driver in his finery in the bush, and here he lies an hour dead and naked in the field. The night is red with devil-work.' A fear came on him and his teeth knocked together. Nevertheless he went back to the bush, laid hold of that other man's feet, and pulled him through the bush to the field, and there he looked at the face of the man he had slain.

"*He looked at the face of the man he had slain!*"

The syllables of the loud repetition went away across the sleeping floor of the square and played among the invisible arcades, echoes deep-toned, momentous, tragic. And in the glow of the embers I saw the lip of that oblivious clay pulsing, pulsing, with the same laggard and monotonous beat. I continued to stare at it. You may be certain now that I stared. The short hairs at the back of my skull stood up and pricked the skin. For the wonder of it. Even to that Senegal orator himself the saga he repeated remained fabulous, an epic of equatorial rivers. Chanted first by son and then by grandson at a hundred feasts and under a hundred village council trees and grown into the body of mid-African legendry, not till this night had it come to ears that heard; to eyes that saw with the eyes of that ancient, moribund, blind, black wanderer. For now I knew that I had heard the tale of that incendiary night on a "Djoja planting" before, not once, but many, many times; not in the glow of a Sahara campfire, but in the emberlight of a Hancock County chimney nook, where my own grandmother Peyton used to sit before bedtime thirty years agone, reciting a saga of her own.

The narrator's voice was heard again, rushing staccato.

"Then Djeba ran through the bush to find that woman, his one thought that he might now slay her too. For he perceived now that she must be a witch doctress, thus by compassion to have blinded his eyes. He ran with all his power. How long he ran, what man can say? Sometimes he seemed to see that woman as a shadow in the bush before him and sometimes as a bird flying before him through the trees. In him there was no hunger save the hunger for her killing, no thirst save the thirst for her blood, no weariness save the weariness of the damned soul.

"And then there was a time when it seemed to Djeba that he was in the midst of many men. He saw that they were white men and that they moved in a thousand ranks. Ruin lay behind them and thunder ran around. And he remembered the words of Moz: 'The Yankis are like the leaves of the pepper tree; they are small, but their number is beyond count.' And when the nights came Djeba saw their campfires, and even their fires were beyond count.

"A forgetfulness came on Djeba. He ran from fire to fire, crying, 'Where is Moa?' And those men mocked him, saying, 'Moa what?' But Djeba screamed at them and ran on. Or sometimes they named him *Samboh*, saying, 'Hold, *Samboh*. Sit down with us now and sing!' Then Djeba thanked them, and sat down with them and sang, and the war chant of the Yankis filled the sky.

"And after many days Djeba came with the war party to the banks of that lake, and there he beheld a bearded chieftain sitting on a horse, and he fell down on his face and wept. And he implored, 'That I come again to my own country beyond this water, where Moa, my brother, has returned, and where he awaits me in the village of my tribe!' And that chieftain heard.

"In after days then was Djeba placed in a boat, together with many of the River and the Cameroun, and he returned across that lake where the waters lay to the sky like the sands in the desert of Djouf. Then they made a village on the shore. But Djeba left them. He penetrated the bush through which he had marched many years before, bound to that chain. He penetrated the country of enemies and he passed through. Then Djeba came to his own village again. There were old men there who knew him when he spoke his name. They rejoiced and made a feast. All night they feasted. And one of the old men said to Djeba, 'Moa, thy brother of the milk, was taken with thee. Where then is Moa?'

"And Djeba said, 'I do not know.' And he took none of the feast.

"And in the years afterward, when Djeba had taken wives and got sons, there came into our country the missionaries of God (to whom be the prayer) and of his Prophet (may his bliss never decrease).

"*La illah il allah!*

"And they spoke the word of the Koran to Djeba, and Djeba's heart turned in his breast. And he said then, 'My heart can no longer contain a lie. Hark all to the truth. Moa, my brother of the milk—which bond is sacred—Moa, my brother, him I slew with my own hands in that land which is beyond the great water. I slew him, being tricked by a witch woman. And that witch woman I was not able to slay! That then is my sin!'

"That then is the sin of Djeba. I have spoken, I, Belkano, who am the son of his son!"

In the hush that followed that deep-toned verbal signature my breath whistled small in my throat.

"Lord! Lord! Oh, my Lord!"

Borak eyed me with a smirk and a grunt. The black fellow showed his shining teeth again. He took another breath into his lungs.

"For the length of thirty Ramadâns the father of my father has not opened his mouth to any man in speech. Because of that sin, because he would not look at any man, his eyes have become blind. He would not hear, and his ears are deaf. Thus men know that he is holy. So they come for many marches to touch his hand. Sometimes then his lips are opened, and for their ears he will sing again that war chant of the Yankis. And then those men will give him offerings against his pilgrimage, that he may see Holy Mecca and ease him of that sin and die."

The voice was rising.

"They give him offerings of broad copper! They throw down pieces of silver before him! *They throw down gold!*"

I heard the wind going out of Borak's chest at that; an obscure thoracic collapse. A snort.

"At last! At last the plot unfolds. Now the old bird will render that popular ditty entitled 'The Unwritten War Song of the Wild Yankis of Yankisland,' and the company will contribute. And strangely enough the ringmaster's eye is fastened unerringly on *you.*"

"For God's sake, man——"

"Yes, but you'll see," he persisted. "You'll note that his toe even now is prodding the old one in the ribs."

It was true. I saw the nudging and peremptory toe. I stared at that lip hanging in the ember light. I beheld a disorder and quickening of that fleshy pulse. I heard an obedient sound issuing forth. It was a very small, shallow, creaking sound. It emerged from that emotionless mask of senility; it rose and fell in mechanical lengths of tone like a bent wire and went away and was lost in the night of the packed Sahara square. It was a queer chant.

"Cock and bull!" grunted Borak.

"For God's sake, man, hush!"

I stared and I listened. Yes, it was a very queer chant indeed. The short hairs were beginning to stand up again at the back of my skull.

On the ground, red with the firelight, a copper sou was tossed. I saw another fall, and another. I took out my wallet and found a hundred-franc note, and I let it flutter into the circle over the shoulder of Bou Dik.

Borak got hold of me.

"*Lord!* I say, now! What's *that* for?"

"To help and ease him of that 'sin.' "

"But my dear simple chap—all that rigmarole——"

"Of the greatest of all African wars——"

He tilted his head at me with the absurdest suspicion about my wits.

"Come away!" he said.

I got up and went with him out into the black ruck of the camels. He was groaning audibly over that squandered bank note. "Man, man, and you were really taken in by that beggar's claptrap. Why—look you—in that old chap's day there weren't enough white men in Central Africa all put together——"

"Borak!" I said. "*Will* you listen to that song!"

In the hollow of the market, above the grunt and snore of the caravan, the thin war chant of the "Yankis" wound on, repeating, repeating:

> "*John B'own's body lahs amoldin' in the g'ave,*
> *John B'own's body lahs amoldin' in the g'ave,*
> *John B'own's body lahs amoldin' in the g'ave,*
> *But his soul goes mahchin' on . . .*"

In that Sahara darkness where the pale courses come from beyond the south I saw Atlanta burning. Sherman was on the march.

*The Man Who Saw Through Heaven**

PEOPLE HAVE WONDERED (THERE being obviously no question of romance involved) how I could ever have allowed myself to be let in for the East African adventure of Mrs. Diana in search of her husband. There were several reasons. To begin with, the time and effort and money weren't mine; they were the property of the wheel of which I was but a cog, the Society through which Diana's life had been insured, along with the rest of that job lot of missionaries. The "letting in" was the firm's. In the second place, the wonderers have not counted on Mrs. Diana's capacity for getting things done for her. Meek and helpless. Yes, but God was on her side. Too meek, too helpless to move mountains herself, if those who happened to be handy didn't move them for her then her God would know the reason why. Having dedicated her all to making straight the Way, why should her neighbor cavil at giving a little? The writer for one, a colonial governor general for another, railway magnates, insurance managers, safari leaders, the ostrich farmer of Ndua, all these and a dozen others in their turns have felt the hundred-ton weight of her thin-lipped meekness—have seen her in metaphor sitting grimly on the doorsteps of their souls.

A third reason lay in my own troubled conscience. Though I did it in innocence, I can never forget that it was I who personally conducted Diana's party to the Observatory on that fatal night in Boston before it sailed. Had it not been for that kindly intentioned "hunch" of mine, the astounded eye of the Reverend Hubert Diana would never have gazed through the floor of Heaven, and he would never have undertaken to measure the Infinite with the foot rule of his mind.

It all started so simply. My boss at the shipping-and-insurance office gave me the word in the morning. "Bunch of missionaries for the *Platonic* tomorrow. They're on our hands in a way. Show 'em the town." It wasn't so easy when you think of it: one male and seven females on their way to the heathen; though it was easier in Boston than it might have been in some other towns. The evening looked the simplest. My friend Krum was at the Observatory that semester; there at least I was sure their sensibilities would come to no harm.

On the way out in the streetcar, seated opposite to Diana and having to make conversation, I talked of Krum and of what I knew of his work with the spiral nebulae. Having to appear to listen, Diana did so (as all day long) with a vaguely indulgent smile. He really hadn't time for me. That night his life was exalted as it had never been, and would perhaps never be again. Tomorrow's sailing, the actual fact of leaving all to follow Him, held his imagination in thrall. Moreover, he was a bridegroom of three days with his bride beside him, his nerves at once assuaged and thrilled. No, but more. As if a bride were not enough, arrived in Boston, he had found himself surrounded by a very galaxy of womanhood gathered from the four corners; already within hours one felt the chaste tentacles of their feminine dependence curling about the party's unique man; already their contacts with the world of their new lives began to be made through him; already they saw in part through his eyes. I wonder what he would have said if I had told him he was a little drunk.

In the course of the day I think I had got him fairly well. As concerned his Church he was at once an asset and a liability. He believed its dogma as few still did, with a simplicity, "the old-time religion." He was born that kind. Of the stuff of the fanatic, the reason he was not a fanatic was that, curiously impervious to little questionings, he had never been aware that his faith was anywhere attacked. A self-educated man, he had accepted the necessary smattering facts of science with a serene indulgence, as simply so much further proof of what the Creator could do when He put His Hand to it. Nor was he conscious of any conflict between these facts and the fact that there existed a substantial Heaven, geographically up, and a substantial Hot Place, geographically down.

So, for his Church, he was an asset in these days. And so, and for the same reason, he was a liability. The Church must after all keep abreast of the times. For home consumption, with modern congregations, especially urban ones, a certain streak of "healthy" skepticism is no longer amiss in the pulpit; it makes people who read at all more comfortable in their pews. A man like Hubert Diana is more for the cause than a hundred. But what to do with him? Well, such things arrange themselves. There's the Foreign Field. The blacker the heathen the whiter the light they'll want, and the soldier the conception of a God the Father enthroned in a Heaven of which the sky above them is the visible floor.

And that, at bottom, was what Hubert Diana believed. Accept as he would with the top of his brain the fact of a spherical earth zooming through space, deep in his heart he knew that the world lay flat from modern Illinois to ancient Palestine, and that the sky above it, blue by day and by night festooned with guiding stars for wise men, was the nether side of a floor on which the resurrected trod.

I shall never forget the expression of his face when he realized he was looking straight through it that night. In the quiet dark of the dome I saw him remove his eye from the eyepiece of the telescope up there on the staging and turn it, in the ray of a hooded bulb, on the demon's keeper, Krum.

"What's that, Mr. Krum? I didn't get you!"

"I say, that particular cluster you're looking at—"

"This star, you mean?"

"You'd have to count awhile to count the stars describing their orbits in that 'star,' Mr. Diana. But what I was saying—have you ever had the wish I used to have as a boy—that you could actually look back into the past? With your own two eyes?"

Diana spoke slowly. He didn't know it, but it had already begun to happen; he was already caught. "I have often wished, Mr. Krum, that I might actually look back into the time of our Lord. Actually. Yes."

Krum grunted. He was young. "We'd have to pick a nearer neighbor than *Messier 79* then. The event you see when you put your eye to that lens is happening much too far in the past. The light waves thrown off by that particular cluster on the day, say, of the Crucifixion—*you* won't live to see them. They've hardly started yet—a mere twenty centuries on their way—leaving them something like eight hundred and thirty centuries yet to come before they reach the earth."

Diana laughed the queerest catch of a laugh. "And—and there—there won't be any earth here, then, to welcome them."

"*What?*" It was Krum's turn to look startled. So for a moment the two faces remained in confrontation, the one, as I say, startled, the other exuding visibly little sea-green globules of sweat. It was Diana that caved in first, his voice hardly louder than a whisper.

"W-w-will there?"

None of us suspected the enormousness of the thing that had happened in Diana's brain. Krum shrugged his shoulders and snapped his fingers. Deliberately. *Snap!* "What's a thousand centuries or so in the cosmic reckoning?" He chuckled. "We're just beginning to get out among 'em with *Messier*, you know. In the print room, Mr. Diana, I can show you photographs of clusters to which, if you cared to go, traveling at the speed of light . . ."

The voice ran on; but Diana's eye had gone back to the eyepiece, and his affrighted soul had re-entered the big black tube sticking its snout out of the slit in the iron hemisphere. . . . "At the speed of light!" . . . That unsuspected, that wildly chance-found chink in the armor of his philosophy! The body is resurrected and it ascends to Heaven instantaneously. At what speed must it be borne to reach instantaneously that city beyond the ceiling of the sky? At a speed inconceivable, mystical. At, say (as he had often said to himself), *the speed of light*. . . . And now, hunched there in the trap that had caught him, black rods, infernal levers and wheels, he was aware of his own eye passing vividly through unpartitioned emptiness, *eight hundred and fifty centuries at the speed of light!*

"And still beyond these," Krum was heard, "we begin to come into the regions of the spiral nebulae. We've some interesting photographs in the print room, if you've the time."

The ladies below were tired of waiting. One had "lots of packing to do." The bride said, "Yes, I do think we should be getting along, Hubert, dear; if you're ready——"

The fellow actually jumped. It's lucky he didn't break anything. His face looked greener and dewier than ever amid the contraptions above. "If you—you and the ladies, Cora—wouldn't mind—if Mr.—Mr.—[he'd mislaid my name] would see you back to the hotel . . ." Meeting silence, he began to expostulate. "I feel that this is a rich experience. I'll follow shortly; I know the way."

In the car going back into the city Mrs. Diana set at rest the flutterings of six hearts. Being unmarried, they couldn't understand men as she did. When I think of that face of hers, to which I was destined to grow only too accustomed in the weary, itchy days of the trek into Kavirondoland, with its slightly tilted nose, its irregular pigmentation, its easily inflamed lids and long moist cheeks, like those of a hunting dog, glorying in weariness, it seems incredible that a light of coyness could have found lodgment there. But that night it did. She sat serene among her virgins.

"You don't know Bert. You wait; he'll get a perfectly wonderful sermon out of all that tonight, Bert will."

Krum was having a grand time with his neophyte. He would have stayed up all night. Immured in the little print room crowded with files and redolent of acids, he conducted his disciple "glassy-eyed" through the dim frontiers of space, holding before him one after another the likenesses of universes sister to our own, islanded in immeasurable vacancy, curled like glimmering crullers on their private Milky Ways, and hiding in their wombs their myriad "coal pockets," star-dust fetuses of which—their quadrillion years accomplished—their litters of new suns would be born, to bear their planets, to bear their moons in turn.

"And beyond these?"

Always, after each new feat of distance, it was the same. "And beyond?" Given an ell, Diana surrendered to a pop-eyed lust for nothing less than light-years. "And still beyond?"

"Who knows?"

"The mind quits. For if there's no end to these nebulae——"

"But supposing there is?"

"An end? But, Mr. Krum, in the very idea of an ending——"

"An end to what we might call this particular category of magnitudes. Eh?"

"I don't get that."

"Well, take this—take the opal in your ring there. The numbers and distances inside that stone may conceivably be to themselves as staggering as ours to us in our own system. Come! That's not so farfetched. What are we learning about the structure of the atom? A nucleus (call it a sun) revolved about in eternal orbits by electrons (call them planets, worlds). Infinitesimal; but after all what are bigness and littleness but matters of comparison? To eyes on one of those electrons (don't be too sure there aren't any) its tutelary sun may flame its way across a heaven a comparative ninety million miles away. Impossible for them to conceive of a boundary to their billions of atomic systems, molecular universes. In that category of magnitudes its diameter is infinity; once it has made the leap into our category and become an opal it is merely a quarter of an inch. That's right, Mr. Diana, you may well stare at it: between *now* and *now* ten thousand histories may have come and gone down there. . . . And just so the diameter of our own cluster of universes, going over into another category, may be—"

"May be a–a ring–a little stone–in a–a–a–ring."

Krum was tickled by the way the man's imagination jumped and engulfed it.

"Why not? That's as good a guess as the next. A ring, let's say, worn carelessly on the–well, say the tentacle–of some vast organism–some inchoate creature hobnobbing with its cloudy kind in another system of universes–which in turn . . ."

It is curious that none of them realized next day that they were dealing with a stranger, a changed man. Why he carried on, why he capped that night of cosmic debauch by shaving, eating an unremarkable breakfast, packing his terrestrial toothbrush and collars, and going up the gangplank in tow of his excited convoy to sail away, is beyond explanation–unless it was simply that he was in a daze.

It wasn't until four years later that I was allowed to know what had happened on that ship, and even then the tale was so disjointed, warped, and opinionated, so darkly seen in the mirror of Mrs. Diana's orthodoxy, that I had almost to guess what it was *really* all about.

"When Hubert turned irreligious . . ." That phrase, recurrent on her tongue in the meanderings of the East African quest to which we were by then committed, will serve to measure her understanding. Irreligious! Good Lord! But from that sort of thing I had to reconstruct the drama. Evening after evening beside her campfire (appended to the Mineral Survey Expedition Toward Uganda through the kindness—actually the worn-down surrender—of the Protectorate government) I lingered awhile before joining the merrier engineers, watched with fascination the bumps growing under the mosquitoes on her forehead, and listened to the jargon of her mortified meekness and her scandalized faith.

There had been a fatal circumstance, it seems, at the very outset. If Diana could but have been seasick, as the rest of them were (horribly), all might still have been well. In the misery of desired death, along with the other contents of a heaving midriff, he might have brought up the assorted universes of which he had been led too rashly to partake. But he wasn't. As if his wife's theory were right, as if Satan were looking out for him, he was spared to prowl the swooping decks immune. Four days and nights alone. Time enough to digest and assimilate into his being beyond remedy that lump of whirling magnitudes and to feel himself surrendering with a strange new ecstasy to the drunkenness of liberty.

Such liberty! Given Diana's type, it is hard to imagine it adequately. The abrupt, complete removal of the toils of reward and punishment; the withdrawal of the surveillance of an all-seeing, all-knowing Eye; the windy assurance of being responsible for nothing, important to no one, no longer (as the police say) "wanted!" It must have been beautiful in those few days of its first purity, before it began to be discolored by his contemptuous pity for others, the mask of his inevitable loneliness and his growing fright.

The first any of them knew of it—even his wife—was in mid-voyage, the day the sea went down and the seven who had been sick came up. There seemed an especial Providence in the calming of the waters; it was Sunday morning, and Diana had been asked to conduct the services.

He preached on the text: "For of such is the kingdom of Heaven."

"If our concept of God means anything it means a God *all*-mighty, Creator of *all* that exists, Director of the *infinite*, cherishing in His Heaven the saved souls of *all space and all time*."

Of course; amen. And wasn't it nice to feel like humans again, and real sunshine pouring up through the lounge ports from an ocean suddenly grown kind? . . . But—then—*what* was Diana *saying?*

Mrs. Diana couldn't tell about it coherently even after a lapse of fifty months. Even in a setting as remote from that steamer's lounge as the equatorial bush, the ember-reddened canopy of thorn trees, the meandering campfires, the chant and tramp somewhere away of Kikuyu porters dancing in honor of an especial largesse of fat zebra meat—even here her memory of that impious outburst was too vivid, too aghast.

"It was Hubert's look! The way he stared at us! As if you'd said he was licking his chops! . . . That 'Heaven' of his!"

It seems they hadn't waked up to what he was about until he had the dimensions of his sardonic Paradise irreparably drawn in. The final haven of all right souls. Not alone the souls released from this our own tiny earth. In the millions of solar systems we see as stars how many millions of satellites must there be upon which at some time in their histories conditions suited to organic life subsist? Uncounted hordes of wheeling populations! Of men? God's creatures at all events, a portion of them reasoning. Weirdly shaped perhaps, but what of that? And that's only to speak of our own inconsiderable cluster of universes. That's to say nothing of other systems of magnitudes, where God's creatures are to our world what we are to the worlds in the atoms in our finger rings. (He had shaken *his*, here, in their astounded faces.) And all these, all the generations of these enormous and microscopic beings harvested through a time beside which the life span of our earth is as a second in a million centuries: all these brought to rest for an eternity to which time itself is a watch tick—all crowded to rest pell-mell, thronged, serried, packed, packed to suffocation in layers unnumbered light-years deep. This must needs be our concept of Heaven if God is the God of the Whole. If, on the other hand——

The other hand was the hand of the second officer, the captain's delegate at divine worship that Sabbath day. He at last had "come to."

I don't know whether it was the same day or the next; Mrs. Diana was too vague. But here's the picture. Seven women huddled in the large stateroom on B deck, conferring in whispers, aghast, searching one another's eye obliquely even as they bowed their heads in prayer for some light—and of a sudden the putting back of the door and the in-marching of the Reverend Hubert . . .

As Mrs. Diana tried to tell me, "You understand, don't you, he had just taken a bath? And he hadn't—he had forgotten to——"

Adam-innocent there he stood. Not a stitch. But I don't believe for a minute it was a matter of forgetting. In the high intoxication of his soul release, already crossed (by the second officer) and beginning to show his zealot claws, he needed some gesture stunning enough to witness to his separation, his unique rightness, his contempt of match-flare civilizations and infinitesimal taboos.

But I can imagine that stateroom scene: the gasps, the heads colliding in aversion, and Diana's six weedy feet of birthday suit towering in the shadows, and ready to sink through the deck I'll warrant, now the act was irrevocable, but still grimly carrying it off.

"And if, on the other hand, you ask me to bow down before a God peculiar to this one earth, this one grain of dust lost among the giants of space, watching its sparrows fall, profoundly interested in a speck called Palestine no bigger than the quadrillionth part of one of the atoms in the ring here on my finger . . ."

Really scared by this time, one of the virgins shrieked. It was altogether too close quarters with a madman.

Mad? Of course there was the presumption: "Crazy as a loon." Even legally it was so adjudged at the *Platonic's* first port of call, Algiers, where, when Diana escaped ashore and wouldn't come back again, he had to be given over to the workings of the French Law. I talked with the magistrate myself some forty months later, when, "let in" for the business as I have told, I stopped there on my way out.

"But what would you?" were his words. "We must live in the world as the world lives, is it not? Sanity? Sanity is what? Is it, for example, an intellectual clarity, a balanced perception of the realities? Naturally, speaking out of court, your friend was of a sanity —of a sanity, sir——" Here the magistrate made with thumb and fingers the gesture only the French can make for a thing that is matchless, a beauty, a transcendent instance of any kind. He himself was Gallic, rational. Then, with a lift of shoulder: "But what would you? We must live in the world that seems."

Diana, impounded in Algiers for deportation, escaped. What after all are the locks and keys of this pinchbeck category of magnitudes? More remarkable still, there in Arab Africa, he succeeded in vanishing from the knowledge and pursuit of men. And of women. His bride, now that their particular mission had fallen through, was left to decide whether to return to America or to go on with two of the company, the Misses Brookhart and Smutts, who were bound for a school in Smyrna. In the end she followed the latter course. It was there, nearly four years later, that I was sent to join her by an exasperated and worn-out Firm.

By that time she knew again where her husband-errant was—or where at least, from time to time in his starry dartings over this our mote of dust, he had been heard of, spoken to, seen.

Could we but have a written history of those years of his apostolic vagabondage, a record of the towns in which he was jailed or from which he was kicked out, of the ports in which he starved, of the ships on which he stowed away, presently to reveal himself in proselyting ardor, denouncing the earthlings, the fatelings, the dupes of bugaboo, meeting scoff with scoff, preaching the new revelation red-eyed, like an angry prophet. Or was it, more simply, like a man afraid?

Was that the secret, after all, of his prodigious restlessness? Had it anything in common with the swarming of those pale worms that flee the Eye of the Infinite around the curves of the stone you pick up in a field? Talk of the man without a country! What of the man without a universe?

It is curious that I never suspected his soul's dilemma until I saw the first of his mud sculptures in the native village of Ndua in the province of Kasuma in British East. Here it was, our objective attained, we parted company with the government safari and shifted the burden of Way-straightening to the shoulders of Major Wyeside, the ostrich farmer of the neighborhood.

While still on the safari I had put to Mrs. Diana a question that had bothered me: "Why on earth should your husband ever have chosen this particular neck of the woods to land up in? Why Kavirondoland?"

"It was here we were coming at the time Hubert turned irreligious, to found a mission. It's a coincidence, isn't it?"

And yet I would have sworn Diana hadn't a sense of humor about him anywhere. But perhaps it *wasn't* an ironic act. Perhaps it was simply that, giving up the struggle with a society blinded by "a little learning" and casting about for a virgin field, he had remembered this.

"I supposed he was a missionary," Major Wyeside told us with a flavor of indignation. "I went on that. I let him live here—six or seven months of it—while he was learning the tongue. I was a bit nonplused, to put it mildly, when I discovered what he was up to."

What things Diana had been up to, the major showed us in one of the huts in the native kraal—a round dozen of them, modeled in mud and baked. Blackened blobs of mud, that's all. Likenesses of nothing under the sun, fortuitous masses sprouting haphazard tentacles, only two among them showing nodules that might have been experimental heads. . . . The ostrich farmer saw our faces.

"Rum, eh? Of course I realized the chap was anything but fit. A walking skeleton. Nevertheless, whatever it is about these beasties, there's not a nigger in the village has dared set foot inside this hut since Diana left. You can see for yourselves it's about to crash. There's another like it he left at Suki, above here. Taboo, no end!"

So Diana's "hunch" had been right. He had found his virgin field indeed, fit soil for his cosmic fright. A religion in the making, here before our eyes.

"This was at the very last before he left," Wyeside explained. "He took to making these mud pies quite of a sudden; the whole lot within a fortnight's time. Before that he had simply talked, harangued. He would sit here in the doorway of an evening with the niggers squatted around and harangue 'em by the hour. I knew something of it through my houseboys. The most amazing rot. All about the stars to begin with, as if these black baboons could half grasp *astronomy!* But that seemed all proper. Then there was talk about a something a hundred times as big and powerful as the world, sun, moon, and stars put together—some perfectly enormous, stupendous, awful being—but knowing how mixed the boys can get, it still seemed all regular—simply the parson's way of getting at the notion of an Almighty God. But no, they insisted, there wasn't any God. That's the point, they said; there *is no* God. . . . Well, that impressed me as a go. That's when I decided to come down and get the rights of this star-swallowing monstrosity the beggar was feeding my labor on. And here he sat in the doorway with one of these beasties—here it is, this one—waving it furiously in the niggers' benighted faces. And do you know what he'd done?—you can see the mark here still on this wabble leg, this tentacle business—he had taken off a ring he had and screwed it on just here. His finger ring, my word of honor! And still, if you'll believe it, I didn't realize he was just daft. Not until he spoke to me. 'I find,' he was good enough to enlighten me, 'I find I have to make it somehow concrete.' . . . 'Make what?' . . . 'Our wearer.' 'Our *what, where?*' . . . 'In the following category.' . . . His actual words, honor bright. I was going to have him sent down country where he could be looked after. He got ahead of me though. He cleared out. When I heard he'd turned up at Suki I ought, I suppose, to have attended to it. But I was having trouble with leopards. And you know how things go."

From there we went to Suki, the major accompanying. It was as like Ndua as one flea to its brother, a stockade inclosing round houses of mud, wattles, and thatch, and full of naked heathen. The Kavirondo are the nakedest of all African peoples and, it is said, the most moral. It put a great strain on Mrs. Diana; all that whole difficult anxious time, as it were detachedly, I could see her itching to get them into Mother Hubbards and cast-off Iowa pants.

Here too, as the major had promised, we found a holy of holies, rather a dreadful of dreadfuls, "taboo no end," its shadows cluttered with the hurlothrumbos of Diana's artistry. What puzzled me was their number. Why this appetite for experimentation? There was an uncertainty; one would think its effect on potential converts would be bad. Here, as in Ndua, Diana had contented himself at first with words and skyward gesticulations. Not for so long, however. Feeling the need of giving his concept of the cosmic "wearer" a substance much earlier, he had shut himself in with the work, literally—a fever of creation. We counted seventeen of the nameless "blobs," all done, we were told, in the seven days and nights before their maker had again cleared out. The villagers would hardly speak of him; only after spitting to protect themselves, their eyes averted, and in an undertone, would they mention him: "He of the Ring." Thereafter we were to hear of him only as "He of the Ring."

Leaving Suki, Major Wyeside turned us over (thankfully, I warrant) to a native who told us his name was Charlie Kamba. He had spent some years in Nairobi, running for an Indian outfitter, and spoke English remarkably well. It was from him we learned, quite casually, when our modest eight-load safari was some miles on its way, that the primary object of our coming was non-existent. Hubert Diana was dead.

Dead nearly five weeks—a moon and a little—and buried in the mission church at Tara Hill.

Mission church! There was a poser for us. *Mission church?*

Well then, Charlie Kamba gave us to know that he was paraphrasing in a large way suitable to our habits of thought. We wouldn't have understood *his* informant's "wizard house" or "house of the effigy."

I will say for Mrs. Diana that in the course of our halt of lugubrious amazement she shed tears. That some of them were not tears of unrealized relief it would be hardly natural to believe. She had desired loyally to find her husband, but when she should have found him—what? This problem, sturdily ignored so long, was now removed.

Turn back? Never! Now it would seem the necessity for pressing forward was doubled. In the scrub-fringed ravine of our halt the porters resumed their loads, the dust stood up again, the same caravan moved on. But how far it was now from being the same.

From that moment it took on, for me at least, a new character. It wasn't the news especially; the fact that Diana was dead had little to do with it. Perhaps it was simply that the new sense of something aimfully and cumulatively dramatic in our progress had to have a beginning, and that moment would do as well as the next.

Six villages: M'nann, Leika, Leikapo, Shamba, Little Tara, and Tara, culminating in the apotheosis of Tara Hill. Six stops for the night on the road it had cost Diana as many months to cover in his singular pilgrimage to his inevitable goal. Or in his flight to it. Yes, his stampede. Now the pipers at that four-day orgy of liberty on the *Platonic's* decks were at his heels for their pay. Now that his strength was failing, the hosts of loneliness were after him, creeping out of their dreadful magnitudes, the hounds of space. Over all that ground it seemed to me we were following him not by the word of hearsay but, as one follows a wounded animal making for its earth, by the droppings of his blood.

Our progress had taken on a pattern; it built itself with a dramatic artistry; it gathered suspense. As though it were a story at its most breathless places "continued in our next," and I a reader forgetting the road's weariness, the dust, the torment of insects never escaped, the inadequate food, I found myself hardly able to keep from running on ahead to reach the evening's village, to search out the inevitable repository of images left by the white stranger who had come and tarried there awhile and gone again.

More concrete and ever more concrete. The immemorial compromise with the human hunger for a symbol to see with the eyes, touch with the hands. Hierarchy after hierarchy of little mud effigies—one could see the necessity pushing the man. Out of the protoplasmic blobs of Ndua, Suki, even M'nann, at Leikapo Diana's concept of infinity (so pure in that halcyon epoch at sea), of categories nested within categories like Japanese boxes, of an over-creature wearing our cosmos like a trinket, unawares, had become a mass with legs to stand on and a real head. The shards scattered about in the filth of the hut there (as if in violence of despair) were still monstrosities, but with a sudden stride of concession their monstrousness was the monstrousness of lizard and turtle and crocodile. At Shamba there were dozens of huge-footed birds.

It is hard to be sure in retrospect, but I do believe that by the time we reached Little Tara I began to see the thing as a whole—the fetus, working out slowly, blindly, but surely, its evolution in the womb of fright. At Little Tara there was a change in the character of the exhibits; their numbers had diminished, their size had grown. There was a boar with tusks and a bull the size of a dog with horns, and on a tusk and on a horn an indentation left by a ring.

I don't believe Mrs. Diana got the thing at all. Toward the last she wasn't interested in the huts of relics; at Little Tara she wouldn't go near the place; she was "too tired." It must have been pretty awful, when you think of it, even if all she saw in them was the mud-pie play of a man reverted to a child.

There was another thing at Little Tara quite as momentous as the jump to boar and bull. Here at last a mask had been thrown aside. Here there had been no pretense of proselyting, no astronomical lectures, no doorway harangues. Straightway he had arrived (a fabulous figure already, long heralded), he had commandeered a house and shut himself up in it and there, mysterious, assiduous, he had remained three days and nights, eating nothing, but drinking gallons of the foul water they left in gourds outside his curtain of reeds. No one in the village had ever seen what he had done and left there. Now, candidly, those labors were for himself alone.

Here at last in Tara the moment of that confession had overtaken the fugitive. It was he, ill with fever and dying of nostalgia—not these naked black baboon men seen now as little more than blurs—who had to give the Beast of the Infinite a name and a shape. And more and more, not only a shape, but a *shapeliness*. From the instant when, no longer able to live alone with nothingness, he had given it a likeness in Ndua mud, and perceived that it was intolerable and fled its face, the turtles and distorted crocodiles of Leikapo and the birds of Shamba had become inevitable, and no less inevitable the Little Tara boar and bull. Another thing grows plain in retrospect: the reason why, done to death (as all the way they reported him), he couldn't die. He didn't dare to. Didn't dare to close his eyes.

It was at Little Tara we first heard of him as "Father Witch," a name come back, we were told, from Tara, where he had gone. I had heard it pronounced several times before it suddenly obtruded from the native context as actually two English words. That was what made it queer. It was something they must have picked up by rote, uncomprehending; something then they could have had from no lips but his own. When I repeated it after them with a better accent they pointed up toward the north, saying, "Tara! Tara!"—their eagerness mingled with awe.

I shall never forget Tara as we saw it, after our last blistering scramble up a gorge, situated in the clear air on a slope belted with cedars. A mid-African stockade left by some blunder in an honest Colorado landscape, or a newer and bigger Vermont. Here at the top of our journey, black savages, their untidy *shambas*, the very equator, all these seemed as incongruous as a Gothic cathedral in a Congo marsh. I wonder if Hubert Diana knew whither his instinct was guiding him on the long road of his journey here to die. . . .

He had died and he was buried, not in the village, but about half a mile distant, on the ridge; this we were given to know almost before we had arrived. There was no need to announce ourselves, the word of our coming had outrun us; the populace was at the gates.

"Our Father Witch! Our Father Witch!" They knew what we were after; the funny parrotwise English stood out from the clack and clatter of their excited speech. "Our Father Witch! Ay! Ay!" With a common eagerness they gesticulated at the hilltop beyond the cedars.

Certainly here was a change. No longer the propitiatory spitting, the averted eyes, the uneasy whispering allusion to him who had passed that way: here in Tara they would shout him from the housetops, with a kind of civic pride.

We learned the reason for this on our way up the hill. It was because they were his chosen, the initiate.

We made the ascent immediately, against the village's advice. It was near evening; the return would be in the dark; it was a bad country for goblins; wouldn't tomorrow morning do? . . . No, it wouldn't do the widow. Her face was set. . . . And so, since we were resolved to go, the village went with us, armed with rattles and drums. Charlie Kamba walked beside us, sifting the information a hundred were eager to give.

These people were proud, he said, because their wizard was more powerful than all the wizards of all the other villages "in the everywhere together." If he cared to he could easily knock down all the other villages in the "everywhere," destroying all the people and all the cattle. If he cared to he could open his mouth and swallow the sky and the stars. But Tara he had chosen. Tara he would protect. He made their mealies to grow and their cattle to multiply.

I protested, "But he is *dead* now."

Charlie Kamba made signs of deprecation. I discerned that he was far from being clear about the thing himself.

Yes, he temporized, this Father Witch was dead, quite dead. On the other hand he was up there. On the other hand he would never die. He was longer than forever. Yes, quite true, he was dead and buried under the pot.

I gave it up. "How did he die?"

Well, he came to this village of Tara very suffering, very sick. The dead man who walked. His face was very sad. Very eaten. Very frightened. He came to this hill. So he lived here for two full moons, very hot, very eaten, very dead. These men made him a house as he commanded them, also a stockade. In the house he was very quiet, very dead, making magic two full moons. Then he came out and they that were waiting saw him. He had made the magic, and the magic had made him well. His face was kind. He was happy. He was full-fed. He was full-fed, these men said, without any eating. Yes, they carried up to him very fine food, because they were full of wonder and some fear, but he did not eat any of it. Some water he drank. So, for two days and the night between them he continued sitting in the gate of the stockade, very happy, very full-fed. He told these people very much about their wizard, who is bigger than everywhere and longer than forever and can, if he cares to, swallow the sky and stars. From time to time, however, ceasing to talk to these people, he got to his knees and talked in his own strange tongue to Our Father Witch, his eyes held shut. When he had done this just at sunset of the second day he fell forward on his face. So he remained that night. The next day these men took him into the house and buried him under the pot. On the other hand Our Father Witch is longer than forever. He remains there still. . . .

The first thing I saw in the hut's interior was the earthen pot at the northern end, wrong side up on the ground. I was glad I had preceded Mrs. Diana. I walked across and sat down on it carelessly, hoping so that her afflicted curiosity might be led astray. It gave me the oddest feeling, though, to think of what was there beneath my nonchalant sitting portion—aware as I was of the Kavirondo burial of a great man—up to the neck in mother earth, and the rest of him left out in the dark of the pot for the undertakings of the ants. I hoped his widow wouldn't wonder about that inverted vessel of clay.

I needn't have worried. Her attention was arrested otherwheres. I shall not forget the look of her face, caught above me in the red shaft of sundown entering the western door, as she gazed at the last and the largest of the Reverend Hubert Diana's gods. That long, long cheek of hers, buffeted by sorrow, startled now and mortified. Not till that moment, I believe, had she comprehended the steps of mud images she had been following for what they were, the steps of idolatry.

For my part, I wasn't startled. Even before we started up the hill, knowing that her husband had dared to die here, I could have told her pretty much what she would find.

This overlord of the cosmic categories that he had fashioned (at last) in his own image sat at the other end of the red-streaked house upon a bench—a throne?—of mud. Diana had been no artist. An ovoid two-eyed head, a cylindrical trunk, two arms, two legs, that's all. But indubitably man, man-size. Only one finger of one of the hands had been done with much care. It wore an opal, a two-dollar stone from Mexico, set in a silver ring. This was the hand that was lifted, and over it the head was bent.

I've said Diana was no artist. I'll take back the words. The figure was crudeness itself, but in the relation between that bent head and that lifted hand there was something which was something else. A sense of scrutiny one would have said no genius of mud could ever have conveyed. An attitude of interest centered in that bauble, intense and static, breathless and eternal all in one—penetrating to its bottom atom, to the last electron, to a hill upon it, and to a two-legged mite about to die. Marking (yes, I'll swear to the incredible) the sparrow's fall.

The magic was made. The road that had commenced with the blobs of Ndua—the same that commenced with our hairy ancestors listening to the night wind in their caves—was run.

And from here Diana, of a sudden happy, of a sudden looked after, "full-fed," had walked out——

But no; I couldn't stand that mortified sorrow on the widow's face any longer. She had to be made to see *what she wanted to see.* I said it aloud:

"From here, Mrs. Diana, your husband walked out——"

"He had sunk to idolatry. *Idolatry!*"

"To the bottom, yes. And come up its whole history again. And from here he walked out into the sunshine to kneel and talk with 'Our Father Witch——' "

She got it. She caught it. I wish you could have seen the light going up those long, long cheeks as she got it:

"Our Father which art in Heaven, hallowed be Thy Name!"

We went down hill in the darkness, protected against goblins by a vast rattling of gourds and beating of heathen drums.

*The Dark Hour**

THE RETURNING SHIP SWAM swiftly through the dark; the deep, interior breathing of the engines, the singing of wire stays, the huge whispering rush of foam streaming the water line, made up a body of silence upon which the sound of the doctor's footfalls, coming and going restlessly along the near deck, intruded only a little—a faint and personal disturbance. Charging slowly through the dark, a dozen paces forward, a dozen paces aft, his invisible and tormented face bent forward a little over his breast, he said to himself, "What fools! What blind fools we've been!"

Sweat stood for an instant on his brow and was gone in the steady onrush of the wind.

The man lying on the cot in the shelter of the cabin companionway made no sound all the while. He might have been asleep or dead, he remained so quiet; yet he was neither asleep nor dead, for his eyes, large, wasted, and luminous, gazed out unwinking from the little darkness of his shelter into the vaster darkness of the night, where a star burned in slow mutations, now high, now sailing low, over the rail of the ship.

Once he said in a washed and strengthless voice, "That's a bright star, Doctor."

If the other heard, he gave no sign. He continued charging slowly back and forth, his large dim shoulders hunched over his neck, his hands locked behind him, his teeth showing faintly gray between the fleshy lips which hung open a little to his breathing.

"It's dark!" he said of a sudden, bringing up before the cot in the companionway. "God, Hallett, how dark it is!" There was something incoherent and mutilated about it, as if the cry had torn the tissues of his throat. "I'm not myself tonight," he added, with a trace of shame.

Hallett spoke slowly from his pillow.

"It wouldn't be the subs tonight. You're not that kind, you know. I've seen you in the zone. And we're well west of them by this, anyhow; and as you say, it's very dark."

"It's not that darkness. Not that!"

Again there was the sense of something tearing. The doctor rocked for a moment on his thick legs. He began to talk.

"It's this *war*——" His conscience protested: "I ought not to go on so—it's not right, not right at all—talking so to the wounded—the dying—I shouldn't go on so to the dying." And all the while the words continued to tumble out of his mouth. "No, I'm not a coward—not especially. You know I'm not a coward, Hallett. You know that. But just now, tonight, somehow, the whole truth of the thing has come out and got me—jumped out of the dark and got me by the neck, Hallett. Look here; I've kept a stiff lip. Since the first I've said, 'We'll win this war.' It's been a matter of course. So far as I know, never a hint of doubt has shadowed my mind, even when things went bad. 'In the end,' I've said, 'in the end, of course, we're bound to win.'"

He broke away again to charge slowly through the dark with his head down, butting; a large, overheated animal endowed with a mind.

"But—do we want to win?"

Hallett's question, very faint across the subdued breathings and showerings of the ship, fetched the doctor up. He stood for a moment, rocking on his legs and staring at the face of the questioner, still and faintly luminous on the invisible cot. Then he laughed briefly, shook himself, and ignored the preposterous words. He recollected tardily that the fellow was pretty well gone.

"No," he went on. "Up to tonight I've never doubted. No one in the world, in our part of the world, has doubted. The proposition was absurd to begin with. Prussia, and her fringe of hangers-on, to stand against the world—to stand against the very drift and destiny of civilization? Impossible! A man can't do the impossible; that's logic, Hallett, and that's common sense. They might have their day of it, their little hour, because they had the jump—but in the end!

In the end! . . . But look at them, will you! Look at them! That's what's got me tonight, Hallett. Look at them! There they stand. They won't play the game, won't abide at all by the rules of logic, of common sense. Every day, every hour, they perform the impossible. It's like clockwork. It's like a rehearsed and abominable program——"

"Yes—a program."

The wounded man lay quite still and gazed at the stars. When he spoke, his words carried an odd sense of authenticity, finality. His mind had got a little away from him, and now it was working with the new, oracular clarity of the moribund. It bothered the doctor inexplicably—tripped him up. He had to shake himself. He began to talk louder and make wide, scarcely visible gestures.

"We've laughed so long, Hallett. There was *Mitteleuropa!* We always laughed at that. A wag's tale. To think of it—a vast, self-sufficient, brutal empire laid down across the path of the world! Haha! Why, even if they had *wanted* it, it would be——"

"If they *wanted* it, it would be—*inevitable*."

The doctor held up for a full dozen seconds. A kind of anger came over him and his face grew red. He couldn't understand. He talked still louder.

"But they're *doing* it! They're doing that same preposterous thing before our eyes, and we can't touch them, and they're—— Hallett! *They're damn near done!* Behind that line there—you know the line I mean—who of us doesn't know it? That thin line of smoke and ashes and black blood. Behind that line they're at work, day by day, month after month, building the empire we never believed. And Hallett, *it's damn near done!* And we can't stop it. It grows bigger and bigger, darker and darker—it covers up the sky—like a nightmare——"

"Like a dream!" said Hallett softly.

The doctor's boot soles drummed with a dull, angry resonance on the deck.

"And we can't touch them! They couldn't conceivably hold that line against us—against the whole world—long enough to build their incredible empire behind it. *And they have!* Hallett! How *could* they ever have held it?"

"You mean, how could we ever have held it?"

Hallett's words flowed on, smooth, clear-formed, unhurried, and his eyes kept staring at the star.

"No, it's we have held it, not they. And we that have got to hold it—longer than they. Theirs is the kind of *Mitteleuropa* that's been done before; history is little more than a copybook for such an empire as they are building. We've got a vaster and more incredible empire to build than they—a *Mitteleuropa*, let us say, of the spirit of man. No, no, Doctor; it's we that are doing the impossible, holding that thin line."

The doctor failed to contain himself.

"Oh, pshaw! *Pshaw!* See here, Hallett! We've had the men, and there's no use blinking the truth. And we've had the money and the munitions."

"But back of all that, behind the last reserve, the last shell dump, the last treasury, haven't they got something that we've never had?"

"And what's that?"

"A dream."

"A *what?*"

"A dream. We've dreamed no dream. Yes—let me say it! A little while ago you said 'nightmare,' and I said 'dream.' Germany has dreamed a dream. Black as the pit of hell—yes, yes—but a dream. They've seen a vision. A red, bloody, damned vision—yes, yes—but a vision. They've got a program, even if it's what you called it, a 'rehearsed and abominable program.' And they know what they want. And we don't know what we want!"

The doctor's fist came down in the palm of his hand.

"What we want? I'll tell you what we want, Hallett. *We want to win this war!*"

"Yes?"

"And by the living God, Hallett, we will win this war! I can see again. If we fight for half a century to come; if we turn the world wrong side out for men, young men, boys, babes; if we mine the earth to a hollow shell for coal and iron; if we wear our women to ghosts to get out the last grain of wheat from the fields—we'll do it! And we'll wipe this black thing from the face of the earth forever, root and branch, father and son of the bloody race of them to the end of time. If you want a dream, Hallett, there's a——"

"There's a—nightmare. An overweening muscular impulse to jump on the thing that's scared us in the dark, to break it with our hands, grind it into the ground with our heels, tear ourselves away from it —and wake up."

He went on again after a moment.

"Yes, that's it. We've never asked for anything better; not once have we got down on our naked knees and prayed for anything more than just to be allowed to wake up—and find it isn't so. How can we expect, with a desire like that, to stand against a positive and a flaming desire? No, no! The only thing to beat a dream is a dream more poignant. The only thing to beat a vision black as midnight is a vision white as the noonday sun. We've come to the place, Doctor, where half a loaf is worse than no bread."

The doctor put his hands in his pockets and took them out again, shifted away a few steps and back again. He felt inarticulate, handless, helpless in the face of things, of abstractions, of the mysterious, unflagging swiftness of the ship bearing him willy-nilly over the blind surface of the sea. He shook himself.

"God help us," he said.

"What God?"

The doctor lifted a weary hand.

"Oh, if you're going into *that*——"

"Why not? Because Prussia, Doctor, has a god. Prussia has a god as terrible as the God of conquering Israel, a god created in her own image. We laugh when we hear her speaking intimately and surely to this god. I tell you we're fools. I tell you, Doctor, before we shall stand we shall have to create a god in *our* own image, and before we do that we shall have to have a living and sufficient image."

"You don't think much of us," the doctor murmured wearily.

The other seemed not to hear. After a little while he said, "We've got to say black or white at last. We've got to answer a question this time with a whole answer.

"This war began so long ago," he went on, staring at the star. "So long before Sarajevo, so long before 'balances of power' were thought of, so long before the 'provinces' were lost and won, before Bismarck and the lot of them were begotten, or their fathers. So many, many years of questions put, and half answers given in return. Questions, questions: questions of a power loom in the North Countries; questions of a millhand's lodging in one Manchester or another, of the weight of a head tax in India, of a widow's Mass for her dead in Spain; questions of a black man in the Congo, of an eighth-black man in New Orleans, of a Christian in Turkey, an Irishman in Dublin, a Jew in Moscow, a French cripple in the streets of Zabern;

questions of an idiot sitting on a throne; questions of a girl asking her vote on a Hyde Park rostrum, of a girl asking her price in the dark of a Chicago doorway—whole questions half answered, hungry questions half fed, mutilated fag ends of questions piling up and piling up year by year, decade after decade. Listen! There came a time when it wouldn't do, wouldn't do at all. There came a time when the son of all those questions stood up in the world, final, unequivocal, naked, devouring, saying, 'Now you shall answer me. You shall look me squarely in the face at last, and you shall look at nothing else; you shall take your hands out of your pockets and your tongues out of your cheeks, and no matter how long, no matter what the blood and anguish of it, you shall answer me now with the whole answer—or perish!' "

"And what's the answer?"

The doctor leaned down a little, resting his hands on the foot of the cot.

The gray patch of Hallett's face moved slightly in the dark.

"It will sound funny to you. Because it's a word that's been worn pretty thin by so much careless handling. It's 'Democracy'!"

The doctor stood up straight on his thick legs.

"Why should it sound funny?" he demanded, a vein of triumph in his tone. "It *is* the answer. And we've *given* it. 'Make the world safe for democracy!' Eh? You remember the quotation?"

"Yes, yes, that's good. But we've got to do more than say it, Doctor. Go further. We've got to dream it in a dream; we've got to see democracy as a wild, consuming vision. If the day ever comes when we shall pronounce the word 'democracy' with the same fierce faith with which we conceive them to be pronouncing 'autocracy'—that day, Doctor——"

He raised a transparent hand and moved it slowly over his eyes.

"It will be something to do, Doctor, that will. Like taking hold of lightning. It will rack us body and soul; belief will strip us naked for a moment, leave us newborn and shaken and weak—as weak as Christ in the manger. And that day nothing can stand before us. Because, you see, we'll know what we want."

The doctor stood for a moment, a large, dark, troubled body rocking slowly to the heave of the deck beneath him. He rubbed a hand over his face.

"Utopian!" he said.

"Utopian!" Hallett repeated after him. "Today we are children of Utopia—or we are nothing. I tell you, Doctor, today it has come down to this—Hamburg to Bagdad—or Utopia!"

The other lifted his big arms and his face was red.

"You're playing with words, Hallett. You do nothing but twist my words. When I say 'Utopia,' I mean, precisely, impossible. Absolutely impossible. See here! You tell me this empire of theirs is a dream. I give you that. How long has it taken them to dream it? Forty years. *Forty years!* And this wild, transcendental empire of the spirit you talk about—so much harder—so many hundreds of times more incredible—will you have us do that sort of thing in a *day?* We're a dozen races, a score of nations. I tell you it's—it's impossible!"

"Yes. Impossible."

The silence came down between them, heavy with all the dark, impersonal sounds of passage, the rhythmical explosions of the waves, the breathing of engines, the muffled staccato of the spark in the wireless room, the note of the ship's bell forward striking the hour and after it a hail, running thin in the wind: "Six bells, sir, and—*all's well!*"

"*All's well!*"

The irony of it! The infernal patness of it, falling so in the black interlude, like stage business long rehearsed.

"*All's well!*" the doctor echoed with the mirthless laughter of the damned.

Hallett raised himself very slowly on an elbow and stared at the star beyond the rail.

"Yes, I shouldn't wonder. Just now—tonight—somehow—I've got a queer feeling that maybe it is. Maybe it's going to be. Maybe it's going to be; who knows? The darkest hour of our lives, of history, perhaps, has been on us. And maybe it's almost over. Maybe we're going to get it done in time. I've got a queer sense of something happening—something getting ready."

When he spoke again, his voice had changed a little.

"I wish my father could have lived to see this day. He's in New York now, and I should like——"

The doctor moved forward suddenly and quietly, saying: "Lie down, Hallett. You'd better lie down now."

But the other protested with a gray hand.

"No, no, you don't understand. When I say—well—it's just the shell of my father walking around and talking around, these ten years past. Prison killed his heart. He doesn't even know it, that the immortal soul of him has gone out. You know him, Doctor. Ben Hallett; the Radical—'the Destroyer,' they used to call him in the old days. He was a brave man, Doctor; you've got to give him that; as brave as John the Baptist, and as mad. I can see him now—tonight—sitting in the back room in Eighth Street, him and old Radinov and Hirsch and O'Reilly and the rest, with all the doors shut and the windows shut and their eyes and ears and minds shut up tight, trying to keep the war out. They're old men, Doctor, and they must cling to yesterday, and to tomorrow. They mustn't see today. They must ignore today. Today is the tragic interruption. They too ask nothing but to wake up and find it isn't so. All their lives they've been straining forward to see the ineffable dawn of the Day of Man, calling for the Commune and the red barricades of revolution. The barricades! Yesterday, it seems to them now, they were almost in sight of the splendid dawn—the dawn of the Day of Barricades. And then this war, this thing they call a 'rich man's plot' to confound them, hold them up, turn to ashes all the fires of their lives. All they can do is sit in a closed room with their eyes shut and wait till this meaningless brawl is done. And then, tomorrow—tomorrow—some safely distant tomorrow (for they're old men)—tomorrow, the barricades! And that's queer. That's queer."

"Queer?"

"It seems to me that for days now, for weeks and months now, there's been no sound to be heard in all the length and breadth of the world but the sound of barricades."

The voice trailed off into nothing.

To the doctor, charging slowly back and forth along the near deck, his hands locked behind him and his face bent slightly over his breast, there came a queer sense of separation, from Hallett, from himself, his own everyday acts, his own familiar aspirations, from the ship which held him up in the dark void between two continents.

What was it all about? he asked himself over and over. Each time he passed the shadow in the companionway he turned his head, painfully, and as if against his will. Once he stopped squarely at the foot of the cot and stood staring down at the figure there, faintly outlined, motionless and mute. Sweat stood for a moment on his brow, and was gone in the steady onrush of the wind. And he was used to death.

But Hallett had fooled him. He heard Hallett's whisper creeping to him out of the shadow:

"That's a bright star, Doctor."

*Bubbles**

CAROL LIVED IN HOTELS, AND HER governess was always being mistaken for her mamma. Or it might be her trained nurse or it might be Daddy's secretary who was mistaken for her mamma. Most often it was governess. Miss Flower, Miss Runkle, Madame Dunaye, respectively in Nice, on the Isle of Man, and in Deauville, were governesses. But Miss Tolley, in Florida, was Daddy's secretary. And Mrs. Kenyon (with long silky legs and an amount of pale-gold hair) was Carol's trained nurse for nearly three months at Capri, though fortunately Carol was not ill a day of the time.

It was a little confusing at first, each time, for in a way they all seemed much alike. One had to remember arbitrarily, that was all, just as one had to remember that whereas two "f's" hitched together make "double-f," two "v's" hitched together make a "double-u." Moreover, Coddie helped her. "Do mind now, child; if anyone's to ask you, Miss Runkle is your governess. *Not* Daddy's secretary, this time, but Carol's *governess*." Coddie was severe about this, unnecessarily so it seemed to Carol, upon whom would be lost the glitter of an ironical amusement in the nurse's sea-gray eyes.

Coddie was middle-aged, and broad, and ate with Carol and not with Daddy. No matter who was governess, Coddie did the governing; no matter who was trained nurse, Coddie did the nursing; and even if it happened to be a secretary Mr. Bonaparte was having, it was Coddie who got the letters from the concierge, the commissionaire, or the desk clerk, and arranged them on the table in his room. And beyond all, Coddie was permanent.

It had never occurred to Carol to wonder what would have happened to the world had Coddie not been permanent. Perhaps it had to Mr. Bonaparte. Perhaps that was why he was always so polite to Coddie, poor man, walking lightly among his words with her, as a man (and a little ashamed of it) walking on tiptoe past a sleeping dog.

Mr. Bonaparte was of medium height, well set up, with fair hair and mustache waxed at the points, and blue eyes which had a way of widening abruptly sometimes, like the eyes of some people who suffer from the pangs of unadmitted maladies. At forty-one he had habitually a deep line which, springing from between his eyes, divided into dozens of creases all over his forehead, as fine as threads and as tangled as the hunting of the Wandering Jew. This wasn't always, to be sure. Sometimes his brow was as smooth as a boy's. Such were the times when Carol admired him most, and Coddie, knowing by the signs what was in the air, admired him least of all.

Coddie admired him most when she was seeing him most, that is, when there were but the three of them, and Mr. Bonaparte cleaved grimly to the apartment, and grew white of conscience and rumpled of soul and clothing, alternately tender and sharp with Carol, and (for once) defiantly spleenish with Coddie herself, till he was like a lean wolf prowling the windows by day, and by night, in his slippers, the bedroom floor.

Carol admired him most when she was seeing him least. Not for more than scattered minutes in whole days. A "good morning" perhaps, and late in the morning too, after she had been brought back from her walk in Central Park or Kensington Gardens or along the Croisette or the Lido sands, and he still in bed, like all the princes charming of Coddie's tales rolled in one, with his brow smoothed out and an adventurous kindness in his big, blue, far-off eyes. And after that only in chance glimpses—Daddy in the distance in High Street helping a lady into a motorcar—Daddy in a vista of the Casino gardens at tea with a lady under a striped umbrella—or after the lights were lit and Carol in her bed, a blur of Daddy in the hallway in shining black and white and tails.

Oh, how splendid he was! It was queer: Carol was proud and jealous all in one. She wished she were dying, so he couldn't go but must stay and be distracted about her. Yet just as fiercely she wanted him to go—out where the clustered lights were and the admiring throngs. "Do look: who *is* that wonderful *man?*" . . . "But don't you know? You know the girl with the red-brown curls and the green jacket and gaiters—well, *that's her father!*" Between the two wants she wept, and often she would be asleep before she could make up her mind which one she was mostly weeping for. . . . And presently, one day, "I shouldn't be surprised," she would confide to Coddie, "if Daddy were looking out for somebody for me—like a governess."

Why did Coddie make it sound so odd when she echoed, "I shouldn't be surprised."

So they weren't surprised when the trunks appeared in the rooms, and when Daddy, as if he had been on the point of forgetting to mention it, called back from the door on his way to luncheon, "By the way, might just pack things up, you know; we're leaving for the South tomorrow" (or "for Scotland" or "for America"). Nor were they surprised when, arriving at the station, they found one seat in their compartment occupied by a lady, and the lady was Carol's governess.

Or in America, of course, it would be in the Pullman. That was where Miss Tolley was, in the bright low cave of the two seats and the berth made up above, and porters and other passengers stepping on one's heels, and Daddy with his face pressed to the window as if trying to think what he might have forgotten, while he said in the back of his mouth, "This is Miss Tolley, Carol. Miss Tolley is going to do some secretarial work for Daddy down in Florida."

Miss Tolley was small and dark and quick and she had enthusiasms. She adored things. She adored the sea. She spent lots of time at Miami on the beach in an old-rose bathing costume, but she never went into the water. Coddie had funny ways of saying things to herself aloud. Later on she said to herself that Daddy had "let the Tolley go" for just that—that she "never went into the water." . . . Miss Tolley liked perfumes.

Mrs. Kenyon did not like perfumes. She liked black coffee, black cigarettes, black Italian shawls, which was interesting, since she was so distinctly un-black herself, all creamy and pale gold in the hot white Capri sun.

They were all different in little ways. Madame Dunaye disliked anything flavored with pistachio and wore a ribbon across her forehead to make it look wide and low, and she and Daddy went to the races.

Miss Flower was an English girl. Sometimes she grew red and at other times she cried. At the Manx Arms, where she was with them, she asked Coddie to let her have one of Carol's lesson books, and sometimes when people looked at her she would come and get Carol, and they would sit in the gardens and read together, much to Coddie's amusement later on. Miss Flower wouldn't go near the water (though it wasn't like Miss Tolley—it was sadder). On the steamer all the way across to New York she would hardly look at the waves, and unless she was tramping the deck with Daddy she was always hidden away somewhere inside, alone. Carol asked her why. Then she told Carol:

"My father and my two brothers were fishermen. They were all lost at sea."

One night Miss Flower stole into the stateroom while Coddie was out. She got on her knees by Carol's berth and put her face in the blankets and sobbed. "Is it because you are frightened of being drowned?" Carol asked her.

Miss Flower was a slow, big, hale person, and there was a silk of down on the arms she flung around Carol suddenly, without a word.

"Or why then?" Carol persisted, feeling puzzled and responsible.

"Nothing! Nothing! Except that I—I—I *wish you were mine!*"

That's an odd kind of a governess.

Miss Flower wept too at the High Ridge House in the White Mountains. One night she wept nearly all night long. It must have been over something she and Daddy were discussing late, for she was in Daddy's room, where Carol could hear her sobbing. She could hear Daddy too. Once she heard distinctly what he said. "You've got to be quieter, I *beg* of you, Clare! Good God, this isn't the Continent, remember—this is America!" And once he too sobbed.

He took Carol for a long tramp next day. When they got back home to the High Ridge House, Miss Flower was gone.

Times like that—just when someone was gone, and before Daddy had begun to grow fidgety—were the times above all that Carol loved. It didn't mean just the one tramp. There were dozens. Up hill and down dale, hand in hand, woods like Persian rugs where autumn was commencing, little clouds in the clear, and blue shadow splashes; boot nails ringing on the rocks, Daddy in rough tweeds, a big brown pipe going, instead of so many cigarettes.

There was a hillside facing the sun, a field running down to a pine forest that, in its turn, ran down into a shining river. There was the ruin of a house, and on an outer corner of the old foundation they sat and let their legs hang over. And Carol began to feel queer.

"Old Girl," Daddy was saying, "what are you going to remember about your dad? What ever do you suppose you think you really think of him?"

Think? Oh, she couldn't *think*. Somehow, the way she loved him —the way she was thrilled by his bigness and kindness and handsome strength, so that sometimes she was almost scared to know that he was there with her, undivided, monopolized—somehow or other, it was more than she cared to tackle in words. There are times in the heart of woman when lightness is the only way out.

"I like," she said (though she was feeling queerer all the while), "the way your mustache does at the ends, like the lances knights level at dastard cravens." She squeezed his hand to make him understand this was whimsicality. "And I like the way this suit smells."

Daddy burst out laughing, twisting still tighter the mustache ends. "Ah, woman, woman!"

But then he stopped and his face grew red. After that it turned a greeny white, like the faces one sees in deck chairs. For a while he sat and hugged his knees. So he hadn't understood after all.

He said, "Old Girl, Daddy needs something. Daddy needs people. Daddy's not much good in this world without—somebody."

Oh, but couldn't he *see?* Idiot! There were teardrops in his eyes.

But now Carol was feeling queerer than ever.

"Daddy," she said before she knew it, "have we ever been here before?"

"Here?" He stared at her blinking. "No!" Then he looked down the pasture to the woods and river, and gave a sort of start. "I see what you mean."

If he saw what she meant, certainly Carol didn't.

"Daddy, listen to me. Was I ever—did I ever have a mamma?"

Daddy kept on looking steadily at the river. "By George, I see what you mean," he repeated to himself. He slid from the wall and put his hands up. "Come, jump." But *her* face was the funny color now. "Lord!" he said. "What's wrong? Tummy?"

That was it. Presently she was ill-and-up-with-it in a corner of the wall.

They laughed over it as they tramped back across the world.

"What a silly thing to do!" . . . "What a perfectly!" Yet it was a little because they felt they had to. There was a change. That was the last of their walks just then.

Daddy went under again. Anyone could see how vilely he hated to. The looks he gave Carol sometimes! It was as if he were a wolf in a forest, but the forest was enchanted, and even while he prowled and growled his horridest he was all the while trying to tell one with his dumb eyes that he wasn't really a wolf at all but a prince under the spell of an evil sorcerer.

It was growing late in the season and the hotel was nearly empty, and there was nothing but the hotel in miles. Carol and Coddie discussed governesses.

"He'll hardly find one *here*," Carol decided, and Coddie concurred.

Bored! It was a more positive thing; more like a disease he had to fight, and tried to fight, sometimes angrily and sometimes in dull despair. His trousers bagged at the knees, and the ends of his mustache came undone. The hotel followed his mood; servants were laid off; the wooden corridors sounded hollower and hollower.

Then one morning Coddie, bringing up the mail, said to Carol, "Here they are." She meant the folders. Cunard, White Star, United Fruit, Royal Mail. Carol looked them over superficially, then turned to the letters, which it was her privilege to sort, Mr. Bonaparte's from Miss Eliza Codd's.

"Here's one for Daddy from someone who's a doctor and who's at home. 'Doctor Kamp's Home!' Now isn't that too silly to put on the outside?"

Coddie was surprisingly impressed. Snatching the letter from Carol's hand and hiding it behind her, she hardened her eyes at the girl as though it were a crime she had been caught in. And within two minutes after she had taken the mail into Daddy's room, here was Daddy out in his pajamas.

"Codd, I want you to get the trunks packed immediately. I've this letter from——" He hesitated, more and more distracted. "Carol, Old Girl, will you run along down and play on the veranda for a while? Dash!"

Carol played on the veranda for a while, but she had nothing to play with and a while is rather indefinite. Returning to the rooms she heard Coddie saying, "Yes, Mr. Bonaparte, we're both right: *I* would *hardly* do."

And Daddy, at his wit's end, "Well, how to manage? I suppose my best plan would be to wire the agency to send somebody down direct to 'The Pasture.' "

Carol felt things a good deal more than she knew things. She could feel a shadow coming before she could see it. All the way to the station in the hotel car that afternoon—she didn't know why—but it was dreadful. What made her cling so hard to Coddie's hand? And why was Coddie, who hadn't a cold, forever blowing her nose on the sly?

Why was it so queer when they got into the parlor car? There was no new governess there, but that wasn't the half, nor the hundredth. It happened just before the train started to move. Coddie bent of a sudden, dabbed a kiss on Carol's temple, cried, "Be a good girl, now, always," and in another wink there she was outside on the platform, waving, and the landscape was sliding, and Daddy and Carol were awkwardly all alone. . . .

It was late at night and it was a strange house, a strange room, and a strange bed. Strangest of all was the getting to bed. The only one there was to preside over it was Daddy (there were servants of sorts in the strange downstairs, but of course *they* wouldn't do), and Daddy was bungling and distraught, and Carol was inept and distrait, and the whole affair was getting to be a dream which she wished she didn't have to have.

How could she ask where such a thing as her nightie was, when she couldn't ask where Coddie was? In ways it was quite as hard for Daddy. With him it took the form of an embarrassment which grew with the child's numbness and dumbness, till it seemed he would have to yell and shake her if she persisted in it ten minutes more. This going on as if nothing had happened!

He did shake her presently, and give her a fumbling kiss on top of her head, so that she couldn't see his face.

"Don't know what it's all about, do you, Old Girl? You'll be so happy, though, when you know the surprise."

"When is the surprise?" Her voice was as dead as dead.

"Tomorrow."

"Is it Coddie?"

Daddy looked worse than exasperated: he looked hurt. Painstakingly, like one counting twenty before he spoke, he turned down the bed. Then he stared at the farther wall and said, "You're getting too old for simply a nurse now, Carol. Tomorrow your regular governess will be here."

"Oh-h-h-h!"

Carol got in, pulled the covers to her chin, and lay quiet, studying him as he bent in circles picking up things that didn't need picking up.

"Oh-h-h-h! So-o-o-! I see-e-e-e!"

Daddy jerked up, his face flaming.

"No, you *don't* see. And it's a *real* surprise—and can't you take Daddy's word for it—and not look like that—and—go to sleep like a good girl?"

He rushed around. "Want a drink of water on your table? No?"

He vanished, and presently he was back again in triumph, bearing a kitten captured somewhere, a gray little creature with fluffy cheeks and pert eyes.

"Look! Isn't it cunning? Want to pet?"

"No, thank you."

Unfortunately the kitten had taken matters into its own paws. No sooner had Daddy put it beside the pillow than it was gone under the covers, and no sooner was it curled in a lump on Carol's chest than it began to purr.

Carol would do nothing about it. Daddy stood and scratched his head.

"Well, I don't suppose it's at all the right thing. However—just tonight——" He sighed, opened the window, put out the light, and fled.

Carol lay and stared into the dark. "So-o-o-o. I see-e-e-e."

The first sob was hard to get up, the second was easier, and then the wild tears came. The ball in her arms wriggled in protest, not liking to be hugged so joltingly. . . . There, that was better.

Not since she could remember had Carol been in one place long enough to be allowed to have a pet. Kittens were amazingly soft and warm. As little by little the sobbing wore itself out, so did the purring. Neither kittens nor kids can stay awake forever.

Carol had a start when she awoke in the morning. It came back with a thump: "*Coddie isn't here.*" Then, hearing someone in the room, she turned her head, and for a wink she thought it was Coddie. The same square figure, a broad back, a head with a topknot. But when the person turned it was a stranger.

Her name, she said, was Mrs. Lephant and, although it wasn't her fault Carol had mistaken her for Coddie, Carol hated her. It didn't help that Coddie would have cried, "A *kitten* in *bed!*" and flung up her hands in just as holy a horror; no, somehow or other it wouldn't have been the same. Nor would her "Up you get now, Carol: don't be a lazy thing!"

The thing that was the hardest to bear, as Carol went about her dressing with averted eyes and heavy hands, was that Daddy had told her a deliberate fib. "Too old for simply a nurse now." If that wasn't to say she wasn't to have a new nurse in poor Coddie's place, she didn't know what it was. Of course it never occurred to her that Mrs. Lephant might be the governess he had spoken of. Governesses don't have red wrists and grizzling hair; if Carol knew anything in the world at going-on-seven, she knew *governesses.*

When Carol looked out of her window she had another start. Last night, whirling up in the car, it had all been dark. Now the sunshine of the clear morning discovered to her eyes an oblique and rocky pastureland falling away to a pine wood, and at the foot of the wood the broad Connecticut.

"Come along to your breakfast, child; don't be lagging there."

Carol had felt queer once before. Was she going to have a "tummy" again?

Mrs. Lephant came treading back. There would need to be some discipline.

"Did you hear me, Carol, when I— Why, what ails the child?"

"Mrs. Lephant, I've been here before."

"Been here before? Gracious! It's your home, isn't it?"

"My—home?"

"I thought your papa told me you were born here. . . . Now whatever the game is, please leave it till after breakfast, my dear, and take my hand and come."

At breakfast, after a long time, Carol asked, "Where is my daddy?"

"He has gone out for a while. He didn't say when he would be back."

from her heart, "I love you, and you're so beautiful, and you're my mamma, and my own, forever and ever—promise me you are!"

But because she was shy she had always to hang back. She had to make believe to be interested in nothing on earth but the kitten that tumbled across the garden at the end of her string. She had to pretend it was secrets, when it was only "She's my own, my really mamma!" that she whispered over and over into Bubble's ear till the creature was nearly frantic with the tickle, and the lovely lady smiled.

It was when they were out for the sunset that Mamma smiled. She stopped dead still and flashed a look at the child, knee-deep with Bubble in a thicket of old snapdragon stalks. She started to speak, then closed her lips tight, and wound her fingers into her palms, as people do who are very nervous at hotels in Italy. Then she smiled, and it was a funny, slow, thin smile, and she said in a tone playfully wistful on top and something mysteriously else beneath, "I wish *I* had a string, little daughter. Would you be my little kitty then, and —and—play with me?"

Carol was allowed to stay down to dinner at table that evening, and if there had been any doubts left, that would have settled it. One doesn't stay down to dine with governesses.

It was wonderful. There were candles on the table, tall ones, whose fat flames wavered softly in miniature in silver and crystal and china such as Carol had never seen in all the hotels in the world. They wavered in Daddy's eyes too, and in Mamma's: they must have been in Carol's own; the three faces and Mamma's neck and Daddy's shirt front were bright, and all was gloom behind.

There was a pale wine in glasses. Daddy lifted his and leaned forward.

"Stacia?"

Mamma was like a lady, Carol decided, sitting in a crystal tower. He had to speak again before she heard and lifted her glass to clink on his.

Daddy's trembled a little. "Here's to—God bless all of us, Stacia."

Mamma sipped and said nothing. When one came to think of it, Mamma had said nothing all that afternoon, or nearly nothing. It was always Daddy.

"Stacia," he went on, musing at his glass, a twisty smile about his lips that was both sad and gay, "I was never built for—going it alone. I'm not the lone wolf. I feel as if I'd been through——" He shook himself, bright teardrops starting. "Never mind! I feel as if I'd come back to life today!"

What Mamma felt she didn't say. Dreaming down at the fires in her wineglass, perhaps she was thinking of nothing at all as she twirled the stem of it idly in the fingers of her left hand, somnambulist still.

Carol couldn't help bouncing (it was a mercy she didn't gasp out loud) when she felt the *other* hand coming through the darkness under the table. She would have liked to get her own two quickly in safe sight above the cloth, but it was so weird somehow, and she was so confused, she didn't know what to do. And then it was too late; the unseen thing that searched had come to her fingers and slid around them, swift as whips and tight as tentacles.

Carol had never been so abashed in her life. It was really more like terror. Of course it wouldn't have been anything at all if the others at table had known about it. But Daddy didn't seem to, and no more did Mamma, sitting there above the serene white damask (miles and miles away) in her tower of glass. And it wasn't just that it was clandestine, that subterranean grasp; it wasn't even a grasp, but more like a grab, a static violence, gradually tightening.

"I'm going to do lots of things now, Stacia," Daddy was musing. "I'm going to buy back into the firm, and I'm going——" From Mamma's face his eyes came abruptly to Carol's. "Why, Carol, Old Girl, what's wrong?"

Carol swallowed, and was red. "N-n-nothing. Really and tr-tr-truly."

In a panic she averted her eyes. She peered busily into the shadows in the corners. "Only I—I am a—a little worried about Bub-Bubble. I wonder where Bub-Bub-Bubble is."

There! If only she had thought of that sooner. Under the table the grab had suddenly ungrabbed and flown away, and almost in the same wink of time Mamma, come out of her tower, was smoothing with her right hand a wisp of her lovely chestnut hair. She appeared to have rediscovered Carol.

"Bubble is the kitten?" she asked, smiling the same funny, slow, thin smile she had used once before.

Daddy laughed. "Yes, and kittens aren't allowed in dining rooms, Old Girl."

In the living room, after dinner, with Mrs. Lephant waiting rather sniffily in the doorway (for after all, she was a governess, not a nurse), Carol was allowed to bid her parents good night. For the first time in her career and for no known reason, she shook hands gravely with her father. Then she turned with a kind of shiver of stage fright to deal with the other one.

On the flare-backed couch before the new fire in the chimney Mamma half reclined, obliquely, one knee over the other, one elbow up and a hand supporting her head, which was tilted a little so, like a bird's in half-preoccupied interrogation. There was a perfume about her that Carol had never known or dreamed of—as if it weren't of earthly flowers—exquisitely faint. Scent and sight worked backward with Carol. A lovely fragrance made her eyes film; to make her nostrils dilate it took an entrancing vision, like the soft flames running and playing in Mamma's hair.

The eyes in the face that was more beautiful in its set pallor than all the roses in the world were turning blacker and blacker as the seconds ticked. Carol felt herself being intoxicated. In the "V" of Mamma's gown she saw the hollow of the white bosom beginning, and it came to her that what she wanted fiercely was to lay her head there, her cheek and temple, and press tight. On the hidden side of her, lying on the couch in the shadow her crossed knees threw, Mamma's other hand was moving. Carol saw it in a corner of her eye, the long fingers coiling and uncoiling restlessly.

"I hope you sleep very well indeed, Mamma," she heard herself saying. "Good night, Mamma."

But then her feet were glued, not knowing how to go. Bubble saved her. When she saw the kitten cleaving to a table leg and making her eyes green she managed a gasp of joy and skipped.

"Now, child!" Mrs. Lephant called from the doorway.

But Carol had to catch that kitten first. She had to fall on her knees and hug her, kiss her on the whiskers and blow into her ear a "Don't you think she is beautiful, Bubble; don't you think she's darling; don't we love her almost to *death?*" Otherwise she would have had to burst with a rubbery shriek, like an overblown balloon.

In the hall Mrs. Lephant said, "Now drop your kitty, that's a good girl."

"Mightn't I have her just a little—just a weency-weency while?"

"Upstairs! What an idea! Bedrooms are no place for animals, not at night. Neither are houses. They're much better off outdoors."

"Oh, but Mrs. Lephant—you—wouldn't. You couldn't! She'd *freeze!*"

"Cats? What do you suppose they've fur for? Let her down; that's right. Scat, kitty; I'll tend to you later. Take Mrs. Lephant's hand now, my dear."

Carol couldn't go to sleep. The tighter she closed her eyes the wider she was awake. A procession of "she's" ramped through her mind. With venomous sarcasm: "She seems to know a great deal about cats!" With a surge of the heart: "She *wanted* me to put my head there in her neck; I *know* she did! She loves me. Tomorrow—oh, to—morrow!" With a guilty, almost forgotten hollow feeling: "I wonder if she has gone to be some other girl's nurse, now I've a Mamma and she can't be mine." And with a sudden eye on the window, wide open and blue-green-black and chill: "She *hasn't* enough fur; I don't care! If she *doesn't* freeze, she'll catch her death. Oh, dear!"

It was at the same time ironic and tragic. For the first time with so many responsibilities, for the first time there was no one in reach to share them with. The room grew as big as the house, the house grew as empty as the whole black outdoors; the time grew hours.

Then came temptation and the fall.

At first it was creepy, like burglars. No door had been opened, but someone or something was in that room. Whether she heard it or simply felt it, she didn't know: she only knew she mustn't stir and mustn't open her eyes.

When she flopped over and popped open her eyes, Bubble said "Prraouw" from the window sill, where she was busy tidying herself after her trouble with the woodbine by which she had come. Presently, vanishing in lower darkness, she arrived on the bed with a thump.

Carol was firm. "You wicked! You heard what Mrs. Lephant said as well as I did." Bubble rubbed, filling the lecturer's face with fluff. Carol sat bolt up for authority. As she did so Bubble took advantage of the lifted coverlet, dived beneath, whipped into a fat knot, and began to purr.

Carol sat and thought.

"Mrs. Lephant thinks she knows everything, but she doesn't know as much as Daddy. She says Bubble shouldn't be here, but last night Daddy said——"

She curled back into the warm place under the covers and got hold of the kitten. Thinking of that window (it's much more dangerous to go down vines than up them–and no matter what Mrs. Lephant thought she knew about cats), she got still better hold, her arms double all the way around.

It was the light that awakened her, falling through an open door. She would have said it must be nearly morning, but it wasn't, for Daddy and Mamma were just coming up to bed. Daddy was in the doorway and Mamma was near the bed.

"Is she sleeping?" Daddy asked in a low voice.

"I don't know." It was hardly above a whisper, in case. "Carol, dear?"

Carol, peering through sleepy lashes at her there, felt all the things she had felt in the whole of the day in one lump now, and the lump was in her throat. There was something that ravished her in that silhouette of a mother, the shoulders bent a little and the head held still, like hovering. Carol needn't wait till tomorrow after all to fling up and cry, "Mamma! I love you, and I'm glad."

She would have done it that moment, had something dreadful not occurred. She wasn't the only one awakened. Bubble stretched under the bedclothes and began automatically to purr. It rumbled, nothing less.

There was no time to plan. Carol opened her mouth and snored. She never snored; she didn't even know how to snore; but she snored.

Mamma hadn't moved. Or if she had, it was only her neck and head, by a fraction of an inch, and so swiftly that nobody would have known. Like an Indian in the dark when his brother touches him for "Did you hear?"

Had she heard? Carol snored in despair. Oh, *had* she heard?

Daddy reiterated his question from the door, but with another emphasis, of mirth: "*Is* she *sleeping!*"

"One would think so, wouldn't one?"

Mamma turned like a shadow, stiffly but without a sound, and moved away toward the bright rectangle where Daddy was waiting, one arm crooked out and a smile trembling about his lips and eyes.

The door was closed and it was dark again. Thank heaven, Bubble

Bonaparte! They were both young in crime yet, and it had been a pretty narrow squeak.

It was late when Carol awoke in the morning; it wasn't indeed until Mrs. Lephant came; and it was a clear warm day full of sun. Still blinking, Carol pawed about under the covers. Then she lay suddenly as still as scared mice and studied Mrs. Lephant out of the corners of her eyes.

"Mrs. Lephant," she began in a small voice, when the woman wouldn't stop her bustling and wouldn't end the suspense by opening her mouth (providing, of course, that she *knew*).

"Yes, child, what is it? Why don't you get up as I told you?"

"Mrs. Le-Lephant, you—you didn't—you haven't seen anything of my—of Bubble—this morning?"

"If you're still talking about that cat, no, I haven't. And now if I have to speak again——"

But Carol had to lie one more moment, staring at that open window. "The little monkey!" she thought to herself with what tried to be amusement.

She was wild to get out of doors. Tugging at the monitor's hand on the way down to breakfast she attempted stratagems. "I don't seem to be very hungry this morning, Mrs. Lephant. Must I eat breakfast, please?"

She wouldn't take even the Lephant's look for answer, but appealed from it to Daddy, who was just getting up from his coffee and eggs. Daddy laughed. "You sit down there and cram!"

"Where's Mamma?" Carol inquired in a smaller tone.

"Not up yet, the lazy. I'm sending her a tray; imagine that!" He was full of animation. All his motions were big, even the way he filled his pipe. "This is the life, eh, Old Girl! Now gobble. It's no day to be inside."

Carol got a piece of string from the maid and a piece of paper from a basket and set forth. She tried the east side of the grounds. "Kittikittikitti——" She combed the cover as far as the toolhouse there and cast back along the front hedge toward the drive, bareheaded in the sunshine. Daddy stood talking with the doctor of yesterday.

"A bit nervous and quiet last evening—but she slept like an angel,

Doctor, and this morning she looks like one. Doctor—I think it's a go."

Failing in the east, Carol trailed her bait into the south, the backyard region, where the land began to slope and the outbuildings were. She didn't go to the valley side till the last. She wouldn't, that was all.

She didn't make a sound for a full half minute after her eyes had found Bubble in the long grass. But when she did, it brought Daddy around the corner at the double, and the doctor behind.

"What is it, Carol? Oh, I see. Oh, poor kitty! *Isn't* that a *shame!*"

"The old *fool!*"

It rasped Carol's throat. It was rage. Grief hadn't had time as yet.

Daddy stared at her. "Who's a fool?"

"Mrs. Lephant. She is! She t-t-told me a k-k-kitten couldn't hurt itself f-f-falling."

"Where'd Bubble fall from?" Daddy craned up. "That your window there?"

Now the sobs began to rack and the tears to roll.

"It wasn't Bu-Bu-Bubble's fault. She came to bed with me—but—bu-but *I* let her st-stay. And of course she wanted to g-g-get up early—and the doors were sh-shut—and she sl-sl-slipped on the v-v-vine and—— Oh, Daddy!"

Daddy caught her up in his arms. His attention, though, was curiously divided, more than half of it still fixed on the gray little body in the grass.

"It's odd," he mused, "but I didn't suppose, myself——" He spoke aloud to the doctor, who had bent to prod with a professional finger. "Neck broken, is it?"

"Broken, yes." The doctor snapped his own neck back of a sudden to look up at Carol's window, but nothing was there. "Broken, yes." His lips moved in a funny way. "I'm afraid a little worse than broken, Bonaparte. *Wrung.*"

Somewhere aloft someone was laughing. It was low but unmuffled and pure, wandering, softly jubilating, soliloquizing, a little saraband of mirth.

Carol couldn't help it, she shook her hands at the high windows. "Mamma, no! . . . Oh, Daddy, but poor Mamma, she won't laugh when we—when we t-t-tell her—that."

Daddy, getting his face in another direction, carried Carol away, while the doctor lingered a moment to break a bit of brush down over the place where Bubble lay. . . .

If yesterday had been upsetting, it was as nothing to today. Carol was too prostrate with woe even to try to make it all out. Trunks, bags, boys on bicycles arriving and departing with yellow telegrams, everybody in a hurry, everything in a mess, Mrs. Lephant going about with a flounce and a sniffle, Mamma still invisible, still a lazy, Carol guessed.

It wasn't till Carol and Daddy were in the station taxi that afternoon that a suspicion of the possible truth came into the child's head.

"Daddy, it wasn't so, after all. I mean, it was all a–a kind of a joke–or I mean a kind of fooling. She *was* a governess, after all?"

Daddy sat and stared at the driver's back. Something distressing had happened to his shoulders between the morning and now. To his color too. It couldn't have been worse if he had been suffering one of his conscientious bored spells for weeks and months; no, it couldn't have been so bad. It made Carol uneasy. She got hold of his hand.

"She *was* a governess, Daddy, *wasn't* she?"

Daddy's gray-looking mouth moved with difficulty. "I suppose we might as well call it–why, yes, Carol, yes. And now–it wasn't long –we'll just forget."

On the platform at the little station, where the train was coming at them with a rush and roar, Carol got hold of his fingers again and tugged.

"Where are we going–this time?"

Daddy stared at the engine. He seemed distraught. He got the question mixed up with the answer he must have meant to give.

"Where are we going," he echoed, "this time?"

A wild wish was trying to dare to spring in Carol's heart. She quit tugging and began to stroke the wooden fingers she held.

"Daddy, couldn't we—— Daddy, mightn't we, don't you suppose——"

But she didn't need to finish. As the coaches rocked by to a grinding halt her eyes had caught a flicker of a face.

Carol shrieked.

"*Daddy! Coddie is on this train!*"

*Blue Murder**

AT MILL CROSSING IT WAS ALREADY past sunset. The rays, redder for what autumn leaves were left, still laid fire along the woods crowning the stony slopes of Jim Bluedge's pastures; but then the line of the dusk began and from that level it filled the valley, washing with transparent blue the buildings scattered about the bridge, Jim's house and horse sheds and hay barns, Frank's store, and Camden's blacksmith shop.

The mill had been gone fifty years, but the falls which had turned its wheel still poured in the bottom of the valley, and when the wind came from the Footstool way their mist wet the smithy, built of the old stone on the old foundations, and their pouring drowned the clink of Camden's hammer.

Just now they couldn't drown Camden's hammer, for he wasn't in the smithy; he was at his brother's farm. Standing inside the smaller of the horse paddocks behind the sheds he drove in stakes, one after another, cut green from saplings, and so disposed as to cover the more glaring of the weaknesses in the five-foot fence. From time to time, when one was done and another to do, he rested the head of his sledge in the pocket of his leather apron (he was never without it, it was as though it had grown on him, lumpy with odds and ends of his trade—bolts and nails and rusty pliers and maybe an old horseshoe) and, standing so, he mopped the sweat from his face and looked up at the mountain.

Of the three brothers he was the dumb one. He seldom had anything to say. It was providential (folks said) that of the three enterprises at the Crossing one was a smithy; for while he was a strong, big, hungry-muscled fellow, he never would have had the shrewdness to run the store or the farm. He was better at pounding—pounding while the fire reddened and the sparks flew, and thinking, and letting other people wonder what he was thinking of.

Blossom Bluedge, his brother's wife, sat perched on the top bar of the paddock gate, holding her skirts around her ankles with a trifle too much care to be quite unconscious, and watched him work. When he looked at the mountain he was looking at the mares, half a mile up the slope, grazing in a line as straight as soldiers, their heads all one way. But Blossom thought it was the receding light he was thinking of, and her own sense of misgiving returned and deepened.

"You'd have thought Jim would be home before this, wouldn't you, Cam?"

Her brother-in-law said nothing.

"Cam, look at me!"

It was nervousness, but it wasn't all nervousness—she was the prettiest girl in the valley; a small part of it was mingled coquetry and pique.

The smith began to drive another stake, swinging the hammer from high overhead, his muscles playing in fine big rhythmical convulsions under the skin of his arms and chest, covered with short blond down. Studying him cornerwise, Blossom muttered, "Well, *don't* look at me then!"

He was too dumb for any use. He was as dumb as this: when all three of the Bluedge boys were after her a year ago, Frank, the storekeeper, had brought her candy: chocolates wrapped in silver foil in a two-pound Boston box. Jim had laid before her the Bluedge farm and with it the dominance of the valley. And Camden! To the daughter of Ed Beck, the apple grower, Camden had brought *a box of apples!*—and been bewildered too, when, for all she could help it, she had had to clap a hand over her mouth and run into the house to have her giggle.

A little more than just bewildered, perhaps. Had she, or any of them, ever speculated about that? . . . He had been dumb enough before; but that was when he had started being as dumb as he was now.

Well, if he wanted to be dumb let him be dumb. Pouting her pretty lips and arching her fine brows, she forgot the unimaginative fellow and turned to the ridge again. And now, seeing the sun was quite gone, all the day's vague worries and dreads–held off by this and that–could not be held off longer. For weeks there had been so much talk, so much gossip and speculation and doubt.

"Camden," she reverted suddenly, "tell me one thing: did you hear——"

She stopped there. Some people were coming into the kitchen yard, dark forms in the growing darkness. Most of them lingered at the porch, sitting on the steps and lighting their pipes. The one that came out was Frank, the second of her brothers-in-law. She was glad. Frank wasn't like Camden; he would talk. Turning and taking care of her skirts, she gave him a bright and sisterly smile.

"Well, Frankie, what's the crowd?"

Far from avoiding the smile, as Camden's habit was, the storekeeper returned it with a brotherly wink for good measure. "Oh, they're tired of waiting down the road, so they come up here to see the grand arrival." He was something of a man of the world; in his calling he had acquired a fine turn for skepticism. "Don't want to miss being on hand to see what flaws they can pick in 'Jim's five hundred dollars' wuth of expiriment.' "

"Frank, ain't you the least bit worried over Jim? So late?"

"Don't see why."

"All the same, I wish either you or Cam could've gone with him."

"Don't see why. Had all the men from Perry's stable there in Twinshead to help him get the animal off the freight, and he took an extra rope and the log chain and the heavy wagon, so I guess no matter how wild and woolly the devil is he'll scarcely be climbing in over the tailboard. Besides, them western horses ain't such a big breed; even a stallion."

"All the same—— Look the other way, Frankie." Flipping her ankles over the rail, Blossom jumped down beside him. "Listen, Frank, tell me something: did you hear–did you hear the reason Jim's getting him cheap was because he killed a man out West there, what's-its-name, Wyoming?"

Frank was taking off his sleeve protectors, the pins in his mouth. It was Camden, at the bars, speaking in his sudden deep rough way, "Who the hell told you that?"

Frank got the pins out of his mouth. "I guess what it is, Blossie, what's mixed you up is his having that name, 'Blue Murder.' "

"No, sir! I got some sense and some ears. You don't go fooling me."

Frank laughed indulgently and struck her shoulder with a light hand.

"Don't you worry. Between two horsemen like Jim and Cam——"

"Don't *Cam* me! He's none of *my* horse. I told Jim once——" Breaking off, Camden hoisted his weight over the fence and stood outside, his feet spread and his hammer in both hands, an attitude that would have looked a little ludicrous had anyone been watching him.

Jim had arrived. With a clatter of hoofs and a rattle of wheels he was in the yard and come to a standstill, calling aloud as he threw the lines over the team, "Well, friends, here we are."

The curious began to edge around, closing a cautious circle. The dusk had deepened so that it was hard to make anything at any distance of Jim's "expiriment" but a blurry silhouette anchored at the wagon's tail. The farmer put an end to it, crying from his eminence, "Now, now, clear out and don't worry him; give him some peace tonight, for Lord's sake! Git!" He jumped to the ground and began to whack his arms, chilled with driving, only to have them pinioned by Blossom's without warning.

"Oh, Jim, I'm so glad you come. I been so worried; gi' me a kiss!"

The farmer reddened, eying the cloud of witnesses. He felt awkward and wished she could have waited. "Get along, didn't I tell you fellows?" he cried with a trace of the Bluedge temper. "Go wait in the kitchen then; I'll tell you all about everything soon's I come in. . . . Well now—wife——"

"What's the matter?" she laughed, an eye over her shoulder. "Nobody's looking that matters. I'm sure Frank don't mind. And as for Camden——"

Camden wasn't looking at them. Still standing with his hammer two-fisted and his legs spread, his chin down and his thoughts to himself (the dumbhead), he was looking at Blue Murder, staring at that other dumbhead, which, raised high on the motionless column of the stallion's neck, seemed hearkening with an exile's doubt to the sounds of this new universe, tasting with wide nostrils the taint in the wind of equine strangers, and studying with eyes accustomed to far horizons these dark pastures that went up in the air.

Whatever the smith's cogitations, presently he let the hammer down and said aloud, "So you're him, eh?"

Jim had put Blossom aside, saying, "Got supper ready? I'm hungry!" Excited by the act of kissing and the sense of witnesses to it, she fussed her hair and started kitchenward as he turned to his brothers.

"Well, what do you make of him?"

"Five hundred dollars," said Frank. "However, it's your money."

Camden was shorter. "Better put him in."

"All right; let them bars down while I and Frank lead him around."

"No, thanks!" The storekeeper kept his hands in his pockets. "I just cleaned up, thanks. Cam's the boy for horses."

"He's none o' my horse!" Camden wet his lips, shook his shoulders, and scowled. "Be damned, no!" He never had the right words, and it made him mad. Hadn't he told Jim from the beginning that he washed his hands of this fool Agricultural College squandering, "and a man killer to the bargain"?

"Unless," Frank put in slyly, "unless Cam's scared."

"Oh, is Cam scared?"

"Scared?" And still, to the brothers' enduring wonder, the big dense fellow would rise to that boyhood bait. "Scared? The hell I'm scared of any horse ever wore a shoe! Come on, I'll show you! I'll show you!"

"Well, be gentle with him, boys; he may be brittle." As Frank sauntered off around the shed he whistled the latest tune.

In the warmth and light of the kitchen he began to fool with his pretty sister-in-law, feigning princely impatience and growling with a wink at the assembled neighbors, "When do we eat?"

But she protested, "Land, I had everything ready since five, ain't I? And now if it ain't you it's them to wait for. I declare for men!"

At last one of the gossips got in a word.

"What you make of Jim's purchase, Frank?"

"Well, it's Jim's money, Darred. If *I* had the running of this farm——" Frank began drawing up chairs noisily, leaving it at that.

Darred persisted. "Don't look to me much like an animal for women and children to handle, not yet awhile."

"Cowboys han'les 'em, Pa." That was Darred's ten-year-old, big-eyed.

Blossom put the kettle back, protesting, "Leave off, or you'll get me worried to death; all your talk. . . . I declare, where *are* those bad boys?" Opening the door she called into the dark, "Jim! Cam! Land's sake!"

Subdued by distance and the intervening sheds, she could hear them at their business—sounds muffled and fragmentary, soft thunder of hoofs, snorts, puffings, and the short words of men in action: "Aw, leave him be in the paddock tonight." . . . "Damn fool, eh? Try getting him in at that door and see who's the damn fool!" . . . "Come on, don't be so scared." . . . "Scared, eh? Scared?" . . .

Why was it she always felt that curious tightening of all her powers of attention when Camden Bluedge spoke? Probably because he spoke so rarely, and then so roughly, as if his own thickness made him mad. Never mind.

"Last call for supper in the dining car, boys!" she called and closed the door. Turning back to the stove, she was about to replace the tea water for the third time when, straightening up, she said, "What's that?"

No one else had heard anything. They looked at one another.

"Frank, go—go see what—— Go tell the boys to come in."

Frank hesitated, feeling foolish, then went to the door.

Then everyone in the room was out of his chair.

There were three sounds. The first was human and incoherent. The second was incoherent too, but it wasn't human. The third was a crash, a ripping and splintering of wood.

When they got to the paddock they found Camden crawling from beneath the wreckage of the fence where a gap was opened on the pasture side. He must have received a blow on the head, for he seemed dazed. He didn't seem to know they were there. At a precarious balance—one hand at the back of his neck—he stood facing up the hill, gaping after the diminuendo of floundering hoofs, invisible above.

So seconds passed. Again the beast gave tongue, a high wild horning note, and on the black of the stony hill to the right of it a faint shower of sparks blew like fireflies where the herding mares wheeled. It seemed to awaken the dazed smith. He opened his mouth: "*Almighty God!*" Swinging, he flung his arms toward the shed. "*There! There!*"

At last someone brought a lantern. They found Jim Bluedge lying on his back in the corner of the paddock near the door to the shed. In the lantern light, and still better in the kitchen when they had carried him in, they read the record of the thing which Camden, dumb in good earnest now, seemed unable to tell them with anything but his strange unfocused stare.

The bloody offense to the skull would have been enough to kill the man, but it was the second, full on the chest above the heart, that told the tale. On the caved grating of the ribs, already turning blue under the yellowish down, the iron shoe had left its mark; and when, laying back the rag of shirt, they saw that the toe of the shoe was upward and the cutting calk ends down, they knew all they wanted to know of that swift, black, crushing episode.

No outlash here of heels in fright. Here was a forefoot. An attack aimed and frontal; an onslaught reared, erect; beast turned biped; red eyes mad to white eyes aghast. . . . And only afterward, when it was done, the blood-fright that serves the horse for conscience; the blind rush across the inclosure; the fence gone down. . . .

No one had much to say. No one seemed to know what to do.

As for Camden, he was no help. He simply stood propped on top of his logs of legs where someone had left him. From the instant when with his "*Almighty God!*" he had been brought back to memory, instead of easing its hold as the minutes passed, the event to which he remained the only living human witness seemed minute by minute to tighten its grip. It set its sweat-beaded stamp on his face, distorted his eyes, and tied his tongue. He was no good to anyone.

As for Blossom, even now—perhaps more than ever now—her dependence on physical touch was the thing that ruled her. Down on her knees beside the lamp they had set on the floor, she plucked at one of the dead man's shoes monotonously, and as it were idly, swaying the toe like an inverted pendulum from side to side. That was all. Not a word. And when Frank, the only one of the three with any sense, got her up finally and led her away to her room, she clung to *him*.

It was lucky that Frank was a man of affairs. His brother was dead, and frightfully dead, but there was tomorrow for grief. Just now there were many things to do. There were people to be gotten rid of. With short words and angry gestures he cleared them out, all but Darred and a man named White, and to these he said, "Now first thing, Jim can't stay here." He ran and got a blanket from a closet. "Give me a hand and we'll lay him in the icehouse overnight. Don't sound good, but it's best, poor fellow. Cam, come along!"

He waited a moment, and as he studied the wooden fool the blood poured back into his face. "Wake up, Cam! You great big scared stiff, you!"

Camden brought his eyes out of nothingness and looked at his brother. A twinge passed over his face, convulsing the mouth muscles. "Scared?"

"Yes, you're scared!" Frank's lip lifted, showing the tips of his teeth. "And I'll warrant you something: if you wasn't the scared stiff you was, this hellish damn thing wouldn't have happened, maybe. Scared! You, a blacksmith! Scared of a horse!"

"*Horse!*" Again that convulsion of the mouth muscles, something between irony and an idiot craft. "Why don't you go catch 'im?"

"Hush it! Don't waste time by going loony now, for God's sake. Come!"

"My advice to anybody——" Camden looked crazier than ever, knotting his brows. "My advice to anybody is to let somebody else go catch that—that——" Opening the door, he faced out into the night, his head sunk between his shoulders and the fingers working at the ends of his hanging arms; and before they knew it he began to swear. They could hardly hear because his teeth were locked and his breath soft. There were all the vile words he had ever heard in his life, curses and threats and abominations, vindictive, violent, obscene. He stopped only when at a sharp word from Frank he was made aware that Blossom had come back into the room. Even then he didn't seem to comprehend this return but stood blinking at her, and at the rifle she carried, with his distraught bloodshot eyes.

Frank comprehended. Hysteria had followed the girl's blankness. Stepping between her and the body on the floor, he spoke in a persuasive, unhurried way. "What you doing with that gun, Blossie? Now, now, you don't want that gun, you know you don't."

It worked. Her rigidity lessened appreciably. Confusion gained.

"Well, but—oh, Frank—well, but when we going to shoot him?"

"Yes, yes, Blossie—now, yes—only you best give me that gun; that's the girlie." When he had got the weapon he put an arm around her shoulders. "Yes, yes, course we're going to shoot him;

what you think? Don't want an animal like that running round. Now first thing in the morning——"

Hysteria returned. With its strength she resisted his leading.

"No, now! *Now!* He's gone and killed Jim! Killed my husband! I won't have him left alive another minute! I won't! *Now!* No, sir, I'm going myself, I am! Frank, I am! Cam!"

At his name, appealed to in that queer screeching way, the man in the doorway shivered all over, wet his lips, and walked out into the dark.

"There, you see?" Frank was quick to capitalize anything. "Cam's gone to do it. Cam's gone, Blossie! . . . Here, one of you–Darred, take this gun and run give it to Camden, that's the boy."

"You sure he'll kill him, Frank? You *sure?*"

"Sure as daylight. Now you come along back to your room like a good girl and get some rest. Come, I'll go with you."

When Frank returned to the kitchen ten minutes later, Darred was back.

"Well, Darred, let's get at it and carry out poor Jim; he can't lay here. . . . Where's Cam gone *now,* damn him!"

"Cam? Why, he's gone and went."

"Went where?"

"Up the pasture, like you said."

"Like I——" Frank went an odd color. He walked to the door. Between the light on the sill and the beginnings of the stars where the woods crowned the mountain was all one blackness. One stillness too. He turned on Darred. "But look, you never gave him that gun, even."

"He didn't want it."

"Lord's sake; what did he say?"

"Said nothing. He'd got the log chain out of the wagon and when I caught him he was up hunting his hammer in under that wreck at the fence. Once he found it he started off up. 'Cam,' says I, 'here's a gun; want it?' He seem not to. Just went on walking on up."

"How'd he look?"

"Look same's you seen him looking. Sick."

"The damned fool! . . ."

Poor dead Jim! Poor fool Camden! As the storekeeper went about his business and afterward when, the icehouse door closed on its tragic tenant and White and Darred gone off home, he roamed the yard, driven here and there, soft-footed, waiting, hearkening—his mind was for a time not his own property but the plaything of thoughts diverse and wayward. Jim, his brother, so suddenly and so violently gone. The stallion. That beast that had kicked him to death. With anger and hate and pitiless impatience of time he thought of the morrow, when they would catch him and take their revenge with guns and clubs. Behind these speculations, covering the background of his consciousness and stringing his nerves to endless vigil, spread the wall of the mountain: silent from instant to instant but devising under its black silence (who-could-know-what instant to come) a neigh, a yell, a spark-line of iron hoofs on rolling flints, a groan. And still behind that and deeper into the borders of the unconscious, the storekeeper thought of the farm that had lost its master, the rich bottoms, the broad well-stocked pastures, the fat barns, and the comfortable house whose chimneys and gable ends fell into changing shapes of perspective against the stars as he wandered here and there. . . .

Jim gone. . . . And Camden, at any moment . . .

His face grew hot. An impulse carried him a dozen steps. "I ought to go up. Ought to take the gun and go up." But there shrewd sanity put on the brakes. "Where's the use? Couldn't find him in this dark. Besides, I oughtn't to leave Blossom here alone."

With that he went around toward the kitchen, thinking to go in. But the sight of the lantern, left burning out near the sheds, sent his ideas off on another course. At any rate it would give his muscles and nerves something to work on. Taking the lantern and entering the paddock, he fell to patching the gap into the pasture, using broken boards from the wreck. As he worked, his eyes chanced to fall on footprints in the dung-mixed earth—Camden's footprints leading away beyond the little ring of light. And beside them, taking off from the landing place of that prodigious leap, he discerned the trail of the stallion. After a moment he got down on his knees where the earth was softest, holding the lantern so that its light fell full.

He gave over his fence building. Returning to the house, his gait was no longer that of the roamer; his face, caught by the periodic flare of the swinging lantern, was the face of another man. In its expression there was a kind of fright and a kind of calculating eagerness. He looked at the clock on the kitchen shelf, shook it, and read it again. He went to the telephone and fumbled at the receiver. He waited till his hand quit shaking, then removed it from the hook.

"Listen, Darred," he said, when he had got the farmer at last, "get White and whatever others you can and come over first thing it's light. Come a-riding and bring your guns. No, Cam ain't back."

He heard Blossom calling. Outside her door he passed one hand down over his face, as he might have passed a washrag, to wipe off what was there. Then he went in.

"What's the matter with Blossie? Can't sleep?"

"No, I can't sleep. Can't think. Can't sleep. Oh, Frankie!"

He sat down beside the bed.

"Oh, Frankie, Frankie, *hold my hand!*"

She looked almost homely, her face bleached out and her hair in a mess on the pillow. But she would get over that. And the short sleeve of the nightgown on the arm he held was edged with pretty lace.

"Got your watch here?" he asked. She gave it to him from under the pillow. This too he shook as if he couldn't believe it was going.

Pretty Blossom Beck. Here for a wonder he sat in her bedroom and held her hand. One brother was dead and the other was on the mountain.

But little by little, as he sat and dreamed so, nightmare crept over his brain. He had to arouse and shake himself. He had to set his thoughts resolutely in other roads. . . . Perhaps there would be even the smithy. The smithy, the store, the farm. Complete. The farm, the farmhouse, the room in the farmhouse, the bed in the room, the wife in the bed. Complete beyond belief. If . . . Worth dodging horror for. If . . .

"Frank, has Cam come back?"

"Cam? Don't you worry about Cam. . . . Where's that watch again? . . ."

Far from rounding up their quarry in the early hours after dawn, it took the riders, five of them, till almost noon simply to make certain that he wasn't to be found—not in any of the pastures. Then when they discovered the hole in the fence far up in the woods beyond the crest where Blue Murder had led the mares in a break for the open country of hills and ravines to the south, they were only at the beginning.

The farmers had left their work undone at home and, as the afternoon lengthened and with it the shadows in the hollow places, they began to eye one another behind their leader's back. Yet they couldn't say it; there was something in the storekeeper's air today, something zealous and pitiless and fanatical, that shut them up and pulled them plodding on.

Frank did the trailing. Hopeless of getting anywhere before sundown in that unkempt wilderness of a hundred square miles of scrub, his companions slouched in their saddles and rode more and more mechanically, knee to knee, and it was he who made the casts to recover the lost trail and, dismounting to read the dust, cried back, "He's still with 'em," and with gestures of imperious excitement beckoned them on.

"Which you mean?" Darred asked him once. "Cam, or the horse?"

Frank wheeled his beast and spurred back at the speaker. It was extraordinary. "You don't know what you're talking about!" he cried, with a causelessness and a disordered vehemence which set them first staring, then speculating. "Come on, you dumbheads; don't talk—*ride!*"

By the following day, when it was being told in all the farmhouses, the story might vary in details and more and more as the tellings multiplied, but in its fundamentals it remained the same. In one thing they certainly all agreed: they used the same expression —"It was like Frank was drove. Drove in a race against something, and not spared the whip."

They were a good six miles to the south of the fence. Already the road back home would have to be followed three parts in the dark.

Darred was the spokesman. "Frank, I'm going to call it a day."

The others reined up with him, but the man ahead rode on. He didn't seem to hear. Darred lifted his voice. "Come on, call it a day, Frank. Tomorrow, maybe. But you see we've run it out and they're not here."

"Wait," said Frank over his shoulder, still riding on into the pocket.

White's mount—a mare—laid back her ears, shied, and stood trembling. After a moment she whinnied.

It was as if she had whinnied for a dozen. A crashing in the woods above them to the left and the avalanche came—down-streaming, erupting, wheeling, wheeling away with volleying snorts, a dark rout.

Darred, reining his horse, began to shout, "Here they go this way, Frank!" But Frank was yelling, "Up here, boys! This way, quick!"

It was the same note, excited, feverish, disordered, breaking like a child's. When they neared him they saw he was off his horse, rifle in hand, and down on his knees to study the ground where the woods began. By the time they reached his animal the impetuous fellow had started up into the cover, his voice trailing, "Come on; spread out and come on!"

One of the farmers got down. When he saw the other three keeping their saddles he swung up again.

White spoke this time. "Be darned if I do!" He lifted a protesting hail, "Come back here, Frank! You're crazy! It's getting dark!"

It was Frank's own fault. They told him plainly to come back and he wouldn't listen.

For a while they could hear his crackle in the mounting underbrush. Then that stopped, whether he had gone too far for their ears or whether he had come to a halt to give his own ears a chance . . . Once, off to his right, a little higher up under the low ceiling of the trees that darkened moment by moment with the rush of night, they heard another movement, another restlessness of leaves and stones. Then that was still, and everything was still.

Darred ran a sleeve over his face and swung down. "God alive, boys!"

It was the silence. All agreed there—the silence and the deepening dusk.

The first they heard was the shot. No voice. Just the one report. Then after five breaths of another silence a crashing of growth, a charge in the darkness under the withered scrub, continuous and diminishing.

They shouted, "Frank!" No answer. They called, "*Frank Bluedge!*"

Now, since they had to, they did. Keeping contact by word, and guided partly by directional memory (and mostly in the end by luck), after a time they found the storekeeper in a brake of ferns, lying across his gun.

They got him down to the open, watching behind them all the while. Only then, by the flares of successive matches, under the noses of the snorting horses, did they look for the damage done.

They remembered the stillness and the gloom; it must have been quite black in there. The attack had come from behind—equine and pantherine at once, and planned and cunning. A deliberate lunge with a forefoot again: the shoe which had crushed the backbone between the shoulder blades was a fore shoe; that much they saw by the match flares in the red wreck.

They took no longer getting home than they had to, but it was longer than they would have wished. With Frank across his own saddle, walking their horses and with one or another ahead to pick the road (it was going to rain, and even the stars were lost), they made no more than a creeping speed.

None of them had much to say on the journey. Finding the break in the boundary fence and feeling through the last of the woods, the lights of their farms began to show in the pool of blackness below, and Darred uttered a part of what had lain in the minds of them all during the return:

"Well, that leaves Cam."

None followed it up. None cared to go any closer than he was to the real question. Something new, alien, menacing, and pitiless, had come into the valley of their lives with that beast they had never really seen; they felt its oppression, everyone, and kept the real question back in their minds: "*Does* it leave Cam?"

It answered itself. Camden was at home when they got there.

He had come in a little before them, empty-handed. Empty-headed too. When Blossom, who had waited all day, part of the time with neighbor women who had come in and part of the time alone to the point of going mad—when she saw him coming down the pasture, his feet stumbling and his shoulders dejected, her first feeling was relief. Her first words, however, were, "Did you get him, Cam?" And all he would answer was, "Gi' me something to eat, can't you? Gi' me a few hours' sleep, can't you? Then wait!"

He looked as if he would need more than a few hours' sleep. Propped on his elbows over his plate, it seemed as though his eyes would close before his mouth would open.

His skin was scored by thorns and his shirt was in ribbons under the straps of his iron-sagged apron; but it was not by these marks that his twenty-odd hours showed: it was by his face. While yet his eyes were open and his wits still half awake, his face surrendered. The flesh relaxed into lines of stupor, a putty-formed, putty-colored mask of sleep.

Once he let himself be aroused. This was when, to an abstracted query as to Frank's whereabouts, Blossom told him Frank had been out with four others since dawn. He heaved clear of the table and opened his eyes at her, showing the red around the rims.

He spoke with the thick tongue of a drunkard. "If anybody but me lays hand on that stallion I'll kill him. I'll wring his neck."

Then he relapsed into his stupidity, and not even the arrival of the party bringing his brother's body seemed able to shake him so far clear of it again.

At first, when they had laid Frank on the floor where on the night before they had laid Jim, he seemed hardly to comprehend.

"What's wrong with Frank?"

"Some more of Jim's 'expiriment.'"

"Frank see him? He's scared, Frank is. Look at his face there."

"He's dead, Cam."

"Dead, you say? Frank dead? Dead of fright; is that it?"

Even when, rolling the body over, they showed him what was what, he appeared incapable of comprehension, of amazement, of passion, or of any added grief. He looked at them all with a kind of befuddled protest. Returning to his chair and his plate, he grumbled, "Le' me eat first, can't you? Can't you gi' me a little time to sleep?"

"Well, you wouldn't do much tonight anyway, I guess."

At White's words Blossom opened her mouth for the first time.

"No, nothing tonight, Cam. Cam! *Camden!* Say! Promise!"

"And then tomorrow, Cam, what we'll do is to get every last man in the valley, and we'll go at this right. We'll lay hand on that devil——"

Camden swallowed his mouthful of cold steak with difficulty. His obsession touched, he showed them the rims of his eyes again.

"You do and I'll wring your necks. The man that touches that animal before I do gets his neck wrang. That's all you need to remember."

"Yes, yes—no—that is——" Poor Blossom. "Yes, Mr. White, thanks; no, Cam's not going out tonight. . . . No, Cam, nobody's going to interfere—nor nothing. Don't you worry there. . . ."

Again poor Blossom! Disaster piled too swiftly on disaster; no discipline but instinct left. Caught in fire and flood and earthquake and not knowing what to come, and no creed but "save him who can!"—by hook or crook of wile or smile. With the valley of her life emptied out, and its emptiness repeopled monstrously and pressing down black on the roof under which (now that Frank was gone to the icehouse too and the farmers back home) one brother was left of three—she would tread softly, she would talk or she would be dumb, as her sidelong glimpses of the awake-asleep man's face above the table told her was the instant's need; or if he would eat, she would magic out of nothing something, anything; or if he would sleep, he could sleep, so long as he slept in that house where she could know he was sleeping.

Only one thing. If she could touch him. If she could touch and cling.

Lightning filled the windows. After a moment the thunder came avalanching down the pasture and brought up against the clapboards of the house. At this she was behind his chair. She put out a hand. She touched his shoulder. The shoulder was bare, the shirt ripped away; it was caked with sweat and with the blackening smears of scratches, but for all its exhaustion and dirt it was flesh alive—a living man to touch.

Camden blundered up. "What the hell!" He started off two steps and wheeled on her. "Why don't you get off to bed for Goll sake!"

"Yes, Cam, yes—right off, yes."

"Well, *I'm* going, I can tell you. For Goll sake, I need some sleep!"

"Yes, that's right, yes, Cam, good night, Cam—only—only you promise—promise you won't go out—nowheres."

"Go *out?* Not likely I won't! Not *likely!* Get along."

It took her no time to get along then—quick and quiet as a mouse.

Camden lingered to stand at one of the windows where the lightning came again, throwing the black barns and paddocks at him from the white sweep of the pastures crowned by woods.

As it had taken her no time to go, it took Blossom no time to undress and get in bed. When Camden was on his way to his room he heard her calling, "Cam! Just a second, Cam!"

In the dark outside her door he drew one hand down over his face, wiping off whatever might be there. Then he entered.

"Yes? What?"

"Cam, set by me a minute, won't you? And Cam, oh Cam, hold my hand."

As he slouched down, his fist inclosing her fingers, thoughts awakened and ran and fastened on things. They fastened, tentatively at first, upon the farm. Jim gone. Frank gone. The smithy, the store, and the farm. The whole of Mill Crossing. The trinity, the three in one . . .

"Tight, Cam, for pity's sake! Hold it tight!"

His eyes, falling to his fist, strayed up along the arm it held. The sleeve, rumpled near the shoulder, was trimmed with pretty lace. . . .

"Tighter, Cam!"

A box of apples. That memory hidden away in the cellar of his mind. Hidden away, clamped down in the dark, till the noxious vapors, the murderous vapors of its rotting had filled the shut-up house he was . . . A box of red apples for the apple grower's girl . . . the girl who sniggered and ran away from him to laugh at him. . . .

And here, by the unfolding of a devious destiny, he sat in that girl's bedroom, holding that girl's hand. Jim who had got her, Frank who had wanted her lay side by side out there in the icehouse under the lightning. While he, the "dumb one"–the last to be thought of with anything but amusement and the last to be feared–his big hot fist inclosing her imprecating hand now, and his eyes on the pretty lace at her shoulder–– He jumped up with a gulp and a clatter of iron.

"What the––" He flung her hand away. "What the–hell!" He swallowed. "Damn you, Blossie Beck!" He stared at her with repugnance and mortal fright. "Why, you–you–you––"

He moderated his voice with an effort, wiping his brow. "Good night. You must excuse me, Blossie; I wasn't meaning–I mean–I hope you sleep good. *I* shall. . . . Good night!"

In his own brain was the one word, "Hurry!"

She lay and listened to his boots going along the hall and heard the closing of his door. She ought to have put out the lamp. But even with the shades drawn, the lightning around the edges of the window unnerved her; in the dark alone it would have been more than she could bear.

She lay so till she felt herself nearing exhaustion from the sustained rigidity of her limbs. Rain came and with the rain, wind. Around the eaves it neighed like wild stallions; down the chimneys it moaned like men.

Slipping out of bed and pulling on a bathrobe she ran from her room, barefooted, and along the hall to Camden's door.

"Cam!" she called. "Oh, Cam!" she begged. "Please, please!"

And now he wouldn't answer her.

New lightning, diffused through all the sky by the blown rain, ran at her along the corridor. She pushed the door open. The lamp was burning on the bureau, but the room was empty and the bed untouched.

Taking the lamp she skittered down to the kitchen. No one there. . . .

"*Hurry!*"

Camden had reached the woods when the rain came. Lighting the lantern he had brought, he made his way on to the boundary fence. There, about a mile to the east of the path the others had taken that day, he pulled the rails down and tumbled the stones together in a pile. Then he proceeded another hundred yards, holding the lantern high and peering through the streaming crystals of the rain.

Blue Murder was there. Neither the chain nor the sapling had given way. The lantern and, better than the lantern, a globe of lightning showed the tethered stallion glistening and quivering, his eyes all white at the man's approach.

"Gentle, boy; steady, boy!" Talking all the while in the way he had with horses, Camden put a hand on the taut chain and bore with a gradually progressive weight, bringing the dark head nearer.

"Steady, boy; gentle there, damn you; gentle!"

Was he afraid of horses? Who was it said he was afraid of horses?

The beast's head was against the man's chest, held there by an arm thrown over the bowed neck. As he smoothed the forehead and fingered the nose with false caresses, Camden's "horse talk" ran on—the cadence one thing, the words another.

"Steady, Goll damn you; you're going to get yours. Cheer up, cheer up, the worst is yet to come. Come now! Come easy! Come along!"

When he had unloosed the chain, he felt for and found with his free hand his hammer hidden behind the tree. Throwing the lantern into the brush, where it flared for an instant before dying, he led the stallion back as far as the break he had made in the fence. Taking a turn with the chain around the animal's nose, like an improvised hackamore, he swung from the stone pile to the slippery back. A moment's shying, a sliding caracole of amazement and distrust, a crushing of knees, a lash of the chain end, and that was all there was to that. Blue Murder had been ridden before. . . .

In the smithy, chambered in the roaring of the falls and the swish and shock of the storm, Camden sang as he pumped his bellows, filling the cave beneath the rafters with red. The air was nothing, the words were mumbo-jumbo, but they swelled his chest. His eyes, cast from time to time at his wheeling prisoner, had lost their look of helplessness and surly distraction.

Scared? He? No, no, no! Now that he wasn't any longer afraid of time, he wasn't afraid of anything on earth.

"Shy, you devil!" He wagged his exalted head. "Whicker, you hellion! Whicker all you want to, stud horse. Tomorrow they're going to get you, the dumb fools! Tomorrow they can have you. *I* got you *tonight!*"

He was more than other men; he was enormous. Fishing an iron shoe from that inseparable apron pocket of his, he thrust it into the coals and blew and blew. He tried it and it was burning red. He tried it again and it was searing white. Taking it out on the anvil he began to beat it, swinging his hammer one-handed, gigantic. So in the crimson light, irradiating iron sparks, he was at his greatest. Pounding, pounding. A man in the dark of night with a hammer about him can do wonders; with a horseshoe about him he can cover up a sin.

And if the dark of night in a paddock won't hold it, then the dark of undergrowth on a mountainside will. . . .

Pounding, pounding; thinking, thinking, in a great halo of hot stars. Feeding his hungry, his insatiable muscles.

"Steady now, you blue bastard! Steady, boy!"

What he did not realize in his feverish exaltation was that his muscles were not insatiable. In the thirty-odd hours past they had had a feast spread before them and they had had their fill. . . . More than their fill.

As with the scorching iron in his tongs he approached the stallion, he had to step over the nailbox he had stepped over five thousand times in the routine of every day.

A box of apples, eh? Apples to snigger at, eh? But whose girl are you now? . . . Scared, eh?

His foot was heavier of a sudden than it should have been. This five-thousand-and-first time, by the drag of the tenth of an inch, the heel caught the lip of the nailbox.

He tried to save himself from stumbling. At the same time, instinctively, he held the iron flame in his tongs away.

There was a scream out of a horse's throat; a whiff of hair and burnt flesh.

There was a lash of something in the red shadows. There was another sound and another wisp of stench. . . .

When, guided by the stallion's whinnying, they found the smith next day, they saw by the cant of his head that his neck was broken, and they perceived that he too had on him the mark of a shoe. It lay up one side of his throat and the broad of a cheek. It wasn't blue this time, however—it was red. It took them some instants in the sunshine pouring through the wide door to comprehend this phenomenon. It wasn't sunk in by a blow this time; it was burned in, a brand.

Darred called them to look at the stallion, chained behind the forge.

"Almighty God!" The words sounded funny in his mouth. They sounded the funnier in that they were the same ones the blundering smith had uttered when, staring uphill from his clever wreckage of the paddock fence, he had seen the mares striking sparks from the stones where the stallion struck none. And he, of all men, a smith!

"Almighty God!" called Darred. "What you make of these here feet?"

One fore hoof was freshly pared for shoeing; the other three hoofs were as virgin as any yearling's on the plains. Blue Murder had never yet been shod. . . .

*When Hell Froze**

It was the biggest farm on the Footstool; it had smooth swelling fields, like waves; well-tended wood lots, and clean fat cattle. Addie Joslin was part of it. The strength of her eighteen years of married life had gone into it; season by season she had served its needs, spending much on the land and little on herself.

The only really hard time was the week in the fall when her husband was away in New York on his year's business, and especially now that he was taking Ray with him. But it was time their first-born should be learning those other things, remote, but apparently as essential to the growth and well-being of the soil as the things that lay in her knowledge—tillage, drainage, and manure. And after all, no matter how long a week may seem on double and treble duty, it is only seven days.

She had the church, the grange, the Daughters of the Morning Star; she had her diversions if she cared to take them. This she seldom did. Her life had little in it that was separate from the farm. Even Frankie, the four-year-old, her baby, was not separate; little that was not of her or of the fields or cattle was in him. He was made of her and the earth, and she was made of the earth.

She was slow of speech and reason, a slow woman. This was because she saw all things moving in unalterable sequence. Seed, sprout, full stalk, threshed grain—as simply as that unfolded all the thoughts she needed. So her hair stayed brown and there were no wrinkles about her eyes.

This evening she was a little tired. But tonight John and Ray would be home; perhaps in time for the milking. The week was all but done.

A little tired, yes. When she had started the cows up from the lower pasture, instead of following at once she rested her weight on the fence in the shriveled shadow of an aspen and stood dreaming up the land, her eyes moving slowly from field to higher field, reaped and brown.

It all did look pretty, with the sun setting behind the mountain.

It had done well this year; well.

Would they be home in time for the milking? First there was Heather to be milked, then Sally, then Dapple, then Princess, then Snow. She must be getting lazy, she guessed. She had better be starting her boots.

But now there was a sound of music. It was strange to hear music down here. Forgetting the cows for another moment, she turned to look. There was a path beyond the fence, leading up from southwest of the mountain, and a man came along it playing a harmonica. He was tall, redheaded, and lank; under one elbow he gripped a pack while with the other he beat time, a perfect vagabond. Observing Addie, he halted and took off his hat.

"How d'you do? Good evening."

Not being much with strangers, Addie kept her mouth shut, nodded slightly, and looked beyond him at the ridges, powdered pink with sunset. The man came and got up to sit on the fence. He played softly a few more bars. Addie turned to go. He whacked the instrument on his thigh and said: "Excuse me, but do you know a town called Twinshead up this way, lady?"

"Yes." She stopped and eyed him. "I ought to, I was raised there."

"You was? Know a man named House there? Garage man?"

"I ought to—he's my brother-in-law."

"Well, I swear! He's the man I was figuring to work for."

"He is? Well, he's my brother-in-law."

"How far would you call it from here?"

"Over down in the next valley. Around six mile."

"Six mile, eh? Some step! Listen; any place around here a man could get a shakedown for the night, lady? I'm not much chopping wood, but if you got any Lord's kind of a gas engine wants tinkering . . ."

"Well, if my husband gets home as I'm expecting them, there's the seedan's been knocking lately. Though I don't know certain he'll come. But then if he don't there's Hurlbut's, a half mile on down."

He got over the fence. "Well, what do you say we see?"

He came along a little at the trail, busy again with his tunes, as, climbing and clucking, she got the cattle through the successive gates. When they had come up into the last lane she said: "You play pretty. Although I must say I don't know those tunes."

"Latest things. I don't suppose they're up this way yet."

"I don't know. I'm not much on town. When I was a girl though, in town, I used to know all the songs going."

"I bet. Know this one? '*I thought it was a kiss, but it was just an idle dream.*' Remember?"

"Yes, certainly. . . . Frankie!" she called to her child, who, half-way down from the house, had stopped at sight of the stranger. "Come walk with Mama; come!" And as the boy, pouting, edged a few shy steps nearer: "Yes, certainly, I know that and a lot of others: the 'Merry Widow' and '*Come, come, I love you only*,' and all those."

"It's funny how those old ones stick by you. The ones nowadays—though now and then you'll find one—listen to this."

Cupping the toy in both hands, he lifted his brows and drooped his lids. He breathed softly among the reeds. He loved it. When he reached the end he recited the ultimate phrase with the throaty husk of the devotee, watching her eyes for approbation: "*Kiss me, kiss me, aga-i-n. . . .*"

She gave her thumb to Frankie.

"What's the matter with *you*, for heaven's sake?"

"Is he my uncle?" The boy pulled around behind her. She laughed.

"Uncle? Land, no! He's nobody you know."

"What you been givin' him kisses fer then?"

Addie's mouth fell open. "Don't say such things; the idea!" She gave his hand a shake. "I—well—you don't understand, that's all."

The stranger grinned, his amused eyes going from one to the other.

Frankie persisted. "Did you kiss him fer playin' so nice, Mama?"

The man laughed outright, arms akimbo, head up. "Look-a here," he cried, bending suddenly and holding the harmonica out on his palm. "What you say to that, sonny? Like play moosic? Well, take that with my regards; that'll keep you busy, won't it now?"

"Oh, he shouldn't," his mother muttered, as the small fingers edged around her skirt. Once he had hold of the treasure the boy was away like an Indian's shadow, through the fence and into the cover of the dogwood hedge beyond.

The man chuckled. "Oh no, he didn't care for it at all; couldn't find house room for it. Oh no!" He shifted his pack and began to whistle.

When Addie came up to the yard after impounding the cows she found the man sitting on the kitchen stoop, still whistling.

"I guess my husband ain't coming tonight after all," she said, looking up and down the darkening road. Entering the house, she came out again with some pie and cheese and a cup of milk. "Though I shouldn't feel like turning you away without a snack. Then 'tain't far down to Hurlbut's."

As he sat munching, the man began to study her with a new obliquity.

"How long's your husband away for?"

"He goes a week every fall on business to New York City."

"Aren't you ever kind of lonesome?"

"No time for lonesomeness. I ought to be milking right now."

"Still, up here by yourself, everybody away." He took out a cigarette and lit it. "Eh? Don't you ever wish—well—there was some man around the place, nights?"

Addie shook her head. "There's nothing to harm a body up this way."

The man shook his. "I give it up." He wiped his mouth and got to his feet. "Then I guess I'll be on my way. Now I've had supper, thanks to your kindness, I guess I might's well go on through. Is it around this way out?"

She showed him, walking down as far as the gate.

"Still," he mused, "the men have all the fun, don't they? I suppose your hubby always tells you everything he does while he's in New York?"

"I don't see what you mean. If you mean he carries on, then you don't know John A. Joslin. And moreover, he's got Ray along; that's our oldest."

"How old?"

"Going on seventeen. But he's big for his age."

The man slapped his thigh. "I bet!"

"Well," he said, when he was done chuckling, "I suppose if you're dead certain you're not going to want protecting tonight—I might's well be on my way. Thanks very much for the bite, and if you're ever in Twinshead this winter, look me up. . . . Good night."

For another moment Addie leaned there watching him off into the dusk.

What was all that talk of his? Who was he? Where had he come from? From as near as the nearest town? From as far as China? A strange irresponsible fellow riding his legs across the mountains, whistling across the world.

"I want my supper." It was Frankie at her elbow, whining.

"Heavens and earth, what am I thinking of! Those poor cows!"

The men came that night after all, when the chores were done and Frankie in bed. Hearing the car turn into the yard, Addie put a piece of meat in the spider and began cutting up some cold potatoes to brown, so that by the time they came in their supper was half ready.

It gave her a queer turn for a moment when they arrived, like two strangers with their good clothes and their suitcases, and the way, for the first instant, they looked around, as if it were a new hotel. She would have been glad if it could have lasted longer. That was why she had hurried to get things under way and their chairs drawn up to the table.

"If you'll set right down your supper'll be on in no time."

"Well, no." Her husband gave her a kiss on a cheekbone—one of the year's two—and adding, "Might's well be comfortable," passed on upstairs.

She wondered if Ray would kiss her too this year. But just as he was on the point of it he remembered something more important.

"Oh, Ma, d'you know what? We bought you a present to bring home, a couple of nice aprons, and then what'd we go and do but leave 'em in the train. Wasn't that a bright one?" And he too went upstairs.

Above the sputter of the frying meat she could hear their voices, Ray's mostly, fragmentary and muffled. Once Ray laughed. He came down in his corduroys and brown sweater, and in pulling off his shirt he had spoiled his hair. His father was in his nightshirt, over which he had drawn a pair of overalls. They might neither of them have been away.

They ate in silence, chewing like tired men, their elbows guarding their plates and their eyes centered in the flame of the lamp between them. They seemed to be dreaming. Once Ray chuckled, his eyes passing to his father. The old man cast him a dour look. "You calm down."

Addie opened some pears. "Everything all right in the city?" she inquired as she helped them. Joslin nodded at the lamp, protruding his lower lip. "I'd say so, yes, all right. . . ."

She went and got the new *Sentinel.* Joslin wiped his mouth, opened the paper, cast an eye over the deaths, and yawned.

"Frankie all right?" he asked by and by.

"Yes, Frankie's all right."

"Stock all right?"

"Yes, all right. Except a funny thing about Snow's calf——"

"What's wrong with Snow's calf?"

"Nothing, only the way she acts about the red rooster. It was the day you left——" Addie drew up a chair and put her elbows on the table. "No, it was the day *after* you left, I guess; yes, Wednesday morning——"

Joslin's lids drooped. His chin was sinking into his neck. He straightened up when Addie's voice stopped, and muttered: "Been a hard day."

"Been a hard week," Ray added facetiously, staring at the lamp.

His father got to his feet. "You be up and down by four sharp, son, that's all." He took a match and went upstairs. Ray leaned back and began to play a harmonica. It was "The Sidewalks of New York."

"Where'd this thing come from?" he demanded, stopping in the middle of a bar. "I had one like it, but it was an 'A.' "

"It's Frankie's." Addie began to scrape the plates.

"Where'd he get it?"

She didn't feel like talking any more; all that explanation. So she said: "Somebody or other give it to him, I guess."

Ordinarily she would have washed the dishes, but this was the night her husband had come home, so she stacked them and, asking Ray to put out the light when he came, she went upstairs, taking off her apron. Just before she reached their bedroom she had a start. Then she could have smiled, for it was only Frankie, out of bed, half awake, in the dark hall.

He resisted her hand. "I wan' my thing; ut's mine."

"What thing? You're dreaming. Go back to bed."

"Who's 'at ut's got ut, playin'?"

"Playing what? Oh, I see, yes, your——"

"My moosic thing, ut 'at man gin me, ut you kissed."

"Shhh!" Addie stood back on her heels. "Hush your mouth!" It was absurd, but she felt helpless.

Frankie turned sullen. "No, but I wan' ut; ut's mine."

"Yes, all right, yes. You be still and run back to bed like a good boy, and I'll go straight and get it for you." She returned belowstairs.

"Ray, gi' me that. Your brother's woke up fretting, and it's his."

The child was waiting at the top. She led him back and tucked him in.

"Here it is, Frankie, but listen, you shouldn't say that about that man. It's bad—naughty, because I never did. Now go bye-bye and forget it."

Smoothing his hair, she left him. At the door, however, she vacillated. It was so laughable, yet it made her feel so helpless. She was used to dealing with things that had some logic in them. It exasperated her.

Returning to the bedside, she got down and put her lips to his ear.

"If ever you say that again about my such a thing as kissing that or any other man, I'll spank you. I'll take down your panties and spank you with the hairbrush, hard; you hear?"

Then she went to their room. The lamp was turned low. Her husband was in bed, asleep.

Well, he'd had a hard day, this traveling. He'd had a hard week.

She undressed and blew out the light, and, going to the window, stood there awhile. The moon was up, sailing in a cloudless sky; under it the farm lay, sloping away; gently swelling smooth fields in the pale light, like pale breasts on the mountain, against the black hem of the woods below.

Her thoughts were in two layers. In the top layer there were these: "Now they've come home we can get the manure started out on the west plowing and we can decide if we'll change it to rye; we can weed out the pullets, and we can get to work and ditch the waste piece before it freezes."

In the bottom layer, the buried one, was this: "They are not part of it, as I am; I am part of it and it is part of me." The deep reason for her being, the long, habitual, fruitful identity with the soil and its creatures, filled her unconscious thoughts. Who, to this dark Amazonian tenant of her soul, were those two men of whom she was a little awed; those two who went away and had a time, and left her alone at last with the autumnal land, at rest after the summer's travail, at peace for a little while? They owned the farm. Yes, but it was hers. . . .

What she was thinking as she crept under the blankets beside the sleeper was: "I wonder what color aprons they were." . . .

The men were cutting out brush in the waste piece, preparatory to ditching. It was the day which last night had presaged: perfect autumn, chill in the shadows, glassy clear. The mountain stood solid and separate; the sky, no longer weighing on the horizons, showed itself detached and whole, going on around. Beast and fowl made themselves heard, sounds reiterant, monotonous, and good, bawling of young cattle, ruffle and cut-cut of hens, pigs grunting, and Frankie marching to his harmonica, a suck and a blow, a suck and a blow, soul-satisfying, around the barn, around the orchard, around the sheds.

"Mama, kin I go down see Ray yet?"

"Not yet, you'll be in the way; run try and find Speck's nest."

Another circuit. "Mama, kin I go yet?"

"Not yet."

Even the apples Addie was sorting seemed to fall in with the cosmic rhythm: a cider, a cider, a cider, an eating, a pie. Under her breath, inattentively, she hummed fragments of old tunes. "*I thought it was a kiss, but it was just an idle dream.*" For her and for the farm it was the beginning of another year.

Clear reddening sunlight. Cut-cut! Mooo-ugh! A loudening harmonica.

"Mama, kin I go down see Ray yet?"

"Yes, pester you, run along; I'll be down in a second for the cows."

Joslin was just coming up as she entered the lane, an ax over his shoulder and his one remaining forelock plastered on his brow. He was a lean, wiry man, a hard worker, as faithful a worker as there was.

"Where's Ray?" she asked. He told her Ray was coming along. "Stopped a minute to set down, trot Frankie. Hurry him up and hurry up them cows."

Crossing the upper pasture, she heard music. It came from the brush in the corner of the waste piece, and it was "The Sidewalks of New York." In the midst of it there arose a disturbance. Howls. Yowls of young rage. Words exchanged, high, low, unintelligible at that distance. Addie halted in the bare field. She felt distracted. It was that sudden rent in the fabric of the day, the break in the smooth great throb of all creation.

She fingered her cheeks. "I'll show 'em!" She started that way. Before she had gone far the squabble had quieted and her older son, pushing out of the thicket, climbed over the fence twenty yards away. At sight of her he fetched up, his head ducked a little and his mouth half open.

"Where's your brother?" she demanded with a hint of sharpness.

No answer. Ray looked queer. He looked fascinated, embarrassed, and sullen, and his face was turning a mottled red. He was large for his age and hardly knew how to handle himself.

Addie's feeling of distraction deepened.

"What's ailing you? Why don't you answer me?"

Ray closed his mouth, opened it, closed it again. Turning at right angles, he started walking heavily and swiftly.

Frankie had appeared now, harmonica in hand. He too stopped short at sight of his mother. Then with a gulp of terror he scuttled back through the fence. She called after him into the brush: "Frankie, you come straight here." The whole thing shamed and scared her in an unaccountable way; there was nothing to get hold of, no beginning, no why, no wherefore.

Lowering her eyes and pretending to think of something more important than naughty children, she turned back toward the lower lane. At the bars she couldn't help peeping. On the stony profile of the pasture Ray had stopped to watch her, a hulking, sulking silhouette; Frankie, sneaking out of the waste piece farther down, was scuttling up the hill to join him.

But why? But why?

As she brought the cows up in the gathering dusk, her feet felt heavy. Nothing any longer kept time; the animals' hoofs clattered on the stones till the wooden jangle got on her nerves and she picked up a stick and drove them.

"Frankie wouldn't come to me; he ran and went with Ray. Why? Why?"

She tried to throw it off at supper, talking more than her habit and laughing at nothing, so that Joslin began to study her, a little puzzled. But it wouldn't work. Ray wouldn't look at her. Chewing to himself, he kept his eyes on his plate, his face sallow and dark red by turns. And Frankie lay as low as a mouse in a corner, an uneasy good little boy.

After his dessert Ray went upstairs. When his father had gone to the barn he came down in his serge suit and began hunting for his hat. Addie stood watching him. For the first time in her life she wanted to scream.

"Where you aiming to go to?"

He had his hat in his hand and the door open, his back to her. "Down to the store, see some life; that's where I'm going to."

"Did your pa say so?"

"What diff's that make to me?" He spit out on the stoop. Then, as though that act had fortified him: "What the hell's it to me? If he says anything you can fight it out with him; it's up to you, see? It's up to you!"

Was he turning crazy? Was the boy sick? When Addie tried to get her mind to think, she began to grow frightened. Frightened of what?

She went at her dishes. Joslin came in by and by.

"Was that Ray I see going out? Where's he think he's going to?"

"Well, I wanted a spool of cotton down to the store."

"Cotton! Cotton, eh? And him having to be up and down at four!"

Where was Frankie? Addie went upstairs. She found the boy in bed. Gone of his own accord, undressed without a whine, and fast asleep. When she had been standing there a moment she saw he wasn't asleep at all.

"Please, please," he wailed of a sudden, "please don' spank me wuth no hairbrush!" He pulled the sheet over his head. "I never said ut, honest; I never tol' Ray ut; I never says you kissed 'at man; I never, I never!"

He screeched. But she was only sitting down, weak as water.

So that was the secret. She felt like laughing. Poor Ray! Poor mixed-up fellow, hurt and scared and scandalized! No wonder! Yet what a relief it was to know the why and the wherefore!

She couldn't spank the child; that was too much to ask of her. Giving him a pat and a tuck, she returned to the kitchen to wait for Ray. She could almost see his face when she should tell him.

She sat with her hands in her lap and waited. Half hypnotized by the still flame of the lamp, she thought and thought. She remembered Ray as a baby; then as a little boy of Frankie's age following her around; then his going away with his father last year on the trip. She hadn't realized till now that from that trip he had never come back. Nor ever would. She remembered him standing there tonight, spitting out, then swearing in a new angry audacious bass. She began again to have that feeling of helplessness. Little by little it crept and claimed her; why, she couldn't say.

Ray was in and had the door closed before she saw him. Studying his narrowed, bloodshot eyes, she got up with a sudden misgiving.

"Come here, le'me smell your breath; you gone and been to Hearn's."

He rubbed a sleeve over his mouth and made for the stairs.

"Ray! Wait!"

Oh, she had never been afraid of anything—of tramps, of bulls, not even of death. But it was this helplessness.

"*Wait!*" she cried in her deep panic. "You listen to me, I know what's ailing you—don't you think I don't!"

He paused on the stair, glowering back. "I betcha."

"Well, you been listening to your brother, I know that, and I know just precisely what he's been feeding you."

"I betcha do." He went on upstairs and slammed his door.

Well, he wasn't himself. Addie sat down on the nearest chair.

Well, she would tell him in the morning.

She didn't tell him in the morning. How to bring it up; how to begin? She was so slow. Nor in the afternoon. She began to find she couldn't get near him except when his father was there. Well, why not with his father there? She was so confused, so helpless about it—so worn out by it—well, why rake Joslin in?

Time grew. It grew from hours to days. Five of them.

"What's ailing Ray?" her husband asked her. "He eats light and he goes around like he's swallowed a pill. Suppose he's coming down with something?"

If only she could have said then, matter-of-fact: "Well, he's got it into his head from something his brother said that a man that was here while you were away, that I kissed him——" But just there something in her rebelled.

"I don't know," was all she could say.

Another time: "I'm getting uneasy about that boy. Couple times today I caught him looking like he wanted to murder somebody. What's ailing him?"

"I don't know."

That was true. What did she know any longer about that brooding fellow, that averter and avoider, stranger than the strangest stranger? What did she know about anything? It used to be you plant a seed and reap a crop; you commit a crime and go to prison. Now she had done nothing, yet here she stood from day to day and held her breath. Every time Ray looked at his father, every time Frankie so much as passed his father, blowing that infernal toy, she held her breath.

Yet after all it wasn't to come directly from either Frankie or Ray.

Addie was sorting the last of the apples one afternoon. Joslin had been to the store. She heard the car return and a moment later he came into the shed. He sat down and began to eat an apple, a thing he never did; after a bite or so he threw it on the ground and rushed out, only to return, his face contorted and his eyes narrowed. He stood with arms folded.

"Wife, what's all this talk I hear down to the Crossing?"

"Who?"

"I want you should tell me what you got to tell me, plain out."

His voice was obstructed. He spoke slowly, evidently determined to get to the bottom of this thing in a cold-blooded, judicial way. It was worse than any rage. It took all Addie's wits out of her.

"Wh-why, I don't know wh-wh-what–wh-wh-what talk?"

All right. He had done his part, given her her chance, fulfilled his obligations as a reasoning man. Let unreason have its way.

"Who was he? You tell me that, or Goll-damn it!" Then he gave her no time. Pointing a fist at her, he lifted his lip, showing the points of his teeth. "I want you to tell me, wife; how long was he here with you, on my farm?" All of his teeth became visible, brown at the bases. "I want you to tell me: what else did you give him besides your kisses?"

Addie wouldn't have known him; he wouldn't have known himself. Wheeling, he walked out of the shed and around the corner of the barn.

No one could blame him. It's terrible enough to ferret such things out in the home: but to get the first inkling at second hand outside—common property, common gossip bandied over a counter or around a stove!

Addie nailed up the last box of the "Selected." She walked across the yard. Frankie came out of the kitchen door with doughnut crumbs on his cheek and, seeing her, began to play furiously on his rusting instrument. She took it and threw it on the steps and stamped on it. The child opened his mouth; presently the howl came out. Still knowing as little what she did, Addie grabbed him, sat down, held him in her lap, and patted his arm.

"There, there; but now see what you gone and done."

Ray came across the yard. She turned her voice on him.

"Now see what you done. Hearkening to foolishness; running to the store and gabbing lies. Now see what you gone and done."

"What *I* done!" Ray sunk his head between his shoulders. "*I* done! That's a good one, that is." He spit to his left and went on in.

The first half of supper passed in silence; it took all that time for Addie to get her words in order. She got up and stood by the sink.

"Listen, the whole lot of you's just going on something Frankie took into his head, and I should think it had come to a pass when you'll swallow for gospel what a baby his age says, and won't even hark to a grown woman you've lived with going on nineteen year."

Joslin raised his eyes for the first time. He looked lined and gray.

"That's just the damn part of it. Out of the mouths of babes and sucklin's." He leaned heavily on his elbows and drummed with a knife. "For instance, if I and Frankie there, we'd been to town, and you was to ask me who I'd seen, and I says nobody, and he was to chirp in, 'Oh, no, Papa, I guess you're forgetting that woman in the red hat you followed out back of the church shed and put your arm around her'—which'd you take for the gospel, Addie?"

Addie turned and screamed at Frankie: "Tell 'em the truth! Tell 'em everything happened! Go on tell 'em every last thing you seen!"

Joslin pointed the knife. "Yes, Frankie, now, everything. Mind now, *everything!* Or else, you know, you could go be put in prison."

The child looked at his mother, then at his father, then at his brother; and his brother too was scowling at him in the same silent, awful way. He began to quaver: "I don' want 'at ol' mouf organ—I never—I never——" and then he was under the table in a heap of fright and woe.

Joslin looked at his plate. He pushed it away from him and got up.

"It tastes dirty." He took his hat and went out. Ray followed.

If Addie could have seen anything she might have been able to see red. But for a while she saw nothing. She stood at the window that night looking out; there was no moon, and the stars were clouded, and she couldn't even see the farm. Joslin's farm. "How long was he here with you, on *my* farm?" Was the reason she couldn't see it from the window that, in the superhuman violence of his anger, he had torn it up and taken it away?

Her mind had been knocked down; it lay stunned and subservient to the beliefs of others. What was this sin she had committed? How had she, Addie Shoemaker, ever come to do it?

Addie Shoemaker! As she crept in between the blankets, chill with emptiness, the one thing she knew was nostalgia. The house had grown frightening in its silence, hung there over the mountain void from which the farm had been torn away in a shamed man's wrath. If she could only have heard Mama Shoemaker's voice downstairs, reading the *Sentinel*, or Papa Shoemaker's horses stamping in the livery stable out back.

Joslin slept with his son. Addie, coming down half drugged with a snatch of sleep, found they had got their own breakfast and were gone about their business. She heard their axes across in the waste piece when she took the cows down.

The forenoon grew. With each hour that passed she sank deeper and deeper into the lethargy of the lost. Habit worked her hands. She got a good dinner—home sausage, mashed potatoes, stewed tomatoes, squash pie, backing-powder biscuit last. It was ready to the minute. She let Frankie ring the bell.

Ray was in the yard, but he didn't come. Then she remembered

Joslin had gone off in the car at eleven. He was returning just now. They came in together, the father carrying two paper bags and a can.

"Well, dinner's on." She fastened Frankie's bib and sat down.

The men went to the sink. Joslin opened his can of pork and beans. In one bag there were crackers, in the other cup cakes. Standing there by the drain board they made their meal.

Addie sat and stared. There was something about this act that took away what little she had left of her powers. Her husband's face fascinated her. Under its stubble the skin looked hot and dry. But never a word.

Ray wasn't the man his father was. His mouth full of cracker paste, he couldn't keep his eyes from slipping to the fleshpots on the table. Caught by his mother, he reddened and lost his poise. "Taste dirty, 'twould."

His father gave him a look to slay him. "Hush your mouth!"

Then Joslin hushed his own; he stopped chewing. He stared at the pump. He had suddenly envisioned the years to come. His mouth still full, he went outdoors, to return presently with a peach-butter can he had found in the dump. Bringing from the pantry a jar of concentrated lye, he emptied it into the can, which he then proceeded to fill from the pump. All his movements were deliberate. He turned to his wife.

"See this? This is lye water. Well, if so be you want to go on cooking for this family, come wash your hands."

"Come—what?"

"Come wash your hands."

Addie didn't "see red"; she saw white. Where the other blow had stunned her mind, this cleared it. Clear as zero ice. Her voice sounded flat.

"You say you want I should wash my hands in that?"

Joslin inclined his head. Her eyes left his and played over the table, resting for a moment on the heavy castor, for another on the broad blade of the meat knife. Strange, rushing impulses. Fearful speculations. Lusts.

She heard her husband's voice: "Here 'tis; I'll leave it here."

"You can leave it there till hell freezes over."

Frankie gasped at the word. Joslin went to the door. "If it takes that long, so be it, wife."

When he and Ray were gone she got Frankie from his chair. She couldn't keep her hands from shaking. She pushed him out of the door, away from her. "Go with 'em! Catch 'em! Stay with 'em! Play down there!"

She put the knife away in the drawer. Then she scraped the untouched plates, carried the food out to the sows and watched them swill it.

She went to her room and lay down. She remained there staring at the ceiling till she was exhausted with the muscular strain of rigidity; then she got up and prepared supper. She worked all around the peach-butter can but did not disturb it. She set the table with cold meat, potato chips, pickled beets, raspberry sauce, cookies, pie, doughnuts, cheese, and put the kettle on for tea. Into the kettle she stuck her thumb.

Frankie was eating all alone when she came in after milking and the others had gone to the store. She took all the food to the sows, put Frankie to bed, and went to bed herself after bolting the door. Once in the night a terrible loneliness came over her. She went on tiptoe and got Frankie. Almost as soon as she had him in bed, however, she began to shake all over again with the murderous license of her thoughts, and returned him to his room. When she awoke in the morning it was broad day. What matter?

So it went.

Hitherto, even when the men were away she had been surrounded by, and one with, the multitudinous life of the farm: the fields, the stock, the child. But now she felt so queerly about Frankie that she grew afraid; and as for the farm, she hated it. It *was* Joslin's farm; it had been his before she came; it believed what he believed and looked at her askance with its hundred kinds of eyes as she went up and down—the foolish town girl, the wicked one.

She was alone on the farm. She hadn't had time yet to think of the outside world. One afternoon, however, two separate parties of her friends drove that way along the road. They didn't stop at the gate, only slowed down, necks craned and eyes slanting back at the house in morbid fascination.

And that evening at dusk when she went for the cows there were three men at the bottom of the pasture. They climbed in as she approached, and when she would have turned back and avoided

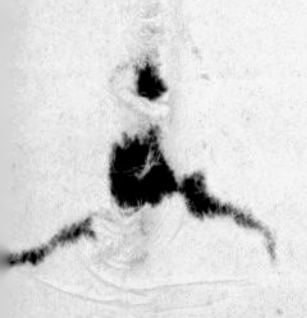

them, one took hold of her arm. Though it wasn't cold they had on overcoats with collars turned up, and their hats pulled down, so she could make nothing of their faces.

It was so fantastic she wasn't actually frightened. When the first one spoke, she said: "You're Albert Pease, from Lower Falls."

"You're mistaken," he growled. "We're more-less strangers this side of the county. But we know Joslin by reputation; we know what he's done with this farm; we know what he stands for in this community; and there's times outsiders can do more'n neighbors can. What we want to say is, this here's always been a God-fearing, law-abiding community, and it ain't going to begin winking at goings on behind husbands' backs at this late date, nor at homes going to rack and ruin and men interfered with in raising this nation's crops, by no stubborn, unholy, un-Christian goings on."

The second man broke in: "A word to the wise is sufficient."

The third: "Get along in the home, or get out of it."

When they let her go and went back toward the fence she looked about in a sort of daze. There was a chunk of rock near her feet; she picked it up and threw it. It struck one man in the small of the back. With the shock and hurt of it he wheeled and started for her, fists clenched, but the others caught him, expostulating in whispers. He puffed at her: "You–you–we'll get you yet, you––" But then one got a hand over his mouth.

She left the cows and ran home. With every step it grew darker and the footing steeper; her chest ached with the bursting of her lungs. When she came into the kitchen her face was red, her lips white, her hair in strings; she looked drunk; she had it in her mind to scream, scream, scream, and nothing more. Then she didn't. Flopping down on the nearest chair, she surveyed the room. Of the supper she had left on the table not even Frankie's portion was touched, and the boy himself hid in shadow halfway up the stairs. Joslin sat against the farther wall with his hands in his lap and his best coat on over his overalls. Ray wore his too, and sat with his hands folded. And in a third chair, with his hands folded, sat the minister.

Addie had never been so embarrassed. She tried to stop panting and she couldn't; her face flamed; she dropped her eyes to the table legs.

"How d'you do?" she mumbled. "Please' to see you."

"I'm pleased to see you, Sister Joslin, I'm sure. As I was saying . . ."

He was a hard-working fellow, their minister, a lean man on a meager living, a little worried head and a big worried heart.

"As I was saying to Brother Joslin, I just dropped in going by. I often drop in on one or another of my people's homes, just simply without any fuss to kneel down in the family circle for a minute and talk with God, as you'd talk with your neighbor. It seems to me there's no prayer in any great tabernacle with stained glass and gilded steeple so helpful, so curative, nor so acceptable to our Father in heaven as that." He got up suddenly and straightened his vest. "Might we pray?"

Addie couldn't budge; something held her. Tears burned her eyes. She choked: "I never done a thing—it's all lies, I keep telling you, telling you." The minister's hand fell on her shoulder, firm and kindly.

"You and God know the truth of that, sister, surely. But anyway, what about just talking it over with God? That's never harmed a living soul since the world was made. . . . Well, men?" He looked at the others, who, appearing sober, impressed, and scared, got down with him by their chairs.

Still Addie couldn't budge. The minister popped up again, darted at the stairs and, catching Frankie with a reassuring chuckle, brought him down and planted him on petrified knees with his elbows in his mother's lap. Then he got back to his place and began: "O God, our Heavenly Father . . ."

Those backs! It was too queer and too awful. Freeing Frankie's elbows, she slid to the floor. She didn't kneel—just hunkered there, her arm on the chair seat. The good man's voice, husky with the habit of supplication, filled the room with its immemorial sedative phrases. From beyond it, beyond the walls, came the supplication of the unmilked cows, lowing at the bars. Addie's muscles slackened. Under the influence of the harmonious repetitions her thoughts slackened too, lost focus, and became a hodgepodge.

"In Thine infinite mercy" . . . "Mooo-ugh! Mooo-ugh!" . . . "goings on behind husbands' backs" . . . "Mooo-ugh! . . . "Vouchsafe that which ever of us is in darkness" . . . The lamp was smoking. . . . The kettle was singing. . . . Somebody was sobbing.

. . . "Mooo-ugh!" . . . She had hit him with a chunk of rock. Good! . . . "Father be good to us, little children that don't know their A-B-C's. Teach us, O Great Teacher" . . . Somebody was sobbing. . . .

Addie lifted her head. Something had happened. What had happened was that a spirit had come into the room. The minister had forgotten in his worriment what he was doing; forgotten his calling, forgotten his husk; his voice had grown strident, insistent: "God, let's wipe it clean; let's look each other in the eye and see the truth and tell it and have the dirty business over with and begin all new again. There, that's right, that's right."

It was Ray sobbing. Frankie blubbered. Addie put her hand on his head. Little Frankie, little baby! And all of them! All gathered around the table again discussing the fields, the smiling fields, the fattening stock. All straight in the loving light of God again; all new.

"Amen."

They got up, all new. Joslin blew his nose. How worn to the bone he looked! It was funny to see his face wet with tears. He walked to the sink, still blowing his nose. He looked at the peach-butter can, still there, still full. Was he going, was he going—— Oh, Glory, was he going to dump it out?

"There, yes, brother, vengeance is mine, saith the Lord, there, there . . ."

"Mooo-ugh! . . . Mooo-ugh!"

Joslin didn't dump it. Before they knew what he was about, there went both his own hands into it, right down to the coat cuffs.

"There's for anything I may've done ever," he whistled through his teeth as he withdrew the hands, gray with the caustic that dripped on the linoleum. "Son," he said, turning to Ray, "if so be you got anything——"

The overgrown boy had been through an overgrown hell these weeks. His diaphragm collapsed; he too ducked his hands to the cuffs; he too stood with them streaming. What deliverance! What brightness! Supper tonight!

And Addie was thinking, her eyes blind with water: "Supper tonight!"

"Well, wife?"

Through the blur she saw them watching, waiting. Their eyes

went to the peach-butter can and came back to her again. Well, Ma? Well, wife?

While she stood there trying to fathom it the minister came softly and, taking one of Frankie's hands, curled its fingers around her thumb.

"'A little child shall lead them.'"

"*Not on your life!*"

For an instant after that their faces looked so blank it was comic. Then the heavenly bubble that filled the room was shattered and the air was thick.

"You won't, won't you!" Joslin spread his smarting hands on the table. Ray bawled: "You double-crosser, you!" And Joslin again: "*You won't, eh?*"

"*Not till hell freezes over, I won't!*"

Before the distracted arm of the minister could catch her she had the door opened and slammed again behind her as she ran.

She stood panting in the middle of the yard, her knees half bent. A crescent moon in the west threw a phantom light across the world. She saw the white faces of the cows all staring at her across the bars at the lane, their black mouths all gaping at her. "Mooo-ugh!"

Turning, she fled around the corner of the house and down the path and out the gate and down the road that led to the valley of the Twinskill where she was born. . . .

Winter came and covered the mountain. In the short days the sun shone and there were occasional sounds. The long nights were silent. For a while in the early evening there was a light in the farmhouse on the ridge, but by eight it was gone. In the town of Twinshead, miles away but distinct in the bodiless air, lights burned in clusters till nine and ten and eleven.

November, December, January, February, March.

In late March a snow flurry met a cross wind and fell as rain. Another week and the gullies were running water. Around the rags of drifts the earth seemed visibly to puff up, reawakened and wishful. One evening when Ray had got a mock of supper huddled together on the table and was about to light the lamp, he looked and blew out the match instead; a shaft of pale magenta standing in at the windows from the west was enough to eat by. Spring had come.

With the coming of spring and the prying of light, the ravages of winter began to show themselves—to the eye, the nose, the cheated palate; even to the ear. When the beasts began to bawl, Frankie, who had been stupid all through the cold like any little animal that hibernates, began too. First to sniffle and then eternally, causelessly, to wail. Threats did no good.

His wailing wasn't the worst. He began to talk about his mother.

"When's my mama coming home?"

"Hush your face and eat your supper."

"When's my mama coming home?"

When nothing else served they sent him to bed. But next night as soon as it darkened he was at it again: "When's my mama coming home?"

His father was a man; he could set his face like frozen leather and sit quiet behind it. But Ray couldn't. His nerves set him on the child.

"Your mama? You ain't got no mama, didn't you know that?"

"Ray," said his father, "eat! Think we want to be up all night?"

"Nothing I'd like better." Ray hulked over his plate for a few mouthfuls. But his nerves only got worse. An embittered restlessness pushed him to bravado. "Nothing I'd like better'n staying up all night once. I betcha one thing; I betcha Ma ain't going to bed no half past seven or eight these nights in Twinshead. Huh-huh! Not Ma."

It kept at him. Doing the dishes later, he resumed the attack.

"Not her, no sir! She knows when she's well off, I warrant you. Seeing everybody, tending shop for Aunt Hattie in the hat store, hearing everything going. And Aunt Hattie gives parties, too. Know what I heard to the store? Aunt Hattie give one party that Uncle Albert had every car from his garage lining the sidewalk to take the folks home. Don't you forget it, Pa!"

His father was reading the *Sentinel*.

"I won't forget it," he said in a steady careful voice, "if *you will*."

Forget it! Ray had planted the wind in his own soul; the whirlwind had him. Parties and cars, bright lights and goings on. He couldn't sleep for thinking of them; all next morning was wishful bitterness. Springtime! It was he that ought to be out with the fellows and girls, and looking well, instead of penned in this makeshift life of two-legged pigs. With the afternoon a wild and weakling resolve took form. Well, he didn't care.

He got away; ran away, he didn't care. He went down to the store at the Crossing where there was a telephone booth. He got his aunt's house. His mother was at the hat store. He got the hat store. He didn't care.

"Ma, it's Ray. Ma, you having a good time?"

"Oh, Ray—yes, Ray; how are you, and how's Frankie?"

"He's all right. Ma, you having a nice time down there?"

"How's everything? How's the hay holding out? How's the cows, and have any of 'em come in yet? How are the hens for eggs?"

"All right, yes, O.K.; but you wouldn't fancy it up here, the good time you're having."

"Your pa still got the lye can waiting?"

"Ma, listen here, I'll dump it. I will! I will!"

"Your pa wouldn't like that."

"I'm bigger'n Pa, Ma. I'm stouter'n Pa."

"Where's the use? Maybe you might see me dropping in, though."

"Ma! No! No, honest, Ma! Say, Ma——"

"Maybe it might be soon. Soon's tonight, maybe."

Ray got home breathless, praying his father hadn't yet come in. Luck was with him. For the last time he pawed together the leavings of things for their evening meal. The last time. Last time.

Frankie was at it again. "When's my mama coming home?"

Ray paled. "Didn't I tell you you hadn't got no mama?" His breathlessness wouldn't go. He made a saving to-do of getting his brother to bed, pulling the soiled blankets over him for the last time, for the last time.

His father was reading the *Sentinel;* he had read it seven times through in seven nights. Ray didn't wait to be told, he went at the dishes with a clatter. Puddling in the pan, he hadn't a thing in his mind but one—and that was as big as a mountain. A mountain at his elbow. There it stood, the peach-butter can, still in the same ring of dried slosh on the drain board, still full, each week's loss by evaporation made good with a dipper from the pump, as sure as church.

Hurry! Time was passing; no time to lose. At last he touched it with an accidental thumb. But not yet. He felt blown up like a Fair balloon.

"Pa," he tried at last, his face hot red, "this here can of slop here, it smells. How long we going to keep it, for Goll sake?"

Joslin turned a page and coughed. His bald spot looked sweaty, but his voice was dry. "You heard her say herself. Till hell freezes over."

Time was passing. Ray thought once he heard a car in the distance. He looked at his father over his shoulder. "I'm bigger'n him, and stouter."

It was true, and he had never realized it till today. His father there was an old man. An old man with stooped shoulders and only a few hairs left, and they white, all in a season. A big bluff. He cleared his throat.

"Well, I'll tell you what I'm going to do; I'm going to dump it."

He laid hands on the sacred can. Then he let go, wheeled, and swallowed.

His father was halfway across the floor. He stopped with his feet wide apart and his jaw out. He began swearing in a low voice, words Ray had never heard. His veins stood out on his temples, and his eyes looked crazy. Where was Ray's bulk and muscle now? He hadn't figured on this. He hadn't seen what his father looked like till today; he hadn't seen what his father *was* till now. He went around the other way of the table, wiping his hands on his pants, and sat down; and still he couldn't get away from those crazy eyes or from that low-toned, almost whispering voice.

"You mealy-mouthed sissy; you son of something–no son of mine; you white-gutted skunk; you–you––"

At the full of it the door had opened and Addie stood there in it, a suitcase in either hand.

"Well?" she said.

In the silence, in the dark of the yard there was the sound of an engine and a crackle of frosted mud as tires backed, turned, and gathered way, and at the last a dying hail: "So long, good-by."

"Well?" She set the suitcases down, closed the door, and faced them.

Ray sat there like a lump. He hadn't emptied the can; what could he do or say? Then there came a new dread. If she were to let anything out; if ever his father were to know about that telephone! He sat up. He tried to wink. He began to stammer, "How'd you c-c-come, Ma? If you'd've told me I could've dr-dr-drove down."

"Oh, no bother about that. A friend kindly offered to bring me up. Mr. Hedge, a gentleman that works for your uncle Albert in the garage, he was so good as to drive me up. He's been very good to me this winter, Mr. Hedge has."

She returned her eyes to the wooden image of Joslin.

"Well?"

She looked so queer. So strange. She had on a nice dress that fitted her, a nice hat, and brown kid gloves which she began now to pull off, her hands looking white under them as they appeared. She seemed to have lost some flesh, but she had good color, high color, and her eyes were bright.

"Well?" she said for the fourth time. "Where's Frankie–in bed? I brought him a present; isn't it pretty?" She had it out in her hand, a bright, brand-new harmonica. "I hope he'll like it and be satisfied."

Joslin stirred. He ran a sleeve over his mouth and backed away two or three stiff steps till he stood by the drainboard. His eyes still looked crazy and his voice was still low, almost a whisper.

"Well, you keep on saying 'Well?' Well what? Has hell froze over?"

"Oh yes. Oh, long ago."

If there was anything on her face it was like a smile.

"Well, wife?"

"Oh yes." She walked to the drainboard and, laying her gloves and the harmonica among the dishes, she dipped her hands into the lye, then drew them out and held them away to dribble on the floor. A spot of pink lay on either cheekbone and her eyes were as shiny as dry diamonds.

"Now," she said in a queer light voice, "I hope we're all satisfied."

It was too sudden for Joslin and too complete; the strain of being adamant when he was only flesh-and-blood had been too long. All he could do was blow his nose and mumble: "There, Addie my girl, good girl . . ."

Ray went to pieces too. With him it was all the winter's bitterness. His face down in his hands, he cried: "Aw, if you was going to do it, why for Goll sake couldn't you've done it last fall and had it done with, Ma?"

Addie had a slow brain. She stared at happy Joslin, then at Ray.

"Why couldn't I——" She stopped there. A slow brain, but it arrived.

Another moment and the room was filled with a soft sound of laughter.

She left them and went upstairs. She passed into Frankie's room and stood looking down at him in the little moonlight from the window.

The thought came to her: "You'd say I ought to kneel down." But she didn't; she sat on the bed's edge. "I oughtn't to give him this, or at least I should think I'd think I oughtn't." But she slid the new harmonica under his pillow. "I'd always have supposed I'd have cried for shame." She bent and kissed his hair and went to her own room.

She stood at the window gazing out. Under the moon the farm sloped away, gently swelling smooth fields like pale breasts on the mountain against the black hem of the woods below.

The thought that came to her in the top layer was: "We'll sow it in rye this year; I like the green of rye growing; the oats can go in the waste piece. But that's so–there isn't any waste piece any more."

In the bottom layer of her thought was this: "I'll make it yield because it belongs to me; it's part of me–the land, the stock, the men. But I'm not part of it. I'm not its property; I'm my own. I can go have a time in town with George and them, or I can stay here. And because I want to stay here, I'll stay, and I'll make it yield."

"How'd you like some buckwheat cakes to go to bed on?" she called down presently from the top of the stairs. . . .

*How Beautiful with Shoes**

BY THE TIME THE MILKING WAS finished, the sow, which had farrowed the past week, was making such a row that the girl spilled a pint of the warm milk down the trough lead to quiet the animal before taking the pail to the well house. Then in the quiet she heard a sound of hoofs on the bridge, where the road crossed the creek a hundred yards below the house, and she set the pail down on the ground beside her bare, barn-soiled feet. She picked it up again. She set it down. It was as if she calculated its weight.

That was what she was doing, as a matter of fact, setting off against its pull toward the well house the pull of that wagon team in the road, with little more of personal will or wish in the matter than has a wooden weather vane between two currents in the wind. And as with the vane, so with the wooden girl—the added behest of a whiplash cracking in the distance was enough; leaving the pail at the barn door she set off in a deliberate, docile beeline through the cow yard, over the fence, and down in a diagonal across the farm's one tilled field toward the willow brake that walled the road at the dip. And once under way, though her mother came to the kitchen door and called in her high, flat voice, "Amarantha, where you goin', Amarantha?" the girl went on, apparently unmoved, as though she had been as deaf as the woman in the doorway; indeed, if there was emotion in her it was the purely sensuous one of feeling the clods of the furrows breaking softly between her toes. It was springtime in the mountains.

"Amarantha, why don't you answer me, Amarantha?"

For moments after the girl had disappeared beyond the willows the widow continued to call, unaware through long habit of how absurd it sounded, the name which that strange man her husband had put upon their daughter in one of his moods. Mrs. Doggett had been deaf so long she did not realize that nobody else ever thought of it for the broad-fleshed, slow-minded girl, but called her Mary, or, even more simply, Mare.

Ruby Herter had stopped his team this side of the bridge, the mules' heads turned into the lane to his father's farm beyond the road. A big-barreled, heavy-limbed fellow with a square, sallow, not unhandsome face, he took out youth in ponderous gestures of masterfulness; it was like him to have cracked his whip above his animals' ears the moment before he pulled them to a halt. When he saw the girl getting over the fence under the willows he tongued the wad of tobacco out of his mouth into his palm, threw it away beyond the road, and drew a sleeve of his jumper across his lips.

"Don't run yourself out o' breath, Mare; I got all night."

"I was comin'." It sounded sullen only because it was matter-of-fact.

"Well, keep a-comin' and give us a smack." Hunched on the wagon seat, he remained motionless for some time after she had arrived at the hub, and when he stirred it was but to cut a fresh bit of tobacco, as if already he had forgotten why he threw the old one away. Having satisfied his humor, he unbent, climbed down, kissed her passive mouth, and hugged her up to him, roughly and loosely, his hands careless of contours. It was not out of the way; they were used to handling animals both of them; and it was spring. A slow warmth pervaded the girl, formless, nameless, almost impersonal.

Her betrothed pulled her head back by the braid of her yellow hair. He studied her face, his brows gathered and his chin out.

"Listen, Mare, you wouldn't leave nobody else hug and kiss you, dang you!"

She shook her head, without vehemence or anxiety.

"Who's that?" She hearkened up the road. "Pull your team out," she added, as a Ford came in sight around the bend above the house, driven at speed. "Geddap!" she said to the mules herself.

But the car came to a halt near them, and one of the five men crowded in it called, "Come on, Ruby, climb in. They's a loony loose out o' Dayville Asylum, and they got him trailed over somewheres on Split Ridge, and Judge North phoned up to Slosson's store for ever'body come help circle him—come on, hop the runnin' board!"

Ruby hesitated, an eye on his team.

"Scared, Ruby?" The driver raced his engine. "They say this boy's a killer."

"Mare, take the team in and tell Pa." The car was already moving when Ruby jumped it. A moment after it had sounded on the bridge it was out of sight.

"Amarantha, Amarantha, why don't you come, Amarantha?"

Returning from her errand fifteen minutes later, Mare heard the plaint lifted in the twilight. The sun had dipped behind the back ridge, and though the sky was still bright with day, the dusk began to smoke up out of the plowed field like a ground fog. The girl had returned through it, got the milk, and started toward the well house before the widow saw her.

"Daughter, seems to me you might!" she expostulated without change of key. "Here's some young man friend o' yourn stopped to say howdy, and I been rackin' my lungs out after you. . . . Put that milk in the cool and come!"

Some young man friend? But there was no good to be got from puzzling. Mare poured the milk in the pan in the dark of the low house over the well, and as she came out, stooping, she saw a figure waiting for her, black in silhouette against the yellowing sky.

"Who are you?" she asked, a native timidity making her sound sulky.

" 'Amarantha!' " the fellow mused. "That's poetry." And she knew then that she did not know him.

She walked past, her arms straight down and her eyes front. Strangers always affected her with a kind of muscular terror simply by being strangers. So she gained the kitchen steps, aware by his tread that he followed. There, taking courage, she turned on him, her eyes down at the level of his knees.

"Who are you and what d' y' want?"

He still mused. "Amarantha! Amarantha in Carolina! That makes me happy!"

Mare hazarded one upward look. She saw that he had red hair, brown eyes, and hollows under his cheekbones, and though the green sweater he wore on top of a gray overall was plainly not meant for him, sizes too large as far as girth went, yet he was built so long of limb that his wrists came inches out of the sleeves and made his big hands look even bigger.

Mrs. Doggett complained. "Why don't you introduce us, daughter?"

The girl opened her mouth and closed it again. Her mother, unaware that no sound had come out of it, smiled and nodded, evidently taking to the tall, homely fellow and tickled by the way he could not seem to get his eyes off her daughter. But the daughter saw none of it, all her attention centered upon the stranger's hands.

Restless, hard-fleshed, and chap-bitten, they were like a countryman's hands; but the fingers were longer than the ordinary, and slightly spatulate at their ends, and these ends were slowly and continuously at play among themselves.

The girl could not have explained how it came to her to be frightened and at the same time to be calm, for she was inept with words. It was simply that in an animal way she knew animals, knew them in health and ailing, and when they were ailing she knew by instinct, as her father had known, how to move so as not to fret them.

Her mother had gone in to light up; from beside the lamp shelf she called back, "If he's aimin' to stay to supper you should've told me, Amarantha, though I guess there's plenty of the side meat to go round, if you'll bring me in a few more turnips and potatoes, though it is late."

At the words the man's cheeks moved in and out. "I'm very hungry," he said.

Mare nodded deliberately. Deliberately, as if her mother could hear her, she said over her shoulder, "I'll go get the potatoes and turnips, Ma." While she spoke she was moving, slowly, softly, at first, toward the right of the yard, where the fence gave over into the field. Unluckily her mother spied her through the window.

"Amarantha, where *are* you goin'?"

"I'm goin' to get the potatoes and turnips." She neither raised her voice nor glanced back, but lengthened her stride. "He won't hurt her," she said to herself. "He won't hurt her; it's me, not her," she kept repeating, while she got over the fence and down into the shadow that lay more than ever like a fog on the field.

The desire to believe that it actually did hide her, the temptation to break from her rapid but orderly walk grew till she could no longer fight it. She saw the road willows only a dash ahead of her. She ran, her feet floundering among the furrows.

She neither heard nor saw him, but when she realized he was with her she knew he had been with her all the while. She stopped, and he stopped, and so they stood, with the dark open of the field all around. Glancing sidewise presently, she saw he was no longer looking at her with those strangely importunate brown eyes of his, but had raised them to the crest of the wooded ridge behind her.

By and by, "What does it make you think of?" he asked. And when she made no move to see, "Turn around and look!" he said, and though it was low and almost tender in its tone, she knew enough to turn.

A ray of the sunset hidden in the west struck through the tops of the topmost trees, far and small up there, a thin, bright hem.

"What does it make you think of, Amarantha? . . . Answer!"

"Fire," she made herself say.

"Or blood."

"Or blood, yeh. That's right, or blood." She had heard a Ford going up the road beyond the willows, and her attention was not on what she said.

The man soliloquized. "Fire and blood, both; spare one or the other, and where is beauty, the way the world is? It's an awful thing to have to carry, but Christ had it. Christ came with a sword. I love beauty, Amarantha. . . . I say, I love beauty!"

"Yeh, that's right, I hear." What she heard was the car stopping at the house.

"Not prettiness. Prettiness'll have to go with ugliness, because it's only ugliness trigged up. But beauty!" Now again he was looking at her. "Do you know how beautiful you are, Amarantha, *Amarantha sweet and fair?*" Of a sudden, reaching behind her, he began to unravel the meshes of her hair braid, the long, flat-tipped fingers at once impatient and infinitely gentle. "*Braid no more that shining hair!*"

Flat-faced Mare Doggett tried to see around those glowing eyes so near to hers, but, wise in her instinct, did not try too hard. "Yeh," she temporized. "I mean, no, I mean."

"Amarantha, I've come a long, long way for you. Will you come away with me now?"

"Yeh—that is—in a minute I will, mister—yeh. . . ."

"Because you want to, Amarantha? Because you love me as I love you? Answer!"

"Yeh—sure—uh . . . *Ruby!*"

The man tried to run, but there were six against him, coming up out of the dark that lay in the plowed ground. Mare stood where she was while they knocked him down and got a rope around him; after that she walked back toward the house with Ruby and Older Haskins, her father's cousin.

Ruby wiped his brow and felt of his muscles. "Gees, you're lucky we come, Mare. We're no more'n past the town, when they come hollerin' he'd broke over this way."

When they came to the fence the girl sat on the rail for a moment and rebraided her hair before she went into the house, where they were making her mother smell ammonia.

Lots of cars were coming. Judge North was coming, somebody said. When Mare heard this she went into her bedroom off the kitchen and got her shoes and put them on. They were brand-new two-dollar shoes with cloth tops, and she had only begun to break them in last Sunday; she wished afterwards she had put her stockings on, too, for they would have eased the seams. Or else that she had put on the old button pair, even though the soles were worn through.

Judge North arrived. He thought first of taking the loony straight through to Dayville that night, but then decided to keep him in the lockup at the courthouse till morning and make the drive by day. Older Haskins stayed in, gentling Mrs. Doggett, while Ruby went out to help get the man into the judge's sedan. Now that she had them on, Mare didn't like to take the shoes off till Older went; it might make him feel small, she thought.

Older Haskins had a lot of facts about the loony.

"His name's Humble Jewett," he told them. "They belong back in Breed County, all them Jewetts, and I don't reckon there's none on 'em that's not a mite unbalanced. He went to college though, worked his way, and he taught somethin' 'rother in some academy-school a spell, till he went off his head all of a sudden and took after folks with an ax. I remember it in the paper at the time. They give out one while how the principal wasn't goin' to live, and there was others—there was a girl he tried to strangle. That was four-five years back."

Ruby came in guffawing. "Know the only thing they can get 'im to say, Mare? Only God thing he'll say is 'Amarantha, she's goin' with me.' . . . Mare!"

"Yeh, I know."

The cover of the kettle the girl was handling slid off on the stove with a clatter. A sudden sick wave passed over her. She went out to the back, out into the air. It was not till now she knew how frightened she had been.

Ruby went home, but Older Haskins stayed to supper with them and helped Mare do the dishes afterward; it was nearly nine when he left. The mother was already in bed, and Mare was about to sit down to get those shoes off her wretched feet at last, when she heard the cow carrying on up at the barn, lowing and kicking, and next minute the sow was in it with a horning note. It might be a fox passing by to get at the henhouse, or a weasel. Mare forgot her feet, took a broom handle they used in boiling clothes, opened the back door, and stepped out. Blinking the lamplight from her eyes, she peered up toward the outbuildings and saw the gable end of the barn standing like a red arrow in the dark, and the top of a butternut tree beyond it drawn in skeleton traceries, and just then a cock crowed.

She went to the right corner of the house and saw where the light came from, ruddy above the woods down the valley. Returning into the house, she bent close to her mother's ear and shouted, "Somethin's afire down to the town, looks like," then went out again and up to the barn. "Soh! Soh!" she called in to the animals. She climbed up and stood on the top of the rail of the cowpen fence, only to find she could not locate the flame even there.

Ten rods behind the buildings a mass of rock mounted higher than their ridgepoles, a chopped-off buttress of the back ridge, covered with oak scrub and wild grapes and blackberries, whose thorny ropes the girl beat away from her as she scrambled up in the wine-colored dark. Once at the top, and the brush held aside, she could see the tongue tip of the conflagration half a mile away at the town. And she knew by the bearing of the two church steeples that it was the building where the lockup was that was burning.

There is a horror in knowing animals trapped in a fire, no matter what the animals.

"O my God!" Mare said.

A car went down the road. Then there was a horse galloping. That would be Older Haskins probably. People were out at Ruby's father's farm; she could hear their voices raised. There must have been another car up from the other way, for lights wheeled and shouts were exchanged in the neighborhood of the bridge. Next thing she knew, Ruby was at the house below, looking for her probably.

He was telling her mother. Mrs. Doggett was not used to him, so he had to shout even louder than Mare had to.

"What y' reckon he done, the hellion! He broke the door and killed Lew Fyke and set the courthouse afire! . . . Where's Mare?"

Her mother would not know. Mare called. "Here, up the rock here."

She had better go down. Ruby would likely break his bones if he tried to climb the rock in the dark, not knowing the way. But the sight of the fire fascinated her simple spirit, the fearful element, more fearful than ever now, with the news. "Yes, I'm comin'," she called sulkily, hearing feet in the brush. "You wait; I'm comin'."

When she turned and saw it was Humble Jewett, right behind her among the branches, she opened her mouth to screech. She was not quick enough. Before a sound came out he got one hand over her face and the other arm around her body.

Mare had always thought she was strong, and the loony looked gangling, yet she was so easy for him that he need not hurt her. He made no haste and little noise as he carried her deeper into the undergrowth. Where the hill began to mount it was harder though. Presently he set her on her feet. He let the hand that had been over her mouth slip down to her throat, where the broad-tipped fingers wound, tender as yearning, weightless as caress.

"I was afraid you'd scream before you knew who 'twas, Amarantha. But I didn't want to hurt your lips, dear heart, your lovely, quiet lips."

It was so dark under the trees she could hardly see him, but she felt his breath on her mouth, near to. But then, instead of kissing her, he said, "No! No!" took from her throat for an instant the hand that had held her mouth, kissed its palm, and put it back softly against her skin.

"Now, my love, let's go before they come."

She stood stock-still. Her mother's voice was to be heard in the distance, strident and meaningless. More cars were on the road. Nearer, around the rock, there were sounds of tramping and thrashing. Ruby fussed and cursed. He shouted, "Mare, dang you, where are you, Mare?" his voice harsh with uneasy anger. Now, if she aimed to do anything, was the time to do it. But there was neither breath nor power in her windpipe. It was as if those yearning fingers had paralyzed the muscles.

"Come!" The arm he put around her shivered against her shoulder blades. It was anger. "I hate killing. It's a dirty, ugly thing. It makes me sick." He gagged, judging by the sound. But then he ground his teeth. "Come away, my love!"

She found herself moving. Once when she broke a branch underfoot with an instinctive awkwardness he chided her. "Quiet, my heart, else they'll hear!" She made herself heavy. He thought she grew tired and bore more of her weight till he was breathing hard.

Men came up the hill. There must have been a dozen spread out, by the angle of their voices as they kept touch. Always Humble Jewett kept caressing Mare's throat with one hand; all she could do was hang back.

"You're tired and you're frightened," he said at last. "Get down here."

There were twigs in the dark, the overhang of a thicket of some sort. He thrust her in under this, and lay beside her on the bed of ground pine. The hand that was not in love with her throat reached across her; she felt the weight of its forearm on her shoulder and its fingers among the strands of her hair, eagerly, but tenderly, busy. Not once did he stop speaking, no louder than breathing, his lips to her ear.

"*Amarantha sweet and fair—Ah, braid no more that shining hair . . .*"

Mare had never heard of Lovelace, the poet; she thought the loony was just going on, hardly listened, got little sense. But the cadence of it added to the lethargy of all her flesh.

"*Like a clew of golden thread—Most excellently ravellèd . . .*"

Voices loudened; feet came tramping; a pair went past not two rods away.

" . . . *Do not then wind up the light—In ribbands, and o'ercloud in night . . .* "

The search went on up the woods, men shouting to one another and beating the brush.

" . . . *But shake your head and scatter day!* I've never loved, Amarantha. They've tried me with prettiness, but prettiness is too cheap, yes, it's too cheap."

Mare was cold, and the coldness made her lazy. All she knew was that he talked on.

"But dogwood blowing in the spring isn't cheap. The earth of a field isn't cheap. Lots of times I've lain down and kissed the earth of a field, Amarantha. That's beauty, and a kiss for beauty." His breath moved up her cheek. He trembled violently. "No, no, not yet!" He got to his knees and pulled her by an arm. "We can go now."

They went back down the slope, but at an angle, so that when they came to the level they passed two hundred yards to the north of the house, and crossed the road there. More and more her walking was like sleepwalking, the feet numb in their shoes. Even where he had to let go of her, crossing the creek on stones, she stepped where he stepped with an obtuse docility. The voices of the searchers on the back ridge were small in distance when they began to climb the face of Coward Hill, on the opposite side of the valley.

There is an old farm on top of Coward Hill, big hayfields as flat as tables. It had been half past nine when Mare stood on the rock above the barn; it was toward midnight when Humble Jewett put aside the last branches of the woods and led her out on the height, and half a moon had risen. And a wind blew there, tossing the withered tops of last year's grasses, and mists ran with the wind, and ragged shadows with the mists, and mares'-tails of clear moonlight among the shadows, so that now the boles of birches on the forest's edge beyond the fences were but opal blurs and now cut alabaster. It struck so cold against the girl's cold flesh, this wind, that another wind of shivers blew through her, and she put her hands over her face and eyes. But the madman stood with his eyes wide open and his mouth open, drinking the moonlight and the wet wind.

His voice, when he spoke at last, was thick in his throat.

"Get down on your knees." He got down on his and pulled her after. "And pray!"

Once in England a poet sang four lines. Four hundred years have forgotten his name, but they have remembered his lines. The daft man knelt upright, his face raised to the wild scud, his long wrists hanging to the dead grass. He began simply:

"O western wind, when wilt thou blow
That the small rain down can rain?"

The Adam's apple was big in his bent throat. As simply he finished:

"Christ, that my love were in my arms
And I in my bed again!"

Mare got up and ran. She ran without aim or feeling in the power of the wind. She told herself again that the mists would hide her from him, as she had done at dusk. And again, seeing that he ran at her shoulder, she knew he had been there all the while, making a race for it, flailing the air with his long arms for joy of play in the cloud of spring, throwing his knees high, leaping the moon-blue waves of the brown grass, shaking his bright hair; and her own hair was a weight behind her, lying level on the wind. Once a shape went bounding ahead of them for instants; she did not realize it was a fox till it was gone.

She never thought of stopping; she never thought anything, except once, "O my God, I wish I had my shoes off!" And what would have been the good in stopping or in turning another way, when it was only play? The man's ecstasy magnified his strength. When a snake fence came at them he took the top rail in flight, like a college hurdler and, seeing the girl hesitate and half turn as if to flee, he would have releaped it without touching a hand. But then she got a loom of buildings, climbed over quickly, before he should jump, and ran along the lane that ran with the fence.

Mare had never been up there, but she knew that the farm and the house belonged to a man named Wyker, a kind of cousin of Ruby Herter's, a violent, bearded old fellow who lived by himself. She could not believe her luck. When she had run half the distance and Jewett had not grabbed her, doubt grabbed her instead. "O my God, go careful!" she told herself. "Go slow!" she implored herself, and stopped running, to walk.

Here was a misgiving the deeper in that it touched her special knowledge. She had never known an animal so far gone that its instincts failed it; a starving rat will scent the trap sooner than a fed one. Yet, after one glance at the house they approached, Jewett paid it no further attention, but walked with his eyes to the right, where the cloud had blown away, and wooded ridges, like black waves rimed with silver, ran down away toward the Valley of Virginia.

"I've never lived!" In his single cry there were two things, beatitude and pain.

Between the bigness of the falling world and his eyes the flag of her hair blew. He reached out and let it whip between his fingers. Mare was afraid it would break the spell then, and he would stop looking away and look at the house again. So she did something almost incredible; she spoke.

"It's a pretty—I mean—a beautiful view down that-a-way."

"God Almighty beautiful, to take your breath away. I knew I'd never loved, Belovèd——" He caught a foot under the long end of one of the boards that covered the well and went down heavily on his hands and knees. It seemed to make no difference. "But I never knew I'd never lived," he finished in the same tone of strong rapture, quadruped in the grass, while Mare ran for the door and grabbed the latch.

When the latch would not give, she lost what little sense she had. She pounded with her fists. She cried with all her might: "Oh—hey—in—there—hey—in there!" Then Jewett came and took her gently between his hands and drew her away, and then, though she was free, she stood in something like an awful embarrassment while he tried shouting.

"Hey! Friend! Whoever you are, wake up and let my love and me come in!"

"No!" wailed the girl.

He grew peremptory. "Hey, wake up!" He tried the latch. He passed to full fury in a wink's time; he cursed, he kicked, he beat the door till Mare thought he would break his hands. Withdrawing, he ran at it with his shoulder; it burst at the latch, went slamming in, and left a black emptiness. His anger dissolved in a big laugh. Turning in time to catch her by a wrist, he cried joyously, "Come, my Sweet One!"

"No! No! Please—aw—listen. There ain't nobody there. He ain't to home. It wouldn't be right to go in anybody's house if they wasn't to home, you know that."

His laugh was blither than ever. He caught her high in his arms.

"I'd do the same by his love and him if 'twas my house, I would." At the threshold he paused and thought, "That is, if she was the true love of his heart forever."

The room was the parlor. Moonlight slanted in at the door, and another shaft came through a window and fell across a sofa, its covering dilapidated, showing its wadding in places. The air was sour, but both of them were farm-bred.

"Don't, Amarantha!" His words were pleading in her ear. "Don't be so frightened."

He set her down on the sofa. As his hands let go of her they were shaking.

"But look, I'm frightened too." He knelt on the floor before her, reached out his hands, withdrew them. "See, I'm afraid to touch you." He mused, his eyes rounded. "Of all the ugly things there are, fear is the ugliest. And yet, see, it can be the very beautifulest. That's a strange, queer thing."

The wind blew in and out of the room, bringing the thin, little bitter sweetness of new April at night. The moonlight that came across Mare's shoulders fell full upon his face, but hers it left dark, ringed by the aureole of her disordered hair.

"Why do you wear a halo, Love?" He thought about it. "Because you're an angel, is that why?" The swift, untempered logic of the mad led him to dismay. His hands came flying to hers, to make sure they were of earth; and he touched her breast, her shoulders, and her hair. Peace returned to his eyes as his fingers twined among the strands.

"*Thy hair is as a flock of goats that appear from Gilead . . .*" He spoke like a man dreaming. "*Thy temples are like a piece of pomegranate within thy locks.*"

Mare never knew that he could not see her for the moonlight.

"Do you remember, Love?"

She dared not shake her head under his hand. "Yeh, I reckon," she temporized.

"You remember how I sat at your feet, long ago, like this, and made up a song? And all the poets in all the world have never made one to touch it, have they, Love?"

"Ugh-ugh—never."

"*How beautiful are thy feet with shoes* . . . Remember?"

"O my God, what's he sayin' now?" she wailed to herself.

"*How beautiful are thy feet with shoes, O prince's daughter! the joints of thy thighs are like jewels, the work of the hands of a cunning workman.*
Thy navel is like a round goblet, which wanteth not liquor; thy belly is like an heap of wheat set about with lilies.
Thy two breasts are like two young roes that are twins."

Mare had not been to church since she was a little girl, when her mother's black dress wore out. "No, no!" she wailed under her breath. "You're awful to say such awful things." She might have shouted it; nothing could have shaken the man now, rapt in the immortal, passionate periods of Solomon's song:

" . . . *now also thy breasts shall be as clusters of the vine, and the smell of thy nose like apples.*"

Hotness touched Mare's face for the first time. "Aw, no, don't talk so!"

"*And the roof of thy mouth like the best wine for my belovèd . . . causing the lips of them that are asleep to speak.*"

He had ended. His expression changed. Ecstasy gave place to anger, love to hate. And Mare felt the change in the weight of the fingers in her hair.

"What do you mean, I mustn't say it like that?" But it was not to her his fury spoke, for he answered himself straightway. "Like poetry, Mr. Jewett; I won't have blasphemy around my school."

"Poetry! My God! If that isn't poetry—if that isn't music——" . . . "It's Bible, Jewett. What you're paid to teach here is *literature*."

"Dr. Ryeworth, you're the blasphemer and you're an ignorant

man." . . . "And your principal. And I won't have you going around reading sacred allegory like earthly love."

"Ryeworth, you're an old man, a dull man, a dirty man, and you'd be better dead."

Jewett's hands had slid down from Mare's head. "Then I went to put my fingers around his throat, so. But my stomach turned, and I didn't do it. I went to my room. I laughed all the way to my room. I sat in my room at my table and I laughed. I laughed all afternoon and long after dark came. And then, about ten, somebody came and stood beside me in my room.

" 'Wherefore dost thou laugh, son?'

"I didn't laugh any more. He didn't say any more. I kneeled down, bowed my head.

" 'Thy will be done! Where is he, Lord?'

" 'Over at the girls' dormitory, waiting for Blossom Sinckley.'

"Brassy Blossom, dirty Blossom . . ."

It had come so suddenly it was nearly too late. Mare tore at his hands with hers, tried with all her strength to pull her neck away.

"Filthy Blossom! And him an old filthy man, Blossom! And you'll find him in hell when you reach there, Blossom . . ."

It was more the nearness of his face than the hurt of his hands that gave her power of fright to choke out three words.

"*I—ain't—Blossom!*"

Light ran in crooked veins. Through the veins she saw his face bewildered. His hands loosened. One fell down and hung; the other he lifted and put over his eyes, took it away again and looked at her.

"Amarantha!" His remorse was fearful to see. "What have I done!" His hands returned to hover over the hurts, ravening with pity, grief, and tenderness. Tears fell down his cheeks. And with that, dammed desire broke its dam.

"Amarantha, my love, my dove, my beautiful love——"

"*And I ain't Amarantha neither, I'm Mary! Mary, that's my name!*"

She had no notion what she had done. He was like a crystal crucible that a chemist watches, changing hue in a wink with one adeptly added drop; but hers was not the chemist's eye. All she knew was that she felt light and free of him; all she could see of his face as he stood away above the moonlight were the whites of his eyes.

"Mary!" he muttered. A slight paroxysm shook his frame. So in the transparent crucible desire changed its hue. He retreated farther, stood in the dark by some tall piece of furniture. And still she could see the whites of his eyes.

"Mary! Mary Adorable!" A wonder was in him. "Mother of God!"

Mare held her breath. She eyed the door, but it was too far. And already he came back to go on his knees before her, his shoulders so bowed and his face so lifted that it must have cracked his neck, she thought; all she could see on the face was pain.

"Mary Mother, I'm sick to my death. I'm so tired."

She had seen a dog like that, one she had loosed from a trap after it had been there three days, its caught leg half gnawed free. Something about the eyes.

"Mary Mother, take me in your arms . . ."

Once again her muscles tightened. But he made no move.

" . . . and give me sleep."

No, they were worse than the dog's eyes.

"Sleep, sleep! Why won't they let me sleep? Haven't I done it all yet, Mother? Haven't I washed them yet of all their sins? I've drunk the cup that was given me; is there another? They've mocked me and reviled me, broken my brow with thorns and my hands with nails, and I've forgiven them, for they knew not what they did. Can't I go to sleep now, Mother?"

Mare could not have said why, but now she was more frightened than she had ever been. Her hands lay heavy on her knees, side by side, and she could not take them away when he bowed his head and rested his face upon them.

After a moment he said one thing more. "Take me down gently when you take me from the Tree."

Gradually the weight of his body came against her shins, and he slept.

The moon streak that entered by the eastern window crept north across the floor, thinner and thinner; the one that fell through the southern doorway traveled east and grew fat. For a while Mare's feet pained her terribly and her legs, too. She dared not move them, though, and by and by they did not hurt so much.

A dozen times, moving her head slowly on her neck, she canvassed the shadows of the room for a weapon. Each time her eyes came back to a heavy earthenware pitcher on a stand some feet to the left of the sofa. It would have had flowers in it when Wyker's wife was alive; probably it had not been moved from its dust ring since she died. It would be a long grab, perhaps too long; still, it might be done if she had her hands.

To get her hands from under the sleeper's head was the task she set herself. She pulled first one, then the other, infinitesimally. She waited. Again she tugged a very, very little. The order of his breathing was not disturbed. But at the third trial he stirred.

"Gently! Gently!" His own muttering waked him more. With some drowsy instinct of possession he threw one hand across her wrists, pinning them together between thumb and fingers. She kept dead quiet, shut her eyes, lengthened her breathing, as if she too slept.

There came a time when what was pretense grew a peril; strange as it was, she had to fight to keep her eyes open. She never knew whether or not she really napped. But something changed in the air, and she was wide awake again. The moonlight was fading on the doorsill, and the light that runs before dawn waxed in the window behind her head.

And then she heard a voice in the distance, lifted in maundering song. It was old man Wyker coming home after a night, and it was plain he had had some whisky.

Now a new terror laid hold of Mare.

"Shut up, you fool you!" she wanted to shout. "Come quiet, quiet!" She might have chanced it now to throw the sleeper away from her and scramble and run, had his powers of strength and quickness not taken her simple imagination utterly in thrall.

Happily the singing stopped. What had occurred was that the farmer had espied the open door and, even befuddled as he was, wanted to know more about it quietly. He was so quiet that Mare began to fear he had gone away. He had the squirrel hunter's foot, and the first she knew of him was when she looked and saw his head in the doorway, his hard, soiled whiskery face half upside down with craning.

He had been to the town. Between drinks he had wandered in and out of the night's excitement; had even gone a short distance with one search party himself. Now he took in the situation in the room. He used his forefinger. First he held it to his lips. Next he pointed it with a jabbing motion at the sleeper. Then he tapped his own forehead and described wheels. Lastly, with his whole hand, he made pushing gestures, for Mare to wait. Then he vanished as silently as he had appeared.

The minutes dragged. The light in the east strengthened and turned rosy. Once she thought she heard a board creaking in another part of the house, and looked down sharply to see if the loony stirred. All she could see of his face was a temple with freckles on it and the sharp ridge of a cheekbone, but even from so little she knew how deeply and peacefully he slept. The door darkened. Wyker was there again. In one hand he carried something heavy; with the other he beckoned.

"Come jumpin'!" he said out loud.

Mare went jumping, but her cramped legs threw her down half-way to the sill; the rest of the distance she rolled and crawled. Just as she tumbled through the door it seemed as if the world had come to an end above her; two barrels of a shotgun discharged into a room make a noise. Afterwards all she could hear in there was something twisting and bumping on the floor boards. She got up and ran.

Mare's mother had gone to pieces; neighbor women put her to bed when Mare came home. They wanted to put Mare to bed, but she would not let them. She sat on the edge of her bed in her lean-to bedroom off the kitchen, just as she was, her hair down all over her shoulders and her shoes on, and stared away from them, at a place in the wallpaper.

"Yeh, I'll go myself. Lea' me be!"

The women exchanged quick glances, thinned their lips, and left her be. "God knows," was all they would answer to the questionings of those that had not gone in, "but she's gettin' herself to bed."

When the doctor came through he found her sitting just as she had been, still dressed, her hair down on her shoulders and her shoes on.

"What d' y' want?" she muttered and stared at the place in the wallpaper.

How could Doc Paradise say, when he did not know himself?

"I didn't know if you might be—might be feeling very smart, Mary."

"I'm all right. Lea' me be."

It was a heavy responsibility. Doc shouldered it. "No, it's all right," he said to the men in the road. Ruby Herter stood a little apart, chewing sullenly and looking another way. Doc raised his voice to make certain it carried. "Nope, nothing."

Ruby's ears got red, and he clamped his jaws. He knew he ought to go in and see Mare, but he was not going to do it while everybody hung around waiting to see if he would. A mule tied near him reached out and mouthed his sleeve in idle innocence; he wheeled and banged a fist against the side of the animal's head.

"Well, what d' y' aim to do 'bout it?" he challenged its owner.

He looked at the sun then. It was ten in the morning. "Hell, I got work!" he flared, and set off down the road for home. Doc looked at Judge North, and the judge started after Ruby. But Ruby shook his head angrily. "Lea' me be!" He went on, and the judge came back.

It got to be eleven and then noon. People began to say, "Like enough she'd be as thankful if the whole neighborhood wasn't camped here." But none went away.

As a matter of fact they were no bother to the girl. She never saw them. The only move she made was to bend her ankles over and rest her feet on edge; her shoes hurt terribly and her feet knew it, though she did not. She sat all the while staring at that one figure in the wall-paper, and she never saw the figure.

Strange as the night had been, this day was stranger. Fright and physical pain are perishable things once they are gone. But while pain merely dulls and telescopes in memory and remains diluted pain, terror looked back upon has nothing of terror left. A gambling chance taken, at no matter what odds, and won was a sure thing since the world's beginning; perils come through safely were never perilous. But what fright does do in retrospect is this—it heightens each sensuous recollection, like a hard, clear lacquer laid on wood, bringing out the color and grain of it vividly.

Last night Mare had lain stupid with fear on ground pine beneath a bush, loud footfalls and light whispers confused in her ear. Only now, in her room, did she smell the ground pine.

Only now did the conscious part of her brain begin to make words of the whispering.

"*Amarantha*," she remembered, "*Amarantha sweet and fair.*" That was as far as she could go for the moment, except that the rhyme with "fair" was "hair." But then a puzzle, held in abeyance, brought other words. She wondered what "ravel Ed" could mean.

"*Most excellently ravellèd.*" It was left to her mother to bring the end.

They gave up trying to keep her mother out at last. The poor woman's prostration took the form of fussiness.

"Good gracious, daughter, you look a sight. Them new shoes, half ruined; ain't your feet *dead?* And look at your hair, all tangled like a wild one!"

She got a comb.

"Be quiet, daughter; what's ailin' you? Don't shake your head!"

"*But shake your head and scatter day.*"

"What you say, Amarantha?" Mrs. Doggett held an ear down.

"Go 'way! Lea' me be!"

Her mother was hurt and left. And Mare ran, as she stared at the wallpaper.

"*Christ, that my love were in my arms . . .*"

Mare ran. She ran through a wind white with moonlight and wet with "the small rain." And the wind she ran through, it ran through her, and made her shiver as she ran. And the man beside her leaped high over the waves of the dead grasses and gathered the wind in his arms, and her hair was heavy and his was tossing, and a little fox ran before them in waves of black and silver, more immense than she had ever known the world could be, and more beautiful.

"*God Almighty beautiful, to take your breath away!*"

Mare wondered, and she was not used to wondering. "Is it only crazy folks ever run like that and talk that way?"

She no longer ran; she walked; for her breath was gone. And there was some other reason, some other reason. Oh yes, it was because her feet were hurting her. So, at last, and roundabout, her shoes had made contact with her brain.

Bending over the side of the bed, she loosened one of them mechanically. She pulled it half off. But then she looked down at it sharply, and she pulled it on again.

"*How beautiful . . .*"

Color overspread her face in a slow wave.

"*How beautiful are thy feet with shoes . . .*"

"Is it only crazy folks ever say such things?"

"*O prince's daughter!*"

"Call you that?"

By and by there was a knock at the door. It opened, and Ruby Herter came in.

"Hello, Mare old girl!" His face was red. He scowled and kicked at the floor. "I'd-a been over sooner, except we got a mule down sick." He looked at his dumb betrothed. "Come on, cheer up, forget it! He won't scare you no more, not that boy, not what's left o' him. What you lookin' at, sourface? Ain't you glad to see me?"

Mare quit looking at the wallpaper and looked at the floor.

"Yeh," she said.

"That's more like it, babe." He came and sat beside her; reached down behind her and gave her a spank. "Come on, give us a kiss, babe!" He wiped his mouth on his jumper sleeve, a good farmer's sleeve, spotted with milking. He put his hands on her; he was used to handling animals. "Hey, you, warm up a little; reckon I'm goin' to do all the lovin'?"

"Ruby, lea' me be!"

"What!"

She was up, twisting. He was up, purple.

"What's ailin' of you, Mare? What you bawlin' about?"

"Nothin'–only go 'way!"

She pushed him to the door and through it with all her strength, and closed it in his face, and stood with her weight against it, crying, "Go 'way! Go 'way! Lea' me be!"

*"Can't Cross Jordan by Myself"**

THERE ARE GHOSTS IN CHARLESTON. At certain hours on some nights on the dwindling peninsula between the Ashley and the Cooper it seems as if there were more of the dead than of the living afoot. Doubt as you can, you can't doubt some of them. You can't doubt the one that, at the hour of the rising of the moon on the first night of its final quarter, hangs by its neck from the Hanging Tree. There's too much evidence. They would never have left that solitary obstacle of a live oak to rear its gray bole in the very center of the pavement of Ashley Avenue all these years if there hadn't been *something*.

The conscientiousness of that "haunt," by the calendar, is its most impressive quality. There are few of us nowadays who know on what date of the month the half-moon comes up at midnight, for few of us ever really see the moon. That sort of spectral punctuality was to be expected in the days when the Tree was still one of the twelve in the short oak avenue leading in to the stately mansion known as "Indigo Landing," and when the rise of the midnight moon, silvering open reedlands and the further river, marked a moment for weirdness, fit for spirit doings. But now that the town is grown thick along that thoroughfare, and the midnight can no longer see the moon for the glows spread out from drugstore and filling stations and the headlights of automobiles wheeling from moment to moment over the trunk of that inconvenient and even dangerous oak, the fact that the shade of the hanged man can still manage to swing in noisy air there under city-bitten leaves (and so have been glimpsed through dazzled windshields by at least three drivers, who thereupon piled up their cars against the dire tree) argues a strength of spectral character beyond the common run.

Indigo Landing, the house, is not to be seen from the Avenue now. In the steep perspective even its tallest relic chimneys are hidden by the screen of early gingerbread and late stucco residences that have come in between. It is still there, however, and it can be reached through an alley at the north side of the Caroilco Service Station, on the corner of which, in fact, they have allowed Joanna to tack a modest business card, "Readings and Séances; Lost Articles Found." For to so low an estate had come in her lean age the one-time Secretary of the South Carolina Spiritist Circle, old Legare's "damn-Yankee" daughter-in-law, Joanna of Hartford—and to so paltry a business the still leaner shade of her famous "control," the Hindoo mystic, Bhundi Ras.

When Judge Legare was alive, forty-odd years ago, when Joanna held one of her "damn-fool table-tapping flimflams" in the house, he got out of it. Another man might have been futilely disagreeable about it. Seeing it was not only his home, but the home of the gentlemen of his blood for five generations gone, he might have been forgiven for flying into a Carolinian temper with the white-trash upstart and psychic carpetbagger that Joanna must have seemed to him. In his younger days he would have. But now, turned in upon himself, first by the marriage and then by the demise of his only son (whom, since the Judge was a stalwart atheist, he had no hope of remeeting in a Beyond, and of upbraiding, as he would have upbraided him, with a ferocious gentleness)—now Percy Legare did neither of these things. Now, on such evenings as Joanna's coterie gathered in the drawing room to scare each other with their silly slates and bells, if the aging rice planter sighed as he beat his retreat out to the twilit peace beneath his scuppernong vine in the rear, it was not in bitterness. It was a sigh compounded rather of the sardonic commiseration of the clear-eyed for the blind that lead the blind, and of relief at having to talk with, instead, two human beings as solid-on-earth, as richly sympathetic, and as comparatively aristocratic as old Sam, the coachman-gardener-butler of these lean days, and his sister, Venus, the cook.

Sole survivors of the Legare servant body of slavery times, they were pulled two ways in their minds. The fiercer, of course, was toward indignation.

"How-come Mis' Joanna do t'ink dis house *she* house?" Sam would protest with the license of one born into the family. "Wha'-foh you do allow that Yankee-woman dribe you out you-own gentleman family house—wid dem sperrit an' t'ing?"

The Judge would smile then his patient, clear-eyed smile. "You ignorant black swamp-nigger, how many times have I told you there *are* no such things as spirits?"

"You mean tell me, suh, dey no sperrit, nor-so no ha'nt, nor no plat-eye or t'ing?"

Now Venus would come in, torn between loyalty and the fearful and obvious fact.

"How-come you too nerbous stay inside de house den, Maussa, night when Mis' Joanna do call de sperrit up?" And before the master could even snort in protest, her ear cocked in terror toward the windows through which the fearful sounds came seeping, the Negress hurried on: "Hear dem ha'nt do holler now. Dat one wid de crack voice, Maussa—Do-Jedus!"

"You know who dat one, suh?" Sam would shiver. "Dat one de Indy sperrit, call um Bhundi Ras, an' he bound obliged do Mis' Joanna's biddin' ober yonduh in tudduh world."

"Hocus-pocus, Sam. There's only one world, the one you're standing in."

"Oh, Maussa! I'd t'ink you frighten sometime Gawd hear you say dat an' strike you dead. What-fashion you gwine git across de Jordan, suh, ef you say such a t'ing?"

Then Venus, feeling the strain, would make haste to turn the conversation into a safer channel.

"*She*," she would mutter, glooming toward the house, "she t'ink she know eberyt'ing, but she don' know eberyt'ing."

They hated Joanna, these two. Why they had never left an employ where they must take orders from such a woman may seem strange. As a matter of fact, though they had been free under the law to do so for twenty years, they had never actually realized it. Nor were they apt to, so long as "Maussa Percy" remained alive. Their own mother had been his "Mauma," and though other niggers might think they could go gallivanting around like poor swamp trash if they cared to, Sam and Venus were not of that kind.

It was unfortunate that Joanna was too Yankee-ignorant to appreciate this Negro reasoning. In the end it was worse than unfortunate; it was catastrophic.

The Judge had been away a few days, visiting his cousin James in Walterboro. The evening of his return was the evening the Spiritist Circle had chosen to hold its weekly "flimflam" at Indigo Landing, and the dusk out back was chill for old bones with the coming of November.

The moment he came into the yard, Percy Legare knew something was wrong, by the dismal note in Venus's singing. What chewing gum is to the modern young woman, their "spirituals" were to Carolina servants. These folk hymns Venus was accustomed to roll between her gums with an enthusiasm that robbed them of all their inherent mournfulness. But tonight there was mournfulness in plenty, where the black woman rocked on the sill of the "slave house."

> *"By myse'f–by myse'f–*
> *Sometime my trouble make me trimble–trimble–trimble,*
> *An' I can't cross Jordan by myse'f. . . ."*

The Judge challenged her. "What's wrong, Venus?" A premonition made a hollow around his heart. "Where's *Sam?* Stop that yowling straight away, and tell me!"

Venus stopped and told him. The pent-up grief and panic of days came pouring out.

The Judge was aghast. "You mean to tell me my daughter-in-law has *turned Sam off?*"

"Yes-suh, gib um he *dis*cha'ge, wha' she say. Tell um he good-foh-nottin', *git.*"

"And he went? But–where?"

"Dat what I say–wheh? Dat poor old ign'unt nigguh, wheh *he* know to go? Mos'-like he got run obuh in de street, or-so he starve to deat', or drownded in de ribbuh. Oh! Oh!"

"Hush up, you black baboon! Do you want me to give you a caning?"

Venus, comforted, moderated her sobbing. The master was "mixed up in his mind," and that was a step in the right direction. As a matter of fact, the Judge was stunned.

"Now this," he muttered, "is too much. I've tried to be patient. But *this*––"

Now that he was angry he was so angry that his old knees shook beneath him. He couldn't march into the house, remonstrant, that way, with knocking legs, and decided that a dram or two would do him no harm. So he started in the opposite direction, out back.

Venus's wail was sharp with new alarm. "Wheh you gwine? You ain't gwine in dat-yah *smokehouse*, wid all dem ha'nt an' hag an' t'ing—*in de dark*—for Lawd Jedus' sake!"

"I am not a child," the Judge growled over his shoulder.

It was true that the floor of the abandoned wreck of a smokehouse out there was unsafe, and the walls so near collapse that any jar might bring one or more of the great rotten rafters crashing down. But now the fact that it was his daughter-in-law who had taken it upon herself not only to warn him, but substantially to *forbid* him (as if he were a child) to go near that "eyesore and deathtrap," only set him in his purpose.

He had been there before, by stealth; that was why he was going now. Joanna was not only a spiritist, but a militant teetotaler as well. The Judge might have continued to argue and quarrel, but essentially he hated haggling. So, instead, he had quietly removed his two-gallon keg of ripe corn whisky from the house cellar and concealed it, on the day he left for Walterboro, under a heap of rubbish in that last of all places where Joanna might be expected to go snooping, the smokehouse.

It was as dark as seven nights inside the rickety shell, but Percy Legare needed no light to guide him as he moved on soles as discreet as ghosts' across the precarious planking. He knew where the rubbish was, and found it with his hands. But then at the feel of it, not satisfactorily swollen, as by a keg, but all rifled and flat, an involuntary deep groan broke from his lips.

What happened then happened swiftly. A wind and screech, like a bat's fright overhead. A crack of timber. Something falling. A stunning concussion. Momentary stars. . . .

From the instant when Percy Legare picked himself up from the smokehouse floor, everything was queer. He wouldn't have known himself. A kind of comic terror; an enormity of panic. Where to go? Joanna? No! Of all human beings, not Joanna. In what seemed to him a perfectly silly way he thought of his nearest of blood kin, Cousin James. What was still sillier, no sooner had he thought of Cousin James than he was over the back wall and bound at a run for Walterboro, fifty miles away. But what was silliest of all, there he was, presently, hardly panting, in Walterboro, on Cousin James's steps.

When he had set his clothing a little straight and smoothed his small but well-trimmed imperial, he pulled at the bell rope several times. He had to go in finally, getting no response. Cousin James *was* napping, before the fire; but his pretty granddaughter, Vi, playing cribbage with her beau at the center table, should have heard the bell.

For all he could do, Percy Legare felt out of place and ill at ease. It showed in the way he rubbed his hands together and chuckled, when he felt so little like chuckling.

"Well, my good friends, you hardly expected to see me so—*James!*" he finished sharply.

The old gentleman in the easy chair twitched out of sleep and blinked around him.

"Here," the Judge directed him. "Right over here I am. Percy. Are you blind?" He appealed to Vi. "Is your grandfather blind, or—or what?"

The girl ignored not only his question but his very existence. "Fifteen-four," she counted on the board; then, to Cousin James: "Cold, Grandfather?"

"I thought I felt a draft," the old gentleman complained, his eyes as blank as a fish's, though they were fixed directly on his cousin where he stood. "I guess, though, it's just one of those—how do they say it?—someone stepping over my grave."

All this queerness was too much for Percy Legare; his mind mixed up and his heart heavy, he left the house and started back home. There was a great to-do there when he arrived; by the sound there must have been more people than were ever in the Spiritist Circle, milling around in the oak avenue out front. Too confused and too depressed to want to face them, he got in by the rear and up the back stairs; his bed was the one thing on earth he needed now. Of all the bad business, though, the worst was still in store. When he got into his bedroom, his cravat already half untied, he found it crowded with people, many of whom he did not even know. Red with confusion and resentment, he made haste to set his neck gear straight again; then he did the only thing a gentleman can do—he stood and stared at them, his brow knotted with interrogation.

Fiasco. No one paid him any attention. All they were interested in was the bed, his bed, and the figure of some stranger with a broken pate they had laid there without even asking his permission. Joanna, down on her knees, was shaking with fearful, angular sobs. Dr. Hatton of Calhoun Street, who had been bending over, unbent with an air of lugubrious finality to say: "I'm sorry, there's nothing to be done. The Judge's death must have been quite instantaneous."

Percy Legare felt a sudden hollowness under his midriff as he craned over the encircling shoulders to study the shape on the bed.

"Why–why, damn it!–it's *me!*"

He got out of the room. He wanted to be alone; wanted some solitude where he could sit down quietly and think this whole distracting business out at length. There was none to be had in this neighborhood; the crowd out front seemed to have increased rather than lessened, and with its numbers its turbulence. So, slipping out again by the river way, now by the light of a half-moon that had risen in the east, the poor fellow set his course in a bee line across St. Andrews Parish.

How far he went he had no way of estimating. It was probably in northern Georgia that he stumbled upon exactly the kind of an abandoned house he was looking for, set in the midst of weed-grown acres. His satisfaction was not to last long, however, for no sooner had he got himself settled down to cogitation in the great dank hall than footsteps on the stair behind him proved his mistake in imagining himself alone in the old mansion.

Confused to find himself even an innocent trespasser, he was doubly so when he perceived that the woman coming down the stair was a lady. She was good enough to accept his apologies graciously, however, and when he made to mend his mistake by leaving she bade him by a gesture not to go.

"I am lonely here," she said with a smile, half wistful, half preoccupied.

The Judge was troubled. She was far from old and very far from uncomely, and if there was a certain awkwardness about her carriage, it should not have been enough to bother him. But it did. It wouldn't let him be. And when, by edging around, he made the discovery that the slight obliquity of her bearing came from favoring an ugly-looking butcher knife whose handle obtruded from her back just under the left scapula, he was new enough in such things to be frankly uncomfortable.

The lady had marked the direction of his glance.

"I suppose you are wondering about—that."

"No—that is—no, no."

"I wonder if you would like to know the story of my——"

"I'm sorry, ma'am, I—I—some other time——"

The Judge was out of the front door by that, and hurrying on faster than ever, west.

He had always wanted to travel, but since the War between the States he had never got much farther than Beaufort, because of the expense. Even upset as he was in his mind now, to find himself crossing the Mississippi gave him a thrill. His first sight of the Rockies gave him another. A veteran of the Tennessee campaign, he had thought he knew mountains, but here were mountains. In a gulch in southern Colorado, beginning to tire a little, he took refuge in the timbered mouth of an abandoned prospect hole. Here again he found himself an intruder, and he would have apologized and left immediately, had the owner's way of trying to scare him off by groaning from the darker end of the tunnel not brought out an almost forgotten streak of Carolinian obstinacy.

And after all, when the fellow found that that did no good, he turned out to be an almost pathetically sociable sort. He had struck it rich in this hill, it seemed, after a lifetime of indifferent luck, but unfortunately in doing it he had starved to death, and he showed it in his cadaverous cheeks, weedy whiskers and rags, and possibly in the one bad habit he had, when interested or in the absence of mind, of eating off a thumb or one or two of his fingers. Otherwise, in the weeks the Judge spent with him at the mine, "Nebraska" Hillhouse proved an ideal companion, so far as his guest was concerned, spending most of his time at the far end of the drift, "in the vein," and so giving the Judge all the time he needed for thinking.

The trouble was that he couldn't seem to think. He could reason to a certain point, and there, by the very logic of the thing, he was balked. "There is no such thing in existence as a disembodied spirit, so I am certainly not a disembodied spirit. What then?"

Nebraska took him up on it one evening, when they were loafing at the mine entrance.

"If you ain't a ghost, then you must be one o' these here second-sighters that can see 'em, spiriters, I guess they call 'em. Otherwise you couldn't see hide nor hair o' *me*."

"*Spiritist! I?*"

"All right, then, Judge, no two ways, ghost you be." Mistaking silence for acceptance, after a moment of rumination in which he consumed all but one of the fingers on his right hand, the prospector went on. "What I can't see, Judge, I can't see what's holding you on earth all this while. With me, with this unregistered claim on my mind, it's one thing. But the way you tell me you've lived, you should've been over the river long ago."

"What river?"

"Why, you know, Judge." Nebraska had been reared in some minor Baptist faith. "Why, across the Jordan, like, to the Promised Land. If you was murdered now, and your murderer not found, that would be a horse of another color. But you wasn't, you say, murdered."

The Judge had to laugh.

"Or if you had a cache of something valuable somewheres about your place, or if there was somebody you should have forgive and didn't, I could understand your hankering to get back there so bad."

The Judge started, the wraith of a flush on his cheek. "What on earth ever put it into your head I'd want to go back *there?*"

"Well, if not exactly want to, feel kind of drawed-like. Eh?" The challenge in Nebraska's eyes was touched with sadness. "I been watching you lately, Judge." And though Percy Legare protested "Fiddlesticks!" he had to turn his own eyes away.

It was true, for some time past he had been aware of a deepening restlessness to be getting East again. He had tried to put it down to simple nostalgia (even with Joanna there), but it was not nostalgia. Nor mere curiosity. Nebraska had hit it; it was more nearly "feeling drawed-like"; and as such, Legare, the rationalist, resented it bitterly.

He was so self-conscious about it that when he capitulated a few nights later he refrained from awakening Nebraska, but leaving a note of good-by thanks tacked on one of the timbers, stole softly out of the gulch and set his face toward Carolina.

Indigo Landing was all quiet when he came in by the rear way, everybody apparently fast asleep. If this was so, Venus must have had a hair-raising dream, for as the Judge passed the "slave house" there burst out through the shuttered window a shriek so powerful that the mistress in the big house waked and called down to know what the matter was.

Percy Legare had not seen his daughter-in-law for a long while. In the bloodless moonlight up there, in the nightgown with the stiff ruching tight around its throat, all the unpleasant qualities of her character were brought back strongly. He felt a chill up his spine as her scrutiny came to where he stood, and sighed when it passed on, unseeing.

"Venus," she repeated, "*will* you open those blinds and tell me *what* is wrong with you!"

Venus did not open the blinds, but her yowlings grew coherent: "Do-Jedus! I hear um!"

"You hear *what?*"

"De Maussa, Maussa Percy, he foot out dah in de yard. Hear um go *tromp, tromp.*"

"Imbecile!" There was in it all the cold scorn of the professional for the amateur. "You and your haunts, you wicked, superstitious old ninny. You hush now, or I warn you!" Retiring, Joanna left the Negress to muffle her wails in her gunny-bag pillow.

The Judge, who had planned to go into the house and have a look around, thought better of it. With that miserable, inexplicable pull of the old home still on him, however, he found he couldn't go away. So, compromising, he shinnied up a drainpipe, got over the eaves, and climbed the slippery slates, intending to sit and rest awhile on the ridgepole.

But there in midroof he was given a start that nearly dislodged him. He had not expected to find another before him in that peaked solitude between the sleeping chimneys.

"Who are you?" he demanded. "And what the devil are you doing here?"

The figure, jackknifed in silhouette on the ridgepole, stared, gasped, and quavered.

"Do-Lawd-in-Hebben! Who dat do speak like my ol' Maussa?"

Astonishment, relief, and happiness sang in the Judge's heart, and moisture prickled his lids.

"*Sam,* you black hound! So it's *you!*"

"Yes-suh, yes-suh, yes-suh; but how-come? Do-Jedus, Maussa, *is you dead too?*"

Percy Legare was too full of joy to go into that now; as he

scrabbled on up, all he could say was: "You thieving old no-account! You miserable scoundrel!"

Tears of beatitude rolled down Sam's face. "Glory to Gawd! I *too* sorry you dead, Maussa. Only tell me dat t'ing, Maussa—how-*come* you dead?"

The Judge flushed. He was still touchy on the score of that fiasco of the smokehouse.

"Speak when you're spoken to! Now be good enough to tell me what under the sun it was that happened to *you?* Speak up!"

An enigmatical embarrassment whitened the old fellow's eyes. The Judge blew out his cheeks. "What's this? Why don't you answer? Sam, you double-faced baboon, what's that you're so anxious I sha'n't see—that thing you've got behind you?"

"Oh, Maussa . . ."

"Out with it!"

"Oh, Maussa!" The fellow's distress was pitiable as he withdrew from its concealment under his sitting portion a length of hempen rope with a noose improvised at its extremity.

"So!" The Judge pursed his lips and gathered his brows. "I've no doubt you deserved it richly. For what *particular* crime, may I ask, did they feel called upon to hang you?"

"I ain't know, suh. Oh, Maussa, beliebe me or not beliebe me, ever I ain't know one Gawd t'ing I do, foh git hang foh. One minute de white folks dey graff ol' Sam, an' nudder minute, *bamm,* dey string um on a tree limb. Angel Gab'rul know dat de Gawd-truth, suh."

"A likely one." The frown deepened. "Blockhead, didn't you know enough to tell them you belonged to the Legares? . . . Mmmm. . . . Throw that blasted thing away!" And when the wretched man had done so (only taking pains to mark with one eye where the rope caught in falling, behind a chimney)—"Now," the Judge said grimly, "let's talk about something else. I've never been up here before. It's astonishing, the view of James Island."

"Yes-suh, Maussa, 'deed-suh."

"The geese are flying late this year."

"Deed-suh, dey is, berry late dis——" But there the old darky interrupted himself. At sound of cart wheels creaking along the outer road he broke off to hearken. Then he stretched out his neck, opened his mouth impulsively, and gave a long, loud groan.

It made Percy Legare jump. He glared at the offender. But when he started to upbraid him, finding that when he opened *his* mouth nothing would seem to come out but a stentorian groaning of its own, he shut it again in dismay and fell into a cold perspiration. Not till the racket of the frightened teamster's flight had died in distance did he speak, and then it was in a small voice.

"Why did I do that?"

"Oh, but Maussa, excusin' me, a ghost bound *obliged* do dat, when he *ha'ntin'*."

The Judge never got over it. There was nothing he could have resented more. At times in the long night watches that followed upon that first one it depressed, at times it infuriated him. "Me, Percy Legare, *haunting!*" He tried to fight it. Squaring his shoulders sometimes, stiffening his spine: "I'm through with this puerile idiocy. Never another groan do they get out of me." But then at the very next footfall vagrant in the dark his good resolutions went to pieces and he fell.

He made a study of this wretched spectral impulse. He proved by experiment that it was quite spontaneous and uncontrollable, and that no personal animus against the passer-by need enter into it. One night it was Venus herself who had the ill fortune to venture out of doors at too late an hour. One was the brother, the other the lifelong master, guide, and friend; neither would have distressed the poor old Negress for anything in the world. In fact both of them were praying she might get back in the house before the last of their self-control was gone. But it was of no use. And when she had screeched to shelter, then half dead with terror of the grizzly salvo unloosed among the chimneys overhead, when the two up there looked at each other, the one face was drawn with remorse, and down the other poured a rain of tears.

The Judge struck down an angry fist. "Why, if we're bound to make public nuisances of ourselves around here—why in the name of human decency don't we-all clear out?"

"Yes-suh, yes-suh. But wheh-to, suh? You don't mean, Maussa—not across de Ribbuh?"

"Across the river, or anywhere. What's to hinder us, Sam?"

"Y-y-yes-suh." The air of nervous depression that the Judge had observed growing on his companion of late seemed to deepen. "Yes-suh—de only t'ing, Maussa, I bound oblige be back here tomorrow night by middlenight."

"Why?"

"Tomorrow night, suh, he de night o' de middlenight moon."

"Yes? What's *that* got to do with it?"

Sam had said too much already. He looked this way, he looked that. When the Judge began to question and berate him, to save himself he retreated down the further slope of the roof and scissored out to a lonely perch at the tip of the Blue Room gable, where the Judge heard him singing to himself for comfort Venus's favorite:

> "*. . . trimble, trimble, trimble,*
> *An' I can't cross Jordan by myse'f. . . .*"

Next night the Judge was prepared to give the truant a going over for that. And then he had to wait. His indignation grew with the hours, until, with the rise of the "middlenight moon," and no Sam yet, it gave place, first to anxiety, and then to a sense of his own aloneness and thoughts of despair. What could have happened to that nigger? He asked himself if it could be that Sam, hurt by last night's words, had gone away forever? By the time dawn grayed its warning in the east he was in so craven a state of despondency at the prospect of having to sit there twiddling his thumbs in solitude throughout the rest of eternity that when Sam did turn up again, all sound, the following evening, he was happy enough to let the whole thing go without comment.

The next time it happened, however (four weeks later), the Judge, being less agitated, was more put out. Between exasperation and curiosity he climbed down from the roof and poked about the grounds, and so it was, shortly after moonrise, that he came on the colored man hanging by his rope from one of the oak trees in the Avenue, his limbs dejected, his neck awry, and a look of patient suffering in his swollen eyes. The rice planter was taken sharply aback, and showed it in the acidity of his sarcasm.

"So this is where you're always running off to, Sam. It must be fun."

"No-suh." It was hard for Sam to talk, on account of the noose around his windpipe. "I don't like um, suh."

"May I inquire, then, what in the name of all asinine damn-foolishness——"

"Suh?"

"*What are you hanging there for?*"

"I ain't know, suh; dey ain't remembuh to told me. I respect I bound obliged to gwine on doin' dis-a-way on de middlenight moon till my sin forgibben."

"What sin?"

"Gawd, he know, Maussa. I *sutten* I don't."

"Either you're a liar or you're a numbskull, Sam; that's all I can say." Washing his hands of the whole ridiculous business, the Judge went back to his haunting on the roof.

It can be cold on winter nights, even as far south as the Carolinas. Both the Judge and Sam were well past their warm-blooded prime, and there were plenty of dark hours that January and February when their bones ached in the winds that ricocheted up the polished slates, and their teeth chattered. Sometimes it seemed to Percy Legare that spring was never to come, and when he let his mind dwell, in that mood, on eternity, he could see nothing but black. Sam was not so bad; in the way of his race he could never stay pessimistic long. "When we-all *is* allowed foh go 'cross de Ribbuh, suh," he prefaced so often that the Judge, who had started by squelching him, ended by simply sighing.

Spring did come eventually, of course. And with it on a warming night in March came a surprise, in the shape of an invasion. Joanna had recommenced her "flimflamming" of late and this was one of her evenings, solemn racketings filling the bottom of the house and leaking up the chimneys to add a salt of mockery to the venom of discomfiture already bitter enough in one old listener's heart. "Nobody but a damn-Yankee female would be so poison low——" the Judge was in the midst of assuring Sam when a scuttle in the roof not far from their feet was opened so unexpectedly, and a figure so strange came climbing out, that all they could do was sit and gape. It was rather a frail-built man of a dark complexion, with a large white turban on, and a robe of flimsy lilac cotton that kept catching on the corners of the uneven slates. Altogether he was so queer that the Judge, to hide the fact that he was startled, took the offensive.

"Who the devil are *you?*"

In place of answering, the other queried: "You are the late father-in-law, are you not?"

"I'm Judge Percy Legare, if that's what you mean. *Who the devil,* I repeat, *are you?*"

The stranger bowed slightly. "My name is Bhundi Ras, at your service, sir. I was the eldest son of a highly placed Brahmin family of Cawnpur, and held the post——" But there he broke off and waited with an urbane patience, on account of Sam, whose teeth had gone to chattering. "Do-Jedus! Oh-my-Gawd! De Indy-man, Maussa, he *him.*"

"Be quiet!" The Judge could have thrashed him. "And you," he reverted, his face crimson, "I don't care who or what you *were!* What I want to know is, what are you doing around *here* so free and easy, *now?*"

Bhundi Ras never lost his air of breeding. "The owner of this property, Mrs. Wallace Legare, who happens to be a–ah–client of mine, has asked if possible, sir, to be put in touch with you. Would you be good enough, I wonder, sir, to step down with me for only a very few moments, so that Mrs. Legare may have the happiness and comfort of hearing——"

"*I will not.*" It was almost a bellow.

"Sorry." The Indian mystic shrugged his slender shoulders and studied the slates. "I'm sure, sir, if you knew how much your daughter-in-law has desired, ever since your death——"

"Death? Bosh!" Now all the obstinate devil in Percy Legare was aroused. "I'm not dead by a damned sight, and you can go straight down there and tell Joanna so. I'm alive, you can tell her, and a great deal aliver than she is. And while you're at it——" The Judge had got up on his heels on the ridgepole, carried away by his own vindictive violence. "And while you're at it, sir, you can tell her, a deal of good I get, being alive around my own house. Tell her, for all the respect and sympathy and companionship I get, if it weren't for Sam here–poor, ignorant swamp nigger that he is——"

But the Brahmin, with a slight start, was withdrawing. "Sam!" he echoed. He stared at the hunched-up colored man above him. "Am I mistaken, then, in—— But there must be some mistake. Tell me, Judge Legare, had you perhaps another servant named Sam?"

"I had not. Why?"

Bhundi Ras got halfway down through the scuttle before resuming. Courageous in some ways, he was timid in others.

"I'm sorry, sir, but I am at a loss at finding this–this association of you two. Pardon me if I'm in error, but is this not the same Sam who –ah–in fact–murdered you?"

"Murdered! *Me! SAM!*"

There was something so menacing in that Gargantuan guffaw that the peace-loving Brahmin let the scuttle down over him with a bang and was gone.

For moments Percy Legare continued to heave and chuckle. "Did you hear that, Sam, you bloodthirsty ruffian? You jailbird! You *gallows-meat!* You—you—gallows-meat! . . ."

That last was airless. Lost in sudden thought, silence fell down upon the Judge. Little by little, as he stared out unseeing across the starlit reedlands and the further river, a horrid arithmetic began to busy his brain. The more he grew appalled, the oftener he put his swiftly clarifying twos and twos together, the heavier that silence lay. Once he hazarded a side glance at his companion, and at sight of Sam's round white eyes glued on him, fascinated, he got his own back quickly.

The most awful part of it was the embarrassment.

They sat and they sat and they sat, side by side. The stars dimmed. The east began to pale before the coming of the "middlenight moon," and for once neither of them knew it and neither cared. It was that embarrassment; that perfectly hideous mortification.

At last Percy Legare could stand it no longer. Self-consciousness made his voice sound cold.

"Sam, what's all this I hear?"

"Whu-whu-what all what you h-h-hear?"

"Sam, where were you on the evening I was—I had the accident—in the smokehouse?"

Now that it was said and done, Sam let go.

"Oh, *do*-Gawd! Oh! Oh! Maussa, was *dat you* in de smokehouse?"

"Stop blubbering. I was—yes—in the smokehouse."

"You *wasn't* a ha'nt or hag, den, gib a groan like dat?"

"How often must I tell you, Sam, that there are no such things as——" Coloring a little, the Judge recommenced: "Calm down. Go on. So you too were in the smokehouse? What, may I ask, were you doing there?"

"Do-Jedus, Maussa, Mis' Joanna done tu'n me out, an' I so lonesome I ain't know wheh-to I got foh go to. I binna walk out in de town, but I ain't easy in my mind. Nigger says: 'Who you?' Buckrah say: 'Moob-along!' So bime-by, Maussa——"

"You came back and hid in the smokehouse. Very well. But did that justify you in——"

"Oh, oh, oh, Maussa, foh Hebben sake—I nebbuh respect it am my Maussa. When I do hear dat foot come creepy in de dark, I respect he a sperrit, or-so a hag or plat-eye, do come foh graff ol' Sam, an' when I hear sucha monst'ous groan do groan, I tek a wood an' I hit um *blamm*, an' I tek my foot in my hand out o' dat place, an' I still do runnin' when de white-folks graff me an' pit a rope 'pon-top me an' hang me on de oak tree."

"So!"

There followed a silence.

"*So!*"

Then Sam's sobbing and wailing broke out: "Don't nebbuh forgib me, so-suh, nebbuh-suh. Eben ef I bound oblige hang on dat tree ebbuh an' forebbuh now, I wouldn't *aks* you ebbuh forgib me foh sucha Gawd-hebby sin I done. No-suh, no-suh, no-suh, Maussa."

"Hmmmm . . ."

"Yes-suh, yes-suh, dah come de middlenight moon do raise up now; bettuh I tek my ol' hang-rope an' go out to de oak tree; my sin too hebby foh ebbuh forgib, suh, ebbuh, *ebbuh*."

Percy Legare wet his lips.

"You good-for-nothing!"

The sense of well-being in his throat grew richer.

"You monkey-faced, flea-brained blunderer!"

He took his time. Like a gourmet, he savored it.

"You crocodile!"

"Oh, Maussa! Oh—Maussa!" Sam began to rise on the ridgepole, teetering, incredulous.

"You poor, ignorant, misbegotten—I don't know what!"

Sam's face was transfigured. He had believed his ears at last.

"Maussa, you *done* forgib me."

"*Good-for-nothing!*"

"Glory-Gawd! I *nebbuh* aks um, an' my Maussa done-*done* forgib me, an' *my soul set free!*"

Percy Legare had no soul; nevertheless he began to feel very queer. Something like a balloon when the tether lines are being loosened. As for Sam, he was another person. He was actually prancing on the roof peak, between impatience and beatitude.

"Glory-Jedus, we-all set free, free, free, an' we-all don't oblige ha'nt dis-yuh place no more, Maussa, nebbuh more. Mek-haste, Maussa Percy, mek-haste an' do come."

The master was too mixed up in his mind to do anything but follow the man down. There was a short stay in the back yard, while Sam sneaked into the "slave house" and out again with a roll of something white under his arm.

"What's that?" the Judge demanded, a little crabbedly, but Sam had no time for it. "Glory, glory!" seemed to be all he could say as he got over the brick wall at the end of the yard and set off across the marshland toward the river, excitement heightening his steps. It was all the Judge could do to keep anywhere near up with him.

The moon had risen, and the night grew diamond-clear. When Sam got to the riverbank he halted and unrolled the thing he had under his arm, and the Judge perceived that it was a best nightshirt, long and clean. The darky put it on and smoothed it down, but then, recollecting something, rehoisted it to unwind from around his waist the dismal rope his shame had led him to wear there, concealed beneath his coat. With a whoop, a grin, and a chuckle, he threw it away on the ground.

But then his eyes, falling on his master, clouded.

"Why–why, Maussa, wheh is yoh snow-white gahment? Why you nebbuh fotch um along?"

"Do you mean my nightshirt? Why should I?"

"More-manners hab a white gahment on, when you do come foh cross de Ribbuh, suh."

"Never heard of such a crazy thing. Wear a nightshirt to cross the Ashley River?"

"Ohhh, *Maussa!*" Sam's eyes were whiter than the shirt. "Ain't you know de Jordan Ribbuh when you *see um?*"

"Jordan my hat! Why, Sam, you driveling idiot!"

There was an emphasis of assurance about it that gave the Negro a momentary catch of doubt. Was he, could he be, wrong? But when he had wheeled and studied the tranquil flood for a wink, he had to shake a sadly puzzled head.

"Sho', Maussa, you only do try foh plague ol' Sam. . . . *Ashley* ain't hab no Hebben City todder-side um, same like dat-yah one obuh dah. Look-a-dah, suh, wheh de wall o' al'baster an' t'ing do h'ist umself up, an' de monst'ous pearly gate, *spang* before yoh-own two eye dah yonduh, an' de gold street inside-um, and Peter do shine up he key an' wave he wing. . . . Do-Gawd, Maussa Percy–you lookin' wheh I lookin'?"

Percy Legare, feeling foolish, stared in the line of Sam's pointing finger.

"Sam, you've been at my liquor again." A crease deepened between his brows. "There's the wood piece over there on the St. Andrews bank where the big bird coveys used to lay, and then the three water oaks at the end toward Old Town Creek, and the marsh where we kept the duck boat, and there's the chimney of the Plum house——"

"Ohhh, *Maussa!*"

The incredulity, the pity and reproach of it, were too much for Percy Legare. All he could do was blow out purpling cheeks, clench his fists, and stare about him hopelessly for some rational help. It was so that he discovered that he and Sam were no longer alone on the margin of the stream. There had been a little arrival of colored people, with one scrawny white woman of the swamp-cracker type among them, and now they were excitedly busy in putting white raiment on. To these he appealed.

The nearest darky touched his forelock decently. "Ashley Ribbuh, suh? Sutten I do know Ashley Ribbuh, spang near Charleston in de state ob Ca'lina. . . . No-suh, Maussa, dis-yuh ribbuh de *Jordan* Ribbuh; ain't you know dat when you see de Hebben City todduh side?"

There was the white one, the cracker woman, as a last resort. But the Judge was too late; already she was rods out from shore, wading to her knees in the brown current. Now they were all in, with a joyful splashing. All but Sam. Like a leashed old hunting dog he trembled as his gaze followed after them, great tears welling between his lids.

The Judge could have slain him.

"Get along with you; go drown yourself with the kit of them, if that's any pleasure."

"Oh, Maussa, suh—you gwine come too?"

"Thank you, no. Quit squirming and blubbering, and *go*. Do you hear me?"

"But M-M-Maussa, what-fashion you gwine git along widout ol' Sam? If I do *do* cross Jordan by myse'f, what you gwine do foh somebody look out foh you, Maussa Percy?"

"Hmmmph!"

The old African wet one foot, then both, in the flood. Sobbing aloud then between grief and glory, he started floundering after the diminishing waders.

Percy Legare stood and watched him for a moment, a white wraith against the dark pediment of—yes, damn it!—of St. Andrews woods. For a flash he was conscious of being tempted; insidious, seductive doubt. "When ignorance is bliss . . ." If he could have been so fortunately credulous—— No; *ignoble* doubt! Putting it behind him, he turned and strode back, stiff-spined, toward Indigo Landing.

The low moon was behind the house, and its rays, thinly penciling the peaks and chimney edges, gave it a look of infestivity beyond any it had ever worn before. No matter. The Judge stuck his hands deeper in his pockets and began to do something he hadn't done since youth—he began to whistle to himself a sprightly tune.

"No-*sir!*" he broke off to growl, at sound of an appealing "*Maussa!*" trailing after him from the direction of the river. "Never!" He tramped fiercely on.

But then, when nearly to the wall of his property, he *had* to turn around.

"What," he gasped, trying his best to frown, "what are you doing *here?*"

The panting darky stood there, abashed eyes on his toes.

"Dat—uh—dat Ashley Ribbuh water, suh, he cold my foot too-much."

"Liar! What's that you've got behind you? Out with it!"

"Do-suh, he nuttin only dis-yuh old rope I gots a debbil trouble findin' again."

A silence, that the Judge tried to make withering. Sam wormed his toes, sucked his lips, and fiddled with the hempen coil.

"You see, suh," he deprecated, "you gots a idea I don't like dis-yuh rope, no-more-so dat-yah tree. But sho'-suh, Maussa Percy, dis nigguh he don' mind um. De more I do ha'nt in dat live-oak tree, suh, de more it seem I don't mind um."

The Judge took out his handkerchief and blew his nose violently, twice.

"You paltry, good-for-nothing, lying black sinner, Sam!"

"Yes-suh, yes-suh!" Contentment rang in the darky's voice. " 'Scuse me, Maussa Percy," he cast back as he scrambled first over the garden wall. "But I bound oblige mek-haste dis-yuh night how. De moon stan' high."

There are still ghosts in Charleston. Doubt as you can, you can't doubt some of them. You can't doubt the one that, incorruptibly, at the hour of the rising of the midnight moon each month, hangs by its neck from the Hanging Tree.

*Conjuh**

THE WOMAN WALKED THE ROAD from Adams Run toward Edisto Island. It was a long way, but she made it a longer. There was a look of fixed confusion on her thin face and in her enlarged eyes. Whenever she heard hoofbeats or footfalls on the road dust she stopped and appeared to brace herself to await the passer-by with an air of unconcern. But then it was no use. Swerving pusillanimously, like a sick animal, she broke into the roadside tangle and made on so for a little way.

It can be hot in May in the low-country parishes of South Carolina. Here in the magnolia-towered thickets of beech and bay and thorn vines it was dead hot. Yet the woman continued to shiver from head to foot of her slender height, as if it were cold. In the open she walked, but here where it was no longer easy, perhaps because it *was* so hard, she tried to run, tried in her panic to fight it. Once, caught in the cul-de-sac of a bamboo brake, she brought up and put her palms to her temples sharply. She stared around her, and as if but just awakened, the whites of her eyes increased. She began to pant heavily.

"What am I doing here?" Her next words were in a blurry French. "*Quelle bêtise!*"

She started back for the opening in the brake by which she had entered. After she had taken three steps a spasm of coughing seized her and shook her light body terribly. She put a handkerchief to her mouth to try to muffle it. When she took it away and looked at the arterial crimson staining the fold she had bitten she wheeled, threw herself in renewed panic against the thick of the bamboos, broke through, and ran on.

When she had slipped down from the train at the little stop back there, in the maze of a moment of hysteria in which the names of these almost-forgotten sea islands had seemed an imperious beckoning, the woman had been well, if quietly, clothed. By the time Bram Tollum saw her, caught without chance of hiding on the road fill going over to the first of the islands, mud-plastered to her knees, dress torn by a hundred thorns, and her hair beginning to look kinky again in its dusty disorder, she made a figure nearly as ragamuffin as one of the native Gullah girls after a day in the wood lots.

Bram Tollum had buried his woman at the Pilkee ground over near Adams Run, and now he was bringing home the mourners, most of them females, packed narrowly in the body of the "nigger-house yard" truck.

When he passed the cinnamon-skinned stranger perched nervously on the edge of the fill he shouted the conventional "Ebenin'!" and would have gone on full-throttle for the rise to the bridge had it not been that he let his eye drag a little in leaving the shape of the wayfarer. Then, because he was alive and bereaved, and because the shape was of a queer, uncommon loveliness, he stopped the truck with a jar that flung his load about, threw in the reverse, and backed back.

The woman was caught. Here there was no cover to hide her from this suddenly leveled curiosity of eleven pairs of eyes. Again, like one shaken awake, she asked herself what she was doing in this place. "It's like an awful dream you can't get out of."

The sense of nightmare increased. Bram's head, twisted around on its glossy, powerful neck, broad-jowled, narrow-browed, the whites of the little eyes showing brown around the circumferences—of all the faces in the truck now this was the only one she could see. But when the mouth in it opened and spoke, the sense of nightmare went away.

"Ebenin', sistuh. Where you gwine to, foot in yuh hand? Mek-so you gwine Appleton Road, gibb you a lift; glad habb yuh company."

It was less the meaning than the music of the words, uttered in that forgotten speech of the Gullahs of the sea islands, that affected the woman so powerfully. She had parted her lips for a "No—thanks" quickly, but then, before she could utter it, it was as if the shape of her mouth had changed. She felt the muscles of her throat flexing like old rusty springs let go, and heard herself answering in a soft, flat-voweled, eager rush:

"T'anky, dat puhzackly where I duh gwine, brudduh. I gwine Appleton House, in de nigguh-house yard, an' t'anky *too* much fuh gibb me a lift."

Venus Burley, relegated to the truck bed to make room for the newcomer on the seat, up beside the widower, was furious.

The big house at the Appleton plantation burned down thirty years ago, leaving only a pair of chimneys to stand in the live-oak avenue. Part of the cotton lands have gone back to jungle; those that are left in tillage, on account of the weevil these times, are planted in corn, spinach, potatoes, and other truck, each field after the whim of its Negro tenant cultivator. The only part of the plantation that has kept a color of animation about it is the row of cabins where these black inheritors live, once the slave quarters, now the "nigger-house yard."

Near sundown the shadows of the cabins, all alike, stripe the sole-packed "street" before them tigerwise, and, going down over the brambly bank beyond it, ray away longer and longer across the tide marsh toward the lift of the barrier beach and the pinky-white lace of the Atlantic combers. Marshward, herons beat their wings in heavy flight; inland the bullbats are waking. The sea wind, beginning to die, blows strong and salt one moment and slacks another, and in the instant of its slacking it is pushed back by the land air, in which are mingled the smoke of piny lightwood from the decapitated chimneys and the scent of trees in flower—magnolia, rose of Sharon, and sweet bay.

Bloom Manigo sat on her doorsill and watched the house shadows pulling themselves out long and thin across the marsh grass, trying for another millionth time to grab the yellow beach sand a mile away with their finger tips before the dusk grabbed *them* and smothered them in the bigger shadow. Bloom knew they never could. She knew a great deal. She was a woman who had had more children than she could easily remember, and so it was a pity, now she was old, the only one left her was the baby, Sukey, a girl not yet eleven and of little use in the potato fields.

Her son Vulcan, her "man chillun," had been dead eight months now; the last of the year's hog was finished months ago; and since one can borrow "bittles" for a while but not forever from even the kindest of neighbors, the pot that little Sukey was rattling in the chimney inside held no more tonight than a thrice-boiled rind, a handful of cowpeas, and another of corn hominy. Tomorrow it would hold less; and Bloom was a woman who had been sleek and fat in her day. So the mumbly song she kept going in her throat as she rocked over her elbows and watched the shadows reaching for the golden sands they could never reach this side of death was a sad one.

"*. . . An' I look on de road, an' de road so lonesome;*
Lawd, I gots to walk dat lonesome road. . . ."

The racket of the truck's arrival with the mourners from Bram's woman's funeral fell in with the melancholy of the spiritual without Bloom's being otherwise aware of it.

"*An' I look in de grabe, an' de grabe so wat'ry;*
Lawd, I gots to lay in dat wat'ry grabe. . . ."

But then one woman, Venus Burley, came running, elbows speared, eyes snapping.

"Aunty Bloom, here come a punkin-skin woman duh say 'e yoh chillun. You ain't habb no punkin-skin gal foh chillun, duh call-umself Delia, gwine away N' Yawk when 'e little. 'E a liar, enty?"

Bloom stopped rocking. "Me habb a chillun duh call-umself Delia? Le' me see. Foh gal-chillun dey Silbia an' *lilly* Bloom an' Promise, an' dey Magnolia an'–an' dey Sukey––"

"Yi-yi-yi! 'E a Gawd liar, a *Gawd* liar, enty? I tell um 'e a Gawd liar."

But now Bloom was looking at the cinnamon-skinned stranger who had come up behind Venus, and when she saw she was a woman grown, and so fit for field work, her memory was revivified and she knew her own child.

"*An' dey my-own Delia!*" Heaving up from the sill, Bloom spread her arms. Tears sprang from her eyes and tumbled down her cheeks. Having done its work of prompting, the material consideration was gone as soon as come, without trace or shame, leaving in the simple old woman's heart only the power and wonder of pure mother love. "Delia chile, t'ank de Lawd Maussa! t'ank de Lawd Jedus! You binna gwine away North wid dem n' Yankee Bukra foh nursemaid, but you done come home to you-own home see yuh maamy befoh 'e dead."

Delia Manigo stood still, not vacillating, but as though her arms were pinioned and her ankles bound. As Bloom studied her the flood of the mother's tears increased. But now they were lustrous things, precious as nothing else to the old country Negro's heart.

"Chile, you dress-up too good. Chile, you gots sin." Nor was there anything illogical in the ecstasy of the sobbing outcry with which she finished: "Praise be to de Lawd!"

"Me, Maamy?" Delia's mouth fell open. "*Me* gots sin?"

Delia looked around her. She looked at the marsh and the striping shadows, the sandy reef beyond it, the breakers still beyond, changing from wink to wink, yet in fourteen years not changed. She looked at the birds moving on the sky, the same great heron, the same fish hawk hung tiny in solitude, the painted streak of a nonpareil, in and out.

She looked at the little cabins and saw them growing big, and the wall of the palmetto tops behind them gigantic. She looked at the dark half circle of the faces of the curious hemming her in.

It was as if her eyes, heavy for so long with her weird, intoxicated dream, were opened clear, and of a sudden she knew them all, these of her flesh and blood and kind. Of a sudden she knew no one else and nothing else.

Had she sin? She could have laughed aloud. Could these but have envisaged the half, the very hundredth, of her sin's fantastic magnitude. But in the same instant she herself was stricken by the terror of it, and tears began to tumble down her face too.

"Maamy—yessum—I gots it. Maamy, I gots a hebby sin."

Bloom caught the flinging body. "Glory Gawd! Yuh ol' maamy gwine fohgibb you an' tek cyar uh you, an' Jedus sabe yoh soul."

"Maa-a-amy! I'ze uh ailin'. I'ze agwine dead."

"No, no, no; hush yuh cryin', rest yuh trimblin'; you tired, dat all; spang tired out. Come-yere in de house and lay 'pon-top yuh maamy's bed."

Delia slept. After a time she was awakened to take some food, fat hog meat and plenty of hominy with the gravy over it. (Now that labor had come into the house, old Bloom had been able to fill her pan at neighbors' doorways without trouble or shame.) Delia tried to eat of these strange, but less strange than familiar, "bittles," and though she could swallow nothing, made a drowsy show of smacking her lips.

Heavy with sleep and with fever, her one desire was to be let lie unaroused, part and parcel of this tiny, ember-lit room, child and never anything but child of it—the browning newspapered walls, the mud chimney with its medicine bottles and broken Staffordshire treasured in niches, and black pots nesting in the ashes, and Sister Sukey's eyes from the dark of a corner, white-rimmed with awe, and Maamy's big shadow moving softly, like an overcurving black wing.

But once recollection passed like a knife through Delia's brain. She sat bolt up.

"They're after me. Ohhh! They've found out by now; they're after me."

Sukey's eyes grew whiter. Maamy's big brown mouth fell open.

"Where you learn talk Bukra talk lukkah dat, chile? Dat too swongah." Here were dimensions of sin of a sudden beyond the old Gullah woman's powers to deal with, even perhaps beyond her stern "God's" and her kindly "Jedus's." She let misgiving shake her for a moment.

"Who-all duh aftuh you? Chile, wha'—wha'—wha' kinda sin you binna dare fuh do?"

Everything was twisted and magnified by Delia's fever. Fumbling in her bosom with distracted fingers, she brought to the firelight a pouch made of some soft skin, hung by a ribbon around her neck. Before she could do more her mother had wheeled on Sukey, crying: "Git outa yere; git out t'rough dat door an' shut-um behine you an' shut yuh mout' same-time an' *keep-um* shut!" Not till the scared child had obeyed did Bloom move, and then it was quickly, her thick fingers pulling open the mouth of the bag. When she saw that it was full of the sparkle of diamonds and things she began to shiver and groan.

"Gawd habb pity! Dat whuffoh you so trimbly; you duh t'ief, duh t'ief, duh t'ief."

"No, no!" Appalled, bewildered, Delia scrambled back for refuge into the island speech. "I nebbuh t'ief-um; I nebbuh, I sway-to-Gawd.

Dey my my-own. Um gibb-um to me, ebery las' one, Maamy. Maa-a-a-my!"

Bloom's mirth came out of her fright, cackling. She caught a bight of necklace out of the pouch. "Who duh gibb you dat t'ing?" Shrill sarcasm. "Huh–huh–huh! Must be a stingy nigguh tek a wench to de crossroads store fuh buy-um sucha poor lilly present no more-na *dat* t'ing." Poking, she chose a bauble of platinum, a six-pointed star with one great brilliant. "Chile, tell yuh maamy, *who gwine gibb a nigguh-gal dat t'ing?*"

"A king, Maamy—he gibb-um."

"A king! Hi–hi! Whuffoh? Wha' kind uh king?"

"Fuh a dec'ration, he gibb-um, Maamy. A honest-to-Jedus white-folks' *king*."

Bloom strained for words fit for her ultimate sarcasm, her cheeks swollen with her breath, eyeballs pressed out against their lids. But Delia, staring around her in panic, cowed not by her mother's incredulity, but by the sudden onsweep now of her own, buried her face in her hands. "I guess I mussuh-t'ief-um. I yent but a poor lilly nigguh-gal, fuh work in de potato-field 'pon-top uh Edisto; I *done mussuh* t'ief-um, an' dat so."

The cough that was always waiting to catch her when her guard was down caught her and shook her to pieces. At sight of the cruelty, everything else was swept clear away out of Bloom, leaving nothing but the mother of mothers. She put her arms around the bucking body, held it fiercely against the large, soft warmth of her breast, moaning, crooning.

"Don' you bodduh, my baby. Yuh maamy gots you in 'e arm, an' 'egwine tek cyar uh you. Gi' me dat skin-bag, an' don' you t'ink no more. Tonight I gwine hide-um unduh de loose board in-unduh de bed; tomorruh I gwine t'row-um in de marsh, where no-Gawd-body alibe ebbuh duh find-um. Stop yuh twistin' an' twinin' now; hush yuh cryin'; listen de wind duh blow in de chinaberry-leaf out dey, so sof', so kind. You want yuh rest; you want yuh sleepy, sleepy, sleep, safe where nobody cyan touch you in yuh maamy arm."

Delia slept. For hours it was the black sleep, untroubled. But toward the gray of morning she dreamed.

She walked rapidly, then she began to run, across the shiny floor of her apartment toward the escape of the tall glass doors. But no matter how skitteringly her feet fled, the soft fall of pliant shoe soles behind her she could not shake off. And when she had slipped out upon the iron balcony and would have pulled the door shut behind her, one of those soles was intruded in the aperture, the silky pendant of his whisker making his face seem even longer, his brown eyes nearly black with imploration and concern.

"*Mademoiselle, je répète*—"

There she turned on him, all-let-go, her blurred French blurrier than ever with the ecstasy of her revolt. "You repeat, you repeat, you repeat. I'm to stop all working, go away from Paris, eat this, drink that, sleep so and so. Or else I will to be grave sick and die. But can you not hear me when *I* repeat, that it is equal to me, and that, the devil, what do I care? The devil! who is there that cares?"

"But your world, Mademoiselle Manigault! Your art, your public, your Paris!"

But now she twisted quickly from him.

"Look, Doctor! No, down there! There, where I point. It goes there. There, where I point. It goes there."

And now, in the queer way of dreams, it seemed that for a long while she had been doing nothing but point at a thing below her in the current of the Champs Elysées that she could see, yet dared not see. Like one of those liver spots that race out of the corner of vision and return to re-escape and are never done with it, time after time this dread spot in her dream ran past beneath her and away up the river of holiday cars bound out toward the races, the woods, and all the trysting places of happiness.

"Look where I'm pointing, Foster!" (For, by a dream-trick, it was no longer the doctor's face beside her, but somehow the face of Foster Lake, the manager.)

"Look, for heaven's sake, Jacques!" (It was somehow Jacques Monck of *Le Matin.*)

Her voice rose to a thready scream: "*Look, Edouard!*"

For now it was Edouard Lebrun himself, there at her shoulder, an unwonted flush on his olive cheeks, his eyes queer, his full mouth tightened and oddly twisted. But when she would have grasped his arm with one hand to make him see where the other was pointing, she grasped at nothing but a thing that dissolved and left emptiness and sudden mockery.

And as suddenly, as if her pursuing finger had been given power, the thing that fled was pinned down, and she saw it. An open car (for the day was sunny), mahogany and nickel and crimson leather, and Edouard Lebrun there in it, his face averted from this building, and by his side, snow and gold and happy, Olga Pedesen, the Norse girl, of the Folies Bergères.

Delia laid hold of the curly iron of the balustrade to twist it and shiver it. But that too dissolved under her touch, and so did the floor of the balcony, and the floor of Paris, and where she fell in a heap she lay and gnawed at her lips and sobbed. And sobbing, she awoke, and saw darkness bending over her, with grayness around its edges.

"Dey, dey, dey, chile; dey, dey, dey, my baby."

Reality. The land air was still blowing, heavy with tangled fragrances–myrtle and bay, honeysuckle and dogwood, cows and pigs, raccoon and deer, woodsmoke and harness sweat and axle grease. Bird song ran around the cabin chinks like the shadow of a baton across invisible reeds and violins. There were other stirrings, husky laughter, pad of bare soles. Reality, generations fixed. After the phantasm of a moment's sleep.

Bloom left the bedside and went to the door; around her the gray light warmed.

"Dayclean," she said. "Time de man duh git on de crop, befoh de crow duh git on-um. Mawnin', Haklus. I do lubb see you wid a hoe 'pon-top yoh shoulder. Mawnin', Madlun." At sound of Delia squeaking up and dropping her feet to the floor, the material and the maternal in Bloom closed in momentary struggle. But the mother conquered. "You lay quiet, Delia, chile. Tomorruh you feel more bettuh; mebby we find some work in de crop foh you work. But you ain' had yuh rest yet. Lay quiet 'pon-top yuh back today."

Delia started to cry, "No, I'm all right; I had all the rest I want——"; then, startled by the anomaly of that speech in this place, she did as she had done yesterday and slid back into the Gullah in haste. "I wanta gwine out, work in de crop, dis bery mawnin'."

"We ain't habb no crop uh we-own dis summuh, Delia, neiduh-so no mule, neiduh-so no cow foh work. But *ef* you do *do* wanta work I binna habb a compersation with Bram Tollum las' night, an' Bram he gots a hebby potato field dis summuh, an' he lubb habb a help."

"I don' cyare who-wid I gwine, Maamy, I *duh* gwine, an' I duh gwine now."

If there seemed reality inside, there seemed a deeper and more vivid reality out between sky and land. This illusion of reality held Delia prisoner. As she walked behind Bram's broad back along the cart track, through the light of morning, through the myrtle thickets, through the little pinewoods, it seemed that weariness and fright of death had been stripped from her like the winding sheet left in the tomb in the garden, never to be put on again. It was less a feeling at all—resurrection morning, her sins forgiven and her soul set free.

Nothing weighed. She felt only a kind of Elysian levity when Bram, turning suddenly in the half-light of the pinewoods, asked her to give him a kiss.

"Me gibb *you* a kiss!" She stood and tittered. "A oagly black 'rangatang luk *you!*" She hadn't to search for them; immemorial epithets fit for such dealings ran off her tongue. "You stand too-much lukkuk elephunt an' a alligatuh an' a 'rangatang, all t'ree, an' I is a puhticulah lady, nigguh, an' you cyan't specify."

But when, come to the foot of his field, heavy with her taunts and his three-day widowhood, he renewed his suit, his face contorted and the huge wedges of his chest muscles tensed with his vehemence, Delia felt a chill of misgiving and a thrill of rage.

"What I come here foh, hoe weed an' crabgrass, or listen to field-nigguh sweetmout' all mawnin'?"

"I ain't talk sweetmout'. My todduh woman, 'e dead; I lubb habb you fuh my woman."

Delia's lips curled back. "Va-t'-en!" There was spittle in it. She threatened him with her heavy hoe, then, wheeling, walked out into the potato field and began, at hazard, to knock out the roots of Jimson weed with its dull blade.

All around Bram's patch the woods made a wall. Heat poured into it as the sun mounted, like fluid into a bowl. Delia's hoe lagged. Swiftly the illusion of well-being was dissipated. The flame of the sun, added to the flame of the fever, burned her. The field and the green wall around it swam with the swimming of her eyes. Her knees bent double and let her down on the earth between the potato rows.

This was the end, she thought. But now she considered it without terror, only dully. Bram was nowhere about. He had gone back toward the "yard," for a drink of liquor perhaps. But it would not have mattered one way or the other; Delia had forgotten about Bram.

She lay on an elbow in the furrow, her head hanging, her eyes blank on the earth. In her fingers alone was there activity. They crept in, wriggled, dug in under the powdery crust, blind as worms or as roots, nosing down through the dead part to where the earth was damp and alive, to try to get a grip of it.

Soil and sun and a low veil of leaves.

A potato leaf, cut by some gnawer, fell down to the dust before Delia's eyes. It lay there green on white. Fever played with it, and of a sudden it was white on green, white of newsprint on the green of a table in a restaurant in the Bois de Vincennes.

A clipping from a paper. *Le Matin.* Jacques Monck's column. Jacques Monck's words:

. . . Strauss, Stravinsky, Honegger, yea, giants, molding and naming for yourselves a musical age. Agreed. One stands before you with bowed head. I mean it, reverently.

But what of you others, concerning whom there is no question of reverence, but only of laughter, pulse, diablerie? A new beating of old drums in the antique dark. What of you, Johnnie Bell, with your jungle-remembering banjo; what of you two, Blaise Watterson of Harlem, Honeyboy Zipp in London, with your witch-doctor batons and your evolving "blues"; what of you, Delia Manigault, who, nightly, on the stage of Paris, with the infinitely subtle gaucherie of your dark limbs and the intricate and simple incitement of your jeweled, whispering feet, create and continually recreate the measure of the morrow's dancing of a hundred million feet?

What of you others, I say! Would it not be a thing of irony, then, if looking back one day upon this minute double decade, the historians, not alone of music, but of letters, of sociology, of politics and religion, should find the names of you others, you children of the jungle, of the slave-market?

Soil and sun and a low veil of leaves. And a Gullah girl, come out from the cabin in the "nigger-house yard" to till the earth in her generation, lying there, hoe lost, tilling it with nothing but her fingers now.

A shadow, come and gone. Was that Bram? No, it was more fearful than the shadow of Bram; it was like the shadow of the wing of the angel of a dark, remonstrant God.

"Impious nigger-girl! Presumptuous, temerarious, fantastical! Rub your forehead in the master dust there; cast out the maggots of dreaming from your brain, and repent!"

That shadow again, and another with it. Now there were two buzzards, circling.

When Delia knew that, she scrambled up somehow and ran along the furrow toward the human being, Bram. Bram had had his drink. Corn liquor does things that not even prayer can do. Bram had to laugh aloud with the power of his exultant wonder at sight of this lissome "yalluh woman," but a half hour ago so "no-mannersable," flying to him with wild hands out. He had to laugh at her weight, at her cry: "Oh, fuh Jedus, tek cyare uh me!"

Delia felt herself being carried, and that was enough; she neither knew nor cared that it was toward the farther woods. She knew nothing of it when Bram, sensing a change in the heft of his burden, stopped to study it, swore, scowled, vacillated, shivered a little, muttered: "What I duh do, mek-so de woman gwine dead?" and, turning back on his tracks, started in haste for the "yard."

Through the heat of noon and through the long afternoon Delia lay on her mother's bed in the cabin and knew nothing of it, nothing when she twisted, nothing when she coughed. The sun declined. Men and women and children came back from the fields. The banked fires were awakened with slivers of fat lightwood, and the smell of bacon and corn hominy was blown about with the smoke. Once again the shadows of the cabins in file set out across the mile-wide marsh in their losing race with dusk, the destroyer. Once again old Bloom sat on her doorsill and watched them, rocking to the measure of her mournful song:

> ". . . *An' I look on de mountain, an' de mountain so high;*
> *Lawd, I gots to climb dat mountain high. . . .*"

Fatalist, that the child who had been given back to her bosom yesterday should today be lying there in chance of being snatched away again, was all of a piece with the "lonesome road" which one is born but to follow, whistling, laughing, pranking as gaily as one can. There was no use in running about, wringing hands, pestering fate. How ill Delia was she had no way of knowing: either she would grow better or she would grow worse; Bloom had done all she could, for now.

After dark it would be another matter; there was perhaps another thing she could do. But she was a good member of the " 'Vangelical Baptiss' " at the Three Crossroads, and it was hardly dusk yet, the tips of the shadows still left to reach for the distant sand. So there was nothing to do but sit and wait, rock and croon.

> *"All I wanta know, am my sin' fohgibbun;*
> *All I wanta know, am my soul set free? . . ."*

Now the shadows were gone. Gradually for a few minutes, then swiftly, the black coast night made. Supper was out of the way in all the cabins, but it was Saturday, and no work tomorrow, so no one was going to bed. Shades passed up the "street," some with monosyllabic queries thrown to the old woman swaying on the sill. Others kept up a soft pad-pad of soles along the rear way, behind the cabins.

Sukey, the "baby," penned indoors by her mother's bulk, stood on one foot and then on the other; she too wanted to be up there at the top of the yard, where, on the beaten earth under the solitary, sway-limbed live oak, the premonitory board-thumpings, string-pickings, and can-poundings of the dance were already beginning to be heard.

Sensing the child's restiveness, Bloom turned on her with a guarded vehemence.

"No-suh, you can't duh gwine out dis ebenin'. You stay here; tek cyare yuh sistuh." Bloom arose, dusting her broad skirts. "Yuh maamy 'e gots a errund. Anybody ask you a answer where yuh maamy am, tell-um I gwine be back-here foh-fibe minute."

Now that it was pitch dark out behind the cabin row and everybody with eyes departed, Bloom could walk boldly on her errand to Gran' Liz's, whose cabin stood inshore a little way, in a palmetto grove. If there was any vacillation, it was not in Bloom's feet, but in her mind, nor was the doubt there of the conjurewoman's power to help if she would; it was precisely *whether* she would. A conjure bag, specific against fevers, is a precious and perishable thing, and Bloom came with empty hands.

As the old woman entered the skirts of the grove the upper fronds of the trees were reddening with the rays of the fires the dancers had lighted on the marsh bank a hundred yards away, and the clattering throb of the orchestra began to run in the air.

Behind, at the cabin, Sukey hung in the door for a little while, hearkening. She hung on the step a little while. Then she too was gone.

Delia could not have said when it was that she began to feel the beat of the music. Its first effect was to translate into a definite dismay all the nameless bodily discomforts of which she had been conscious in her unconsciousness—the heat, the binding of her limbs, and the weight on her heart. Now it was explained in terms of confusion and dismay.

Why had she not been given the call—even the first call? Where was that call woman? Sneaked out to a *buvette* to steal a glass with her lover, the second electrician? In that case, where were all the others, the dressing maid, aghast, the stage manager in a tumult, if Manigault had missed her entrance?

For surely she had. Surely it belonged to no act but hers, that rhythm that came jarring, tuneless with distance, repeated and repeated. Appalled, she could see big Sam Pira, his neck craned, his baton agonizing, hoping through another bar and another, and then for yet another time flipping his clarinets and fiddles, his big bull fiddles and his traps and saxophones, back into the opening.

She could see the waxing consternation of her support, the twenty of them already on-stage and at it, their prancing more and more galvanic with each rebuilding of her entrance, their panicky eyes cornering at the high darkness in the wing where her shadow should long since have come within their sight, snaking along the great moss-hung limb that swayed down, as from a live oak, across the stage.

Now the thing took on that quality peculiar to nightmare. It was not alone that she was tardy; it was that she was not dressed, not even *un*dressed *to* dress, not even thinking about beginning; half like a cataleptic she lay here on the divan in her dressing room and did nothing.

She conquered this inaction. She began to tear haphazard at her clothing, plucking it in ribbons; ineptitude still kept half a grip on her. She couldn't find things. Where was her costume, her circlet of trunks, her few bright rags of crepe? Where were her jewels, her flashing things? They weren't in the case, and there wasn't any case. They weren't in the lock drawer, and there wasn't any drawer. Panic added to panic now.

If one who knew the fumbling of her thoughts had been watching Delia's movements in the dark of the cabin, he would have been surprised by their precision, the pulling aside first of the rickety bed, the search on hands and knees, the marking of a board that was loose, its lifting, the quick sweep of an arm beneath it, the sigh of relief, the bag.

Delia had never realized that the runway from her dressing room to the wings could be so dark, so empty, and so long. Where was everybody? Where, tonight, were all the faces she was used to glimpsing at the turnings of the walls—the black-eyed Arab poet, the little bank clerk, Boracque, with his savage shyness and his flowers, the loafing stagehands, the worshipful maids? But where now, when it came to that, were the walls themselves? How had wind and stars got into this swollen corridor?

Was it a prank of punishment for her tardiness, one wide conspiracy? Was that why, without warning her, they had shifted all the mechanics of the wings and then cleared out, leaving her to fumble for strange handholds, clamber unhelped and unguided up incomprehensible distances, abrading her tender skin on new corners as rough as bark, and catching her hair and rags on unremembered twigs that were like living twigs of a tree?

Victor Jimms and his son Hercules pounded on a plank, their shoulders jerking to the time. Jube Appleton picked on an enormous guitar that had but two strings left. Bram Tollum beat on a drum contrived of a ten-gallon keg, with a cowhide over the end. Three or four boys clapped with the flats of their palms on dried gourds.

Men, women, girls, and boys, all ages, they danced, each one solo, sufficient to himself. To see them, flinging their elbows, cracking the heads back on their necks, knocking their knees together, each seeming to follow nothing but the pattern of his own mercurial impulse—and to hear the perverse and incoherent *mêlée* of their outcries—it would have been hard to realize that under the surface complexity there lay a simplicity of movement as prescriptive as any prison step, as formalistic as any ritual, as old as the antique tree that sent its bearded bough down over them to catch the refractions of the bonfires' light; older, even; as old perhaps as the light of bonfires in the night.

Boom-boom-boom . . . "Hi! Crack my foot!"

Boom-boom-boom . . . "Bressèd Jedus! Nyam-uh-gunjuh! Lay-down-die!"

When Delia dropped from among the reddened leaves overhead and landed with a pelvic pirouette, light as a feather in a wind eddy on dust, the dancers shied, yelled, and scattered, some of them never stopping in flight till they had reached the protecting lee of the first of the cabins. The lads in the orchestra dropped their gourds and retreated somersaulting into the wild-oat cover on the marsh bank behind them.

This woman, this strange "chillun" of Aunty Bloom's, come out yesterday out of nowhere, she must have died after all, as folks had said she would. "Sick-to-dead," she couldn't have been flying around in that treetop while no one knew it: "done-dead," she might. Of all the music makers, Bram was the only one to hold his ground. Eyes swollen, mouth wide, legs gathered for jumping, after the first startled hiatus he let his cudgel fall on the cowhide and got hold of the running beat again.

Now how he did beat! He beat with a violence compounded of terror and fascination.

"Mek-so de woman *done*-dead, mek-so 'e *am* a spirit, I don' cyare! Lawd, *my* Lawd Gawd!" *Boom-boom-boom-boom* . . .

Half seen, half veiled in the streaming chiffons her garments were, uncomprehended jewels weaving living fires around her—in his dreams Bram had never dreamed of flesh of woman like this.

"Mek-so 'e a hag-woman, I don' cyare!" *Boom.* "Debbil gwine graff me; let-um!"

A flame of hysterical passion burned him.

"What a woman fuh lubb! *What a woman fuh dance!*"

Now it was no longer Bram that beat the drum. Cudgel, arm, body, and mind, now they were all one instrument, pounding willy-nilly. Now it was Delia that beat the drum.

At first Delia danced simply because it was the hour to dance. Here was the stage, the music, the support, all the familiar preparation. The whirlwind vanishing of her chorus and the stoppage of the orchestra shook her, leaving her for a moment "all in the air."

But she was trained in a hard tradition. With the re-emergence of the dance beat, insecure at first but growing in power, she could throw off the panic that had so nearly laid hold of her, and dance, and wonder.

Near memories ran in with her puzzlement and her deepening suspicion. The want of a call, the deserted corridors, the sly tamperings with the mechanics of her entrance, every familiar move of hers made unfamiliar and difficult. Why? Had she been right; was there premeditation in it? Malice? Now this emptying of the stage by tacit treachery, leaving her to carry on, impossibly, alone. This stripping of the music. This conspiracy of silence out there in the enormous house——

And now—*what* an enormous house! Nightmare must be playing tricks again. Almost as enormous, it seemed to be growing, as the whole of outdoors, the whole black bowl of the towering night, myriad-packed, shadows ringed above shadows till their cigarettes and lighting matches became as high and tiny and many as the stars. All watching concentrically. All waiting unmoved. As dumb as the dead.

Here was something Delia Manigault had never had to know before; it came out of that house against her, as speaking as a wind one can neither see nor hear:

"Well, nigger-girl?"

To her bewilderment was added the beginning of dismay. She cried, panting, while she continued to fling her body, pivot, and bend her limbs: "What do you want, you-all? You know me; you know what I can do. Why all this? How do you get this way?"

"Well, nigger-girl?"

She cried in fury: "What do you think? This is no tryout!" But then, touched by the misgiving that lies forever in the favorite's heart, she wondered if it was. That *second* tryout, the irrevocable and pitiless one—— If it was, it was monstrous for them to have asked it so, without warning, without prop or help, against their silence.

"Well, nigger-girl?" She seemed to hear a fleering, "Is that your stuff?"

"How can you expect anybody to do her best stuff like this?" She turned coward, the supplicant. "Yes! Wait! Watch me now. Now I'm going good. I'm going better now."

But she wasn't going better; she was going worse. She punished herself, but it was of no use; a heaviness began to envelope her limbs. In despair she flung into another figure, more sophisticated and more intricate. This was what they wanted; the other was too naïve and looked too easy. Calling on all her store of virtuosity, she added complication to complication.

Now they would *have* to leap up, acclaim, applaud. The heat around her head would burst it. The drumbeat was getting ahead of her; she had to whip her failing muscles with her tiring nerves to keep up. The thin, hot sweat that ran down into her eyes would blind them, unless she could "get the house," and do it very, very soon.

Now it seemed as though there must be a spotlight searching at random over the tiers of that black immensity out front. Here it hovered, bringing alive for an instant a remembered face; there it ran and stopped again. Petey Pitcher, the almost-white boy, fiddler, St. Louis. How many years was it since he had killed his career so that Delia Manigo's might live? And now there; only shoulders and the top of a head, the face hidden in the hands; that was Monck of *Le Matin*. Disappointed? Fed up? Or asleep?

So they came, so they went, faces, faces, faces. All of them the same size, distinct but distant, so many masks, emotionless. Now there were three together, three in a box, black coats, braided, and ribbons across their breasts. And Delia remembered the three, the messengers of a king.

Greed and fright and bitterness. Had they come back to take it away from her, their "decoration"? With one hand she pawed among the streaming rags at her bosom for the touch of the great six-pointed star, then more wildly still, with both hands. But already the light had passed and the three were gone and no star could she find; all that her fingers had caught was a necklace, a tiny thread of pearls. At that a cry went out of her mouth, "*Edouard!*"

The roving nimbus of the spotlight was arrested, as if an unseen manipulator had heard. There was Edouard Lebrun, as if incalculably far off, but large and vivid, watching her as a stranger might, his face quite immobile, his eyes as dead as glass.

That dance was done. For an instant Delia stood, keeping her balance on her wabbly legs. Holding the necklace high away from her throat, aglimmer in the red light for the glazed eyes to see, she cried with all her might and all her fright:

"*Souviens-toi!*"

It went only a little way and fell; it couldn't cross that distance. "*Remember!*" It couldn't touch Edouard Lebrun. In the widening nimbus he turned to the girl beside him, the white-and-golden Norse girl who sang at the Folies, Olga Pedesen. He smiled, and she smiled in answer. And under the thrust of Delia's hooked thumb the necklace parted. Where it went then she did not know; she had a vivid illusion of baubles turned bubbles and bubbles broken in the air.

She commenced to fall. But a sob caught her and lifted her straight up again.

"*Boom!*" A simple drum note. "*Boom!*" Imperious, powerful.

"Nigguh-gal, you-all t'rough? Cyan't you dance no mo'?"

Another sob took Delia's body and twisted it, flinging the pelvis one way, the shoulders the other. But her feet were tied to the ground.

"*Boom! Boom! Boom!*"

The measure of the beat increased, and with it the measure of the sobs that flung her. But now, what difference, what did she care? She gave them rein. The moment she had done that a queer thing happened. There were no longer sobs, but laughter, Gullah laughter.

"Cyan't I dance! Lookuh de nigguh-gal. Dance? Yi-yi-yi-yi-yi!"

"Gibb-um debbil! T'row yoh elbow! Crack yoh knee'!"

"I gibb-um debbil! I shake-um down!"

The beginning of marvels. Amazement. Exultation. Why had she ever forgotten the power that was in her when she no longer worried or cared or thought of herself as an artist or of dancing as dancing—when, very simply, she could give herself up body and soul to the hollering drum?

"Nigguh-gal," she fleered and gloried, " 'e duh shake de Bukra out uh hebben!"

True it was, she was shaking and shivering them, the tiers of that enormous "house" against the sky. Her laughter rang higher and higher, flouting and fleering. "Nigguh-gal, 'e crack 'e backbone, t'row 'e shoulduh, shake de Gawd-a-mighty white folks down!"

Wizening shadows, like rags of wind-struck cloud she saw them tumbling. The loopings and bendings of her flesh had got beyond her now; she had no feeling of them. Faster, faster, wilder, wilder. And of a sudden they reached the fullness of simplicity, and stopped.

That was done. The floor of the old marsh she saw empty, wound by the channels of the tide; the bowl of the sky she saw hollow, wiped clean of all but the glitter of the Sea Island stars. Her paean was hardly louder than the rustling of the wind: "Done shake-um down!"

The fires were going to embers and their light warmed the earth. Delia was down on her buckled knees on the earth, and she had hold of it with her hands. To have safe hold of the earth is to be part of it, and to be part of the earth is to be imperishable.

Now everything around Delia was part of it. The little cabins, they were not like things built. The slowly tossing wild oats, the trees, the ember-lit watchers ringed in distance, and Bram, nearer, broad-bottomed on the beaten ground, his great spent wrists hanging over the head of his cowhide tom-tom and the sweat of heaven trickling down them as red as blood—they were all parcel with Delia Manigo, but the earth where it moved and breathed and desired. And so was Maamy now, of a sudden, between her two big soft wings of shadows.

"What you duh do dey, chile? Whuf-foh you duh lay 'pon-top de groun'?"

Delia was so heavy-close to the ground now that she heard a breathing. That was the ocean on the barrier beaches miles away. But she thought it was the beginning of the beating of another drum. Boom-boom-boom! The oldest drum of all. And Delia thought she was dancing to it. She thought she was a child on the marsh bank in the cool of "dayclean," with the smoke of breakfast fires blowing down around her seaward, and the stamp and clank of hitching mules and the chitter of rushing birds brittle in the air. Dancing, vagrant as a feather.

Somebody was speaking far off, as far off as the other end of Edisto.

"Look up yoh maamy, Delia. I gots a conjuh from de conjuh woman. Now you gwine be all-well."

Dancing, lighter, lighter, lighter than any feather, laughing, caroling.

"Conjuh, Maamy? Whuffoh conjuh? I *gots* a conjuh. *I yiz* all-well."

*In the Shade of the Tree**

WHEN YOU SEE A VERY OLD PERSON you are apt to think, what can there be in living, for that one? You wonder to yourself, what has he got? Well, he's got this: he's got his memories. So have we all, you say. But memories, you say, are not meat of adventure or wine of hope for daily sustenance; they are but thin stuff, ghost and gone. You don't know the memories of the old.

A cow, walking across the morning pastures, tears her mouthfuls here and there, half in haste, eye on some rich tuft ahead. A boy, a man in his prime—he does the same. Broken grasses, little tasted.

The savor is in the cud. Lying by and by in the shade of the tree of age, redrawing it up the gullet of the years—no, it is no thin stuff, ghost and gone. Now it begins for the first time to surrender its inner juices to the unhurried tongue, presently pungent, vividly sweet. What is this? A tang of wind-tossed stems from the hilltops of excitement. And this? Lush, deep clover of loves accomplished, triumphs won. And this, to sting the appetite? Thistle of passing sorrows and small defeats.

No, no; commonly when a man comes to a certain age he steps right clear of the law. He's eaten his cake, and here's his cake to eat again.

Commonly. But sometimes there's to be found an old man condemned by this or that to live imprisoned in today, this morning, this evening, tomorrow morning, dustily present, pitilessly awake. It's like the predicament of a camel in the desert with his hump cut off. Or it's like that torture devised to drive a man crazy, the trick of denying him sleep for days and nights on end, continually jerking him back out of the beginnings of dreams by a tickle or a buffet or an abrupt loud sound, like the ringing of a bell.

In Leander Killen's case the instrument was, in fact, a bell. The clangor of that bell, hung outside the back door where his garden ran down to the river, had fetched him back to here-and-now so often, so many hours, days, and years, that now he couldn't have dreamed off if it had stopped and let him. It was as if his powers of reminiscence, too long denied, had fallen into atrophy—worse than the powers even—the appetite.

It's one thing to be a young man without a past; it's another to be an old one. Leander had come clear of the law the wrong way. Not only hadn't he his cake to eat; it was as though he never had had it; he hadn't even the lingering taste of it left. He hadn't anything left now but his hatred of that bell.

He hadn't even his garden, and this was because his eyes had been frozen permanently open by the habit of that alarm, and he couldn't close them to repicture what a brave garden it once was; he had no way of seeing it but as a senile, shallow ground, whiskered with fewer flowers, beans, and lettuces than with weeds, now his hoe had grown so dull.

Weeding is not so bad; it's work to do without thinking. The trouble was, Leander thought about the weeds as he went at them, having nothing else with which to occupy his mind.

The two o'clock sun, coming from across the river, lay on his face, a heavy glare. Bang, bang, feebly, with his hoe. How tough the ragweed stems had grown. Stubborn things! Damned things! Bang, bang . . .

Clang! . . . That bell!

Shame that it was, there used to be a moment of mutiny, in other days.

There was none now. Letting the hoe handle fall from his hand, he turned and hastened slowly up the garden. "Yes, yes, I'm coming, ain't I?"

He entered the kitchen. His eyes frozen open, he saw everything there, the mop marks left by the woman who came in in the morning, the towels drying on a string over the stove, the soiled plate of his dinner on the oilcloth-covered table. He had never in his memory seen the room otherwise. As many years as his rusty consciousness ran back, what seemed his whole life, every dingy thing had been just so.

He passed through a dark hallway and came into his wife's room.

"Yes, my dear?"

"I feel like I'm going to die, L'ander. I'm sorry to be such a——"

"Now, now! Pshaw!"

"But I never felt this way before. It's a giddiness."

It seemed to Leander that if he had ever been a boy he must have stood in this room with his little cap off, listening to this old, bedridden woman saying: "I never felt this way before; it's a giddiness." For he couldn't seem to arouse himself to imagine her as ever having been anything but a cadaverous martyr pinioned beneath a stuffy-smelling quilt.

"It scares me, L'ander."

"Now, now! Would you be comfortabler if I put you on your side?"

"I might try it that way. But I don't know."

It began to take his strength these days to get her rolled over.

"There, I'm sure you'll be comfortabler now. You know your giddiness is always better for turning."

"So you don't believe me. You think I'm just putting on, for sympathy." The woman twisted her mouth in a wan, secretive smile. "I'm glad you can. After all, what good is it, your getting upset any sooner than you have to?"

"Oh no, no, Mama, you don't think for a minute——"

The invalid bit her lip and turned her face away. "Go back to your garden, L'ander, out into the air and sunshine. I–I shall be all right."

"If you're not, all you have to do is pull the bell; I'll come in quick."

"Will you? I hate to–but–you used to come quicker. I suppose——"

"No, now, don't you worry, I'll come on the run."

Leander went outdoors, took up the hoe, and banged at a weed.

It was Saturday. Young Mr. Cotton, next door, was out in his garden. He had rank rows of beans and a strong stand of cabbages. He smiled to himself as he studied the antique figure beyond the pickets. "Myra," he said to his wife, "wouldn't it kill you? Look at him standing there, innocent as bliss, square in the middle of the only decent button chrysanthemum he's got, whacking for the past five minutes at one old sunflower stalk!" Mrs. Cotton smiled too, but there was a shine of moisture in her eyes.

"Poor man, we oughtn't to laugh at him. If ever there was a saint on earth!" There were ten very old frame houses in the row, Gibb's Terrace, and he spoke for nine of them. "I hate to think what'll happen to him when *she* goes."

Her husband looked sober. "When she passes on, you mean?"

"He won't last long beyond her, Jack. They don't, not when they've been together as long as those two, so devoted, wrapped up in each other, like a pair of lovers. If there were more like him today!"

Cotton didn't know whether there was a dig at him in that. He hunkered down, creasing his brow. "Here's a worm got into this cabbage."

"It's because he does love her." The woman's eyes were wetter than ever as she went back to her perennial borders.

Over in the next yard Leander said to himself: "I hate her!" It made him jump. He had never shaped the thought before. Only a monstrous disaster could have provoked it now. Plodding in circles after weeds, here he had come on the one ewe lamb among his button chrysanthemums laid in ruin. He stood with his chin hanging. The work of a vandal! There lay the footprints bold to see among the broken stems. Whose? Leander hadn't an enemy he could name. Had he? Had he given anyone cause, without knowing it— It was too upsetting; he wrested his mind away. Let it go for just one of those things that are always happening. Concentrate on something else.

Now he could concentrate on the larger aspects of his bitterness. It was not that plant alone, it was the whole garden. How could he be expected to make a decent garden, when, no sooner had he a plan matured or an action started, it was shattered and scattered beyond memory's recall by that damned bell?

Till today he had been at pains to keep his anger centered on that bell. Unconsciously afraid of shame, he had tied a knot in the bell cord over which his passionate resentment could not slide, to run along it and come to the ringing hand. Now it was like a bolt from the blue of truth:

"I hate her!"

He tried to undo it by forgetting he had said it. He threw himself against the weeds. His hoe must have wondered at the renewed violence of his hands.

Batter and bang—what odds what his blade hit? If he could but have kept it up at that pace! Perspiration, thin as water, broke from his skin. He found of a sudden that all the while he had been holding his breath.

He stood to breathe. He felt strangely terror-smitten. His gaze, turning this way and that, came to the masts of the shipping, sticks as fine as spider thread a mile away down the river, and remained there dully. It marks the complete atrophy of his imagination, that those sticks which for the normal man, wherever seen, will set fancy straightway towering, golden cloud in a blue wind, ebullient hail of up-anchor, freed heart, swift keel, the narrow room of trouble forgotten, the ineffable, perilous embrace of space—it marks it, that in old Leander's sight they stood but lesser brothers of the clothes posts running in ranks down the diminishing yards. If they aroused any emotion at all, it was one of querulous protest: "Why do people want to keep moving about; why not be quiet and rest?"

As a matter of fact nine tenths of his mind was fixed on the business of breathing. Once he let up on it, here he was, holding his breath again.

Why? Something was amiss. What? Something in the world of this afternoon was so weirdly changed that his lungs wouldn't, or couldn't, do their work. Perhaps it's so a fish feels, taken out of water into the air.

He opened his mind a crack. Was it that he had said: "I hate her!"?

He tried to close it again, but now a pair of figures coming up the riverbank prevented him. A sailor and a girl.

It was a favorite stroll for sailors wanting to get girls out into the country the shortest way. Leander's eyes followed them past the bottom of the garden. Though the lass was not the prettiest in the world, nor her lad the most prepossessing, there was something in the hunger of the arm he threw about her swiftly at the lilac cover at the fence corner that had a beauty quite unrelated to either of them—even despite them—as if willfully mingling with their amorphous young excitement a tenderness, a larger yearning, a nobler groping of its own.

"How lucky he is," thought Leander. "Head over heels in love with her." He struck his hoe on the dust with a sudden ferocity. "Why wouldn't he be?" He wheeled and faced the backs of the kindly, neighborly houses, like an animal cornered. "No, I won't take it back, nor you can't shame me into it!"

As he recommenced his hacking at the weeds he muttered to himself: "Why should a man be ashamed for looking at the truth?"

He seemed to be getting an immense amount done this afternoon. Freshly pecked-at soil ran in long snake trails around him. At a price, though. Whether it was this continued holding of his breath, or what, he grew as wobbly with weariness as if he had done the work of three ordinary shifts. Yet now he was so nervous he couldn't stop till he was stopped.

Unconsciously, all this while that seemed the length of hours, he was waiting for that bell to ring.

A ray of the lowering sun struck under his lids.

So it wasn't that it seemed hours. It *was* hours.

There was a clump of dandelions. It was in the turf border of a bed, so he couldn't use the hoe. But every time he took hold of the sticky leaves to try and pull its roots out they broke in his fingers.

He straightened, wheeled, and cried aloud at the bell.

"What's the matter with you? Why don't you ring?"

He hurried slowly up the yard. He passed through the kitchen and the hall.

"Mama," he said, at the doorway to her room.

No answer. It was not like her to sleep so soundly.

"Mama!"

He went in and shook her by the shoulder. But she didn't wake.

The sun rested on the woods beyond the river; indoors it was already dusk. So many neighbors had come in to manage things for the old man, the house seemed crowded to suffocation with their tiptoeing business. They had the wisdom of the humble. They occupied themselves with practical matters, tidying the place, especially the room where the body lay, calling up the elected undertaker, preparing supper for the bereaved one, when he refused dumbly to go out for it to another house. So overtly—while privily their one preoccupation was in that figure seated bolt up in a chair in a corner of the death chamber, hands folded, motionless as wood.

"When he *does* come to!" they whispered among them. "When

he *does* begin to cry—oh, dear!" But there were some who thought differently. "No, this is the worst—this while he's stunned yet. Crying eases the pain."

Leander sat there staring at the sheeted bed for upwards of an hour without a sign of emotion of any sort changing the muscles of his face.

It was dreadful, this waiting for him to break.

"He don't realize yet. Somebody's got to do something."

One man, nerving himself to it, went in and laid a hand on Leander's shoulder. "Come, Mr. Killen."

Rattled, he began to shake the old man. "The ladies've got some supper for you in the kitchen, Mr. Killen. You ought to eat something—do you good. That's the man!"

In the hall, the others put fingers to their lips and bent their ears. Silence.

"Mr. Killen, now, come. We understand what this means to you, one and all. But you've got to help us if we're to help you."

There was a break at last. Low, harsh, throat-trapped, a sound of brief laughter. A cartilaginous cackle.

Leander came out of the room then faster than they had thought his feet would carry him. It gave them no time to wipe the confusion from their faces. Over his own, at the sight, spread a redness of more blood than they had supposed was in him. There was a savage misery in his eyes. They thought: "How awful. He's too old for it, and he's gone queer." Aloud they said: "There's some supper for you in the kitchen. That's it, take an arm, out this way. Sit down right here and have a bite."

But Leander had another purpose. Cutting loose in mid-floor, he followed the line of his own shuffling momentum and passed out of the back door.

Alarm. "What's he doing? Catch him. Somebody must go with him."

Young Mrs. Cotton had a ray of sense. "Let him be. He just wants to get out in his garden, alone, and maybe it's the very best thing."

Leander went down to the bottom of the garden. It was true, he wanted to be alone and rid of them. He wished passionately they were all dead too. Damned whisperers, damned tear dabbers, why couldn't they have come straight out with it: "Poor, poor fellow, your heart is broken and we know it, so why try to keep the sobs back? It's too stunning a blow, too cruel a loss."

He had an impulse to go back and brutally challenge them: "What loss? Say! Frankly, putting sentimentality aside, describe it to me."

He could see their faces. They'd feel silly enough then. But no, they wouldn't. They'd only signal to one another: "See, it's unhinged his mind."

For that hadn't escaped him, in the hall. The heat of it still burned his cheeks and temples, its redness doubled by the light from the dome of sunset reared above the transriver woods.

What if they were right, and it *was* his mind? He grew aware of a kind of numbness, lying, not in him, but tight around him, like an iron cloak. Was it possible they were the right ones and he the twisted and wrong?

With a scared sincerity he tried to think of some single thing in his life with his wife, the loss of which would have subtracted from his happiness. He'd be reasonable; he wouldn't take today, or yesterday; he'd struggle back into the past. Ten years. Twenty years. It was still yesterday, still today. Twenty-five, then—a quarter of a century. An ache in the brain. Calling on emotional memory for so long a leap was like asking power of a machine wrecked by rust.

Maybe he could begin to do it by and by. Perhaps with time, now he had been given the gift of time. . . .

Clang!

Sweat struck out on Leander's forehead. Ghostly, incorruptible even by death, that bell!

A calm man would have considered that there were outsiders in the room in there, unfamiliar with the purpose of that rope end hung by the bed, curious hands itching to finger and find out. "Goodness, so that's what rings!"

But sweat struck out on Leander's forehead. Vividly, he saw the hand of the dead one on the time-greened cord.

"Come in, my poor dear husband. Don't lag this time, for pity's sake! All I ask is so little, L'ander. To see your tears."

Panic grabbed him. Scuttling through a gap in the pickets, he fled down the path along the riverbank. His soles scratched on the gravel, heavier and heavier, but he wouldn't, he daren't, give in. Not till he had gone a great way (it might be fifty yards) did he pause to breathe. He sank on a bench made of a single board, below the path, facing the river.

He fastened his mind upon the glowing surface. Damned to live in the moment, he would live and lose himself in that maze of reflected sunset. The tide was making, the river ran backwards, with what slowly dissolving, softly flaming whorls, with what crimson ripple nets cast about glimmers caught from the greener top sky, like little, cool, green fishes!

Engrossed so, the one old man did not see the second old man who came up along the path from townward. This was a fellow much of Leander's age, but brighter of eye and ruddier of cheek, where it showed above the white ring of his whisker. And livelier.

No wonder he was livelier; he had eighty years of brave alarums and sweet excursions to regale his gums with and hunger his appetite.

He sat down on the other end of the bench. Leander might be dumb, but this was not one to be quiet long.

"Yessir, by Jolly, I been here before; same identical place, by Jumbo! Comes back to me, plain as plain now. It was when I was a sailor."

Once Leander was assured that this was none of his tormentors, he got back among the fluent whorls. Now the fire from the sky began to pale; the little green fishes caught in the ripple nets grew paler, dying. . . . Here came dismay. What was he to do when they were quite gone? How then keep his mind from the senseless, numb discomfort that lay wrapped tight around him?

To any but an ancient mariner, this abstraction might have been a damper. But after all, the stranger's speech was less conversation than soliloquy. Only as an afterthought did he turn his word on Leander.

"Yessirree, comes back to me. Used to be, right up along there somewheres, a little stage with a boat made fast to it. Eh?"

Leander glowered and shook his head. "Don't ask me."

"Newcomer, eh? Heh-heh! Well, I could tell you things."

Now a shadow ran toward the zenith. To the one old fellow it was the coming of tonight. To the other it was neither day nor night, here nor there; it was the shade in the pasture of the sunny past, cool to lie down in under the tree of age. Now, at his ease, this time-gelded bullock of a man who had been a sailor had up his cud of memories. Ruminant, reminiscent, he worked his jaws, expressing the juices a hundred times savored, but never so sweet, never so vividly actual.

"A sailor, mate, he's got a funny lay. He's got no home where he can stay long. Take girls and women, the best of 'em. It'd surprise you, now and again. Them and sailors. The way I figger it—a sailor—when a sailor he's got on his ship and gone, he's gone a long ways over the water, and they nor nobody's going to hear of him ever again. Heh-heh. . . ."

Chewing and chuckling.

"Good women too. But all women are good, God bless 'em. This one was good, pretty and good. Only she was young, and her husband he was long away. I see her plain as if she stood there now, in her skimpy waist and big long skirt the color of lilacs. Her cheeks they'd go red one minute and white the next—no sir, she didn't know how to handle herself, the way things were. Know what she'd say, mate? 'You mustn't come by here again—with my husband away in the West,' she'd say, with her blue eyes as big as two-bit pieces and her fingers working crisscross on her breast—she was built full in the breast, I remember, like a beauty ought to be—upstanding—mmmm-mmmm—a right armful of a woman for a strong handsome man!"

Leander would have got up and gone away if the weight of his strange numbness had let him. There was no flame left in the water.

The other sucked at his ambrosial pabulum. "I forget her name."

"It's growing cold," Leander thought. "I'll catch my death." The word made him writhe. "I wish I could feel like moaning and crying; then they'd be satisfied."

"Where was I?" the other mused. "I was a seafaring man. I was second mate on the bark *Andrew L. Cram.* I could thrash any man aboard of her. Good-looking too. Always ready for anything. We were taking on spruce logs here, and they came along slow—yes, I remember where I was now—and she'd say: 'If you come by again, I'm sure I shan't speak to you.'

"Then I give her a grin—I was always a cocky one—and I'd say: 'I don't see what's the harm, my helping you with your flowers.'

"She had an almighty lot of flowers—all kinds—asters and pansies and bachelor buttons—all kinds—and rambler roses climbing over the kitchen porch—and everything. How sweet they smelled! Maybe it was because she was messing with 'em so much—but, mate, she smelled like flowers, all kinds mixed up. Ever since, a flower garden's put me in mind of her.

"She had little ways with her, enough to craze a man. The way she could pout. 'You're lucky you're a sailor; sailors have so many ladyloves; ladyloves everywhere.' And she'd run down into the vegetables then and stand with her hands going crisscross on her breast—she was built full in the breast, I remember—and 'I wish,' she'd cry, 'I wish my husband would hurry and come home.'

"I told her the ship was laded and I was going away. 'Tomorrow?' says she. 'Day after,' says I.

" 'My husband he's coming home day after tomorrow,' she says, and she run, and I run after her into the lilacs and caught her and give her a kiss, the first I done. Delicious! Day following, I went by to say good-by.

" 'Here's a boat tied up,' I says, 'and here I am a sailor. Come out on the river for a little row.'

" 'No, no,' says she, 'no, no, no.'

"We got in the boat and I rowed across the river. . . . See them woods over there yonder, mate?"

The woods were no more than a low black wall now above dark water.

"See them woods there?" Ancient Lothario, he rolled between tongue and gum his succulent morsel of memory. "Mate, don't ask me. We walked a ways in the woods. She laughed and cavoorted. Then she'd get white's a sheet and run hide, so's I couldn't find her, and I had to stand and hail for her. 'Ahoy, Marjorie'—by Jolly, I got it, that was her name."

"Marjorie!" Syllables uttered at a great distance in Leander's mind.

"Marjorie!" An echo from beyond a gulf. The numbness that had been as wide as an iron cloak shrank as narrow as an iron hoop around Leander's brain. Where had he known one by the name of Marjorie?

"We walked in the woods. Ah, mate, but there was a lovely woman. Only she'd put her hands to her neck and cry out: 'My husband's coming tomorrow.' "

"Marjorie, Marjorie!" A dam, thick as twenty years, crumbling before the inflood of forgotten memories. . . .

"See them woods over there yonder, mate? Don't ask me. I was a sailorman them days. Yum-yum! When I left her she was crying."

That inflood, tumultuous, instantaneous, complete and vivid. . . . Stench of train smoke. . . . Smell of the earth of a street, years ago now paved. . . . In a gateway the fragrance of a garden of flowers. . . .

Leander opened his mouth. "She was crying when I got here. It was because I'd been away so long and she'd been so lonely. She always had a playful way—could look like a thunderstorm. 'You don't love me any more, otherwise you'd have hurried more. You can be happy away. I suppose I ought to be happy you're so lucky.' "

The weight was gone from the other end of the bench.

"How pretty she was—Marjorie! No, not pretty—beautiful!"

When Leander looked up to see the other old man standing there, his mouth a black hole in his whiskers, he gasped. He got to his feet with a sense of towering.

"You—I'm going to thrash you."

He had to say that. He was a man.

"I'm going to kill you."

What a shame it would be to him if he were to forget it before he could do it, too helpless, too happy?

The hole in the whiskers opened and shut. "I—mate—I thought you says——"

Leander shuffled toward him. Desperately he fought to make it remain momentous, that dirty little pebble in the great white flood. He got his hands on the scoundrel's shoulders. But it was too late. He'd forgotten.

The dams in his tear ducts broke, and water poured out of his eyes.

"She was lovely. Wasn't she lovely? She was so sweet. She was so true, so good, and so beautiful."

He opened his hands and the ancient mariner was gone, a gulp and a shadow. Turning his feet homeward, thirty years of age had vanished too.

Full dark had come, but he needed no light up the yard. It was a garden thronged and fair. The good green smell of brittle cabbages, firm squashes and melons and tall young corn, and mingled now the coming perfume of many, many flowers. Flowers that Marjorie gathered in a great sheaf against her bosom—gay with pride of them—and one for love for young Leander's buttonhole. . . .

He passed into the kitchen. A clean room, a singing, busy room, never so shining a kitchen. . . . Dr. Hathelly drying drug-washed hands by the stove there. . . . "It's a fine baby, Leander, fine big boy." . . .

Chug-chug and cinders. . . . Trip to Niagara. . . . What a sight!

"Jack got ninety in algebra. The Hewett boy got only eighty-five."

"They found him early this morning; he must have fallen in yesterday on his way from school." . . . In this hall here, nothing in words to say to each other, nothing to do but hang tight to one another's hands. . . .

"Your beans have never looked so well as this year, L'ander." . . . "Nor your hollyhocks either, my dear." . . .

Bedroom. There was something under a sheet. A thing that was still and white, full-breasted and young and beautiful.

Leander went down aspraddle on his knees.

Out in the hall they listened, and sighed after the long strain.

"That's better. He's crying now."

*The Body of the Crime**

THE HOUSE IN WHICH DANIEL WAS born was the kind of which we say, as we drive past it in the elm-pillared margin of some New England village: "What a monstrosity!" One day, when the Antique has caught up with the Eighties, perhaps we shall say: "What a beauty! What noble bays and airy cupolas and richness of brown scrollwork! They knew how to build their houses in those days."

Perhaps, too, we shall have matured enough to say of men like Dan Kinsman, who was Daniel's father: "They knew how to build their lives."

When the young Daniel came home from his first year away to prep school and saw with his changed eyes the unchanging house, the weighing cornices and flying towers, squared bays, rounded bays, porte-cochere, all cocoa brown in the shadows of the chestnuts——

"That's it," he thought, "it's not like other fellows' houses."

And when he studied this man, his father, it seemed for a while he had found the answer to the riddle as old in its secret wretchedness as the very beginnings of his memory. "And *he*, he's not like other fellows' fathers."

Other fellows' fathers, Daniel had found in his year, were men who arrived cheerfully from lifting their incomes and departed grimly to lower their medal scores. Forward-moving, tomorrow-thinking young elders, eager, industrious, mobile fellows fearful of nothing but of seeming to stand still.

But here was a father apparently content to be one year where he had been the year before, possessed of but the same possessions, the same small-town friendships, the same leisurely, half-patriarchal judgeship, the same pedestrian pleasures, books and dogs, pruning hooks and garden hoes and fishing rods. And he a strong, straight man alive, not yet fifty, with black hair thick on his head, and lungs to laugh with when he wanted. Strange!

Now it came to Daniel it must be because his father was so wanting in—that's to say, so strange this way—that he had always seemed to his son so—so—Daniel groped for a word for a thing he'd never been able to give a shape or name, and had to finish lamely—seemed so "strange."

Daniel could have laughed for joy to discover, now he was grown up, that the trouble about his father was so little a one as this. For all the weight of his fifteen years, he could have skipped for lightness, to know that here was a difference from other fathers he now could grasp, even learn to condone, yes, even admire, even fight for, with fellows with more—well—say—money-grabbing dads.

Yes, Daniel could have skipped for lightness on the deep cave-green turf of the hydrangea alley, where they walked and talked that first June afternoon at home, he and his father, while Mother watched them with her pale smile from her long chair in her high window.

It was curious; Daniel had always loved his ailing, beautiful mother, easily, and been near her and told her everything tellable, easily, and not thought much about it. The one he would have given his life to be able to love as easily, to be close to, friends with, whole of heart, was this other, this darkly handsome man whom he himself was so absurdly like to look at, his father.

So today it was as if the year of forgetting had worked a good miracle. It was a dream come true to find himself sauntering and chatting with Dan Kinsman as affectionately at ease as though they had been but two fellows gravely estimating the apple yield in the west yard and the hay chances in the back mowing, chuckling together over the antics of Spot's pups on the barn floor, waving answer to the view halloo of Doc Martin racketing by in the antique twin-six, and, wonder of wonders at last, arm in arm, man and man, marching indoors prepared to mount and demand of Mother if supper were ever to be ready—as if she, poor fragile chatelaine, could know anything about that.

But, day of marvels! An elixir must have run in the air. For here in their sight came Mother down the stairs to meet them, walking by herself, suddenly, subtly revivified, the flush on her cheeks and the shine in her eyes not more for their astonishment than for her own.

So tonight there were three at table in place of two, and it was like the sort of dream in which one wakes from an interior nightmare to find everything finished that was horrid, and everything at its beginning that is right and bright. Nor did it end with the supper table; afterward she would go out abroad with them, as if greedy to share in the marvel of those two men of hers who walked of a sudden as one, and by their walking so, seemed so suddenly to have made her walk again.

What a sight it was for the evening sun to see, level and bloody rose beneath the eaves of the chestnuts! Dan Kinsman, bemused, commencing words and swallowing their ends on half-choked chuckles, even as his eyes, quick for once, kept slant track of Vivian's every oddly exuberant gesture. Daniel, beatified, accepting wonders with a new omnivorous trust. And Vivian Kinsman, unbelievable, a princess freed from some evil enchantment in exile, returned to her kingdom, leading them.

In the east yard, hidden for years, the low, excited laugh was on her lips continuously. For this border, it was: "They're too gorgeous, Dan; I love them!" For that bed: "But there never *were* such flowers!" When she came in view of Father's season's pride, the bastion of man-high crimson poppies, all she could do was put her hands to her heart.

Only when she caught sight of Spot and her puppies taking the last of the sun at the barn door was there a shadow of change in the exclamation of discovery.

"You're going to keep them all, Dan!" She drew Father's eyes. "All, Dan!"

He would have temporized, laughingly: "Spot got away this time, and——"

"You're not going to drown them, Dan. I couldn't bear to think——"

The sharpness in her voice brought quickness to his.

"Why, no, of course not, Vivian. I shall keep them, of course—

unless someone should want them very much—who'd give them a good home."

The sun touched distant woods. Father dared worry aloud at last. "It'll be chilly in another second now, Vivian."

She turned back with a queer, mercurial docility, asking only, when they came to the porch steps, that she might have some of the crimson poppies for her room tonight.

"I should so love to see them in the morning, Dan, just three or four."

"You'll have an armful, that's what you'll have, dear; I'll go and get them now."

Daniel took her in on his arm, feeling tall, now his father was gone. She would go only as far as the living room for the moment, where a slender summer fire was laid, ready for the match. When Daniel had lighted it he studied the white figure lying back deep in Dan Kinsman's chair. He said: "You're happy tonight, Mother."

She needn't answer. Her eyes, fixed on the fire, were alight with all its beginning, playing flames. And before he knew why, "Have you always been happy here with Father," he demanded, "and with me?"

This must have seemed to need no answer, at first. But then she sat up and fixed the boy with her straight gaze. "Always, yes!" From vehemence it changed to mirth. "What ever put it in your head, sonny?—yes, yes, yes!" And sinking back, with a little gasp at the end of her laughter: "He's an angel, sonny, your father is, but he's an awful slow-poke; won't you go and hurry him along?"

Father had meant it when he said an armful; he had gathered a whole great sheaf of the poppies, and rather a pity, for the blooms were closed. But what matter if Vivian wanted them; they'd open again at day. So he seemed to be thinking as he stood there, laden and bemused, in the falling night.

And so it was that Daniel, his son, came upon him, deep in a preoccupation of his own, halted a rod away, and, without lifting his gaze from the ground, said: "Has Mother liked it here in Kennelbridge, Father?"

Dan Kinsman had had a day of astonishments. Without turning anything but his head, and that slowly, he studied his dim questioner.

"It has liked your mother here," he said quietly.

The boy, given a riddle, raised his eyes to the man, who was no more than a shadow shape in the dusk now—and, as shadows may be, something distorted and magnified—between the blackening blood of the poppies he carried and the dike he had torn them from. And Daniel forgot his riddle and widened his eyes. The father knew the sign of old. All afternoon he had been waiting for it, pulled between dread and the beginnings of an incredible hope. Now he wheeled, cried, "Ah, Daniel, son!" and held out his arms, careless of their sanguinary burden. And his son turned and ran.

What good is it to be fifteen and a man, instead of ten and a boy, or five and a child? When Daniel, fleeing, needles in his legs and an icicle up his backbone, reached the firelight where he had left his mother sitting, it was on the knees of veriest childhood he tumbled down, to hide his face in the chair bottom beside her, wind his fingers in her skirts, and sob it out in words aloud, at last:

"Mother—why am I—why am I sometimes—sometimes so fr-fr-frightened of my—my fa-fa-father?"

Mother had always answered his questions, till he asked this question. Her failure now, her complete, unstirring silence, doubled the magnitude of a terror till now his own shamed secret. And the doubled was redoubled by the sound of that man's feet on the piazza, coming toward the door.

He groveled. "Mother, please, hurry—hurry and tell me, tell me, Mother! What—what's there about my father—what's he done that's such a—a horror?"

Still, for answer, no word, no gesture. And it was too late; a quiet door had opened and the feet were in the room. As Daniel scrambled up and wheeled, a defending courage suffused him. He stood his ground, and, not knowing why, spread his arms across the man's way, and not knowing what, cried: "No! Don't! Don't come!"

Through the water in his eyes he began to see his father's face hung there before him, oddly gray, the stare of it fixed, not on him, but on her behind him. And he grew aware of two things fighting in that stare, the greater one like a stunned sorrow, the lesser like a reawakening hope.

As sometimes in crisis, it was of the lesser one the man spoke now.

"This, then, Daniel, is why you said what you said out there, and sobbed, and ran away back here? It wasn't that old queerness of yours coming back then, after all?"

The husband's shock was gentler than the son's, for all evening he had had in his mind as he watched Vivian the thought of a candle when it gutters, how it will flame to its old brightness for an instant at the last.

Not so with Daniel. When he turned and knew that the reason his mother had sat there and not answered him was that all the while she had sat there in the deep chair dead, he fainted.

Doc Martin had to mop his bald head with a troubled handkerchief many times in the following days. On the third, the afternoon after the funeral, stopping in at the Kinsmans' by right of the oldest and closest friend and finding Dan there all alone, he asked: "Where's Daniel hiding himself?" And if it sounded casual, and was meant to, already in the soil of the doctor's mind uneasy little roots of wonder had begun to set.

"Don't know; not far off, I guess." The answer was given with an averted face.

Why shouldn't it be? Men's faces, when they've just buried their wives of twenty years—why may they not wish to keep what's written on them to themselves? The physician mocked himself for a worrying idiot as he went on home.

But he had his head to mop again when he got to his own house and found Daniel fidgeting up and down the piazza, inarticulate and miserably mantling. It was all mysterious and awkward. He didn't know what he was to do or say, and especially was this so when the boy's dumbness, laboring, brought forth some mouse of words about the weather or the baseball standings. But finally, "Dr. Martin," it came at a rush, "was my mother happy, living here in Kennelbridge, with Father—and me?"

It is unfortunate that at such moments men seem to think they have to speak in the manner of oracles. As Dan Kinsman, three days before, now Doc Martin:

"Well, son, she *lived* here in Kennelbridge, with you and your father, almost exactly ten years longer than I gave her to live. Does that mean anything?"

And thereafter he wondered why the boy's eyes, savagely troubled, followed him slantwise everywhere. He wondered more. Seeing the sun go and the dusk come, he wondered why the sensitive, naturally unobtrusive lad stayed on, apparently aimless and plainly wretched, and stayed, and made no move to go. It was after dark when Doc Martin appeared at the Kinsman place, to find Dan out in the east yard, standing, chin down, hands locked behind him.

"I thought, Dan, you might wonder where the kid was. He's over at my house. I'm afraid I've been—uh—keeping him."

Dan listened, stock-still, without comment. It became an ordeal.

"I don't know just how to say it, Dan. The boy seems badly upset. He has a lot of his mother in him, Dan—a lot of the thing that made us all love her—and—want to spank her, sometimes. That sentimental defenselessness—it went with her ailment, I've no doubt. That making a mountain of emotion out of a molehill of—not that I mean this is a molehill—but—damn it, old man! The boy—this house—this night after the funeral—I've a hunch he'd more than half like to stay over with me. Thought I'd ask you."

"Yes."

The one syllable, it sounded rough in the throat. As he went away the doctor turned twice to study the figure posted there in darkness, head heavy, face hidden. Anger? Sorrow? What? Headless, tailless business! He told himself he wished he were dead and well out of it.

He wasn't. After that night, any half plans there may have been of father and son going off for a summer of travel together were dropped. There was a camp in the Green Mountains where Daniel's school went, and he was packed for it by the second morning. Dan came to Doc Martin, unhappy, unused to lying.

"I wonder if you'll do something for me, old man? Drive Daniel over to the main line this noon. I shall be busy."

The doctor did it. What their parting was he never knew, for the boy had his bags out at the gate when he drove by, and the father was "busy." If the friend of them both was profanely troubled he kept it quiet and set himself for a gallant hour of cheer and small talk. The problem of a book for the journey seemed a godsend. They went over the newsstand's library with a mutual pretense of care, but as if it were not bad enough that all the novels were detective novels, Daniel discovered after brief browsings that there was none he could be certain he hadn't read. As he accepted one at last—entitled *Murder!*—the physician had to stare.

"Lord, son! To look at you anybody'd think you were as mild as a lamb. And here you turn out a glutton for crime. Don't you ever read anything else?"

Daniel went red—even redder, the doctor thought, than was asked for.

"Oh, I forget 'em faster'n I read 'em. If you asked me one single thing that had happened, a week after, I couldn't any more remember it than I could——"

He got no further. He had touched by chance on a pet dogma of the other's; and Doc Martin, figuratively, squared off.

"Couldn't remember? Bosh! Ever tried?"

"Tried?" Daniel was confused by this vehemence.

"*Really* tried, I mean. Rolled up your mental sleeves and taken pick and spade to the humus of memory, to try and turn up some one particular thing that's buried there? It's surprising. There are authenticated records of long-term prisoners, men in solitary confinement, who, simply for something for their minds to do . . ."

And here they came, the classic cases, served up with a zealot's gusto; the aged criminals reconstructing verbatim the nursery tales of infanthood; the old fellows repainting in minutest detail places passed through as children and thereafter wholly forgotten. And so forth. And so on.

The man with a hobby is not to be held accountable. Doc Martin, who had toiled to make talk—now his one fear was that the belated train would make up time.

"Can't remember! Actually, you can't *forget!* Nothing you've ever felt, heard, seen, no matter how tiny—you may mislay the record, but you can't lose it. No matter how dim, it's here in your cranium somewhere, indelible, forever."

The bent ear and big eye of his audience it was cruel to give up. The train was in, but there was still the moment on the platform.

"Theoretically, Daniel, you ought to be able to remember the day of your birth. But it would probably take you as many as a thousand years, in a dark cell, and after all——"

After all, after the boy was up the step Doc Martin recollected something he had been two days thinking on.

"Daniel, listen! Your mother *was* happy. Her life here was a clear, quiet, happy life, with those she loved deeply. Believe me, Daniel."

It was good for Daniel he had the book called *Murder!* At the end of his emotional tether he must have escape, and the surest escape was here between these covers; he knew the taste of it beforehand, as the eater of drugs knows the taste of his drug. Escape, yes. And a curious, helpless, rather horrid surrender.

Never remember? "Bosh!" For a little while yet he left the book unopened, and thought of the mild old doctor and his ferocious expletive. But was it true, even a half of what he had claimed, about digging up buried things? . . . If you tried hard enough? . . . Took a pick and spade . . . to buried things?

There were five hours to ride, more than enough for the book. Let it wait.

To remember things forgotten! By dim footprints in the mold of old fantasies, by broken twigs of sensation—this sort of sound disliked for no reason, that odor as inexplicably agreeable—by clues so thinner-than-air to be able to track back relentlessly—what?

"Bosh!" It was Daniel's own bosh this time. But the light in the deeps of his abstracted eyes burned no less steadily, nor did the color of a strange excitation retreat from his cheeks and temples.

There was a station. Express, the train only slowed, going through. On the flickering platform stood an elderly woman, back to, a stoutish figure glimpsed for a split second, gray-clad, with a purple hat with a tulle quill.

"Emma!"

But then the boy lay back and derided himself. It was that purple, forward-tilted hat. Emma, his old nurse, had been dead three—no, two—years. It was three years ago she came to see him, from Albany, and that was the year before she died.

Yes, yes. She came in her nephew's car and brought Daniel a sweater she had knitted for him. He could see her now, when he tried to get into it, there on the big circular side piazza, and her chagrin. "Mercy, when I was here last I never looked to see you grow so in two years. Remember when I was here last time, Dannie?"

"Course I do; what d'you think? And you said I used to be a caution when I was little, and you hoped I'd got over it."

"Bless you, Dannie, and have you?"

Had he? Got over what? Three years ago he'd known what, because three years ago he'd remembered what she'd said two years before that. Something about: "I declare, you always were a caution, Dannie. The first day ever I saw you . . . saw you . . . first day ever I saw you . . ."

Concentrate on it! Try harder!

". . . first day ever I saw you, do you know what you said . . . what you . . ."

In the Pullman, but unconscious of the Pullman, Dannie knotted his brows.

Don't give up. Go at it some other way. . . .

Well, they'd been in his room; he was ready for bed, and Emma had come up—she'd stayed overnight that next-to-last visit—and she'd sat there in the blue rocker and talked and talked. Talked so long that Mother had called: "Daniel, Emma's tired, so you must stop asking her so many . . ."

But now he *had* it—the other thing—it was "question."

It wasn't "what you said." It was, complete: "First day ever I saw you, do you know *the question you asked me?* Well, most three-year-olds, they'll ask you like, 'What's a zebra?' or 'What's a airplane?' But the first thing you asked me was . . . thing you asked me was . . ."

No, after all, not quite complete. Why did the light of recollection close again, just there? Especially when, by thinking on it, that bedtime visit of Emma's had grown as vivid as a thing today.

The expression of the boy in seat No. 5 was a set scowl. A flush colored it, like anger. A "Bosh!" trembled on his lips. He had a book to read, and, by hang, he'd read it now. A book called *Murder!*

"Murder!"

Why, now he'd got that too!

"The first thing you asked me—I was trying to get you to go into the summerhouse and you were howling and pulling—and you asked me, 'What is murder?' And if you don't call that funny for a three-year-old to be asking . . ."

Murder? Three-year-old? Funny? . . . But leave those, for the moment.

Summerhouse! Latticework, probably. Light through it in squares or diamonds, probably. Unless—ugh, it was chilly in the Pullman—there were vines. Vines?

The train carried the corporeal weight of Daniel Kinsman to the White River Junction that summer afternoon. But the part of him that weighed nothing at all had started on an immensely longer journey, an incalculably stranger quest.

At camp, for the first while, they let him go his own gait, without nagging him or themselves. Aware of his shocking loss, they even let down the rules a little—rules, fundamentally, of good fellowship—

in his case. Daniel, with his shut mouth, little appetite, and eyes fixed habitually on nothing, was no good fellow for anyone.

This was all right for a certain period. But when a week and another week had gone, and a normal youngster should have been getting some hold on healthy life, and Daniel was still not less separate, but if anything more so, physically torpid, colorless of expression, unmistakably if incomprehensibly not among those present, the responsible began to think of doing something about it.

At length the Head sat down and wrote a letter to the boy's father, who had shut up house on Doc Martin's plea and gone off with him to the Canadian woods. But that letter was destined not to be posted. Before a stamp was on it, word came in that young Kinsman had not been seen since lights-out the night before. At the end of a day and night of combing the woods, beating the hills, a telegram was despatched to Canada.

Locked, bolted, and shuttered though the house was, Daniel knew a boy's way into it. One of the cellar windows was loose enough to let a lock-pick wire in.

Of all that Daniel had done, of all he was yet to undertake, this one act was the hardest. That he could, in the night, enter into that sealed, empty, pitch-black habitation, of which anyone might be nervous—and he, with his mother dead and his imagination whipped keen by a fortnight's flagellation, was horribly, icily afraid—gives the measure of the thing that was stronger than the house's terror, its pull.

If he were only in the house, only on the scene there, only at home! Day by day, night by night, the brown house of home had kept the dragline taut on him, by innuendo, by promise, by command. Whenever a peephole, opened in memory, had closed again before the glimpsed stage could set itself with half the properties of old actuality, "Ah, yes, but if you were *there* it might be different," something had seemed to whisper.

And now that he was here? Now that he was actually in, his feet weighing on sightless stairs, hands guiding him along blind walls? Now what was he to do?

Nothing. When he had reached his own room, at the end of gropings that brought sweat out of his neck, he pawed for his bed, found it, and laid himself down along the middle of the mattress. There, inert—almost as inert for hours at a time as a cataleptic—he remained. How long?

By calendar it came to four days. In his consciousness the lapse of time was not measurable, it was as well a dream's forty winks as a dungeon's forty years.

Of his rare actual moves he was to all intents unconscious. Luckily it was summer, and the water not turned off; from time to time he drank. Once he bolted raw oatmeal from a box in the pantry and was ill with it. The electric current was cut, but there was the oil lantern he might have lighted long before he did, had he cared. Rather, perhaps, had he dared. Perhaps, more simply, had he felt the need. After all, his eyes were no longer concerned with this shuttered Here and Now.

They were concerned with the half-open door of a summerhouse.

Relatively, it may have been little more than a scratching of the topsoil; actually, in that blank-eyed fortnight away at camp, he had penetrated a surprising depth into the leaf mold of his fallen memories. Most important, he had caught the trick of it, learned the heft and balance of his tools, pick and spade, a dogged mental concentration working at one with a reserveless mental surrender.

So it had become child's play, literally, by fastening on some fag end of sensuous recollection—a barked shin of escapade, sting of a punishment, taste of the sweetmeat of some reward—to restore the outlines of whole episodes in the comparatively recent years of his sixes, fives, even his fours; to relive whole days, repeople whole scenes with shapes which began by having no names, or with names wanting shapes, and watch these phantasmal beings take on identities and lineaments—and lo! Auntie Prichard, of course, the doughnut woman! Or Mary Belle—who could forget the girl with wire on her teeth!

He had learned a lot about the creature of pranks and bush beatings that is the mind. He learned, at a price, that no lead can be too paltry to follow. So it was, retrieving a boy's face plastered with freckles and banged with red hair, he had given three long hours of his last camp morning to trying to find the face a name. A dozen times he nearly had it; the muscles of his tongue knew the feel of it, yet couldn't get the sound. It made him mad. "I won't give it up, not if it takes all day!"

And, "day," there it was. Georgie Day! Who could forget Georgie Day?

Accident? In the weird business Daniel was about, there's no such thing.

Georgie Day. Well, well! Immediately, fruitless hours fruited magically. A house suddenly sprang up around the freckled rascal, and around the house a tin-can-littered yard, and in the yard a tumbling barn, and in the barn, rabbits.

Rabbits? What about rabbits? Look! Here's a rabbit running, bounding high with fright across a greensward in sunshine. No, none of Georgie's; he and his have vanished from the scene. This is a wild one, cottontail, surprised among berry bushes behind the home garden, retreat cut off, scuttling across the west lawn for all its worth, and Daniel running after it.

Run, cottontail! Run, boy! Bounce, bunny! Whoop, Dannie!

"Here, Daisy! Where are you, Daisy? Where's that dog?"

Daisy? Why, Spot's mother, of course, elderly, sleepy, all setter-red.

Yellow sunshine, green grass, little wild blue shadow, hunting, praying, for some hole. And a hole, a hole at last! Squarish aperture among massed leaves. Dive for it, bunny! Stop, boy! Into it, rabbit! Boy, stop dead! Don't go near there, youngster! Frown if you please, stamp, mutter; yes, you know you don't want to go near there. You know you don't.

Why not?

Pandemonium. Out comes rabbit, out comes Daisy, the lazy, surprised asleep in there. And the two of them, fleeing, pursuing, flicker past the transfixed Dannie, and away, into limbo. For it's the squarish aperture in massed woodbine leaves, crosshatch of lattice in their gaps, lattice door ajar—it's this he's staring at.

So it was, by uttering the irrelevant words "if it takes all day," Daniel had found the way back to the summerhouse.

Two weeks it had taken him to reach its viny exterior, those two weeks away at camp. Had he had a hundred years, real ones, in place of the hundred hours he could command, who knows but that he might actually have succeeded in covering the rest of the journey—might have crept or leaped at last across that one remaining rod of grass, gravel, and doorsill, and been inside?

Now he started sanguinely. Only a rod left—the last dash—home stretch. Pooh! Thrown back from it, confused, he started again with the same assurance, only again to be set on his heels by a wall, impalpable as air, but impenetrable as glass. How many times did he relaunch the attack? In one hour of the clock he could live a score in recollection, a hundred toward the end, when hunger and fever had whipped the pace. No longer sanguinely, but desperately, he tried one breach after another.

For now there were several; he had multiplied his points of attack. To the rabbit day he had added quickly the Emma day. It was no task by now to reconstruct that episode entire. He could commence with the breakfast table, where the new nurse was first introduced into the scheme of his cosmos. He could mount then to his room with her, suffer the change into denim play pants, come down, come out, and go towing around the yard at her arm's end, dazzled by the sudden wealth of her "What shall we play? Anything on earth you like, Dannie?"

So, not once, but dozens of times, he came to the spot where something in him balked, he began to howl, cleared Emma's grasp, let her go on. He could see her face in all its mystification now—and see it, more was the wonder, across the width of the rod he couldn't cross—in the doorway of the summerhouse. And he could hear her expostulating still:

"What is it, Dannie? Nothing but a toad here. You're not afraid of a toad!"

And he could feel something in his stomach's pit, that came up, and was words.

"What is murder, Emma?"

Why on earth that? What was it in him, cold and hot—not shame, not rage, not terror, alone, but like a misery of all three compounded? Or like the feeling Daniel had to this day, immensely diluted, whenever anyone in his hearing spoke of cycles or sickles or Seckles.

And, coming to that, why on earth that? Did it all come from "Seckle"? And did that come from the pear tree, down past the east corner of the barn, which, since he was recollecting, he recollected he had never liked? Recollected, in fact, that when they used to play hide-and-seek at his house, and Daniel himself was "it," and one of the boys hid behind that Seckle pear below the barn, he wouldn't go there to spy him, not if he stayed "it" forever.

So? Why wouldn't he? Time and time again he made an effort to follow that trace, but it was of no use; there was nothing there that was important, he had to tell himself; much better buckle down to business with the shovel day.

The shovel day he had added to the rabbit day and the Emma day now. Where it came in the chronology he couldn't say; though he judged from the longer time it had taken him to dig it out it must have been earlier. At any rate, it was the farthest back he could remember being frightened by his father.

He had to work on it. Again, again, stubbornly again, he would stand in a flushed twilight on the perimeter of that arc whose radius was a rod, and watch the woodbine leaves put aside, and see his father emerge from the dark interior, carrying a spade.

Well, what about it? What so fearful was his father doing? Going gardening, probably, in the evening's cool; tools may have been kept in the summerhouse. So, what? Look more deeply into this! But try as Daniel would, he couldn't. Each time, at sight of man and shovel, the child gulped, turned, ran, with goblins grabbing after him, for the house and Mother.

Why? Why, oh, why, oh, why?

And now at last, time lost all count of—grown to months and years, it seemed, in the black house—now at last, let down by the caving of the body beneath it, Daniel's mind began to surrender to exhaustion. Daylight—what was actually the fourth daylight—creeping through the shutter cracks in slim fans of grayness, did not waken him for a long time from the sleep into which he had sunk near midnight.

When it did he failed to fall immediately, as his habit was, into his reminiscent reverie. Lying supine, staring at the ceiling, it was the ceiling he saw this morning. He raised himself on the mattress, intending to go downstairs, but with the act a dizziness took hold of him. He lay back again and listened to his teeth knocking together. It is one thing for a man, adult and idle, to starve himself for a while; for a growing boy it is another thing.

It was the first time there had been room in Daniel's brain for a thought of failure. Was it not possible that the end of the time he could hide and have solitude was approaching? No sooner the idea than he repelled it. With a strength of panic he drove himself back to his task. Dig or die, now!

But the pick and spade, till now so docile, developed the balkings and crotchets of a curious sabotage. Today, when he summoned the old face of a playmate, straightway the features began to twist in the weirdest fashion, magnify, diminish, like the grotesque faces that dissolve in dreams. Or, coming on a new trail of old adventure unexplored, he found it leading him into extraordinary places, out of all color with the rest of his past—and realized with a start that it was something he had read, not lived.

And presently, frustrated, he slept again.

Each other day had been an age; this was but a dozen blinks long, a day wasted. How could Daniel know the incalculable value of that day his mind lay fallow?

It was night once more when he arose, went into his mother's room, and lay down on the bed there. It was nearly, if not quite, somnambulism. Certainly he was unaware of any reason for the move. Whether he fell asleep and woke up, whether he slept at all, or waked at all, whether at any time he was actually, bodily, in the summerhouse, it would be now impossible to say. It can only be said that the thing till the end had all the stigmata of true nightmare.

The will to terror, to begin with. Terror sprung of its own seed, an effect wanting a cause, a shadow condemned to create the object that casts it. And with this, alternately, a weightless, boundless mobility, and a sense of being held from moving, arms pinioned, legs bound.

Nothing was ever clear. Such moments as were lighted—less than pictures; mere rags of sight vignetted on the dark—were whisked away too quickly to be comprehended whole. Nor were these many. The pervading scene was a blackness in which blacknesses moved, giving forth but muffled sounds. Acts witnessed and no more, shadowy, separate, retreating rather than ever coming nearer.

"They're going away from the summerhouse, ma'am," or, "carrying him away"—that adverb, "away," was forever recurring. And generally, somewhere near it, whether before or after, blacknesses moved on blackness with a black burden; heavy breathing, soft feet.

It must be understood there was never an attempt at sequence. No act revealed itself whole at any one time; at divers times divers fractions of it would repeat themselves, mingled with stray fractions of other acts or utterances.

Take the one set of sounds. Sometimes it ran, out there—door creak, oath, blow, scuffle. Sometimes quite reversed. Sometimes—oath, blow, scuffle, door creak.

And that querying cry, coming from close above, thrown down—out of a window?—into the dark, now it would be, "Dan, what are you doing? *Tom!*" Then, like as not, next time it would be: "Tom, what are you doing? *Dan!*"

It is impossible to tell it, by a tenth, adequately. For by the very mechanics of telling, nine tenths of the formlessness is lost; fragments, released from the peculiar bedevilment of nightmare, inevitably fly together. Detached words, fractional phrases, flickering by, flitting back again; before they can be written here they must needs have formed themselves by some degree into sentences, no matter if the sentences are forever changing something of the forms. As, for instance, in the one, "Dan (Tom), what are you doing?" followed by, "*Tom!* (*Dan!*)"

There's the other sentence, into which at last the word "murder" has come. By the time it has crystallized itself into the sequence, "It was murder, Dan; I saw it; murder in cold blood!"—by that time the light around it has crystallized, too, in a pattern, a pattern of diamond-shaped pencils striking in through gaps of latticework. And the strait jacket of nightmare around one's limbs has taken the shape of the arms of the crier-out. And the crier-out is Mother.

"Don't come in that door; I'm afraid of you, Dan! The blood on your hands is blood of brutal murder. Why? Don't tell me. Was it because I loved him? I love my child, here in my arms. Must I be afraid for *him* then? Must he be afraid of his father, now, as long as the two of you live?"

And this cry, too, vibrant with hysteria, has a vision to go with it, a peephole vision of a close lantern, a red-flecked hand, a spade with earth spots on it, and the tight, white, terrible mask of Father's face.

So, in telling, already this big, close lantern light has extricated itself from the little lantern light at a distance. But in the dream, if it was a dream, this very separation of the two became from the first the thing, intuitively, the dreamer fought for. Wrestled for with tied hands, ran after with hobbled feet; cried to with stopped mouth.

In the beginning it was equally the one or the other that might start it; toward the end of an aeon a kind of rule was established; it was the little light far off that began, and the big one then, too soon, that came and swallowed it, only to be swallowed in its turn by that blackness with black things moving in it, or the door-creak sequence, containing the scuffle, the oath, and the blow.

Perhaps it was because of this that the desire of the boy's dread centered more and more fiercely on that weakling spark, and he told himself it was there that whatever was hidden was hidden, and awaited its recurrence impatient of the other shadow plays. And when it came, and the voice of the second woman in the bedroom—a nurse?—began, "It's digging they are, ma'am, down there——," and with that the light began to swell, irresistibly, and stripe itself in the pattern that meant the summerhouse, Daniel fought with all his bitter, puny power against the re-enwrapping arms, the relifting hysteria of Mother's "Don't come in that door! I'm afraid of you!" and the reopening peepshow of the red hand and the white face.

And he cried: "Yes, but go on with the other! Digging down *where*, down *where?*" till in the nightmare the lees of the sweat of his exhaustion ran in icy dribbles down his skin.

It was not till he gave up, beaten by weariness, that it suddenly gave in.

"It's digging they are, ma'am, down there under——"

"Under *what?*"

"—under that pear tree——"

"Pear tree?"

"—with the little pears, below the barn. By the light of the lantern, ma'am——"

Lantern! By the way, where is a lantern? Now, quick!

"—they're digging in the——"

Digging! Pick and spade? Where are they?

"—ground, burying something——"

A thing that is buried!

"—under the pear tree, ma'am."

Ever tried? Rolled up your sleeves, taken pick and spade—to turn up something that is buried there?

When Dan Kinsman and Doc Martin reached the house late that night, and found it black, the one last hope, which neither had dared to confess to, seemed to have followed all its fellows. Red-lidded with sleeplessness, jaws ill-shaven, clothing long worn, they looked the men they felt now, as, unlocking the front door, they went in.

"What's the good?"

It was the doctor that saw it, through one of the living-room windows.

"Hey! What's up out there? Somebody with a lantern, down there behind the barn."

They started out of the door at a walk, but then ran.

They found a lantern, a spade, and a garden mattock under the Seckle-pear tree, and a sprawling trench dug, and a weazen-faced, wide-eyed boy to his knees in it, holding out toward them two brown bones.

Dan spoke. "For God's sake, what are you doing here?"

Daniel spoke. "For God's sake, what are *these* doing here?"

Doc Martin spoke. "For God's sake!" That was all.

It wasn't that Dan was obstinate; it was simply that he was dazed.

"What are you doing here, son? Tell me!"

It wasn't that Daniel was sullen; it was simply that his legs were going to go out from under him at any moment now.

"What are these, Father? You tell me!"

"Son–sonny–you're sick."

"I am sick. Who was Tom?"

"Good lord alive! Dan, look here! Be quiet, Daniel; wait till I get through with him. Dan, how long ago was it–I mean, how old would this kid have been, that night?"

"What night do you mean?"

"Come out of it, man! That night when you heard where Tom had been the week before, and called me, and I brought the chloroform over, thinking maybe, perhaps, the dog might––"

"Dog!" High in the roof of a boy's mouth, the one syllable, echoing.

"–and you, Dan, no maybe or perhaps about it, you got him in the head with the spade, thank God, in time. What I asked you–how old was Daniel then?"

"Not old enough to remember anything. . . . Daniel, who's been telling you––"

But Doc Martin wouldn't have it. "No, man, you talk to me. How old?"

"Two, perhaps. Not three. A baby. A babe in arms, actually, come to think of it. Vivian had him there in her arms."

"Where?"

"There in the summerhouse."

"Vivian—in the summerhouse?"

"Afterward. She—she had come there."

"You've never told me."

"No. I—it's something I—— Look here, Daniel, son, you'd best be——"

"No you don't, Dan. Talk! What's this about Vivian, and Daniel, and the summerhouse afterward? Tell it, and tell it straight."

"She was ill, that's all. Frightened. And—and you know how she was about animals and things—and she didn't understand. Couldn't expect her to, not knowing anything. Hysterical. Went to the summerhouse to see—and bolted herself in."

"But when you explained?"

"That's it. I was a fool, I suppose. I tried to lie, at first. The mastiff was hers, from a pup; she adored him; it was all so sudden; I couldn't bring myself to say the word—hydrophobia. A fool."

"Yes, and a damned one."

"She said she was afraid of me, Doc. She said it was—it was——"

"She said it was murder, Father. And—it was only—— *Father!*"

"Son! Lord! What's the—— Hey! Catch him, Doc, or he'll fall."

"Catch him yourself, he's yours. Pick him up, fool. Starvation; don't worry too much. Bring him along."

"But if he should come to, and me carrying him. I'm afraid——"

"Don't be. Not any more."

*A Bath in the Sea**

MARTY MARTELLO WAS A PIANIST. Her luck was always running out. She got a job playing in a Bronx picture house, but then the neighborhoods went talkie and that ran out. She looked all set with Moe Kaplin's Racketeers at the Pantheon, but Moe's brother Cyril quit law school and took up the ivories, so that ran out. The Goldstone Agency threw occasional fill-ins her way; they were very occasional indeed after the depression came. August was always the tight month. Her life-insurance premium fell due the seventh of July, thirty-four dollars and forty cents. August sixth ended the thirty days of grace, and she had to make it somehow; she had a kid to think of.

Agents have to be patient. But this time when she came up Ben Goldstone's patience was about all gone.

"Broke, and gotta eat, is that your story?"

No, Marty wasn't broke. She showed him two tens and some silver. But she had to have fifteen more to put with it by tomorrow or else her insurance would go to hell. She kept repeating that over and over dully. It was hot. It was ninety-eight in the office. She put her fingers under her hair and held it out so as to let some air up through it. Fifteen dollars by tomorrow or else her insurance would go to hell. "I'm making it your problem, brother."

It was too hot to ask a fat man to laugh. Goldstone got up and picked his clothing away from him. He went out into the outer office and came back with a card in his hand. While he talked he fiddled with it, rapping it against his other knuckles. Marty never took her eyes off that card.

"How old are you, Marty?"

She told him thirty. "What have you got for me there?"

"Thirty. You oughtn't to let yourself go. You need a wave."

"Don't make me laugh."

Goldstone didn't intend to. He let go. People didn't like her, the people she had to work with. Give and take, they liked a sport. "Look at Pearl Fisher; she hasn't got the stuff you have even, yet she gets by."

"Oh yeah?" Marty never took her eyes off the card he was fiddling with.

"Oh yeah is right, dearie. These pluggers know she's willing to be friendly, that's why. If they feel like going over to Child's after work for some cakes and coffee, or over to Stein's or somewhere, Pearl's there with bells on."

Marty flung a shoulder. "When did I ever turn down a chance to eat?"

"So they tell me. Only there's this about Pearl; after she's through eating she isn't all of a sudden tired."

"You're telling me I'm tired! God! Mr. Goldstone, I've got a kid. I can't sleep all day the way they do. I've got a kid."

"I'm only telling you." Goldstone looked at the card. "You know Ed Fine? Here's a six-piece job for three nights down at the old Turner Hall in East Twenty-ninth. Ed's short a pianist. There's five a night in it, fifteen big dollars. I don't know if you can talk Ed into the advance, but he might. Ed's a good fellow. That's up to you."

It was some sort of a Legion thing, shows, chances, and dancing. Marty worked for all she was worth in the heat, "breaking" till her neck ached and sweat ran off her wrists. Ed Fine had a reputation as a funny man. Dull as Marty's head felt she didn't let a single fast one get by her, kept her eyes snapping and her laugh on tap, till Ed wondered why he'd never used her more. He had a pint with him. He and the saxophone and Marty put it away between them in the free ginger ale the management sent around. It was a godsend to Marty.

It got toward the end. "Now come on, this last one, boys and girls!" Ed wiped out his collar. "Let's get hot!"

"Oh yeah?" Marty gave him an eye. He had to laugh; he hadn't realized till then what he had pulled.

"You're all right, sister. Why don't you work with me more?"

"I don't know. Why don't I? Ed, listen, ordinarily I wouldn't think of it, but I've got to meet my insurance tomorrow, and I'm fifteen short. How's chances for an advance?"

"Oh, I don't know. I've been known to, dearie. Le' me think it over. . . . Come on, boys, wake up!" Tap, tap, tap, tap!

Ed had an arrangement of "Home, Sweet Home" that kept Marty on the jump and left her a rag. Ed went and got his money and came back. He asked Poritch, the saxophone, "Where are we, Twenty-ninth? What do you say to a bowl of chili around at the Santa Cruz? Marty and I are going around."

It was only a block and a half, but it seemed a mile to Marty. Her clothes were plastered to her; her feet hit the walk at each step long before they ought to. This wouldn't do. She hummed brightly. She asked Poritch if that wasn't a swell arrangement of "Home, Sweet Home" Ed had. Ed took her arm.

"On top of the world, aren't you, Marty, tonight!"

When they got to the Santa Cruz and she discovered they had stairs to climb, Marty just leaned against the jamb of the entrance door. It struck her funny.

"What's the laugh?" Ed asked.

She was in a hole; she didn't know what to say. Then she had an inspiration. On the walk outside was a drunk, trying to fill a pipe from a tobacco tin he'd forgotten to open. He kept shaking and looking and shaking. Marty pointed. "The Pied Piper."

She started up the stairs. She had made about ten of them before Ed, who was coming up right behind her, got it. "Pied Piper! Kid, you're good!" He reached up and gave her a delighted pinch in the back of the thigh. Next thing he knew he was seeing stars.

It wasn't anything Marty could help. Once done, it wasn't anything she could pass off. It wasn't a slap; it was a solid haymaker with a doubled fist. Ed was back against the handrail, holding on to his ear and calling her a name. She got by him and by Poritch, down and out to the walk.

Poritch came down. "You'd better beat it," he warned her. But Ed was out by that, still holding his ear.

"Yes, and don't come back." He repeated the name. "You're through."

Marty stood. "Where's my money?"

Ed looked fit to holler. He started to turn away, but then thought.

He took out a five-dollar bill and threw it on the walk. "Otherwise I might have to see her again," he said to Poritch.

Marty picked up the bill and walked away. At Third Avenue she hesitated, then went to Twenty-eighth and climbed the stairs to the Elevated. What difference did a nickel make now?

She had always wondered how she would feel if ever the day came when she actually couldn't meet the insurance. She felt clumsy and drowsy, that was all. The blocks going past the train windows almost put her to sleep.

When she got home to Fifty-ninth she had three flights to climb. Everybody in the building was asleep. Slagger, on the second floor, had rigged a screen in the hall door to get a draft through; Marty could hear the whole family snoring. At the Kolacks', on the third, she rapped on the door, waited, rapped again. By and by Mrs. Kolack came bare-footed, in her nightgown, Sandro asleep over her fat shoulder. She looked sulky. Marty stood.

"I'm going to pay you what I owe for minding Sandro in a few days now. I've got a job playing for the Legion." It was the easiest lie Marty could think of. The woman looked skeptical. She eased the child loose for Marty to take. Marty just stood.

"Please–look–this once–would you carry him up the stairs?"

One would have expected Marty to lie awake, but she didn't, she passed right out. She had four good hours before the dread began. It could get her even in her dreams. In her dreams now she thought it was only the familiar daily dread of that moment, along about eight, when she would no longer be able not to hear Sandro's suckings and blowings.

He had been taught not to cry or whimper or move around, and he was very good. But he would make sounds with his mouth, sucking in and blowing out by the hour; either he couldn't remember or he couldn't help. This morning Marty fought it even in her sleep, tossed and mumbled, "Please, please!" Finally she woke up. Then she remembered what the matter was.

She dressed Sandro while the cereal was cooking. It's an ill wind –he could still get on with the same old rompers, for though he was seven he hadn't grown any, except his head size, since he was three. Sometimes he didn't seem three, even. He was blind, besides, and that made it worse; Marty had to feed him every spoonful and wipe his mouth.

There was no letup in the heat: it was hotter than yesterday, if anything. After breakfast she gave up for a while. She took off everything and just sat, staring out of the window at the houses opposite. There was a box with geraniums in it on one of the fire escapes. It meant that much work for somebody, and what was the use? What use was anything? What was the use of picking up her stockings from the floor, or her hat from the chair, or bothering to wash up or sweep up, or anything?

Sandro was in the other room. He was making a noise he liked by scraping on a screen with a fingernail. If it was the left-hand window, that screen was loose. If he was on a chair and the screen went, he might go too.

It wasn't the left-hand window, so she had gotten up for nothing. On her way back Marty picked up the stockings, took them into the bathroom, hung them with their feet in the bowl and turned some water on them. Presently she would soap them. She sat with the soap in her hand.

She tried to make herself think. Was there anything she had overlooked she could possibly pawn? She had cleared the place out of personal things. Once she tried to get away with a piece of furniture, she knew well enough that Voltaire, the block janitor, would see her. Then everything would go for nothing, for the rent. She gave up trying to think. By and by she would soap the stocking feet. By and by, though, Mrs. Kolack came up to get her. They had a telephone, and somebody wanted Marty.

When Marty heard Ben Goldstone's secretary on the wire she asked Mrs. Kolack for a chair, she felt so light. But then Goldstone took the phone, and he was mad. "First time you're down this way, Marty, drop in with my piece of that five dollars. That closes you and I out."

Marty wondered if Mrs. Kolack heard him. She was terrified. She tried to sound cheerfully excited. "Oh yes, Mr. Goldstone, and I want to have a talk with you; I'll be right down."

She gave Sandro his noon cereal before she went. "I don't know whether I can come back before I work or not; anyway I'm paying you tomorrow," she told Mrs. Kolack when she left him.

People in the streets were saying there was bound to be a thunderstorm before long, the way it felt. She walked to West Forty-second Street first. The insurance agency was there, and she had to try one forlorn hope. She wanted to see Mr. Byram himself, but couldn't, unless she wanted to wait a couple of hours. She started to wait, then thought of Goldstone and grew nervous.

She appealed to the man at the desk. She explained she knew it was her last day to pay. "I wanted to know if Mr. Byram wouldn't make an exception and take the money tomorrow. Please!"

The man wasn't excited. He said she never could tell. "Sometimes he'll do it; all according to the way he feels."

That was enough for Marty. She hit the sky. She tried to push the twenty-five she had into the man's hand, saying, "If he'll take this much on it now!" But the man pushed it back. "Nothing doing, sister; this is a business." He told her to bring the whole of it in the first thing in the morning and try it on.

People were talking more than ever about a storm. It had grown dark over Jersey. The heat was something thick enough to wade through. At Sixth, Marty went into the drugstore and had a coffee malted. She'd hardly touched breakfast, and had no lunch, and now that she was going up to Goldstone's it was all or nothing.

It was dark in the Goldstone waiting room. Once there was lightning, but no thunder. The secretary wanted the half dollar Marty owed them. Right out before three others who were waiting she told Marty that Mr. Goldstone wouldn't see her, and no use thinking he would.

He did, though, in the end, after the others were gone.

"I know the whole story," he said, before she could speak. "Ed was in here this morning." He gave her a look of disgust. "My God!" He stripped off his shirt and sat in his mesh undershirt. If it bothered Marty she knew what she could do; she *would* come in.

She let him talk himself out. She was like a mule with her ears back.

"Give you half a dollar? Don't make me laugh," she said. "I still need ten–eight-ninety if I don't eat–and you've got to find it for me by nine tomorrow morning. You've got to, Goldstone! Got to!"

Goldstone's jaw hung. "*Me* find it! Didn't I just finish telling you——"

"You've got to find it for me somehow. You don't realize–if anything happened to me–you don't know about my kid."

"Such a cunning boy and you love him so much–I know the line."

"I loathe him, Mr. Goldstone."

The man's jaw really hung this time. He didn't know how to handle this. He got up and stood looking out of the window, wishing to God it would rain. He almost whined. "Yet you won't do anything to make things go, Marty. Here's Ed last night, just trying to be friendly. My God, Marty, Ed's married."

"I'll do anything."

"The trouble with you——"

"I'll do anything."

Goldstone slopped back into his chair. He didn't know how to handle this. *He* didn't want her, if that was what she meant. And if he began advancing her money he knew where that would end.

"I'll do anything, I tell you!"

He had a sudden idea. "You will?" He spoke into his secretary's phone. "Get Bendigo; find out if he's got anybody." He slapped his thigh. He gave Marty a leer. She'd asked for it. He felt like being cruel. "You will? Well now, we'll see. Do you know Bert Bendigo? I mean, does he know you?"

"I should say not. You mean, at the Jack o' Diamonds?"

"Bendigo's raking the town for a hot piano. His own's in hospital with a broken arm, and his fill-in's gone to Detroit. Bendigo's up against it."

"But listen—my God, Goldstone—that's Harlem."

"So you just *thought* you'd do anything, you forgot you draw the color line."

The phone buzzed. Goldstone listened in, nodded, hung up. Marty looked everywhere to avoid his mocking grin. "No," she said, "but *they* do."

"How would they know? Don't kid yourself; they've got dinges up there blonder'n you are, dearie. Don't let 'em see your fingernails too close, that's all; put on plenty of perfume and call Bendigo 'Mister'." Goldstone enjoyed himself. He thought he'd called her bluff. "Well, you asked for it!"

It didn't rain after all. The storm veered away up the Hudson and the sun came out worse than ever. Marty would have given a year of her life for a bath, but she hadn't time to go home. She bought a bottle of perfume at a Woolworth store and took the Elevated for Harlem.

Bendigo made her work. He was a pale olive-skinned man without any fooling about him; she needn't have been nervous; he was sore enough that she was a woman. He kept her at the piano in the airless hall till nearly eight, making her play through some of his arrangements a dozen times.

"Play nigger!" he kept hammering at her. He quit. He walked up and down, polishing his nails. "The trouble with you is, somebody's told you you ought to go over, you could pass anywhere. Well, forget it here. You're nigger here, baby, and you're going to play nigger!" He came back and sat down, put a hand around her, rocked her body to the measure of the break he wanted her to get.

"Now come on, baby, get this!"

They had lighted up, and waiters were laying the tables. A big black buck wandered in from behind, said "Hy" to Bendigo, and stood and looked Marty over. Presently he sat down among the instruments. He tried softly with the heel of his hand the hides of three funny-looking, long-barreled drums. He was Bendigo's big ace. A pure-blooded Gullah from the Carolina sea islands, Cato hadn't the sense for the snare and traps, which were played by a regular drummer. He handled only his own three prehistoric tympani.

He made Marty nervous. Even in this heat he wore heavy clothes, a double-breasted brown broadcloth with a plush collar, beige flannels, and spats. Cato didn't mind sweating; he liked it; it made him feel glossy. He had broad white teeth and bluish gums, which he showed when he caught Marty peeping at him. Out of nothing, during a rest, he said: "I lub yalluh gals."

Bendigo whirled on him. "Shut up, ape!" He had to handle Cato that way, like a tamer with his whip always ready. A few minutes later when Marty went to the girls' dressing room out back for a wash-up, she saw how it was. She had pulled her dress off and was soaping one of the bowls. Of the fifteen show girls changing there, half were stark naked, bodies ranging from cocoa to old ivory. Suddenly they began to yell, some jeering, some swearing. Cato had walked in, unconcerned. He had a large tongue sandwich in his hand. Recognizing Marty when she turned, he came forward, holding it out. "You mustn't go hungry, yalluh gal."

But Bendigo was in the doorway by that. "Get the hell outa here, you big ape! How many times!"

Cato looked muddled and went. Marty put her dress back on

without washing. Getting into privacy, she emptied the whole ten-cent bottle of perfume over her.

It was a slack evening at the Jack o' Diamonds, on account of the weather. There were a couple of colored parties, but the rest were whites. One of these was an elderly man, alone at a table next the orchestra. He couldn't have been less than sixty-five, stoop-shouldered, spare, with a small fat paunch. He wore young clothes though, a coat with square shoulders, and had his hair cut high over his ears. Tipsy when he arrived, he drank steadily, gin and ginger. He could never be at rest. When the girls did their Alligator River, his eyes were in a panic for fear of missing something. They darted from one body to another, flew to another, got the good of none. He tried to get the waiter to take a note to the peach-colored star after her solo act, but the waiter wouldn't do it. Finally he discovered Marty.

Marty couldn't keep her eyes always on Bendigo, especially after he noticed it. But if she didn't, if she turned one way, there was Cato, or if the other, there was the old boy waiting to jiggle and wink. There came a time though, once when she did look, that her heart gave a jump. The man had his pocketbook out. He handed something to the waiter and pointed at Marty. All the while it was being brought to her, he waved, wagged, winked, clapped in dumb show, jiggled up and down like a child. It was a ten-dollar bill.

Once she had it in her hand, Marty was scared. All she wanted now was to get away. She looked around her at the Negroes hemming her in. There was only one more number before closing, but that was one too many; she wanted to get away, get away. Bendigo was already tapping his stand. It was no use. Quickly she pushed the bill down her neck, clipped a corner under her brassière.

She didn't know how she got through that number. She hadn't any instrument to put up afterwards. She got away. She was a fool to have gone for her hat. She knew it too late, in the dressing room. All of a sudden she knew what would happen. Cato would be in the hall when she went out.

He was, but so was Bendigo. It was Bendigo grabbed her wrist.

"What's the matter, sweetheart, what's the rush?"

"Give me my pay—I've got to get home."

"Yeah? . . . First, though, how about coming across? Where's that ten?"

"That ten?" Marty choked, she fought. "He gave it to me; it's mine!"

"About ninety cents is. We pool here, baby; you ought to know that."

Cato was happy, laughed with his big mouth. "Yalluh gal do lub money. I gots a lotta money, yalluh gal."

Bendigo gave him a shove, without letting go of Marty. "Beat it!" Cato retreated to lean against the wall. Bendigo said to Marty: "All right, if you can't find that bill, I can." It was no bluff, he was going to do it. He started to do it. Marty was quick enough then.

"Stop! Wait! There, take it, you–you——"

Bendigo took the bill and kept the hand. "You ought to get mad oftener," he said. She tried to jerk her hand away. "Give me my pay and let me get out of here." She was so mad she sobbed it.

Bendigo began to enjoy this, now he was through work. "Well, well, well!" He stroked the fingers, squeezed blue as milk in his own olive ones. "Well, well, what a pretty little hand!" Of a sudden he bent closer over it. He pinched one of the nails hard. He straightened, gave her a funny look, and felt of her hair before she could duck her head away. He glanced around to see if Cato was still there. He lowered his voice. "Come into the office and get your pay." He let go of her and went ahead; it was only a few steps.

He wasn't the same man. He was excited and miserably eager. He fumbled the door open into the office, pawed and pawed before he found the light. "Come in, come in, miss."

"All right, but leave the door open. Where's my money?"

"Yes, sure, in a minute. I want to talk with you a minute."

"Yes, but don't shut the door."

"I'm light, you've got to give me that. Light enough for anybody. I pass any time. I go anywhere I want to. I can talk——"

"Don't shut that door, I tell you!"

"I can talk Spanish–pass for a South American anywhere. Now listen——"

"*Don't shut that door!*"

Again it wasn't anything Marty could help. It was her muscles; a rat's are the same way. She jumped for what was left of the opening, banged a shoulder, scraped through, ran. She ran and ran. Even when she was out in the open air of the alley she still ran.

She ran out into a street. It was almost deserted; dawn was near.

Fifty yards away a drunk held up an area railing. At the curb a colored taxi driver sat on his running board watching and waiting, patient as a buzzard. When he saw Marty, however, he got in, started his engine, and rolled rapidly backwards toward her, calling, "Taxi, lady?"

She stood and looked at him. She frowned. She passed a hand over her eyes, turned and looked back at the alley. "How silly!" A funny titter got away from her. "Because, of course, I've got to go back in there."

But now the drunk had got clear of the railing. The sidewalk brought him. It was the same old boy. He fell against Marty. She tried to shake him off, but he clung to her arm. "Thought you never come—where been—Creo' belle?"

"Taxi, lady? Taxi, sir?"

The man stopped clinging, began to tug. "Tha's right—taxi—Creo' belle."

Marty looked at the alley. She looked at the taxi. "I've got to have ten dollars; they took the other away."

When they were in the taxi the driver looked back and waited.

"Anywhere," said Marty. "Just drive."

The fellow hesitated, frowned, grinned, touched his cap. "I know a place."

"Mind your business and drive!" Marty leaned forward and pushed the glass slide shut. The starting of the car threw her back against the drunk. He would have been asleep in another moment, but that brought him to, and he began to grab. Marty started to pry him off, but then thought, "No, I mustn't." He got an arm around her neck.

"I've got to have ten dollars," she said. "They took the other away."

"Are you an oct'roon?"

"I've got to have ten dollars. Oh, give me ten dollars."

"Now don't you worry, dear—are you what they call oct'roon?"

"Give it to me now in my hands."

He jiggled and jittered. "I'm no sucker. Think I'm drunk? How would I know?"

"How would—how would *I* know?"

Relenting, he pulled out his billfold. "Gi' me a kiss then, li'l kiss."

Marty *had* to help it this time. With an abrupt turn and a quick evasion she bumped her mouth against his cheekbone. He began to yammer. "Tha's no kiss! Real kiss!" She temporized. "What do you want?" She had to think of right words. "What I mean is, don't be silly, the–the night is young."

To her surprise he broke out weeping. The arm around her shoulders sagged and slid. His head went down between her elbow and the back cushion. His body shook with his blurry blubberings. It was the first time he had ever gone with a nigger. What would his boy say? His boy was a big lawyer in Cleveland.

Streets went by. Marty sat forward, and his weight went down behind her. Little by little the blubbering ceased. A snore half strangled but failed to wake the sleeper. He had plenty of money; there must have been fifty dollars in the billfold. Marty took one ten. She put the rest back, poked it into one of his coat pockets, leaned forward and rapped on the glass. When the cab swerved to the curb she opened the door and got out. She put on an act.

"Passed out, the dirty bum! Whadda y'u know if that ain't just my luck!"

The last she saw, from half a block away, the driver was on the sidewalk, prodding into the cab.

It was pink dawn when she got home. She went up quietly, tiptoeing past the Kolacks' door; she didn't want Sandro yet. Upstairs she let the bath run, but only at a trickle so they wouldn't hear it below. She was starved. She ate a handful of cereal flakes dry out of the package. The next time she remembered the bath it was full and gurgling in the waste pipe. She started to take off her clothes. But then she thought, "I've just eaten." It wasn't really that. It was simply that a bath didn't seem to matter enough. Besides, she hadn't the time. She had to keep hurrying. She went out and sat on the stairs, halfway down. It was at least an hour before Mrs. Kolack opened the door to see if anybody might have brought the milk up. There was a chance Sandro was awake inside; Marty beckoned her up and spoke in a whisper. She had to go down to the Whitehorn Building to pay her insurance, she explained, but she didn't want Sandro till she came back. Mrs. Kolack had been going to blow up, but the Whitehorn Building put her off, because her husband used to work there sometimes. He'd worked there as late as the middle of June; it was a nice building.

Marty walked. It was only seven. She looked in windows. Three times she went and sat in the Grand Central waiting room awhile; it was darker there and the day was going to be another scorcher. She was up in the hall in the Whitehorn Building half an hour before the first clerk opened Byram's office.

Mr. Byram arrived about half past nine. Marty got up from her chair in the outer office and put a smile on. Mr. Byram had a man with him, though, and passed on through. The clock went to ten, then to a quarter past. Marty broke out against the man at the desk.

"You told me I could see him first thing this morning. You told me!"

The man was busy on his phone, arguing, protesting to somebody, "What the hell–this is a big building–there's other insurance people." He tried to wave Marty off, but she wouldn't wave off.

"You told me nine sharp! You told me!"

He looked up at her suddenly. "You don't happen to be a Mrs. Martello, do you?" He saw by her expression. "Wait, here's the party," he said into the phone. He handed her the receiver. "Some dame's excited."

Marty listened a second. She spoke then on a high note. "I told you never to let him on the street with the children. Why?" She listened. She began to go white. The man at the desk studied her face, then turned and beckoned one of the girl stenographers to come. From white, Marty turned green. The receiver clattered to the desk. Marty's mouth fell open. Sobbing laughter came out. The girl stenographer and another got her into a chair, but they couldn't hush her hysteria.

"There was a manhole. They were working in the sewer. He fell in the sewer and broke his neck."

Three days later, Marty was on a train, in the rear coach. Though there were plenty of vacant seats she stood and looked out of the open half of the rear door. Trees, fences, crossings, houses, everything, rushed back from either side, closed up small, and, curve by curve, were obliterated.

Near Southbrook she had her first momentary glimpse of the water. There was a marsh that ran about a quarter of a mile, beyond that a beach, lifted like a dike, and beyond that the sea. It was just at sunset; the flat light reddened the sands and the lines of whitecaps rolling under a southeast wind.

It was dark when she got down at the Little Great Point station. She needed no help with baggage, for she had none, not so much as a handbag, not even a purse, only a crumpled handkerchief. She was the only one for there; it was a weekday. An elderly man dragged a mail sack along the platform toward an elderly Chevrolet. He peered, hesitated, stopped, peered again.

"Ain't you Martha Matthews?"

"Yes, Mr. Ring."

"I vow! Been away some while, ain't you? I'd've thought your father——"

"Father's here, is he?"

"I vow! Well, I'll be glad to ride you far's the Point road anyways."

She thanked him. She thanked him again when she got down after nearly a mile. He went on along the tar toward town and she turned into the gravel leading down the Point under a tunnel of trees.

The first house was the Greers'. There were lights in the living room and out the kitchen way, cigarette points in the deep of the veranda. A voice called out, "Hy, Terry, is that you?" She wondered if it meant Terry Brinker as she walked on.

The second house was the Brinkers'. After that there was a fence of white rails at the left. Martha heard a whicker. A shadow wheeled beyond. On impulse she turned aside, leaned with her hand out over the top rail and called, "Mac?" Only after she saw in the starlight that this colt had two white stockings in place of four did she realize how foolish she'd been to think it might be Mac. She dabbed a finger on the satiny, inquiring nose, turned again and went on.

The last house was under the last of the big elms, before the grassy end of the Point ran down. The living-room windows were yellow; the black pillars of the veranda marched across them as she moved. She came up on the veranda, found the door knocker and let it fall. Presently the light came on overhead, the door was opened, and a bent man peered at her myopically.

"May I speak with Mr. Matthews?"

"Mr. Matthews is out for the moment. Whom shall I say——"

It scared her. "Why, Seifer, it's Martha, can't you see?"

The long-bent shoulders actually unbent. The wrinkled patterns in the old face changed shape. "My gracious!" Water sprang to the eyes. Seifer opened the door wide. "I'll ring the Greers, Miss Martha; your father stepped over. . . . Aren't you—aren't you coming in?"

"Not yet. Seifer, will you do something for me? Get me a bath towel?"

When he came back, perplexed, she took the towel and turned away down the steps. "I'll be back in a little while."

Out on the grass of the Point she stood still a moment. She listened to the sounds the wind made, the trees threshing above and behind her, the water threshing on either hand below. She took off her hat, shook out her hair, and went on down.

She stripped with a few quick motions and walked into the black water. A low shadow grew high, grew higher, toppled and fell. She took it on the breast, didn't fight, let it carry her backwards, loose-limbed, over and over in foam and sand. Cast on the beach she lay a moment to get her breath, then arose and walked back in. Three times more she did this; three times the rollers rolled her out again, foam-lathered, weed-whipped, sand-scoured. A fourth time she got up from the washboard. But this time she ran in, rather than walked, dived when the comber came, swam strongly under the water till she could feel the suck of the shore no longer, turned over on her back and lay still. How deep she lay she neither knew nor cared. She spread out her arms and legs, felt the power of the tide turn her slowly over, first from side to side, then heels over head. She moved her head and felt it dragging at her hair roots. She opened her eyes and let the black salt wash the eyeballs and the lids, opened her mouth and let it wash the gums and teeth and tongue. After what seemed a great while then she stroked, came to the surface and saw the stars. "That's that," she said aloud.

On the one broad rock on the shore she stood and rubbed and rubbed herself with the towel, rubbed her hair as dry as she could, set it on end with combing fingers, and put on her clothes.

She saw a figure standing at the foot of the veranda steps when she came back under the trees. She stopped when she had come within half a dozen paces.

"It's me, Father. I'm here."

The cleanly chiseled head was inclined an inch, in silhouette.

"I've been for a swim, Father. . . . Father, are you glad to see me?"

"Have you left Martello?"

That startled her so she nearly laughed. She could only nod.

"Divorce?"

"No. He died seven years ago, in Bellevue."

Level as he kept his voice, there was yet bewilderment and a question in his echo. "Seven years!"

"I had a child—a boy. I buried him yesterday."

There was a moment's silence. Then: "I lost your mother seven years ago."

"I know."

Another silence, his eyes on the ground in front of him, hers on the ground in front of her. She lifted her head at the same moment he lifted his.

"You're looking well, Father. Except that you've grayed a little——"

But he broke in sharply. "You're not looking well, Martha. You're thin!" He studied her with his quick, characteristic glance. His impatience always had sounded like anger. "Martha, you're hungry! You haven't dined!"

"I had something earlier—about five I had a——"

"Don't be an ass!"

All of a sudden he was sitting on the gravel. She ran to him, caught hold of his hands, shook them roughly, crying, "Father! Father!" He shut his eyes, opened them, looked at the veranda light, shut them again, looked at the gravel beyond his knees. "It has been lonely." Knowing him, she knew he didn't know he said it. When she cried, "I'm going to call Seifer," he came around, a crease between his brows. "I tell you, don't be an ass. I turned my ankle, that's all. Give me a hand up."

She gave him one. He brushed the gravel from his trouser leg.

"Why are you standing there, Martha? Good God! Come in!"

Left for a moment in the hall, she heard him in the dining room, speaking to Seifer. "Miss Martha will dine in half an hour. Thin soup, chops, and a salad. Cress in the salad. She's fond of cress, you'll remember."

Martha looked in the other way, across the living room. She saw the broad table in its place, with red and brown books between the book ends, and the back of the deep couch beneath and beyond it, and beyond that the piano, as at a great distance, with the rust-brown 'cello case leaning against it at the hollowed side, and still beyond these things the sheer white curtains in the windows, bellying. And she remembered that she had remembered more vividly than anything else how the curtains in the windows moved with the sea wind.

*An American Comedy**

JOHN RUFFO GOT OUT AMONG THE rubble of stone and steel at the approach to the bridge. "Well," he said to his chauffeur, "you can wait for me here; I'll be back pretty quick; I got to see Koulous a second, that's all."

This was a fiction and quite gratuitous, as if it mattered to the chauffeur, who was thinking only of the stone dust and the smoke from the work tugs that hung red in the sunset light, presently to want removal from the glittering surfaces of his employer's imported limousine. The contractor might as well have been frank. "I got to have a look at my bridge because I'm proud."

The stone foreman wasn't there anyway; five o'clock had blown long since. No one was about but the watchman, unslinging his supper pail in the shadow of one of the piers, as Ruffo, nodding, walked on along the causeway which, curving gently upward between its granite parapets, swung out high above the muddy-brown reach of Iron River. Come nearly to the middle, where unfinished stonework left a gap of raw steel to go on, he lit a cigar and looked around him, to the east, to the south, then westward, lastly to the north.

This was really what he had come for. He did it often of an evening, after the workmen were gone and before it grew too dark to survey, in solitude so, and from a height, the strong, beautiful, gigantic thing he had made.

Eastward there was the city of Iron River, the sun's last rays flaming a deeper red in the smoke from the ranked chimneys in the North End, where John Ruffo had come as a boy of five to live with his parents and five brothers and sisters in two rooms in Switch Street, above a grain store where there were rats.

To the south, half a mile down the truncated pyramid of the stream, was one of the two shames of Iron River, the McKinley Avenue Drawbridge (the other, the Tenth Street, was as far to the north). Adequate in their days—their days had been respectively fourteen and twenty-four years ago—it was a decade since the peak of their usefulness had passed, and, ceasing to be assets, they had become drags on the limbs of the giant that should have grown.

To the west were the Claybury Hills. Against the fires of evening they lifted half opaque, like a drift of smoke, in which all things, far and near, were of the same weight and substance, equal strokes of a brush full of a dilute shadow color. A terrain roughly three miles by two, he didn't need to peer; he knew it in cartographic detail. Meadville, terminus of the McKinley trolley, two thousand souls, car barns, a few stores, and a filling station. Withered ganglia of suburban bungalows lost in wastes of cabbages and cans. Foelker's Woods.

"Fairyland" at South Claybury, with its skeleton scenic railway and its rotting ferry barges. Claybury Center. Once, with its new carriage factory, Claybury had set out to be a city; now, huddled down beside the abandoned works, it eyed the real city across the water with the dull eyes of a starveling child. It didn't seem to know even yet what John Ruffo was about.

But as Ruffo dreamed from his height above the river he saw it all transfigured in the magic of the deepening dusk. He saw the woods razed, the fields obliterated, and the silence routed by the irruption of pavements and foundations, the clangor of bells, beat of machinery, all the voices of the habitation of men. He saw towers growing, factories and tall office towers cutting up through the twilight first with skeleton blades of steel, then overclothed with granite, brick, and glass. The smoking shadows turned to smoke.

When he was a boy a patch of that far blue wasteland stood framed in the river end of Switch Street, and he remembered how his father and mother, natives of the Carraras, used to stand in the litter and racket sometimes and gaze at it sadly. How little they had dreamed that in the day when that shore had become life or death to the city and to the race they had made their own, it would be no Son of the American Revolution from the Middle Fields who should reach out an arm boned with steel and sinewed with stone to grasp it, but a ragged-panted and dusty-haired Giovanni, their son!

Ruffo knocked off the ash and set the fire end of his cigar to glowing. He was not a poet. He wore a close-cropped mustache, a serge suit, and a derby hat, and he got things done. Done honestly, too, now, after the years of pinching and paring and nip and tuck. It was amazing what a sense of dominance it gave a fellow to be able at last to watch, not the margin of profit in a pier, but the beauty of its strength as it grew. They would remember him for this bridge when he was dead. Indeed, now, he would not die. This bridge was John Ruffo, his body stretched in an arc of power across the beaten stream. He felt the traffic of twin cities, generations to come, sweeping over his indomitable body. Where there had been hundreds there were thousands, born of this bridge, fed and reared by it, the line of John Ruffo in the destiny of the Western race.

He turned to the north. On a stone scow, moored not far away, a slightly built man in well-fitting but long-worn and ill-pressed tweeds was just getting up from a campstool, a portfolio and a box of water colors in his hands. Bareheaded, he stood for a moment gazing up at the nearest of the arches, reared cathedral-big from where he stood. A lemon-yellow light still glowed in the height of the sky, but already the river, the bridge, and the figure of the sketcher grew dim. From above the fellow looked Lilliputian.

"Now, who the devil?" Ruffo wrinkled his forehead and peered more intently. Then he unwrinkled it abruptly, threw his cigar butt away, and laughed. It wasn't a loud laugh, but it was trenchant and full-flavored. It had taken thirty-three years to make.

Leaning over the parapet, he spread his arms wide. "Davie! Ay, you! David Winter! Hallo!"

The water-colorist, already picking his way shoreward across the neighboring barges, looked up, wrinkled his own brow, then wagged an arm in return.

Ruffo surrendered to an impulse. "How do you like the bridge? Pretty fair, ain't it? Well, it's all yours, David; you built it, not me!"

Getting back from the edge, he laughed again, softly. The joke tickled him as nothing ever had before, and this was because he alone knew that what he had bawled down was true. Almost literally, that unpretentious little shade, barge-hopping shoreward down there, had built the Centennial Bridge.

The more Ruffo thought of it . . .

In the days when he was eleven, in the fourth grade in school, Davie Winter was the dude kid from the Middle Fields. He made fellows want to spit. His lunchbox, for one thing, the sandwiches all done up in tissue paper. The way he washed his hands with his handkerchief after doing this or that. The habit he had of sitting off by himself and watching, a quiet smile moving his lips from time to time, as if something funny had happened that no one else in the gang had seen. It made a guy want to haul off and belt him one.

There were marbles one recess time. They had got Davie in. And suddenly there he was, his silly bare-kneed legs astride the ring.

"No, you don't touch 'em, John Ruffo; you fudged a mile."

"I never!"

"You did too, you cheat; six inches, and I saw you."

"You lie like *hell;* you ast any of 'em. Tony, did I? There! Yah!"

Davie's face grew pinched and green. "If you touch one of these marbles——"

"Ya-a-ah! What'll *you* do?" John humped and shuffled in a war dance behind his famous "guard." "Come on, ya yellah! Want t' fight? *I'll* put a head on ya!"

Howls and yowls. Davie's voice sounded frail among them.

"We fight now and Miss Rucker'll stop us, and you know it. You're bigger than me; it'll take me some time to lick you. Come to the Dumps after school."

The word ran. After school it seemed as if everybody lived out the Dumps way. The caravan lengthened. Having to cross the residential district known as Middle Fields, it took advantage of all back streets and alleys possible. And this, as it turned out, was its undoing.

John, his heart swollen and his face red with the worship of his backers, saw the danger first. Sometimes, between spells in the mills, his father went about doing people's gardens, and there he was now in the flesh, bargaining with a householder over an alley gate not twenty yards ahead.

"Jigger!" breathed John, bringing Davie and the whole parade to a stand. The sanguine glow drained from his cheeks as he saw the parental eye upon him. "Jigger, there's my old man! Listen, guys, if he asts ya——"

The guys had fled, however, leaving the two champions transfixed in emptiness to answer for themselves whatever "astin' " there was to be.

Then the wonder occurred. Ruffo Senior came toward them, but he wasn't the first; the householder, a slender gentleman in an old soft-woven suit, got his legs over the gate and led the way, a look of humorous inquiry in his eyes.

"Well, well," he said in a museful baritone, studying the dust of them that fled. "What seems to be the matter, David, my son?"

John gasped a good one. What a hole *this* was! He hoped Davie could lie. But then he must gasp again. "This kid and I," Davie was saying, "are going to have a fight, and we don't want anyone interfering. So please don't, Dad."

It was the Italian that interfered. Scandalized, he made a grab at his presumptuous offspring. "Fighta, eh? Fighta with a gentlaman's boy? You littla devil, I learna you. You say excusa me, queek!"

But Davie's father lifted a hand. He was silent himself for a moment, studying the two youngsters with pursed lip and a gravely twinkling eye.

"What's the trouble between——" He stopped, flushed slightly, and inclined his head. "I'm sorry! I beg your pardon. Well," he addressed himself to the confounded laborer, "what could be simpler? Shall we go in?"

The house was of old brick, serenely proportioned, its cornices showing in high cream-white flecks through the foliage of the trees in the spacious yard. The room into which they were ushered was such a one as John had never dreamed of; no darkness anywhere, yet rich in shadows, the things in it, massive but uncrowded, shining with a dull old luster, and not as furniture that is varnished shines.

There was a decanter on a sideboard; from it Mr. Winter poured two glasses of a wine as brown as November leaves and offered old Ruffo one. The gardener, deeper than ever in the maze, drank in abashed gulps; Mr. Winter sipped his with the leisure of appreciation, talking cordially about plants the while. Only when it seemed he had quite forgotten the grim business in hand did he bow to the waiting enemies, produce from a closet a cardboard box, and from the box four brown-leather pillows with thumbs.

It was a godsend for the morale of the rattled Switch Street kid. "Boxin' gloves!" he railed to himself. "Pew! That ain't no fightin', that ain't."

There was something queer about Davie's father. Stopping short in his handling of the gloves, almost as if he had heard John's thoughts, he glanced at him quickly and shrewdly. "Oh!" he said then. "Quite right." Restoring the pillows to the box, he returned it quietly to its old place in the closet.

The same thing happened in the yard. It was about rounds this time.

"Shall we call the rounds a minute each, Mr. Ruffo?"

Ruffo nodded and grinned with uncomprehending enthusiasm. John glowered at the grass. Rounds! He wanted to spit. That was a silly dude way for two guys to fight it out between them.

Once more Mr. Winter divined. After a moment's study he asked: "Which one of you is the challenger?"

"Huh?" It was the first time John had opened his mouth, except to gape.

"I mean, which one of you—— But never mind. After all." Mr. Winter put his watch away with a stiff little nod. "We'll eliminate the rounds. Stand up to it, boys. Get it off your souls."

Bare-knuckled, then, and without mete or measure. But still it wasn't like a scrap. Sunlight through broken foliage of pear and cherry trees, dappling the smooth-rolled turf. It wasn't like the Dumps. Parents standing, deliberately hands-off. It wasn't like the gang. John's appetite was gone.

David kept hitting him. He ought by rights to have been slaughtering this weedy-limbed, thin-necked sis of a kid; he couldn't get over it. Batting ineptly at the white wrists that kept somehow weaving in to tap him with their sharp-knuckled fists, as he began to sweat and grunt he grew furious, but furious only with himself, and of what use is that to a fellow in a scrap?

There's no telling how long it would have gone on so, had it not been for old Ruffo's anxiety to bend before his betters.

"By gosh, gentlaman," he exulted aloud in specious zeal at one of Davie's shrewder thrusts, "datta keed he gotta sci'nce, he gotta! He putta it all ova my Giovanni, by gosh!"

John dropped his hands. "He *what?* Put it over *me!* Why, you old fool!"

Heat struck his heart and redness cleared his eyes. Now he was different; this was another thing. Lowering his head, scowling furiously, he charged, athirst for gore. He roared in his throat, swinging windmill arms.

Where had he been? Good Pete, he *had* been dumb. Wise in the lore of alley battle, trained in the rough-and-tumble of gang wars, in his stage fright he had been acting like a guy without any legs. Where, pray, were his feet?

Science? Bah! Pipestem arms shooting here and there in lead and feint and parry? Bah! Here's a trick worth ten times your science. Out with a foot, unseen, curved like a flash at the back of the enemy's ankle; a jerk; and as your man, tripped, claws at the air for a balance the air can't give, a good easy bang in the jaw to lend him something to dream about, lying on the grass.

"Put it over *me*, eh? *Ya-a-ah!*"

In the hush of victory there was one sound, the whistle of Davie's father's intaken breath. It wasn't loud, but there was that about it which brought the street cub about-face, knees bent to dodge either right or left as the need might be. Mr. Winter hadn't stirred, however; he had only put his hands out of sight behind him, clamped his lips together, and gone gray.

Ruffo Senior rushed into palliative protest. "That ain'ta right; my Giovanni, he gotta alla the luck, alla the luck."

Mr. Winter opened a slit in his mouth, and, still without removing his narrowed eyes from his son's conqueror's, he said in a harsh voice: "David, get up."

David obeyed, uncertain of knee. His father groped, got hold of his shoulder, and fetched him to his side, tight.

"No, son! Not a word!"

That was all. On the way to the gate, still holding the boy to him by a blue-knuckled grip on a collarbone, he talked gravely and politely about plantings, and inquired of the elder Ruffo what the weather was going to be.

The poor man could hardly answer, for his eagerness now to be away. After all he was flesh and blood; he couldn't be expected to throttle forever his pride in the battling prodigy Heaven had given him for a son. No sooner were they beyond whisper shot across the street than it began to issue in little jets from the safer side of his mouth: "Gooda boy! Ha-ha! That reecha kid, what he theenk, he can fighta my Giovann'? Ho-ho! Ya want some cand'?"

Towed along, chattel of triumph, John twisted his head and looked back. In the white gateway Davie and his father still stood, two slender figures erect, the one holding the other to his side grimly, as if still saying: "No, son! Not a word!"

Not a word about what? Something mysterious and horrid began to happen to the apple of victory; it began to taste like ashes in John's mouth. "Cripes! I licked 'im, didn't I? I put a head on 'im good, didn't I, the poor puke?"

The loudening elation of his father maddened him. He jerked his hand free. "Y' old fool! What ya think ya swellin' about, huh? That boy's went and put it onto me—I dunno how, but somehow. You guineas make me sick!"

What had he done, or what hadn't he done; where was the catch in it all? It looked as though he were never to know, for when he turned again the Winters had withdrawn into the peaceful green twilight of the old yard and the gate had swung to with a wooden clack.

"All right, you wait!" He knotted his fists and winked his burning eyes. "You wait, ya dude ya, you're so smart! You wait; I'll show ya a thing!"

"I'll show you a thing!"

It was amazing now, looking back from the top of the Centennial Bridge, to see how John Ruffo's whole life had been shaped and dominated by that cry. For years, piling buildings on top of one another, cutting streets, playing politics, he had not thought of it; momentum carries on sometimes long after the impulse that gave it birth is gone.

Davie wore the cleanest shirts in the school. "I can wear cleaner'n him; I'll show you if I can't." With John, his mother in the mills, a clean shirt meant a new one. Indolent by nature, he worked at any catchpenny job. Sometimes, if he was lucky, he could sneak a coveted garment off a Jew's barrow in North River Street. The moral problem was no problem to the North End kid. It was the same with his studies. Davie got good marks without seeming to try or care.

"You watch; I'll show 'im!" How John studied; how he sweat and swore and persecuted his simple lump of a brain! How he peeped at the papers of brighter children, hearkened to whispers, hunted out marked books—anything, any way, so long as the answer was got! There he had it on Davie, if he could but have known. He could do things that Davie couldn't; he could laugh at molehills that were mountains to the Elm Street lad; for the battle of the new America he was infinitely better fitted, for he was stripped to the buff.

And he did get the answers and the shirts. Raw, uncomfortable new shirts, bulging out stiff from his pants top: what a fierce joy it was to crackle to his seat past Davie's! What a thrill it was that ran in his arm that day in algebra class when, to a question of Mr. Olliphant's, Davie Winter had to shake his head! To John Ruffo it was like the end of a marathon. It wasn't like lifting his hand; it was like breaking out a banner in the wind. The one trouble was that he might not be able to answer after all, for the lump of triumph in his throat.

He had to peep once in Davie's direction. Davie was looking at that waving hand of his, not ruefully, as might have been expected, but musingly, something as he used to do when he sat off by himself and watched the gang. Touched by a mistrust as instinctive and as old, John stared up at it himself. For the first time in his life he looked at his own hand. And then he knew. It was the fingernails. The very whiteness of the shirt cuff made them only the blacker. The lump in his throat turned poison. His elbow buckled and the hand that had been a banner came tumbling down.

"Damn him and double damn him! You wait; I'll show him yet!"

And he did show him, in the matter of Celestine Lafarge.

John had never thought much about Celestine till David began going with her. Nobody had. There were dozens that seemed prettier and more fun to the eyes of eighteen than the French-Canadian girl who dressed nearly always in brown or black and lived behind a harness shop in North Water Street. The reason was that she was the kind one had to look at in a certain mood and more times than twice before one began to see what she really was.

John never would have seen if it hadn't been for David. He never really did, indeed, till the summer evening when he sat in the Lafarge parlor, perverse and uninvited, and watched her waiting for the tony beau from the Middle Fields who was that night not destined to come.

"Lookin' for anybody'n particular, Celia?"

"Oh no." She yawned. Then, the polished surface of her self-control broken for a moment as her eyes ran from the clock to the deepening dusk outside: "Didn't I tell you once, *no,* for heaven's sake?"

"Well, then, why don't we slide over to Fairyland and shoot some chutes or dance a few? Huh?"

"Well—thanks—but I'm—I'd have to ask Father, and he's not at home."

"Oh, he ain't, ain't he?" John could have chortled. It had been so simple, a matter of a little innuendo here, a half-stopped sentence there, in the harnessmaker's hearing: "Wonder what that tailor-made pet's after, smellin' around down here in the North End? Mmmm. Well, that kind's the kind can get it—and get away with it—them good family boys."

It had been even simpler with the gang. No need of indirection there.

"You guys hang out at Casey's and when you see the dude gettin' off the car you nail 'im and nail 'im good enough to last the night. Let old man Lafarge do the showin'; you do the work."

"Lookin' for anybody'n particular, Celia?"

"Didn't I tell you—oh, haven't I told you ten times—*no?*"

"Well, how about over to Fairyland?"

It grew dim and it grew dark. John enjoyed himself. Back at his ease on a sofa, he contented himself for the time with studying the cold, still loveliness of Celestine. And the sweetest of it was that it was David himself who had "put him onto it"; opened his eyes. And once tasted with the eyes, the quality of her beauty, which was like that of flowers seldom seen, growing in shady places, left not much for a fellow to run after in the brighter allurements of such as Rita Nero and Myrtle O'Hare.

Then, too, there was something that went deeper than this sensuous satisfaction of the eye; there was a fillip to the imagination and a challenge in her smoldering stillness and her sullen, edged, fastidious separation. John supposed that he was just discovering it this summer, not knowing that it wasn't till this summer that it had come.

He hadn't an idea, of course, of the confusion, the doubt, and conflict of that last vacation when David "went with" Celestine Lafarge. When he saw David getting down from the car to walk into the littered purlieus of North River, he couldn't guess the gantlet David ran—curiosity, fascination, chivalry, bewilderment, self-questioning. Nor any more could he comprehend the ordeal the summer was for Celestine, asked to believe in fairy tales, asked to stand on tiptoe, till her head swam, in order to seem taller than she could really ever be.

And so, not knowing this, John never fathomed why she acted as she did when, enough time wasted, he crossed the dark parlor and grabbed her in his arms. Her choking, clawing, and tugging he expected and understood. But when they ceased of a sudden and when she came lopping down full weight against his chest with what sounded like a sob, he never knew in his jubilation that the lopping was down from tiptoe, and the sob nine tenths a sigh.

She seemed as dull as sleep, making no protest when he kissed her. But when he demanded: "How about over to Fairyland *now*, eh?" she was alive again.

"Yes! Quick! Come on! Yes! Yes!"

The ferry barge, jeweled with lights. The Ferris wheel, the car whirled high against the summer stars. The nectar of soda fountain, the ambrosia of hot-dog stand. The triumphant hug. The wild, strong kiss in the dark.

"Did that doll-face ever kiss you like *that*, huh?"

A peal of mirth, threaded thin with hysteria. "*Kiss* me? *Him?*"

John was in the parlor next night when David came. He held her hand while she talked with the loser through the veil of beaded strings at the window.

"Did you mistake your nights, or what? This ain't Tuesday." (Yesterday it would have been "isn't"; the "ain't" was sullenly stressed.)

David stood with his shoulders slightly contracted in the dusk outside. He spoke with an almost painful care, as he did always, for some reason, with Celestine.

"I'm sorry, but I was—I was unavoidably detained."

"Well, I'm sorry, but——" Celestine closed her eyes, but the sudden tears squeezed out. "I'm sorry," she cried roughly, "but I've unavoidably got another date *this* evening, that's all!" As David turned away she came down like lead on John's knees and hid her face away. "Let's go to Fairyland—quick!"

David didn't come to their wedding; he had gone off to college the day before. He sent them a gift, however.

It was a picture under glass, in a narrow mahogany frame. It was a small picture at that, and what was worse it hadn't cost him a cent, for it was a thing he had done by hand, Celestine's head in profile, drawn in pencil on the day of the seniors' picnic at Rocky Point, half a dozen lines of an utter simplicity. Perhaps David himself would have smiled at it now after these years. Or perhaps he wouldn't have.

John did more than smile, that morning of his wedding day. The one thing he had never suspected in David was niggardliness; the discovery was balm to his self-esteem. Holding the little sketch up against the background of that room full of solid treasures, cut glass and rugs and china, silver pie knives and brass beds, given lavishly by those who could ill afford to give at all, he saw the humor of his years of self-abasement, and he laughed aloud.

But then something curious happened; the laugh died in his mouth, and he was glad of a sudden that he was alone in the room. He didn't know what it was; he only knew that somehow, with David, he always laughed too soon. Oppressed, he laid the sketch down and went away and handled richer things. But willy-nilly his eyes would stray back to it, lying as simple there in the glittering rout of possessions as a daisy picked in a field of memory.

He flung around and doubled up his fists.

"You–you——" Words stuck in his throat and his face grew purple. "You–you just wait!"

The sketch hung in their room as long as they had only their room in North River. Then it hung in the parlor of their tenement in Corbett Street. Celestine arranged the furniture, and what could John say? And after all, perhaps, no better thing could have happened for the health of John's career. In the past David had only come and gone; now he was with them, in that picture of the girl Celestine, all the while.

"Yes, but I'll show you yet!"

A man *can* lift himself by the bootstraps, given the anger and the will.

More than once he caught his wife idle, when she should have been busy, brooding at that picture on the wall. He knew what she was thinking, what she was dreaming amid the racket and squalor of her North End home. It whipped him to a dark fury of deeds. He took chances no man should take, with his mortal limbs and his immortal soul, and with the law. "Never you mind; you wait! A house in Middle Fields! What's Middle Fields? I'll take you somewhere that's somewhere, and you'll wear your diamonds before I'm done!"

And what in truth was Middle Fields? Fifteen years after that wedding gift had been lost in the shuffle of progressive movings and forgotten in the beginnings of their success, they drove one evening across the region once known as Middle Fields. It was the day of their last removal; they were on their way to the big limestone residence on Bellevue Heights. By a simple chance of geography their way led them through Elm Street itself.

At either end of David's block apartment buildings had gone up long before, had housed a reputable society for a while, and then, as industry rolled southward, had given up the battle of gentility and become little better than warrens of the office-working class. The Winter place in the middle was no longer a place, but a well. John was startled, the house seemed to have shrunk so. It looked dingy, too, and pitifully out of fashion in its overshadowed huddle of dying trees.

Neither he nor Celestine spoke as they whirled by. There was nothing to say: it was all said. John didn't even feel like exulting. He was a little scared in his heart by what life can do when it tries.

That was three years ago. It was nearer thirty-three years ago that he had stood and shook his fists after the aristocratic lad he had somehow not "put a head on" and cried: "I'll show you a thing!" Tonight, leaning out with his arms spread across the twilight heavens, he had showed a middle-aged dabbler in water colors the Centennial Twin City Bridge.

Throwing the butt of his third cigar away, Ruffo thought of his chauffeur. "Guess he thinks I must've fallen off or something." The sky, apple green in the west, was turning deep blue above the town. There were footfalls on the raw concrete behind him. Supposing it to be the watchman (puzzled too by his employer's loitering), he did not turn immediately from his good-night survey of the hills. But it wasn't the watchman. It was David Winter.

"Well, John, hullo! It's been a long time, hasn't it?"

Engrossed as he had been in his memories, Ruffo turned with a start, instinctively defensive. Then, as his gaze ran over the mild, dust-colored form of his old schoolmate he re-remembered, relaxed, and indulged in an inward grin. "Well, well, Davie Winter, I'll be! Put 'er there!" His hand engulfed the other's. A merry thought came. What if he should really *squeeze!* He had a picture of the demigod of his youth squirming like a dishrag in agony at the end of his powerful arm. He was merciful, though; he didn't squeeze.

"How do you like it?" He took his paw back and waved it over the bridge.

David's long, deep-lined face worked for a moment, a light gathering in his eyes. In that light, it seemed to Ruffo, was pay for all that had ever been.

"By jingo, John, it *is* a beauty, though, isn't it?"

"Yes, and not only a beauty, David; it's strong. It's adequate. It's honest." The contractor lifted a foot and brought it down heavily, as if to prove by the ring the proud integrity of the span.

"Every last cubic inch of it, David, an honest bridge."

"You don't need to tell me; I've got eyes. I want to thank you, John."

Wanted to thank him? Why? But then it came to Ruffo that that would be like David, taking it upon himself to speak in the name of Iron River, forgetting that the Iron River of the Middle Fields day was lost from sight in the giant of now. Nevertheless, somewhere between his humor and his self-esteem the builder was touched. There was a curious lightning transformation; a debt was canceled.

He wondered how he had ever managed to hate this quiet, baggy, unassuming fellow, who seemed content to let the world march by. Almost he loved him. The long-buried Latin in him urged him to embrace his ancient enemy; he compromised by slapping him on the shoulder. "Glad you like it, old man! I ain't seen you in a coon's age, David; still living the same old place?"

"Yes, same old place. It's a deep root there."

"I was thinking, maybe—I was passing that way a while ago——"

"I know; it's changed. But when five generations of you have lived and died in the same place, John——"

Ruffo nodded with a false solemnity, enormously tickled. "My family was like that back in the old country, I guess, sticking always the same old place."

"And you, John; you've lived in a dozen already, and built this bridge." But the museful smile, reminiscent of the dude kid, went away. "Built this bridge," David repeated. "It *is* blamed funny about life, John. There we were in school together, scrapping like a couple of terriers—and here, after years and years, out of the hundreds of thousands it might have been, I find it's you that's on the job. It beats a fellow how such things can happen."

"That's easy, how it happened. It happened just because I put in a bid that made the rest look sick. And why? I'll tell you a secret, David. I'm not figuring to make a cent on this particular job. I don't know's I can make you see exactly why I done it, but it's like this.

I've made a few dollars in my time. I've made enough. This bridge here now is my—my—er——"

"I know, John. Every artist has to have one once, at least," David ruminated. "And that makes it all the queerer, doesn't it?"

"Queerer? What?" Ruffo rubbed his hat around on his head. There was a time when he would have been offended by this trick of David's of talking in enigmas, but now he was too wise. He was too indulgent. He passed it off.

"Well, well, David, I'm certainly glad to have seen you again. You must come up and see us some evening—120 Bellevue Road—you must. It's funny I never run across you around town, though, ain't it, though?"

"Oh, me, I'm a bit of a bum; that's the trouble. Of course I'm in New York part of the time with the business, and part of the rest I drift. I'm just now back from eight months' tramping it on the other side."

"Making sketches? I see you busy striking one off down there a while ago."

"Yes, it's rather fun, seeing the likenesses—and the *un*likenesses—between the figment and the fact."

"Uh—yeah—mmmm." Once more Ruffo rubbed his hat around on his scalp. "Do a lot of that, don't you, sketching?"

"I fool around with it, yes. We do, though, don't we, we architects, those of us that are worth our salt?"

Ruffo chuckled. Same old highbrow Davie, his head off somewhere else.

"Got any there?" He poked an indulgent thumb at David's portfolio.

"Pretty dark to see 'em." David was too much the artist, however, not to open it quickly. "Some of them old as the hills." He riffled the unmounted sheets and smiled. " 'Hills' is the right word. Look at this, and this."

He lifted his head and nodded toward the Claybury rise, steep dark blue against what light of heaven there was left. "I've been at them a lot, as you'll see. I'm fond of those hills. We used to have a farm out behind the Corners; I used to go squirrel-shooting there with my grandfather when I was eight. So you can understand. You can see why I've always rather dreaded the day when those hills, those woods and meadows——"

He left it there with an oddly emotional lift of the shoulders and flipped over more sheets. "See here again, John. I've rather cherished those old hills. You'll do it yourself, John; you'll cherish something, someday, when you've lived with it a hundred and fifty years again. In a way I've loved those two old bridges for their very inadequacy, even while I've hated them horribly for what they are. They're about as bad, of course, as they can be, in every principle. If there had to be another bridge, though, I've always prayed we'd go the whole hog; I've always hoped it would be in scale with its landscape and in keeping with its destiny. It must have breadth and depth and power, you know. It must have the weight of what's behind it. But not dead weight. Living! It must move. It must march. No, John, it must *hurtle*. And—it, John Ruffo, I believe it *does!*"

He uncovered still another sketch, done in bold lines and massed shadows. The flush that had grown on his cheeks was creased by a sudden smile, half eager, half whimsical. "How do you think it stands as a portrait, John?"

Ruffo wasn't much at pictures. Moreover, the light was failing. He had to bend and peer. It was his bridge all right. Taken from a nether angle of perspective, it swept down in a stunning arc across the composition, beneath an arch a glimpse of the lower river, sunset-lit; above and beyond it the flame-rimmed wall of the Claybury Hills. Pursing his lips, he nodded judiciously. But then his nods grew slower. There was something wrong.

"Why, looka here, David, where's the steel? You've gone to work and sketched it off as if it was done already."

David beamed. Ruffo wasn't so happy. He felt for a moment the grievance of the man of deeds. "If it was as easy to dash it off in the solid goods," he grumbled belligerently, "as it is with some paints and a little water——" He came to a full stop. "Looka here, you never done this here *tonight!*"

"Hardly. Look at the date, man."

Ruffo bent nearer and peered where David's finger was. Metaphorically, and beginning to feel funny at his midriff, he rubbed his eyes. "What you givin' us? This date here—it's three years old."

"Why—naturally." It was David's turn to be at a loss. "I've got one here somewhere that's nearly five. Why, the Hartley, Blake & Winter blueprints you've been working with are nearly *three*."

Ruffo stood and let the words run through his brain: "Hartley,

Blake & Winter." How many hundreds of times had he looked at that firm's name on the blue sheets of drawings, and never once seen it at all! ". . . *& Winter!*"

David grinned of a sudden, moved by something comic in the big workman's posture.

"Good lord, man, how long did you imagine it took an architect to dream out a bridge like this?"

*Due North**

MAY COBERLY WAS A COWARD. Things that scared her, scared her so much they made her feel sick at her stomach. She was always so proud, though, that nobody knew it. Even as a very little girl she would never let on. The Rock Island tracks ran almost under their back yard in Des Moines, and her older brother, Fred, who would have been ten or eleven then, used to make her sit astraddle of the back fence sometimes when the Chicago flier was coming. It made her scream, and she knew it was going to, but she always managed to hold it till the shaking and roaring were at their worst and drowned out the noise she made, and then she would run away and pretend to play somewhere, and if she was sick Fred never knew it.

The words about fearing God in the Bible never puzzled May as they do most children. God always did frighten her. When she was taken into the Wilder Avenue M. E. Church, when she went up forward to her first communion, the instant she got the grape juice into her mouth she tasted blood and had to go out—somebody showed her to the door under the choir the minister used, and there was his lavatory.

But the time she had the fright which really put her to bed was when she was seventeen, the day they told her that the Grace Church girl who was delegate to the Epworth League Convention at Ocean Grove, New Jersey, couldn't go, because of her father's being suddenly worse in Colorado, and May, who was the alternate, had to go.

Two of May's best friends brought the news to the house, Milla Heiffer, who was president of May's class at high school, and Kathleen Batt, who sang soprano in the choir at Wilder Avenue and went with Sylvester Templin, who sang the baritone solos. They asked May why she looked that way, after they had told her, and she said it was because she had an awful pain in her stomach, which she really had, but it would be all right soon if she lay down. They laughed and said it had better be, seeing she was to leave for the East day after tomorrow.

"You'll see Chicago and Pittsburgh and New York City, think of it!" Kathleen said. May's mother said she would go and write a card to May's cousins in Davenport to be at the station there when May came through, and Milla said: "And you'll see the Atlantic Ocean, think of it, May!"

May did think of it. It seemed to make the pain inside of her ten times worse; she had always been so thrilled when she thought about the seashore and the sea. May's mother was explaining to the girls how interesting that would be for her daughter, since she herself had been born and raised on the coast of Maine, and her father, May's grandfather, had been mate on a sailing ship, although he spent his last days here in Des Moines, passing away in their old house on Slater Street.

"Often he used to spin yarns about voyages and storms while he trotted my daughter on his knee, though of course she was too little at the time to remember."

May, from her bedroom where she'd gone, wanted to call out, "I wasn't—I do!" But it didn't matter enough to pay to make the effort, she was so panic-stricken at the idea of starting out for the East all by herself, and so terrified something might happen and she wouldn't.

Her upset got better soon after she lay down.

Dozens were at the station to see her off. The girls had put up a box for her first luncheon, and Dr. Warren, of Grace, handed over the expense money and the two tickets, the regular one and one for the Pullman. She thought to herself, when the train had started, in a few minutes she could look out and up and see the back fence of the Slater Street house, and think: "How little I could have dreamed, then!" But a man came in and sat down in the seat opposite, where his hat was, and said, "Pardon me," with a kind of humorous smile, and May quickly got out a book she'd brought and read it, so that she completely forgot to watch for the old fence when it passed.

And she saw that the man had sandy hair and gray-blue eyes and broad shoulders, with a kind of tweed suit with a double breast—a man, by his looks, of twenty-three or -four or -five.

So she read until the two conductors came. She had an awful minute then. Her regular ticket was there, but the little berth ticket wasn't. May wanted to die. She tried to tell them that she *had* had it; they could ask the porter. The two conductors smiled and said they guessed it wasn't going to be fatal. There was something about wiring back from the next stop, and what was May's name. She told them, May Price Coberly, and she was going to Ocean Grove—though they knew that already, of course. And just then the man opposite leaned forward and picked up something from under May's seat. It was the berth ticket. Then they all laughed, and the regular conductor patted her shoulder and said, "Change to the Pennsylvania in Chicago, that's all you have to remember," and the two went on.

May didn't know what to do, whether to thank the man or not. If she said anything he might think she would talk. She looked in her book. Then he said, more to himself: "May, that's a pretty name—though I'd have said April."

May read. He said: "It's not my fault, young woman. It's Fate's. Here you are, bound for Ocean Grove, and here I am, for Atlantic City, and both over the Pennsy too, and we simply can't sit here face to face for God knows how many hours pretending each other is not alive. So why don't you start by telling me why you're going to Ocean Grove, of all places! . . . I'm going to Atlantic City because I live right near, and I have a sort of a kind of boat there."

May didn't know what she ought to do. It would have been different had he been strikingly handsome, like Sylvester Templin when he threw his dark hair back and sang baritone, or like the clerk at Stanger's who would try it on with any good-looking girl. But he wasn't awfully handsome, with his rough-combed hair, his wide jaw and wrinkly-cornered eyes, and freckles on his hands—at first sight anyway. And of course, older.

So May said: "The Epworth League national convention is at Ocean Grove and I am a delegate."

He threw up his hands. "Help!" he groaned, though he grinned. May had to ask why. So he told her, a friend of his, a fellow he'd gone through prep and college with, he'd been on a train with a

Y.W.C.A. delegate once, and that was only from Camden to Altoona, but now they'd been married two years.

May felt her face go as hot as fire. He made haste to cover it up by laughing to himself and saying, God help the girl who had to marry him, because he was a sailor. He looked at May, with that, and seemed hurt. "If you don't believe I am, I'll take you up to the baggage car and you can see my duffel bag."

It wasn't that she didn't believe him; it was just the opposite. It was knowing he was a sailor, all of a sudden like that, that fussed her. She opened her book and started to read whatever page happened, but he warned her that reading on trains was a terrible way to treat anybody's eyes, which she hadn't known before. And anyway, he said, getting up, it was away past lunchtime, and they ought to be getting to the dining car.

Fortunately, May had an answer to that, the box Kathleen and the others had put up. The man looked crestfallen. "Well, make sure you clean it up now, for this evening you are dining with me."

And after all, May couldn't eat a bite of the lunch, tasty as the girls had made it. She had hardly opened it when she began to have the same stomach ache she'd had two days before, and it got worse. Finally she pushed the box back out of sight under the seat, and was clenching her hands and almost biting her lip to keep looking right, when the man returned.

"What's wrong with you?" he asked. "Hot in here?"

She let it go at that, and he said they'd better go out back to the observation platform and get some air—"and have a look at several of the United States," he said—although in fact they were still in Iowa.

May began to feel better out there. The train was just leaving a station. May saw the sign at the yard limit, "Marengo." She waited till they were beyond the last of the town, and then she said to the man: "Now I'm the farthest east I've ever been." He just looked at her with those wrinkles of humor out of the corners of his eyes, and kind of shook his head, and got his pipe out.

They sat and watched the rails and he smoked. By and by the pain was gone. May began to feel hungry.

"What did you have for your lunch?" she said. She had almost to shout, on account of the train. He hitched his chair nearer and took his knee between his hands.

"Lunch," he said, "is a thing of the past. Dinner is what I am thinking about intensively now."

May was too. She felt so hollow. "I think for my dinner I'm going to have some——"

He stopped her. "You are an Iowa girl. How do you know what people have for dinner in foreign places like Illinois, any more than you know what they have for breakfast in Ohio or for lunch in Pennsylvania? No, no!" He shook his head. "I am a world-traveled man; I shall just have to take hold of this whole thing. In fact, I have a rough working plan sketched out for dinner already. To begin with, some salami, celery, and olives—green, because the ripe olives they have are canned. We will have some soft-shelled crabs, which will come on at Davenport, the chef tells me, very fresh, and a small but succulent fillet of beef to follow, and an artichoke—and let me think."

He must have been watching May from the corners of his eyes and seen the worried way hers went to the purse she had tight in her hands in her lap, for he gave her a look with his eyebrows pulled together. "I hope you understand, when I say dining with me, I mean dining with me, young woman!"

May kept looking in her lap. "No, I couldn't let you do that."

"You can too. See here, I am an easterner, and therefore a man of great wealth. So, please!"

"No, please, I don't think I ought."

He began to jeer. "You, you're a fine Epworth League delegate, not to know any more about God than that!"

May was so startled that she asked why.

"Because God practically all but put it in the Bible that sailors must buy dinner for girls with pretty eyes. It's called the Law of the Medes and Persians."

May couldn't help it, he looked so provoking and merry. She laughed.

"All right, I guess so then. Just dinner, though."

They were past West Liberty by that time. They sat for a while and watched the rails, while he smoked his pipe. May began to feel funny. She thought it might come from her eyes, the way the rails went. So she looked at the passing fields and then at the sky. But it didn't help much. Her lips felt dry. She wet them with her tongue.

"I'm sorry I'm not more talkative," she said.

He simply grunted. "Thank God! I've spent most of my life running away from the kind of people who can't just sit, sometimes."

Presently he knocked out his pipe. He caught her licking her lips.

"Let's have some lemonade." He called the steward and ordered two glasses of lemonade. When hers was in her hand, May said to herself, "I'm going to drink this!" But next instant the glass got away and she grabbed for the man who was a sailor. All she managed to catch was one of the buttons on his coat, and that was all she knew then.

The next she knew, it was in the station at Davenport, on the platform, and people were saying, "Yes, we are her cousins," and people were saying, "Gangway." He was carrying her. He was looking down at her. Probably he wouldn't have said it out loud, even to himself, if he had realized she had come to.

"Poor girl with the pretty eyes, you never did get out of Iowa."

The next she knew, the second time, she was in bed in a hospital, all tied up around the middle, and they had taken her appendix out.

Her mother had come from Des Moines and was staying with the cousins. They all came in every day. They asked May how she was, and she said she was all right. They asked if there was anything she wanted, and she said no. But at night, when there was no nurse, she cried a good deal.

They brought her belongings one day, the purse and compact and things which the nurse had done up in a package. And one cousin asked, "What's this button, May?"

"What button?"

"Well, you had it tight in one fist, the nurse said. It looks like off a coat or something."

May raised herself quickly and looked. Her breath came hard. "Oh, that button—yes—I know—it's nothing." She got hold of it. "It was just something I had—something I had to make me remember something."

That night when she cried she beat the pillow with her fists, took a wad of it between her teeth to keep her sobs from being heard everywhere. For something told her now. "I know, as certain as certain, if we had gone on all the way . . ."

She dreamed about it often in the following two years. She could never dream it straight, though. She would be somewhere, say in Kathleen Batt's living room, and somebody was shouting outside, and when she looked it was a railway station, and an announcer was walking up and down, calling, "Camden to Altoona!" Or she would be at table somewhere and ask someone to pass the bread. Instead of bread, it was like a cross between a pineapple and a green Easter lily that came toward her, and then she saw it was he who passed it, saying, "And now your artichoke, young woman," and May would wake up crying.

That was about as near as her dreams ever came to getting hold of it. They stopped pretty well altogether when she married Sylvester Templin. She was nineteen then.

It seemed at first as much like lucky lightning as the other had seemed at first, the time the real delegate to Ocean Grove had to go to Colorado instead. May was almost the only girl in the Wilder Avenue who had never run after Sylvester. That's why it went the way it did, perhaps. So often superattractive men, or women, will end by doing exactly that, picking the last person in the world anybody has ever thought of.

For once May wasn't frightened; she was too bewildered even for that. Everybody was too excited, everything went too fast, for her to ask herself if this was what it meant to be in love. It took the five days and nights of their wedding trip to the Kentucky caves for her to begin to realize, and then it didn't come fully until they were home again.

It happened in church, the Sunday after they returned, at the morning service. All that any of the girls could see that day was May, May in her pew and Sylvester in the choir loft. May knew it. She felt their eyes on her, full of envious speculations they couldn't help, and wonder, and awe. Her own eyes she dared not turn or lift, till everybody did, when the choir got up to sing.

Sylvester had on the dark suit he'd been married in, made to measure by a tailoring house. It set off his tall, slender, almost willowy figure to perfection against the many-colored light that came in by the Young St. John window. And when it came his time, and he flung his head back to throw the dark lock off his forehead, and lifted his face and began to sing alone with the organ, May caught her breath. Of a sudden she knew what love and marriage really meant. Not just going around to caves and hotels with Sylvester, and being called Mrs. Templin. It was something so much bigger, so much deeper, marriage, and children, and everything.

May couldn't help it, she didn't care who saw, down went her hands on the pew back ahead and down went her face between them. "O God our Father, grant and let me have a child—grant and let me bear to Sylvester my husband a son in his own image, O God, Amen."

She couldn't help it, she didn't care if the other girls did see that her face was wet when she lifted it.

But as the years began to go by it seemed that her prayer was not to be answered. Whether it was she or Sylvester she didn't know; it didn't matter. And perhaps it was just as well in a way. Sylvester's aim had always been the opera; everybody had always said that there was where he would land. An English opera company from Chicago came to Des Moines the year after he and May were married, and Mr. Agassiz of the Third National Bank, a trustee at Wilder Avenue, got Sylvester a chance to sing for the director and some of the stars at their hotel. He sang well. They thought he had the makings of something. But the director wanted him, if he went with them, to be in the chorus simply—"carry a spear awhile," was the way he put it, "and begin to get a glimmer of the rudiments." The pay, moreover, was practically nothing.

May could have met that part of it. She went so far as to see Mr. Agassiz, and he promised to give her a job in the bank at eighteen a week, and she could have lived with her mother when Sylvester was away. In the end, though, she had to agree with Sylvester that there was nothing in being a chorus man, for him. Something better was bound to come along.

He had a position for a few months with another church member, a concern that handled hides. But he wasn't adept, and he wasn't contented. Music, after all, was the career he was marked for. "Why waste time and energy on a sidetrack?" he told May. Some people said it was a pity the church couldn't pay something, even a little, for choir work. May went to Mr. Agassiz the second summer. He kept his word and gave her a job mailing statements and things like that, which she could do.

May always had been a coward. Little by little as she grew tired she worked out a philosophy, without knowing it was a philosophy, certainly without ever putting it in words. But it was this: if you don't look at a thing, then it isn't there: if you don't say it, it isn't so.

Pride was mixed up with this too. If she met one of her old girl friends (and that meant one of Sylvester's old girl friends) and if she was asked how Sylvester was making out, May would look happily mysterious. "Oh, Sylvester is working on something now that looks so good that we're not saying a word." And if there was any wooden thing handy May would reach and rap on it three times.

May began by liking the Wilder Avenue less and less; she ended by hating it more and more. She explained it to herself by thinking it was because she had to see so many people in whom she was no longer interested, when she went there. Often, of a Sunday, she let Sylvester go alone. If he asked what he should say—whether he should say she was tired or ill—she made haste to tell him no. That was the last thing on earth she would have had Kathleen and Milla and the others thinking, that she was ill or tired. He could say she had gone over to Grace with a friend that belonged there, one of the bank girls.

The last time May set foot inside the Wilder Avenue was the day her mother was buried from there. They moved out to the Viaduct section shortly after.

Once on a time some independents built a packing house in the Viaduct, and two streets of small houses for the labor to live in. The packing business had failed in short order, and now all sorts of people had the houses, which were cheap, renting for sixteen dollars a month. Of course there were the trolley fares, but they didn't make anywhere near the difference. Some months, if nothing special came up, May could add two or three dollars to the account she kept at the bank against the chance which terrified her more than anything else: "Supposing something should happen to me!"

For if anything should happen to her, and if she didn't leave him any money, Sylvester would have to go to somebody, and the only ones he could go to would be their old friends and acquaintances at the Wilder Avenue.

But the best part of living in the Viaduct was that it was so far across town that Sylvester gave up his choir work.

May's first realization of the truth of why she had fallen away from the church came to her by chance, if not by sheer accident, and it came like a bombshell. It was in the spring when she was thirty-one. A girl at the bank had a husband who was a steel worker, and one Saturday afternoon she wanted May to go to Halvert Union Hall with her. Perhaps because she was too tired to want to argue out of it, May went. She wished she hadn't, when she saw that the speaker was dressed like a clergyman. But when he began to speak he took her breath away.

The fear of God and the hope of the Hereafter have always been the drugs, he said, with which the Have's have kept the Have-Nots doped in submission. The Truth has got to put these bugaboos to flight before the workers can hope to come into their own—the Truth that there's actually no such thing as God, no such thing as life going on after the grave. People long for immortality. So the capitalistic church says to a woman: "There's your man that you love—you be good and make him be good, and when you're dead you'll be raised again to live together in a happy land, forever and ever and ever." Then the speaker pounded on his desk and pointed at them all and told them. That husband and wife do go on living after the grave, not because they're good, nor because they're bad, but because they have loved. Married, mingled, in the veins and brain of the child they have made, and of that child's children, together they shall live till the end of time. That is their immortality.

It took May's breath away. She grasped at what he said, grabbed at it, and fiercely believed. When they were out on the sidewalk the other girl asked her what had happened, that she looked that way.

May said: "Thank God, I'm barren. When I die I can call it a day."

It seemed as if tons had fallen from her shoulders. She could carry them straight now. She felt better, stronger, harder, more independent. She spruced up. She bought a new compact the following Monday and put more color on her mouth and cheeks, simply because she felt that way. Before leaving the bank, after hours, when they were in the washroom, the other girl asked May why she didn't put a touch of mascara on her lashes, she had such pretty eyes, that color brown. The girl had some.

May was sorry, though, when she reached home looking that way. She hadn't thought. It got Sylvester started. She couldn't say she was too tired that night; she'd already said she felt fine, though she hadn't told him why.

That night a second bombshell of realization hit May. Sylvester went to sleep quickly, when he went. It was warm weather. He hadn't any pajama top on, and the bedclothes were half off his shoulders and chest, which were as smooth and white as a child's. He never seemed to change. Time, which dragged May down little by little, passed over Sylvester and left no mark. He might still have been twenty. He might have been seventeen.

It may have been some premonition and May didn't know it. All she knew was that horror came to her as she lay there in the dark beside him and couldn't sleep. Finally she couldn't help herself, she lifted on an elbow and stared at the grayness his whiteness made in the gloom. There was something unnatural, unhealthy, unright. Between a boy of seventeen and a man of thirty-four there ought to be a difference, in mind and in flesh. Either a thing is alive or it is dead. If a mind is alive it doesn't quit. If flesh is alive it changes, grows, grows older. If it's dead it's only so much meat, and decays—unless you want to keep it on ice.

Suddenly, all May could see was the glassed-in meat counter at the A. & P. store, rimed with frost around the lower edge. She saw red steaks, pinky-gray chops, greeny-gray sausages, and laid among them on the bed of shaved ice, about of a size with the sausages, perfect and willowy and white, she saw Sylvester. And she knew in that instant what she had fooled herself about for years. It wasn't that she was too tired. It was because her flesh loathed that flesh.

She got out of bed, went into the bathroom, shut the door and turned on the light. She didn't know what, she didn't know why. She sat on the side of the tub and stared at the wall. She said to herself, "I can't be awake."

She got up. "One thing I want, I want to wash my mouth with something." She opened the medicine case above the bowl, pushed bottles around, hardly looking to see what they were. There was one away at the back she hadn't seen or thought of for months, some mercuric cyanide tablets she had got through the bank's insurance doctor two years ago, for some antisepsis. This was just what the drug clerk had warned her against, forgetting and leaving them around where somebody might mistake them for some kind of soda-mints or medicine. They ought to be down the drain, before somebody did.

She sat on the bathtub again and looked at the bottle.

"You'd be dead in a wink," that's what the clerk had said. "You'd never know," he'd said, "what struck you."

May shook herself. What was wrong with her? She didn't know. "Don't be such a fool!" she said.

She returned the phial to the case. She went back and got into bed, lying as far as she could over on her side of it. "Don't be such a fool! Forget it!"

She did forget it, for some weeks. When she remembered it again was when she was beginning to go around her work at the bank with white cheeks, and big eyes that might have been blind, the way she dropped this thing or bumped into that.

One blistering morning in July the other girl said to her: "Look, May, you don't look good. Why don't you see some doctor?"

The head bookkeeper spoke to her the same morning. "Go see Doc Gable, May. Won't cost you anything. I'll ask Mr. Agassiz."

May flew at him. "No you don't! I keep telling you!" She came back to his cage a little later. "Please! It's just this heat."

At noon she got out alone. She took a streetcar and went across to a part of town she didn't know, and found a doctor's sign. She gave the doctor a wrong name and wrong address, she couldn't have said why. It was simply panic. He catechized her and examined her. He told her, yes, she was going to have a baby. He had to remind her, when she got up to go: "That will be two dollars and a half, Mrs. Brown."

Even then he had to call her back. He was looking at the small silver that made up the half dollar, spread on his palm. He grinned in a kind of sheepish way. "I guess you would as soon have this, Mrs. Brown, and I'm sure I'd rather have the nickel." He handed back the luck piece she'd always had a habit of carrying in her purse, a coat button made of horn. She gave him the nickel and went away.

First she thought she wouldn't go back to the bank. Then she decided she must, otherwise they would think there was something wrong with her. Besides, she'd rather be working than thinking.

She needn't have worried. She couldn't think. She felt the heat that afternoon, not as heat, but as a weight without particular temperature pressing down on top of her brain. After closing, while she was waiting for a Viaduct car, a newsboy stuck a paper into her empty hand. It was the *Evening Courier*. She had given him pennies mechanically before she realized what she was doing. She wanted to call after the boy, tell him they took the *Courier*. It would be at home when she got there, on the floor by the stuffed chair, sprawled open at the radio page. But what was the use?—and the car had come.

Then she was glad she had the paper. There was a man sitting next to her, hip to hip with her, who wanted to make a pickup. She knew she would break out screaming if she had to argue, so she just kept looking hard at the paper. It was a Wednesday, and the outside section was the Mid-Week Pictorial. There was a picture of a record baseball crowd in Chicago. There was a picture of a two-masted boat at anchor somewhere, with a man, a woman, and a small boy at work about it, coiling ropes and things. In an oval at an upper corner was a half-length snapshot of a bearded man in a fur parka with the hood laid back. Behind him, in the background, was a stripe of black water and one of white ice. A strong wind beat at his beard and his hair.

A soiled finger came and pointed at the picture. "That wouldn't feel good a day like this—oh no!"

May slammed the paper between the fellow's knees. "Take it, if you're so interested; and let me be!" She got up and went out to stand by the motorman till the car reached Alpine.

May's house was the fifth on the right, up Alpine. It was distinguished by stained glass in the front door, a garish imitation of Della Robbia which some Italian tenant had put in years before. Otherwise one would have had to count.

Sometimes Sylvester had things started toward supper, the potatoes peeled, for instance. Tonight of all nights May hoped to God he would. She hoped to God Fred wouldn't be there. But when she was on the porch she knew that Fred was there. She could hear the music through the closed window. They always kept the window closed for secrecy, because of whatever new "novelty" they were trying to work up.

This one, May knew, was one they called the Mixed Quartette. Sylvester had learned how to throw his voice into a falsetto contralto when he wanted to. Fred could jump back and forth between tenor and soprano so cleverly that you would have sworn it was a man and a woman alternating. Sylvester played on a portable melodion, while Fred doubled in saxophone, steel guitar, and some hand traps. There was going to be money in this one, Sylvester said.

It was a tossup with May. For two cents she would have turned back down the steps and walked around for a while. She was too dead on her feet, though. They stopped singing when she came in, but neither one got up.

Sylvester said: "How are you, May? Feel any better?"

"It's this weather, I guess," said May.

Fred kept his eyes turned out through the window. He was a short, heavy-bodied man with a pock-marked face, an ex-barber, some said Armenian and some Greek. They said he took cocaine too. Like Sylvester, he was in his undershirt, on account of the heat, and had his shoes off. His feet looked smaller than ever so, in nothing but socks, and rounded and soft and moist, like his hands. He said nothing to May. He never did, any more than he ever looked her way when she was in the room.

May started for the passage leading to the kitchen.

"Well?"

The funny way Sylvester spoke made May stop and look at him. "What's the matter?"

He threw the hair off his forehead. "Nothing. Why?"

May picked up the *Courier* from beside the stuffed chair. "Why. nothing." She started on again.

"Well, don't you want to hear the news?"

"News about what?"

"About Fred and me tonight—at WFKA?"

"Not—another audition!"

"I don't know why not. E. F. Mackay wants to hear us, for the Mackay Furniture hour. It looks pretty good, doesn't it, Fred?"

Fred never stirred. May said: "That's fine." She went out into the kitchen.

She wanted nothing but just to be by herself. Of a sudden she got to the chair by the table and sat down, her body felt so heavy. She had realized she wasn't herself. She couldn't be. For months to come she'd never be able to be alone with herself anywhere—month by month, less and less alone.

Her hands moved on the oilcloth of the table and touched the paper she had brought out. She took it up. She reversed the fold to get away from the radio page. That brought the rotogravure section outermost again, but never mind. Anything to look at, anything.

That man in the oval, think of it, furs! Try and think of it, on a hot, hot evening in July, in Des Moines, Iowa! The wind that threshed at his square beard and tumbled his hair was blowing straight off of white arctic ice!

There wasn't any name. It would probably be down below, under the bigger picture of the two-masted boat with its crew of three.

. . . *Ketch "Kestrel," Home After an Adventurous Winter Locked in the Ice off Baffin Land: Mr. Eric Abernathy, of the Smithsonian Institute, His Wife and Son Bobby Bring Back Valuable Drift Data and Rare Arctic Algae for the Instit*——

May's eyes quit in the middle of the word. They went back to the first words, which they hadn't consciously seen, the date line. "Atlantic City, N. J." They moved down obliquely to the caption's end: " . . . *In the Oval: Eric Abernathy in Arctic Gear.*" They went up then and reached the oval. There they stayed, and there they stared.

Presently she made a whimpering sound.

"It's the beard, that's why."

"What's that, May?"

She hadn't heard Sylvester come out from the other room. When he put a hand on her shoulder, to lean and look, she fainted dead away.

She was on the bed in the bedroom when she came to. Her face and blouse were wet with water. Sylvester had a saucepan with more in it, and looked helpless.

"I'm all right now," she said.

"You are? What do you suppose you——"

"Nothing. Just the heat."

Fred was out in the passage, protesting in a lowered voice, "Syl, do you know it's seven thirty-five?"

May took her lip between her teeth and sat up. The room went around and around.

"Go, Sylvester. I'm all right, honest! You mustn't be late."

"I know—but how can I——"

"You must, it's so important. You can get something to eat on your way, at the Green Car. Get me my purse."

There were two one-dollar bills and a quarter in it; May knew without having to look. She put the quarter in his hand.

She cried sharply, when he just stood and looked at it: "There's all the bills this Saturday, and two months' rent, you know that. You can get a hamburger and pie and coffee for that at the Green Car."

He stood. "How about Fred?"

She gave him one of the dollars quickly. Anything! Anything to get them gone! She called after Sylvester in the passage: "I may lie down awhile. Take your things along with you to the Car. I might sleep a little while."

She went into the kitchen when she was sure they were gone, sat down and put her elbows on the table, one on either margin of the picture page.

"So that's your name. Eric Abernathy. I never did know your name."

May had always thought that beards on men were funny. His didn't look funny. It made him look older. "But you are, though. Fourteen years."

The boat in the bigger picture had been taken from a little above, from a dock, perhaps. No furs there. That was Atlantic City, and summer. The boy, balanced monkey-wise on the furled sail on the main boom, looked to be about ten. Like his father, he was in dungarees and singlet.

"He needs a haircut."

Abruptly, May put a hand down and hid them, boat and all. She swallowed at something in her throat. Swallowed and swallowed.

Dusk had come, out of doors. As yet it brought no coolness.

May took her hand up. She looked at the woman. The woman too was in dungarees, with some kind of a jersey on. It was hard to see, that small, how her hair was done, though you knew it was long hair. Thick braids, perhaps, roped around. She was turned the other way: you couldn't see her face.

May had the same impulse she used to have as a little girl, to turn the picture over, so as to see her from the other side. No, she didn't want to, though. She didn't want to see or know. She hid the picture again, this time with both hands. She put her face down on them, biting the knuckles.

"He'd be my boy. I would be her."

Night came down, a hot, black cloud.

May started, and couldn't believe it, when she heard Sylvester at the front door; it didn't seem possible she'd been there in the dark that long. She wondered in a panic whether she could get through the passage to the bedroom and pretend to be asleep. She had seen him come home with his hopes dashed more than once. She could have borne it better if he had borne it worse, been blue or bitter, or gotten swearing mad. Anything but the easy acceptance, the quick forgetting.

It was too late for the bedroom. She jumped up, turned on the light, and pretended to be just looking around, thinking, when Sylvester came into the kitchen. Fred was with him.

"What's that?" May asked. Sylvester had a bottle under his arm.

"Some claret I bought. It's good—seventy-five cents."

"With what?"

"Why?" He gave her a look, up and down. May had never seen him like this before. He threw his head, to toss the hair back from his brow. "What's worrying you—your money?" He took bills from his pocket and put one into her hand. "How about some glasses from the pantry, Fred?"

Fred went. May sat down. She stared from Sylvester to the money she held.

"Where did you get this?"

"Why, off old man Mackay. A little advance. And was he tickled to do it, Fred!"

Fred had brought two tumblers. Sylvester filled them from the bottle. He looked at May. "Why, aren't you having any, May?" When she made no answer: "Don't look so dumb!" he protested. "I told you we would put it over, didn't I?"

"How much?"

"Oh, ninety a week, to split." He sipped at his claret. "Only three months, though, at that money. Mackay wanted to make it six." He touched his mouth with the handkerchief from his breast pocket. "Fred and I are no suckers. Once we get this thing on the air . . . !"

Fred spoke into his tumbler. "We ought to get some white flannel suits."

"Double-breasted."

May commenced to laugh. She caught hold of the back of her chair. Higher and higher she laughed, harder and harder. After the way of hysteria, the thoughts racing through her brain seemed killingly funny. "So I don't have to go on now. . . . Don't have to go on—don't have to have the baby now."

Sylvester looked mystified, then uneasy. "Stop it, May! You're tired."

Fred actually addressed her. "Look, May!"

That was better than cold water. May got hold of herself and got to the door, biting on her teeth.

"Yuh-yes—I—I'm tired, I g-g-guess."

She went, and the two men sat down. It was the heat, Sylvester explained to Fred. A few minutes later, however, May was back in the kitchen.

"Sylvester, I wonder if you'd do something. I feel so kind of all in tonight. I've made up the sofa in the living room and put your things out there, and I wondered——"

Sylvester lifted a hand. "Not another word, little girl—of course. Get a good sleep now. Run on."

May went into the bathroom first, to the medicine chest. In the bedroom, when she had closed the door, she stood till she heard them talking loudly enough to cover the sound, and turned the key in the lock. Snapping the light off, she sat down on the edge of the bed.

She held the phial, half full of tablets, between her hands, on her knees. It wasn't horrible, it was fascinating. May wasn't afraid of death, as death, now that she wasn't afraid of God or of waking up afterwards. She was afraid of pain, but that clerk had said it would be only a wink, said that she wouldn't know what struck her.

When an auto or trolley went past the foot of Alpine, eastbound, a faint light fanned around the bedroom walls, in reverse. Again in reverse, in miniature, it ran around the inside of the phial. May could have laughed, no longer in hysteria, but because she felt so light-as-feathers, so irresponsible and free.

Sylvester and Fred went along the passage. There was the sound of the front door. Sylvester moved about the living room for a while, getting ready for bed. Presently, whether worried or curious, he came out into the passage and stood. What if he were to try the door? What would he think to find it locked? What would he say? Do?

All of a sudden it came to May: "What difference?" She uncorked the bottle and dropped one tablet in her palm. "Why should I care? One wink, and I wouldn't know it even if he broke the door down. Wouldn't know it if the whole house—if the whole world—fell down on my head. Wouldn't know there'd ever been a world, even. Or Sylvester. Or me."

May never heard him when he tiptoed away. She was so engrossed. She, who had always been so cowardly, was so thrilled. For with this in her hand, there was nothing on earth she couldn't do.

She could walk around the cornice of the Baise Building tower, if she wanted to. She could take off every stitch right now and go out and run around the streets, if she felt like it. She should worry! If she wanted, she could murder people. She could go to the living room, where Sylvester would be asleep, and take a chair and beat his skull in.

She remembered when the Chicago train used to scare her as a child. Well, with this in her hand all ready to swallow, she could go and stand between the rails and watch the engine coming at her and never flinch. It could never hit her. Never while she knew.

"But I don't want to, any of those things. I'd rather sit right here and go."

All at once she thought of something. She crammed the tablet back into the bottle and corked it, wiped her palm on the bedclothes, in a panic. She could have cried, it had all looked so simple. What she had remembered in time was this: if they found her here, it wouldn't be just Sylvester and Fred and the neighbors, and like that. The police would want to know about it too. They always did, when people who weren't sick were found dead. They cut them open then; that was the law. Autopsy. There was the woman they found in the Wyant Hotel last year; they knew well enough she had done it herself, but they cut her open just the same, and it was in the papers. They didn't let anything get by them in an autopsy. "*She was in an expectant condition,*" it said at the end.

And that May couldn't have, and wouldn't have. Whatever happened, she wouldn't have Sylvester knowing that.

She got up and walked around the floor. The room of release had turned into a cage.

"Somewhere, where they wouldn't know who I was . . . There's money enough. Over a hundred and forty dollars in the bank. All I need to do . . ."

May turned on the light. She opened the closet door. There was a suitcase on the upper shelf.

But what if Sylvester should be curious, seeing her go out with a suitcase in the morning?

Well, she would just have to tell him it was some cleaning, or some other lie.

Luckily, she didn't have to lie. Sylvester was still asleep when she got out at eight, by the kitchen way.

She left the suitcase in check at the station before she went to the bank. She was afraid of the bank, afraid some of the back-office people might see her and ask questions. She slipped in by the front way and across to the teller she knew the least.

It worked. "I didn't realize your vacation came so early, Mrs. Templin. Going on a regular one this time, eh? . . . How will you have it?"

"I don't care–five twenties, I guess. Thanks!"

That was all she dared draw. She was afraid even that much would seem suspicious. Besides, there was something she wanted to do. At the station she wrote a check to Sylvester for the balance, forty-four dollars and odd cents. It would cover the two-months' rent that had to be paid right away, the light, gas and milk. May wanted to do that.

She had reached the ticket window before it occurred to her that she had no idea where she was going. The man looked at her. She fiddled with her purse. He tapped with a pencil and looked at her.

"Ocean Grove," she said.

"New Jersey?"

"Yes, New Jersey. And I want to go by the Pennsylvania."

The man started along his rack.

"No, wait!" May said. "Make it Atlantic City."

May walked up and down the Boardwalk at Atlantic City, carrying her suitcase. There was no use in going to a hotel, she thought at first. Finally, it was so hot, she checked the case at a checking place in a drugstore. Then she walked and walked, looking at the ocean.

It was a pity it couldn't have been another time, when she could have been thrilled by the strangeness and wonder of it, coming in blue from the horizon to whiten on the sands. All she wondered now was, she wondered where the anchored boats could be. She didn't see a one, though she saw a few under sail, out further. Perhaps it was only at night they came in toward the beach, among the diving floats—though she had to say it looked uncomfortably rough there for anchoring.

May hated to ask questions, for fear of questions. When it got late, however, she approached a policeman. "Do you know of a man named Eric Abernathy, a sailor?"

The way he looked at her when he said no, she almost decided to give it up and have it over with. It was so small a thing after all, just a whim she had taken, just to see his boat once, first, from a dock or beach or wherever it was, even though she didn't see him, which she wouldn't, ten chances to one.

But it was too late; too late, that is, for going on with the other business. The beach was deserted of bathers. The tide was low, a bathhouse man told her, just at the turn; before there was much water again it would be dark, he said. May grasped at the chance his words gave her, for making doubly sure. (She had already, in a roundabout way, asked the Parmalee man crossing Chicago, and a dining steward on the Pennsylvania, and they had both said they thought so.) So now she put on a vague expression and said: "I suppose people that get drowned, if it's when the tide's rising, it'll bring their bodies right back in and you find them. I suppose it's only when it's going out that it carries them out to sea?"

He too looked at her in a funny way. "Why?"

"Oh, nothing, I'm just trying to write a story for a magazine, that's all. If they ever find the body, then there's no point. That's why."

May went away. She got her suitcase. She had to go to a hotel after all. She signed the register as a Mrs. Kathleen Brown from Toledo. Then she had a streak of luck.

"Abernathy?" echoed the clerk. "You mean the Polar man. He'll probably be lying over the other side of the island, in the Inlet, at one of the boat yards. Probably Forston's."

It was after ten next morning when May found the Forston Boatbuilding Company. There was a man sitting on a half barrel in the gateway.

"I'm afraid you're a little late," he said, before May got any further than, "Is this where——" He mopped his head and looked down through the tangle of railways, derricks, hulls, and spars that almost hid the water. "There comes the reporters' boat ashore now. He'll be under way any minute now."

May just stood.

The gateman mopped the inside of his collar. It was ninety-six in the shade. "The crowd's down there at Number Two Ways, if you want to go——" A faint sound of cheering interrupted him. "There!" He pointed into the tangle of wood and iron. "There she goes."

May was bewildered. She felt dumb. She saw whiteness in one of the gaps. It passed slowly to another, and another, a sail beyond them, hardly more than drifting.

The man was grumbling. "Damn foolishness. If he'd ask me, I'd say 'twas no day to be starting out for Great Egg even, say nothing of the Ar'tic Circle. This weather's going to bust wide open, you watch, and not too many hours."

May began to laugh of a sudden. The man, thinking she laughed at him for claiming to know more than Abernathy, glowered and said, "Oh, all right."

But May wasn't laughing at him. She was laughing at everything. "That's done," she thought. "That's that!"

She walked back across town. There was no hurry in getting to the beach. It would be after twelve before the tide began to ebb, she'd seen in a paper. On the way she went into a shop and bought a bathing suit. She didn't feel like renting one, somehow. She chose a deep-blue suit and bought a blue waterproof bag that tied to the wrist, to go with it. She found another bathing place than the one where she'd talked with the man the day before.

When she had undressed in the sultry cubicle they gave her, she looked at herself. It seemed strange to think . . . Then she put on the suit.

She made sure, one last time, there were no marks in the clothes she was leaving. She had already done that for the things abandoned at the hotel. She had gone so far last night as to soak the Harknett Drugstore label off the phial. The phial she had left in the waste-basket; the label she had put down the toilet, together with all but one of the tablets; one was all she would need. She had it loose in her purse now, along with everything by which she might have been identified, her initialed handkerchief, wedding ring, high-school pin, such things. These, before she went out, she transferred to the little rubber wrist bag. There was a dollar bill and seventy cents change left from her hundred. She put the bill back in the purse; there was no reason somebody shouldn't have it; it told no tales. But the silver would help weight the rubber bag, which she meant to take off. There mustn't be any mistake about its sinking.

When she went out on the sand she was faced by an unappreciated problem, and by its solution, almost in the same moment. A boy, a lifeguard with deeply tanned body, was there in a skiff beyond the first of the surf, laughing and nodding to a girl who climbed in over the stern. May ran through the shallow foam. "Wait! Take me out too!" She had hold of the gunwale, and there was nothing he could say.

"I'm going to the offshore float," the girl said with some tartness, looking sidewise at May.

"I am too," said May.

"How about it? Good enough swimmer?" The guard had to know.

Good enough! Apparently, that gave May a good laugh. Any day she couldn't swim a mile! And that meant in fresh water, she said. It ought to mean two, in salt. (May couldn't swim a stroke. She wet a hand over the gunwale and touched it to her tongue when they weren't looking. She'd always known it, but she'd never believed it could be. But it was true. It was salty.)

"The only reason," she explained, "I want to get my sun bath before I get my shoulders wet."

May lay on her stomach on the canvas deck of the offshore float and stared seaward and wished the girl would go away. Before she did go, others had come. They talked, giggled, teetered on the springboard.

Noon was furnace hot. There wasn't a stir in the air. Half a dozen boats, out a way, lay with slack canvas, pointing in all directions. The sun beat down. One of the swimmers, a woman, warned May. "You're going to have an awful burn if you don't look out." May just lay and stared seaward. "All right," the woman said to her companion, "she don't feel it now, but wait a couple of hours!"

May wondered what their faces would have looked like if they had known. It ought not to be more than an eighth part of those two hours before the tide would change.

It grew long. Those swimmers went and left May alone. It seemed as if at least an hour was gone. Yet the low, lazy, glassy swells still came from seaward and went on shoreward, exactly as they had. (In her midland mind May confused the waves with the tide. The tide was already ebbing, but she didn't know.)

A man and a woman came, rocking the float as they climbed on. The man said suddenly: "God A'mighty, Nell, look what's coming!" The woman said: "As quick as that! Just while we've been swimming out! We better beat it."

The man trod nearer to May. "Look what's coming, lady." He laid a hand on her shoulder, on the sunburn. That brought her up, pivoting on a hip. Over the shore, above and beyond the town, a black cloud climbed for the sun. Lightning split it. Thunder thudded.

"Beat it!" the man said to the woman. She plunged and swam. He looked at May. May could have killed him. She could have cried. She looked at the waves, and they still ran as they had run. Among the boats becalmed offshore, sails were dropping down. People on the floats nearer the beach were excited, shouting to one another to get ashore.

The man grew impatient. "That's going to hit quick. You better come."

May felt helpless. She felt angry too. "Yes, yes, I'm coming in a second. I'm a fast swimmer—I'll be there before you two. Go on."

To her relief he turned and dived. She dropped on the canvas behind the butt of the springboard. When he came up and looked back and didn't see her, he thought she was in the water too, turned and swam after the woman, who was well ahead.

May lay where she was till the cloud touched the sun. She sat up and watched the black shadow come, broken by lightning. All at once it made her think of the train when she was little. She laughed. She untied the rubber bag, fumbled out the tablet and held it in one fist. With the other hand she threw the weighted bag as far as she could, away into the water. She stood up. She laughed out loud. Nothing could hurt her. Nothing could hit her while she knew.

Rain hit her in a blinding flood. But that was only rain. Wind hit her and knocked her down to her knees. It was only wind. She scrambled up and stood against it. She could see no more than a hundred feet in any direction, so she didn't know the float had swung right around at its mooring; all she knew was that when she looked at the water the thing had happened; the waves had turned and were running past her the other way.

At last there was no worry. She could have danced while the wind and rain hammered at her and the lightning crackled and couldn't scare her. There was no worry and no hurry, and May could have sung.

It was only by chance she turned and saw a boat coming close through the welter, a boy with a scared face over a brown shoulder, pulling at the oars. Just in time she lifted her fist, popped the pellet into her mouth, tumbled toward the float's edge and the water.

A rending flare, and blackness. Heavy, cold blackness. And May thought: "I did know what struck me."

Then she thought: "How do I know?" She felt herself turning over in slow somersault, touching nothing. How could she feel that if she was dead? There was something on her tongue. It was the tablet. She hadn't swallowed it. She tried to swallow it, tried and tried and couldn't. She tried to bite it, and couldn't seem to. She was under the sea, and she wasn't dead.

Terror came and got her. "O my God!" She fought out with arms and legs. "O God!"

She tried to climb. "Oh, please!" But there was nothing to climb by. "O God, please!"

Her lids paled. Her lips parted, and for an instant air came between her teeth. But water followed. It grew dark again as she went down.

By and by she stopped praying. She stopped thinking, stopped caring. The muscles about her mouth tired and loosened. Water leaked in.

If there was another paling of the dark, May didn't know it. She knew nothing till she opened her eyes and saw a city of gold.

It was far off and quite small, painted on a ribbon of sun-shot mist beyond water the color of lead.

Around May the dark still racketed, wind and rain. Voices

shouted and were small. "Ease her off, Bobby—keep some way!" . . . "Off it is, sir!" . . . "No more!"

By turning her head a little May could see the second of the speakers, a boy of ten or so, braced at a wheel at the other end of a cockpit sharply aslant, a taut rag of sail above him. He had his jaw clamped, for courage, and his eyes narrowed, for mastery, and he needed a haircut, May saw. She couldn't see much of the other speaker, only, out of the bottoms of her eyes, a bit of the forearm with which he held her, half lying, half jammed, against the cockpit combing. But that was all she needed. She knew.

Strangely, she hadn't time yet to think how strange.

There was something in her mouth. She had to think about that.

"Let me!" she gasped. He didn't hear. She got one hand free and stuck her fingers in, down between tongue and gum. She got the tablet out and looked at it. It wasn't a tablet. It was a button made of horn.

"Let me!" she gasped. She strained. The arm gave. She leaned out over the combing, over the side. She looked down into rushing foam. She opened her mouth, and water and sickness emptied out.

"There you are, young woman!"

She was lifted to her feet, thrust toward an opening in a low house with a ladder of three steps inside. When she was in and down she turned to look back. Eric Abernathy was leaning, one hand on either side of the companionway, looking down and in. It was enough like the rotogravure picture to be funny, the wind battering his beard and hair and his eye corners puckered—though of course it was against the wetness now, not the cold.

May said to herself: "He doesn't know me from Adam." Then she thought: "How would he, in a bathing suit?"

He said to her: "It's about blown out now. You lie down awhile, while Bobby and I get some sail on."

May looked around her. Of a sudden she caught a big breath. She thought: "Where is she?"

Eric was gone. There was only the boy at the wheel to be seen, and he wasn't looking, and she didn't feel like asking, anyway.

In the narrow cabin where she stood there seemed to be everything: bunks, books, boots, oilskins, dishes, charts, quadrants, binoculars—everything but a Mrs. Abernathy. A door at the other end opened into a passage. May dreaded to go, but she did. There was nobody in the passage. There was nobody in the galley at its other end. There was nowhere to go beyond the galley.

May wondered till she was giddy. She tried to lean in the doorway, but the doorway knocked her about and threw her down. She had to get up. There were still two doors, both closed, behind her in the passage. She opened the first. She closed it quickly, feeling abashed, even though there was no one. It was the lavatory. She opened the second. There was a stateroom with two berths, made up with nautical neatness, one on either side. When she saw there was nobody even here May felt like a rag. She lay down on one of the berths. She hadn't slept for what seemed weeks. She slept.

It seemed to May she had been asleep for weeks, when she waked. Some of the bits of dreams she remembered were like things years and years away, and even they, once she was wide awake, went like mist in the morning when she tried to see them again.

At first she had no idea where she was. Her eyes were on the window, and the window was funny. It wasn't rectangular, it was round. Then a sight of sea tipped up and filled it, the blue-green flank of a comber, spangled with foam and sunshine, and she remembered.

She remembered she'd been in her wet bathing suit when she threw herself down. She was in the bed now. She looked at her arms, felt at her throat. Soft Shantung. When she moved her legs, under the sheet, she knew it was pajamas. She turned quick eyes to the other berth. It had been slept in. A hotness swept her cheeks.

"Where could she have been when I was looking for her?"

The door from the passage opened a crack. It opened wider. May hated to look, but she had to. And it wasn't the woman, after all; it was the boy.

"Well," he said, "have you had enough at last?"

When he smiled he grinned. When he grinned, he wanted a tooth here and there—he was at that age—and he had quantities of freckles.

May's mind played a queer trick on her for one instant. It thought: "If I don't get the shears at that mop of his today!" She was confused, and that was why she failed to answer.

Bobby seemed not to mind. "Captain!" he shouted aft along the passage. "Lash the wheel and come and see!"

Eric came. "Well, Commodore, feel better?" That was funny. Commodore?

He came and knelt down beside the berth, all woolly in a big windbreaker. May thought her heart was going to stop when he laid a hand on her forehead. But then: "Maybe I've had a fever," she thought, "maybe it's that."

It seemed, though, as if he only did it to smooth the hair back out of her eyes. He looked into them hard for a while. "Lazy May," he said, "get up and stand your trick now."

It came to May: "It's the eyes—he remembers my eyes." She got them away from his, and past Bobby, in a panic to the open door. "What would she think if she came and saw!"

Aloud, May said: "Yes—now—go—I'll get up quickly."

She got up when they were gone and slipped out of her pajamas. She looked at herself. She looked at her hair, that hung down over her shoulders. With a strange regret she looked out of the port at the water, crisp with crests. "I suppose I'm too late for my bath—they hove to hours ago and had theirs. That's for being lazy."

She pulled open the middle one of the three drawers let in beneath the berth. She took out something of primrose georgette. She wondered. Again she looked out at the water, at the color of it. "No," she said, "I think I'd better . . ." Replacing the georgette, from another layer she took a garment of Scotch wool, almost as sheer as the crepe itself. This she put on. There were dungarees, worn but clean, in the big drawer at the bottom, and a bright yellow jersey with a turtle neck, and sneakers. When she had washed in the bowl that let down from the cabinet by the porthole, she combed her hair before the mirror. She looked at the small framed photograph that stood on the shelf below it, and smiled half a smile, with a fleeting wistfulness.

"How far away and how long ago. That was taken in my senior year at high school." The wistfulness was gone, and the smile was purer merriment. "He thought I thought I'd lost it, when we both changed at Philadelphia. As if I didn't know he had it in his bag!"

May had got to the door before she thought. She stopped. She brushed a hand over her eyes, turned and looked back at the picture. "What am I thinking of? How did that come here?" Again she ran fingers over her eyes. "What difference!" A coat button of horn lay near her feet on the stateroom deck; she picked it up and put it in the top drawer under the berth before she went on out.

She had a fright in the cabin. Somebody was in one of the bunks there, rolled in a blanket. But then May saw it was Bobby. Without thinking, she thought: "Poor lamb, he must be tired." For she thought: "They've been standing watch and watch while I've been ill."

She stood on the ladder, halfway out of the companion. A fine morning, a fine, tingling, blue-and-white wind out of the west; gulls high above the wake rode like sleep on the wind. A mile off on the port beam a basalt reef stood on the ocean, surf-laced and lonely.

May said: "Why, there's the Pope and Cardinals! Already?"

Eric, riding the wheelbox, laughed. "We've come along. Seven days from Nantucket Shoals to Cape Race of Newfoundland—tell me *that's* not coming!"

"Whew!" May whistled.

But then she was all confused again, as if her whistling had waked her up. Quickly she twisted in the opening, peered along the house, along the narrow decks, all the way to the bow. She got back down into the cabin. Once and for all, she made certain there was nobody else but Bobby in that cabin. She went forward into the passage, looked in at the stateroom, made certain there. She knocked on the door of "the Head," opened it. Empty. And the galley was the same.

There was a half door in the forward bulkhead of the little sea kitchen. May went and pulled it open. She peered in. She reached in. She brought out part of a side of bacon, some coffee, tinned milk, flour for making griddle cakes, lime juice in a bottle. She fired the vapor stove and put the coffee on. She sliced the bacon with a heavy, sharp knife and beat up the batter for the cakes.

When all was ready she set the table for two in the cabin. She touched the boy on the shoulder. "Wake up!"

He rolled over, opened his eyes, shut them, rubbed them, opened them again. Presently he would outgrow those comical tooth gaps, outgrow his freckles perhaps. Thank God, May thought, he could never outgrow those eyes.

"Wake up, breakfast, Bob!"

Suddenly the eyes were like Christmas morning. "You called me 'Bob'! That means I'm grown up, doesn't it?—growner-up than 'Bobby.' Won't you ask Father to call me it too?"

May leaned and kissed him between those eyes. There was something in her throat that made her laugh. "Yes—and drink your lime juice."

"Bobby wants you to call him Bob," she told Eric as she relieved him at the wheel. "Do, and go before your breakfast's cold. . . . Is this right, nor'-by-west-a-half-north?"

"Due north," said Eric.

Mechanically, May's hand swung the wheel. Half a point the needle in the binnacle swung.

"By the way, Eric." He looked back from the ladder. "Where's your old tweed jacket, the gray-brown one with the double breast? I've found that button."

Eric started to answer, and then didn't. He looked at her.

"Why, May, what's the matter? Why are you crying?"

She took her lip out from between her teeth. "I don't know." She felt like simply blubbering. "I love Bobby so. I love you so. . . . No, go on before your coffee's cold."

The Pope and Cardinals had gone down astern. The sea ran unbroken. Trough and crest, trough and crest, with an ordered, almost monotonous motion, the *Kestrel* drove. The steady wind blew cool against May's cheek, blew cool through her body and mind, and the white wings of the gulls astern rode the wind like sleep.

There began a twittering. Then a racket of sailcloth as the boat came up under a limp rudder and the canvas lost the wind.

May winked back half awake as man and boy came tumbling out. They took it well when they saw how it was, both laughing. But May was flustered, and she was ashamed.

"It's all this air, I guess," she mumbled as Eric carried her below in his arms. While he was undressing her, pulling jersey off one way and dungarees the other, she kept at it like a drunk with one idea—drunk with sleep. "All this air—I must get used to it."

May waked in the middle of some night and sat up in bed. She didn't know what night it was. She only knew it was the middle of it because they grew so short now and it was black dark out of the port. The only light came in at the door from the lantern in the passage.

Half in the ray, Eric was getting ready for his four-hour turn of sleep, stripping the heavy woolen shirt over his head, off his square-built, hard-muscled body, still brown from southern suns.

"It'll be all right tonight," he said, when he saw May sitting up. "It's clear, the glass high, and hardly any sea running, and I've told him to call me right away if he sees any ice. He's a great sailor, and he's a great kid, isn't he, May?"

When there was no answer he stepped nearer and saw that May wasn't looking or listening. She was looking down at the two loosely braided ropes of her brown hair, which fell forward, one over either shoulder, to lie together in the valley of her breast. Now, and again, she raised a hand and almost touched them, and let the hand drop. There was a mist of trouble mixed with sleep over the surface of her eyes.

Eric said, "May dear!" almost sharply. That brought her out of it. She reached with her arms and her hands.

"Eric, please, here!" He was beside her quickly, hunkered down by the berth. "Put your arms around me, Eric. Tighter! I've had such dreams. Eric, I dreamed I hadn't you and Bobby. It was as if I was back in Iowa, Eric, and I couldn't wake up, and I couldn't get away, and there was no air. And the awful thing, Eric—it seemed as if I was married to somebody that wasn't you—and Eric—I was going to have a baby—and it was—oh, it was—— Look at me, Eric, I'm all of a shiver still."

Eric got in bed and held her against him to stop her shivering. With his strong hand he caressed her brow and smoothed her hair, till that made her remember something, with a caught breath.

"And my hair, Eric—that was what I was dreaming when I waked—my hair was short—they'd bobbed my hair."

He held her head a little away and looked at it and smiled.

"That would be a pity!"

The way he said it, the way he smiled, all at once the shiver was gone, and she laughed in her breath as she pulled one braid through under Eric's neck and the other over it and was busy with their ends beyond. "Wouldn't it! For how could I tie you up with it then, so you couldn't get away?"

Eric looked in her eyes. "Pretty eyes," he said.

"Take care, Mr. Abernathy!" May's heart was filled with an enchanted merriment. "You got yourself into an awful pickle once, if you'll remember, with this talk of pretty eyes."

"Do you mean, Mrs. Abernathy, that time on that train?"

May simply gazed at him, shaking her head as if with pity. As if with pity, he shook his.

"And you, poor dolt of an Iowa girl, you imagined I meant it."

"I didn't imagine. I knew. Right then."

"Right when?"

"Remember that first evening in the dining car, after Davenport? I do—because it was the first artichoke I ever had. Well, I think it was then that something *really* told me."

"Be explicit! Told you what?"

"That if I could get you across Chicago without losing you, then Bobby would have brown eyes."

"Indeed? . . . I think I shall kiss you, May."

But May was busy untying the knot in the braids she had tied.

"Go shut the door first," she said.

The storm at noon hadn't broken the weather after all, as people in Atlantic City had hoped it would. It was hot again that evening, hot even in the morgue. A police sergeant and a police surgeon stood by the body of the unidentified woman that lay under a sheet on one of the slabs.

The doctor mopped his head with a handkerchief. "Drowned?"

"No, and that's funny, Doc. The guard did pretty work, even to get out there in that squall, and when he was almost to the float he saw this dame kind of stumble and slide overboard. He got her the second time she come up, still breathing some, he says, and he figured he'd pulled the trick. But when he got her ashore she was dead—and I mean dead too."

"Try the pulmotor?"

"We did, till we found there wasn't hardly any water in her. . . . Funny. . . . Heart failure or something, could it be? Or maybe poison?"

"Tell you better about that after the post-mortem—that and everything." The doctor touched the hand that lay outside the sheet, on the slab. "Almost be nice to be as cool as that for a while, dogged if it wouldn't."

The sergeant wiped his neck. "Be heaven," he said.

"Do you believe in heaven, Sergeant?"

"Life eternal? Don't you, Doc?"

Cornered, the boy struggled up on an elbow. "Why do I have to tell you? You can't force me, if I don't want to!"

The intern put his card and pen away quickly and got up. "Of course not. Heavens! Don't you bother one bit more now. Come, nurse."

The boy took what comfort he could in the belief that he had fooled them. But he couldn't fool the awful embarrassment, the awful loneliness. Nor had he fooled the others. The nurse, returning with a glass of something to make him sleep, smoothed his brow after he'd drunk it.

"Don't worry, son. It often happens after things like scarlet fever, the kind of a siege you've been through. But it's an amnesia that passes. As you grow stronger, things will come back to you."

They didn't, though. Out of quarantine at last, lodged in the convalescent division, the fellow became a problem. They tried all sorts of sudden things; flashed on him the clothes he'd been picked up in, sweat shirt, dungarees, and sneakers, worn but clean from their disinfection. These meant nothing, stirred no memory. Doctors of one breed and another dealt with him. One, a young man with a crazy eagerness to know the hidden sides of things, refused to quit.

"For you see, if we could get you to want to remember, you'd remember. . . . No, now, wait," he pleaded, over the protestations of the lost one, by now as jumpy-wild as a rabbit caught in the open, no thicket to hide in. "By 'you' I don't mean this you that's talking, thinking here, with the top side of your cranium. No, it's the other guy, the you that lives 'way down under, boss of the filing cabinet where every least act and word of your life is on record, for merely the riffling of his thumb to find. He's the guy that takes a memory and declares it out of bounds, taboo, and he's the guy I want to talk with—if there's any God's way of getting through the wall of hysteria he's thrown around your consciousness."

"I'm not hysterical! I'm not!"

"That's all that amnesia is—hysteria of a type. Hypnotism will sometimes help. If you're willing to let us have a shot at it——"

"No! Let me be! Let me go now!"

"Easy, friend—no one's going to bother you. But you can do it for your own self if you'd rather—probably *do* it every night you sleep. Because it's that other guy that does your dreaming—if only you could remember when you waken the parts of the dream he doesn't want you to. . . . Listen, here's something can't hurt you. Will you, for me, give it a try?"

So it was that the boy was shifted to a private room to sleep that night, and wasn't let sleep—not for a while, anyway. Propped up on triple pillows, he was given a sheet of paper to stare at, blank and blinding in the ray from a hooded bulb, "for that guy to write on when he's ready," the doctor said over and over. "Like a signboard. Think of it as a signboard, to point you the way."

Over and over, ruthless, each time the boy's eyes wandered or the lids dropped—until it must have been that words did actually take shape, on a signboard grown enormous. Words fleeting, but half written, and all gibberish, were they? Or were they words solid, sober, and sequent in the idiom of dreams? The boy could never say, for he was asleep and remembered not a bit of it.

The first thing he himself knew, and nine-tenths fantastic, was a fragrance heavy in nose and mouth, and ecstasy. If only he could have hung on, lain there longer in the drift of perfume that was like nothing on earth but heavy, hot, wet lilies, shaken by fright and bliss. But now the doctor's face was above him, bringing him wide-awake.

"Have I been asleep?"

"About five hours. Tell me, did you watch the signboard? Do you remember what you dreamed?"

"No. I guess I didn't dream." Of what had been dreaming, but half waking, the boy saw no need to speak "Why?" he asked.

"Nothing. I'll put the light out now. Go on back to sleep."

But the next day the doctor let him know what actually had happened. He had a notebook, scantily penciled. "I got you to talk in your sleep last night—if you can call it talking. I want your help now. Does any of this mean a darn thing to you?"

The boy took the loose leaf the other detached from the notebook. He read aloud the fragmentary jottings, blank mystified.

"*Signboard? . . . Signboard?* [At intervals, as prompted.] . . . *The White Friars. . . .* [Prompted: Who are the White Friars?] . . . *The white rocks. . . . They are killing the natives—no, it's the Friars—no—I don't know. . . . Some were killed Thursday and I hear the bell. . . .* [What bell?] . . . *I daren't go out by the bell till dark—lay low till dark, in behind the sisters. . . .* [What sisters?]

. . . The Three Gray Sisters. . . . Cocoa, nutmeg, cinnamon—spices, spices, everything nices. . . . What will the wages be? . . . Maybe death? No, no! . . . Dark and the bell is still. . . . The White Friars are small and black with the moon behind them. . . . To hell with death! I will dare! [Vehemently, and no more.]"

"You must realize," the doctor hastened to explain, "not a word of it awake may have the sense it had dreaming. That guy in the subconscious has a thousand dodges, double meanings, association hookups, farfetched puns. Read it again; see if there isn't some one thing can touch a spark. For instance, your White Friars, evidently rocks of some sort—I find there's a reef in the Irish Sea, the *Gray*-friars. Still, the insistence on the word 'natives'—I don't know—it's hard to say. Mayn't the Three Gray Sisters, taking the bell as a buoy——"

But the boy cried sharply, "Let me think!" His rereading had brought him as far as "Cocoa." Mightn't it mean "coco"—coconut? Nearly it seemed there was a spark. "Coco, nutmeg, cinnamon . . . spices, spices." Excitement shook him as he recalled the fragrant fright-and-bliss of his waking. But no, not spices; more like heavy lilies it had been.

The doctor, watching his face, asked: "Caught something?"

"I thought for a second—but not quite. Could I keep this and——"

"Surely, yes, do!"

But when the boy was returned to his room all thought of the paper in his pocket was whisked out of mind. A middle-aged, stoutish man with a queerly tight gray face was waiting there. The boy stopped dead, blinked once or twice, and said: "Dad! You here?"

"Hullo, Merrill."

"My—yes—my name is Merrill. Merrill—August—Mygatt. How's everything in—back in—you know——"

"Des Moines."

"I mean, Des Moines."

There are all sorts of keys; Merrill Mygatt's key was visual. Just as physical sight of his father had unlocked recognition instant and complete, so it was to go with everything.

He had said, "I mean, Des Moines," but it had really been only echo to his father's prompting, and not until they got off the train at the station days later did he remember what his home town was like, and who his friends were. Even then it was only such friends as were gathered there that memory accepted, face by face, and fitted back into the pattern of life; Uncle Ben and Aunt Ella; Waite Koy, basketball captain; Belle Wingate, such a peach; Walt Finn, boss toolmaker; so on, one by one, face by face. And so it was with the city, each street; one look along it on entering, and in a wink: "Of course—I know all this."

So too with the house that was home; Cousin Natalie, white-haired housekeeper, smiling weepily in the doorway; then room by room, unknown before the threshold, and in a flash familiar since babyhood; and the picture of a pretty woman, and Merrill knew, and what had been a secret wonder was cleared away. His mother. She'd died when he was little.

For Merrill's father had not quite understood about him, and shyness born of shame had kept the boy under a strain of watchful waiting through the long trip on the train, careful to ask no question till some chance word of his father's had prepared him for the answer.

It was so he learned, without asking, that he was seventeen, and it was well over a year since he'd gone away. "Run away," he read between the lines. What they'd done about it at home was left a blank, other than that it was only through police publicity, set going by the hospital, that his father had learned of his whereabouts.

"Even then I doubted it," he told Merrill. "They made such a point of your being, probably, a sailor."

Coloring, frowning with embarrassment, the boy hitched up a sleeve. The man frowned in turn as he studied the crossed anchors.

"Where ever did you get a thing like that done to you, son?"

"Oh—er—I dunno."

The way he tried to throw it off, sulky-sounding, threw the father off. They were too much alike, shy to the point of prickliness, overquick at hiding a hurt. And there'd been too much of this flushing and eyes turned away at any least attempt to draw Merrill out about his year of wandering. If he could once have looked his father in the eye and said straight, "I'd tell you if I knew, Dad, but I don't know, that's all," it would have been different. As it was, the father ended by feeling puzzled, evaded, and rebuffed. He certainly wasn't going to pry, he told himself, and space and silence had grown between them.

The irony of it was that Merrill himself had a question he'd wanted very much to put. It recurred to his mind after he'd gone to bed in the heaven of his own bed that first night, with a day of recovered kin and friends and common graciousness behind him; came with such a press of necessity that he got up, went out barefooted to his father's door, knocked, entered, and asked quickly before pride and timidity should catch up with him: "Dad, why was it I ran away from here?"

To the parent it was happy miracle, contact remade. His brow cleared, his eyes misted; he made a gruff pushing-off motion with his hands.

"That's all water under the bridge, son; let's both forget it."

That was just what Merrill didn't want, but what could he say?

A few days later, Mygatt got down to business, with characteristic awkward lightness.

"Well, my man, how about it? Still feel the same—don't want to go to college? Straight into the works, from bench up?"

Could something about that have been the "water under the bridge"? Absurd! Not knowing what to say, Merrill said: "Yep, I still do."

It was a hot summer, the air through the windows of Mygatt's metal-stamping works heavy with the dust and pollen of the midlands. But the apprentice toolmaker didn't mind; he was too content to have his hands busy with solid substance and measurable angles, and foreman Finn's quaint profanity to bring his mind back when sometimes it would stray.

The straying would begin like this, sparked by a glimpse of the anchors on his forearm: "My palms are hard and my fingers quick to catch the hang of things. How come?" On what seas, what coasts, had the skin learned to callous without blistering; what queer knacks did his fingers know that he didn't know they knew?

One day Finn found him truant from his bench, seated idle among the odds and ends of a rubbish shed, two bights of greasy old rope across his palms, his eyes fixed on nothingness, resolutely blank.

"Whaddaya think you're doin' here, me fine felluh?"

"Aw, nothin'—I dunno." It was a lie. Had Merrill answered the truth, it would have been: "I was waiting to see if knots would tie."

Foreman Finn began to worry. "Give him time," Old man Mygatt put him off. "Merrill's been a sick fellow, remember." And because it went all against his business religion his voice grew sharp: "Boys will be boys!"

Merrill was a boy as boys will be in any country city, any summer. Waite Koy, ex-basketball captain, home from the CCC; Belle Wingate, with her job in Fliegenheimer's, such a peach; Winona, Emil, two or three others of the old class; movies, dancing sometimes, long discussions in dog wagons, or a boat on the park lake while the band played. A thin-tin boat and Merrill rowing, his hands uneasily disdainful on the plaything oars in their patent oarlocks, the red-and-blue-inked stigma on his forearm winking in and out between the rays from the bandstand arcs and the moon. . . .

"Heave ho, whaddaya know—our Merrill run off to be a sailor!"

"And here *I* used to think he was set for the *baking business!*"

A gasp of merriment at this sally of Belle's; something of the past known to them, cryptic to Merrill.

"Where all did you sail and what all did you see—no kiddin', Merrill, why won't you ever loosen up and tell us?"

"With one in every port? You don't get that guy to talk. He's too wise. He 'don't remember.' "

"Shiver my topmast, look at our bloody pirate—is his face red!"

Red, yes, ducked down, chin in neck; and in the fury of his heart the boy who had mislaid a chunk of his life wanted above all things to be alone, free of them and their picayune prairie-bound railleries about things he couldn't remember and about things they couldn't guess.

That night he got down a bundle from his closet shelf, sweat shirt, dungarees, and sneakers, felt in a pocket and found a folded paper.

"*Signboard? . . . Signboard?* [At intervals, as prompted.] . . . *The White Friars* . . . [Prompted: Who are the White Friars?] . . . *The white rocks. . . . They are killing the natives—no, it's the Friars—no—I don't know. . . . Some were killed Thursday and I hear the bell* . . . [What bell?] . . . *I daren't go out by the bell till dark—lay low till dark, in behind the sisters* . . . [What sisters?] . . . *The Three Gray Sisters. . . . Cocoa, nutmeg, cinnamon—spices, spices, everything nices . . . What will the wages be? . . . Maybe death? No, no! . . . Dark and the bell is still . . . The*

White Friars are small and black with the moon behind them. . . . To hell with death! I will dare! [Vehemently, and no more.]"

To the taunting of the words the cheap, frayed, adventurous garments spread there seemed to add their own. "Here at home you have three suits for play and two for work and one for Sunday, and every day three big soft meals, security, and a thin-tin boat with patent oarlocks on a park pond where a band plays. You—who once lived and cried vehemently: 'To hell with death! I will dare!' "

When Merrill did go to sleep it was with the bedside light on and the paper held against his peaked knees, "signboard," though without much faith. Yet it worked, in a way. He dreamed laboriously, the same dream over and over. He sailed a pitch-black water, but with no ship under him and no ship's wheel in his hand; instead, three tiny figurines of pressed coco fiber—the hear-not, see-not, speak-not monkeys they seemed at first, till a disembodied bell went by and they were three gray-robed nuns. And one said, "Keep clear, it's none of your affair," and one, "And you're too young," and one, "And too afraid."

Then there would come in sight a line of rocks, ill-formed, far off. Now they were white with fountaining surf, now black with the moon behind them, and now to end with, every time, they became a smooth concrete rim with park benches above it, packed with dim people listening to a band. And as for the gray sisters, they were three little dark spiced cakes with coconut frosting he was eating, and when he started to wake at last the taste of the spice was in his nose and mouth. Half awake, he thought with a cloudy excitement: "I had hold of it!" But, wide-awake then, he realized that the stuff of the dream had only been what his consciousness had given it to play with: once more he recalled that it wasn't spice that should have lingered, but a frightening sweet stench of lilies.

The following Saturday Merrill turned up at the public library. Awkward with shyness as he was, the girl who waited on him had to wait.

"Something about islands in the South Seas?" she echoed dubiously.

"Well—er—yes."

He was the more vacillant because the girl troubled him. Young, slight, grave almost to plainness, mouse-colored and mouse-quiet, it was only when she glanced back at him on her way to the racks and, caught by his eye, flushed hotly and bit a smile, that he half placed her. When she returned with a trial offering, *White Shadows on the South Seas*, he beat around the wretched bush. "Haven't I—somewhere——"

"Washington High." She swallowed, pink again. "But I was only a junior—I didn't suppose you'd remember me."

"Alice——"

"—Doane. . . . Er—Mr. Mygatt—we are all happy you are back in town again. I don't know if *White Shadows* will do, but you can try it."

Merrill tried it. From three till the library closed at six he lost himself in the sad green heaven of the Marquesas.

"Would you like to take it home to finish?" Alice Doane suggested, seeing the excitement that widened his eyes, and the carriage of his shoulders, as though his stature had increased by inches.

Merrill shook his head. "It's not it. There aren't any spices, and there have to be spices. And lilies."

"I'll see what I can do—if you'll drop in next week sometime."

Wednesday was the evening the library kept open. Wednesday evening: "I don't know, of course, Mr. Mygatt, but do you suppose the Moluccas might do? They've been known as the Spice Islands for centuries."

"Where?"

"Here's an atlas. See, the Celebes and Dutch New Guinea, and here between them all the Moluccas—the group called the Bandas is somewhere here in the Banda Sea."

"The Bandas? I don't see them."

"They're too small. But of all the spice islands they are *the* spice islands—Gunong Api, Banda Neira, Lontor, Pisang and Suwangi, Wai and Run. And in this old travel book I found in the storage racks—have you time?—here's the passage I mean: 'With dusk the force of the northwest monsoon had abated, and though our ship lay well out, to seaward of the dazzling reef called Te Takeh, yet there was borne to us on the soft night air from Lontor a fragrance of nutmeg forests, mingled with the lesser perfumes of mace and cinnamon and stench of copra from the natives' drying yards.' "

"Copra?"

"That's the meat of coconuts they dry."

"It says there 'the dazzling reef'?"

"Here, see? 'The dazzling reef.' "

"It doesn't say if lilies grow on Lontor, does it? Would there be any way of–er–could you find out?"

"I'll try."

Looking up at her, Merrill knew that "Why?" trembled on her lips. But she didn't ask it. Instead: "Would you like to take the book home?"

Merrill let his breath out, grabbed the book, and went.

The next evening he was back, not inside but on the steps, when the library closed at six–all because she hadn't asked why. He was surcharged and stammering. "W-w-would you like–er–why don't we walk by the Ideal and–I dunno–have a soda?"

Nearly there, Alice stopped. She said, like a teacher: "No true lilies. But *Agapanthus formosi* grows in profusion on Lontor and Banda Neira, a cousin of *Agapanthus umbellatus*, the so-called African Lily. Heavy-flowered, its scent––"

"I know," said Merrill; and who was she to ask how he knew? "Look," he said, "here's the Ideal, but do you feel like a soda–or–how about we go somewhere and–well–eat?"

But though they passed a dozen eating places, on a bench in the park was where they found themselves, the sun gone down, and Merrill pressing a piece of paper into the girl's hands with a diffident violence.

"I woke up last night, wrote it straight off, in bed. It's not poetry, just written like poetry. Read it!"

Alice read it, half aloud:

"*I hold my breath. The bell is still.*
The dazzling reef is dark with murder and the moon behind.
They come out to me from Lontor, swimming, murmuring.
Three Sisters, murmuring, swimming round and round me.
With lilies in their hair."

Alice swallowed. "It *is* poetry!" She reddened and looked away. Who was she, little more than adolescent and altogether unextraordinary, to be telling Merrill Mygatt what was what?

"No, it isn't," he protested. "But wait. Alice, you don't even know the beginning of it. . . . Look at this."

Another paper, dingy, creased, nor head nor tail to be made of its babble of friars and white rocks and natives, sisters, spices, death, and a bell. . . . The girl kept her eyes on it, moving back and forth, back and forth; she couldn't think what else to do.

Nor could Merrill wait. "Nobody understands, not even Dad. But Alice, honest, from before I left here, up to the day in Frisco . . ."

Here came the story at last, a rush and tumble, words end over end. " . . . If I could just only *know,* Alice! Whether it was something criminal I did, or something yellow, or *what!* For instance, look."

Rush and tumble, words end over end. Dusk was long gone. At a distance below, the lake reflected the yellow apple of the stand where the band was playing. Maybe Belle was there, and Winona and the fellows. Strange that Merrill should be out here, telling everything to this kid he hardly knew. But how explain, even to himself, how it was he couldn't have told it to a peachy-looking girl or anybody quick with all the comebacks?

The thread of his words broken, confusion took him. "Good gosh, here I invited you to eat—and look!"

"I'm not hungry. Wait, won't you?"

Silence for a while. Had it not been so dark he might have seen the girl's face whitening with the effort to be old. Then: "Merrill. You say it's only when you see faces and places you remember things?"

"It seems to work that way, yes. . . . Wh-what, Alice?"

"There's no two ways, Merrill. You've got to go."

Sunday noon. Merrill's father looked tired and bewildered and his hands that lay on the table before him in the den were suddenly veined and old.

"Well, son, I suppose there's no two ways. If you want to go——"

"But I *don't!* It's not that I *want* to, Dad, can't you understand?"

"I'm dull some ways. I fit in Des Moines, Iowa, U.S.A."

"And I ought to. I want to. Remember, I've one more generation of it in me than you have, Dad. If I could be any good here, do my work, feel right! Haven't you ever in your life looked over your shoulder and caught a shadow of something frightening that you couldn't quite see, and known you couldn't go on till you found out what it was?"

"Why 'something frightening?' Now you're out of it, obviously safe."

"But how *came* I out of it safe? Did I quit on it, all mouth, no guts? Why doesn't the subconscious want me to remember what it was all about and how I acted? I've got to know, Dad, I've got to know!"

"I guess you have. You better drop in at the American Express tomorrow, look up transportation. I want you to go decently this time."

The boy caught at it. "The other time, why did I go? You've never told me."

The man's eyes went down to his hands on the table. Red came out of his collar and covered his face. "I guess it was because you didn't like the licking I gave you, with a trunk strap."

"But *why* did you lick me? What *for? Tell* me, Dad!"

Deeper and deeper red. "Because I forgot a couple of things. I forgot you were nearly sixteen, son. And I forgot I was nearly sixteen once, myself, in this same town, and my old man didn't fancy some of the company I kept, either. . . . As I say, see the Express people, work out the way that's quickest—we'll find the funds. . . . Come, there's Cousin Natalie calling and she doesn't like her Sunday dinner to go cold."

Merrill went up to his room after dinner, shut himself in, sat on the bed. "So I'm going, honestly, actually going." He waited for his heart to beat faster. It didn't. Beat slower, if anything. Something was wrong. An impulse came to him to rush down to the den, throw open the door, cry: "Nonsense! Where did we ever get this fool idea?"

But he didn't. He sat there. It wasn't nonsense. It was settled—he was going. Alice ought to know. After all, it was her doing in a way. Merrill got to his feet before he recollected that the library was closed, and he didn't know where Alice lived, the funny kid.

Funny? Officious was more like it. What call had she to mess up his life this way? The life he wanted and was fit for.

He went to a window and looked out at the neighbors' roofs. Now the uneasy thing that had budded the instant his father had said he should go came full to homesick bloom. Friendly roofs. Friendly, ugly, beautiful town. The work and the workmen. Evenings and the gang. Dad, Cousin Natalie, this house, this room. . . . Merrill moved about the room, touching objects, worn, homely, part and parcel of him. As he reached up to straighten a picture of himself as a baby with a St. Bernard, his sleeve slid down from his wrist; cross anchors looked him in the eye and brought him roughly right-about. "What am I doing, going soft?"

Quick to the closet and the shelf, out he brought the bundle. Gear of what adventure, frayed by the winds, rimed with the salt, blistered by the white-hot decks of what far seas? Chiding, deriding him.

"What's wrong?" he parried. "It's settled. I tell you–I'm going."

Skeptic: "Yes? When? Right now?"

"The minute I get the transportation fixed and the money——"

"Money for what? Had you money the other time? . . . And transportation where?"

Merrill flung the bundle back on the shelf, slammed the door, sat on the bed, red playing tag with white across his face. But still, through the shut door, it seemed to him the bundle went on mocking.

"White Friars, black with blood and the moon behind them; night of spice and lilies, ecstasy and terror; do you think for a minute a bank and a travel bureau know where such things be? Zephyr trains and gold-braid liners, do they ride the roads of the aching sole and the begging thumb, steer by the wakes of tramp and schooner, junk and proa? No, lad, there's only the one way there; you found it once. But you'll never in God's world find it twice if you wait for money and tomorrow."

The only thing Merrill did that was different was to leave a note on his dresser before he went down quietly the back way. Though, after all, how could he know it was different? Maybe he'd left a note the other time.

It was dusk when he stood at a crossing of Potter Avenue; why Potter Avenue he had no notion, except that it ran west. And though he had money in his pocket, above eight dollars of his own earned money, yet he knew his ticket would have to be his thumb.

Cars, cars, cars, went by without a flutter; a wishful youth in sweat shirt, sneakers, and blue jean pants was too old a story. Finally a T-model coupé with a home-built pickup body slowed in to the curb.

"Where you want to get to, buddy?" the driver called.

Dazed and dumb as he felt, Merrill had to smile. "The Moluccas."

"The–where did you say?"

"The other end of the Pacific Ocean."

"Yeah? Take a trolley!" Off went the T-model, the joke on Merrill.

And here, in fact, came a trolley car. Merrill got aboard, rang a precious nickel in the box; with that the whole thing became fantastic. How many trolley rides, divided into halfway around the world? He returned along the aisle of the nearly empty car and peered in around the curtain, forward. "How far do you go?"

The motorman turned a face immediately familiar to Merrill. "Yeah? Go on, sell your papers!"

The roadbed was none too good; the platform pitched and swayed. Hanging to a rail, tongue-tied, the boy stared ahead at the oncoming avenue. It was the first time he'd been out this way since he came home. It happened as always, with each successive landmark as it took shape in the twilight: "Why, of course, of course."

A dark big building. "Washington High! I went there."

"No kiddin'!" The motorman had overheard. "How's every little thing by you, Merr'l? Ain't seen you for a coon's age."

"I–I've been away."

"So I heard."

The houses grew smaller and sparser. Some to the right backed on the avenue and faced the river it paralleled. Merrill felt queer.

By and by, "Hogan," he said, "I used to ride out this way with you–after school sometimes–when I was in high school."

"You're tellin' me?"

The houses were thickening again, down toward the river, and the river farther and farther off downhill. Day was only a ribbon in the west now.

Hogan mused, "I wish I was you, your age, night off, with a moon like that comin' up. Give it a look, Merr'l."

Moonrise was on the far side from Merrill. He started to duck, to look, but his eyes never got to the moon. At a distance ahead, on a corner among the vacant blocks, an open-faced shack stood empty, a sign reared above it, obliquely, to catch the outbound traffic. It caught Merrill. As he watched it grow, prickles came up his legs and up his spine. And of a sudden—of course! How many times he'd watched and waited for that sign, all prickles.

Brakes, and the south of the door behind him folding back open.

"Want off here, don't you, Merr'l? . . . With that moon—oh, baby!"

Merrill got out, and the car moved on. He stood in the dimness and stared up at the signboard:

SAMBOWSKI'S ROADSIDE
GARDEN TRUCK, POULTRY, EGGS
SPECIAL
FRESH KILLED EVERY THURSDAY
NATIVE WHITE ROCK FRYERS

Of course. Waited and watched for it, high-school kid, not because of vegetables or eggs or Thursday frying chickens, but because it signaled the cross street here, leading down to the corn-canning suburb on the river.

Merrill turned into it. Halfway down the hill, the note of the bell came up to him faintly. Someone had just gone into the Grace place, or else just come out.

Come out. And coming up the street a pair. The moonlight was stronger than the vestige of day now, and behind Merrill. To them he was only a silhouette; to him they were plain. The fellow didn't matter; he was anybody. But Merrill thought to himself with the shock of one who has been away: "How sharp and bitter she looks!"

But why shouldn't she, at her age? Of the three Grace sisters, Rose was by far the oldest. Twenty-four—five—she must be twenty-six now. Sharper than ever, in that pointed little hat like a horn, more sarcastic, picky, interfering. Jealous, knowing her time was by.

It was not till Merrill was past that she looked back, stopped short.

"*You* again, you damn kid! I thought you went away."

"Hullo, Rosa."

"Come on, now, turn around, beat it somewheres else, hear me? If you think we want your old man out here givin' us hell again——"

Her gent had had enough and dragged her. "Cut it! Come along!"

Merrill went on down to the dead end in the suburban business street.

LORELEI BAKERY
JOHANN GRACE, PROP.

The windows were weakly lighted, showing Saturday's staling bread and cake. Merrill turned the knob and pushed the door open, to the tinny clang of the bell overhead. The remembered air met him full in the face, a mingled redolence of slab gingerbread, cinnamon buns, coffee rings, rye-and-caraway, apple cake brown with nutmeg, cookies a half inch deep with coconut, gone a little rancid.

Johann, ancient of the Rhine, legless prisoner in his chair high in a corner, brooded with puttering fingers over his till box. Only by chance, or some instinct, did he become aware someone had entered. He gazed at Merrill with the infant eyes of senility.

"Haf you hear now in Germany vat dey do mit dot Jew-people?"

There was nothing to do but shrug and nod; Johann was stony deaf. That was the reason for the bell, so that the girls could hear when customers entered.

One was coming now, slap-footed down the stair beyond the rear partition. It was Columbine, the middle of the three Grace sisters and the sloven, always shouldering at a strap beneath her blouse or hiking up a stocking or, with a spit-finger, curling the hair back out of her large, brown, ready eyes.

"What can I do for——" She broke off, mouth open. "O my God!"

"Hi, Columbine."

"You Mygatt kid, get outa here! If your old man was to find out! Look, I'd think you'd had your bellyful once. Didn't he give you a beatin' up? That's the way we heard it—with a trunk strap—and you run away from home, West or somewheres. Whyn't you *stay* run away?"

Merrill didn't say. He'd hardly heard. As he moved toward her and the partition door, Columbine's voice broke high. "Lily ain't in! She's went out, I tell you! . . . Papa, Papa! Tell him Babe ain't here. . . . No, now, wait, Merr'l, while I tell you 'bout Lily. . . ."

The boy passed through the doorway as if there'd been nothing in it but air, passed on through the back part where the mixing tables were, and came out on the terrace above the river at the rear.

Underfoot, bricks some places, other parts cement. Overhead, lean poles supporting a vine's old age. Beyond and below, sloping to the water, a moraine of cans: sirup, fruit, pumpkin, baking powder. To Merrill's right, at the far end, there was swung a Gloucester hammock, dilapidated by wear and weather. He went and sat down in its riverward corner, back to the water.

He was busy wondering. He repeated out loud, "Grace sisters, Grace sisters," first slowly, then fast. Had it been that he'd babbled in his watched sleep, mistaken by the jotting doctor? Or had the subconscious warder in him slurred it to "gray sisters" in pure craft and cussedness?

He raised his eyes. The terrace was longer than the building was wide, this end clear of its corner, so that he had only to raise them to see out between the bakery and the neighboring barbershop, up the hill of the street he'd come down, to the signboard small at the crest, black against the moonrise sky.

He had only half heard the murmurous goings on inside the back door, anxiety and protest. The youngest of the girls was out and nearly to the hammock before he realized and looked.

"Hullo, Lily."

"Hullo—but listen, Merr'l, you can't do this!"

Lily must be close on twenty now. The heavenly plumpness of a while ago began to take on more plumpness, less heavenly. The childish face was still a childish face, though, and a strange thing to see now as it tried to struggle with adult dismay.

"Look, sweetie, I—I—I'm glad to see you back and all that—but things're different—I'm a married woman. If he come home and—and you was here, see? . . ."

The scent of her came and lay around him, got into his nose and mouth, humid, heavy, blent of armpits and ten-cent-store perfumery. The extraordinary thing was that the perfume wasn't lily, but heliotrope. It was her name that was Lily.

" . . . was differ'nt then . . . you were just a kid . . . like a kid . . . then . . . but me bein' married now . . ."

It ran on and on like a worried beebuzz, but Merrill's brain took none of it. Something inside had parted with a soundless pop. A clear wind ran all the way down through memory. . . . The bell, and Dad's feet coming through the bakery, a Dad he wouldn't have known. The ride home. The incredible strap. The tail of a truck that night into Dubuque . . ."

He wanted to laugh, he felt physically so light. He pulled the belly of his sweat shirt out in a peak to see. "You, I remember where I bought you new; Minneapolis, on that relief job sorting rubbish." He picked at a dungaree thigh. "Salvation Army, Denver; they got me work, too, carrying sandwich boards for that tattoo parlor."

He was on his feet. Lily's face was a study–pulled two ways.

"Not that I–I don't mean to rush you off, Merr'l. Maybe–I dunno –after all–listen, dearie–Eddie–that's my husband–he don't get off till ten at the cannin' works–and––Wh-what's this?"

Merrill had her by a hand, pumping it up and down.

"You don't know what you've done for me. Thank you very much, and good-by!"

He didn't stop running when he was through the shop and clear; he kept right on up the cross-street hill. He thought he heard the trolley coming, inbound. Maybe he wouldn't make it in time.

But, he thought, what difference? Feeling as light as he did, he wouldn't mind running all the way home.

*Survivor**

IN THE HOLLOW OF THE BLOCK west of the State House, Dobson was putting his studio shutters on, for it was class evening, and though the model posed only in the "semi," this was Denver, not Paris. The shutters were heavy and high from the ground. The elderly sculptor was glad when the job was done and he could sit down on the box he had been carrying around, breathe for a moment, mop his temples and sparsely whiskered cheeks, and look at the mountains behind which the April sun was already a half hour down.

When he built the studio, in his early days out here after he had begun to get the better of his lung trouble, he could see a great spread of the snow range that way across vacant lots; but the city had grown in the quarter-century, and all that was left him now was a glimpse of the twin peaks, Grays and Torreys, framed in an alley notch.

How many thousands of nights had the alien sat and watched the darkening of that bifurcated giant upland, cut out in the dilute air so cleanly that even at half a hundred miles the ear strained for the note of the incessant wind whining between the pinnacles, and the whisper of ice dust polishing the rocks of the inhuman solitude! And how many times had the exile started with a wince of nostalgia, wondering what he was doing on this strange side of the world, dreaming his years away, and where were his eyes of waking!

Where were the lanes and hedgerows, the meadows and folded moorlands of his native Oxfordshire? Where his friendly, dingy London? And where his working, fighting, rollicking runways of Montmartre, smelly of turpentine and bus horses, in a lilac haze?

Now that Dobson had cooled off he was cold. It was almost dark, and around on the cement of the court he heard the feet of his pupils arriving. He went indoors. He spoke to Lincoln Hussack, as always the first at his stand. The young man had been given a page in color to do at the *Post* for the Sunday after the following, and the news tonight brought a glow to the heart of his instructor. "Bravo, my lad! Good! Push on!"

Dobson spoke to Miss Lukes, the serious schoolteacher; to Roy Dickens, the governor's nephew; to the two sisters from the convent, and to the ranchman, Kraus. But Mary Shannon had not yet come. He took his time posing the model, the Indian, Frank Shoe, stripped to the waist for the anatomy of the torso. He tried him first with one hand shading the eyes in the immemorial gesture, then with both hands on his hips and his face slightly lifted. But still Mary Shannon had not come. It was like her, Dobson reflected; it was the atmosphere of the studio she liked, not the hard fashioning of a beautiful thing. And since her mother was a widow without a fortune, Mary would have to be more than an amateur at something or other before very long.

Now Dobson knew of a sudden what he must do tonight, and he tasted wormwood in his heart. He went into his own shop to get away from it, turned on all the lights, removed the damp covering from the great unfinished figure of his "Arapahoe," and gathered his tools with an impatience that was rare in him. As he stood before the clay, the shape of the aboriginal plainsman, noble in its nakedness, erect, implacable, stoic, shading its gaze toward the doomful east (the commission was for the eastern entrance to the Capitol grounds), Dobson tried to turn his misery into a temper against the Philistines against whom he had fought so long.

They would be coming again tomorrow. Again, with their dull eyes and their stupid impatience, they would argue, protest, and threaten, the politicians, the storekeepers. Three years ago this Art Committee of the Legislature had begun its grumbling: "Looks like a finished statue to us; why don't you go ahead with it?" Two years ago there had been a note of exasperation: "Don't see how you can expect to improve it any more, fussing with it. And if we're satisfied you should be. Frankly, Dobson, what's holding it up now?"

To look at them was enough to know there was no use in trying to explain. How could they comprehend that, so long as a last knuckle wanted a least wrinkle to make it right, though it might seem good enough in their eyes, in the artist's the whole creation remained but an attempt, and a foiled one, so much dead clay? They seemed not to realize that it was to last a great deal longer than they. But they were like that, forever building things in a hurry so as to be able the sooner to tear them down, in a greater hurry to build newer ones. And Mary Shannon was like that.

The circle had brought him back, and immediately, as he fell to tooling a vein on the "Arapahoe's" ankle, he set off on another circle. Reminiscence this time; dismayed by here and now, he made haste to escape it; daydreaming, he ran back into there and then.

Paris, and youth, and the haze of lilac. The court called the Impasse Carre. The mountainous woman with three moles and three whiskers, concierge at Number Eleven. At nine, Sven Lie's studio panes shining with the sky. Old Mique and his barrow of snails in front of the *librairie*. Alan Dumergue's diggings. Then the café tables under the soiled glass awning of the Masque d'Or, carrying the corner around into the loud Rue Lac.

Alan and his girl there, Sven and his. Loaves, cheese, smoked fish, half liters of blond beer. Ivan Morvitch and Alan's brother, the young playwright, and Freddy Webster from Des Moines, hatless, arm in arm, in from the clattering dusk. "*A bas l'Académie!*" they chant. "*Mort aux vieux!*" they roar. The battle cry of the comrades of the Impasse Carre. Yes, down with the old ones and their old order, those established, rich, stupid ones who think that there will never be another light in art but their light! Away with the solemn fogies; tumble them off from the shoulders of the genius that now at last will cure the sickness of the world! Down with romanticism! It had its rope and hanged itself. Up impressionism! youth's new last word.

Beer and sausages for thirty centimes. " 'Allo, Tom Dobson! 'Allo, Johnnie Bull!"

"What do you think that old donkey of a dealer said to my canvas, 'Loire Midi'? 'I can see only that it is a hodgepodge,' says he. 'My little boy with chalks does better; at least I can see what his drawing is meant to tell.' "

"Moneybag, potbelly, let him wait ten years, and weep."

Dancing. Warm, eager, and wild. Céleste, Marie, Sven's Lilla with her large bosom and her straw braids, Orma, Puvis's new model, and Madeleine! And Madeleine!

"Tom Dobson, how is it say *en anglais*—'Ai lawv you'?"

Beastly sulks, angelic gaieties; Madeleine. An immeasurable, inexhaustible vitality. That is her beauty, her vitality. The long slope of her shoulders, the ivory pillar of her strong neck, the full red overturn of the lip, the brown hair, so massive in growth—the devil! That's not Madeleine. Madeleine was as blond as a Swede girl. Who is this dark one, then? It's Mary. Mary Shannon.

Dobson was cornered. He went to the window. There was a full moonlight. Fifty miles away on the scallop between the twin peaks the ice rim glittered. The wind would have died in that high, white night; there would no longer be even the whistling of the thin wind to distract the solitude. Dobson turned his back on it.

He went out to the class, for it was time. To young Hussack there was not much to say, hardly more than "Good! Push on!" There was not much to be said to Roy Dickens either, but for the opposite reason. This nephew of the governor was not serious. Educated in the East, now that he had come home he was at a loss what to do with himself. He was here in the modeling class simply because Mary Shannon was here. Dobson made no mistake about that. As for the two sisters, they listened and tried, listened and tried again. That was something. But Mary Shannon neither listened nor tried.

What to say to Mary? For an instant, now that it no longer mattered, Dobson had the impulse to mutter, "Good! Push on!" without even looking at the clay she had clapped hastily upon an armature ill bent. But then it was like a fever; he broke out chiding.

"It's because you'll not look. What's the model there for, Mary? You used to study at least the fundamental proportions before committing them, but nowadays—— But even if there were no model, you should know from simple anatomy that, the shoulder line being so, the axis of the head cannot possibly be so. A head is not an egg. You'll fix it up later, you tell yourself. But I'll tell you—look, my child—by the very block-in of those arms I can predict you this, the weight of the hands resting on the hips will never rest on them, never. For all your 'fixing' later on——"

What was the use? Mary's ear might be for him, but her eye was for Roy Dickens.

"Oh, dear," it seemed to sigh, "the same old line. When he's through jawing . . ."

Dobson had to swallow, and it was a bitter swallow. "Well, push on!"

But at the third and final criticism of the evening he broke out with it:

"Now you see, Mary, once wrong, always wrong. That head, it is an egg. And do you see what's happened to the arms? Where is the weight? Not down. They don't push, they pull. See, there's Frank Shoe, the redskin, poised, at ease, gazing up at the mountain-tops, let's say. And what have you given me here? You've given me a poor egg-head doing nothing but trying rather desperately to hold his own trousers up. 'The Broken Braces,' you must call it. You can see this one of yours thinking: 'Well, you've given me this plaguy garment, and now what in the name of the happy hunting grounds am I supposed to do with it?' Tell me, Mary, looking at Frank Shoe as he stands there—— But I see, he's got down. Next time, then——" Dobson put his teeth into the flesh of his lip. "Mary, will you be so good as to come into the shop for a moment? I've something to say."

In the privacy of the shop he went straight at it, his eyes fixed on the "Arapahoe's" great toe and a wrinkle of misery between his brows. "Mary, I've been talking with your mother. I'm fond of you, Mary. It's because I'm fonder of you than of anyone that I'm willing to be brutal. Child, you're wasting your time; you'll never get anywhere with the modeling; you haven't got it. But you've so many other gifts, you ought to be busy finding them out while you're still a girl, Mary. So–you're not to come here, Mary, any more."

It was no good, his staring so desperately at the toe of clay; his ears were worse than his eyes, to follow the havoc. "Oh! Oh!" he heard her stifling the gasps wrung from her affronted pride. "Oh! Oh!" Incredulity, bewilderment, comprehension, fury. But then when he did turn his wretched eyes he saw that her resentment had passed with those breaths. From the doorway she was looking back at his hunched figure with a smile altogether enigmatical and a light curiously mingled of mockery and ruth in her gaze.

She did a thing that confounded him. Returning at a dart, she bent over his head and brushed the bald spot with her lips, a feather-weight caress, then ran.

It would have helped if he could have groaned, but he hadn't even that defense against the silence. Presently, around the corner outside, he heard the fall of four feet on the cement, and he knew by that that Roy Dickens had waited for Mary. He could almost see the girl with the finger of warning to her lips till they were out to the open of Broadway. It was from the distance of the street then that he heard the release of their rebellious mirth.

It was springtime. Dobson felt it of a sudden a trap in which he was imprisoned, a cell walled by the dry suns and sapless winds of the tableland of the raw young West.

He tried to re-escape. He sat and tried to remember. The lilac haze. Blond beer, hard bread, gray sausages. Young mutiny when youth was clear-eyed and mutiny fateful. "*Mort aux vieux!*" Death to the old ones! Wild daylights, and clay on the hands; wild gaslights, and dancing. And Madeleine! Mary!

Dobson got up and ran out into the other studio to look at the travesty of childish clay that Mary had thrown together. It was gone. Turntable, armature, everything. He understood now why one pair of the retreating footfalls had sounded heavier than the other. At last he could groan, for the pity of those youngsters.

Once in the following winter Mrs. Shannon, Mary's mother, came to the studio. Though she did not utter it in words, her attitude said it: "It was you that started all this; you've got to help me end it."

Dobson had asked: "What's Mary doing with herself, now she's given up the modeling?"

"Given it up?" The sluice gates of the widow's trouble were opened then. It had been bad enough when her daughter had been studying with Dobson, and so in a measure justified. But now it was simply mulishness, the child's hurt vanity.

"My one best room, Mr. Dobson, always cluttered up with her 'masterpieces.' Not that she really cares about them; if she did she'd try and do them better, and make them look like something under the sun. No, it's just that Mary's got the idea she must be in on this artist life—'bohemian,' I suppose you'd call it. And I wish you'd see the kind of friends she's got now. Where she ever found them——"

"I'll come and see her," Dobson said.

He should have set an hour. When he went, next day, Mary was out. He spent the waiting time in examining the "studio" and its prodigies. They would have been pathetic if they had not been laughable, and laughable, he told himself, if they had not been tragic. Steeled as she had believed it, the mother's pride mutinied once. One piece, shrouded in the working cloth, she would have passed over, getting Dobson on to another. When he persisted and uncovered the figure, she could, as she said, have died.

"Yes, die. It isn't even as if it was of a model; I've got hardened to that. But it's actually one of Mary's friends, May Paige, and wouldn't you think she'd be ashamed, and, on top of ashamed, furious? May's really quite a passably pretty girl, in life."

Dobson's humiliation was deeper than the mother's in a way, for it was he that had had the faith. Blinded (he could see now) by the appeal of her youthful vitality, he had been persuaded for nearly a year that Mary was capable of more than ordinary things. She had progressed up to a certain point. And now! The way the stick of that rocket had come down. It was not merely that she had forgotten what she had learned; she had forgotten more than she had learned. Given even a half-pretty girl for model, that the best Mary could do now was this naïve distortion of the human form, lopsided, faceless, save for prehensile-looking lips bent in a V-shaped smirk, with the neck of a vulture and the dugs of a cat—for a moment as Dobson dropped the cloth back over it he felt sick.

After that one, the purloined figure of Frank Shoe had nothing to offer but ridiculousness. Pigheaded, Mary had not taken his word for it; she had thought to right its wrongness by dint of superficial polish, till she had polished even the little that was human of it away, leaving nothing but glazed cylinders. Empty egg-head to an empty sky, there this "Indian" stood, shoulder blades flared out like porcelain shelves, long, thin, tired grasshopper arms and bewildered clod fists holding up the weight of pants as hard and round as lengths of stovepipe, patiently.

Mrs. Shannon was pouring out her troubles. "And of course this riffraff, seeing they could never get into any other decent house in town—except of course the Dickens boy, with his uncle the governor—of course it's their game to pretend to encourage Mary. And she'll swallow it. Now do you know what? Mary owns a bond her uncle left her, and now she's all for selling it, so she can get these blobs cast into brass or bronze or whatever it is. Oh, Mr. Dobson, isn't there something?"

"I don't know," he groaned, suddenly worn out. "I give you my word I don't know."

He couldn't wait forever. After two hours, when Mary had not returned, he had to go. Outside he saw a figure making off hurriedly, as if to avoid meeting him, and it looked like Roy Dickens.

Dobson finished the "Arapahoe" with a rush that winter; by spring it was in the marble, Colorado stone. It was up in its place in its swathings nearly a month before Decoration Day, when it was to be unveiled in connection with the annual art exhibition held in the State House basement.

The Exhibition Committee, bewildered lawmakers from the mountains, followed a precedent of twenty years' standing and came to Dobson. "Here are the folks," they said in effect, "that want to get their pictures and things in. You know them. You tell us."

Halfway down the list stood the item: "Mary Shannon, sculpture, 17 pieces."

For the first time in years Dobson saw red. It was a good thing, he had to confess to himself; there had been times when he had run a dotard's danger of mixing this child up too confusedly with his sentimental reminiscences. Now he was simply exasperated beyond bounds. If he had had her here he would have turned her over his knees and given her a spanking. Stubborn, wayward, blind—to persist in her vain innocence in wanting to make a laughingstock of herself.

He controlled his voice before the committeemen. "This item you will do well not to accept," he said, drawing his pencil through the line.

The following day one of them was back at the studio. "The governor, he wants to know if what is out about this item is that there's too many pieces. Would it be better to cut it down from seventeen to maybe eight or ten, Mr. Dobson? Or do you mean it 'out,' the whole shootin' match?"

"I mean it 'out,' decisively. Let there be no mistake in that."

Oh, miserable Mary, bad Mary! Happily, by and by, Dobson saw the comic side of the thing. He sat down alone in his emptied shop and chuckled.

"*Enfant terrible!* Incredible child!"

The awful thing happened. Dobson had dealt with politicians before, so he should have misdoubted. As it was, the first he knew of it was when, surrounded by the notables on the afternoon of the unveiling, in glancing through the leaflet cataloging the annual exhibition inside, he saw: "Bureau of Claims Room: Shannon, Mary A., sculpture, 17."

"The governor!" He remembered. "The governor's nephew, Roy!" Dobson saw the ugly light.

His day of days was spoiled. Throughout the length of Senator Woodson's speech he could think of nothing but the catastrophe brewing in the basement behind him. His own few words sounded remote and inane, and so did the applause at the actual uncovering of the "Arapahoe." There was no thrill in it for the perturbed man.

Afterward it was worse. He ought to have gone inside. There were works of old pupils of his on exhibition, and they would think it queer of him not to. He made an effort to listen to the kind things that prominent people were saying to him, the indulgence of Mrs. E. D. Bragford, the parrot patter of Mrs. Winn Constable, the gush of Mrs. Colbine. It came as a relief, though, when Abrahams, the art dealer, stopped to add his congratulations.

"I'm glad to see you, Abrahams. I heard you were back—yesterday, wasn't it? Tell me about your trip. Did you find anything worth while?"

Abrahams sketched his fifty days, Chicago, New York, London, Paris, Provincetown.

"And back here for today and your 'Arapahoe,' best of all, old friend."

"Thank you, Abrahams. No, I've not been in yet; I'll go presently. By the way, I see your truck parked out there on Colfax; have you a loan in the show in there?"

The dealer laughed. "What a man! For one thing, there's your own 'Young Circe,' as usual. What would their show be without that?"

It was a comfort to Dobson to reflect what would Abrahams' own gallery be without that same "Young Circe"? What would his window in Seventeenth Street have done any time in these past ten years without its mainstay and keystone in the marble shard of loveliness, the masterpiece of Dobson's later middle life? It would be pleasant if it would sell, of course, but sometimes Dobson was almost glad it hadn't been taken and shut away in privacy. There in Abrahams' window it did its bit in leavening with beauty the daily ugliness, a monument almost as public as the others, the "Grizzly at Bay" before the courthouse, the "Scout" in City Park, and now the "Arapahoe" here.

People who had been in to the exhibition were coming out again, and now the worst of the ordeal began. Dobson could keep his eyes wherever he wanted them, but against derisive or scandalized whisperings he could not stop his ears.

"Did you ever in your life! Who is this Shannon person?"

"Isn't there someone supposed to handle these exhibitions, someone responsible?"

"But what I can't understand—I'm told she's actually a pupil of Mr. Dob——"

"Shhhhh! (Right there.)"

Ears crimson, eyes averted, Dobson kept silence, and denied Mary once.

There was the voice of Mrs. Dickens, the governor's wife: "Why, of course Earle didn't realize—never had laid eyes on the girl's work. It was simply that Roy, his brother's boy (he has a crush on the girl), plagued him—and believing she was a protégé of Mr. Dobson's —Roy made that up out of whole cloth, as we can now see . . ."

Deeper crimson, farther away, Dobson denied Mary twice.

"I'd rather be anything than embarrassed." That was Mrs. E. D. Bragford, president of the State Confederation. "I think this will teach them that it should be strictly limited to entries having some art education, and by that I mean in some recognized course devoted to it, such as Mr. Dobson's——"

It was startling then. It was the sculptor himself, red-jowled, bright-blue-eyed.

"If you are speaking of Mary Shannon, Mrs. Bragford, she is something of a protégé of mine."

It had nothing to do with Dobson's intelligence or with his will. It was simply a year's accumulated explosives going off disastrously. Snickering at Mary Shannon, were they? Sneering at Mary! Wheeling, he marched into the basement of the Capitol.

He knew he was being an idiot, and worse than an idiot, a renegade. He knew it with his head, though not with his heart or his feet.

He had not seen Mary for months till he saw her across the shoulders of the people there in the Bureau of Claims. Her head up, her face a mask, her stubborn shoulders squared against the affront of muffled gasp and giggle, she stood withdrawn in a farther corner, hemmed in by shadowy figures. Whether they were the figures of the living or of her own distorted bronzes Dobson could not have said; Mary, cornered, was all he could see. Miserable child, she had nothing to thank for it but her own vain folly. But who cared?

Half a quiet had fallen at his appearance in the doorway, a gesture of the crowd's curiosity and vague illness at ease. It became a whole one as he began to make a circuit of the exhibit. Halting heavily before each successive prodigy, he appeared to study it with deliberation; he scarcely saw it, as a matter of fact. He was too upset. The strongest impression he carried out of it all, indeed, was not of the dead casts but of the living faces that watched his as he deliberated, some of them hard, dull, and old, some, scattered here and there, the faces of the strangest youth, intractable and vigilant.

"Who are these?" Dobson found himself wondering.

There was one face triangular and sallow, save for a hectic feather on either cheek ridge, and with long black hair. Another, a truculent young fellow, had mine dust bitten into his neck pores. They were all different, but somehow or other they were less different than they were alike.

"Where did they come from," Dobson wondered, "and what are they doing here?"

Against almost the last of the pediments in the gantlet a placard was propped: "Survivor." When Dobson lifted his eyes to find the figure above it that pipe-limbed, egg-headed travesty of an Indian holding his pants up patiently, he shivered a little, said "God forgive me!" to himself, and closed his eyes tight. But then he opened them.

His voice was harsh and loud, for he spoke, purposely, across the width of the room.

"Splendid, Mary! Do your own thing in your own way, and don't bother about the fatheads. They come to scoff now. They'll remain to pray." On impulse he raised one hand to his temple. It was a funny little old-man salute, as prim as it was unpracticed, and by so much the more impressive. "Good!" he cried. "Push on!"

He nearly collided with Abrahams in the doorway, but cleared himself and escaped into the corridor. His legs, he found, were as rickety as an old rag doll's. Outside he avoided the crowd and followed the building's shadow around, wanting no more of his day of days, wanting only to get home.

He tried his rooms, above the drugstore, but found no peace there. Driven out to his studio, it was little better. If he had had something to work at, something to beat and mold with his hands, in place of the vacancy left enormous by the "Arapahoe's" departure, it would have helped. Helpless, he wandered or sat.

He could see now. He had made a fool of himself.

To what end? Thinking in his quixotic zeal to fend off mockery from Mary, what he had done in all probability was only to double it by his transparent clowning.

And at what price? At the price of the oldest and deepest loyalty he had, his faith in the virtue of beauty and in the dignity of its creating.

The sun went down, leaving for a moment between the peaks a glitter in the shape of a curving sword. "The coward does it with a kiss," he recollected, "the brave man with a sword." He had done it with a kiss.

As it grew dark he made an effort, jumped to his feet, shook himself. "What the devil! All this stew over nothing, practically. It's late and I haven't eaten: I'm hungry; that's the trouble." Hurrying to his rooms, he began to tidy himself, and decided abruptly on evening clothes. "What the devil! I have finished a piece. Such days don't come too often. Tonight I'll have nothing but the best. I'll go to the Laville Café, order a sole and little beans and white wine. Swank it." On the way, turning into Fifteenth Street, the ferrule of his stick faltered in its resolute tattoo. "People. There'll be a crowd there." But then with relief and a little shame he recollected: "It's too late and too early; I'll have the place to myself; quiet, that's the ticket," and strode on.

White wine? This night itself was white wine as he walked. Still spring, already summer. Moonlight and arc light, weaving beauty between them out of raw brick ugliness. And people had liked the "Arapahoe" uncommonly.

On Dobson's right was the better commercial quarter, on the left the poorer. From the poorer came the greater noise of life, gossip, hails, fall of feet, muffled music, instrument and voice. It bothered the sculptor, affronted him somehow. He increased his pace, turning his silk-hatted head a little away. Soon he would reach the cross street where he could make to the east.

But now there was a sweaty yellow window to get past, a cheap restaurant, full of hubbub. The door opened and a fellow came out, loafing, perhaps for a breath of air. Starting at sight of Dobson, leaning to peer, he turned back and began to bellow.

"Hey, everybody, out here! Look! It's himself—the old man."

A rush, hurly-burly, violence. There was no room for defense, no chance for protest, hardly time for dismay. And Dobson was inside.

A few tables dressed in greasy oilcloth at one side, at the other a lunch counter backed by gas burners and a hot plate, on which a stout woman, worried and none too clean, was busy turning wheat cakes. Steam of cooking, steam of life.

A body leaping, athletic, reaching in one leap the height of the counter, erect, arms spread. Whose voice was that? It was Roy Dickens's.

"Come on now, all together, three long, loud, lusty cheers for the grand old man!"

Like the crashing of avalanches.

Confusion of the ears, confusion of the eyes. Who was that foreign-looking blond girl with the thick brows, sliding pie into a magenta mouth with one hand and waving a cup of milk-muddied coffee in the other? Why, it was the girl from the afternoon and the Bureau of Claims room, no longer sulkily vigilant, but almost a wanton for triumph now. And there above his plate of cakes doused with sirup was the fellow with the long black hair and the triangular, consumptive face, exulting: "Fatheads, you were right, sir; they've had the earth, and look what they've done with it; out with 'em; give us the room!" And back there was the mine-dust-bitten boy, his shoulders rounded over an accordion and his eyes as rapt as if it were real music he was playing for the dancers, not jazz.

And who danced? Who was this coming from the dancing, luminous with perspiration, eyes shining, hands out, this strong angel, wild and young? Mary Shannon, Mary herself.

"This is our day, Mr. Dobson, yours and mine. Won't you ask me to dance?"

What did she mean, her day? Had she been taken in? Consternation, exasperation, pity. Or—or was it he that was being "had"? His face aflame, he dropped his eyes.

"I am too old for dancing."

He turned and fought his way out, as though someone were trying to stop him. Not till he was clear away on the sidewalk was a hand laid on him. It was Mary's.

"Please; I must tell you. They may talk, Mr. Dobson, but I am the only one that really knows how brave you've been. How wise and brave when you turned me out on my own when you did, and how fine and brave today." Bending quickly over the hand she held, she kissed the back of it, squeezed it, and let it go. "I thank you, sir," she said.

It was the bitterest thing he had ever known, the misgiving that went with him as he went away. If it was all malice, tongue in cheek —and certainly, flushed and self-deluded as they were, they couldn't all have been fooled by his folly of the afternoon—then this of Mary's was the blackest worst.

Where was he going, dropping one wooden foot in front of the other so? He had forgotten. Passing by the Laville Café without even seeing its rosy globes, he let himself be carried on to the east. When he reached Seventeenth he turned down it, north. Espying the white illumination in Abrahams' Art Gallery a block ahead, he realized what had brought him drifting, the want of something to see in the wilderness that was his own thing.

The dealer had been in late in consequence of his loans to the exhibition. He was locking the shop door when he saw the sculptor approaching, twenty yards or so away. He hurried toward him, his hand thrust far out.

"Well, Dobson, old friend, where are you bound in your splendor? If nowhere in particular, why not come along with me to—back to— the Laville? I haven't dined."

"Thanks, I will. One moment, though. You—you've got your pieces back from—my piece—back from the show?"

Abrahams could find no way to hold him from going forward. He followed, agitated, stumbling among his words. "I—I've been thinking, Dobson—I've decided it's poor selling policy to keep that marble of your always on view, on the street practically. Why buy it—that's the psychology—when you can see it every day just by——"

But there the sculptor stood before the shop, pale to the temples, mouth ajar.

"What the devil, Abrahams!"

Where from a time that began to seem immemorial Dobson's "Young Circe" had been wont to grace the center of that big window with her pure-white, tristful loveliness, Mary Shannon's dark atrocity, the "Survivor," stood. To the right was the smaller bronze of what might have been meant for a tiger, but looked like a mangy cat. To the left was the bust of an apparent idiot, apparently done with a mason's trowel.

"What the devil, Abrahams!" The old man's voice broke high. "You too?" The dealer looked everywhere. "Well—you see—old friend——"

"You don't mean to tell me you swallowed that today? You can't be simple enough to have believed I saw anything"—Dobson pointed a shaking finger at the nearest, the idiotic bust—"anything but the fumbling of a kindergarten child in that thing of Mary Shannon's there?"

Abrahams gasped. "Heavens, that isn't a Shannon, man. That's an Epstein I picked up in London, and they made me go to the bottom of my pocket for it, don't forget. The other, the animal piece, is an Ed Villon; but tell me, you must have seen the plate of that one in *Studio* this spring. I had to dig for that one too. Deep."

Perceiving Dobson dumb, Abrahams rushed on: "A gamble, of course, in this town. I shall not sell them this month nor next. But by Christmas I shall have sold them; wait and see. I know my people: I can predict definitely. The Ed Villon I shall sell to Mrs. E. D. Bragford, and she will pay for it—through the nose. The Epstein, Mrs. Earle Dickens, the governor's wife, will take; Mrs. Bragford will have told her to by then. The Shannon piece I shall not offer here, but in Chicago. A prophet in his own country, you know."

Abrahams had been talking against a thing that failed him now. With a catch in his throat, "Old friend," he cried, stepping forward to throw an arm around the smaller, grayer man, "as for me, myself, I see more truth and worth and beauty in your 'Circe' than in all of these. That is my taste. Added to that is my loyalty. But these days are other days, and my old taste will not pay my assistants' wages, nor loyalty my rent."

Dobson shook the arm off and stood away. He tried to keep his voice level, but it trembled for all of that, like a blade in an infuriated hand.

"I have owned up that I have made an ass of myself, Abrahams. It seems to me that you at least might accept it at that, and drop the ragging." Dobson wheeled round, stiff-legged, and marched away.

It grew midnight and past midnight in Dobson's workshop.

It is curious what the human mind can be when it is driven to defend itself. He no longer thought of Abrahams, but he had not yet managed not to think of Mary Shannon. It seemed to him he would have given anything to be able to forget her as he had last seen her, flushed with what seemed to him her self-delusion of achievement, surrounded by bragging riffraff, in that squalid eating place. Flapjacks and raisin pie, fried-egg sandwiches and muddy coffee, stamping, wild hallooing, perspiration, jazz. Ugh!

By an effort of the will, in panic, Dobson ran away into his memory. Ah, but this was better! Loaves and cheese, smoked fish and gray sausages, under the flaking gilt trelliswork of the Masque d'Or. Alan and his girl there, Sven and his Lilla. Ivan Morvitch and Freddy Webster from Des Moines with his half a shirt and patched trousers, bellowing "*Mort aux vieux!*" Down with the old fogies! Up youth! "What do you think that old donkey of a dealer . . . a hodgepodge," says he. "My little boy with chalks . . ." "Moneybag, potbelly, let him wait ten years . . ." Dancing, when dancing was dancing, warm, eager, and wild. Gas-lit nights of dancing, lilac-lit days of working—working when work was a true, fierce, rebellious matter, sweet clay on the hands.

Work! Dobson got out of his chair, stood on his two feet, and began shaping with a thumb before his eye the vacancy where the "Arapahoe" had been.

"Tomorrow I will go about it. A—uh—the—'Indian Mother.' So. And so. Yes, 'Arapahoe Mother'—companion piece—the west approach will want something now to fill it. So. And so. Marching toward the sunset, bowed a little, burdened. But unbeaten, untired. So."

With a sweep of the thumb the old man finished the line of the shadow of a noble beauty.

"Good! Push on!"